SURPRISINGLY

sarah

SURPRISINGLY sarah

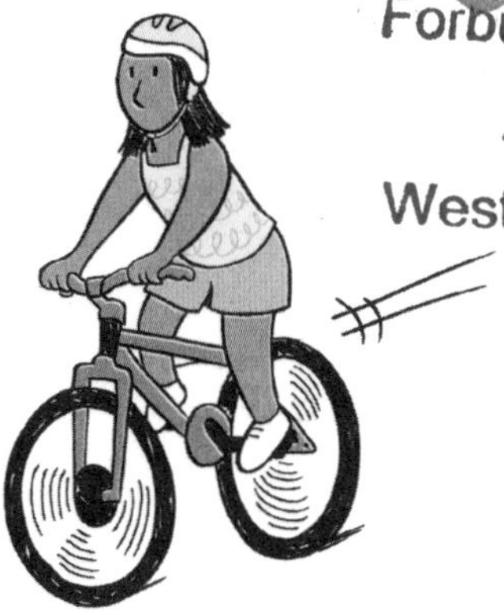

TERRI LIBENSON

BALZER + BRAY
An Imprint of HarperCollins*Publishers*

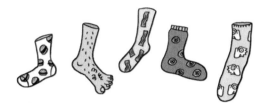

Balzer + Bray is an imprint of HarperCollins Publishers.

Surprisingly Sarah
 For information address HarperCollins Children's Books, a division of HarperCollins Publishers, 195 Broadway, New York, NY 10007.
www.harpercollinschildrens.com

Library of Congress Control Number: 2022949256
ISBN 978-0-06-313922-0 (hardcover) — ISBN 978-0-06-313921-3 (pbk.) —
ISBN 978-0-06-332344-5 (special ed.)

Typography by Terri Libenson and Laura Mock
23 24 25 26 27 PC/WOR 10 9 8 7 6 5 4 3 2 1

First Edition

To Michael:
I think I chose well.

PROLOGUE
SARAH

You know that girl in the cafeteria who's surrounded by a ton of friends? Whose phone always blows up with texts? Who goes to parties every weekend?

Well, that's not me.

I don't really have a lot of friends—but I don't mind. I'd rather have a few close friends than a big group of not-so-close ones. Also, the ones I **do** have, I hold on to tight (specifically, three of them). Maybe it's because I see so many kids at school go through friends like paper towels. They use them, crumple them up, and move on to others.

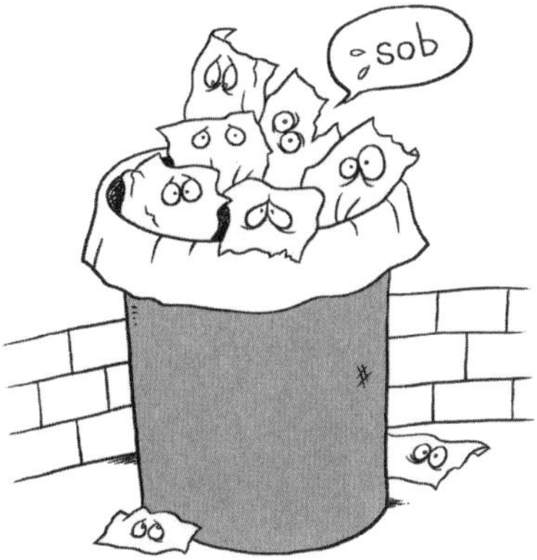
sob

I feel the same way about other things: hobbies, books, stuffed animals. I have a small bunch that I love and stay loyal to. But, other than family, my close friends are the most important thing to me.

I have one oldest friend ("old" as in longtime, not "old-old"). His name is Leo Catalino (I love how that flows!), and he lives right next door to me. We've been neighbors forever and best friends practically since we were born.

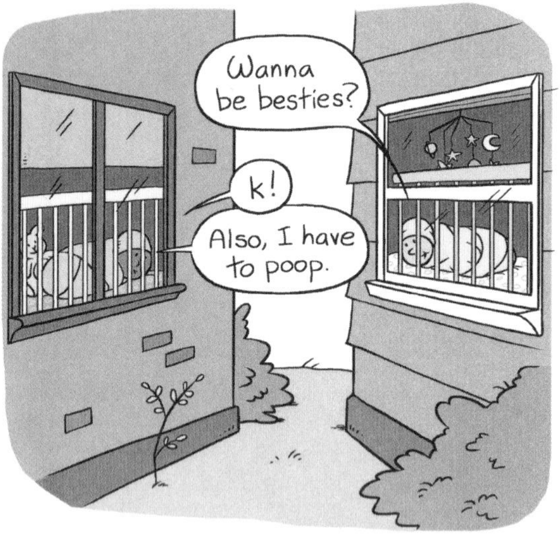
Wanna be besties?
k!
Also, I have to poop.

Leo is in seventh grade like me. He loves being outside . . . a lot. I do, too, but not as much as he does. He likes to play basketball or Hacky Sack in his driveway. I usually sit on my stoop and draw fabric patterns and clothing designs while we talk and shout to each other. Sometimes he'll take a break, sit on the steps, and eat snacks with me.

Our houses aren't big, and they're pretty old, but they do have large covered front porches. We like to hang out on mine because it's so cute and homey. My mom decorated it with plants and flowerpots, little wood chairs, a small table, and a multicolor outdoor rug. Leo and I like to play Bananagrams on the rug or sit on the steps, talk, and people watch. But the best thing?

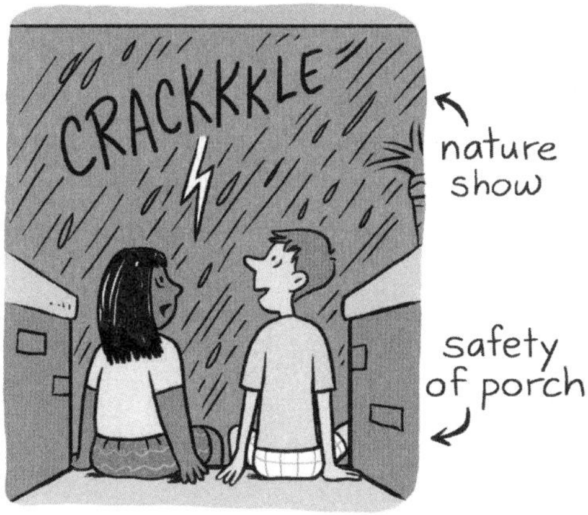
CRACKKKLE
nature show
safety of porch

My mom isn't thrilled that the porch has turned into:

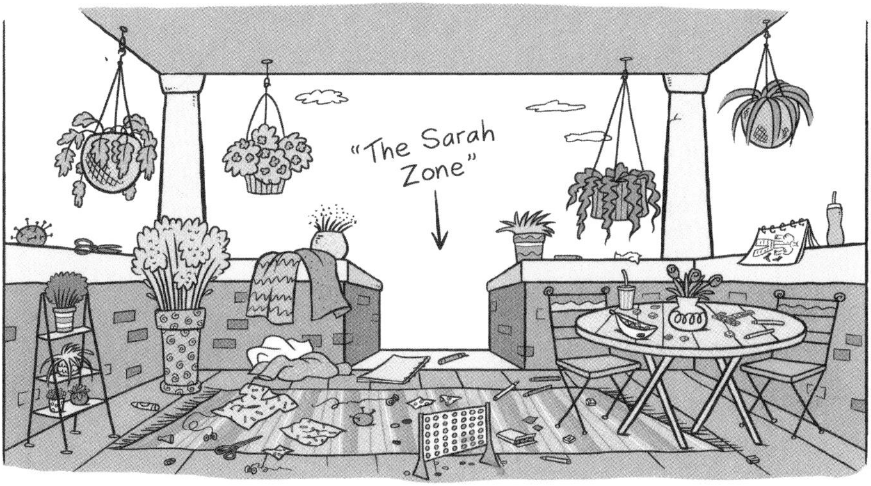
"The Sarah Zone"

But as much as she grumbles, I think she's secretly happy I use that space. Especially when Leo is around. She loves Leo.

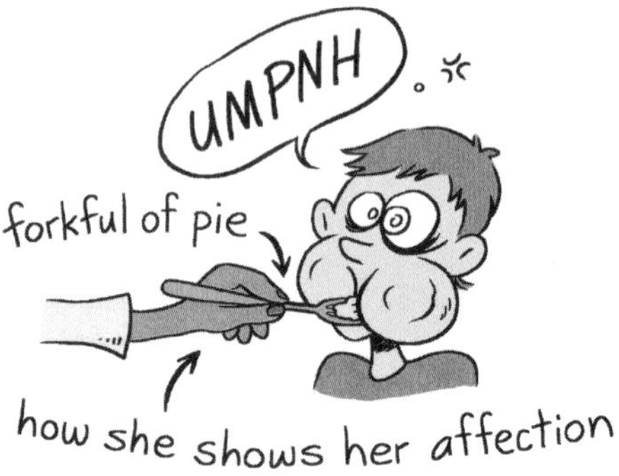
UMPNH
forkful of pie
how she shows her affection

Today, we're not on the porch because we have school. The good news is we can walk to the bus stop together. The bad news is Leo goes to a different school. So when we get to my stop, I stay there and he keeps walking. He goes to a private school, Ellings Way. (He likes to sound out its initials, "EW," which used to make me giggle.) Ellings is really big, really old, and really pretty.

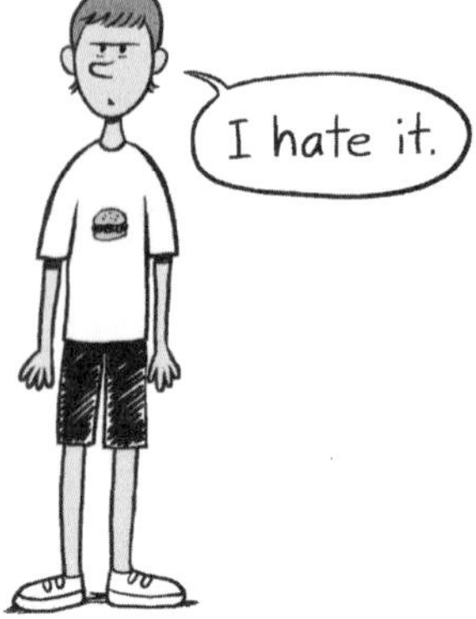
I hate it.

Leo would rather go to school at Lakefront Middle with me and some of his other elementary school friends, like Ben Friedman. But Leo's parents think EW is better and will "pave the way for college." I get it. They want the best for him. He doesn't want to disappoint them, so he feels kinda:

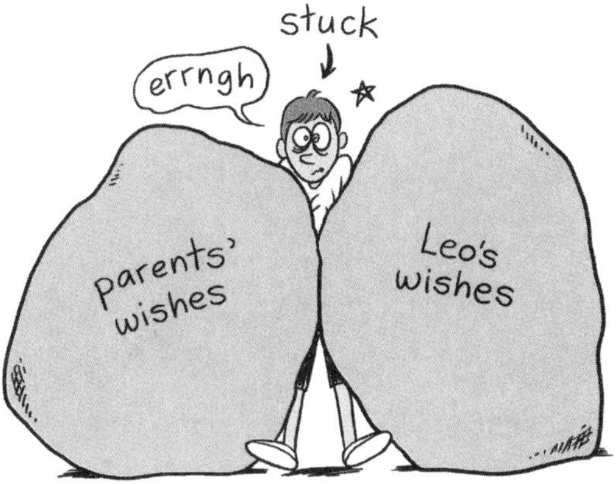
stuck
errngh
parents' wishes
Leo's wishes

It's a warm day in May, my favorite month. We're walking to my stop while eating homemade breakfast burritos (my mom made a huge batch—Leo's favorites).

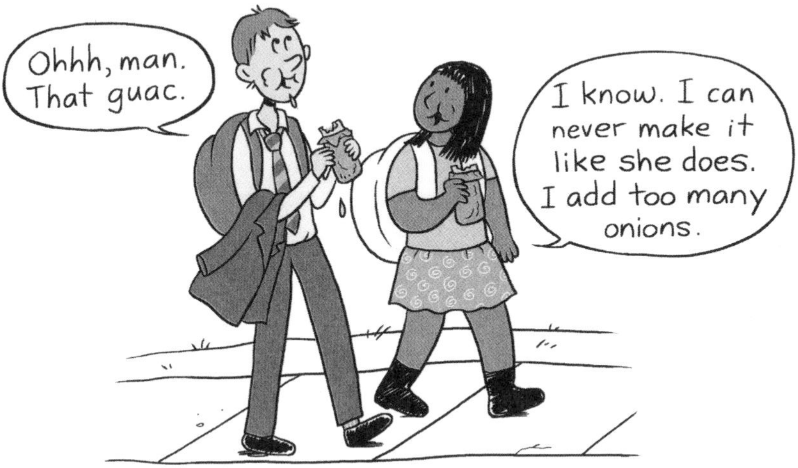
Ohhh, man. That guac.
I know. I can never make it like she does. I add too many onions.

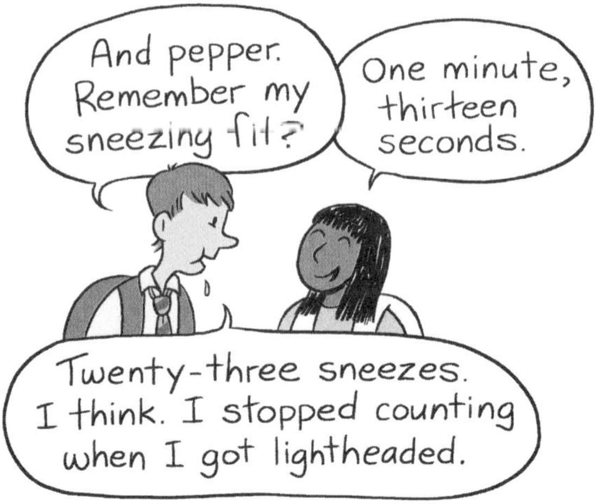
And pepper. Remember my sneezing fit?
One minute, thirteen seconds.
Twenty-three sneezes. I think. I stopped counting when I got lightheaded.

There's already a bunch of kids at the bus stop. Everyone's in shorts and tees and talking a lot. I love that it's spring. The big school dance is coming up. If there's anything I like almost as much as warm weather and designing clothes, it's dancing. I used to take hip-hop and Mexican folk until I realized I liked making my costumes more than being in recitals.

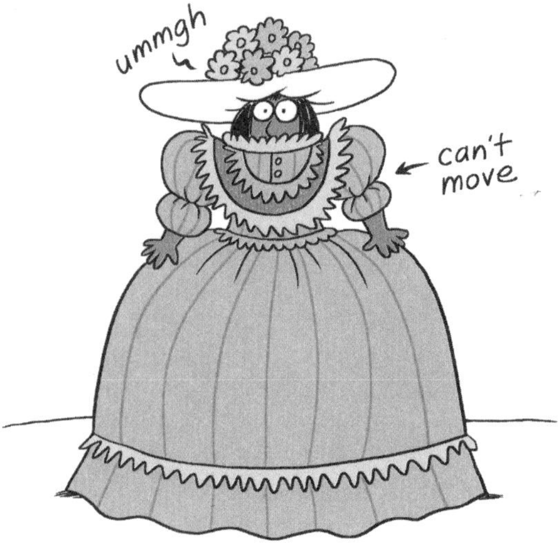
ummgh
can't move

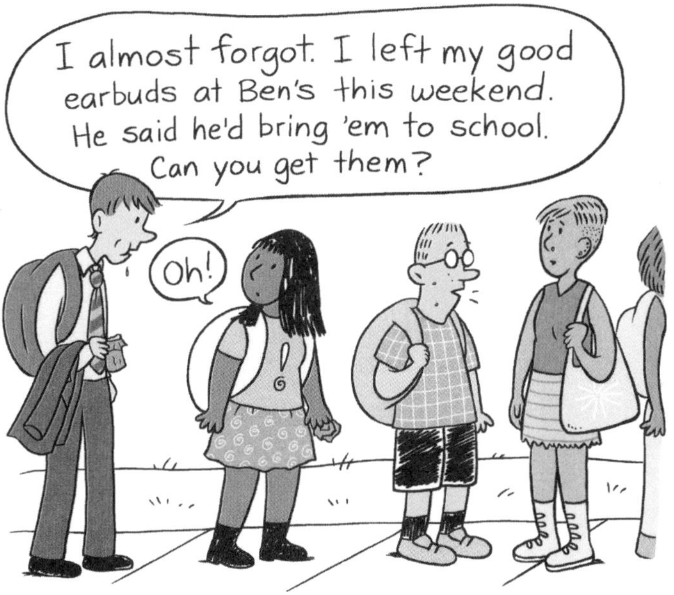
I almost forgot. I left my good earbuds at Ben's this weekend. He said he'd bring 'em to school. Can you get them?
Oh!

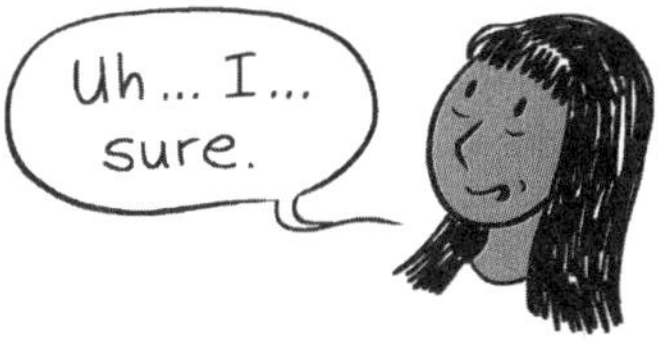
Uh... I... sure.

He gives me a weird look.

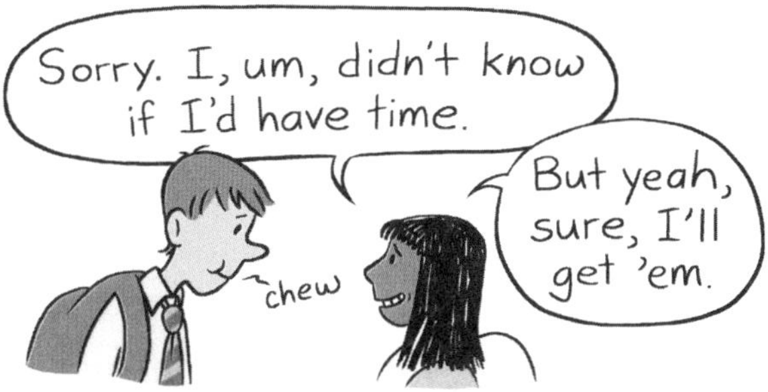
Sorry. I, um, didn't know if I'd have time.
But yeah, sure, I'll get 'em.
chew

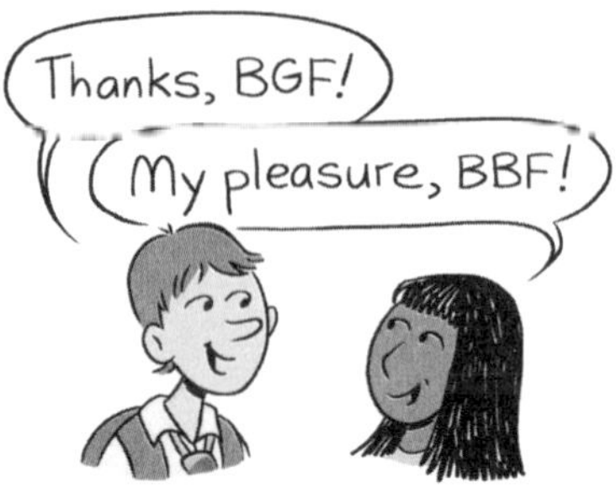
Thanks, BGF!
My pleasure, BBF!

That's what we call each other: BGF for Best Girl Friend (**not** girlfriend) and BBF for Best Boy Friend (definitely **not** boyfriend).

The bus pulls up and I get on. I wave at Leo through the window as he walks. There's guacamole on his backpack. No idea how it got **there**, but that's pretty typical.

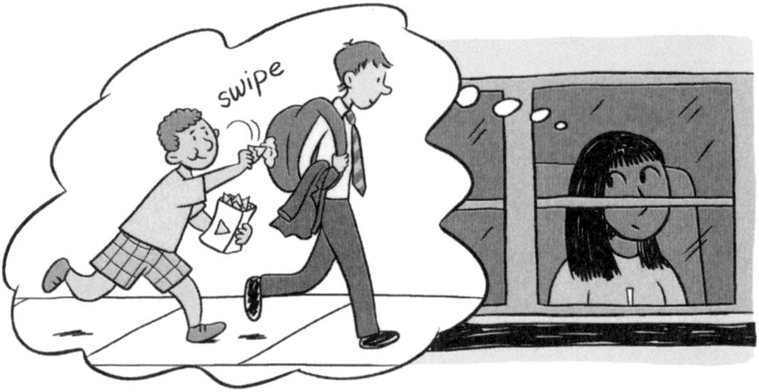
swipe

When I get to school, I see Ben right away.

Here's the thing. I have a massive crush on Ben. Every time I see him, I feel like I'm a victim of a horrible-yet-dreamy disease.

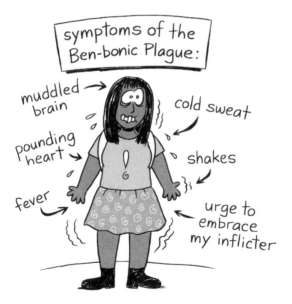

symptoms of the Ben-bonic Plague:

muddled brain

cold sweat

pounding heart

shakes

fever

urge to embrace my inflicter

I didn't always feel this way. But about a year ago, some

seismic shift took place in my heart and now here we are.

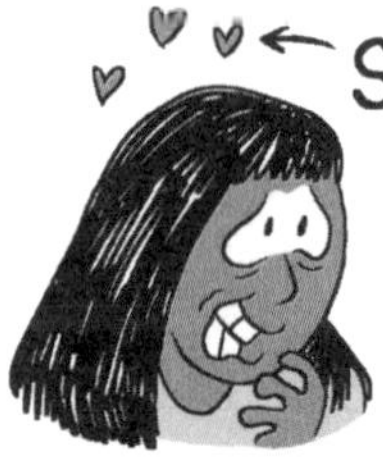
Smitten Sarah*

*alternative title to this book

I take a deep breath and walk over.

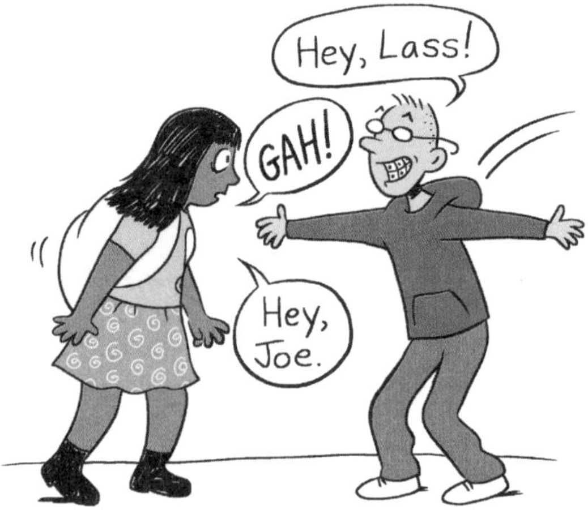
Hey, Lass!
GAH!
Hey, Joe.

Joe Lungo and I have weirdly become almost . . . well, I wouldn't say **friends** or anything. But definitely friendlier. Ever since the Student Showcase. That was a great night. I won the comics contest and then we went to Taystee's in a big group and had so much fun.

Ever since then, Joe says hi to me in the halls and calls me

"Lass" (his nickname because of a jumper I wear, which looks like a kilt). But he actually treats me like a human being now instead of teasing me or acting out.

I think it's because I treat him like a human being, too. I guess that's the solution. I should tell the others.

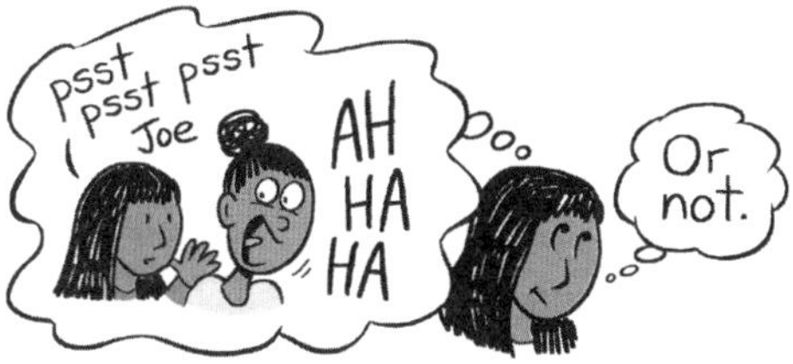
psst psst psst
Joe
AH HA HA
Or not.

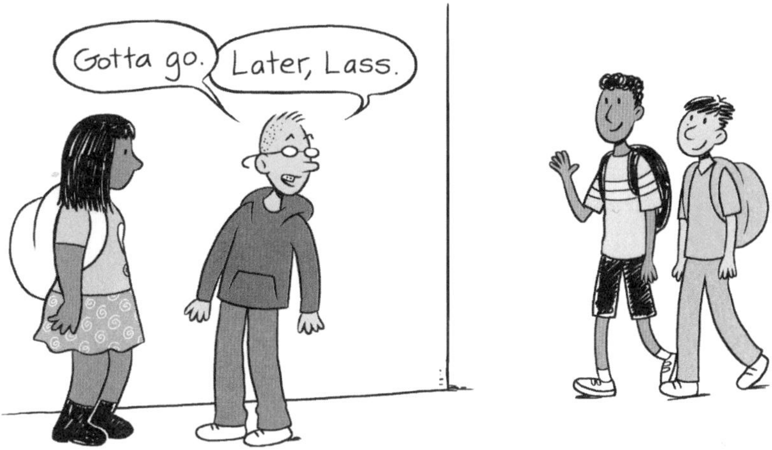
Gotta go.
Later, Lass.

He jigs away.

I try to clear my head. I take another deep breath (my friend Emmie's mom calls this a "cleansing breath deep from your root chakra") and start walking slowly toward Ben. I'm both relieved and terrified that he's still there. And still alone.

Before I can think, he slams his locker door shut and I jump.

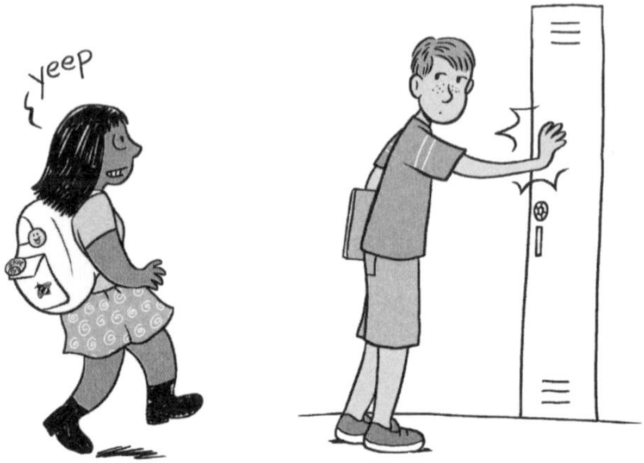
yeep

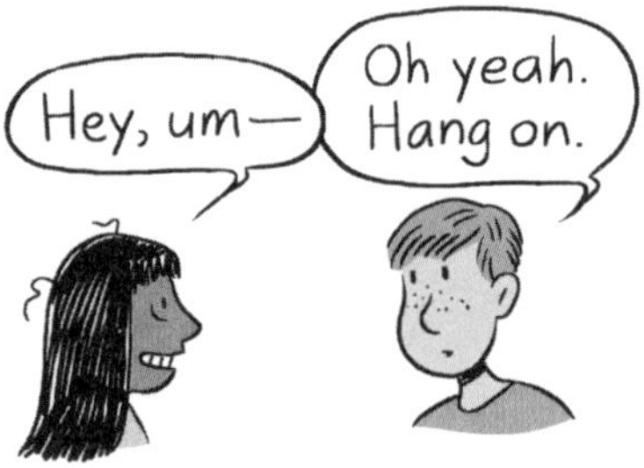
Hey, um—
Oh yeah. Hang on.

He opens his locker again and pulls out something from the top shelf. His gym shoes fly out. They just miss his head. He hands me a small black earbud case with a fuzzy—and peeling—burger emoji sticker. Leo loves burgers.

Ben quickly bends down to pick up his stinky-looking shoes while I stand there. My hands are getting sweaty, and my feet feel like cinder blocks. I can't move.

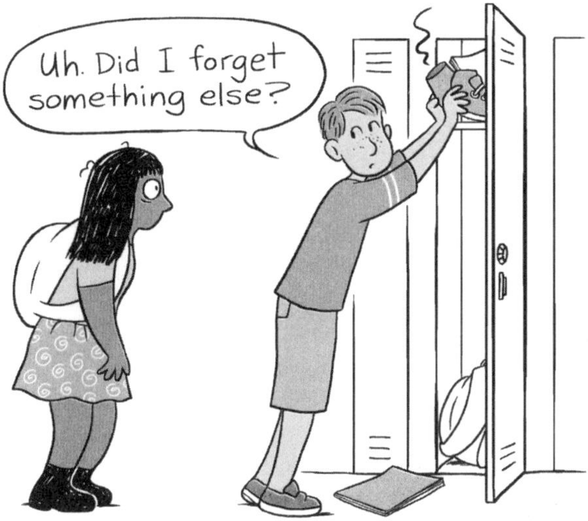
Uh. Did I forget something else?

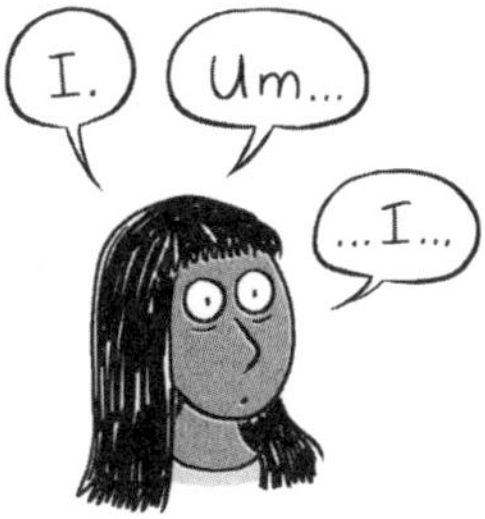
I.
Um...
...I...

My hands are all shaky and clammy. Does he notice? OMG, I should've worn a cotton shirt, not this nylon one. I'm sweating right through it. And I did such a bad job stitching the hem. What was I thinking . . . ?

Okay, never mind that.

I take one last deep, shaky breath.

And then . . .

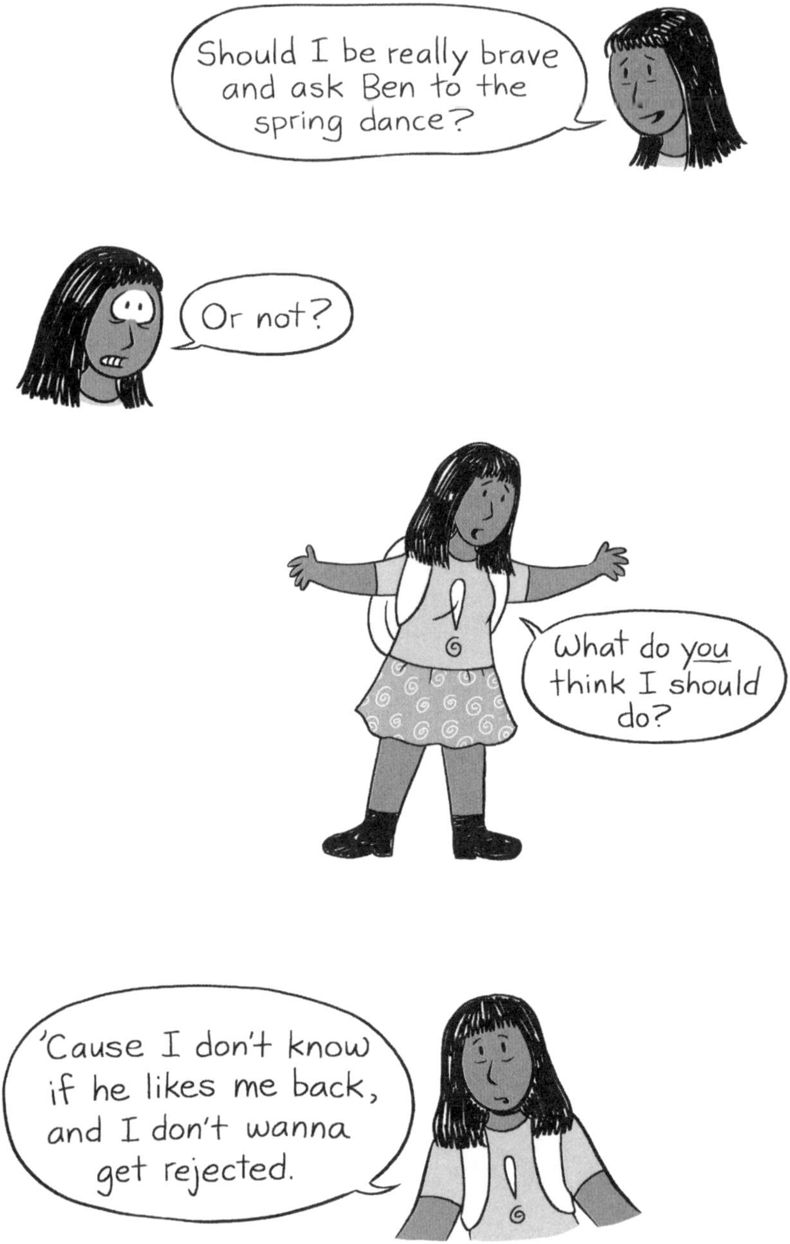
Should I be really brave and ask Ben to the spring dance?
Or not?
What do you think I should do?
'Cause I don't know if he likes me back, and I don't wanna get rejected.

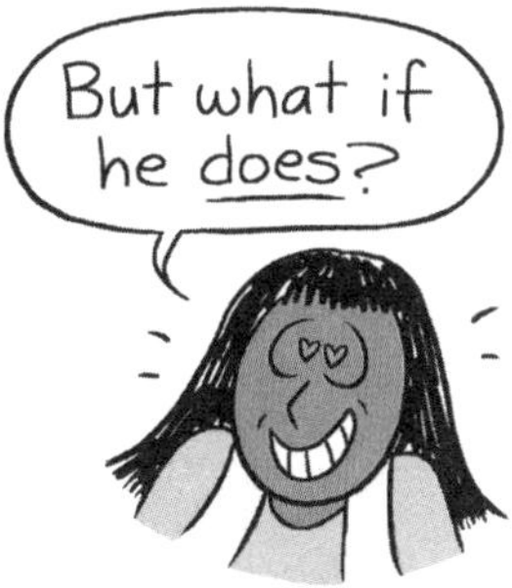
But what if he does?

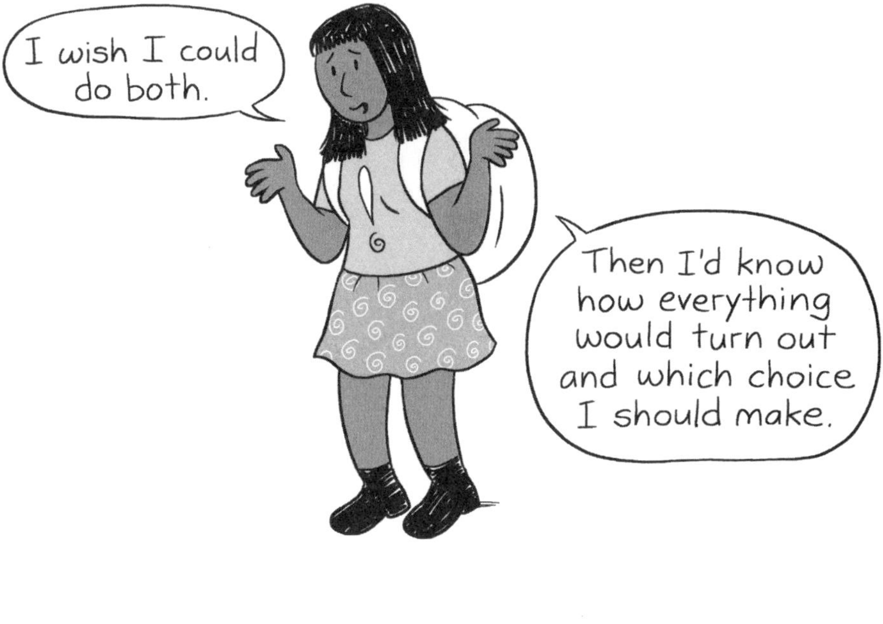
I wish I could do both.
Then I'd know how everything would turn out and which choice I should make.

SARAH

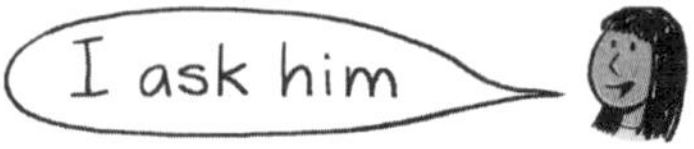
I ask him

I take one last deep, shaky breath.

And then . . .

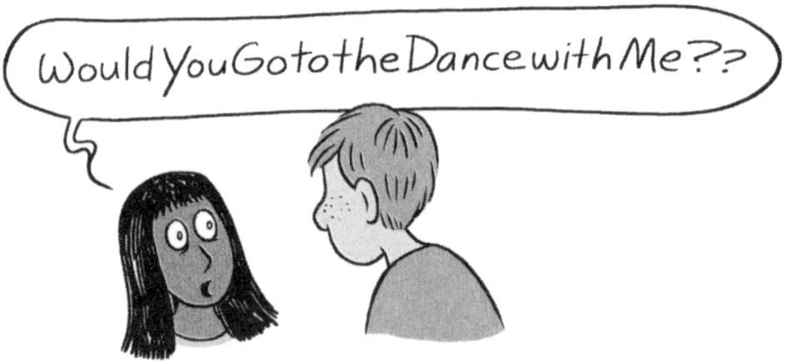
WouldYouGototheDancewithMe??

Ben looks like I hit him in the head with a bag of rubber chickens. (I once saw that in a cartoon and the character had the same expression.)

He turns bright red and quickly looks toward his left, down the hall. It's not that crowded yet. Then he looks at his feet. Converses. Or maybe the fake ones.

Meanwhile . . .

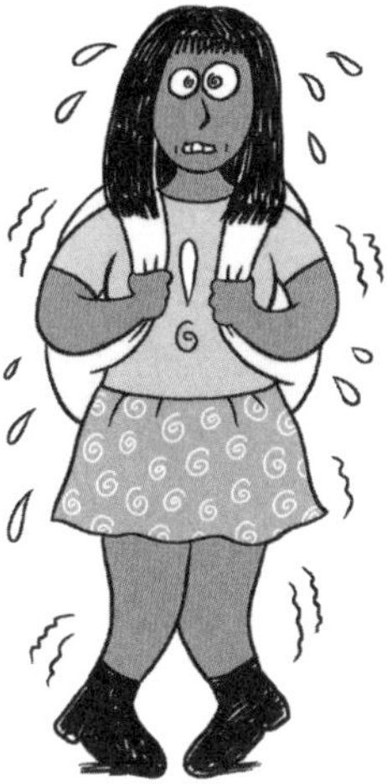

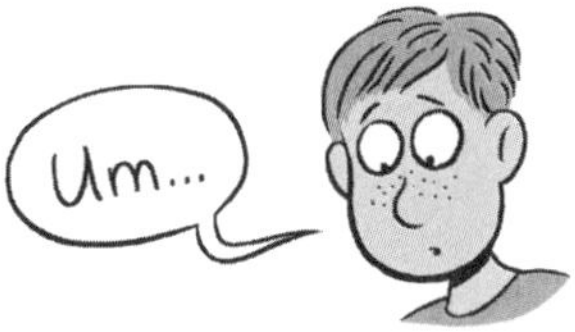
Um...

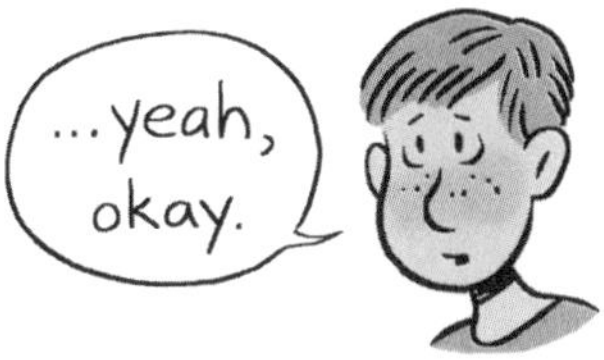
...yeah, okay.

I exhale. I realize I was holding my breath for a long time. It comes out in one long

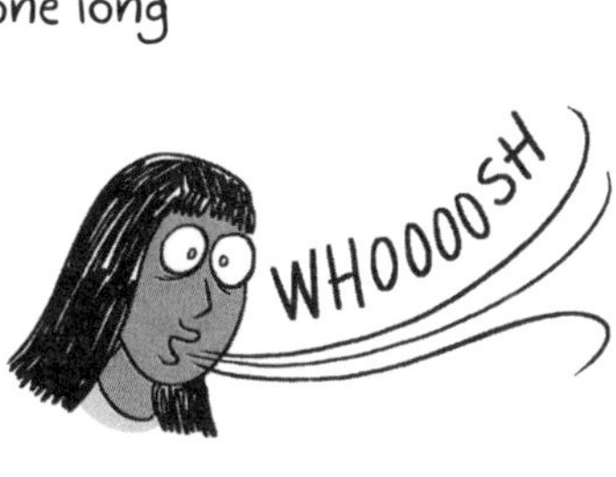
WHOOOOSH

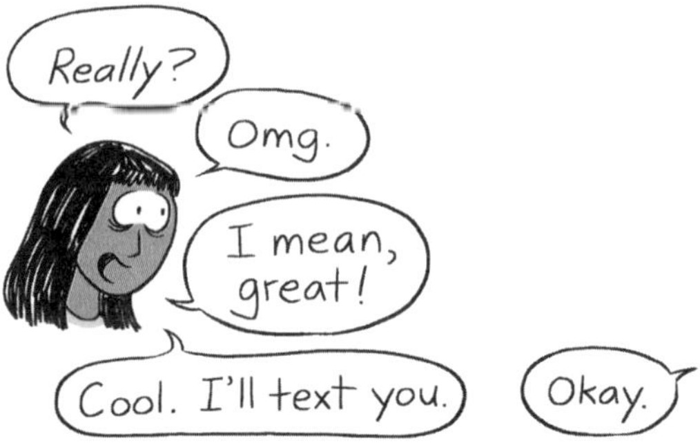
Really?
Omg.
I mean, great!
Cool. I'll text you.
Okay.

I rush away, smiling and waving. He waves back.

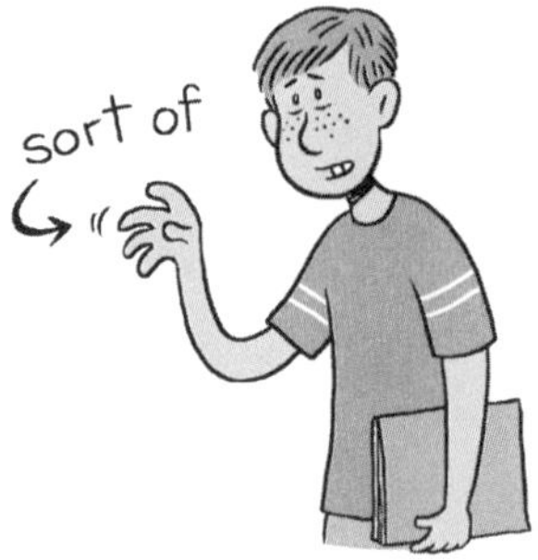
sort of

I try and keep it together until I round the corner. Then I see Emmie and Brianna.

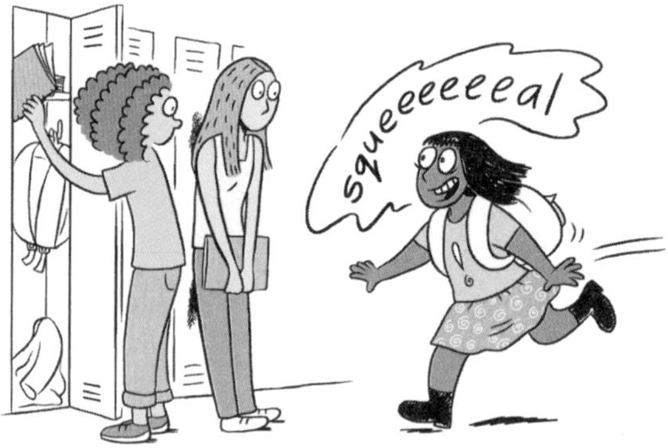
squeeeeeeeal

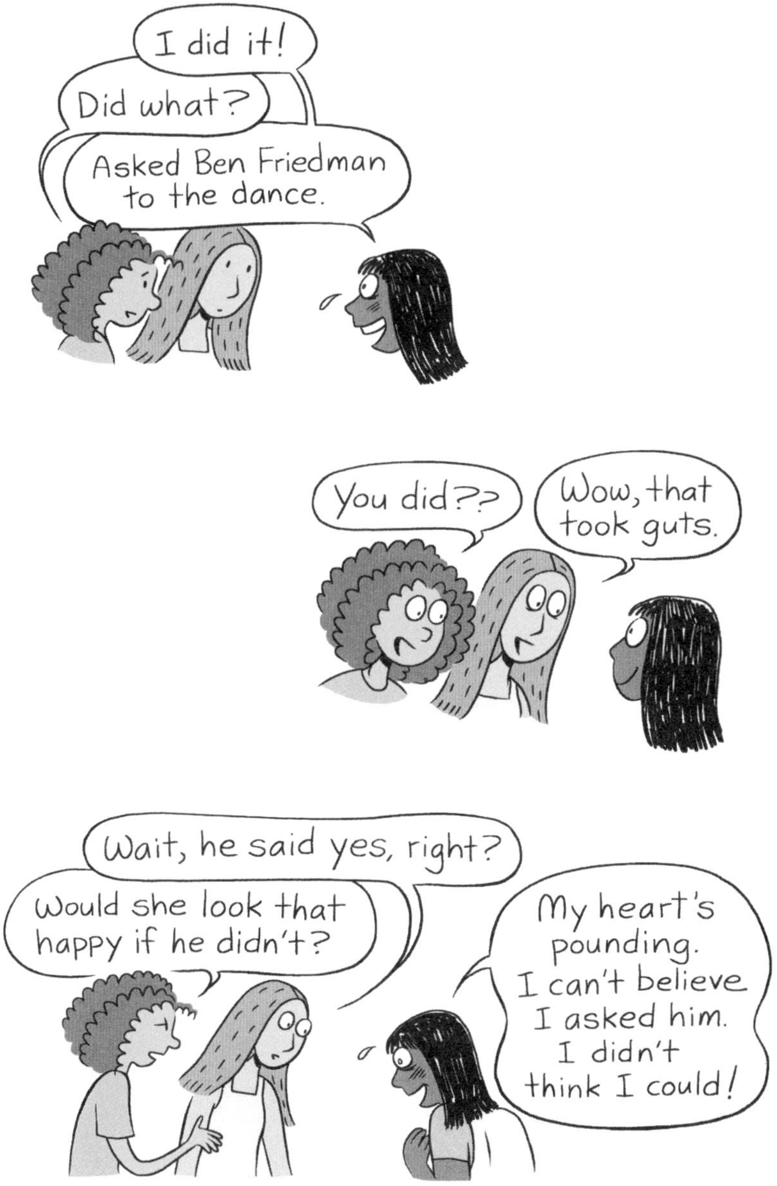
I did it!
Did what?
Asked Ben Friedman to the dance.
You did??
Wow, that took guts.
Wait, he said yes, right?
Would she look that happy if he didn't?
My heart's pounding. I can't believe I asked him. I didn't think I could!

We all squeal loudly until I see Ben and his friends head down the hall.

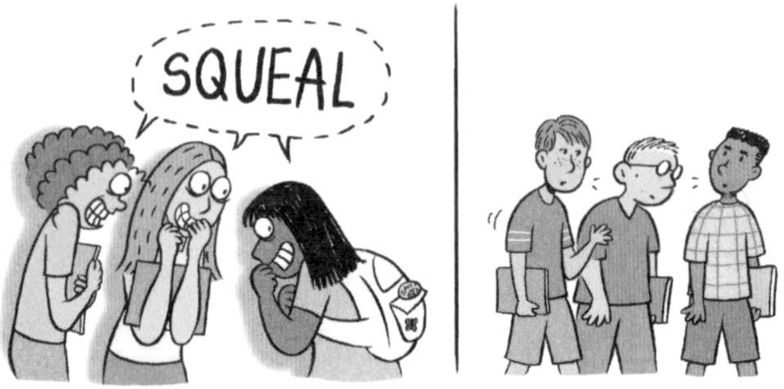
SQUEAL

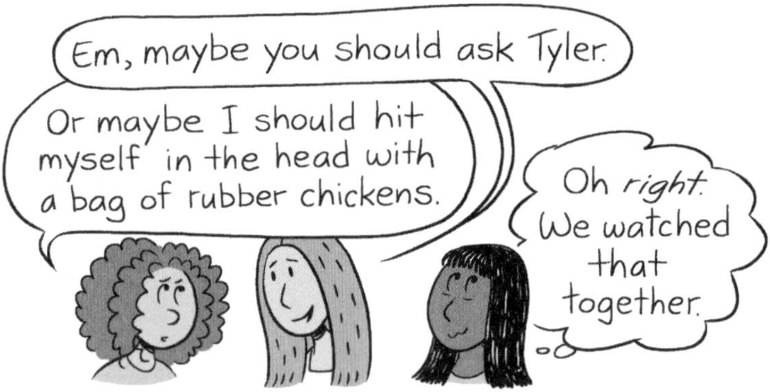
Em, maybe you should ask Tyler.
Or maybe I should hit myself in the head with a bag of rubber chickens.
Oh *right.* We watched that together.

I'm squeezing Bri's arm in excitement without realizing it. She clears her throat, and I let go. I forgot she's not the touchy-feely type. I'm the total opposite, but I'm really trying to respect boundaries. We learned all about that in Health. Mr. Bauman also taught us about consent. It was kinda eye-opening for a girl who likes to express herself by squeezing arms, grabbing hands, and giving atomic hugs. Emmie's shyer than me (like with a capital S), but she doesn't mind.

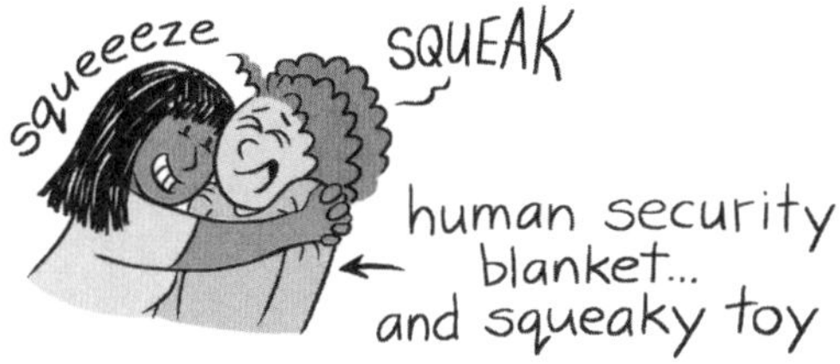
squeeeeze
SQUEAK
human security blanket...
and squeaky toy

Leo's like me. Everyone thinks we're boyfriend and girlfriend because we're always hugging and holding hands, but it's just how we are. We're family.

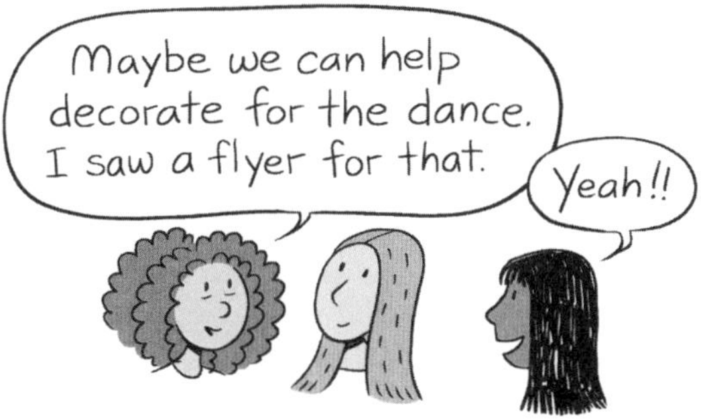
Maybe we can help decorate for the dance. I saw a flyer for that.
Yeah!!

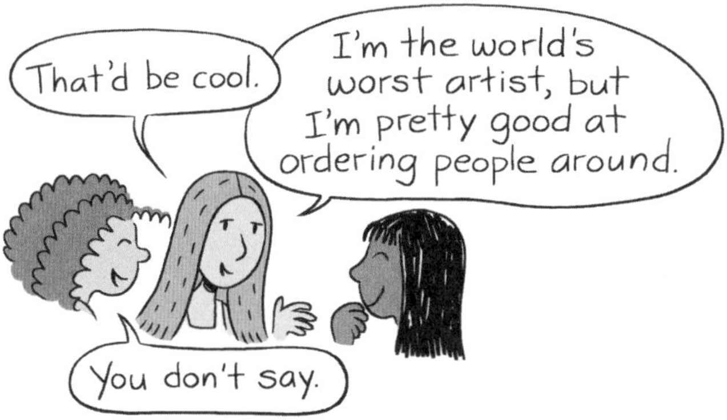
That'd be cool.
I'm the world's worst artist, but I'm pretty good at ordering people around.
You don't say.

We all walk to our homerooms together. I feel like the luckiest girl alive. I've got my best friend, Leo. And in the past few months, I've gotten really close with Em and Bri (although it took a while for Bri to warm up to me). And they are the most loyal friends ever. And now I'm going to the dance with Ben Friedman, the boy I've crushed on for a year!

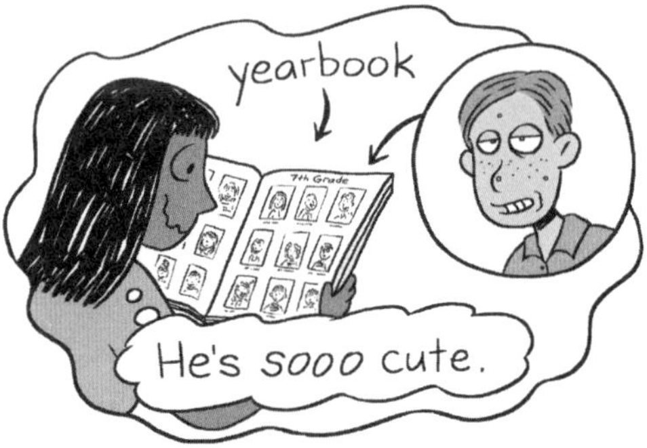
yearbook
7th Grade
He's *sooo* cute.

Only . . .

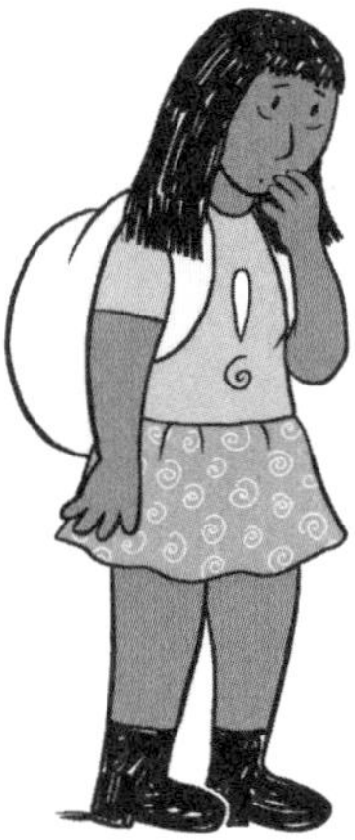

Leo knows nothing about my crush. At least I don't think so. I've never told him. And I have no idea how he'd react to my taking Ben—one of his closest friends—to the dance.

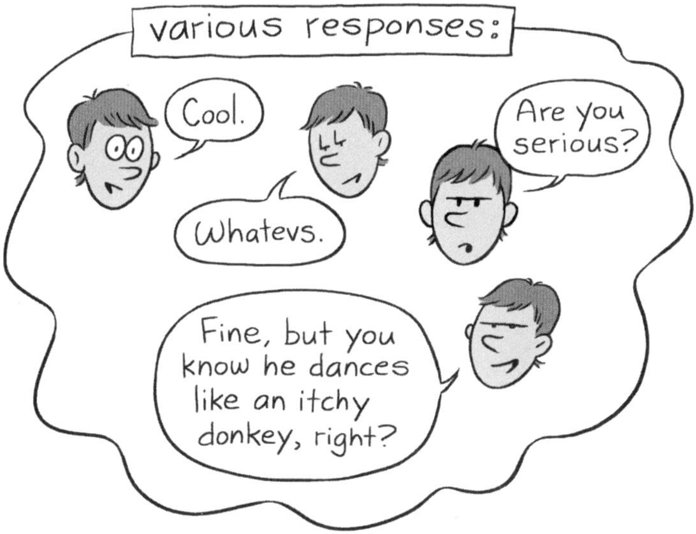
various responses:
Cool.
Whatevs.
Are you serious?
Fine, but you know he dances like an itchy donkey, right?

We all used to go to elementary school together. Me, Leo, and Ben. I never really talked much to Ben, though. I was scared of all boys except for Leo. I know that seems weird, but it's true.

I was raised only around women. My mom, of course. But I've also grown up with my aunt, Tía Elena, who's single, and my abuela (grandma). They live close by. My parents divorced when I was little. My dad lives in California, and I rarely see him. We talk only about once a year.

Leo's dads are really nice. They're probably the best examples I have of what fathers are like. They sometimes treat Leo and me to ice cream on weekends. But they work full-time, so I don't see a lot of them.

And as for Leo, he's more like a brother than a guy. So, yeah, I'm not exactly smooth around boys.

the time
I lost all my
vowels

H! Ygyz
plyng bskbll?

I glide through the day in a great mood. I haven't seen Ben since this morning, but that's okay. I'm still floating from his answer.

After the bus drops me off, I walk home alone. My mom is already in the house, cooking up a storm. That's her passion. She makes the best food in the world. She also shares my love of clothes. She helps me with my patterns and designs. Together, we make the most amazing outfits.

fashion model vibes

Mamá works two jobs: her main one is as an executive assistant. But she also has a "side hustle" as a pastry chef. She makes desserts at home and delivers the orders by car—aka "Julia the Jalopy" (her oldish-but-reliable Toyota).

← old car

Mamá Maricel's Sweets 2 Go

new sign

We don't have a lot of money, but we don't really need much. My abuela gave us her house after my abuelo died (before I was born). It's roomy enough for two, and other than repairs (which my mom can do, too!), it's all paid for.

"M" for "Marvelous," "aMazing," and "Masterful" Mamá (NEVER "Mean" or "Malicious")

My aunt and abuela live in a newer, one-story house nearby. Tía Elena is some kind of scientist (Mamá says she does research), and she takes care of my grandma, who can't work at all since she has really bad arthritis. I love visiting them. Tía Elena has a huge backyard screen for movies and a built-in firepit. In the warm months, we sit in her yard, watch movies together under blankets, and toast marshmallows. Leo joins us all the time. We like to chase fireflies around the yard, which makes my abuela laugh.

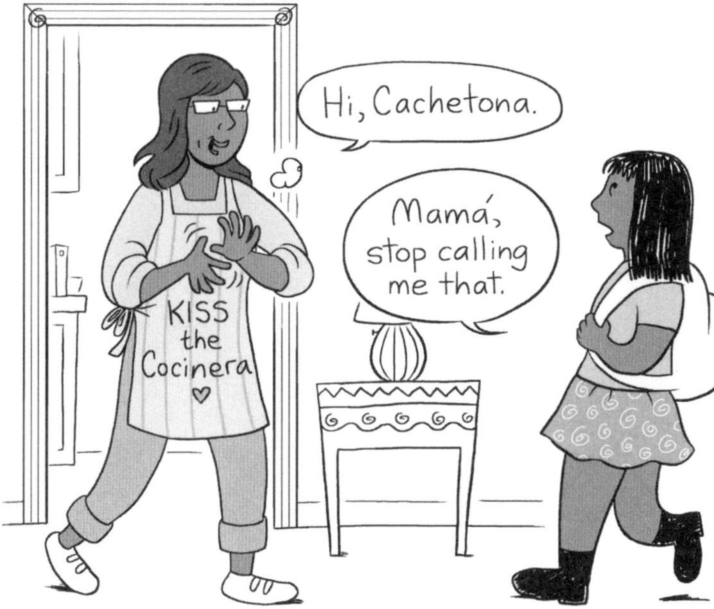
Hi, Cachetona.
Mamá, stop calling me that.
KISS the Cocinera

"Cachetona" means "chubby cheeked" in Spanish. When I was little, women used to grab my cheeks between their fingers and pinch **hard**. I'm scarred for life.

They're still kinda chubby. But I don't want to be reminded.

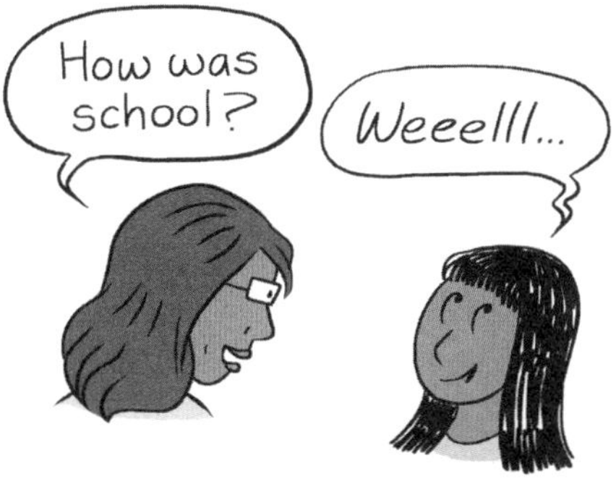
How was school?
Weeelll...

I tell her about Ben, and she squeals, too.

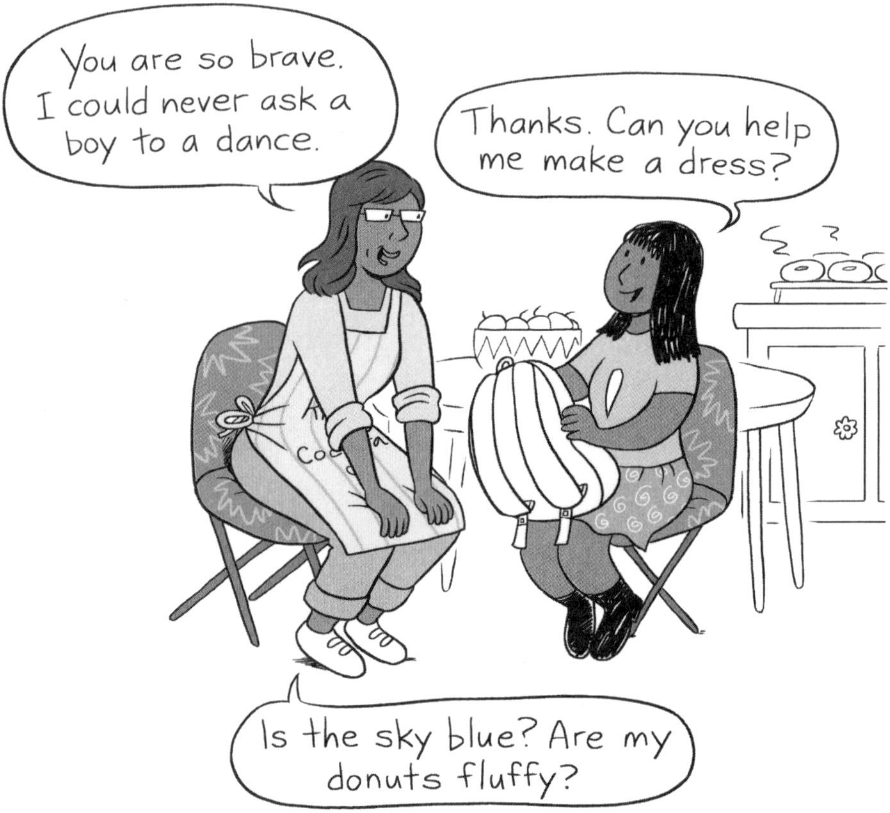

You are so brave. I could never ask a boy to a dance.
Thanks. Can you help me make a dress?
Is the sky blue? Are my donuts fluffy?

They are. I grab one.

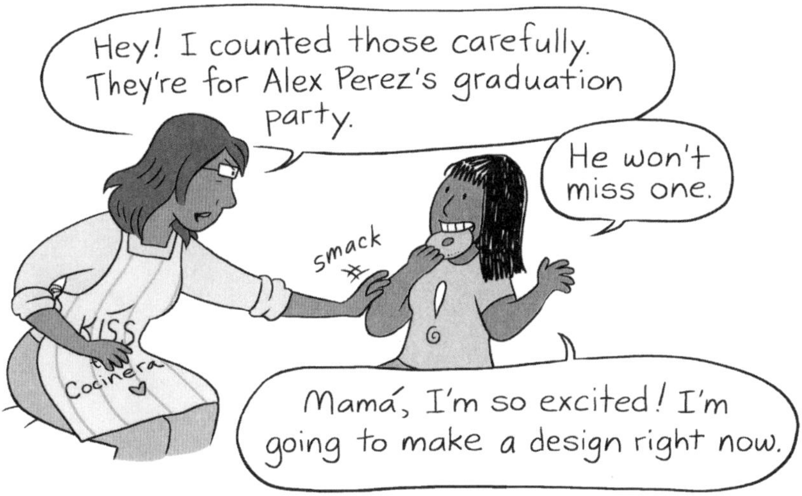
Hey! I counted those carefully. They're for Alex Perez's graduation party.
He won't miss one.
smack
KISS
Cocinera
Mamá, I'm so excited! I'm going to make a design right now.

She laughs while I run out the front door and grab my sketchbook and colored pencils off the porch table. I sit on the stoop and start drawing right away. I love it. I'm in art class and art club with Emmie and Tyler Ross. We all like to draw different things, though.

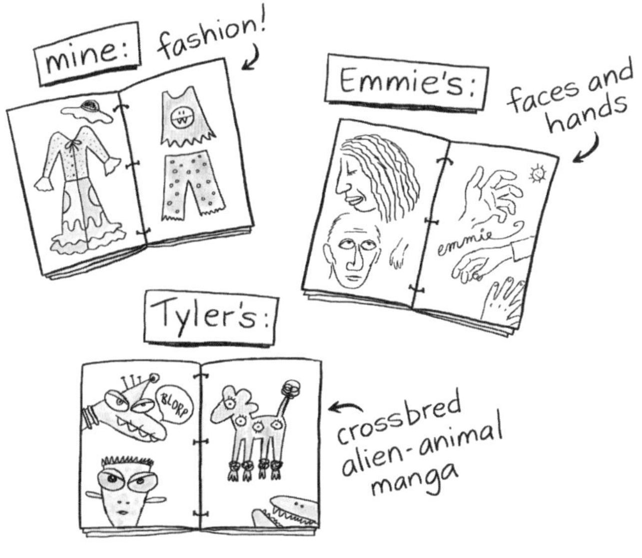
mine:
fashion!
Emmie's:
faces and hands
emmie
Tyler's:
BLORP
crossbred alien-animal manga

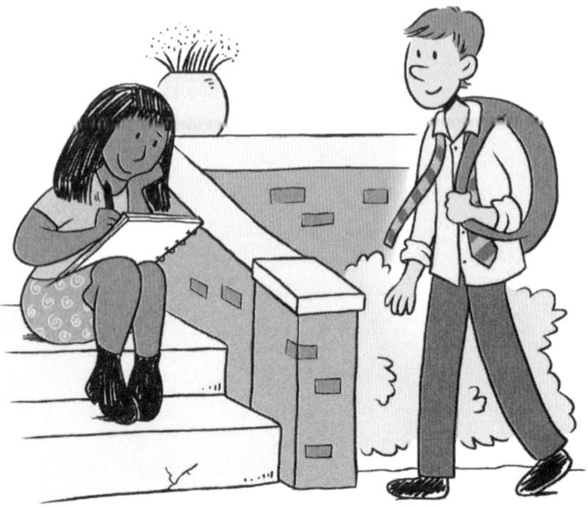

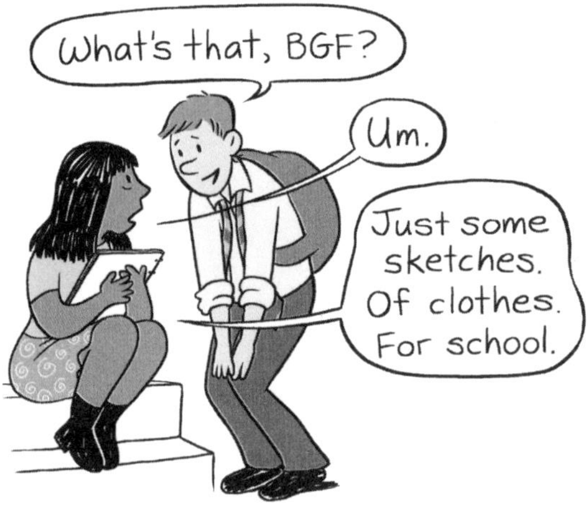
What's that, BGF?
Um.
Just some sketches. Of clothes. For school.

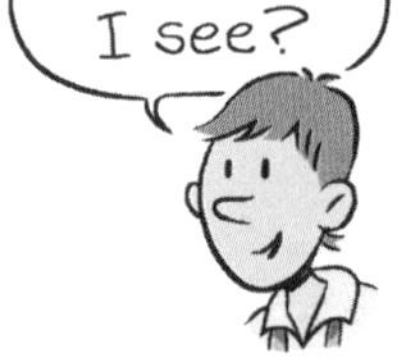
Cool. Can I see?

Reluctantly, I lower the sketchbook. There are a few small drawings of brightly colored, swingy dresses ("skater dresses"). I love the ones that swish around.

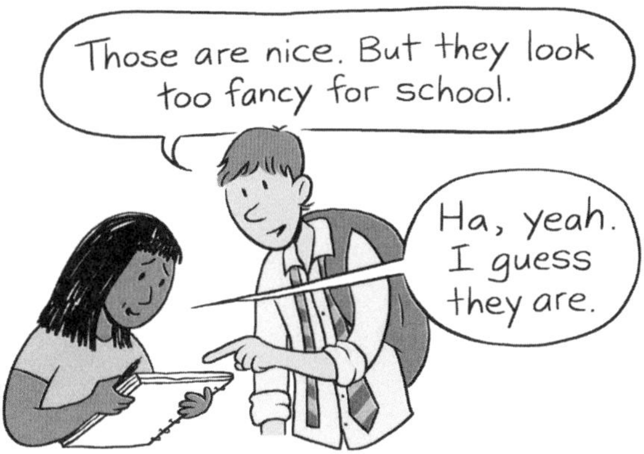
Those are nice. But they look too fancy for school.
Ha, yeah. I guess they are.

I put my sketchbook down.

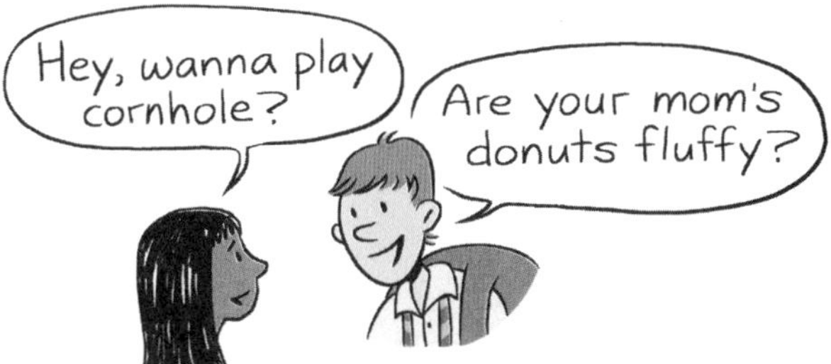
Hey, wanna play cornhole?
Are your mom's donuts fluffy?

He runs into his house to change and put away his backpack. I remember his earbuds and go inside to get them. Leo comes out in shorts and a striped T-shirt, with a big bag of chips tucked under his arm. We head through the rickety fence to his backyard and grab the little red and blue beanbags. Soon, we're playing the game, chomping on chips, and goofing around.

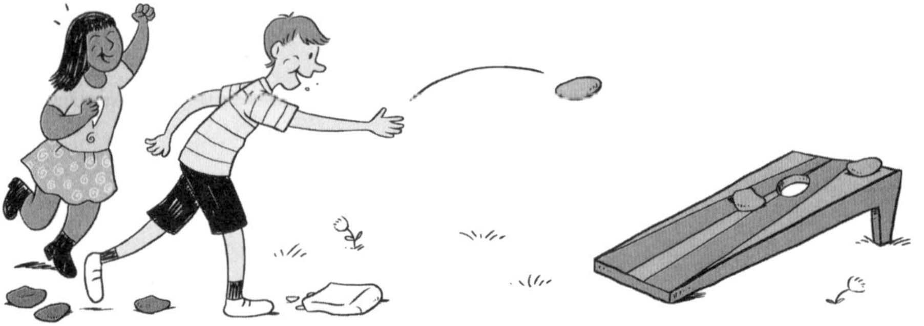

I'm glad he didn't ask me more about the dress designs. I don't know why I didn't tell him about Ben and the dance. He's gonna find out, anyway. If I don't say anything, Ben sure will.

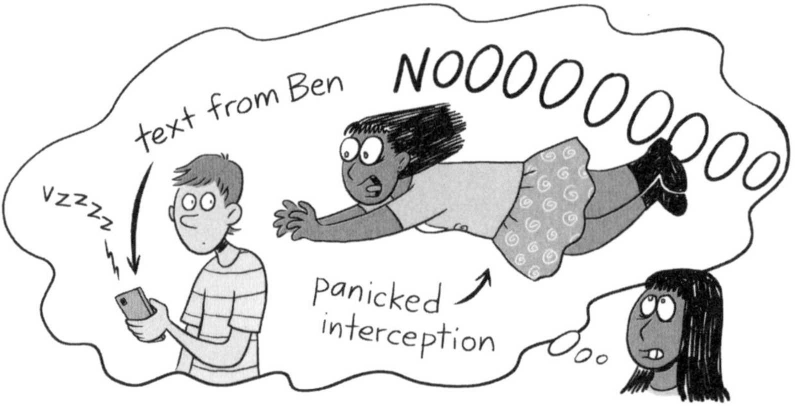
text from Ben
NOOOOOOOOOOOO
VZZZZ
panicked interception

I **will** tell him. Just not now. Not yet. But soon. Like after this game.

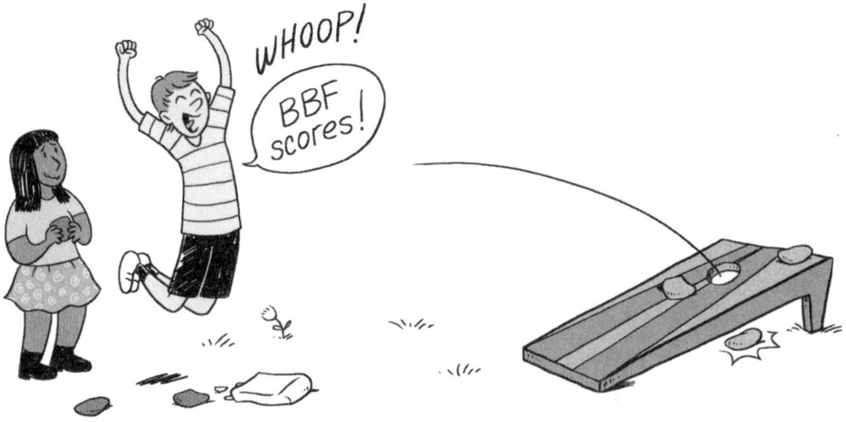
WHOOP!
BBF scores!

Or maybe tomorrow.

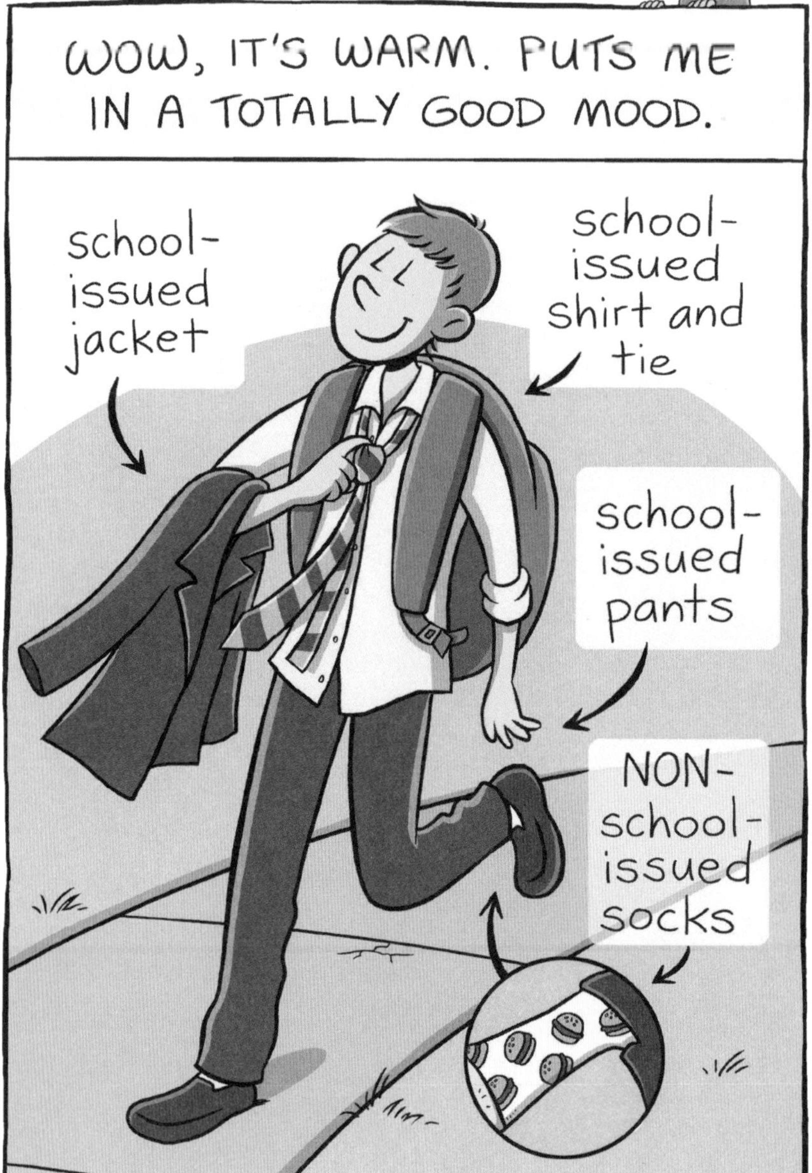
WOW, IT'S WARM. PUTS ME IN A TOTALLY GOOD MOOD.
school-issued jacket
school-issued shirt and tie
school-issued pants
NON-school-issued socks

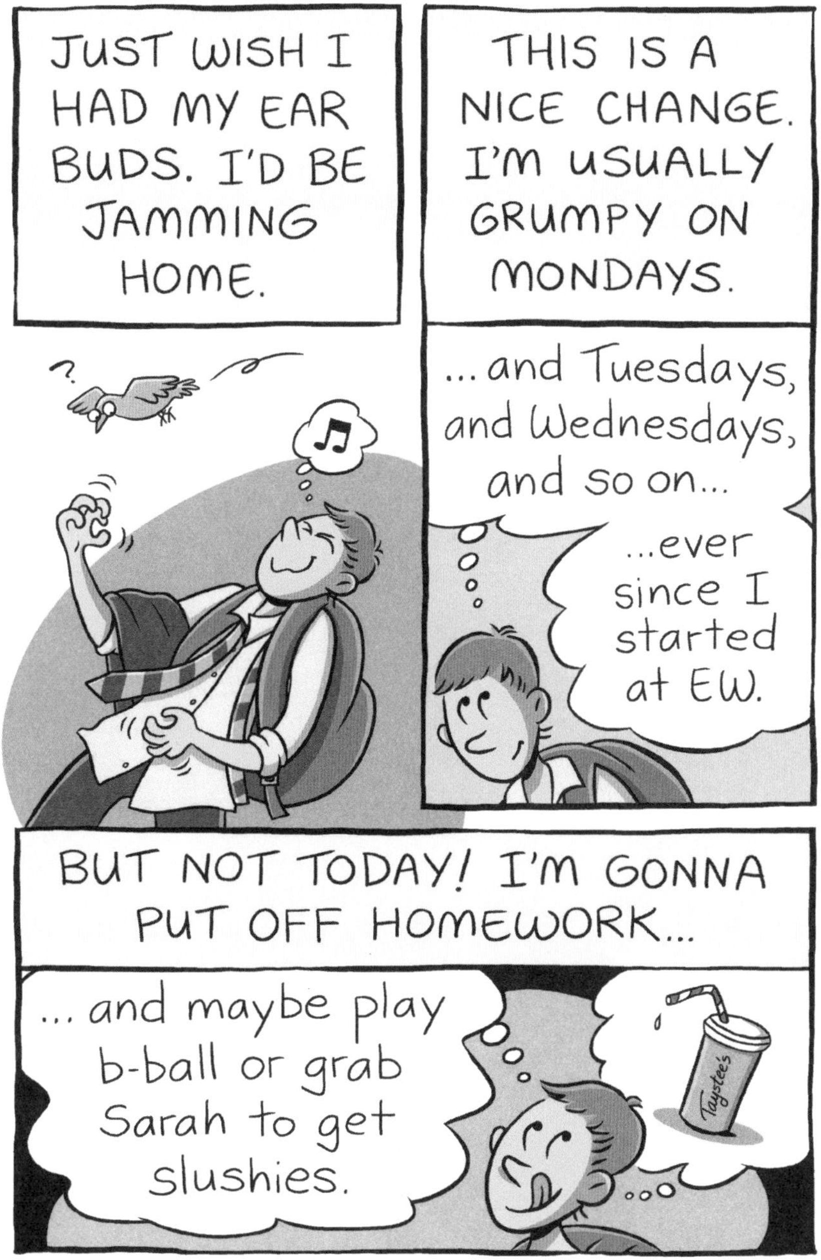
JUST WISH I HAD MY EAR BUDS. I'D BE JAMMING HOME.
THIS IS A NICE CHANGE. I'M USUALLY GRUMPY ON MONDAYS.
...and Tuesdays, and Wednesdays, and so on...
...ever since I started at EW.
BUT NOT TODAY! I'M GONNA PUT OFF HOMEWORK...
...and maybe play b-ball or grab Sarah to get slushies.
Taystee's

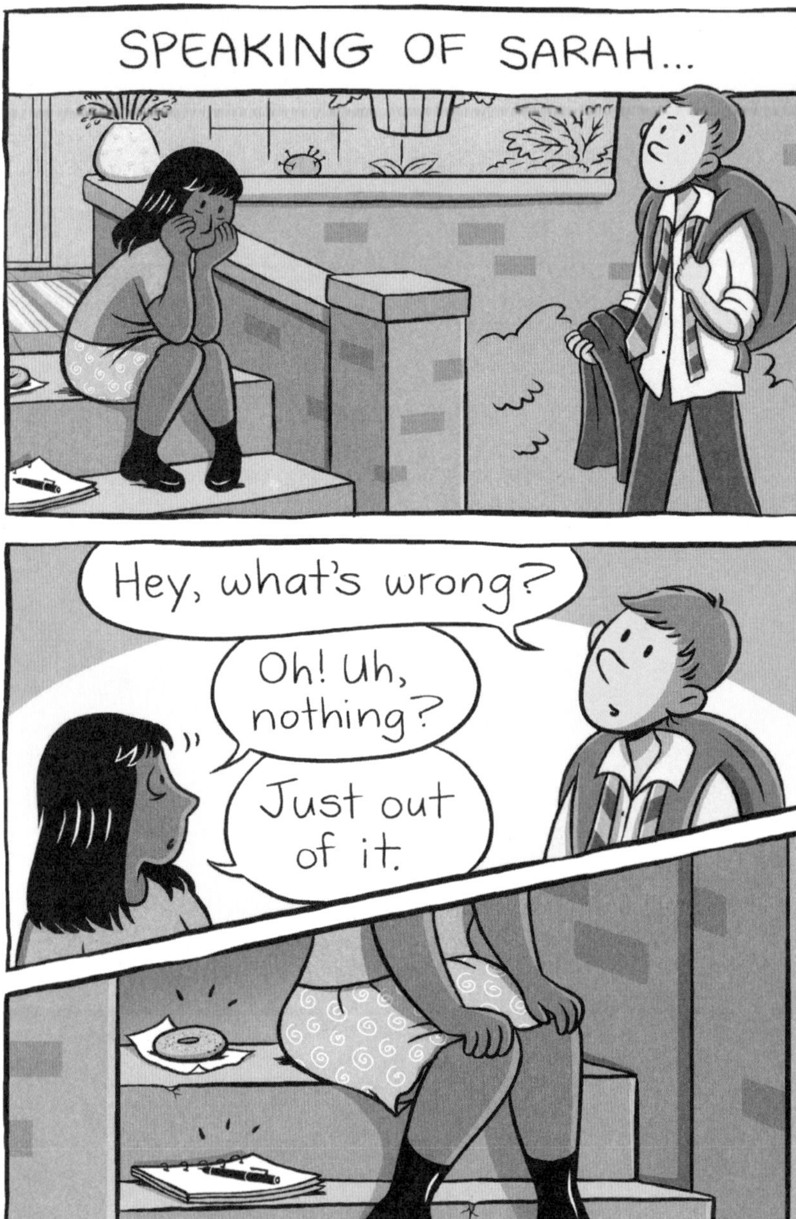
SPEAKING OF SARAH...
Hey, what's wrong?
Oh! Uh, nothing?
Just out of it.

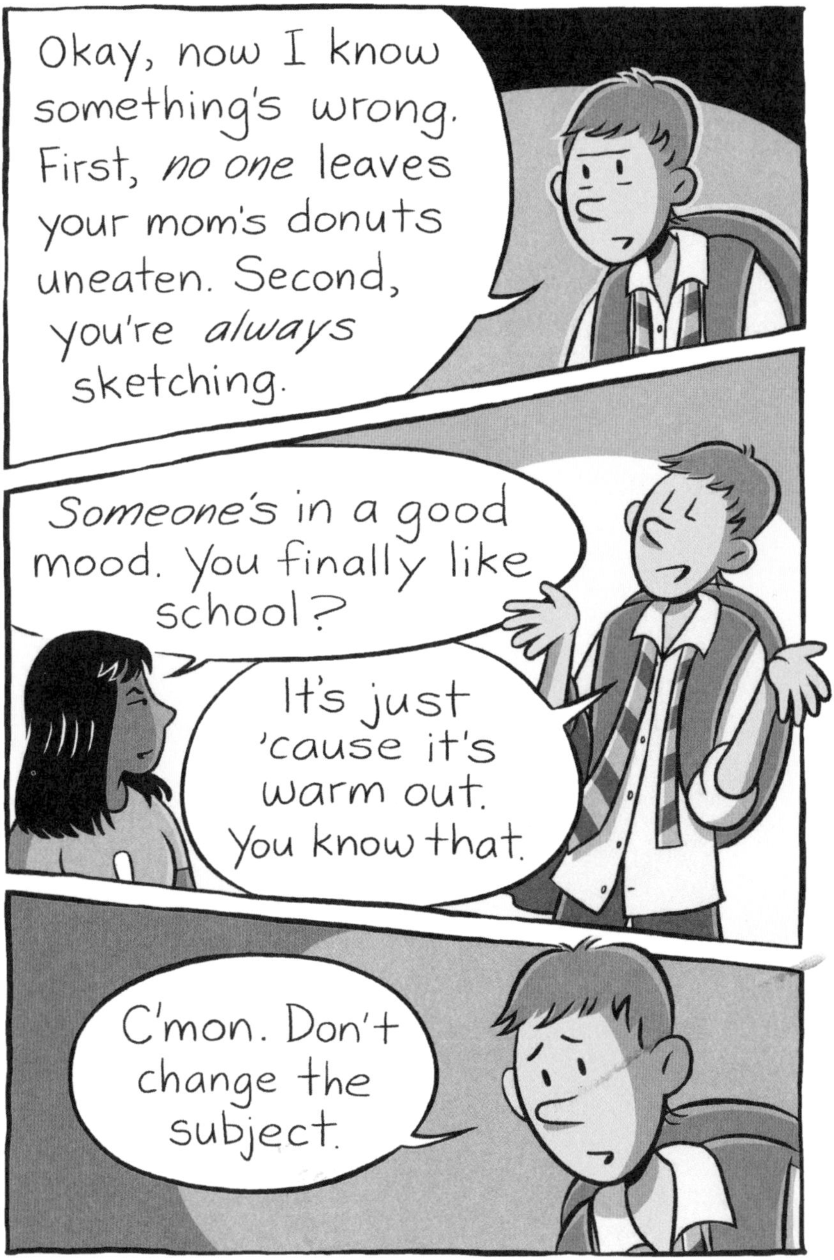
Okay, now I know something's wrong. First, *no one* leaves your mom's donuts uneaten. Second, you're *always* sketching.
Someone's in a good mood. You finally like school?
It's just 'cause it's warm out. You know that.
C'mon. Don't change the subject.

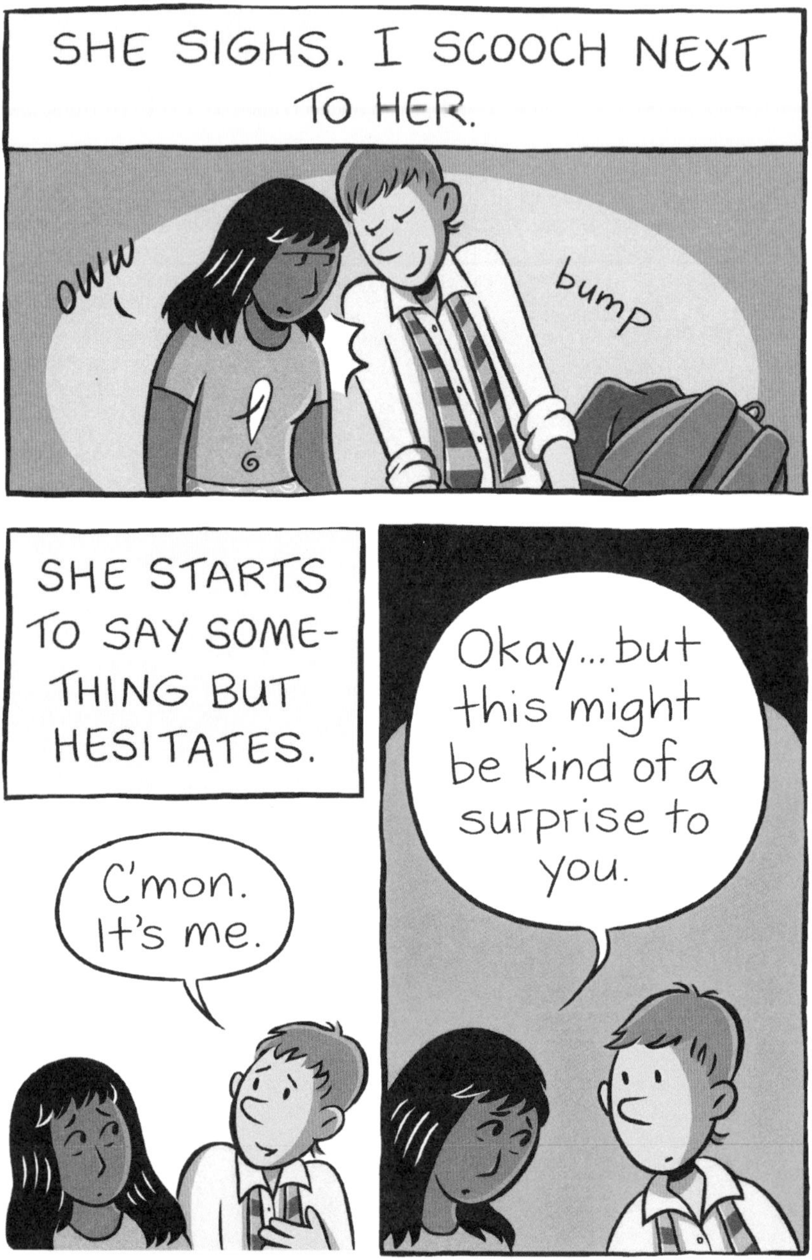

SHE SIGHS. I SCOOCH NEXT TO HER.
OWW
bump
SHE STARTS TO SAY SOMETHING BUT HESITATES.
C'mon. It's me.
Okay... but this might be kind of a surprise to you.

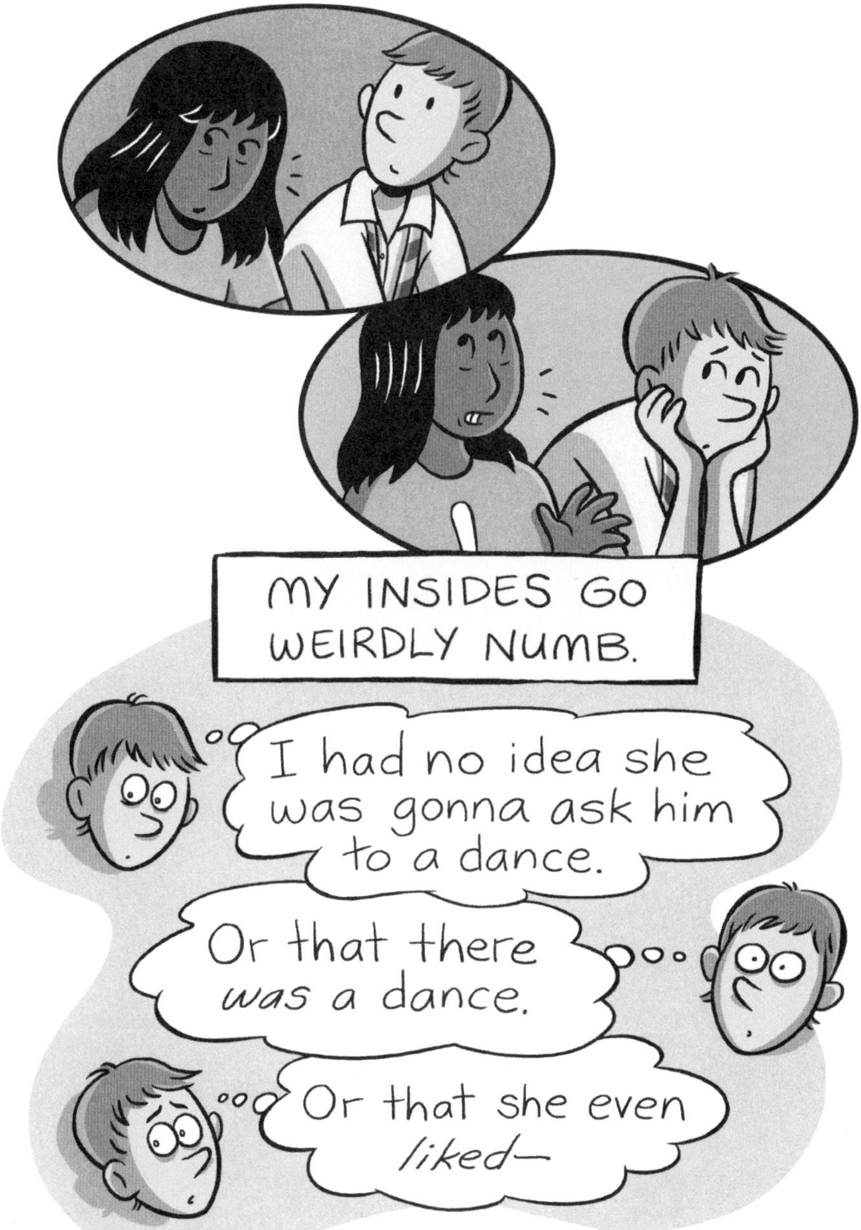
MY INSIDES GO WEIRDLY NUMB.
I had no idea she was gonna ask him to a dance.
Or that there was a dance.
Or that she even liked—

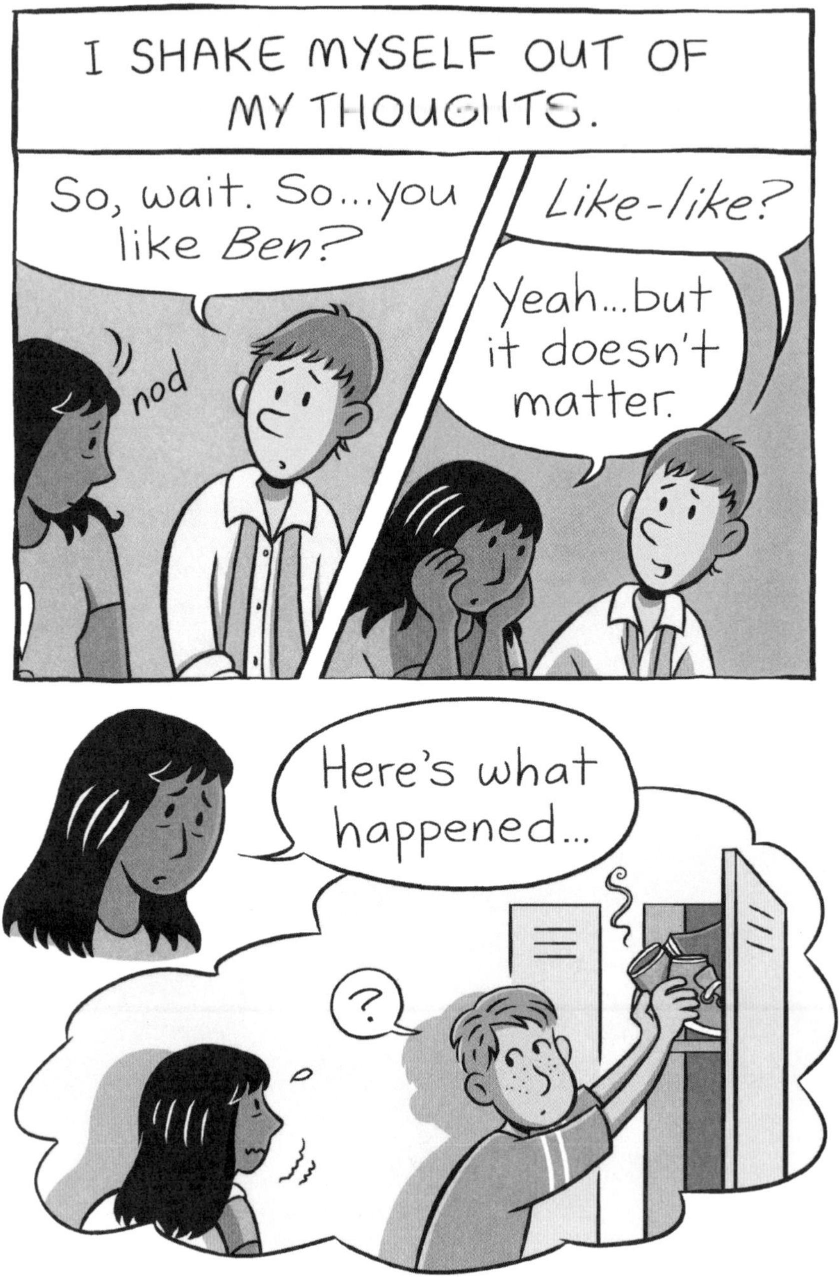
I SHAKE MYSELF OUT OF MY THOUGHTS.
So, wait. So...you like *Ben*?
nod
Like-like?
Yeah...but it doesn't matter.
Here's what happened...
?

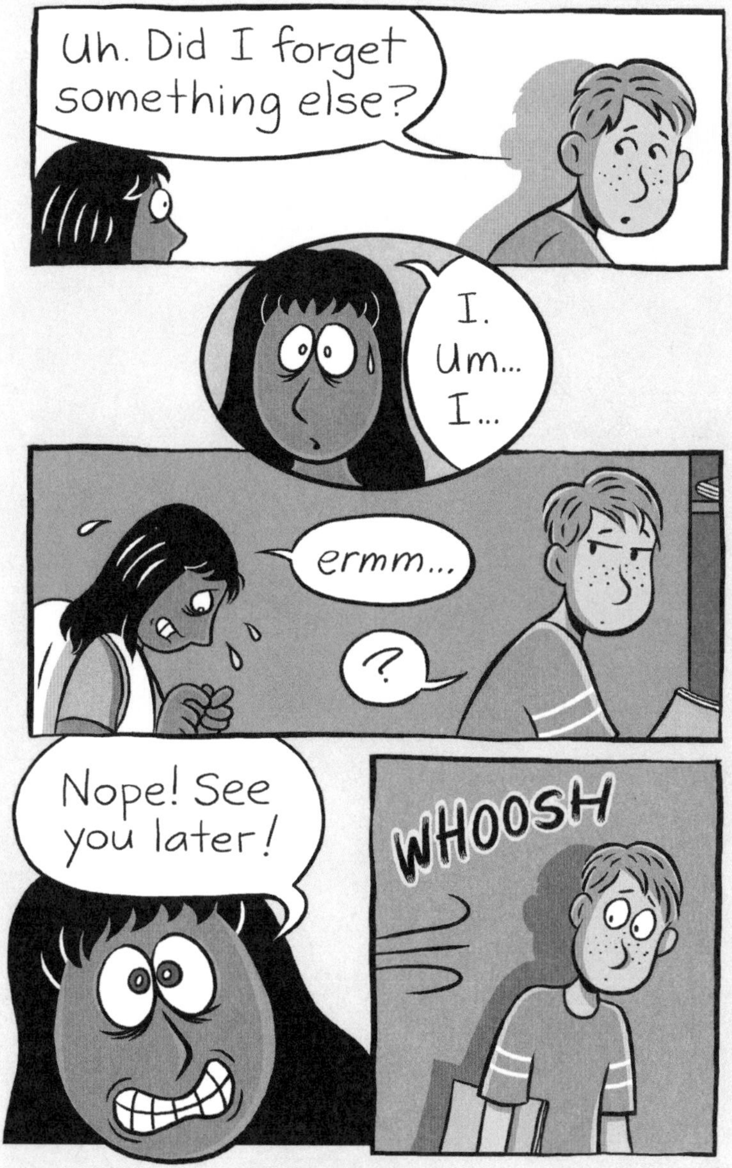

Uh. Did I forget something else?
I. Um... I...
ermm...
?
Nope! See you later!
WHOOSH

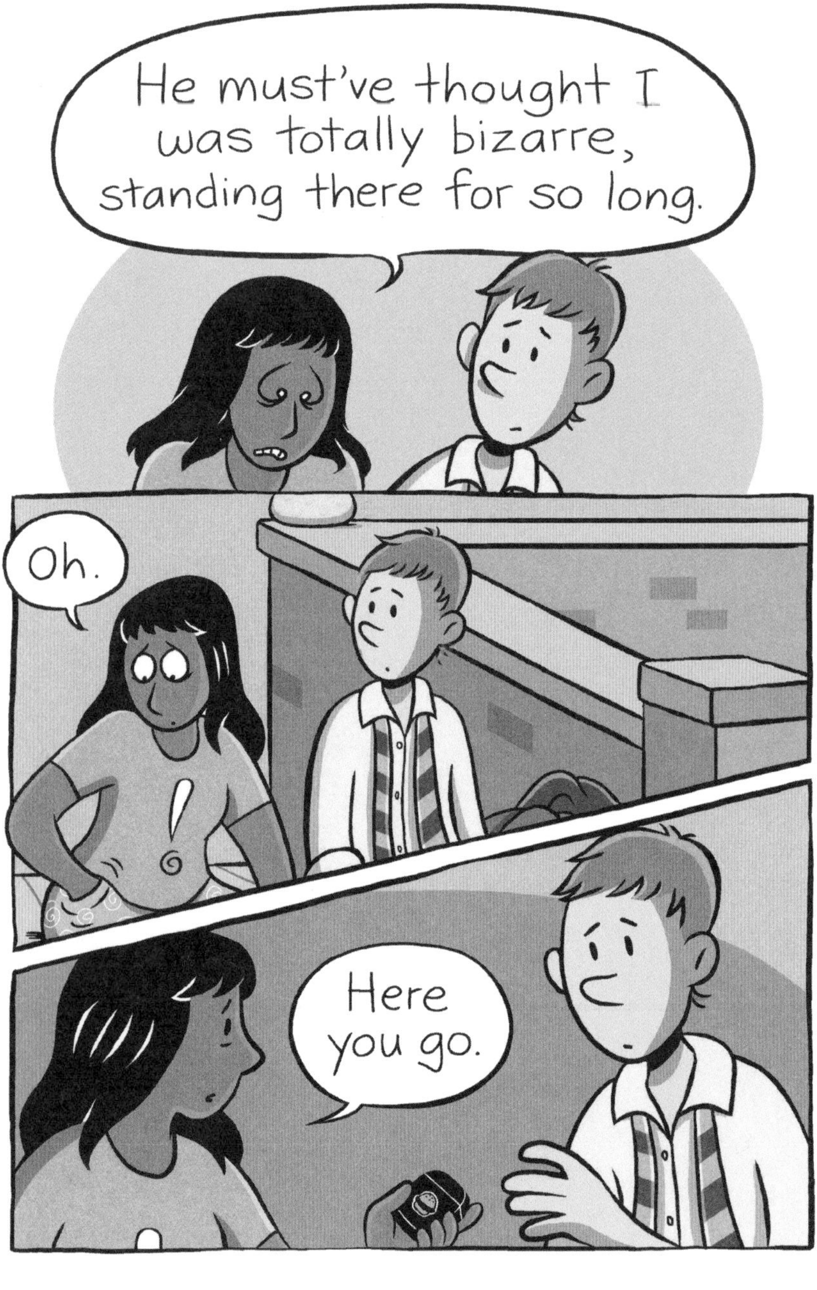
He must've thought I was totally bizarre, standing there for so long.
Oh.
Here you go.

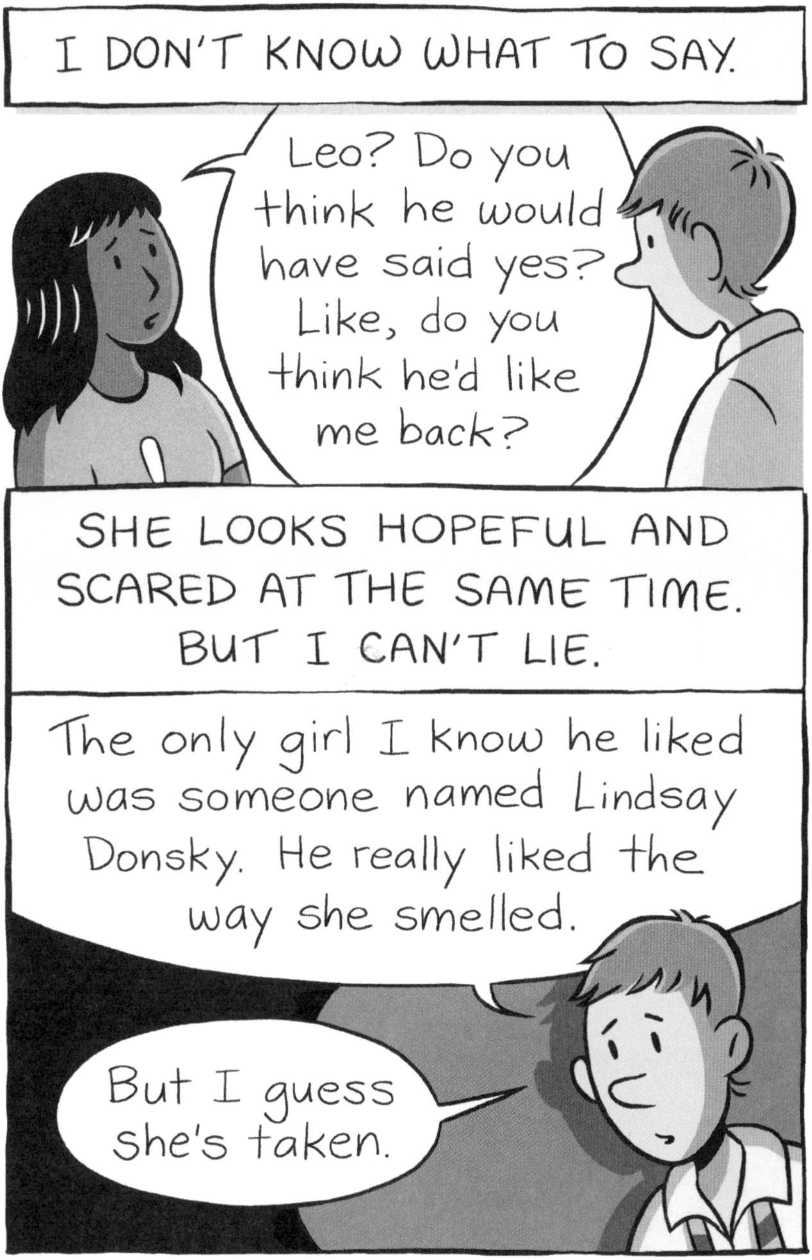
I DON'T KNOW WHAT TO SAY.
Leo? Do you think he would have said yes? Like, do you think he'd like me back?
SHE LOOKS HOPEFUL AND SCARED AT THE SAME TIME. BUT I CAN'T LIE.
The only girl I know he liked was someone named Lindsay Donsky. He really liked the way she smelled.
But I guess she's taken.

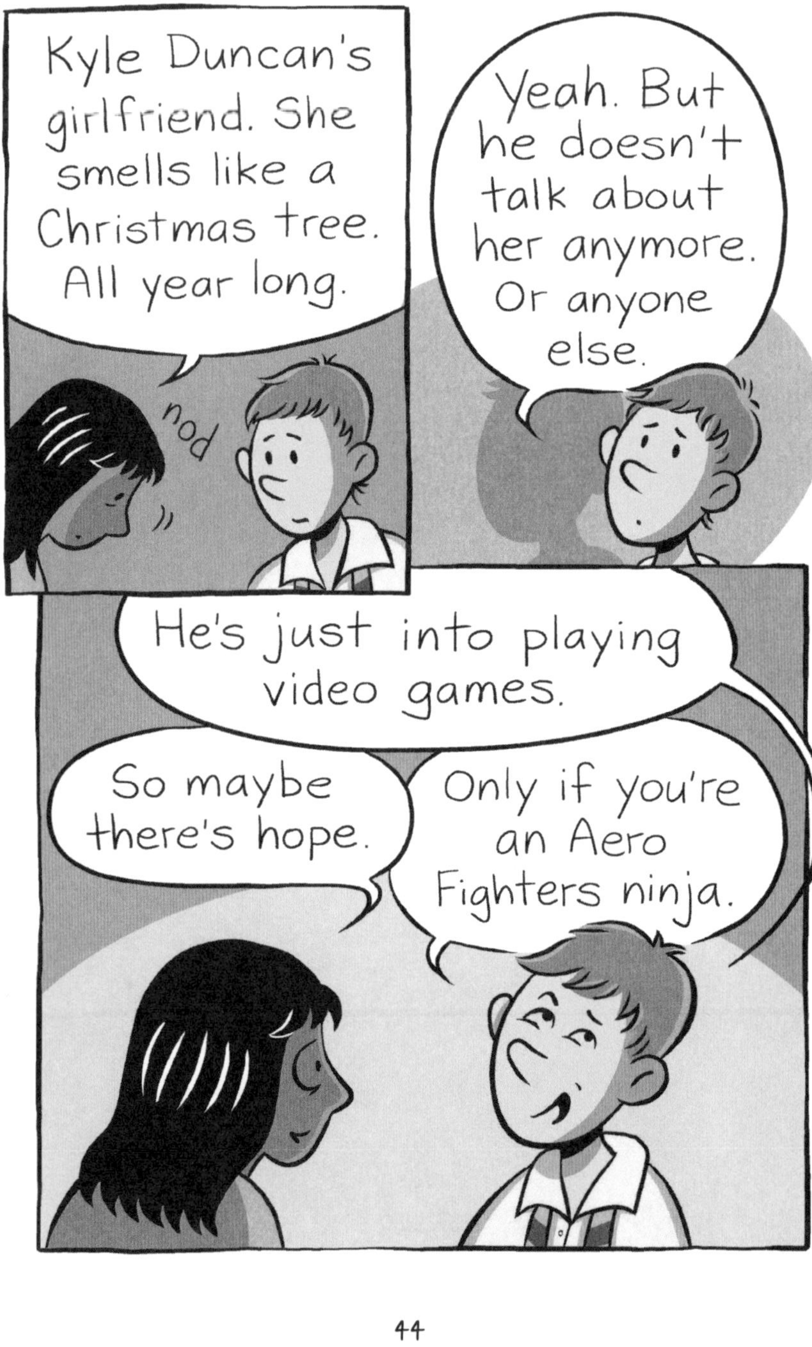
Kyle Duncan's girlfriend. She smells like a Christmas tree. All year long.
nod
Yeah. But he doesn't talk about her anymore. Or anyone else.
He's just into playing video games.
So maybe there's hope.
Only if you're an Aero Fighters ninja.

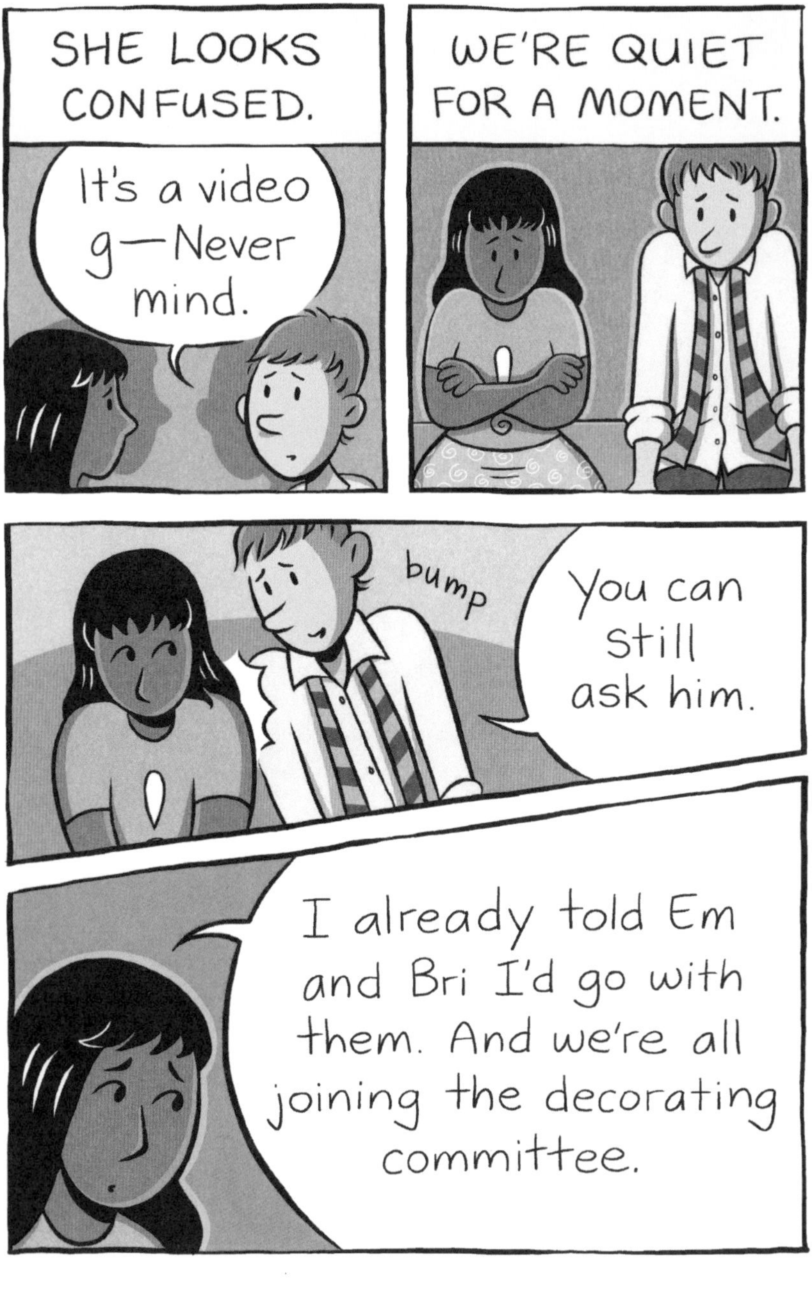
SHE LOOKS CONFUSED.
It's a video g—Never mind.
WE'RE QUIET FOR A MOMENT.
bump
You can still ask him.
I already told Em and Bri I'd go with them. And we're all joining the decorating committee.

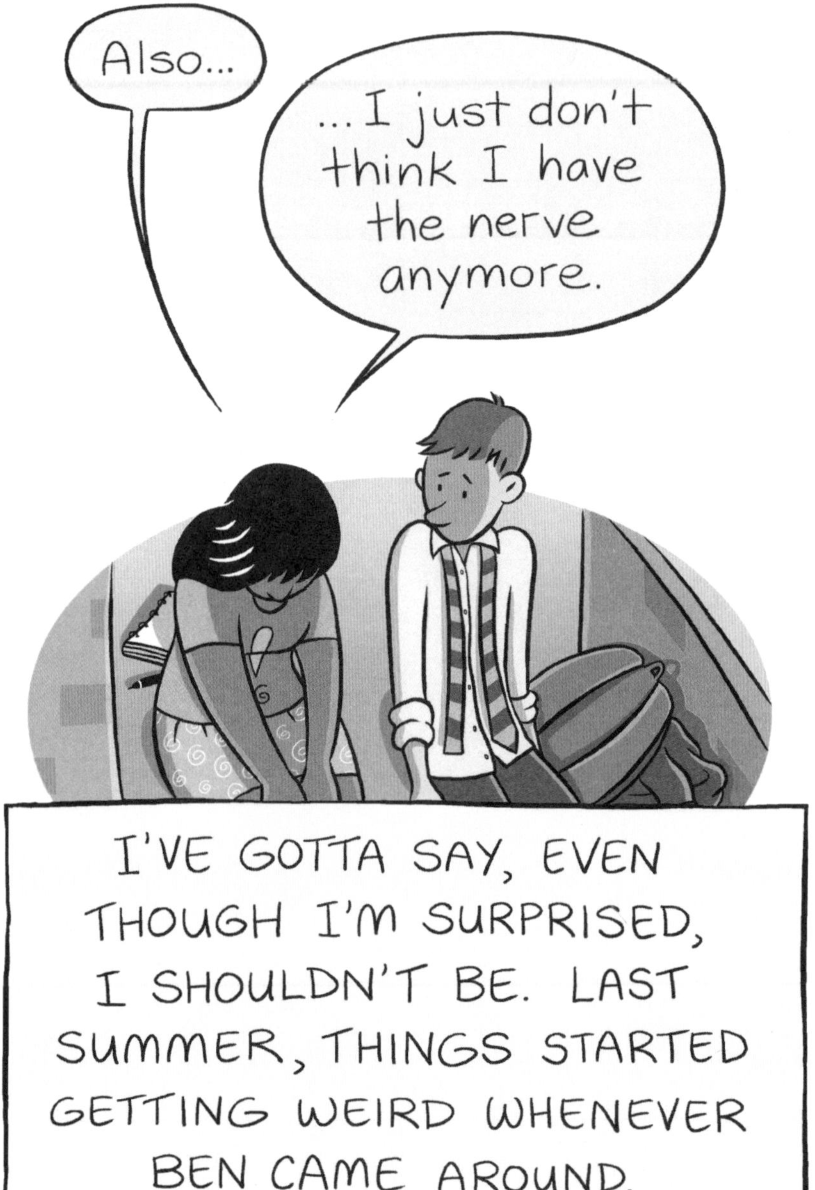
Also...
...I just don't think I have the nerve anymore.
I'VE GOTTA SAY, EVEN THOUGH I'M SURPRISED, I SHOULDN'T BE. LAST SUMMER, THINGS STARTED GETTING WEIRD WHENEVER BEN CAME AROUND.

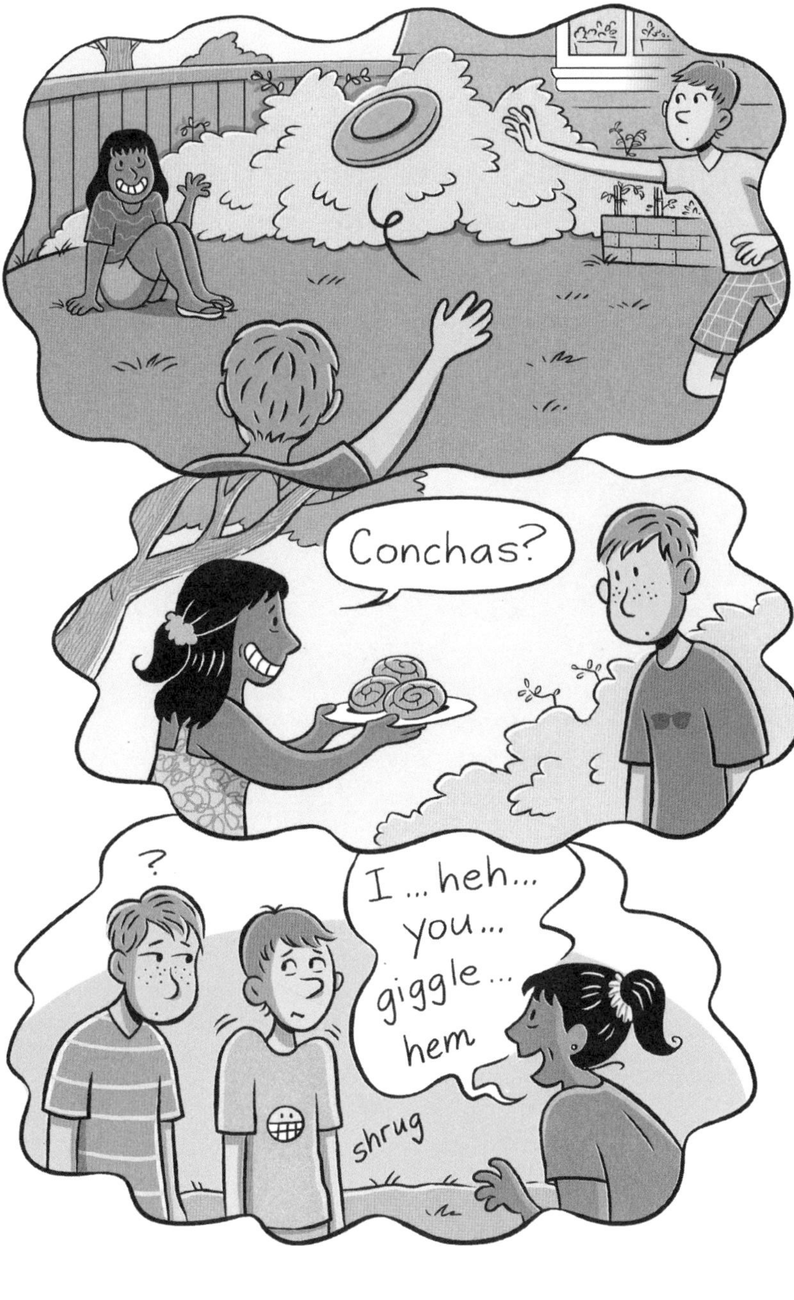
Conchas?
?
I ... heh... you... giggle... hem
shrug

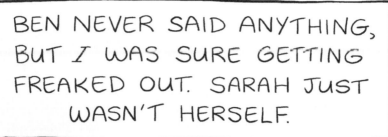

BEN NEVER SAID ANYTHING, BUT *I* WAS SURE GETTING FREAKED OUT. SARAH JUST WASN'T HERSELF.
Conchas?
whatever alien took over her body
TRYING NOT TO BE A JERK, I HINTED *MAYBE* SHE SHOULD TAKE IT DOWN A NOTCH.
that made it worse

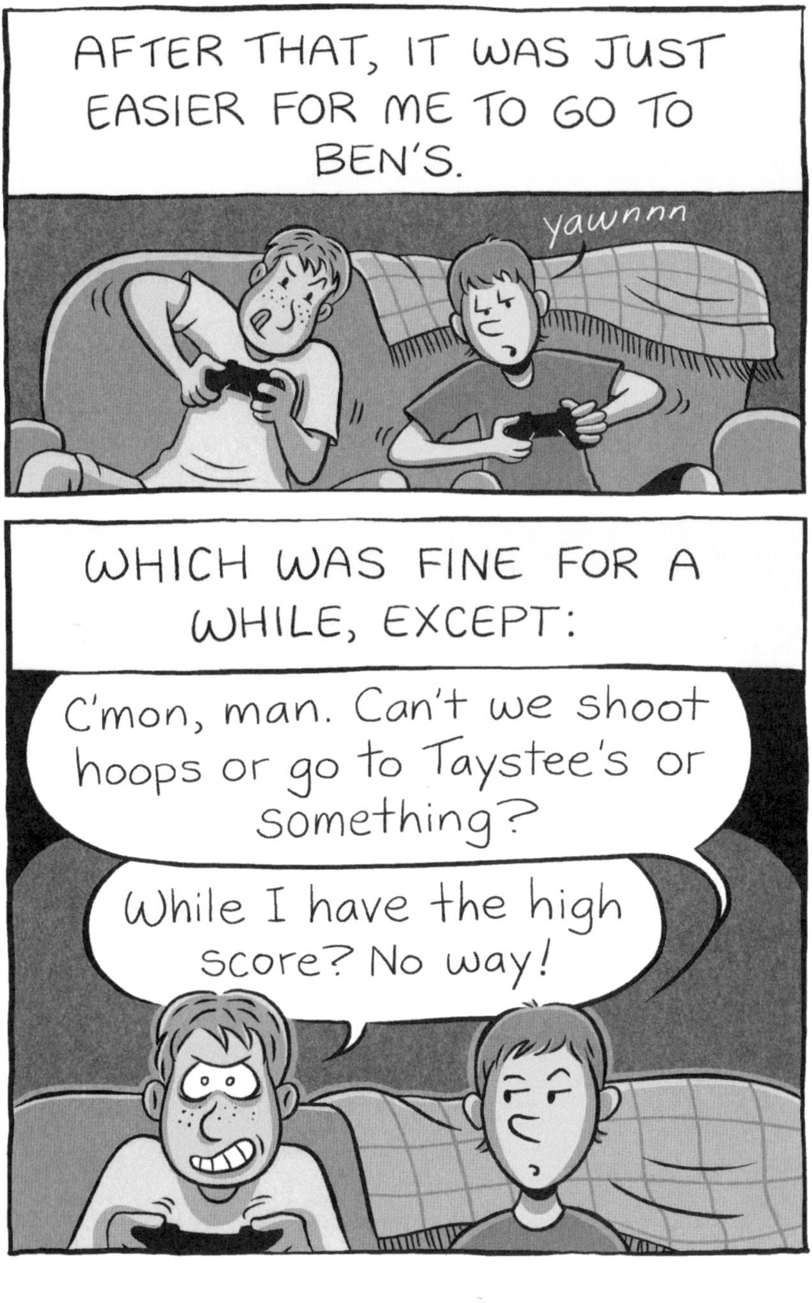
AFTER THAT, IT WAS JUST EASIER FOR ME TO GO TO BEN'S.
yawnnn
WHICH WAS FINE FOR A WHILE, EXCEPT:
C'mon, man. Can't we shoot hoops or go to Taystee's or something?
While I have the high score? No way!

IT WASN'T ALWAYS LIKE THIS. BEN USED TO LIKE DOING THE SAME STUFF AS ME.

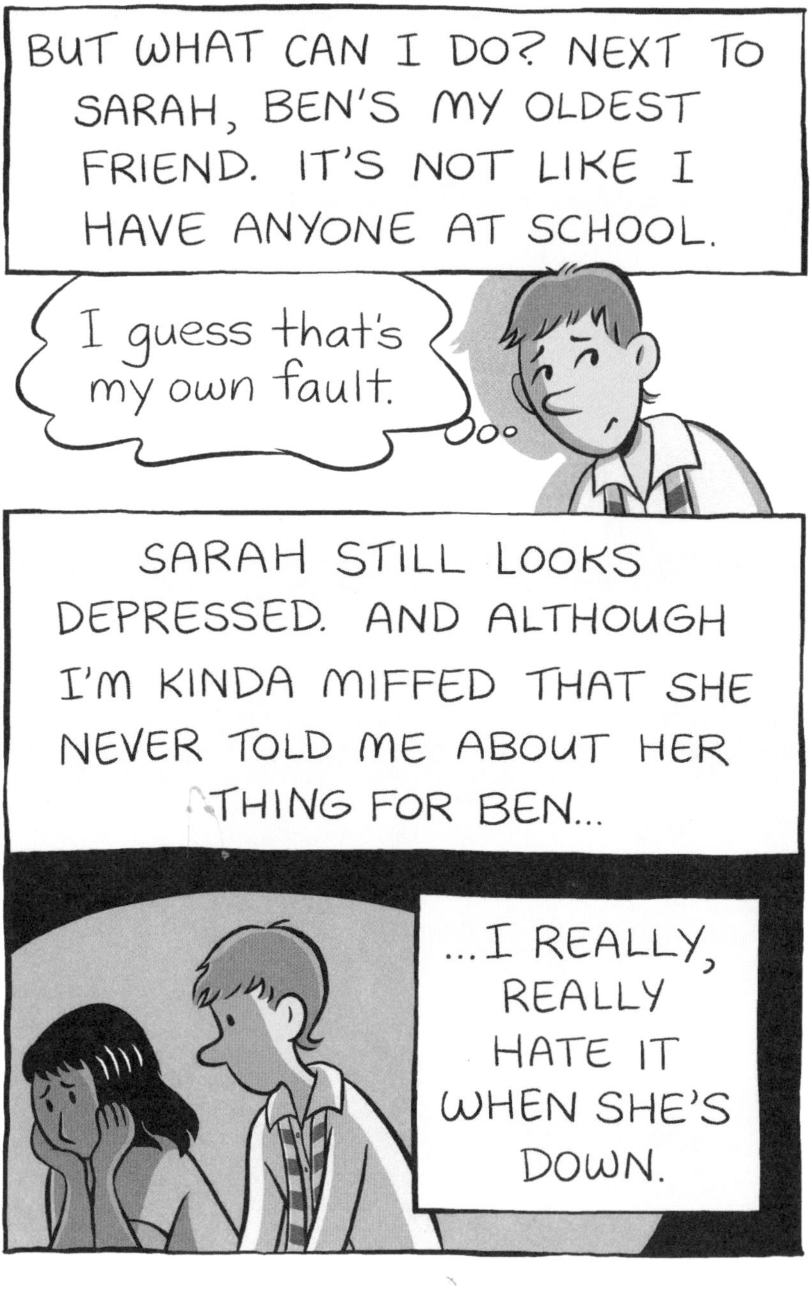
BUT WHAT CAN I DO? NEXT TO SARAH, BEN'S MY OLDEST FRIEND. IT'S NOT LIKE I HAVE ANYONE AT SCHOOL.
I guess that's my own fault.
SARAH STILL LOOKS DEPRESSED. AND ALTHOUGH I'M KINDA MIFFED THAT SHE NEVER TOLD ME ABOUT HER THING FOR BEN...
...I REALLY, REALLY HATE IT WHEN SHE'S DOWN.

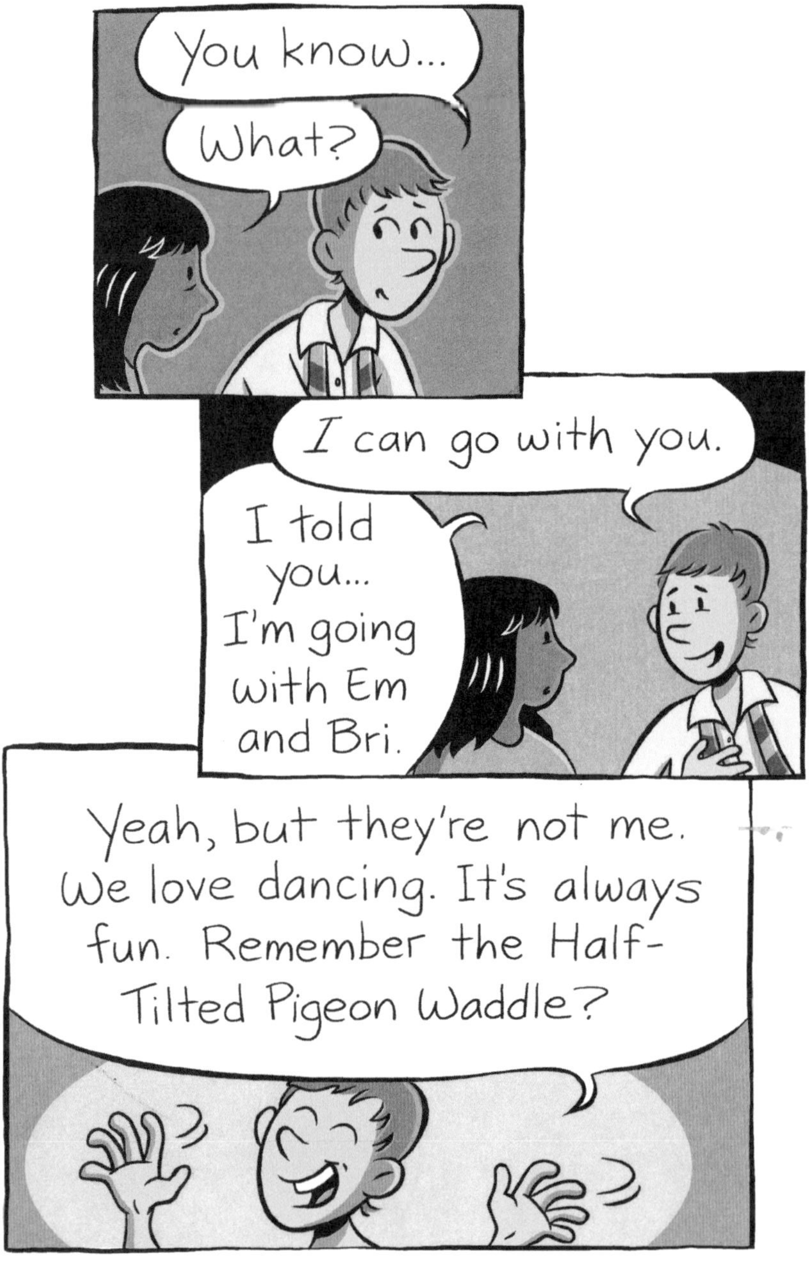
You know...
What?
I can go with you.
I told you... I'm going with Em and Bri.
Yeah, but they're not me. We love dancing. It's always fun. Remember the Half-Tilted Pigeon Waddle?

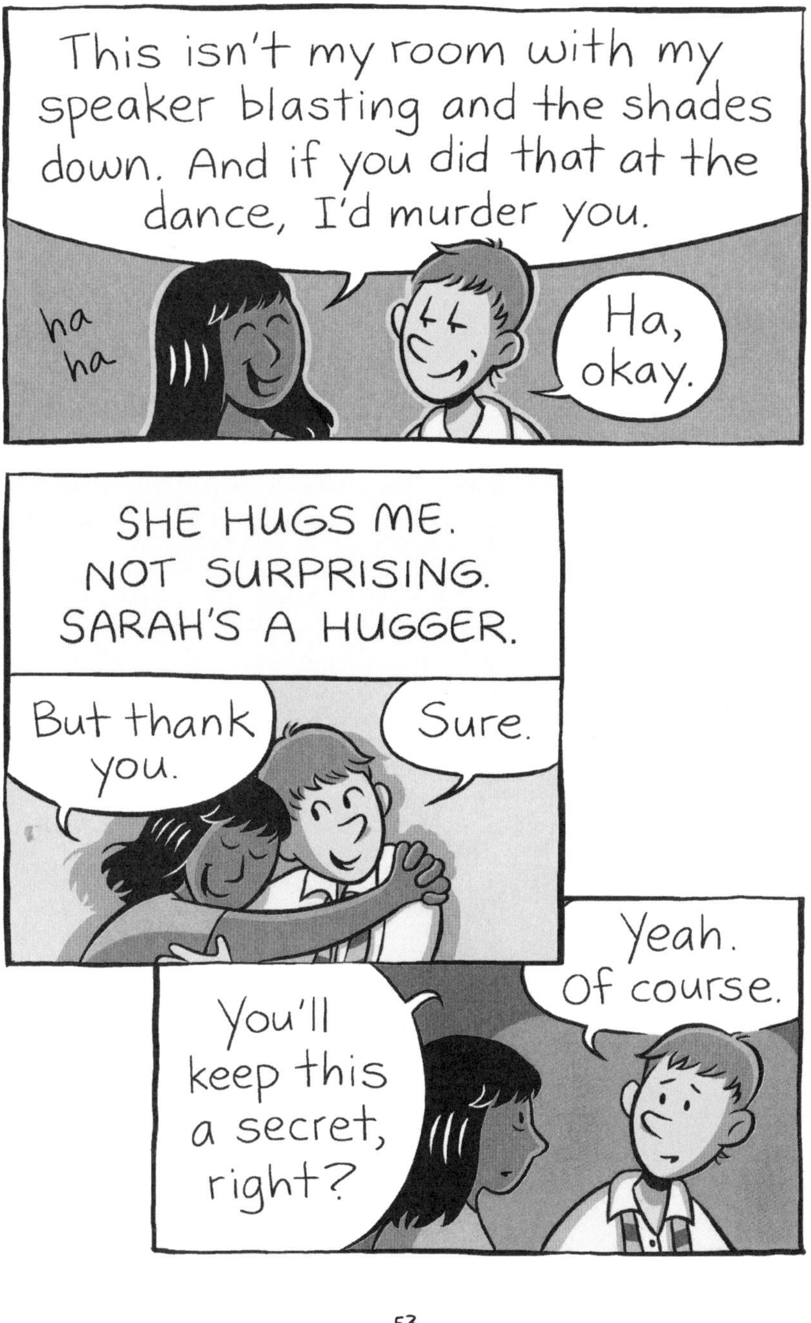
This isn't my room with my speaker blasting and the shades down. And if you did that at the dance, I'd murder you.
ha ha
Ha, okay.
SHE HUGS ME. NOT SURPRISING. SARAH'S A HUGGER.
But thank you.
Sure.
You'll keep this a secret, right?
Yeah. Of course.

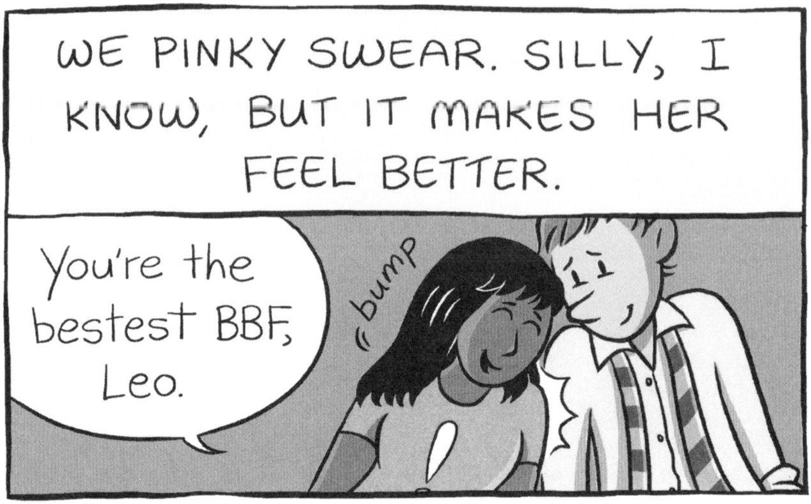
WE PINKY SWEAR. SILLY, I KNOW, BUT IT MAKES HER FEEL BETTER.
You're the bestest BBF, Leo.
bump

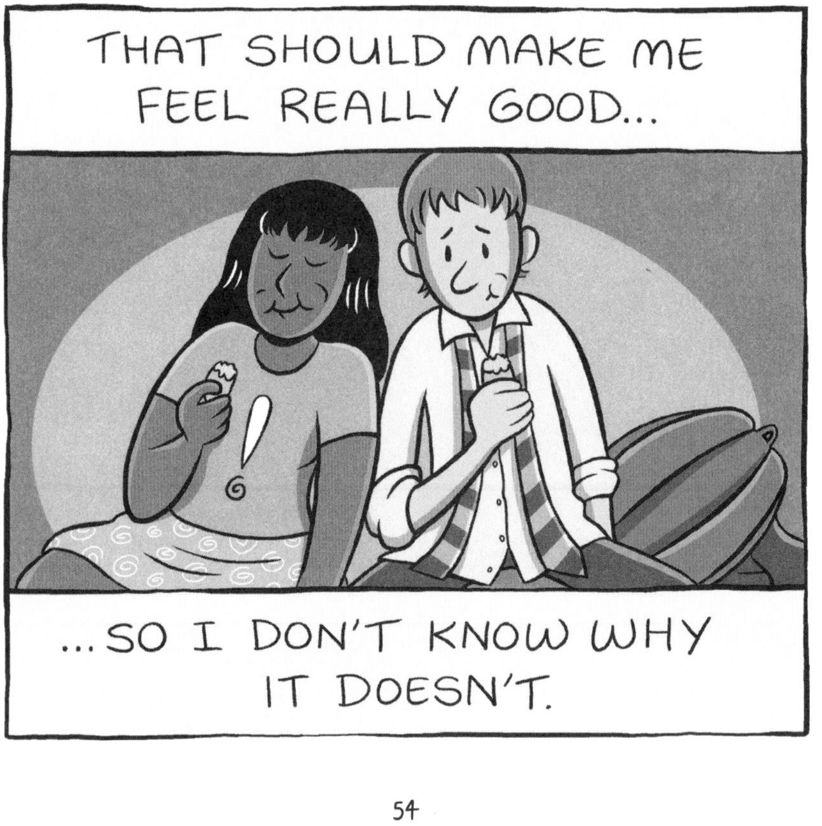
THAT SHOULD MAKE ME FEEL REALLY GOOD...
...SO I DON'T KNOW WHY IT DOESN'T.

SARAH

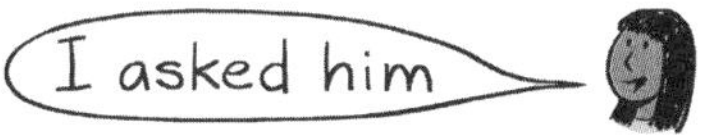
I asked him

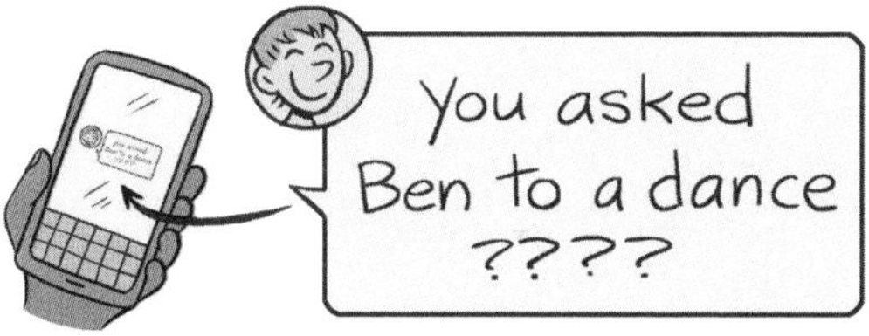
you asked
Ben to a dance
????

News travels fast.

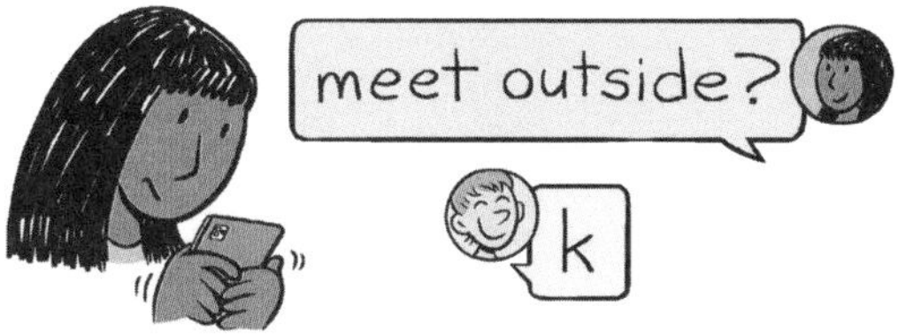
meet outside?
k

A minute later, we're on my stoop. It's dark out. Our street isn't busy, so we can hear the usual chorus of crickets. And every so often, the low **wrrrrnnn** of a motorcycle pack on the highway.

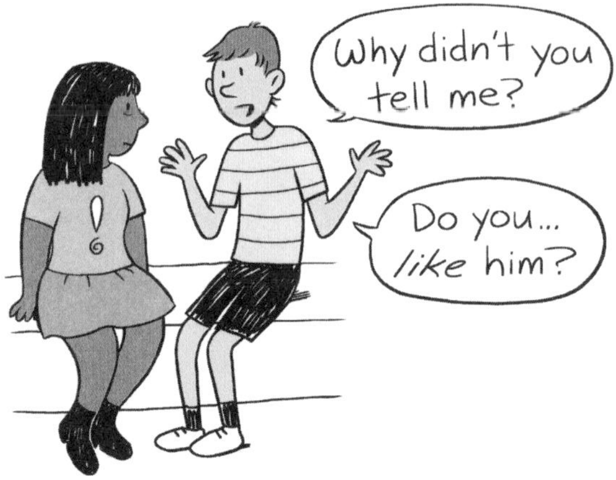
Why didn't you tell me?
Do you... *like* him?

I don't answer at first (which, I guess, is an answer in itself).

But for some reason, I don't want him to know about my crush. First, Leo could let it slip out accidentally. Second, I don't want to put him in the middle in case Ben doesn't like me back. Sure, Ben said yes to the dance, but maybe he was just being nice.*

And third? Actually, I don't know what the third reason is. It's there, but I can't name it.

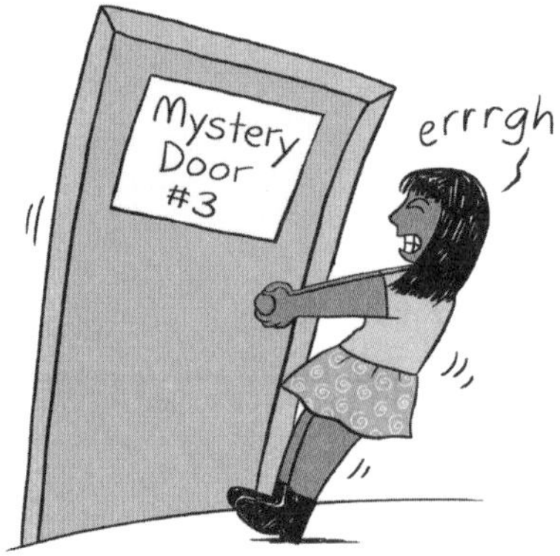
Mystery Door #3
errrgh

*Either way, I still want to go with him. 'Cause there's always a chance that by the end of the dance, he **will** like me back!

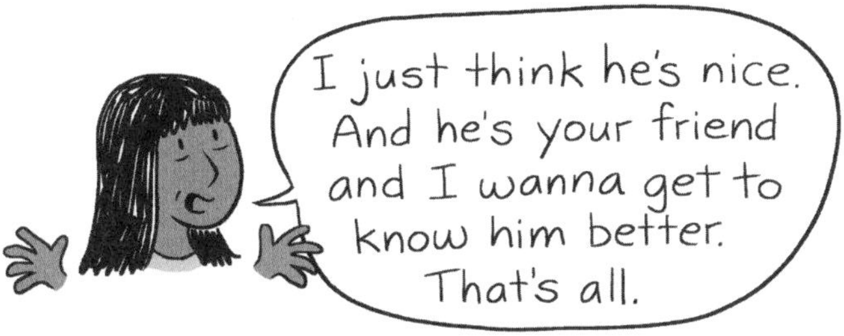
I just think he's nice. And he's your friend and I wanna get to know him better. That's all.

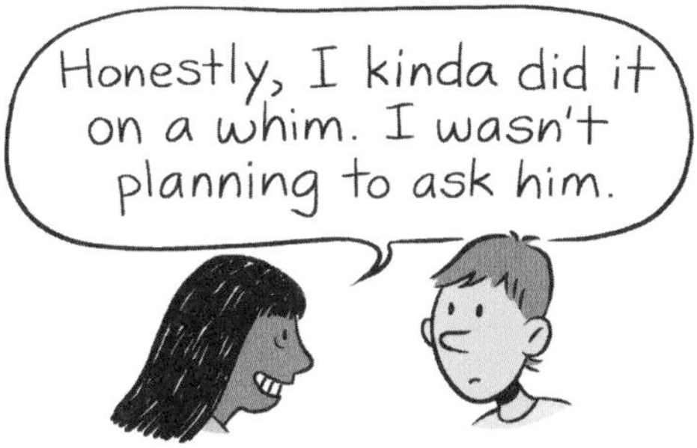
Honestly, I kinda did it on a whim. I wasn't planning to ask him.

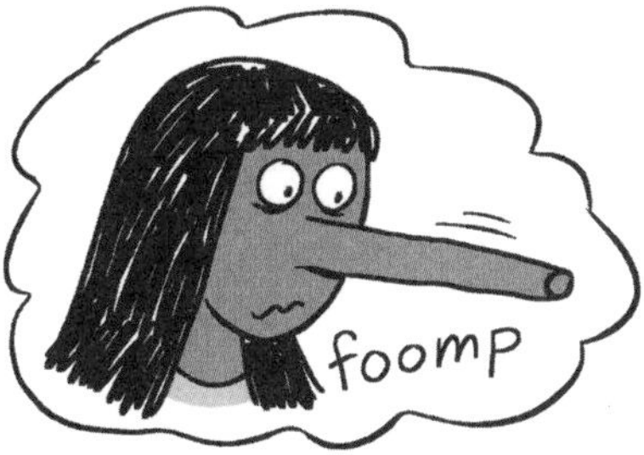
foomp

I think I figured out the third reason. Leo would think I'm ridiculous, crushing on someone like Ben. Okay, so he's just a regular guy, not Mr. Popularity or anything, but he's still cooler than me.

Leo just stares at me.

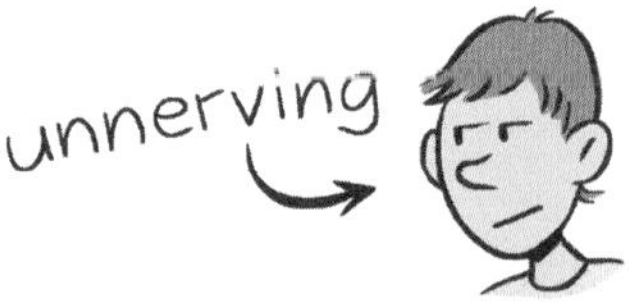
unnerving

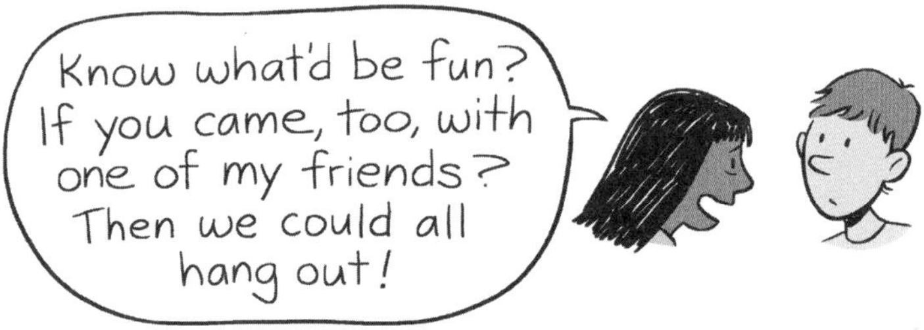
Know what'd be fun? If you came, too, with one of my friends? Then we could all hang out!

Leo looks down and mutters:

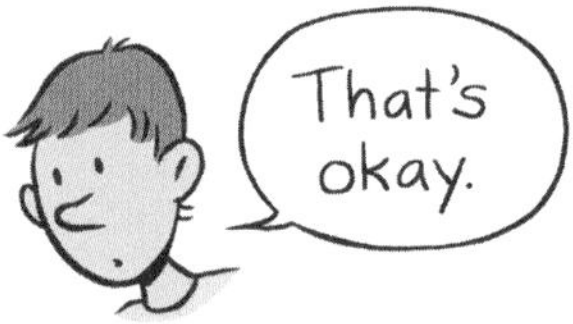
That's okay.

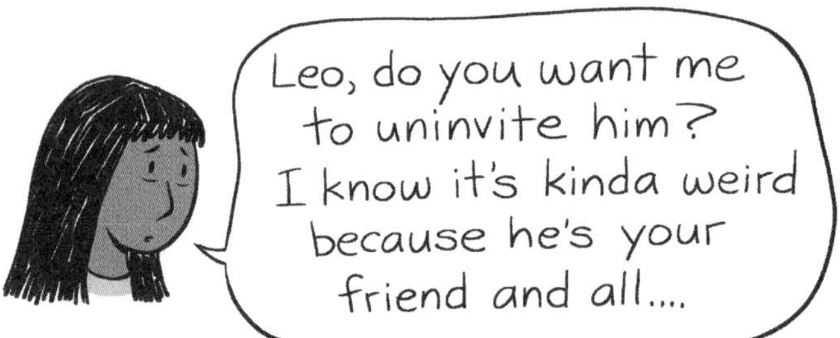
Leo, do you want me to uninvite him? I know it's kinda weird because he's your friend and all....

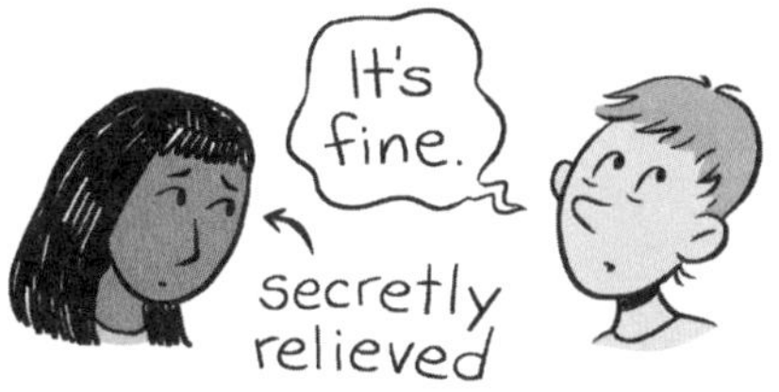
It's fine.
secretly relieved

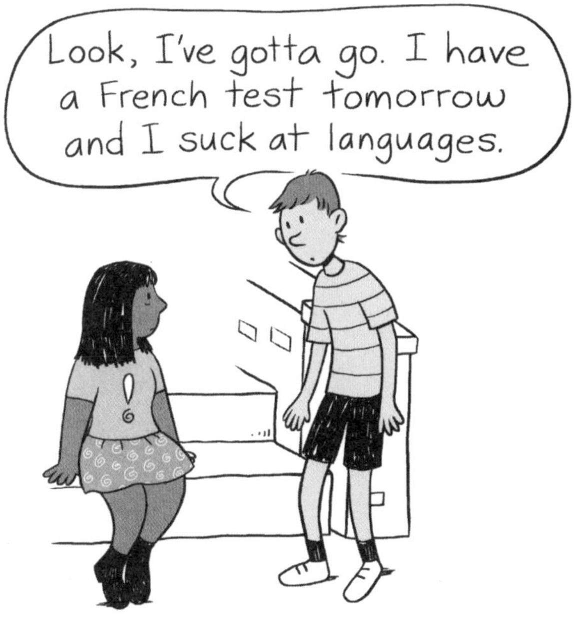
Look, I've gotta go. I have a French test tomorrow and I suck at languages.

Before I can react, he's already running up his porch steps.

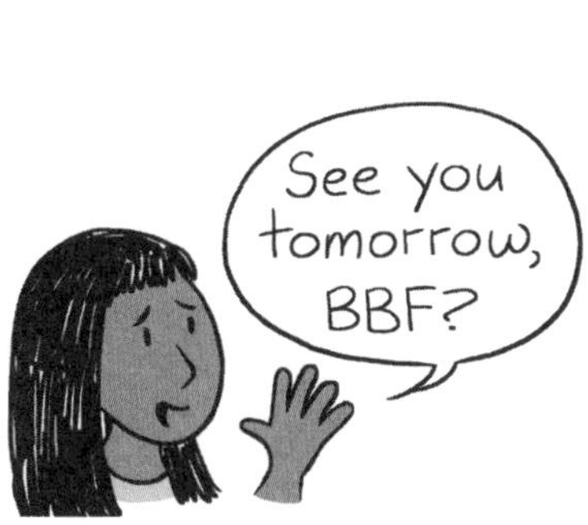
See you tomorrow, BBF?

He doesn't smile. He just gives me a little wave and goes inside.

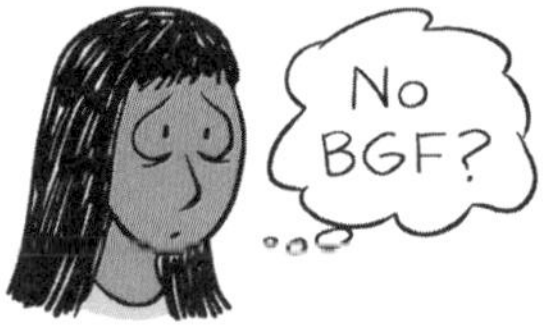
No BGF?

It's not the first time Leo's been upset with me. We've had lots of fights, usually about stupid things.

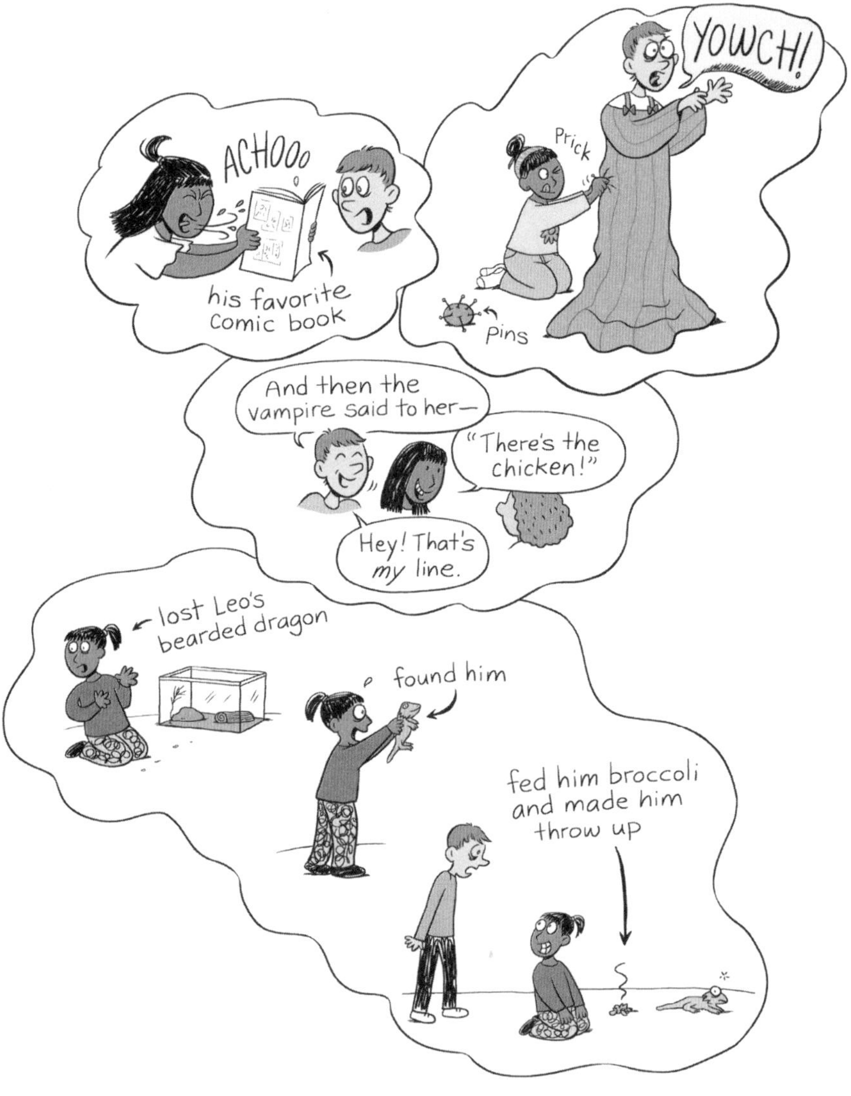
ACHOOo
his favorite comic book
YOWCH!
Prick
pins
And then the vampire said to her—
"There's the chicken!"
Hey! That's *my* line.
lost Leo's bearded dragon
found him
fed him broccoli and made him throw up

But this is the first time I don't know the **reason** he's upset with me. Is it 'cause I didn't tell him about asking Ben to the dance? Or 'cause he thinks I'm stealing his friend behind his back? Or that I'd want to hang out with Ben over him?

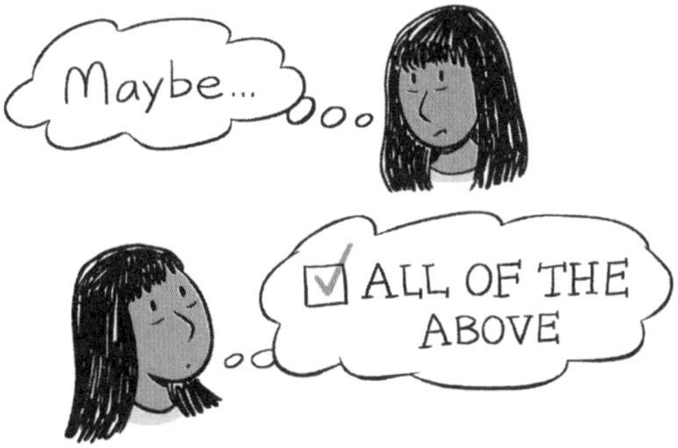
Maybe...
ALL OF THE ABOVE

I go back inside and plop down on my abuelo's old recliner. It's comfy and comforting. I don't know what my grandfather actually smelled like, but the chair has a faint aroma.

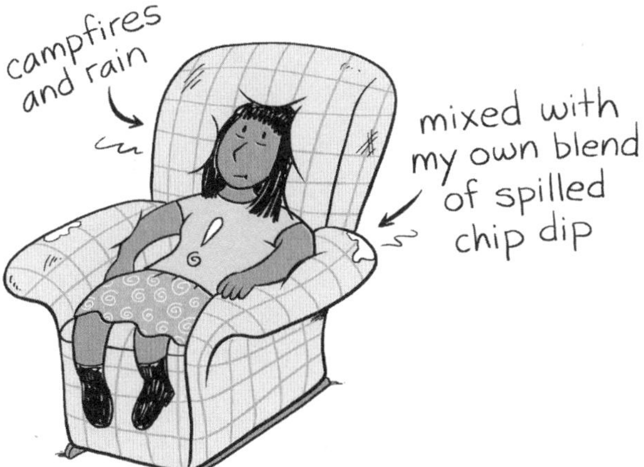
campfires and rain
mixed with my own blend of spilled chip dip

Mamá said he was an avid outdoorsperson. I wish I had known him.

liked fishing and hiking

loved giving Abuela surprises from nature, like flowers and dead fish

had my eyes (or vice versa)

Are boys really so complicated? At least I know where I stand with my dad (nowhere). I could always count on Leo, but I went and messed it up, and now I don't know what he's thinking.

Only thing I do know is:

He needs to cool off.

That's it! He just needs to chill and then he'll come around again. He always does.

I'm baaaack!

I heave myself off the plushy chair and head to the kitchen. Mamá is cooling more donuts.

That must be a big party.

I finally made some extra. Do you want to run a few to Leo's?

Not now.

He's doing homework.

She shoots me a look while I nibble.

You okay?

It's so hard to hide my feelings. Tía Elena calls my face "expressive." But it's my downfall. I can't hide anything.

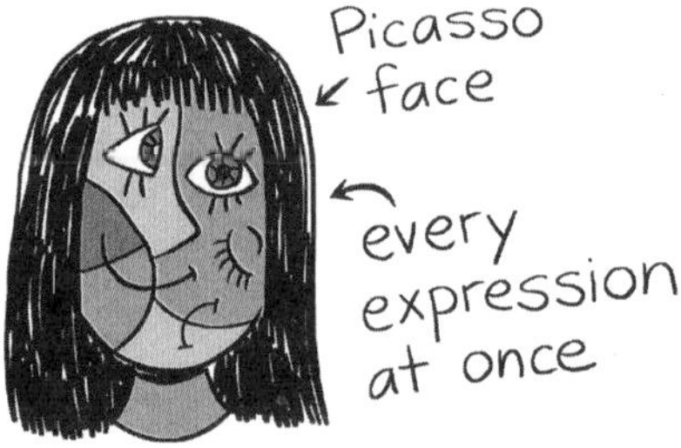
Picasso face
every expression at once

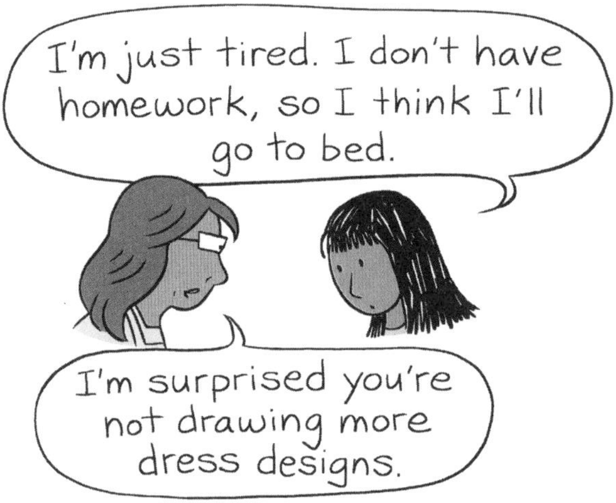
I'm just tired. I don't have homework, so I think I'll go to bed.
I'm surprised you're not drawing more dress designs.

Yeah. Leo squashed my enthusiasm. Guess I need some cooling off, too.

I head upstairs. Em and Bri love my bedroom because there's a crawl space in one of the walls. It's practically a whole other room! There's just enough space to sit in (even though I've bumped my head on the ceiling more times than I can remember). I strung up fairy lights and keep my small collection of graphic novels and old stuffed animals in there. I also tacked colorful fabric to the walls. Emmie and Bri have even added their own touches.

Bri's glow-in-the-dark stickers

Emmie's drawings

We use it as a little clubhouse. My mom can't hear us in there, so we can talk as loud as we want. I think I've lost count of how many times I've giggled about Ben or Emmie's gushed about Tyler or Bri's rolled her eyes at us.

Leo won't go in there because he's claustrophobic. That's probably why he loves being outside. It's too bad . . . but then again, it's nice to have a space just for my "newer" friends and me.

The
SAREMBRI
SISTERHOOD
≥ Keep OUT =

I don't go in there right now. Instead, I flop on my beanbag and text Emmie.

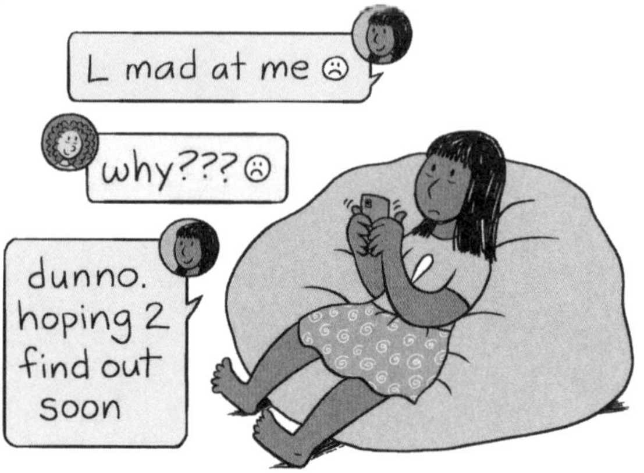

L mad at me ☹
why??? ☹
dunno. hoping 2 find out soon

I hesitate.

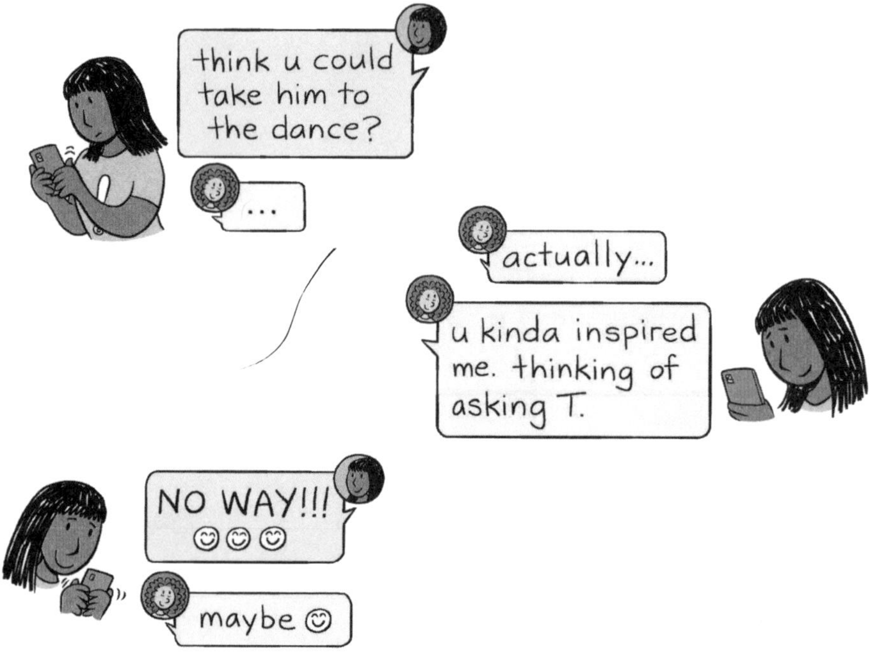

think u could take him to the dance?
...
actually...
u kinda inspired me. thinking of asking T.
NO WAY!!! ☺☺☺
maybe ☺

We text for another minute. Then I plug in my phone in the hallway (Mamá's strict) and get ready for bed. But before I crawl under the covers, I decide to tiptoe back in the hall to check my phone one last time. Leo usually sends me funny videos or memes at night.

← no messages

I have a hard time falling asleep. I can't stand it when anyone's upset with me. Especially when I don't know why. I don't like leaving things . . . um . . .

"Unresolved"

Winn Word of the week

← English teacher

Or "hanging in the air," as Leo once called it when his parents had a fight and didn't speak for two days. He practically lived at my house to get away from the tension.

But I finally do fall asleep.

Because here's the last thing I remember before drifting off: despite the stuff that's hanging in the air . . .

. . . I'm sure we'll be okay.

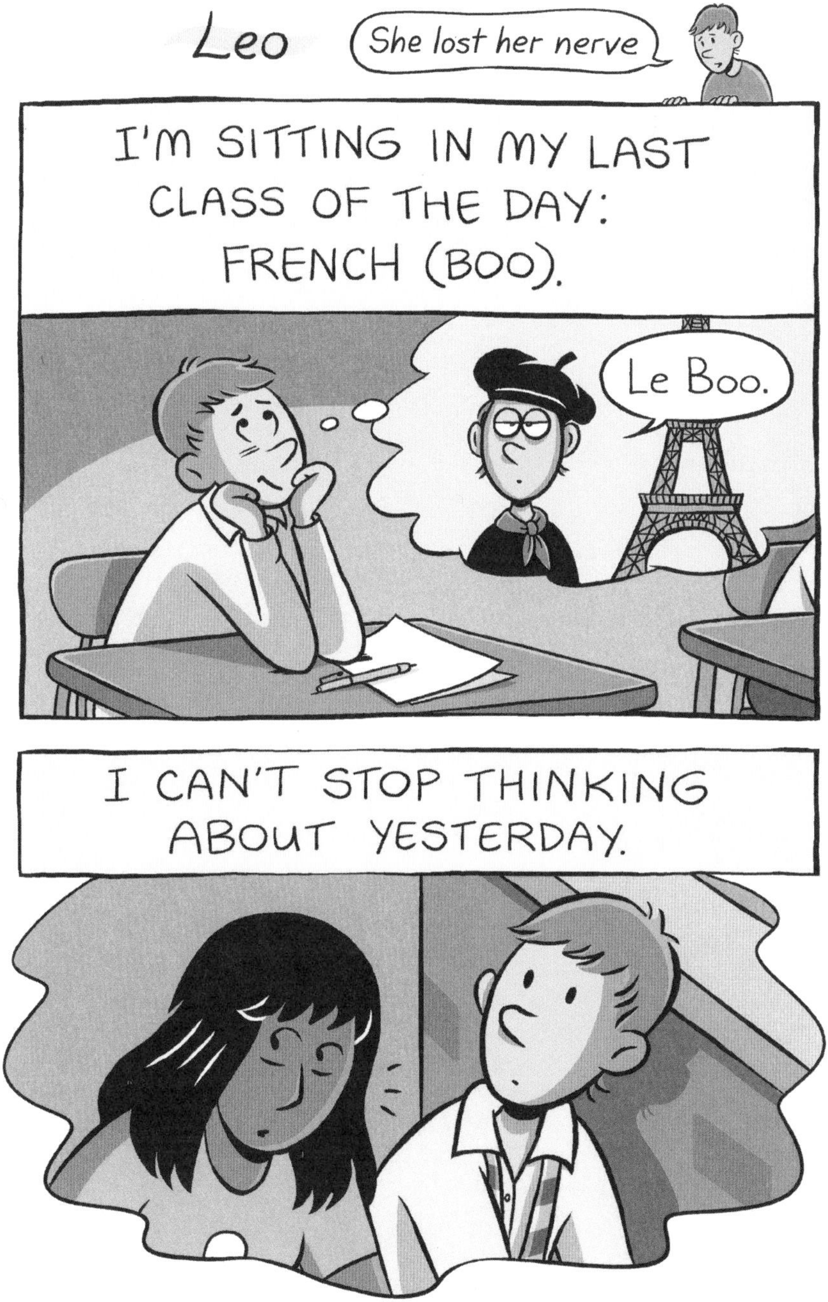
Leo
She lost her nerve
I'M SITTING IN MY LAST CLASS OF THE DAY: FRENCH (BOO).
Le Boo.
I CAN'T STOP THINKING ABOUT YESTERDAY.

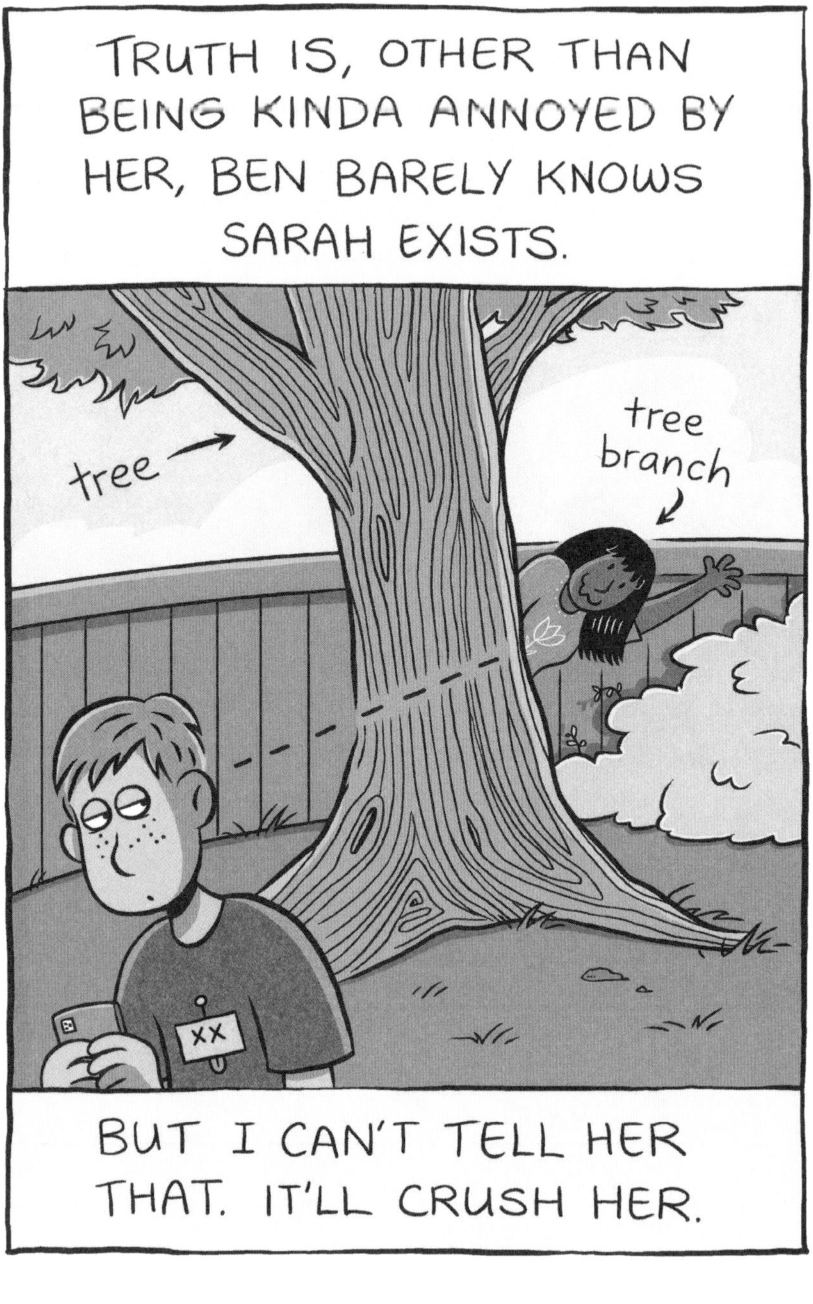
TRUTH IS, OTHER THAN BEING KINDA ANNOYED BY HER, BEN BARELY KNOWS SARAH EXISTS.
tree
tree branch
XX
BUT I CAN'T TELL HER THAT. IT'LL CRUSH HER.

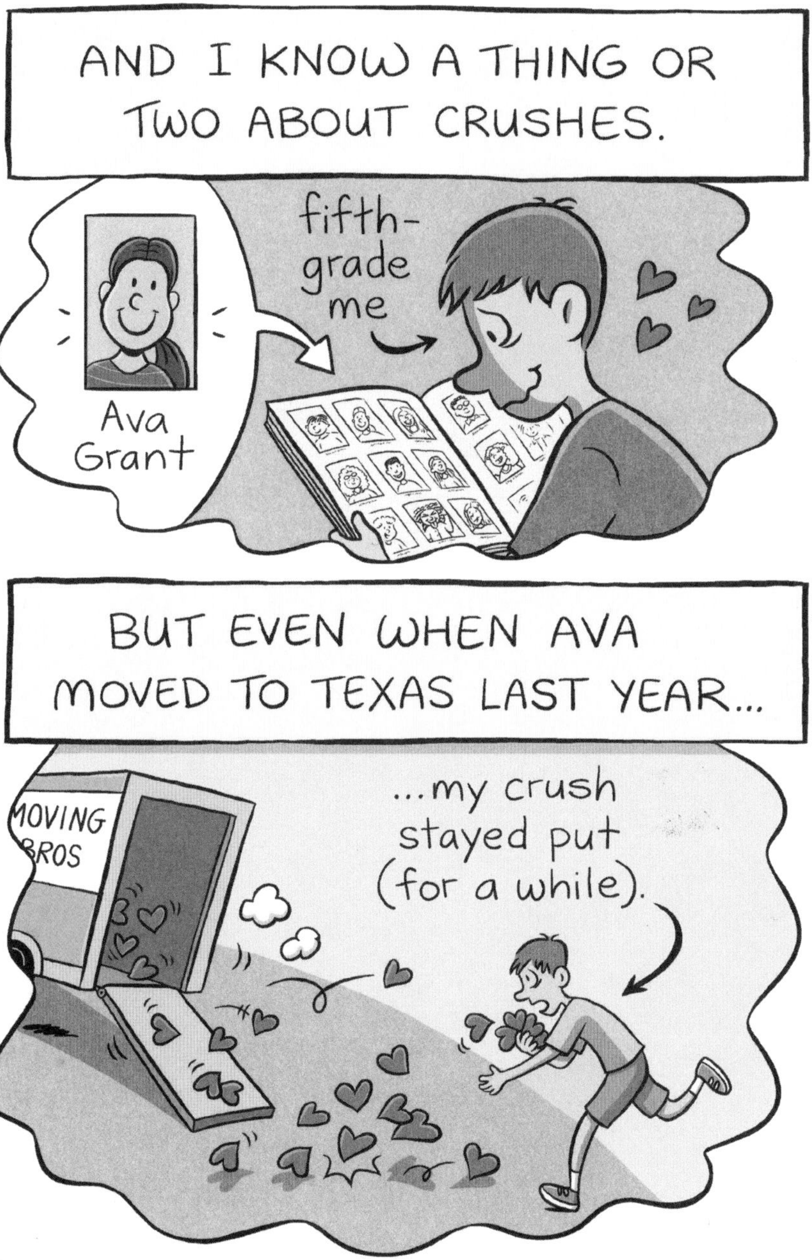
AND I KNOW A THING OR TWO ABOUT CRUSHES.
fifth-grade me
Ava Grant
BUT EVEN WHEN AVA MOVED TO TEXAS LAST YEAR...
MOVING BROS
...my crush stayed put (for a while).

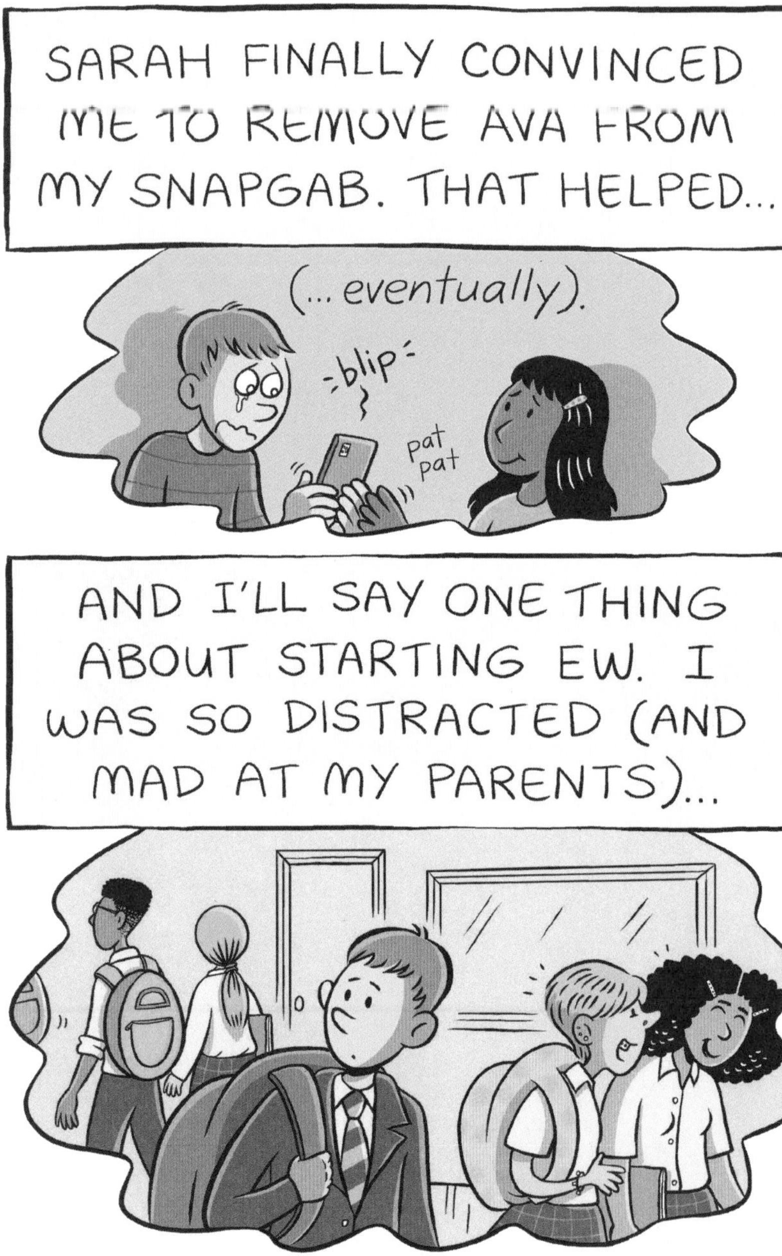
SARAH FINALLY CONVINCED ME TO REMOVE AVA FROM MY SNAPGAB. THAT HELPED...
(...eventually).
blip
pat pat
AND I'LL SAY ONE THING ABOUT STARTING EW. I WAS SO DISTRACTED (AND MAD AT MY PARENTS)...

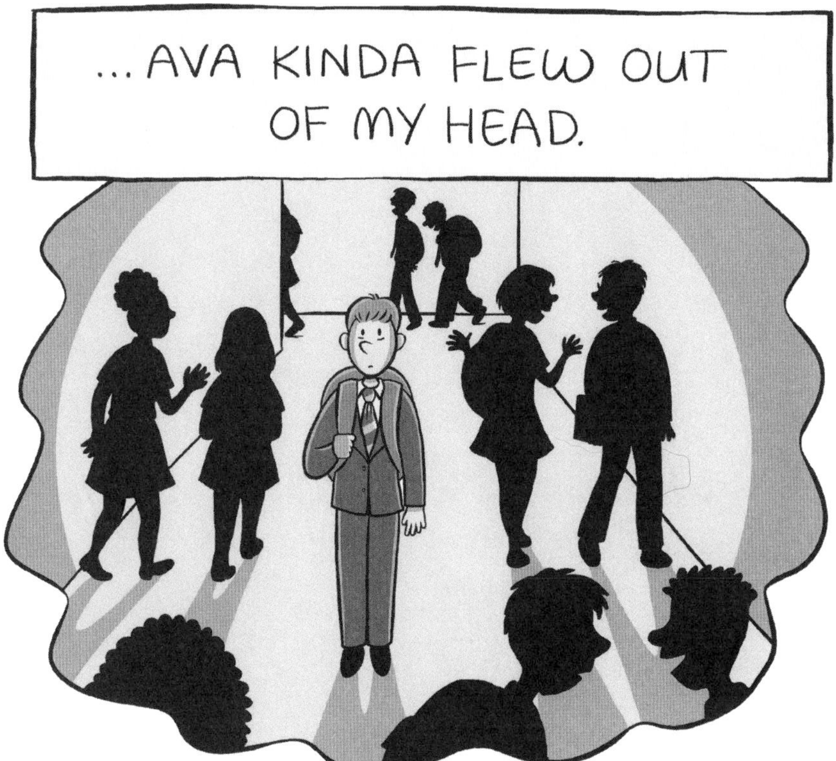
...AVA KINDA FLEW OUT OF MY HEAD.

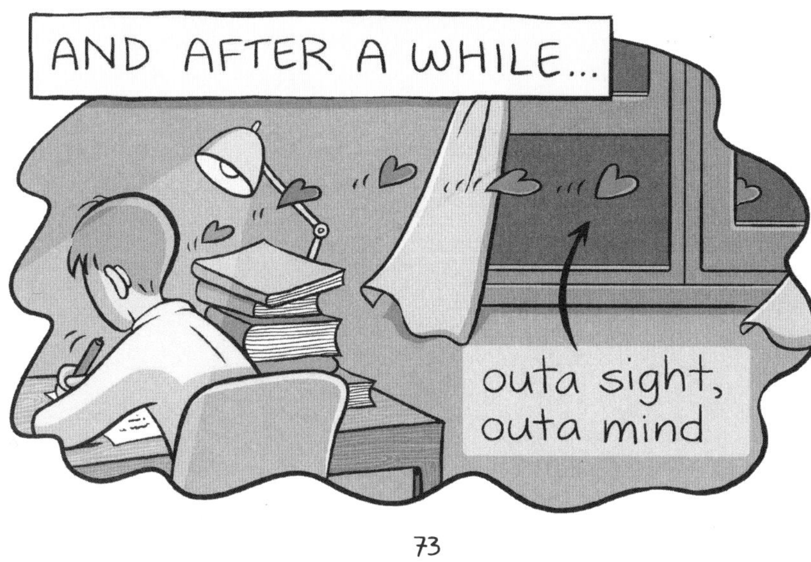
AND AFTER A WHILE...
outa sight, outa mind

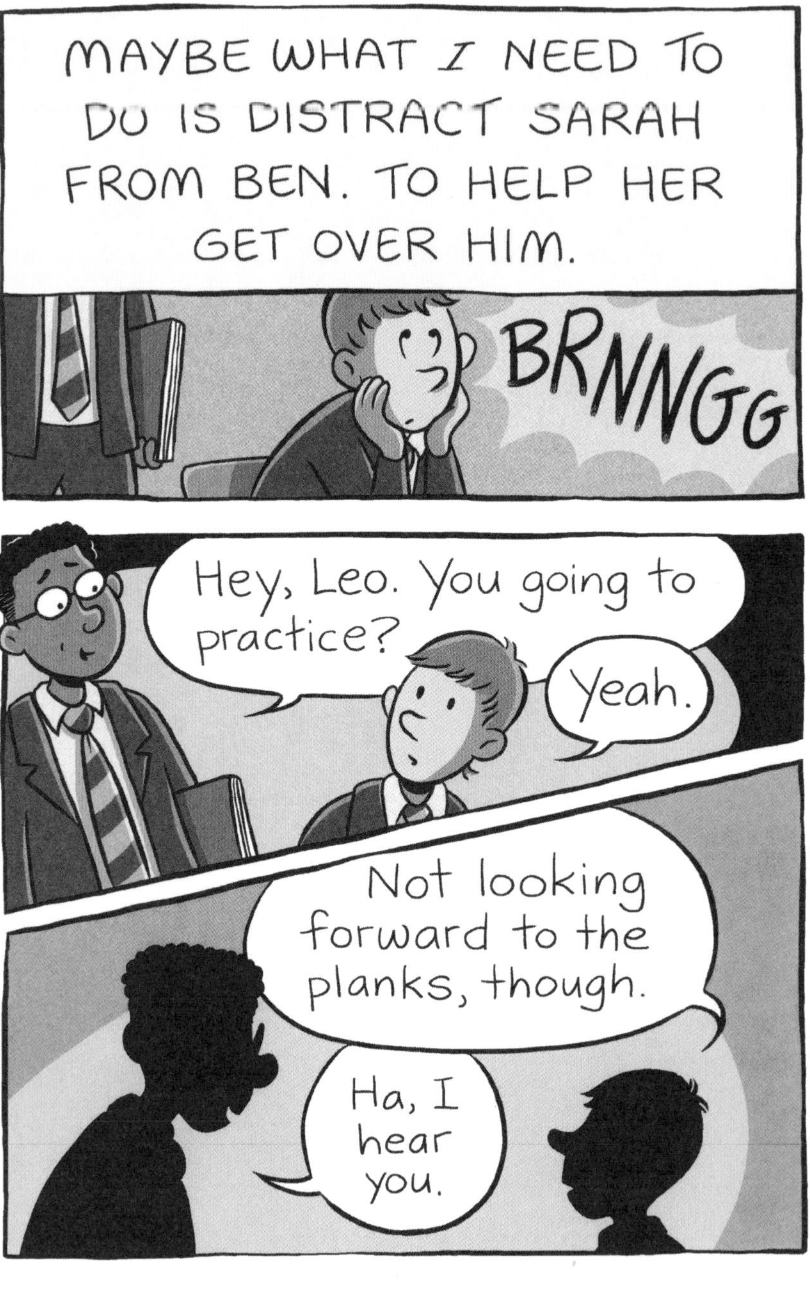
MAYBE WHAT I NEED TO DO IS DISTRACT SARAH FROM BEN. TO HELP HER GET OVER HIM.
BRNNGG
Hey, Leo. You going to practice?
Yeah.
Not looking forward to the planks, though.
Ha, I hear you.

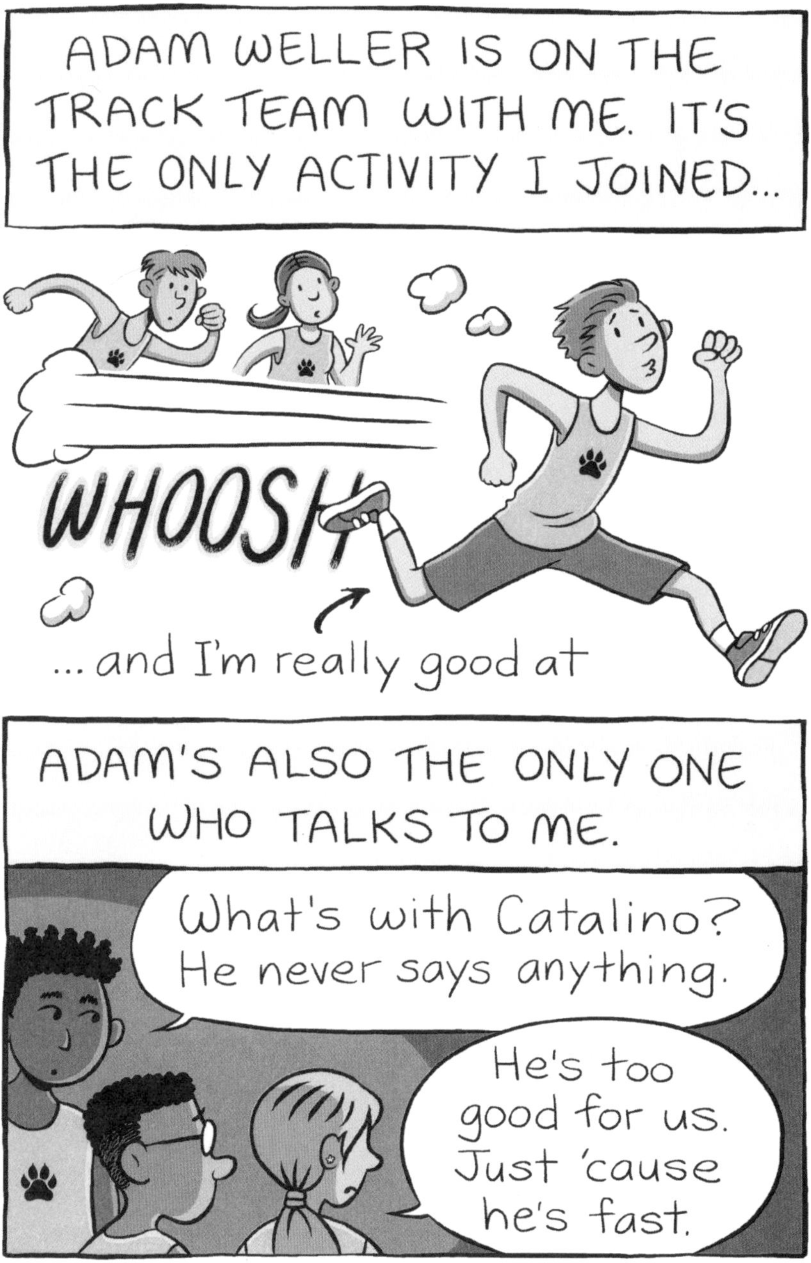
ADAM WELLER IS ON THE TRACK TEAM WITH ME. IT'S THE ONLY ACTIVITY I JOINED...
WHOOSH
...and I'm really good at
ADAM'S ALSO THE ONLY ONE WHO TALKS TO ME.
What's with Catalino? He never says anything.
He's too good for us. Just 'cause he's fast.

He's actually pretty nice.
Whatever.
HONESTLY, PART OF ME *WANTS* TO MAKE AN EFFORT. BUT PART OF ME...
Why don't you at least try to make friends?
What's the point? I'm not sticking around. I hate it there.

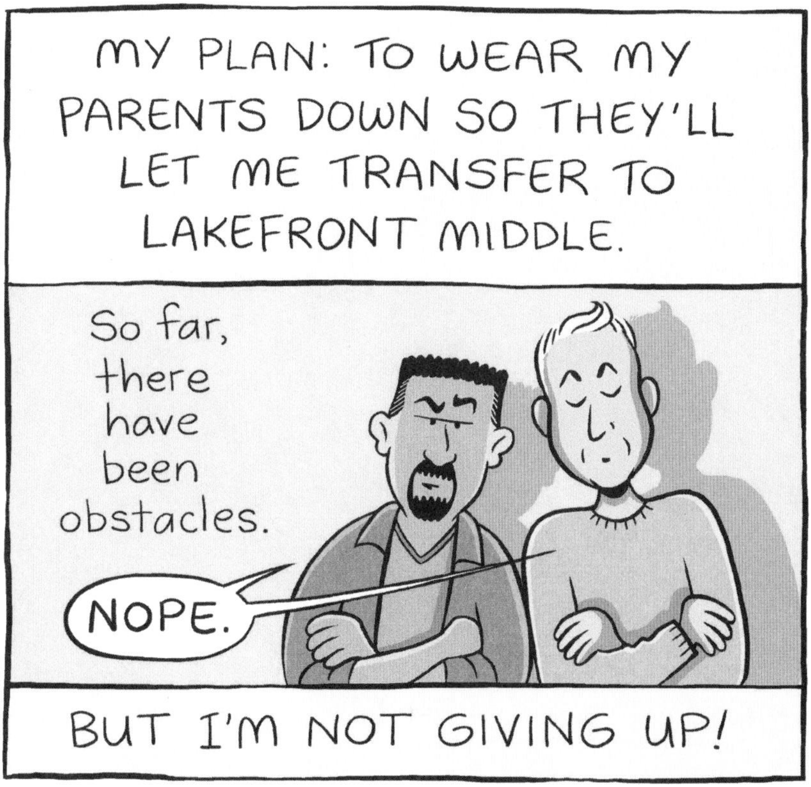
MY PLAN: TO WEAR MY PARENTS DOWN SO THEY'LL LET ME TRANSFER TO LAKEFRONT MIDDLE.
So far, there have been obstacles.
NOPE.
BUT I'M NOT GIVING UP!

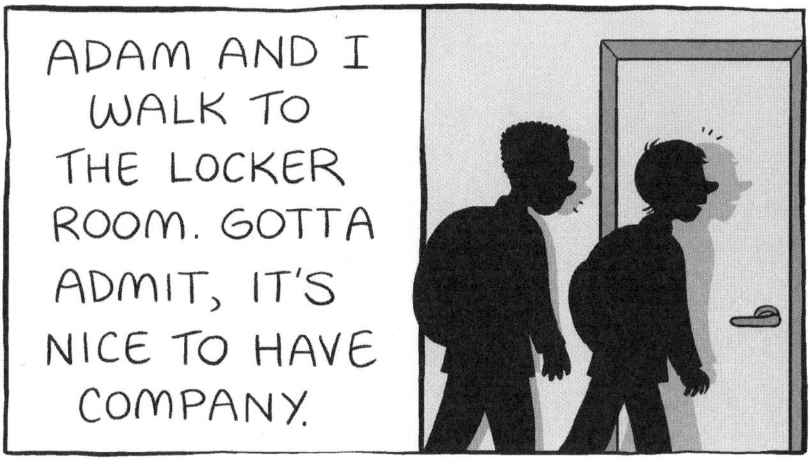
ADAM AND I WALK TO THE LOCKER ROOM. GOTTA ADMIT, IT'S NICE TO HAVE COMPANY.

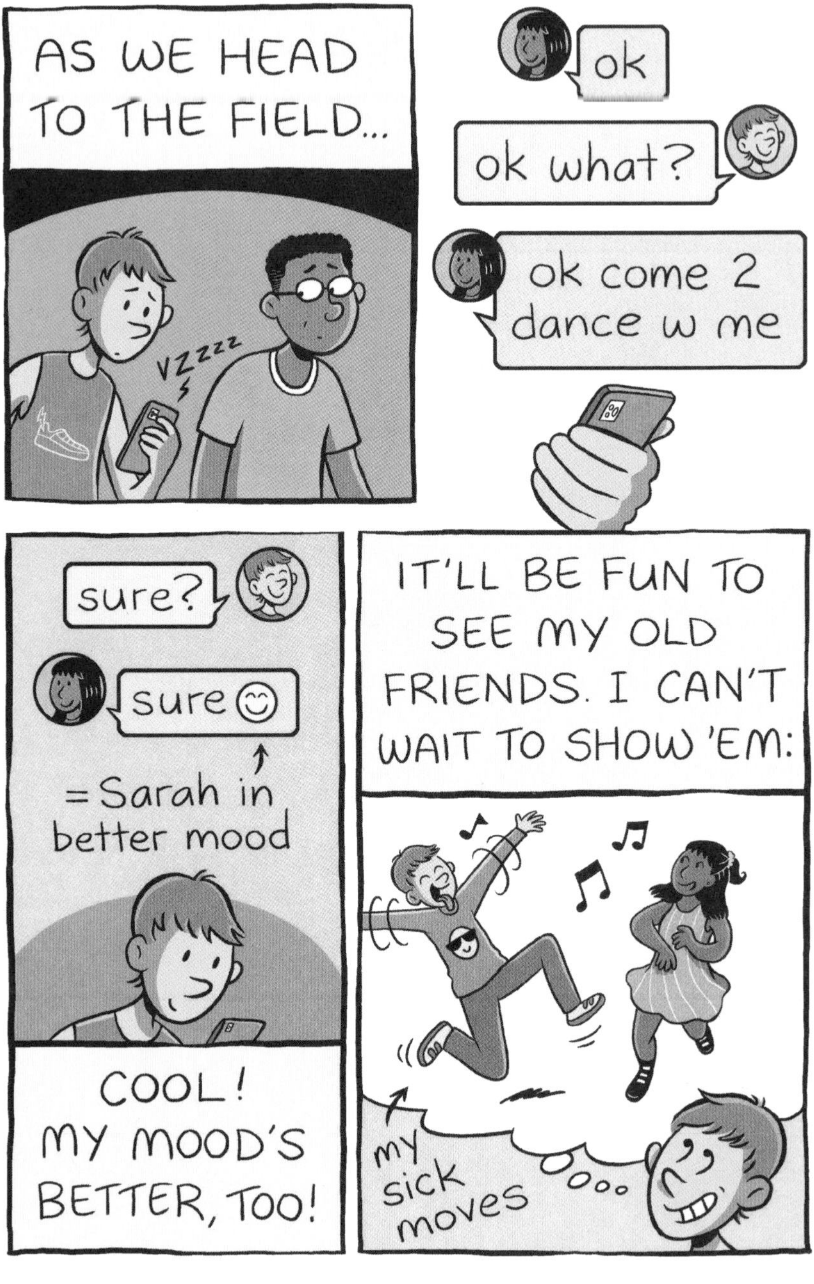
AS WE HEAD TO THE FIELD...
VZZZZ
ok
ok what?
ok come 2 dance w me
sure?
sure ☺
= Sarah in better mood
COOL! MY MOOD'S BETTER, TOO!
IT'LL BE FUN TO SEE MY OLD FRIENDS. I CAN'T WAIT TO SHOW 'EM:
my sick moves

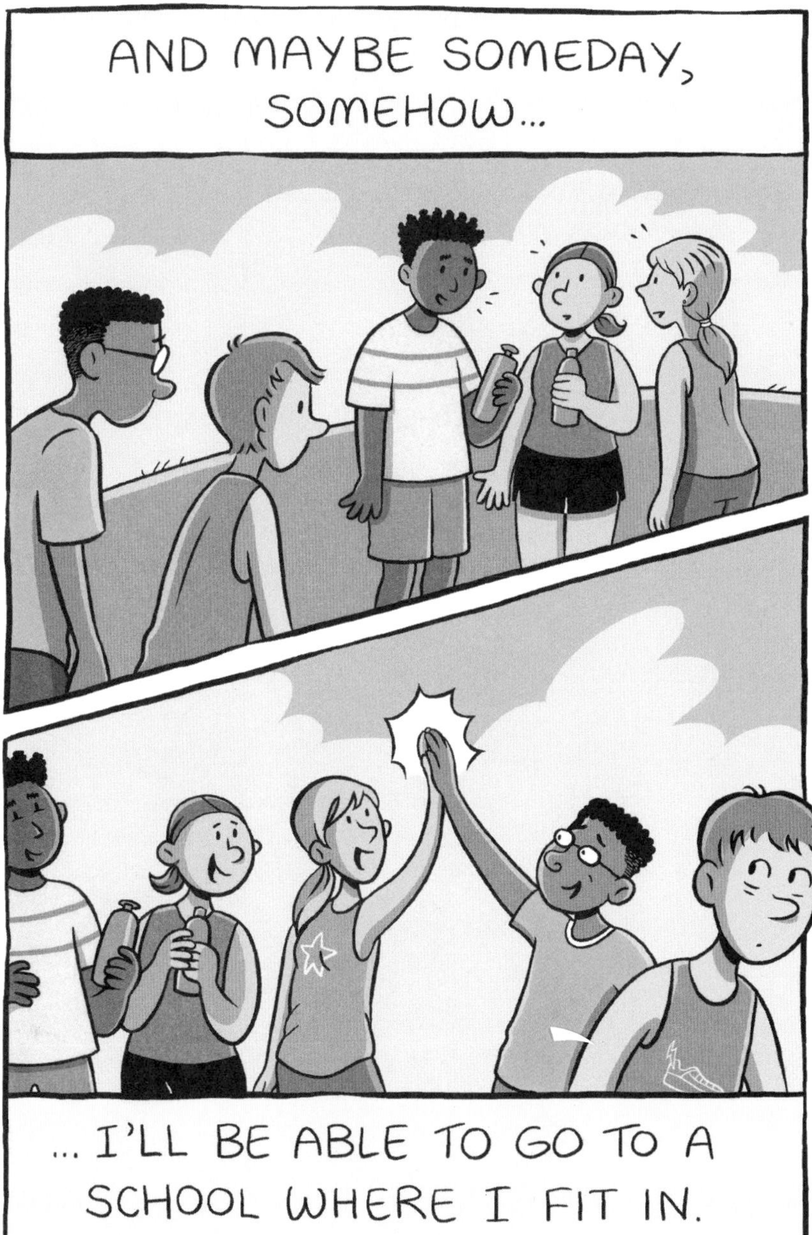
AND MAYBE SOMEDAY, SOMEHOW...
... I'LL BE ABLE TO GO TO A SCHOOL WHERE I FIT IN.

SARAH

I asked him

Leo hasn't texted or stopped by in two days.

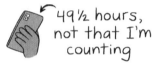
49½ hours,
not that I'm
counting

Okay, he responded after I texted **him**, but that doesn't count.

u mad?

u talking
2 me?

wanna come
ovr? my mom
made yoyos*
☺ ☺

* Mexican pastry
that looks like the
toy it's named for

homework

This is the weirdest. First, because I can always lure Leo with sweets.

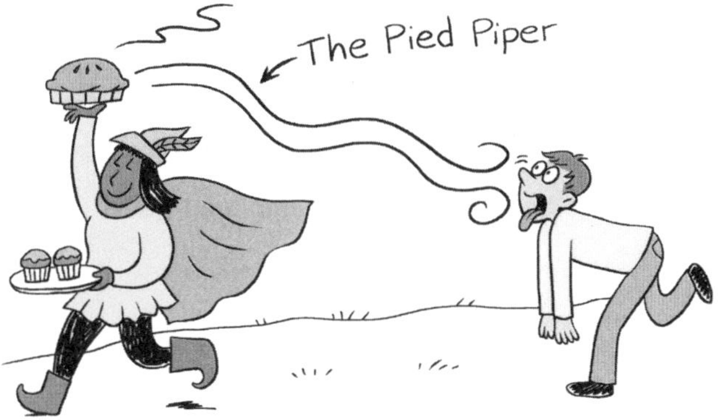
The Pied Piper

Second, because we've never been apart for more than a day, unless you count vacations. And for those, one of us usually tags along.

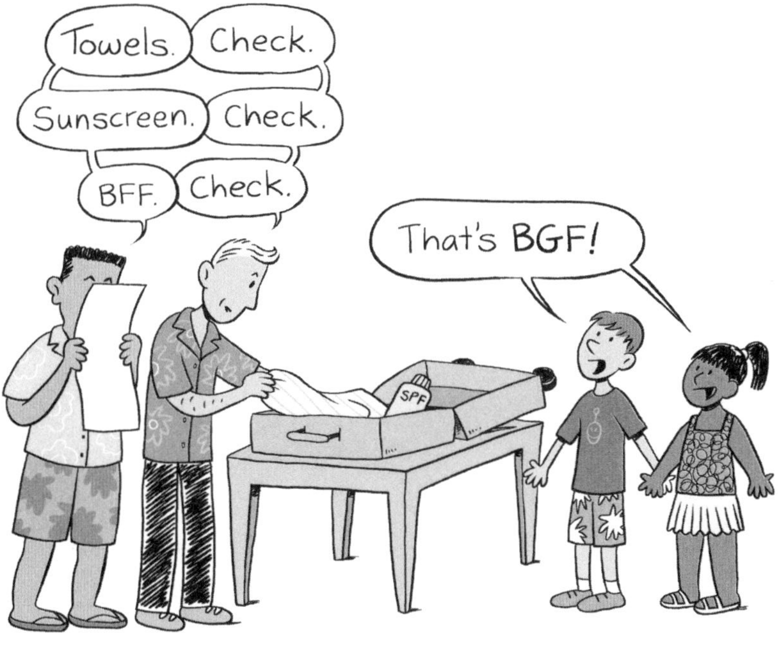
Towels.
Check.
Sunscreen.
Check.
BFF.
Check.
That's BGF!
SPF

Then I notice the weirdest thing of all.

The heck?

They're in running clothes, so they all must be on the track team.

I should be glad, right? I mean, Leo's always resisted making friends at EW. Maybe he's finally broken down and gotten some.

I've been encouraging it. After all, his parents aren't gonna cave on private school. But he's stubborn. For a while, he let his grades drop, too (on purpose!). But that didn't help—in fact, his dads got nervous and just hired tutors around the clock . . . so Leo was cooped up all last fall, which drove him batty.

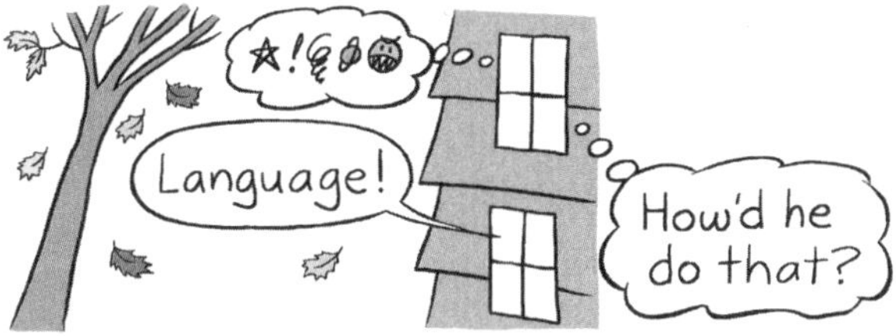
Language!
How'd he do that?

His grades finally improved, and he joined track. But that's where it ended. He still refused to make friends. And you've gotta understand . . . unlike me, Leo is pretty outgoing. I guess that's what drove me bonkers. Because where it takes extra effort for me to make and keep friends, this is something that comes naturally to Leo and he was **wasting** it.

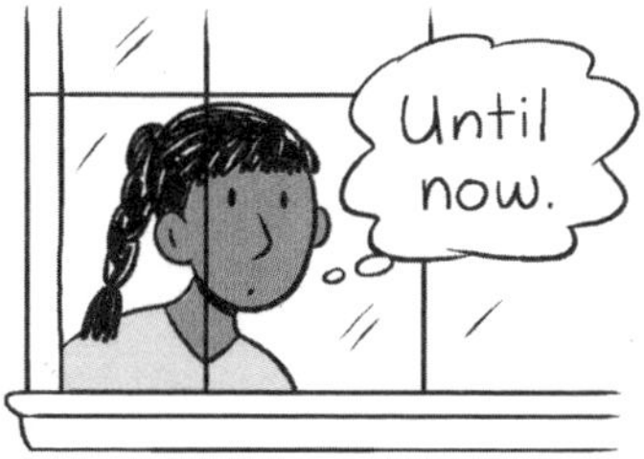
Until now.

It took me all of sixth grade and part of seventh to finally find school friends I'm comfortable with. It wasn't easy. Leo was only one of two friends I had in elementary school. Kerri

Kowalski was the other, and she pretty much abandoned me for the cool crowd in middle school.

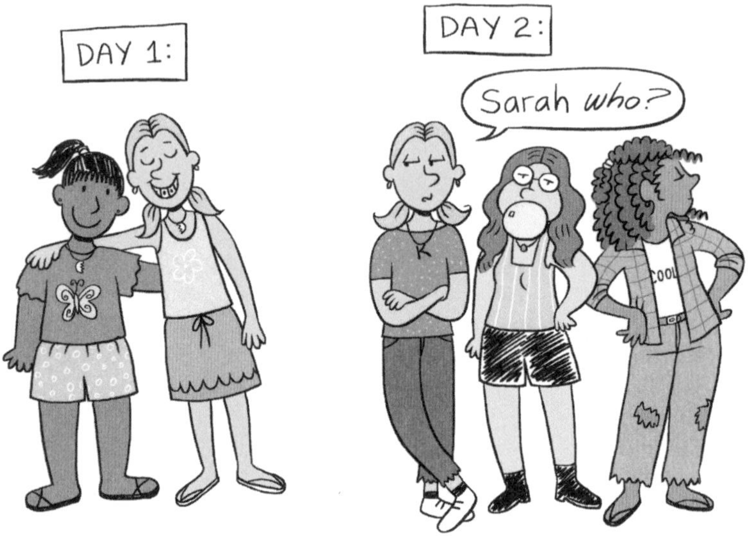
DAY 1:
DAY 2:
Sarah *who?*
COOL

I floated around for a while, mainly hanging out with some kids from art class and dance club, but I never really connected with anyone. Until Emmie. I was the one who reached out—not an easy move for me—and I'm so happy I did.

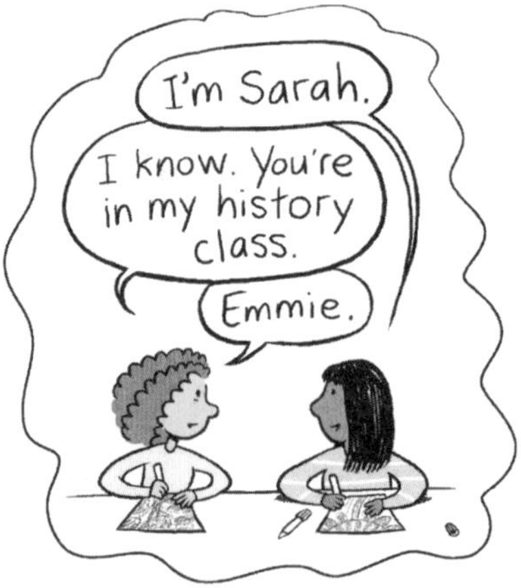
I'm Sarah.
I know. You're in my history class.
Emmie.

probably heading
to Taystee's

Maybe he still needs to cool off.
Maybe it's good for us to take a little break from each other.
Maybe it's also good he's making friends.

Then why am I feeling
miserable and confused?

I can't just sit here and be miserable, though. I get up and
head outside myself.

Where are
you going,
Cachetona?

To Emmie's.
And stop
calling me
that!!

I hear her laugh. Grr.

I grab my bike and ride to Emmie's. She's not far. I usually text first, but this is just Plan A. Plan B is heading home and sketching more dress designs. An' if I'm not inspired, Plan C is helping my mom clean the dishes (normally Plan Z, but I'm pretty antsy).

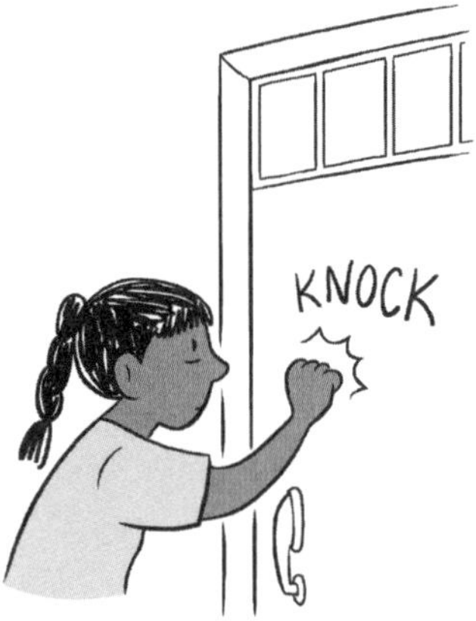
KNOCK

Luckily, Emmie is home.

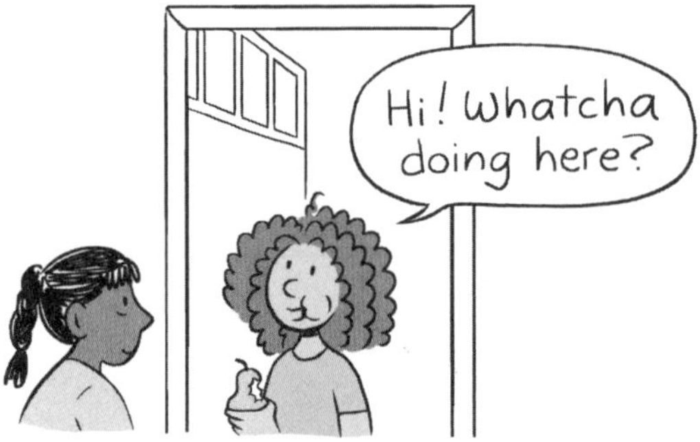
Hi! Whatcha doing here?

I was just riding around and...

Inspiration strikes.

... I thought it might be fun to start brainstorming decorations!

For the dance?

Yeah. I mean, I know the committee doesn't meet until Monday, but I thought we could get a head start.

Okay! Come on in.

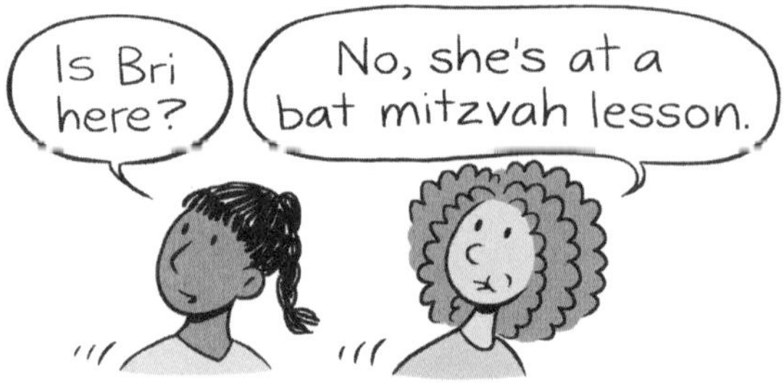
Is Bri here?
No, she's at a bat mitzvah lesson.

Poor Bri. Her bat mitzvah is less than a month away, and she's nervous.

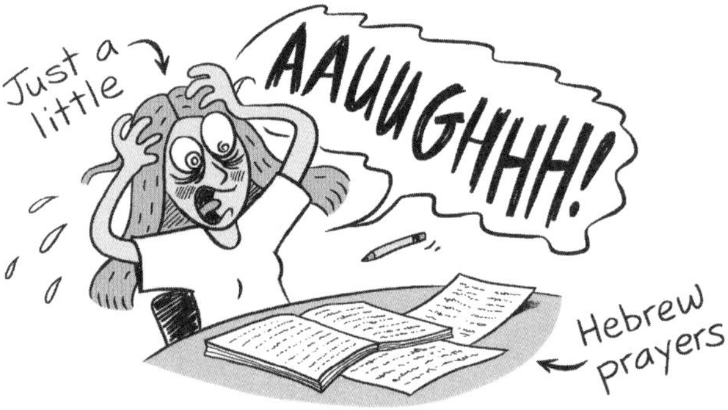
Just a little
AAUUGHHH!
Hebrew prayers

I sit at Emmie's kitchen table while she finds us snacks.

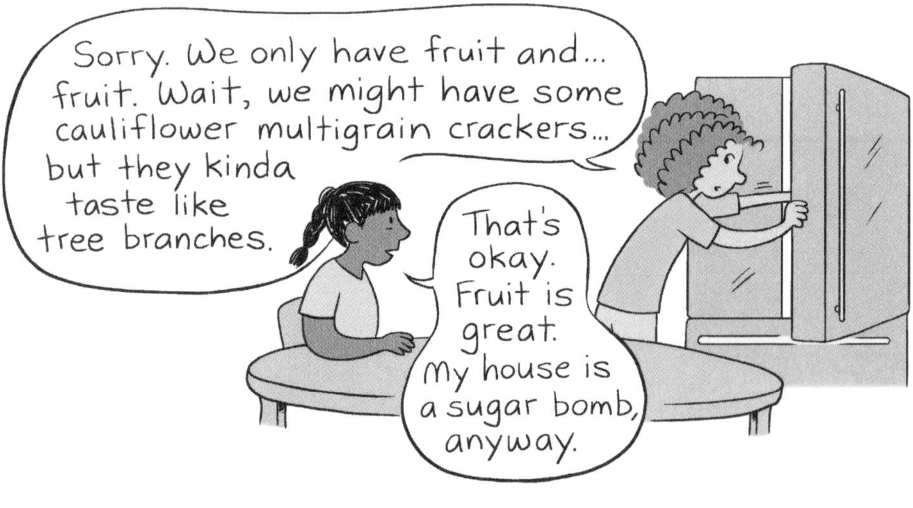
Sorry. We only have fruit and... fruit. Wait, we might have some cauliflower multigrain crackers... but they kinda taste like tree branches.
That's okay. Fruit is great. My house is a sugar bomb, anyway.

Truth is, Mamá and I have gotten so used to being around sweets, we barely touch 'em anymore (except for those—mmm—donuts).

We talk and sketch and munch on orange and pear slices. It doesn't take long to forget about Leo.

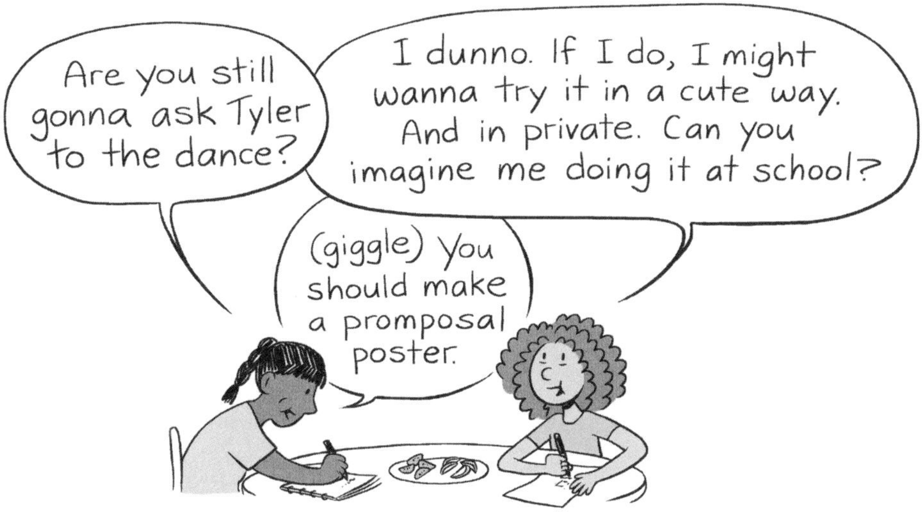
Are you still gonna ask Tyler to the dance?
I dunno. If I do, I might wanna try it in a cute way. And in private. Can you imagine me doing it at school?
(giggle) You should make a promposal poster.

We get back on track and come up with a few ideas for dance decor. Not too many in case it goes in a different direction, but enough to get people enthusiastic. So far, the theme is "Get Glowing" (glow-in-the-dark), which should be really fun.

I head back home before dinner, feeling twenty thousand times better. I even think of another dress design while riding. I wanna knock Ben's socks off.

regular, not burger-themed

About a block away from home, still lost in dress thoughts, I practically run over Leo and his two new friends.

Whoa!

Omigosh, I'm so sorry!

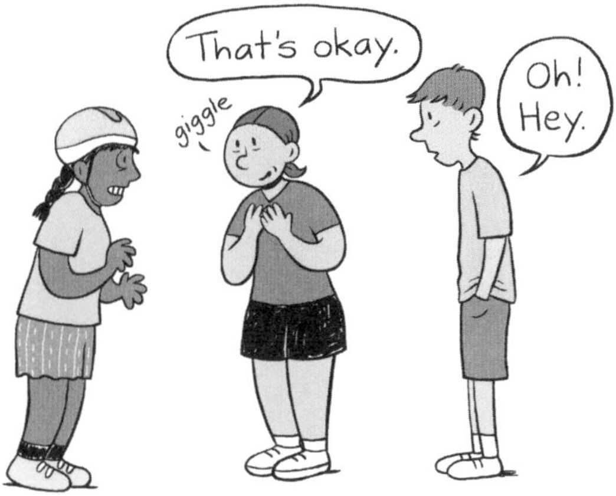
That's okay.
giggle
Oh! Hey.

We stand there awkwardly for a moment.

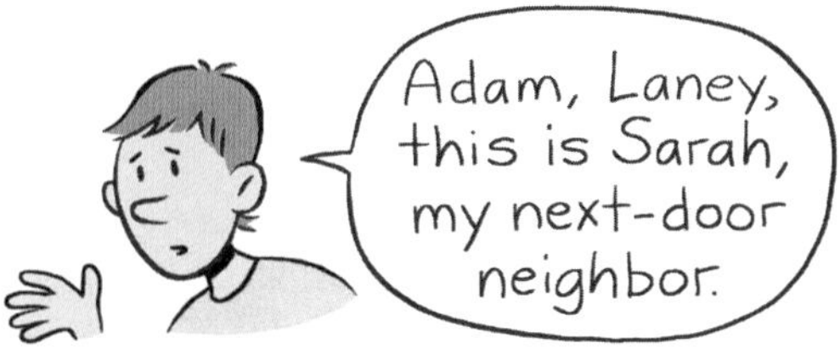
Adam, Laney, this is Sarah, my next-door neighbor.

Next-door neighbor??

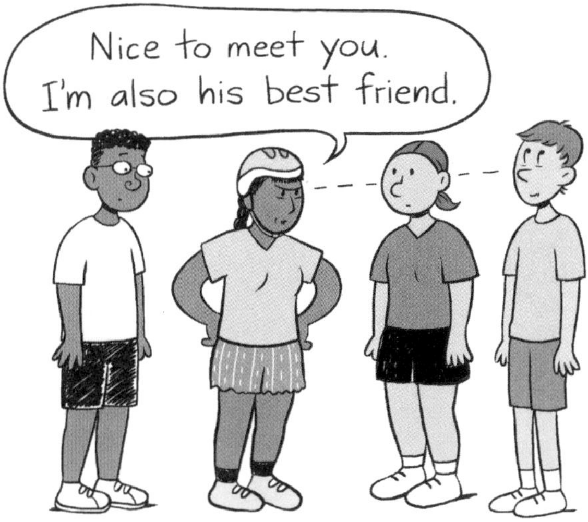
Nice to meet you. I'm also his best friend.

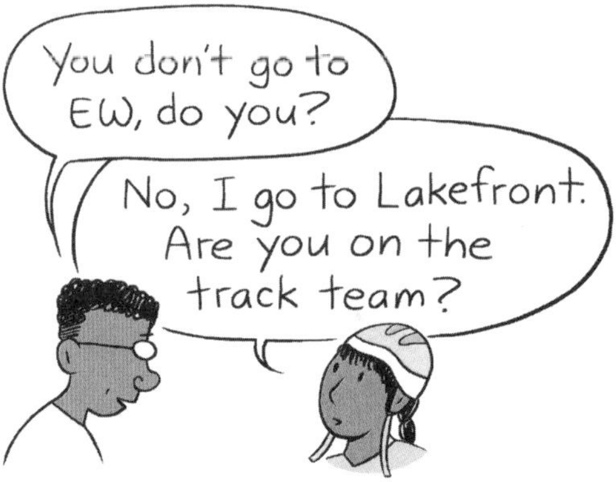
You don't go to EW, do you?
No, I go to Lakefront. Are you on the track team?

They nod.

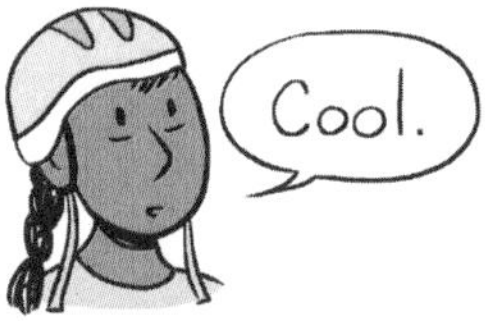
Cool.

I don't know what to say after that.

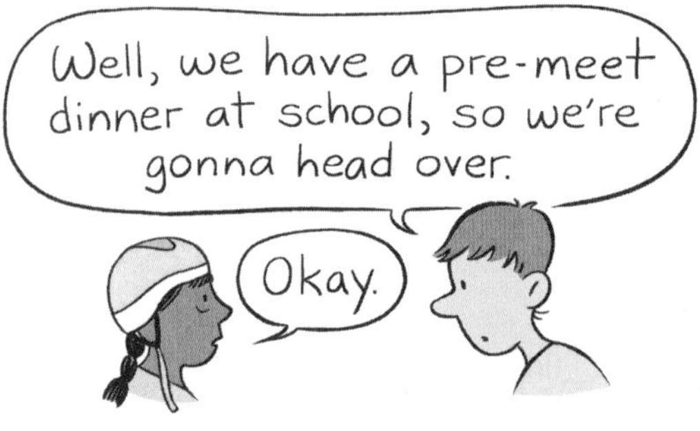
Well, we have a pre-meet dinner at school, so we're gonna head over.
Okay.

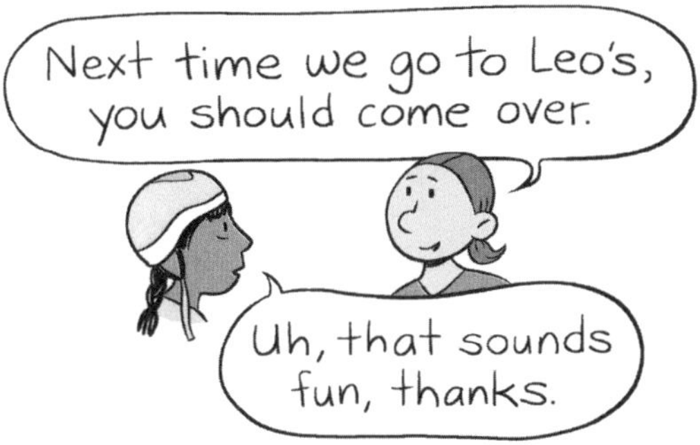
Next time we go to Leo's, you should come over.
Uh, that sounds fun, thanks.

I probably should've sounded more enthusiastic, but Leo's standing there, looking uncomfortable. Also, his house might as well be my own—I'm always running back and forth without permission—so it's weird to get an invite.

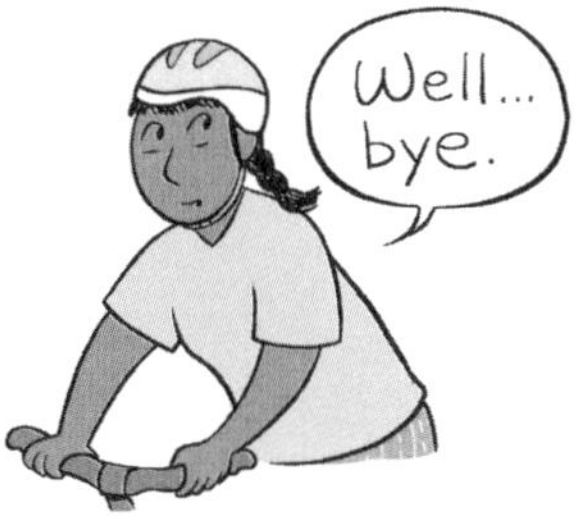
Well... bye.

I go straight home and don't look back.

So, that's it, then?

I'm now just a **next-door neighbor**?

Fine. He can be that way. After all, I have other things I can do until he comes to his senses. Not just the decorating committee, but there's art club, poetry club, and now a dress to design and sew! I have a full, busy life, close friends, and a potential bf (please, please, please).

At least, that's what I tell myself.

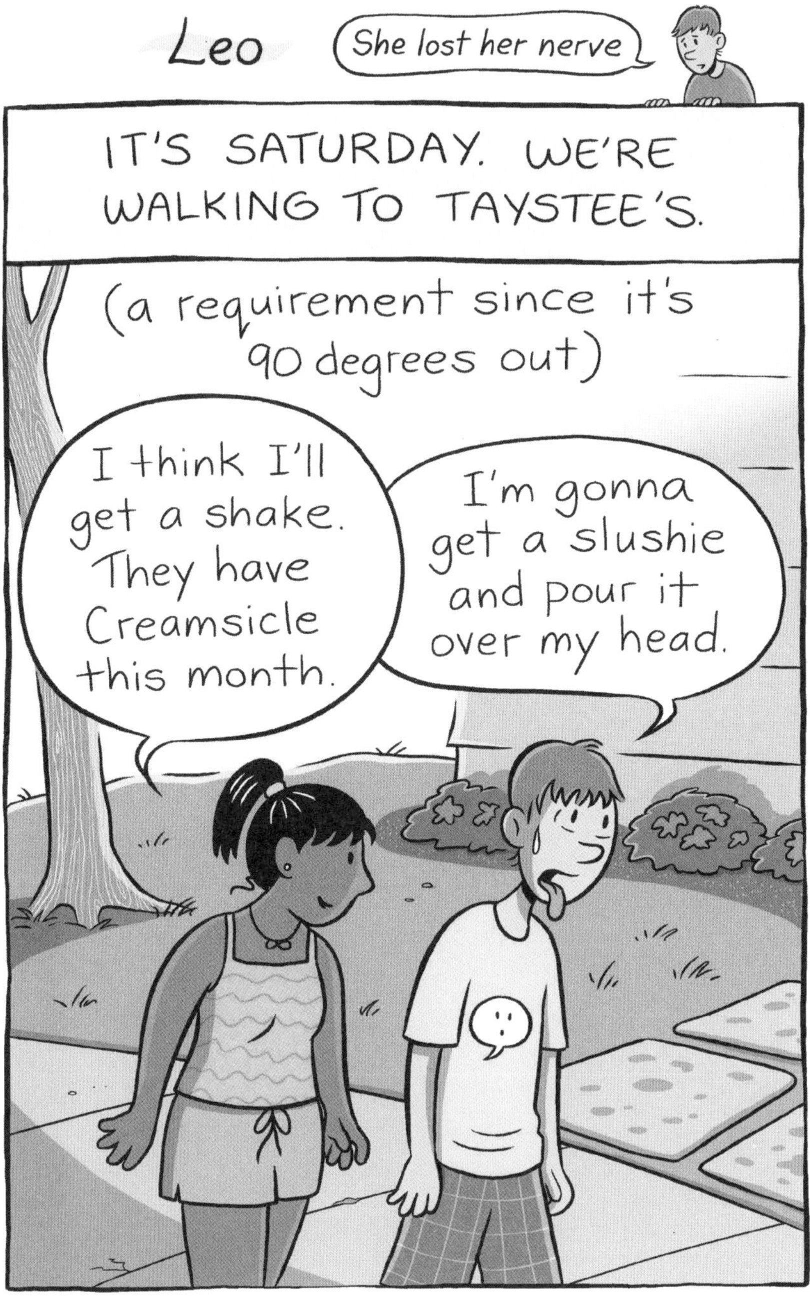
Leo
She lost her nerve
IT'S SATURDAY. WE'RE WALKING TO TAYSTEE'S.
(a requirement since it's 90 degrees out)
I think I'll get a shake. They have Creamsicle this month.
I'm gonna get a slushie and pour it over my head.

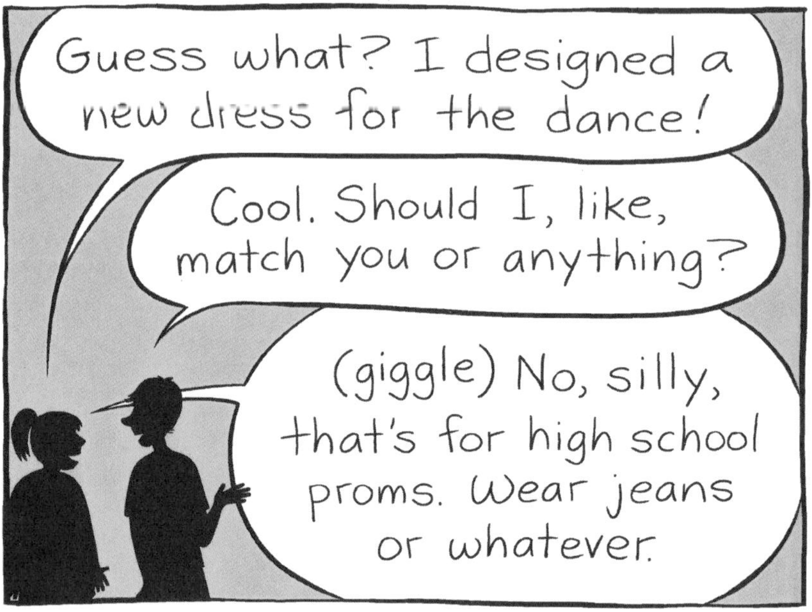
Guess what? I designed a new dress for the dance!
Cool. Should I, like, match you or anything?
(giggle) No, silly, that's for high school proms. Wear jeans or whatever.

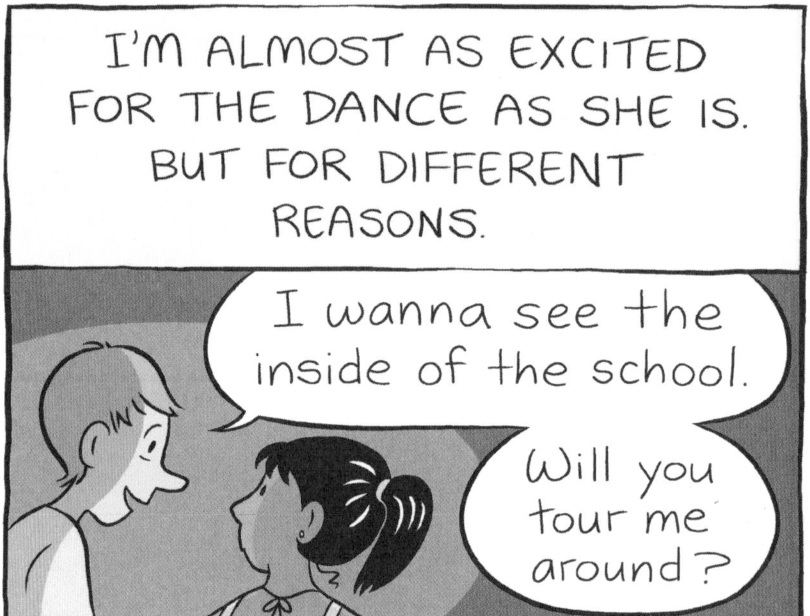
I'M ALMOST AS EXCITED FOR THE DANCE AS SHE IS. BUT FOR DIFFERENT REASONS.
I wanna see the inside of the school.
Will you tour me around?

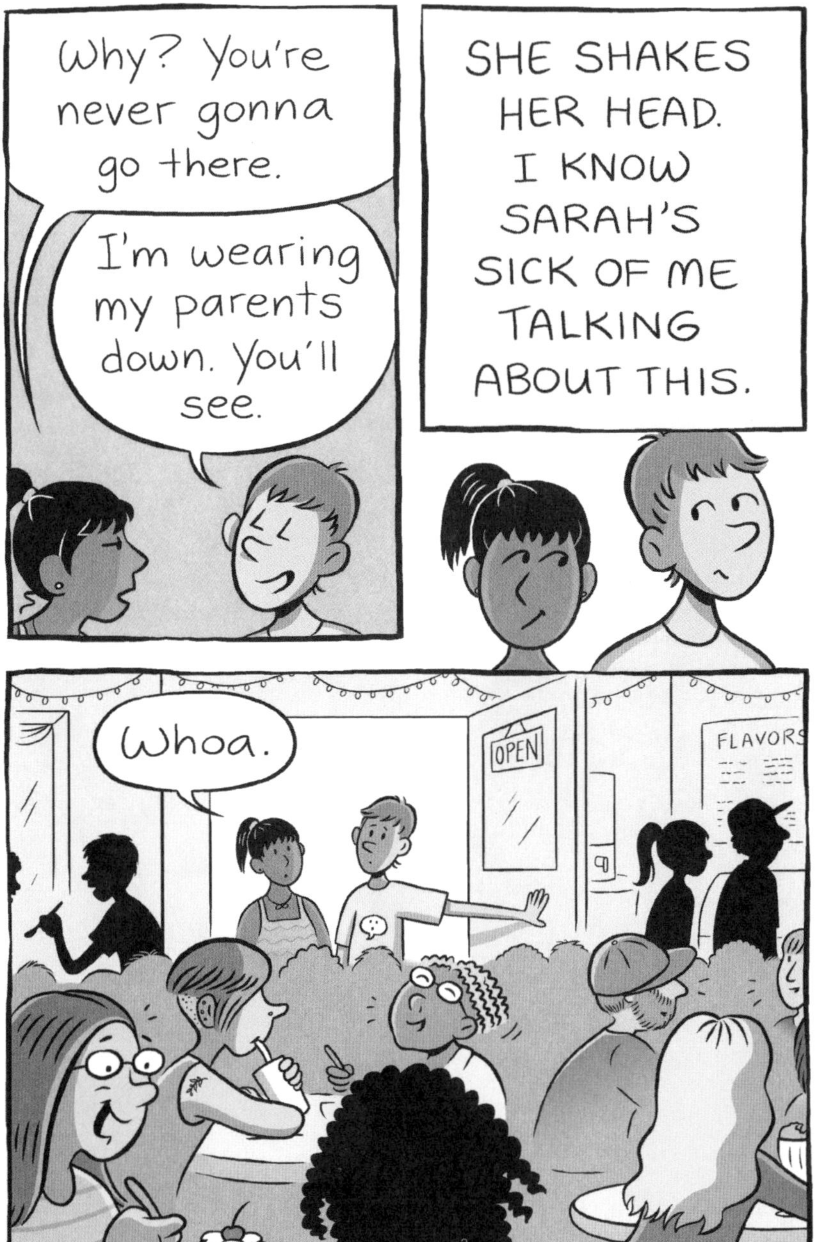
Why? You're never gonna go there.
I'm wearing my parents down. You'll see.
SHE SHAKES HER HEAD. I KNOW SARAH'S SICK OF ME TALKING ABOUT THIS.
Whoa.
OPEN
FLAVORS

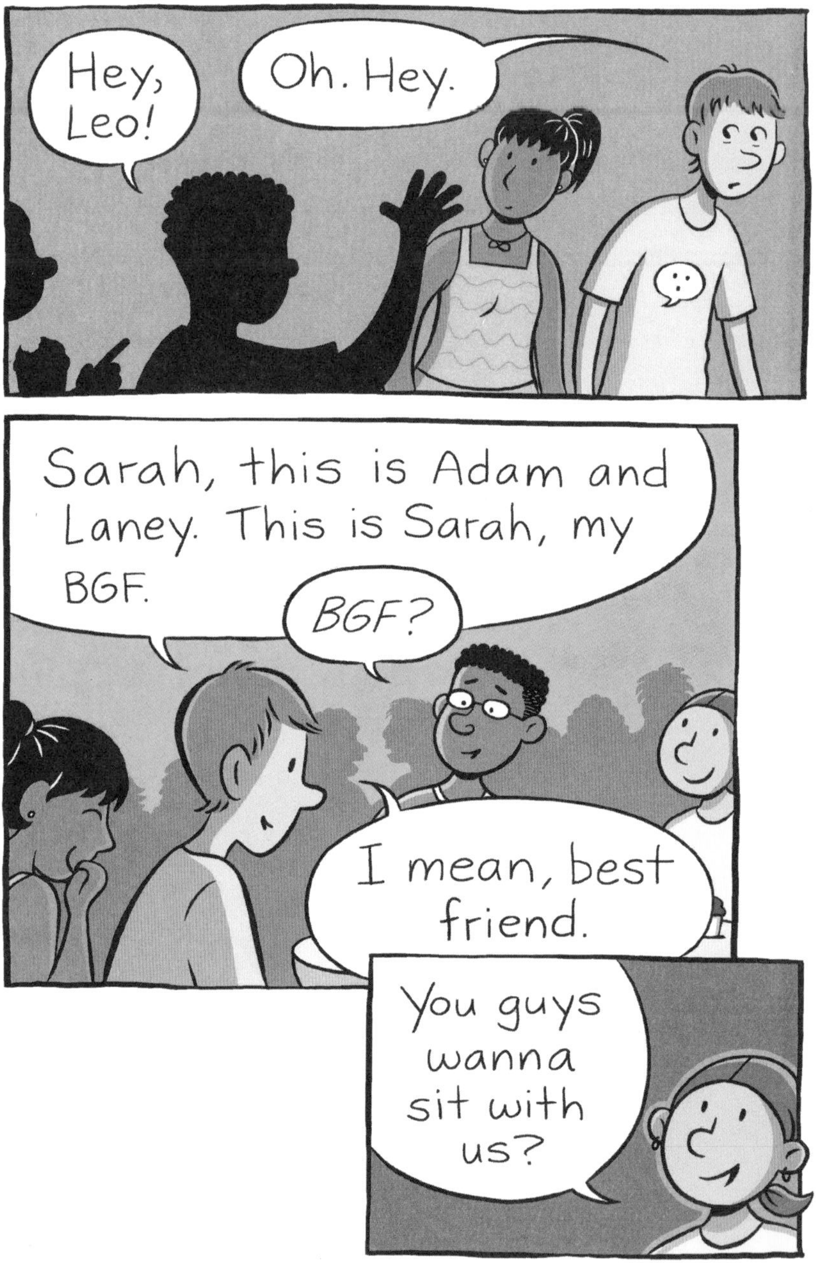
Hey, Leo!
Oh. Hey.
Sarah, this is Adam and Laney. This is Sarah, my BGF.
BGF?
I mean, best friend.
You guys wanna sit with us?

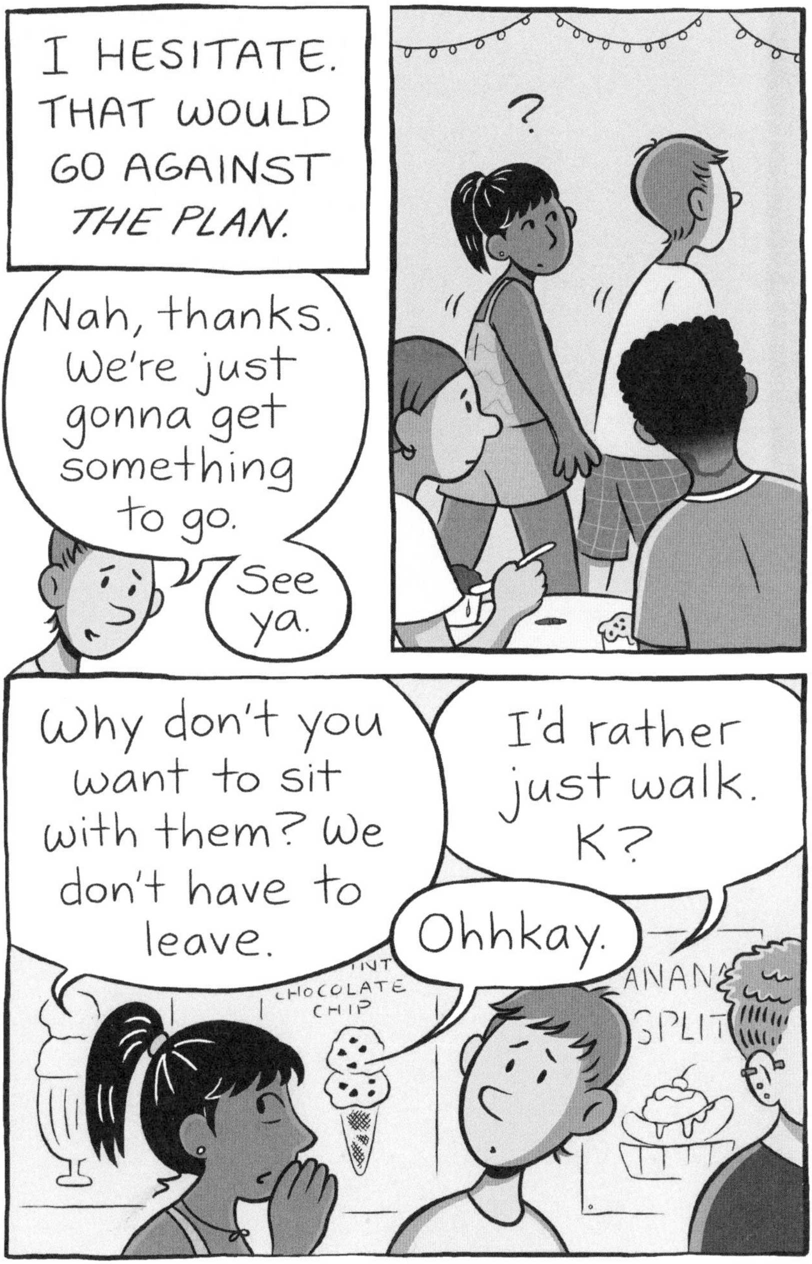
I HESITATE. THAT WOULD GO AGAINST *THE PLAN.*
Nah, thanks. We're just gonna get something to go.
See ya.
?
Why don't you want to sit with them? We don't have to leave.
I'd rather just walk. K?
Ohhkay.
CHOCOLATE CHIP
SPLIT

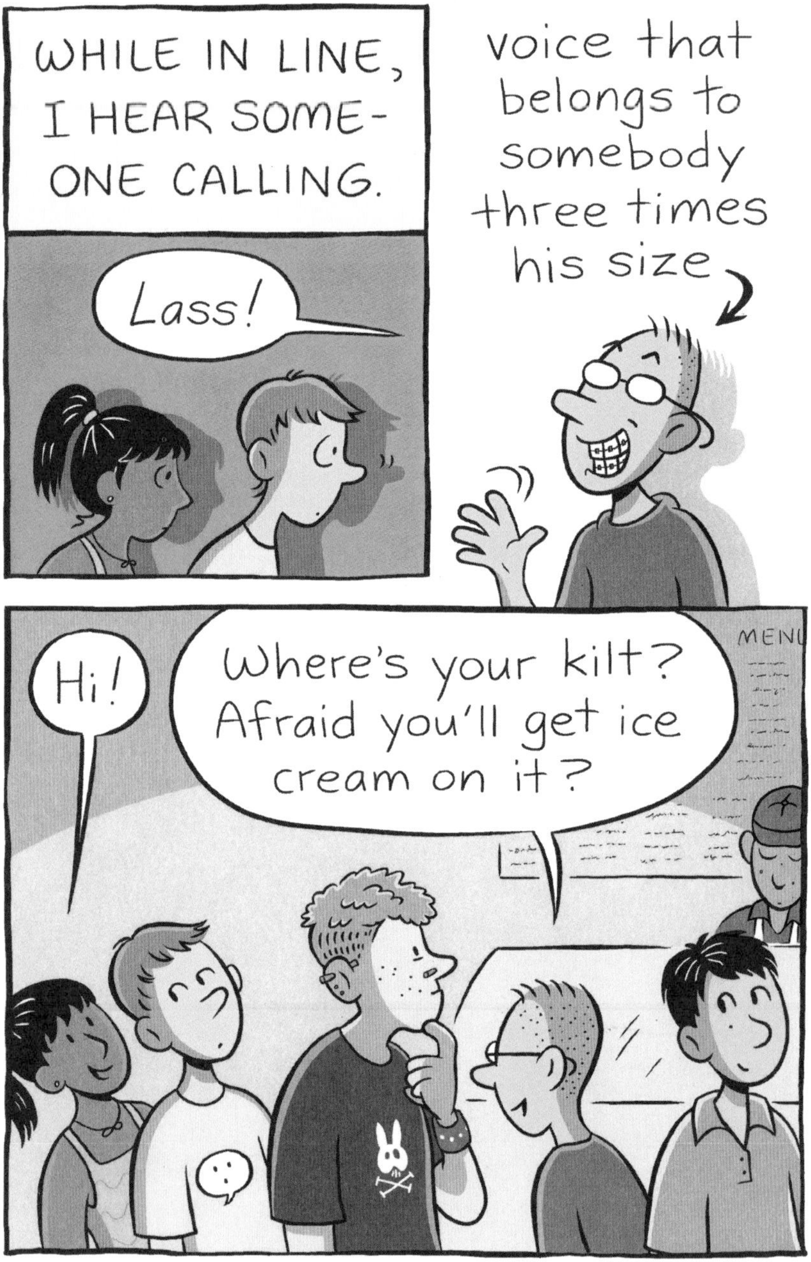
WHILE IN LINE, I HEAR SOME-ONE CALLING.
Lass!
voice that belongs to somebody three times his size
Hi!
Where's your kilt? Afraid you'll get ice cream on it?
MENU

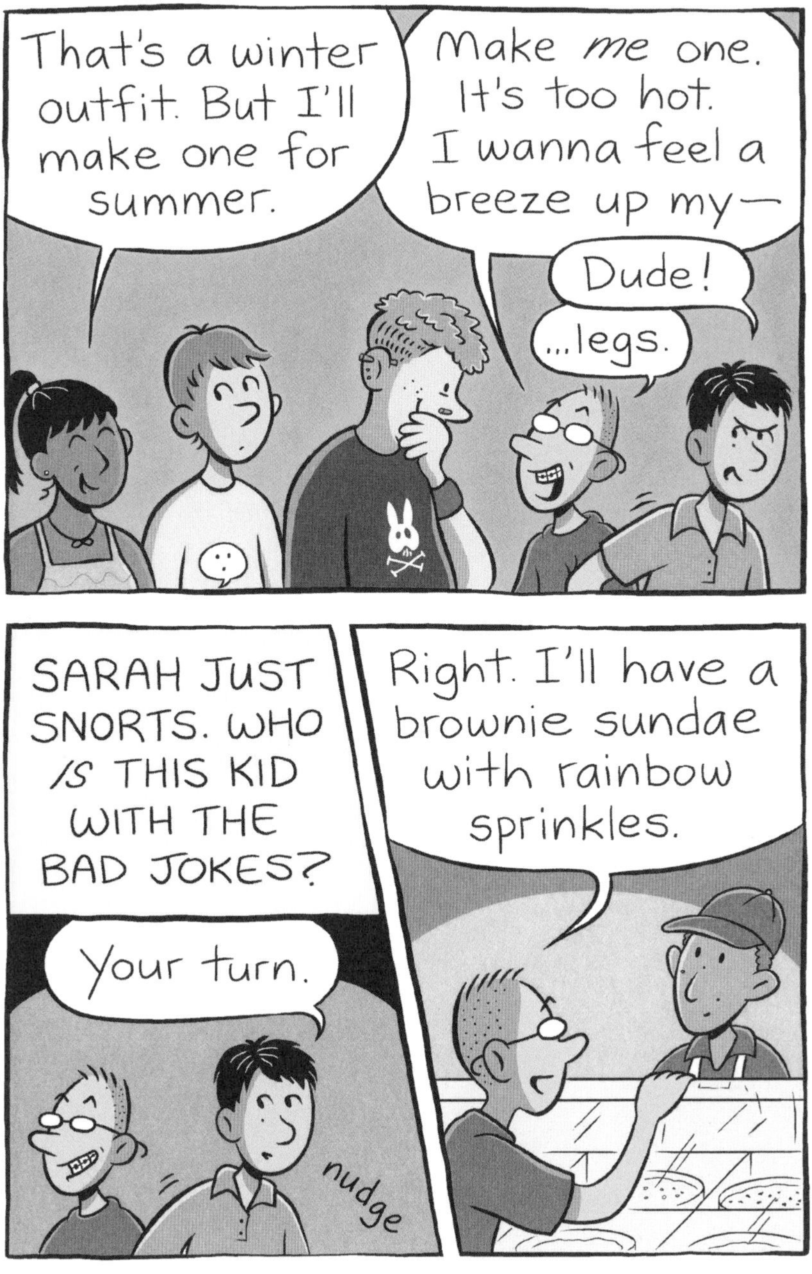
That's a winter outfit. But I'll make one for summer.
Make *me* one. It's too hot. I wanna feel a breeze up my—
Dude!
...legs.
SARAH JUST SNORTS. WHO *IS* THIS KID WITH THE BAD JOKES?
Your turn.
nudge
Right. I'll have a brownie sundae with rainbow sprinkles.

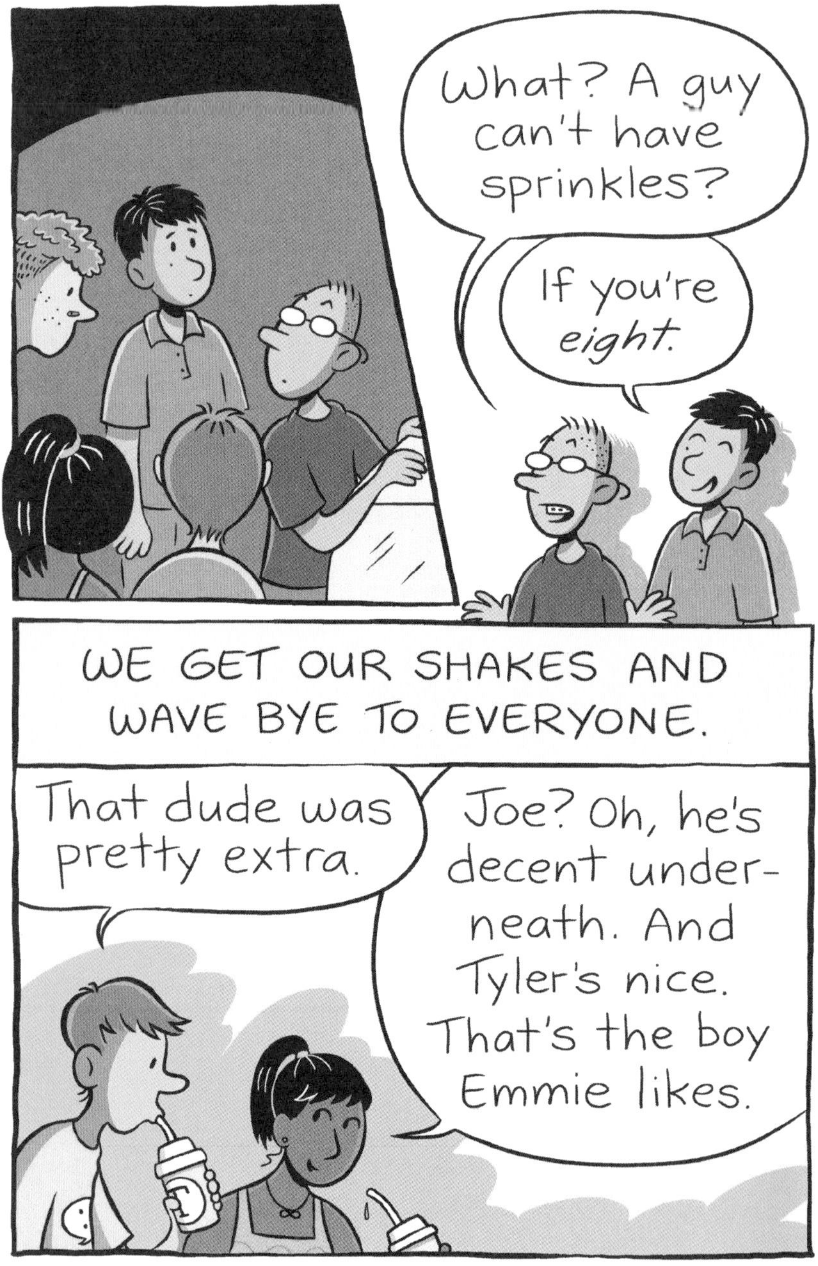
What? A guy can't have sprinkles?
If you're *eight.*
WE GET OUR SHAKES AND WAVE BYE TO EVERYONE.
That dude was pretty extra.
Joe? Oh, he's decent under-neath. And Tyler's nice. That's the boy Emmie likes.

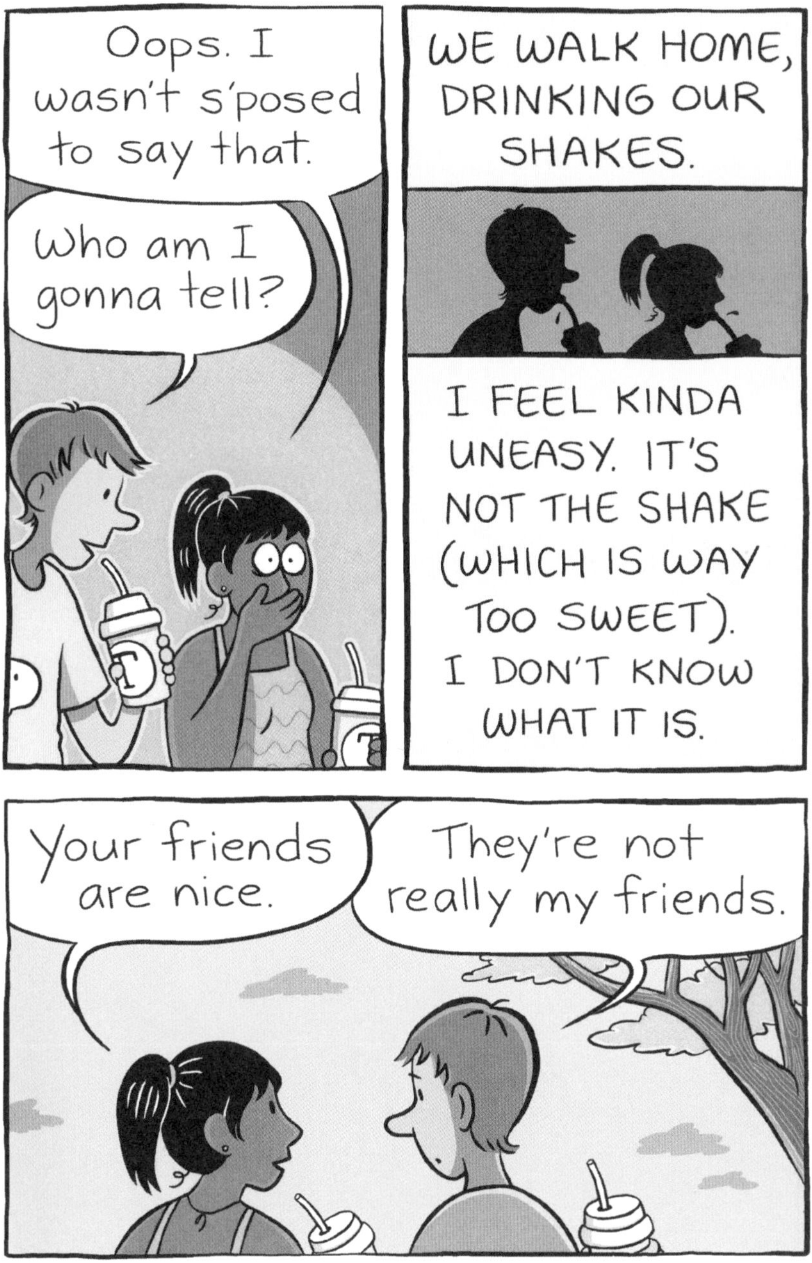
Oops. I wasn't s'posed to say that.
Who am I gonna tell?
WE WALK HOME, DRINKING OUR SHAKES.
I FEEL KINDA UNEASY. IT'S NOT THE SHAKE (WHICH IS WAY TOO SWEET). I DON'T KNOW WHAT IT IS.
Your friends are nice.
They're not really my friends.

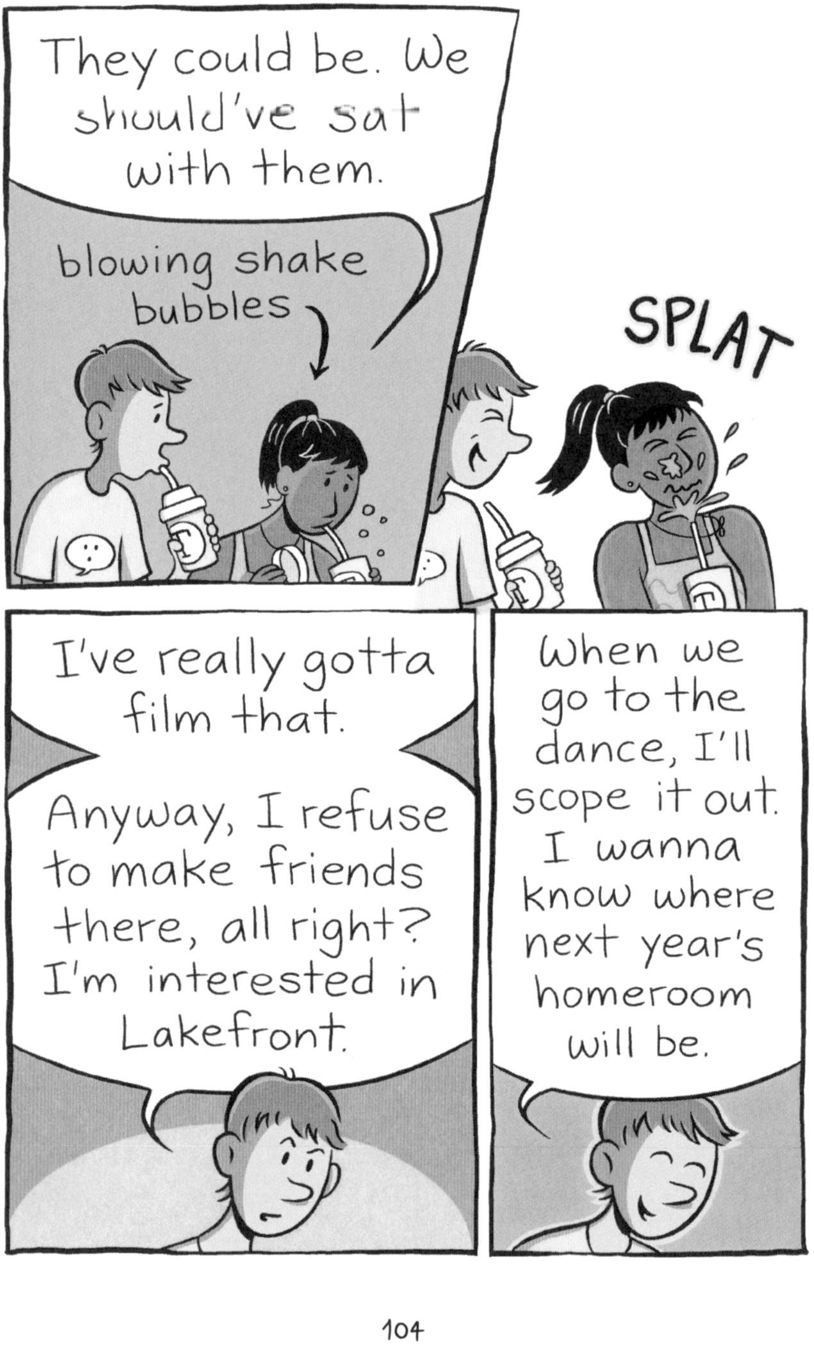
They could be. We should've sat with them.
blowing shake bubbles
SPLAT
I've really gotta film that.
Anyway, I refuse to make friends there, all right? I'm interested in Lakefront.
When we go to the dance, I'll scope it out. I wanna know where next year's homeroom will be.

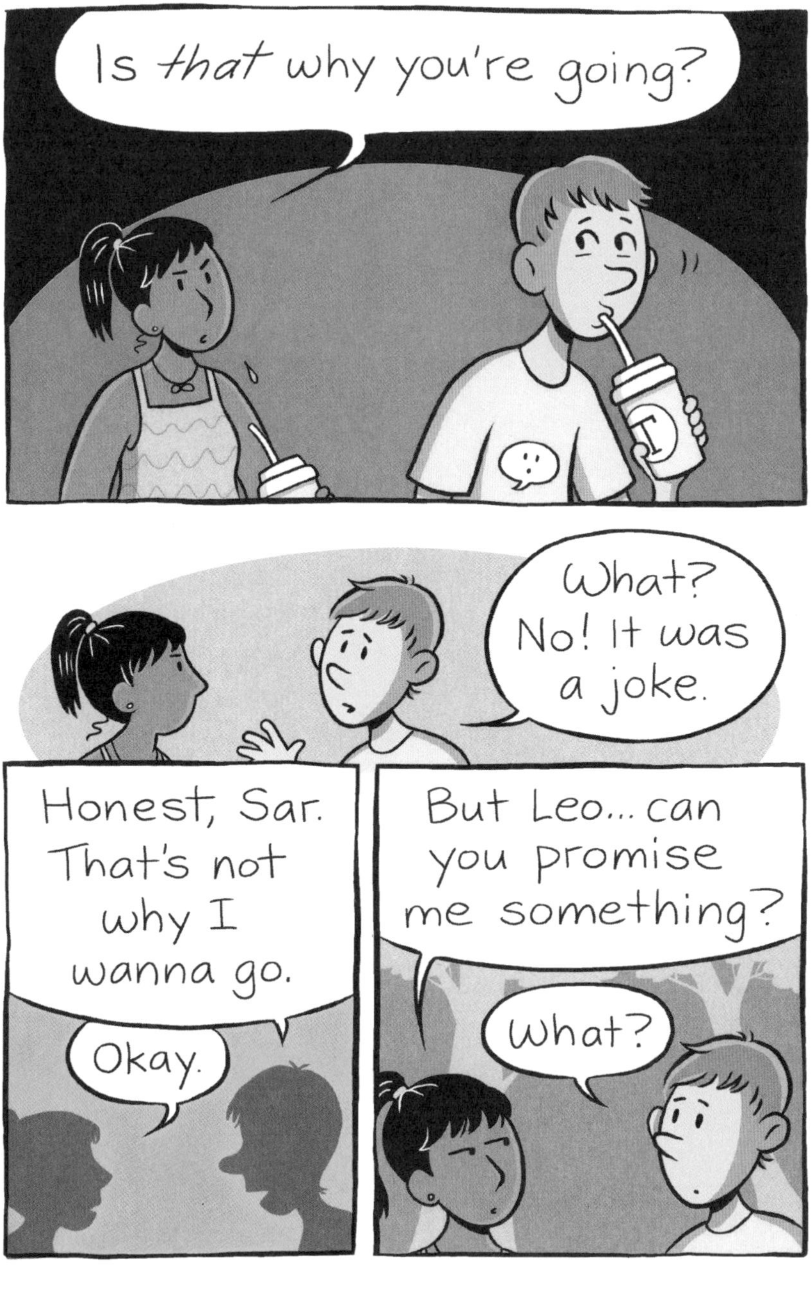
Is *that* why you're going?
What? No! It was a joke.
Honest, Sar. That's not why I wanna go.
Okay.
But Leo... can you promise me something?
What?

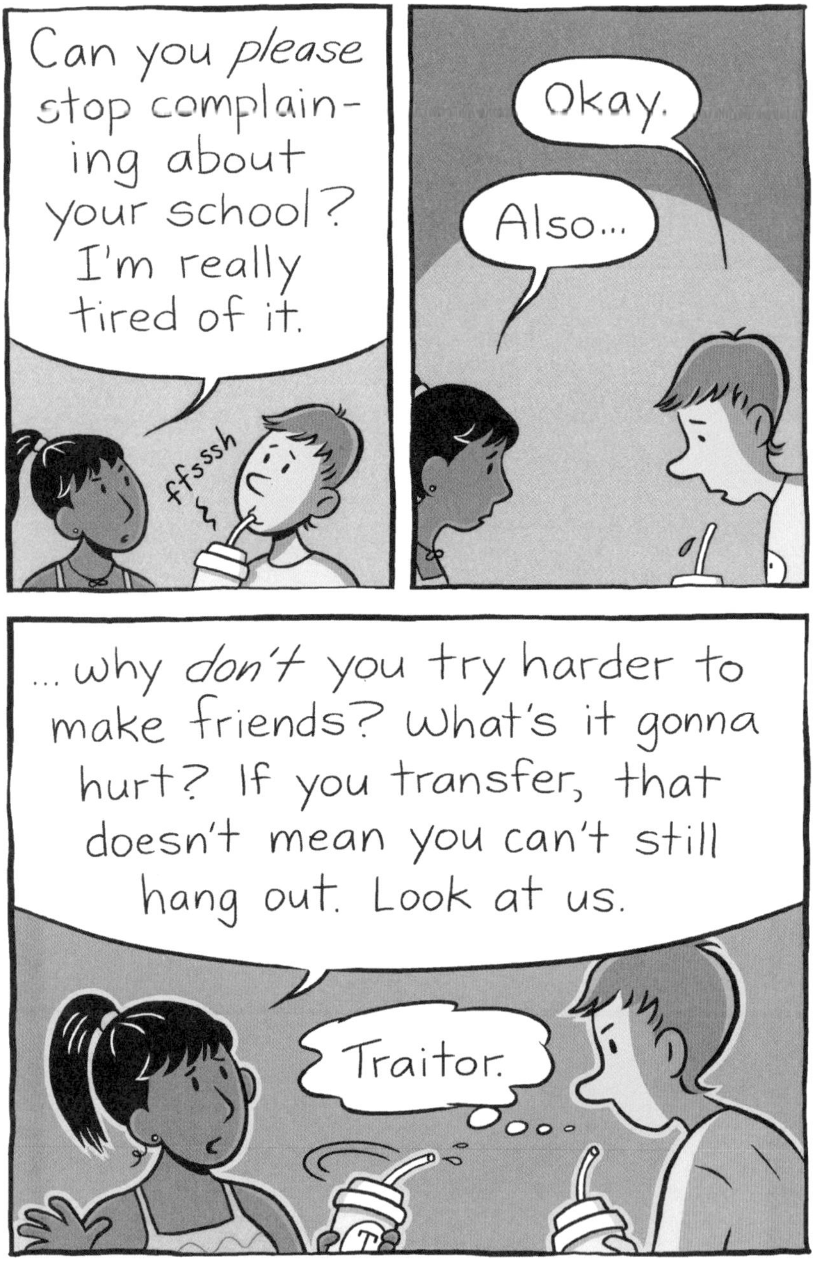
Can you *please* stop complaining about your school? I'm really tired of it.
ffsssh
Okay.
Also...
...why *don't* you try harder to make friends? What's it gonna hurt? If you transfer, that doesn't mean you can't still hang out. Look at us.
Traitor.

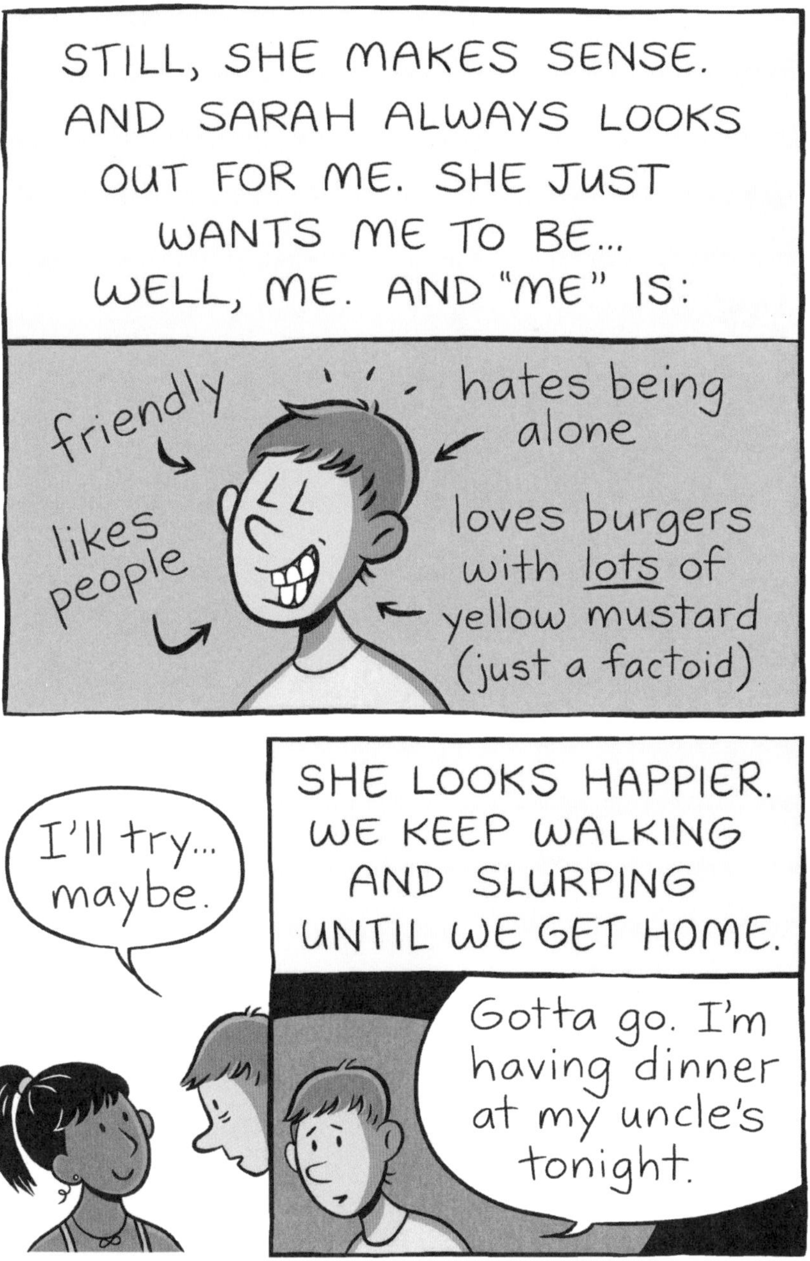
STILL, SHE MAKES SENSE. AND SARAH ALWAYS LOOKS OUT FOR ME. SHE JUST WANTS ME TO BE... WELL, ME. AND "ME" IS:
friendly
likes people
hates being alone
loves burgers with lots of yellow mustard (just a factoid)
I'll try... maybe.
SHE LOOKS HAPPIER. WE KEEP WALKING AND SLURPING UNTIL WE GET HOME.
Gotta go. I'm having dinner at my uncle's tonight.

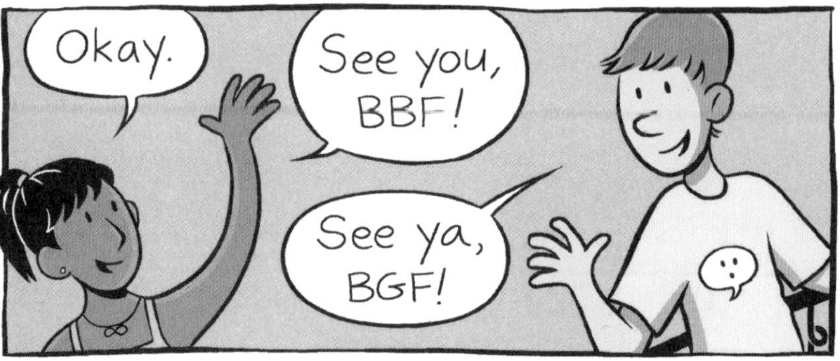
Okay.
See you, BBF!
See ya, BGF!

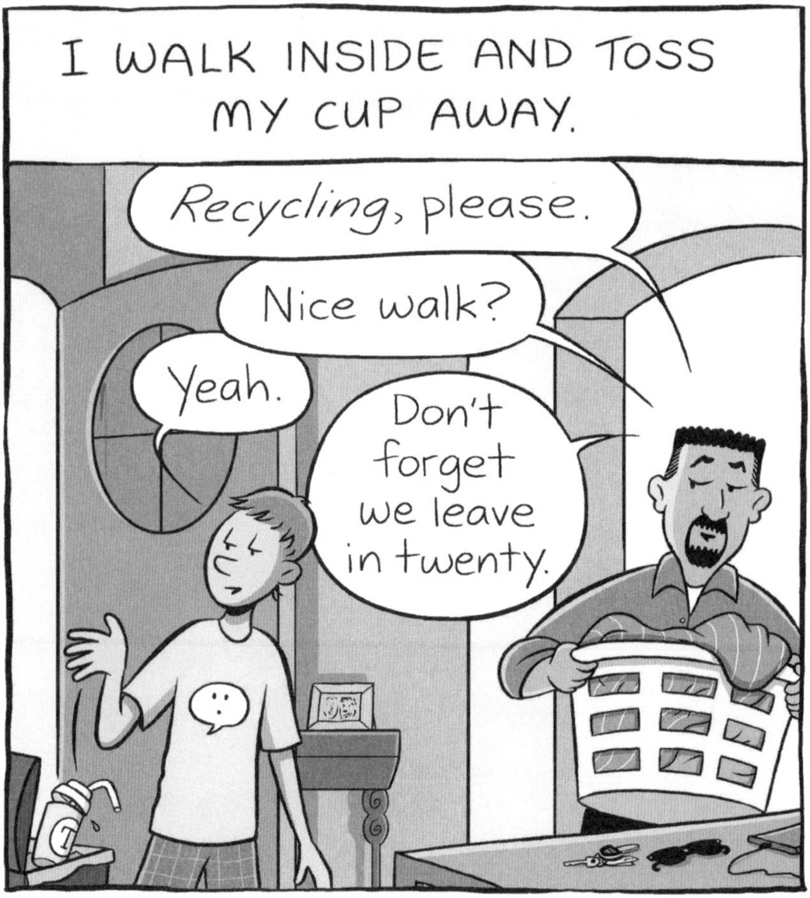
I WALK INSIDE AND TOSS MY CUP AWAY.
Recycling, please.
Nice walk?
Yeah.
Don't forget we leave in twenty.

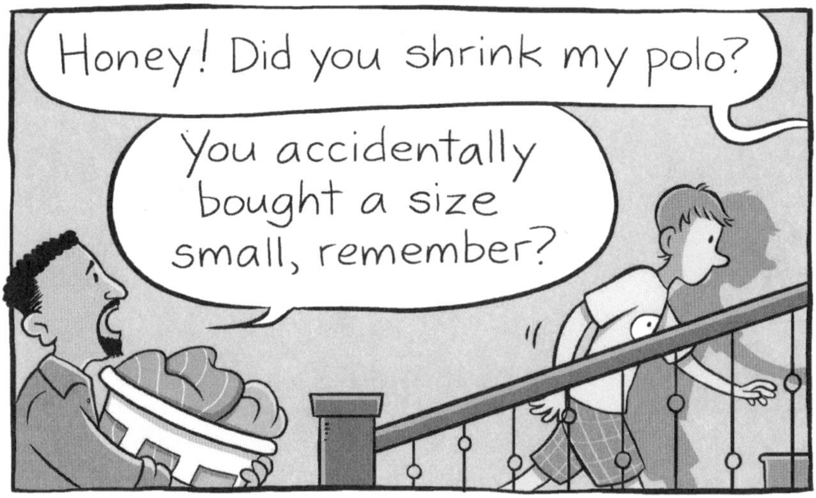
Honey! Did you shrink my polo?
You accidentally bought a size small, remember?

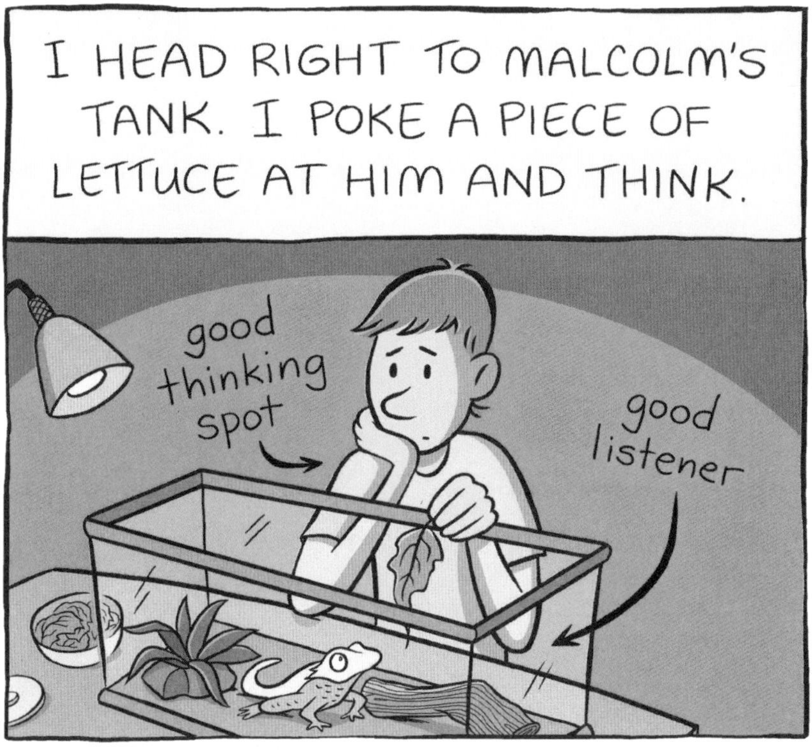
I HEAD RIGHT TO MALCOLM'S TANK. I POKE A PIECE OF LETTUCE AT HIM AND THINK.
good thinking spot
good listener

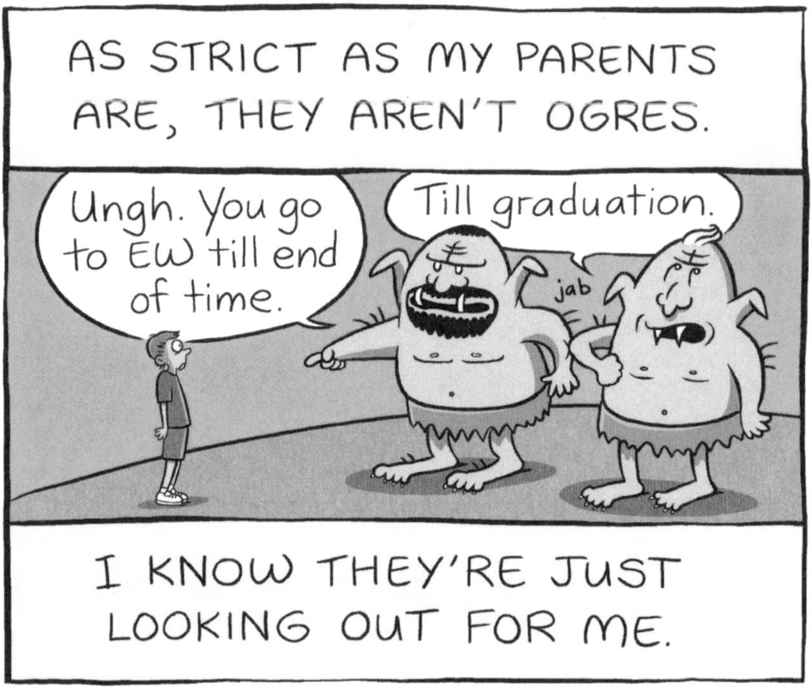
AS STRICT AS MY PARENTS ARE, THEY AREN'T OGRES.
Ungh. You go to EW till end of time.
Till graduation.
jab
I KNOW THEY'RE JUST LOOKING OUT FOR ME.

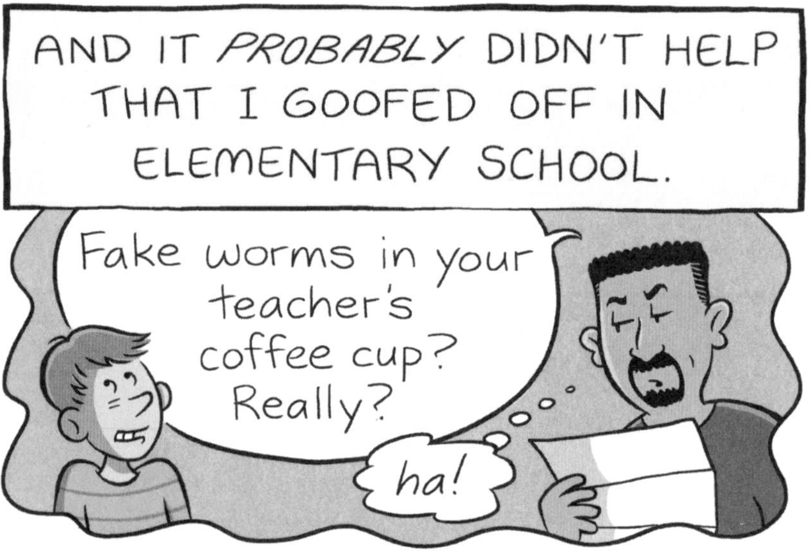
AND IT *PROBABLY* DIDN'T HELP THAT I GOOFED OFF IN ELEMENTARY SCHOOL.
Fake worms in your teacher's coffee cup? Really?
ha!

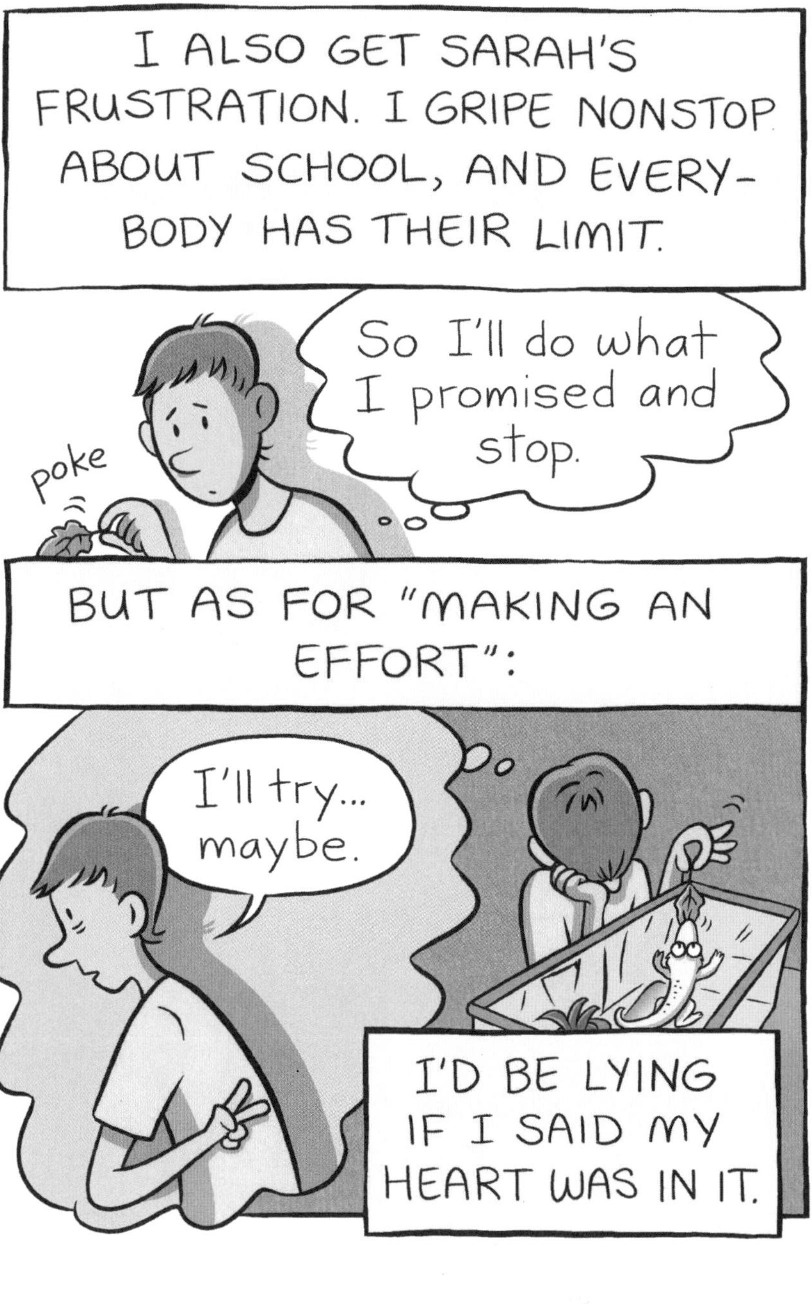
I ALSO GET SARAH'S FRUSTRATION. I GRIPE NONSTOP ABOUT SCHOOL, AND EVERY-BODY HAS THEIR LIMIT.
poke
So I'll do what I promised and stop.
BUT AS FOR "MAKING AN EFFORT":
I'll try... maybe.
I'D BE LYING IF I SAID MY HEART WAS IN IT.

SARAH

I asked him

As I said, it started about a year ago.

It was like one minute Ben was just some kid at school who happened to be:

← Leo's friend

The next:

sigh

← swoonworthy hotcake

I never developed a crush that fast. Okay, I'd never had a crush, period. I guess I just didn't know it could hit like a ton of . . . What's heavier than bricks?

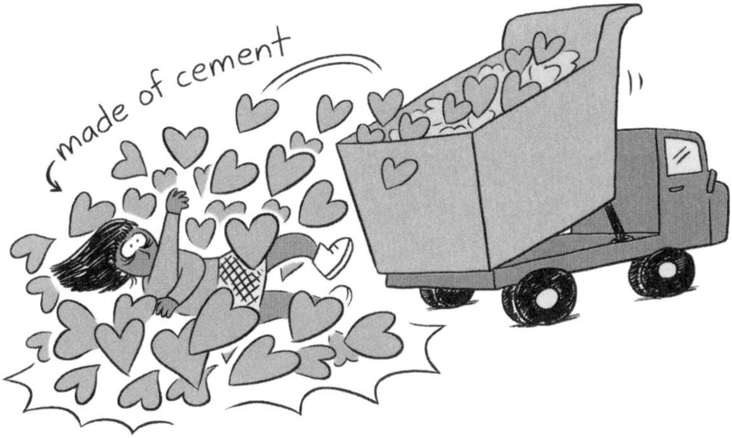
made of cement

It's no fluke that it coincided with Ben's growth spurt and the fact that he finally grew into his ears and stopped tucking his shirt into his shorts. Not that looks matter that much to me (they don't), but it changed him in my eyes. He seemed older somehow, not the squeaky-voiced, silly, freckly little kid who played tackle-tag with Leo in the elementary school playground.

He got cooler, too. Or maybe quieter, hard to tell. I like that he's:

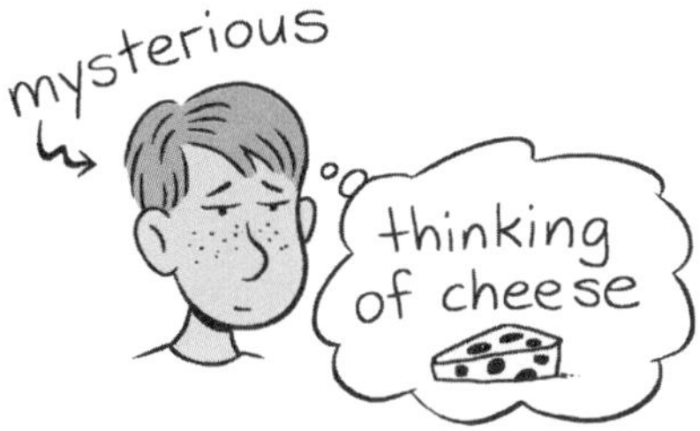
mysterious
thinking of cheese

Bri thinks that it's more important for a potential bf to be open, enthusiastic, and know how to make good conversation. But I prefer someone I can just be with.

Okay, I have no idea how I'd be with him, but at least I'll find out next Friday!

We've already started meeting for the decorations. There are about a dozen of us on the committee. Emmie and I presented the ideas we had come up with.

Okay, I presented them

eep

Everyone loved them! Ms. Laurie had us all brainstorm some more ideas. Then we divvied up what we're going to do. Emmie, Bri, and I will make cutout neon shapes to hang on the cafeteria walls. Everybody else will be in charge of:

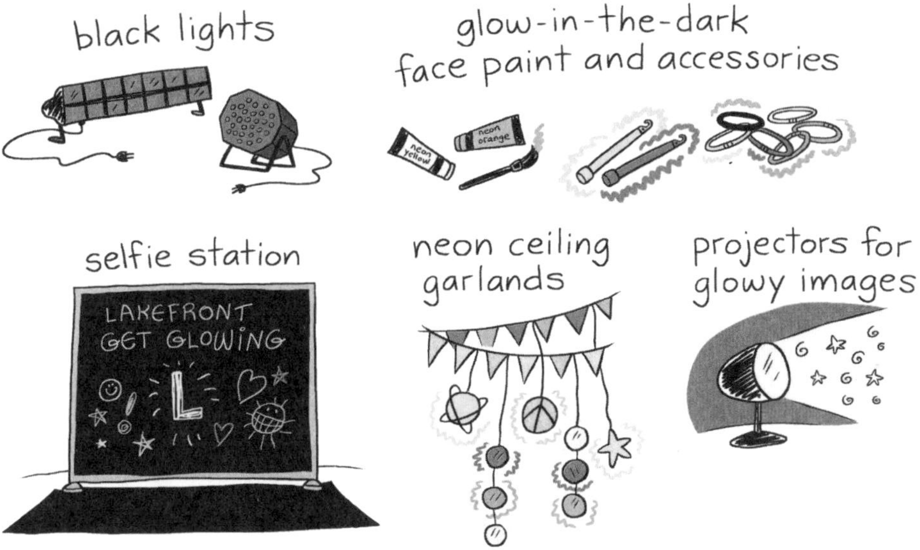
black lights
glow-in-the-dark face paint and accessories
neon yellow
neon orange
selfie station
LAKEFRONT GET GLOWING
L
neon ceiling garlands
projectors for glowy images

There's even enough in the budget for glow-in-the-dark punch and snacks!

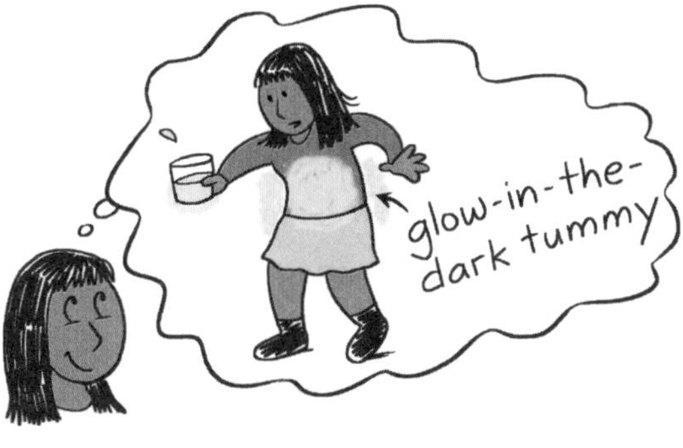
glow-in-the-dark tummy

We got permission to skip classes and decorate the cafeteria on the afternoon of the dance. Em is planning to come to my house afterward to get ready. I asked Bri if she wanted to come, too, but she's going to the dance straight from dinner at her aunt's.

(PS Emmie still hasn't asked Tyler.)

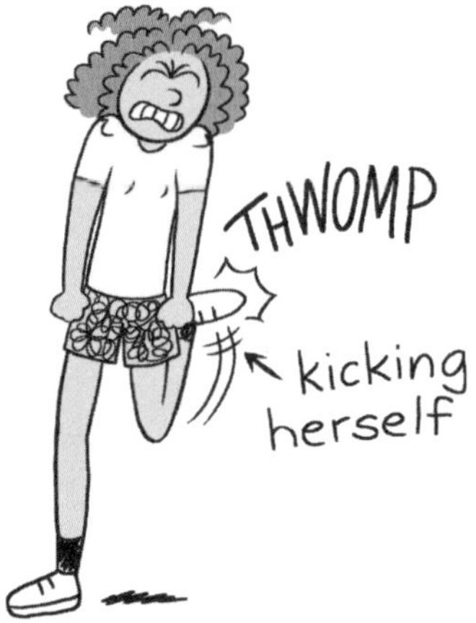
THWOMP
kicking herself

All this would have me totally giddy except for a couple of things.

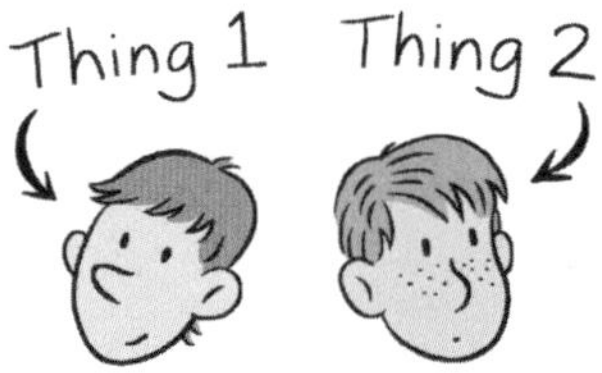
Thing 1
Thing 2

First, Leo is still avoiding me. It's now been a week, and he's barely acknowledged my existence. It's actually giving me bad flashbacks of sixth grade.

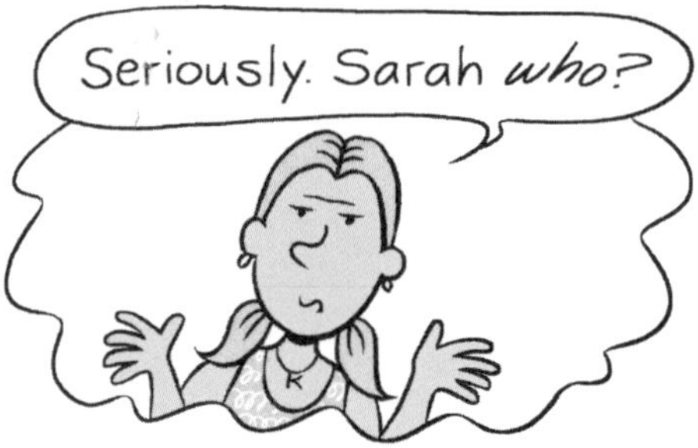
Seriously. Sarah *who?*

Every time I try to talk to him, he tells me he has too much homework ("private school load") or that he's tired from track. I'd **almost** buy it except I've seen him with his new friends—twice.

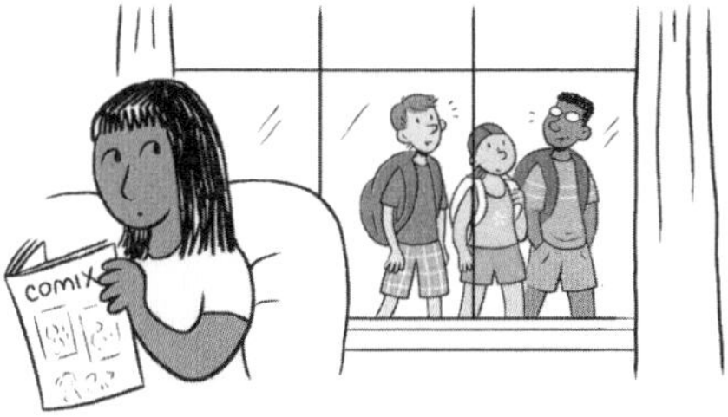
COMIX

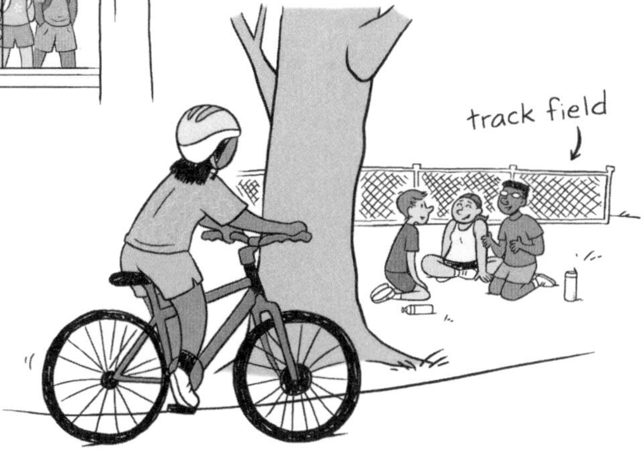
track field

I'm trying not to worry about it until after the dance, when I'll have more time to figure things out and he'll have had more time to cool off.

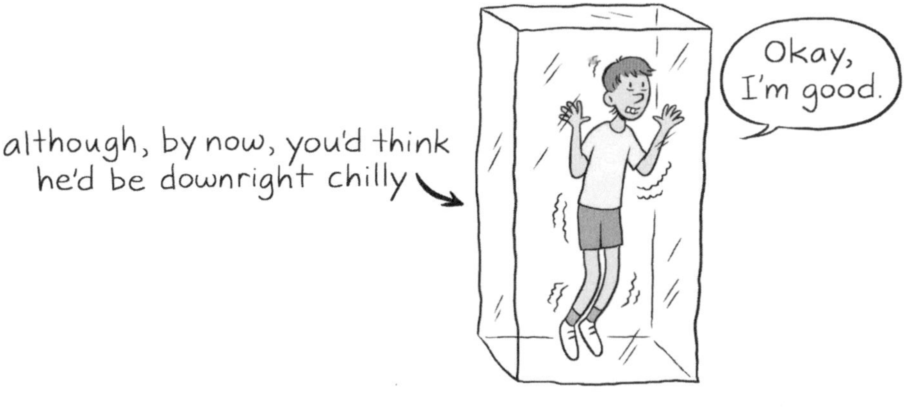
although, by now, you'd think he'd be downright chilly
Okay, I'm good.

And then there's Ben. Ever since I asked him to the dance, he hasn't exactly gone out of his way to ask me about plans. I've seen him in the halls, but either he hasn't seen me or he's been in a hurry. I did text to check if he wanted to be picked up for the dance or meet at school. He never responded. At first, it didn't bother me, 'cause even Leo gets frustrated about his text avoidance.

So I tried again two days later.

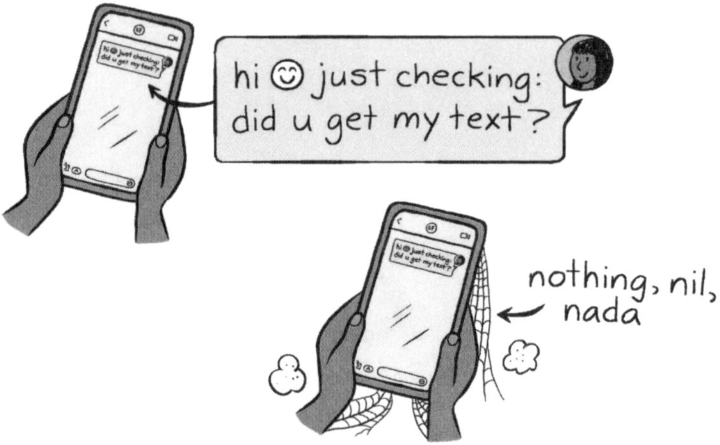
hi ☺ just checking:
did u get my text?
nothing, nil,
nada

If only I could talk to Leo about it, he might have some advice. But how do I talk to my best friend about boy problems when my best friend . . .

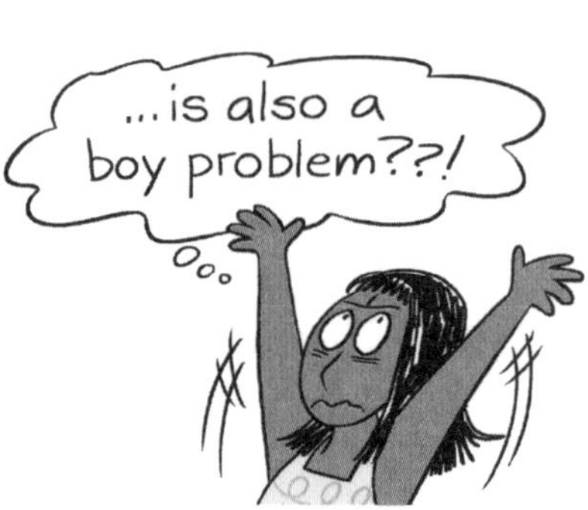
...is also a
boy problem??!

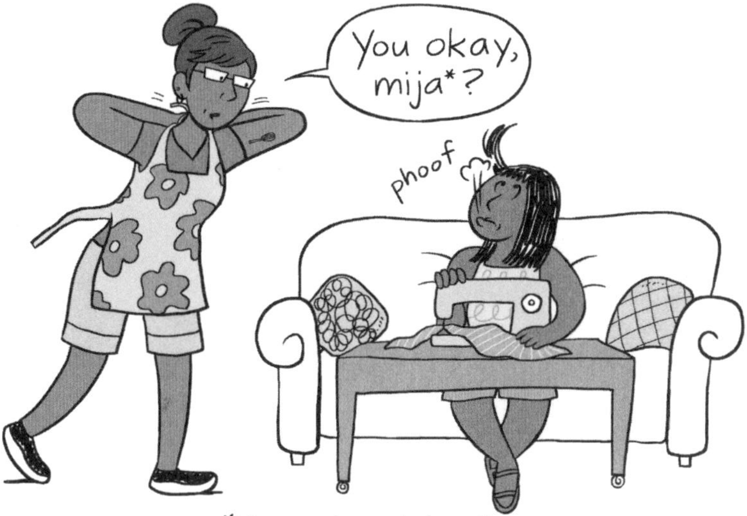
You okay, mija*?
phoof

*"my daughter"
(much better than Chubby-Cheeked)

I stop sewing.

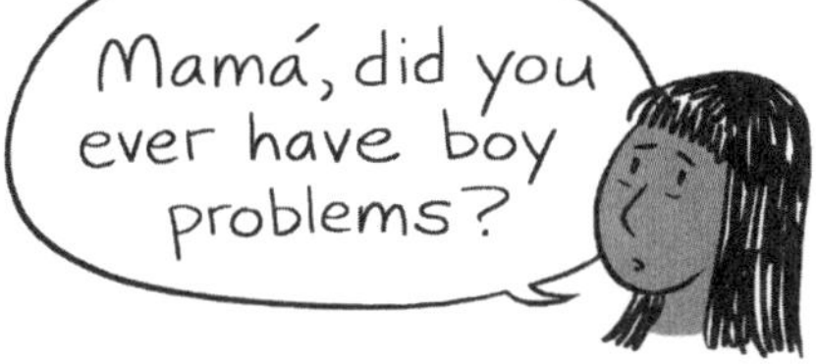
Mamá, did you ever have boy problems?

She raises an eyebrow.

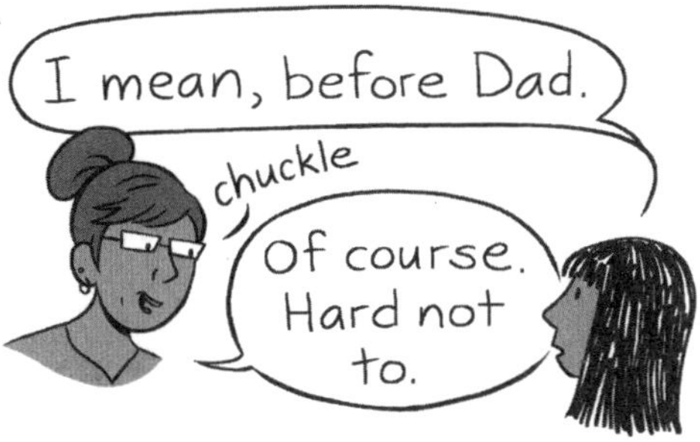
I mean, before Dad.
chuckle
Of course. Hard not to.

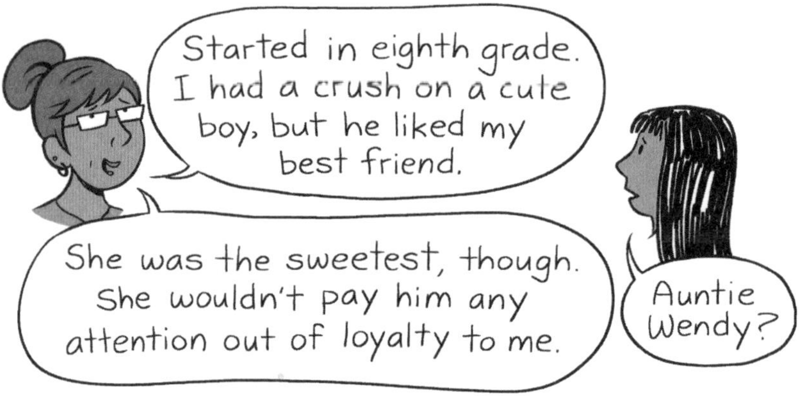
Started in eighth grade. I had a crush on a cute boy, but he liked my best friend.
She was the sweetest, though. She wouldn't pay him any attention out of loyalty to me.
Auntie Wendy?

That's Mamá's best friend. She lives in another state, but they're still close. Mamá nods.

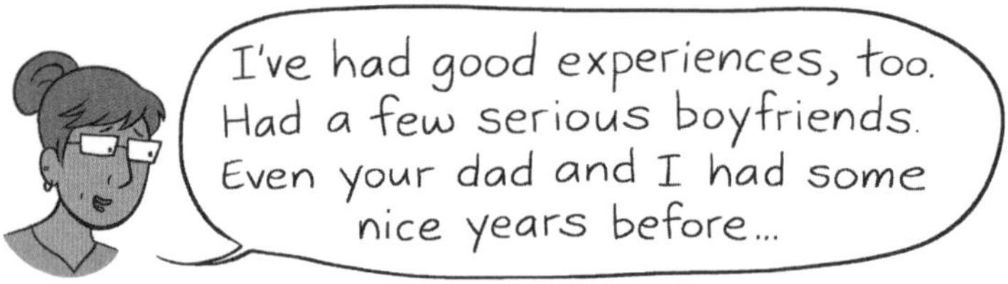
I've had good experiences, too. Had a few serious boyfriends. Even your dad and I had some nice years before...

Her voice trails off.

We don't talk about him. Like, ever.

My parents divorced when I was two. They married and had me really young—my dad right out of college and Mamá while she was still there (where they met). Mamá said they were infatuated and rushed in against their parents' wishes.

invisible cartoon hearts

Money soon got really tight. My dad couldn't find a good job here, so he went to the West Coast to live with his parents, work, and save up. It was supposed to be temporary. But months turned into a year, and a year turned into:

meeting the "true" love of his life

walking off into the (California) sunset

Her name is Sheila, but I call her "She-Devil" to Leo. Mamá wouldn't like that. She says it's not her fault, and anyway, we've all moved on. I even took Mama's last name.

Dad now has a good job (he owns some sporting-goods stores) and sends us money, but practically the only time I ever hear from him is when I get a card on birthdays. And he always signs it, "—Brett."

<u>not</u>:

Love, Dad **OR** xo, Pops **OR EVEN** ☺ Brett

So I try to forget him.

Mama's had dates since my dad but nothing serious. She says she likes it being just the two of us. Her big dream is to go back to college (since she dropped out), get her business degree, and open an actual bakery.

Then I'll worry about a boyfriend... if I even want one.

She's already making her dream come true. Not just the catering business, but she's started taking classes. Only one per semester, since she works two jobs, but it's a start.

I'm so, so, so proud of her.

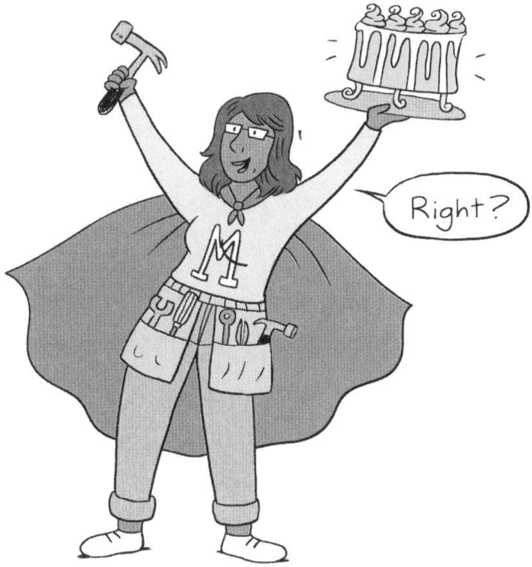
Right?

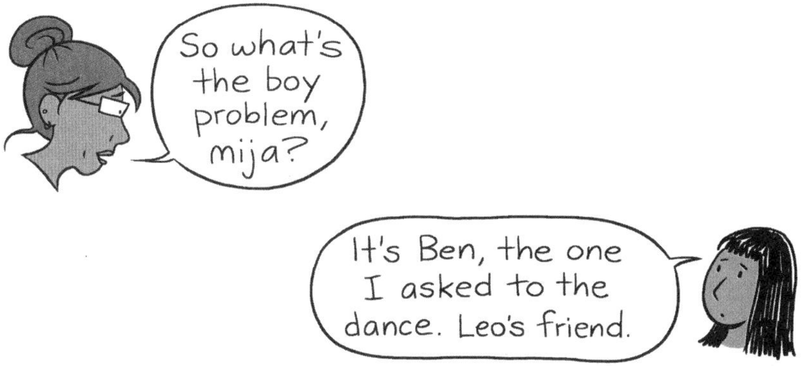
So what's the boy problem, mija?
It's Ben, the one I asked to the dance. Leo's friend.

I tell her about the texts.

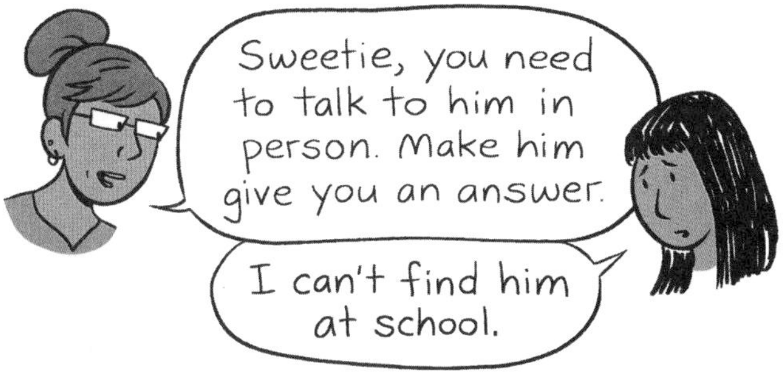
Sweetie, you need to talk to him in person. Make him give you an answer.
I can't find him at school.

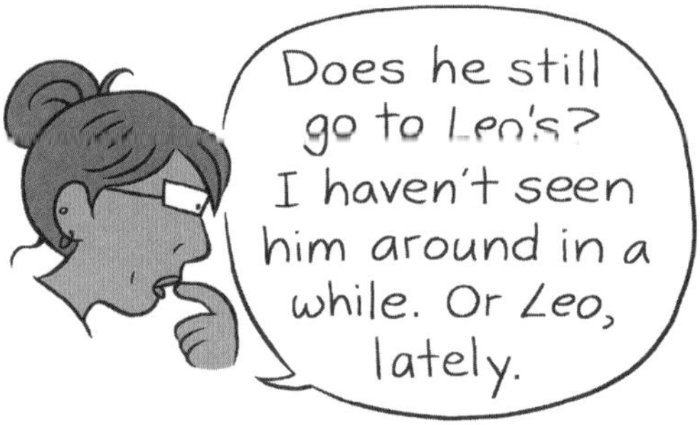
Does he still go to Leo's? I haven't seen him around in a while. Or Leo, lately.

She frowns.

I'm not ready to talk about that, so I just ask:

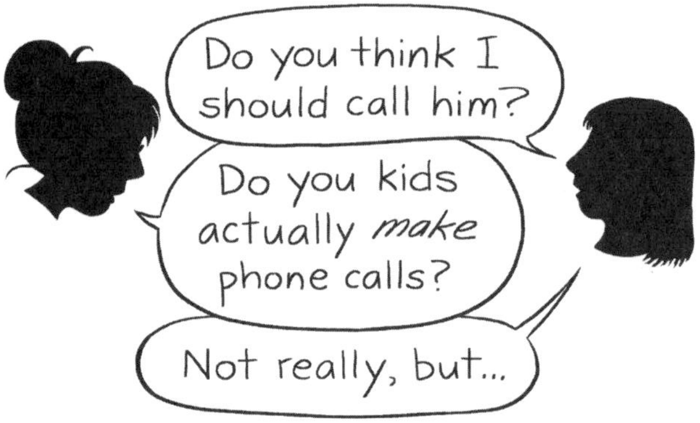
Do you think I should call him?
Do you kids actually *make* phone calls?
Not really, but...

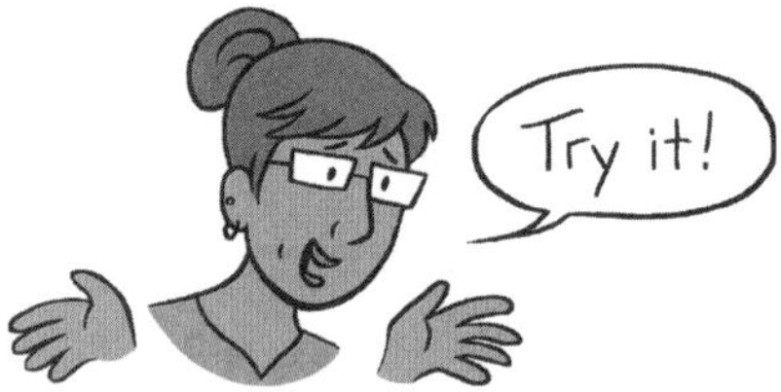
Try it!

She goes back in the kitchen to clean up for dinner, humming something I don't recognize.

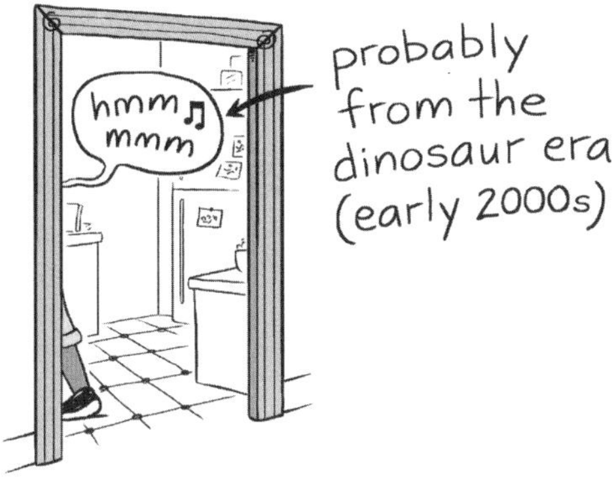
hmm ♫
mmm
probably from the dinosaur era (early 2000s)

I don't intend to call Ben (who **does** that?), but I have an idea. I race upstairs, taking my phone with me.

I plop on my beanbag. I'm determined to do this before I lose my nerve.

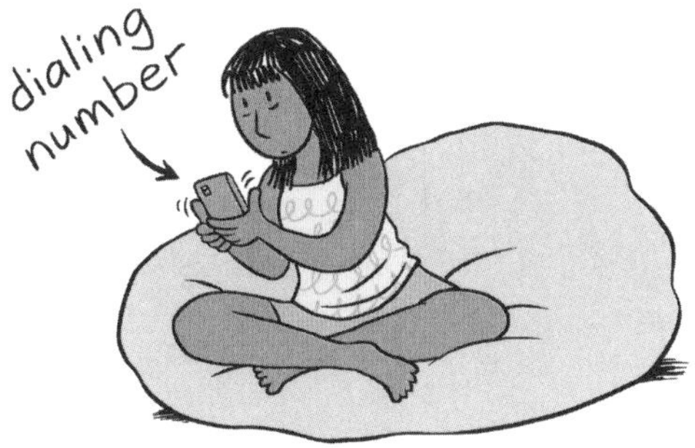
dialing number

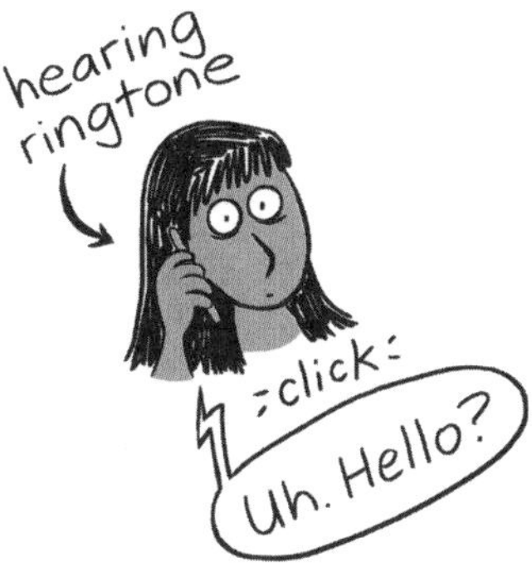
hearing ringtone
:click:
Uh. Hello?

I hang up immediately.

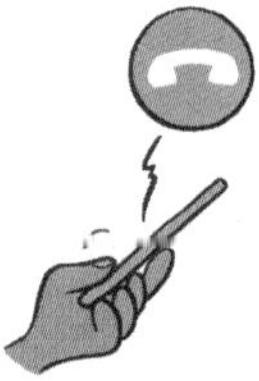

I wait exactly thirty seconds.

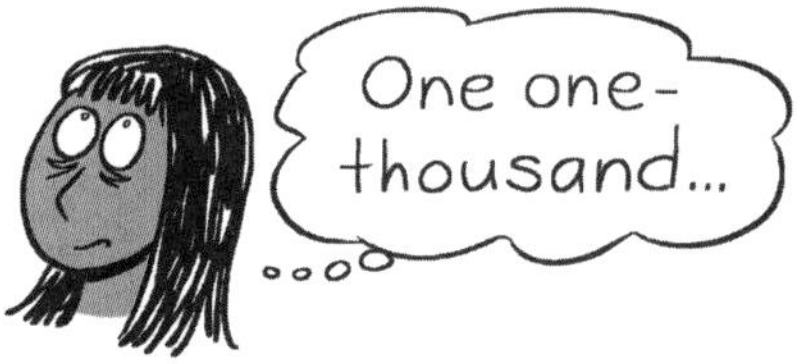
One one-thousand...

And then . . .

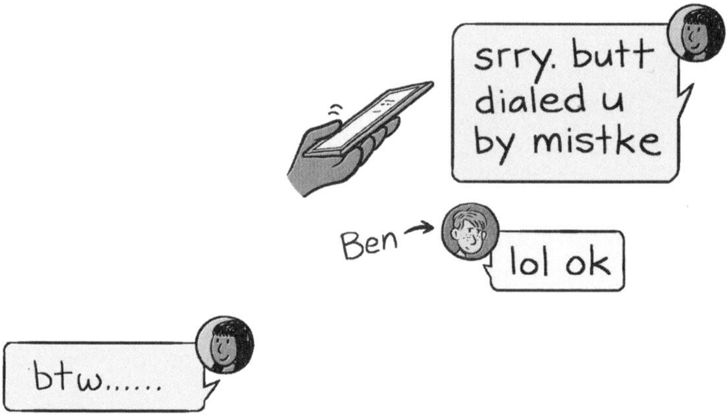
srry. butt dialed u by mistke
Ben
lol ok
btw......

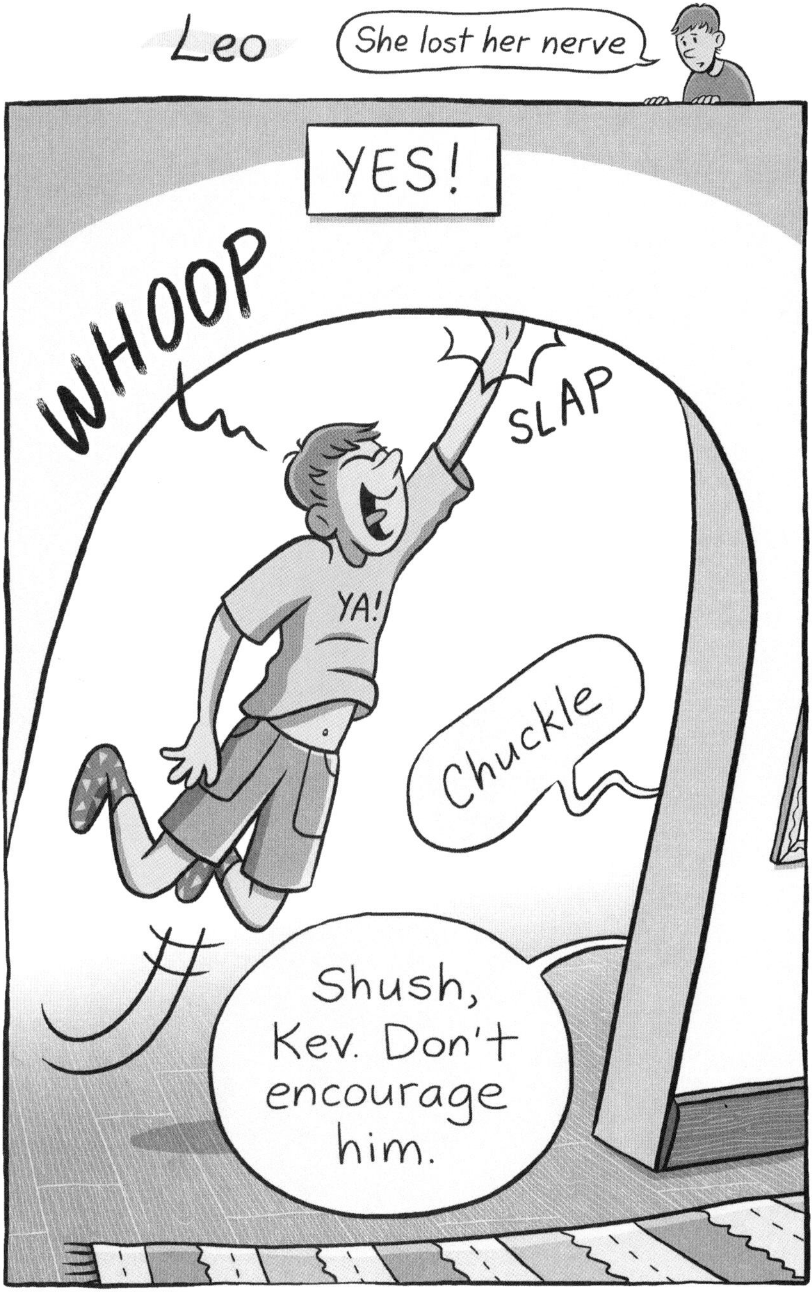
Leo
She lost her nerve
YES!
WHOOP
SLAP
YA!
Chuckle
Shush, Kev. Don't encourage him.

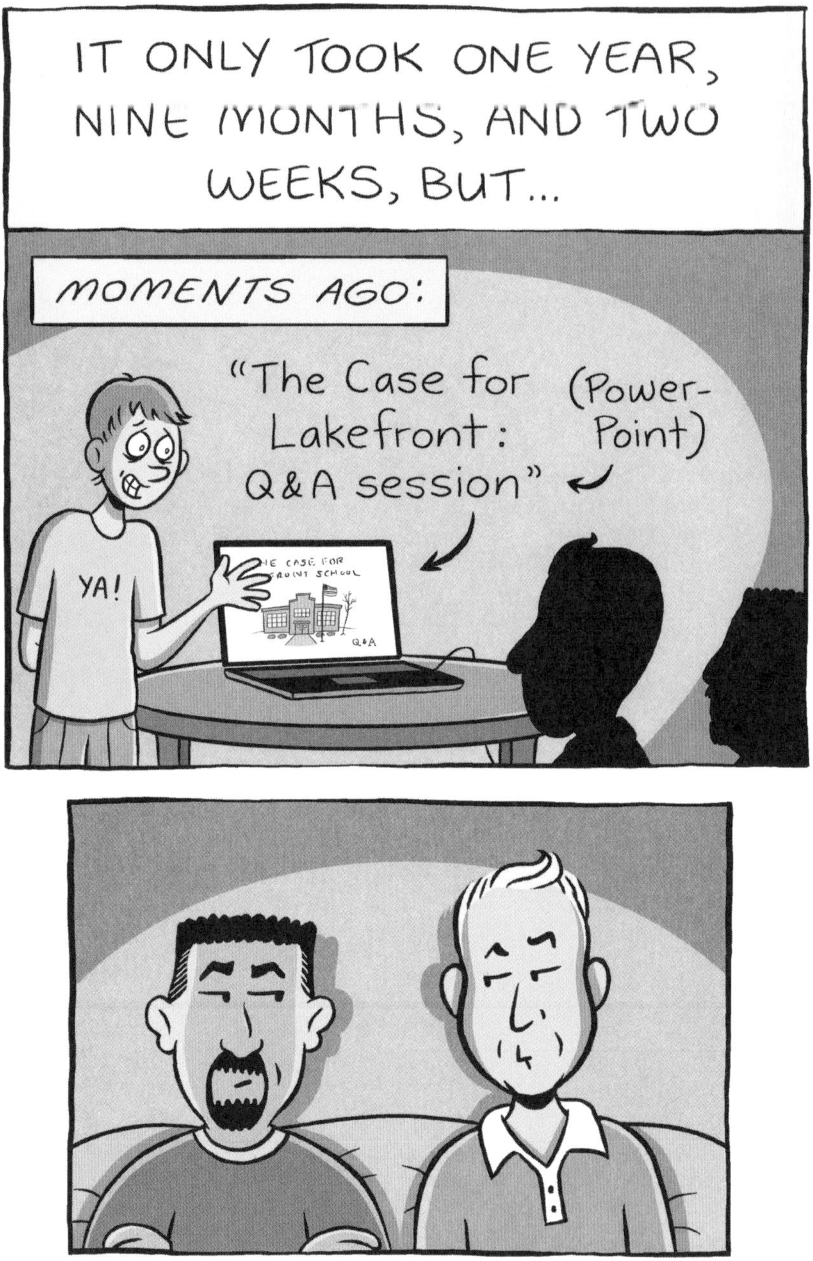
IT ONLY TOOK ONE YEAR, NINE MONTHS, AND TWO WEEKS, BUT...
MOMENTS AGO:
"The Case for Lakefront: Q&A session"
(PowerPoint)
YA!

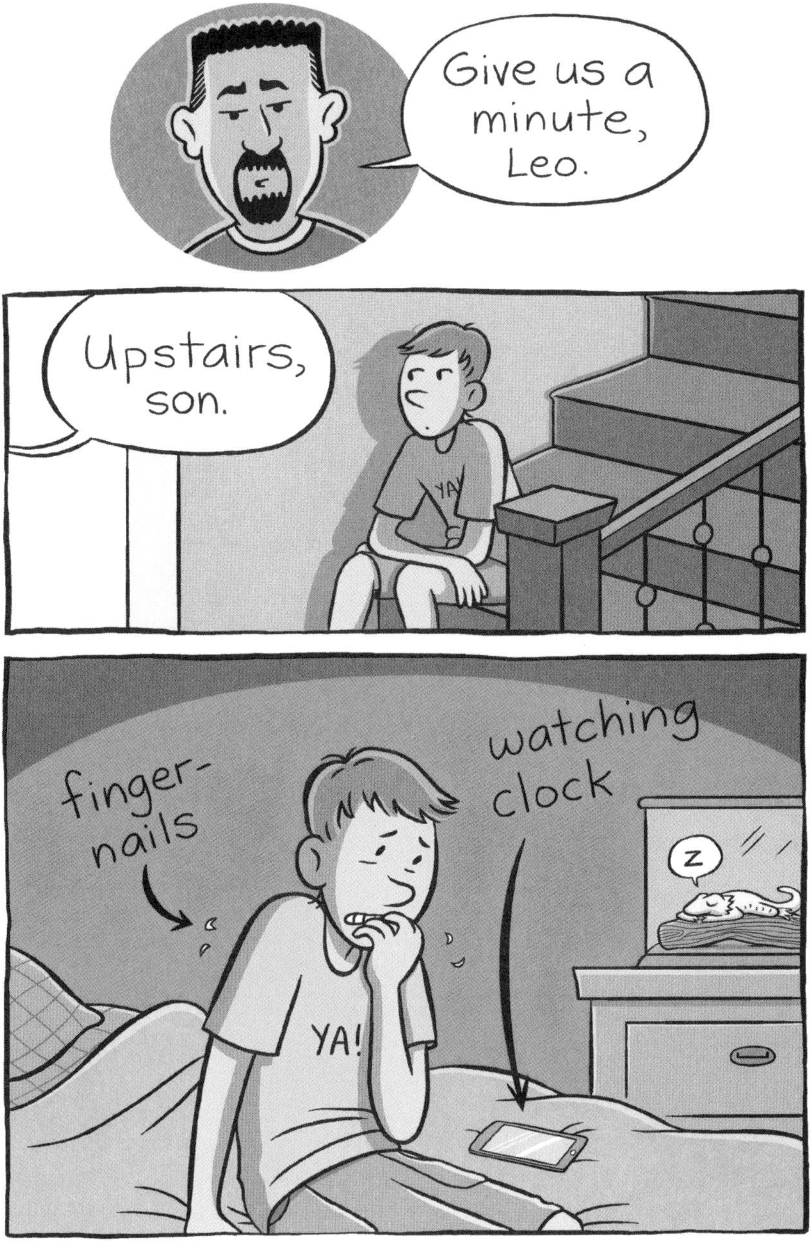
Give us a minute, Leo.
Upstairs, son.
YA
finger-nails
watching clock
Z
YA!

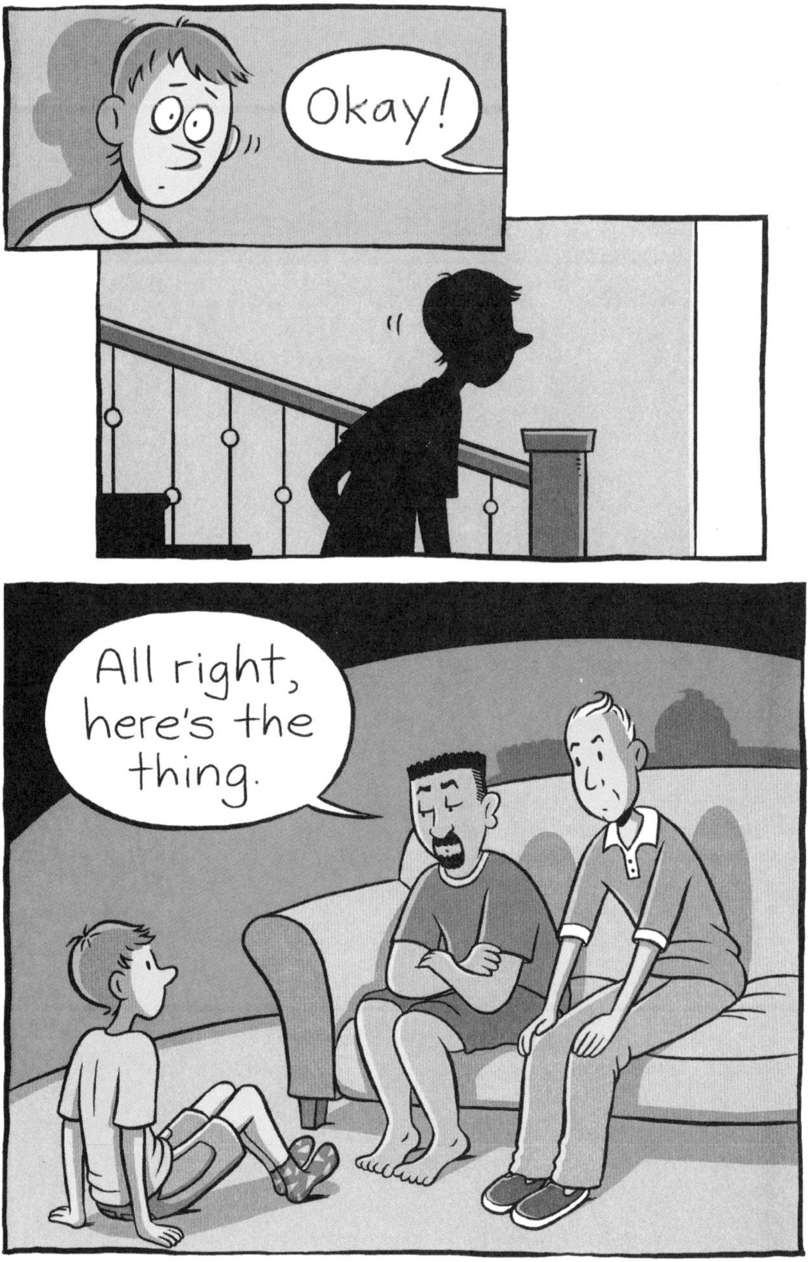
Okay!
All right, here's the thing.

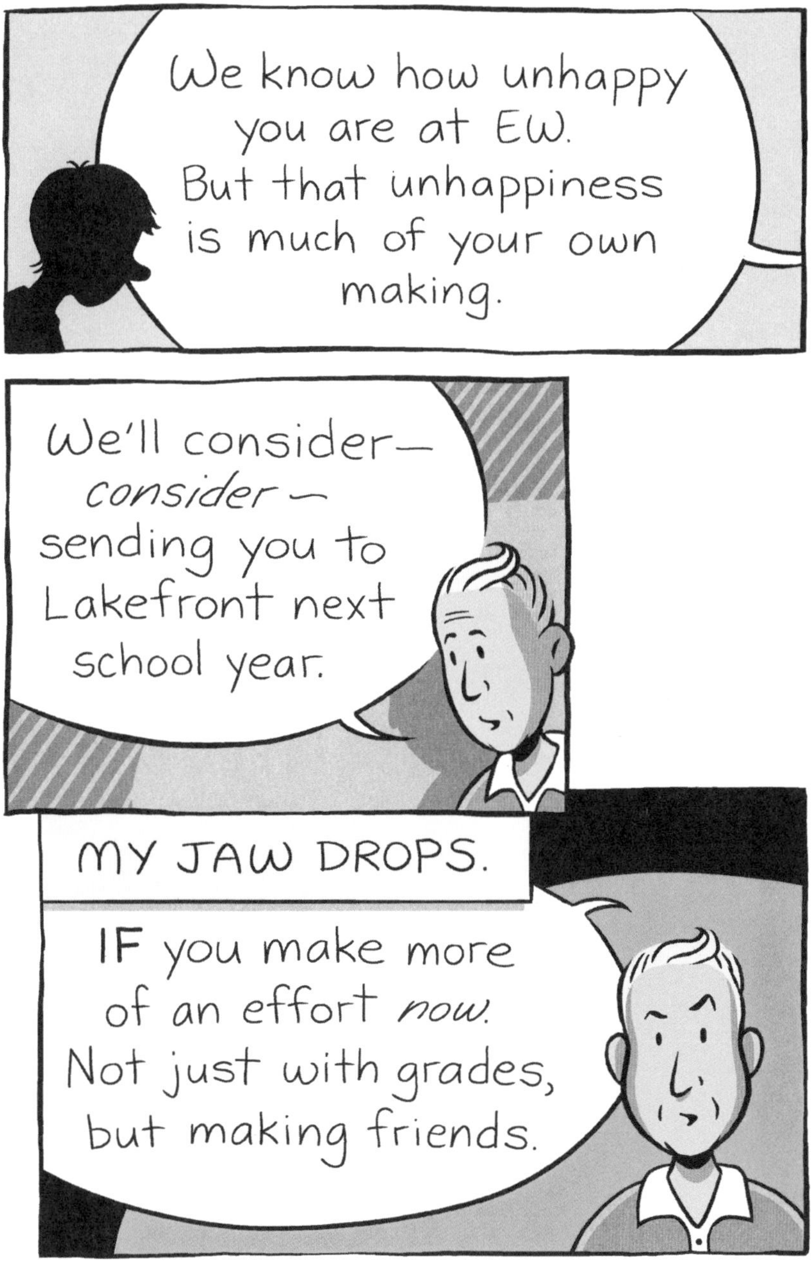
We know how unhappy you are at EW. But that unhappiness is much of your own making.
We'll consider—*consider*—sending you to Lakefront next school year.
MY JAW DROPS.
IF you make more of an effort *now*. Not just with grades, but making friends.

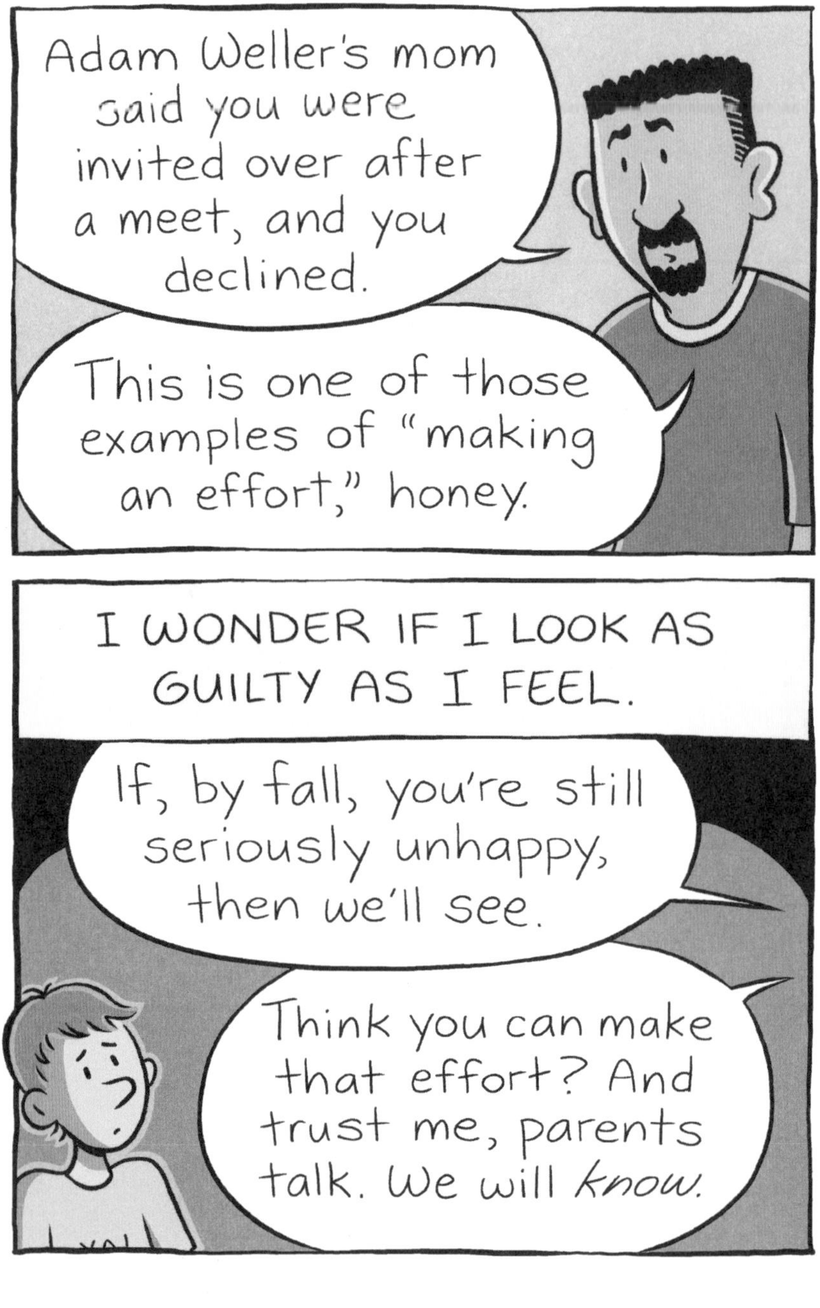
Adam Weller's mom said you were invited over after a meet, and you declined.
This is one of those examples of "making an effort," honey.
I WONDER IF I LOOK AS GUILTY AS I FEEL.
If, by fall, you're still seriously unhappy, then we'll see.
Think you can make that effort? And trust me, parents talk. We will *know.*

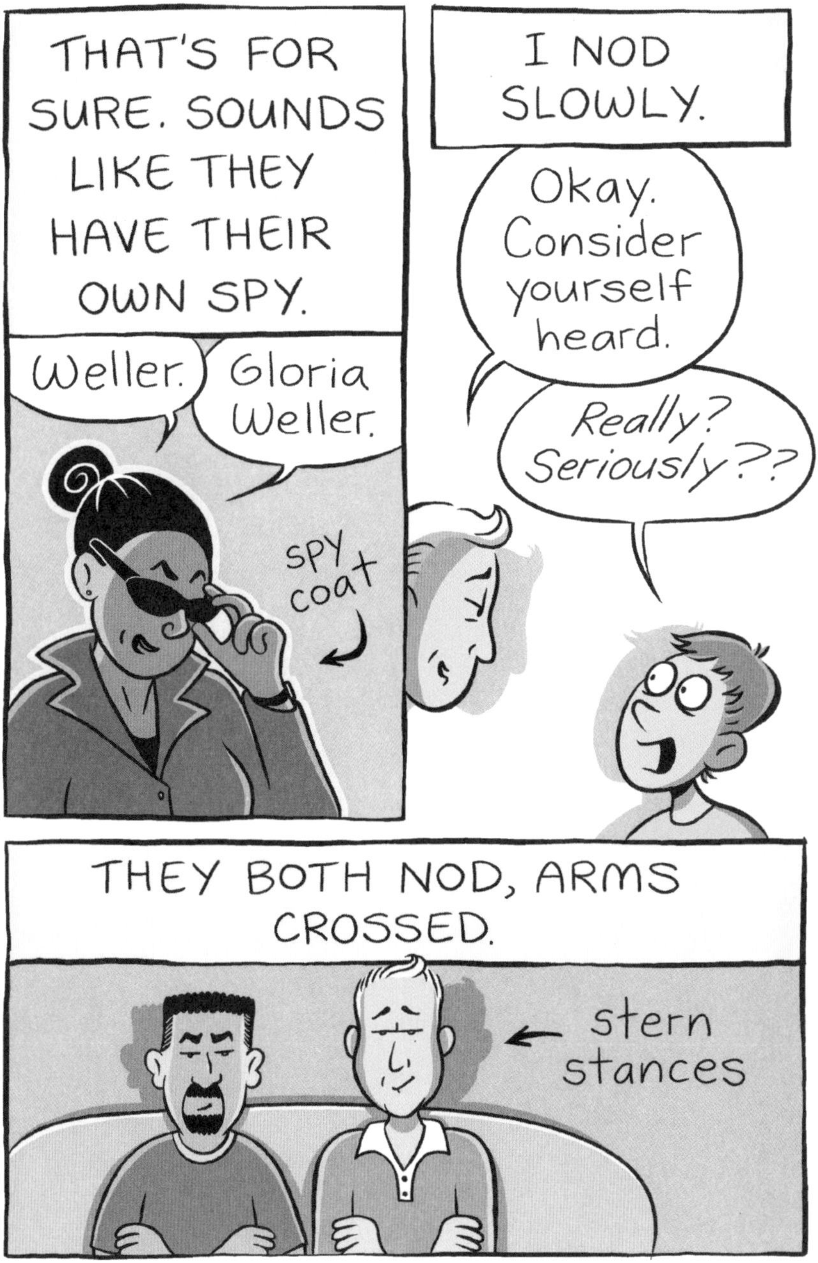
THAT'S FOR SURE. SOUNDS LIKE THEY HAVE THEIR OWN SPY.
Weller.
Gloria Weller.
spy coat
I NOD SLOWLY.
Okay. Consider yourself heard.
Really? Seriously??
THEY BOTH NOD, ARMS CROSSED.
stern stances

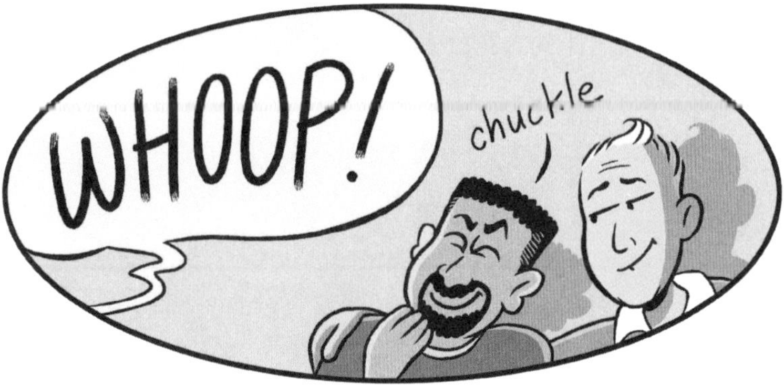
WHOOP!
chuckle

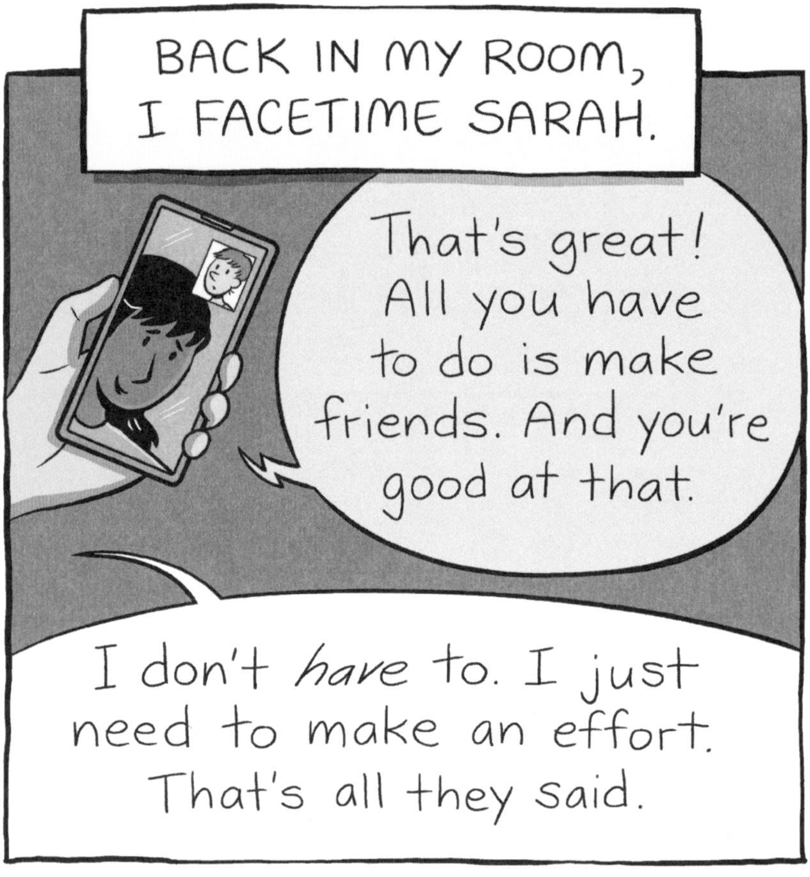
BACK IN MY ROOM, I FACETIME SARAH.
That's great! All you have to do is make friends. And you're good at that.
I don't *have* to. I just need to make an effort. That's all they said.

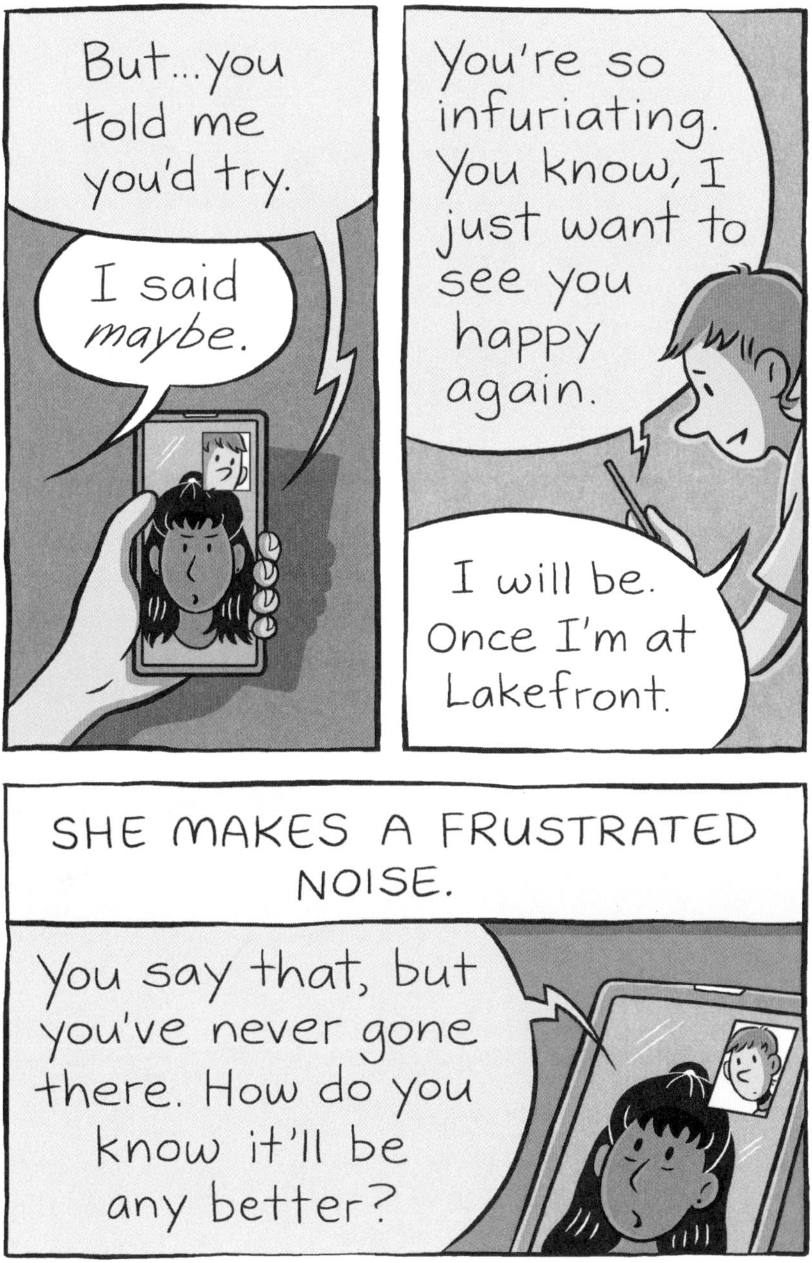
But...you told me you'd try.
I said *maybe*.
You're so infuriating. You know, I just want to see you happy again.
I will be. Once I'm at Lakefront.
SHE MAKES A FRUSTRATED NOISE.
You say that, but you've never gone there. How do you know it'll be any better?

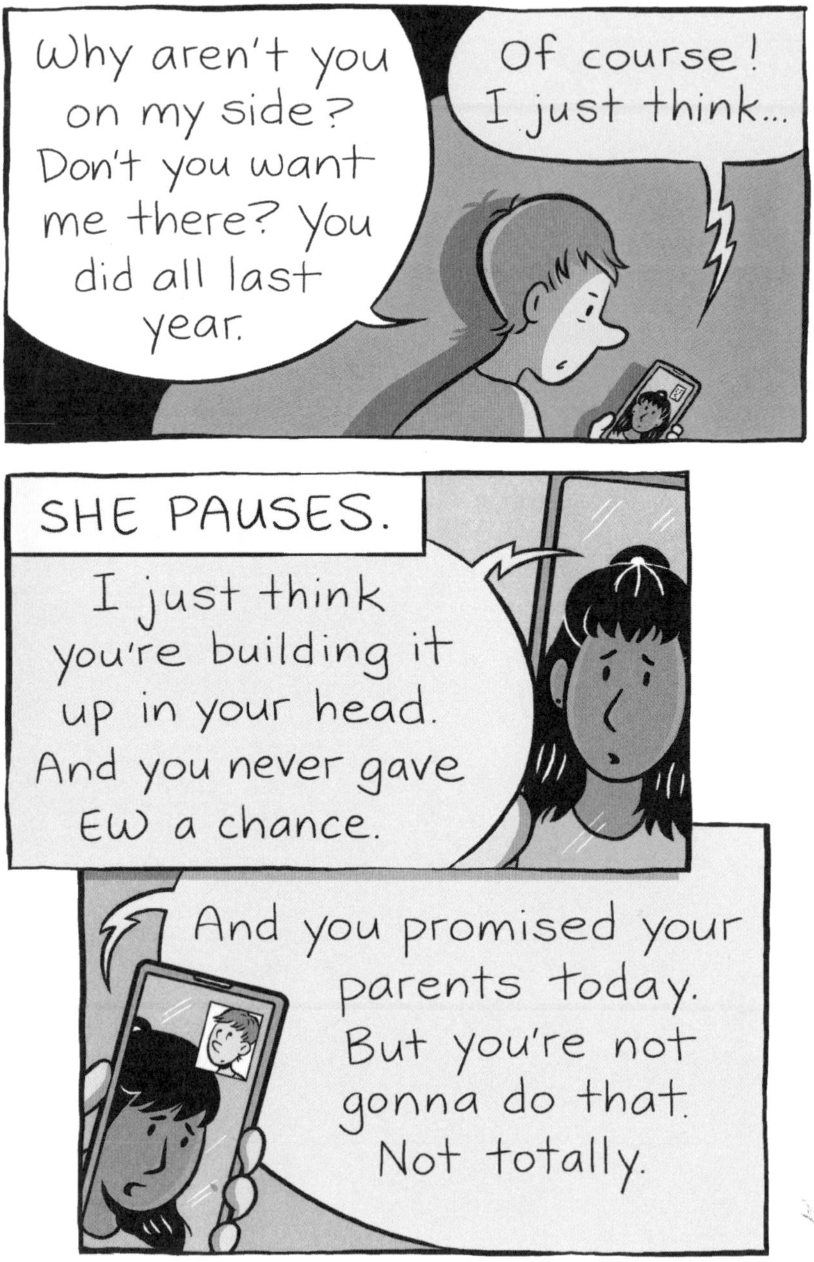
Why aren't you on my side? Don't you want me there? You did all last year.
Of course! I just think...
SHE PAUSES.
I just think you're building it up in your head. And you never gave EW a chance.
And you promised your parents today. But you're not gonna do that. Not totally.

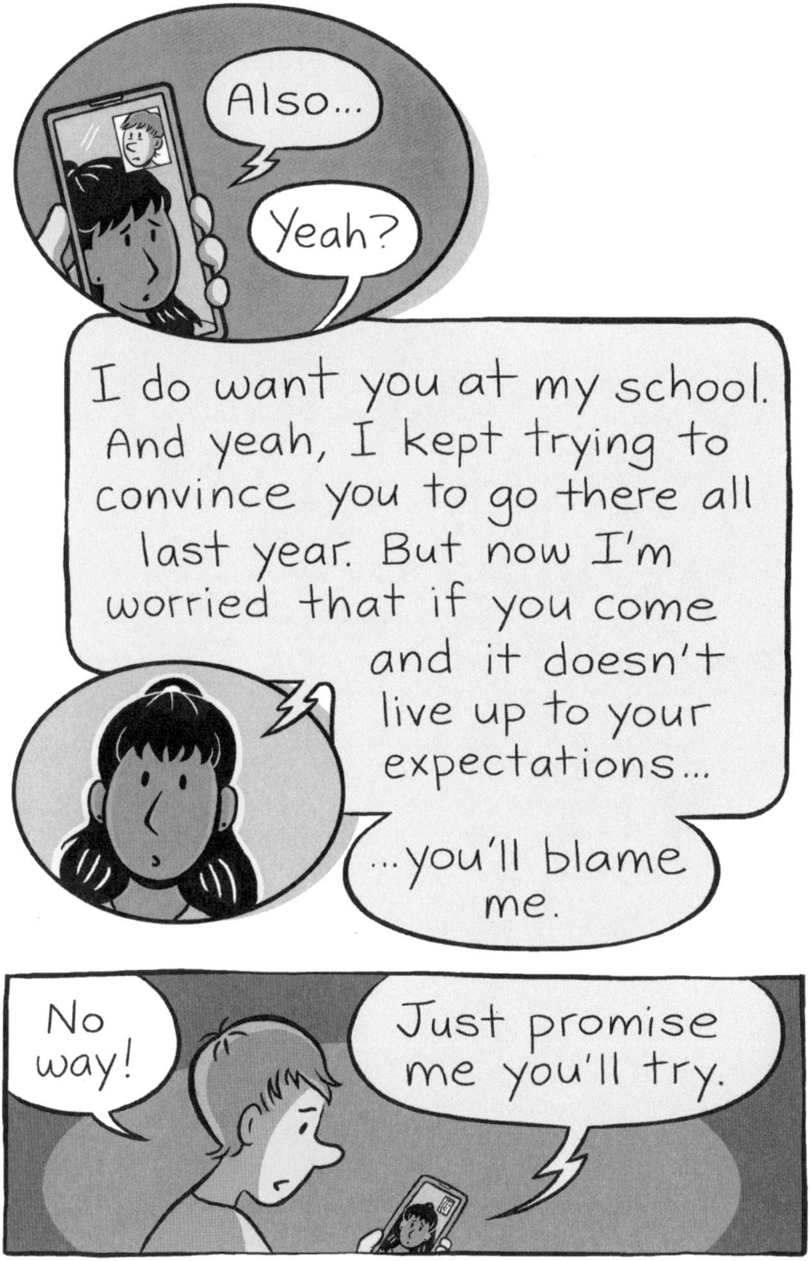
Also...
Yeah?
I do want you at my school. And yeah, I kept trying to convince you to go there all last year. But now I'm worried that if you come and it doesn't live up to your expectations...
...you'll blame me.
No way!
Just promise me you'll try.

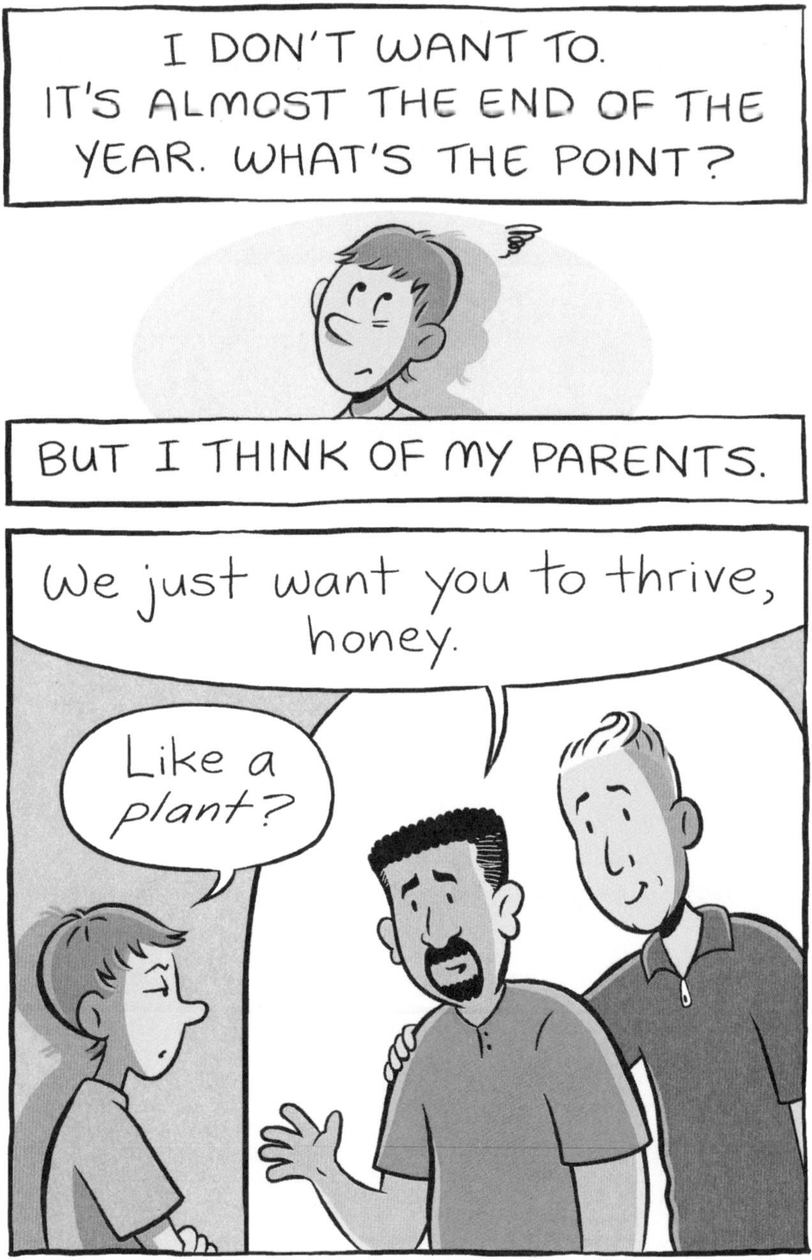
I DON'T WANT TO. IT'S ALMOST THE END OF THE YEAR. WHAT'S THE POINT?
BUT I THINK OF MY PARENTS.
We just want you to thrive, honey.
Like a *plant*?

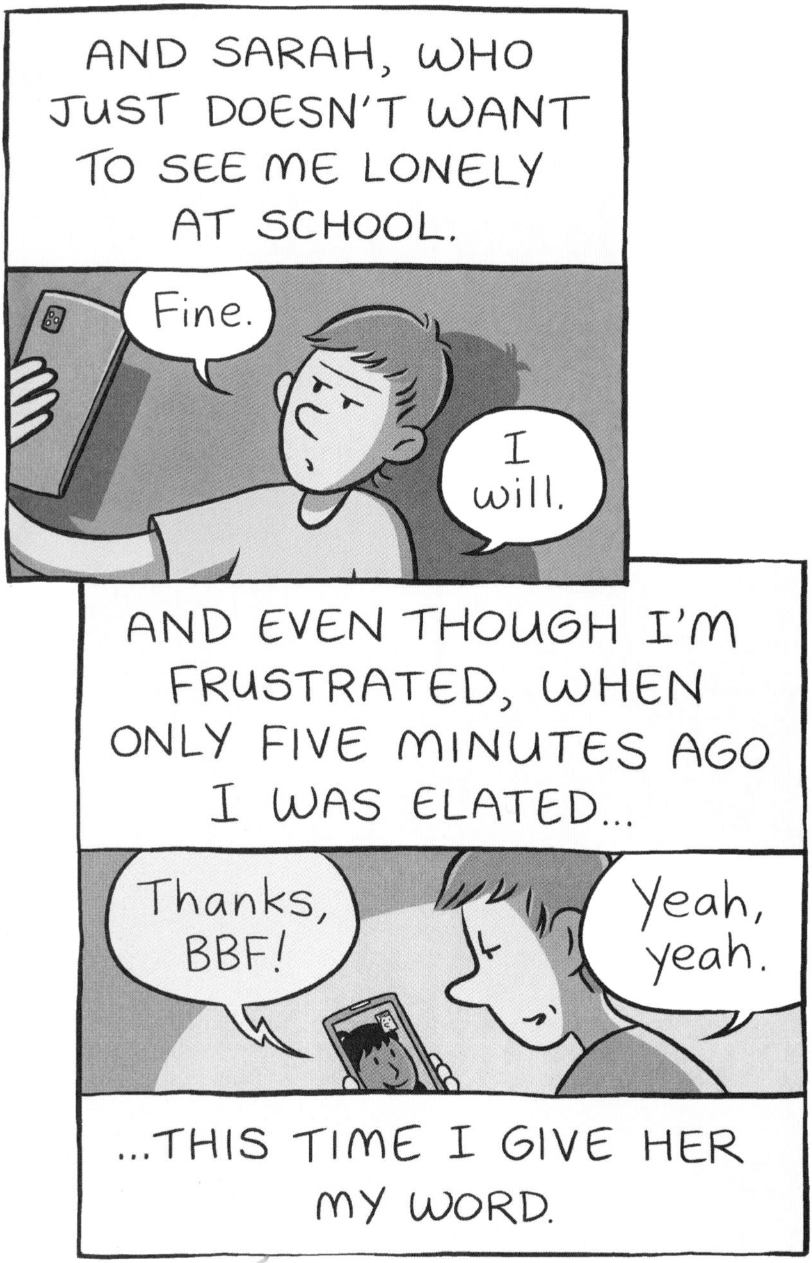
AND SARAH, WHO JUST DOESN'T WANT TO SEE ME LONELY AT SCHOOL.
Fine.
I will.
AND EVEN THOUGH I'M FRUSTRATED, WHEN ONLY FIVE MINUTES AGO I WAS ELATED...
Thanks, BBF!
Yeah, yeah.
...THIS TIME I GIVE HER MY WORD.

SARAH

I asked him

YES!!

   I whoop and kick up my legs, accidentally hurling my phone into my fake plant, Fiona.

gulp

buuurp

   It worked! I got Ben to answer my text. And now we have **definite** plans for the dance.

desk calendar
↓

Friday

PICK UP BEN
at 6:52 pm
!!! ☺

Saturday

sleep
in! Ⓩ

↑
triple-highlighted

I barely see Ben the following week. But that's okay. I look forward to our magical night together. I don't even worry so much about Leo. I still figure he'll come around, and I promise myself that I'll talk to him right after the dance.

In the meantime, I do the usual stuff: go to school, hang out with Emmie and Bri, do homework, and go to art and poetry clubs. I'm **really** enjoying poetry club. I've sort of made some new friends there, too.

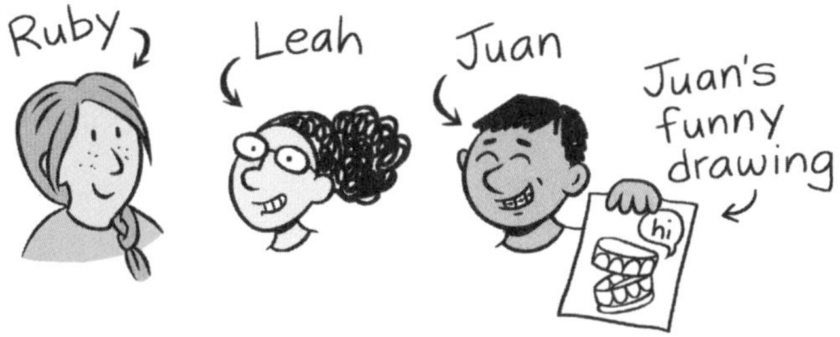
Ruby
Leah
Juan
Juan's funny drawing
hi

Which makes me wonder if Leo is still friendly with those kids from his track team.

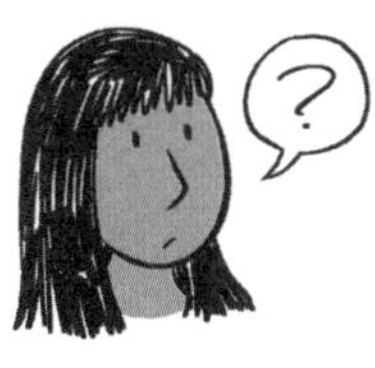
?

It makes me feel weird. Like, almost . . . jealous? I don't know why, 'cause we both have other friends and still manage to be BFFs.

Or **did**.

Maybe that's why I feel weird. Maybe it's 'cause our friendship is on shakier ground and I'm worried.

rumble

friendship earthquake

I remind myself—again—that I'll talk to him after the dance.

Besides, I'm super busy with all that stuff I mentioned, **plus** I'm working on the decorating committee and putting the final touches on my dress.

It looks so good. Mamá and I decided to model it after a Chiapas dress (traditional costume from Mexico):

off-the-shoulder

flower embroidery (used pre-made ones)

flowy skirt

← favorite color combo: charcoal and pink

It's funny: even though I'm kinda quiet and don't really try to stand out, I **love** experimenting with fashion. I know I get weird looks sometimes, but that's how it goes when you wanna be "cutting edge" (Mamá's words).

In a strange way, it also helps me weed out the people I don't want to be around. If someone doesn't like what I'm wearing, then I don't bother with them. So, I think it's good that Kerri Kowalski ditched me (I can say now), 'cause she started giving me looks and whispering to her friends all the time. She didn't think I knew, but I did.

psst
psst
Sarah ← not even
psst   that subtle

giggle
(choke)

Anyway, my real friends always compliment my creations.

Including Leo. But then, he likes wearing fun things, too. That's another reason he complains about EW—he has to wear a uniform all the time. At least he's allowed to show his personality with:

novelty socks!

eye-
balls

Malcolm,
Leo's bearded
dragon
(custom-made)

bacon

burgers

ugly feet

I've really gotta take my mind off him.

I already finished homework, and I'm getting kinda antsy. Mamá used to say I have ants in my pants if I don't have something to do all the time.

I text Emmie.

wanna
come ovr?

...

k

Huh. She seems down—or as down as I'm able to read in a text.

She rings the doorbell
about ten minutes later.

Hi.

What's wrong?

We go up to my room and enter the crawl space. I close the door for privacy and turn on the fairy lights. It's a little hot in here (hot in the warm months, chilly in the winter), so I peel off my hoodie.

So...I tried to ask Tyler to the dance.

Really?

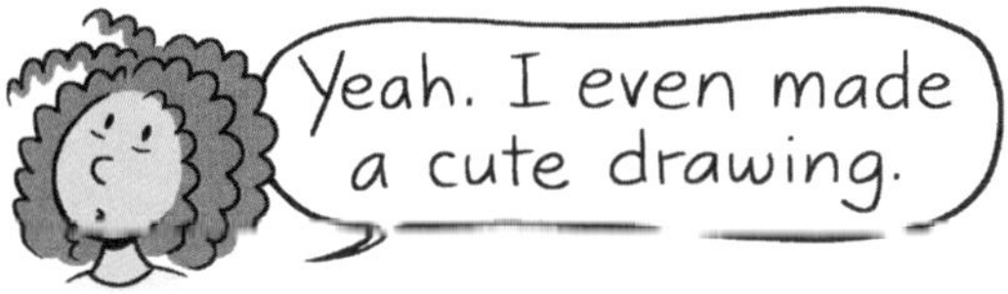
Yeah. I even made a cute drawing.

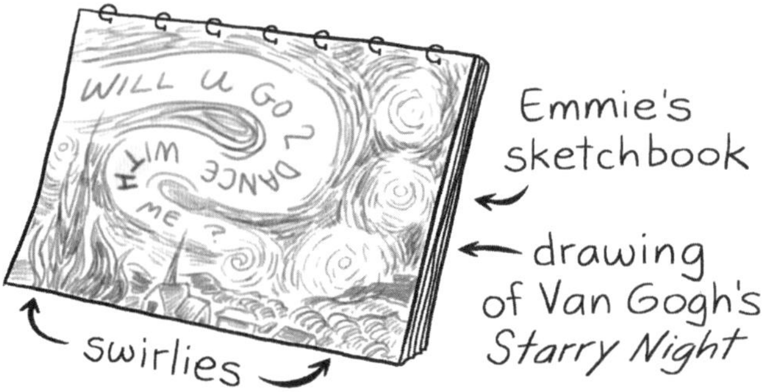
WILL U GO 2 DANCE WITH ME?
Emmie's sketchbook
drawing of Van Gogh's *Starry Night*
swirlies

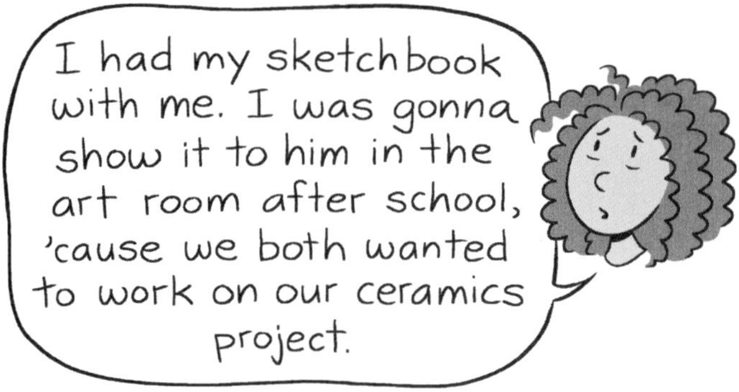
I had my sketchbook with me. I was gonna show it to him in the art room after school, 'cause we both wanted to work on our ceramics project.

Ms. Laurie is having us make all these crazy pinch pots. Mine are funny animals with giant square teeth.

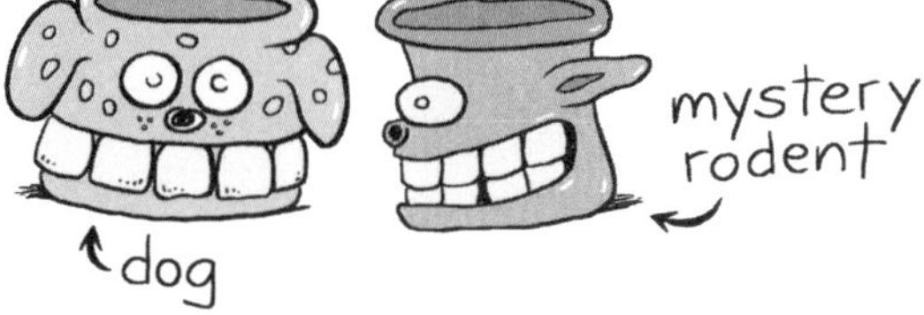
mystery rodent
dog

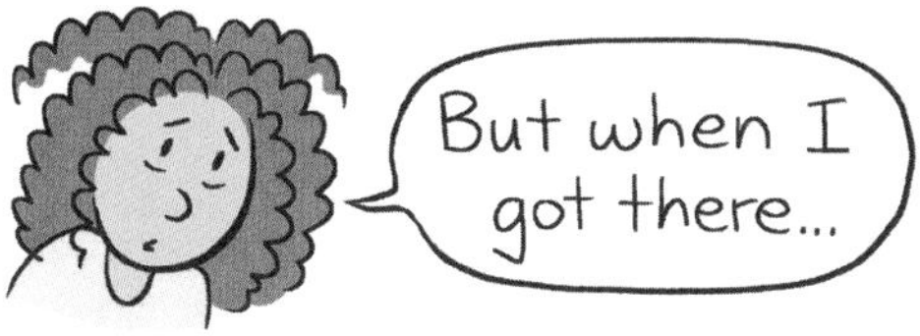
But when I got there...

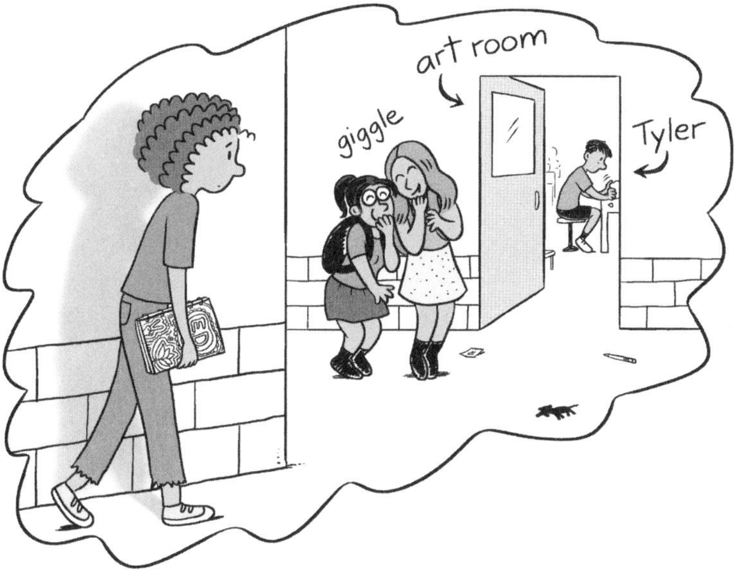
art room
giggle
Tyler

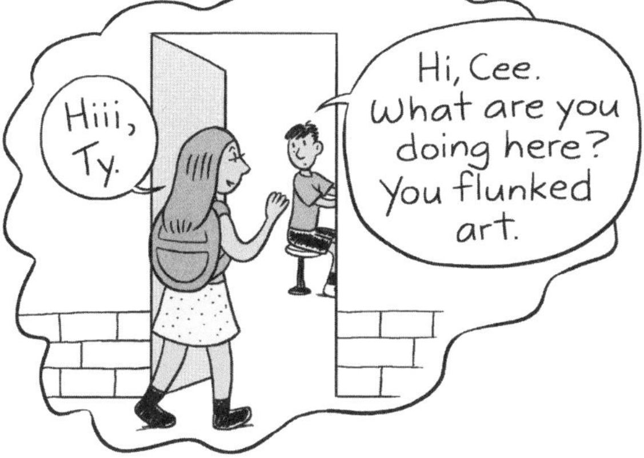
Hiii, Ty.
Hi, Cee. What are you doing here? You flunked art.

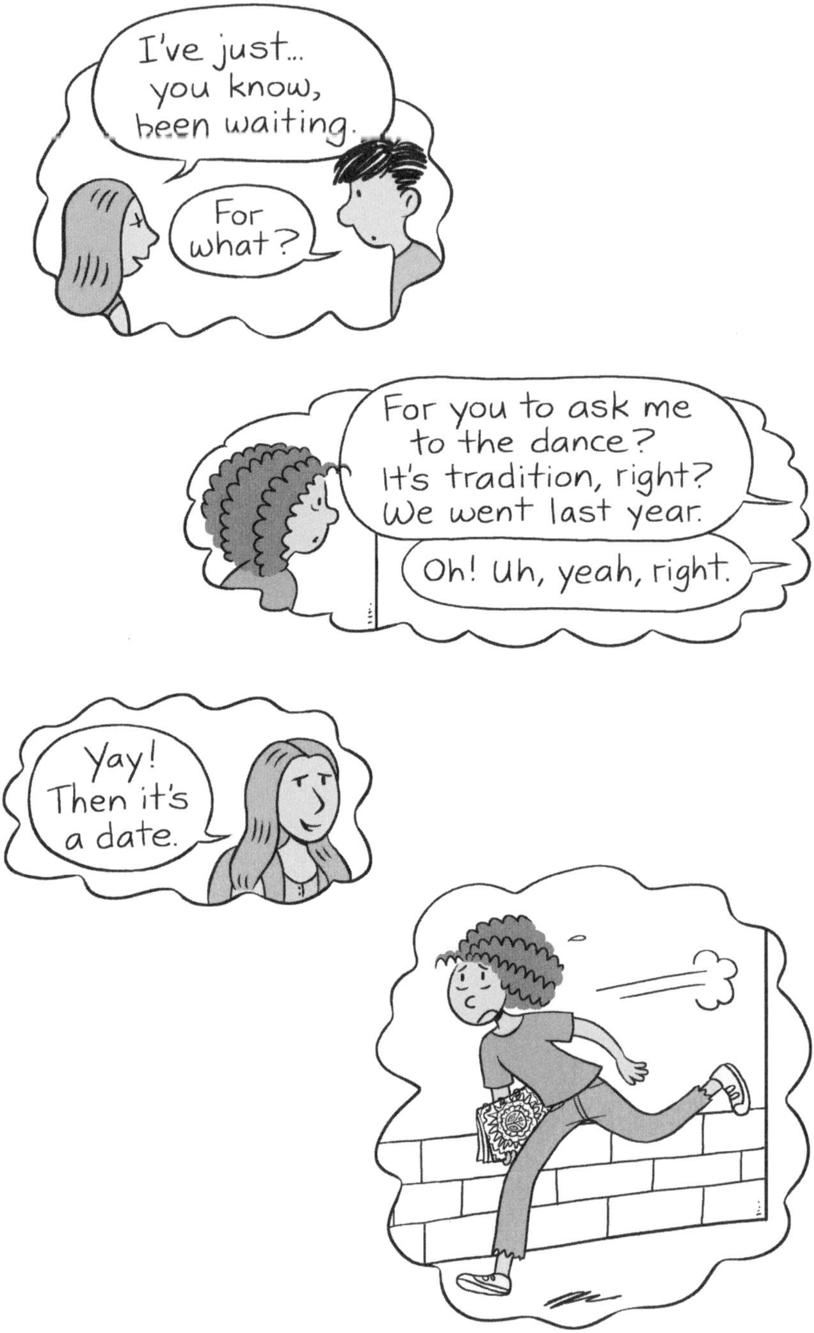
I've just... you know, been waiting.
For what?
For you to ask me to the dance? It's tradition, right? We went last year.
Oh! Uh, yeah, right.
Yay! Then it's a date.

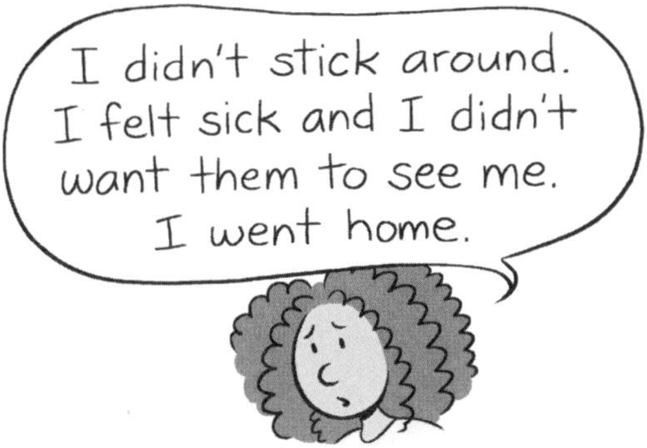
I didn't stick around. I felt sick and I didn't want them to see me. I went home.

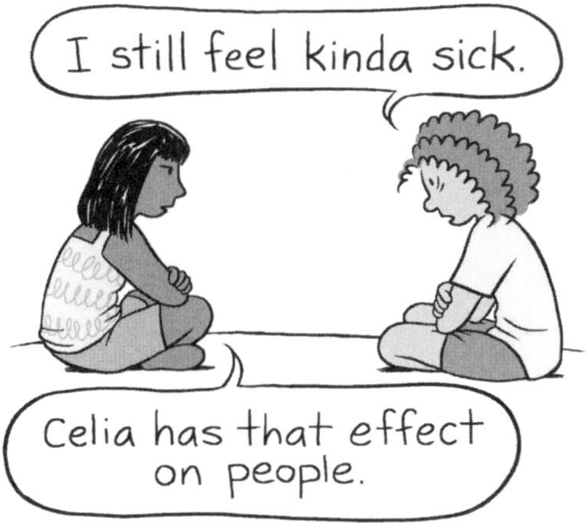
I still feel kinda sick.
Celia has that effect on people.

Emmie breaks into a little smile. But it's gone in an instant.

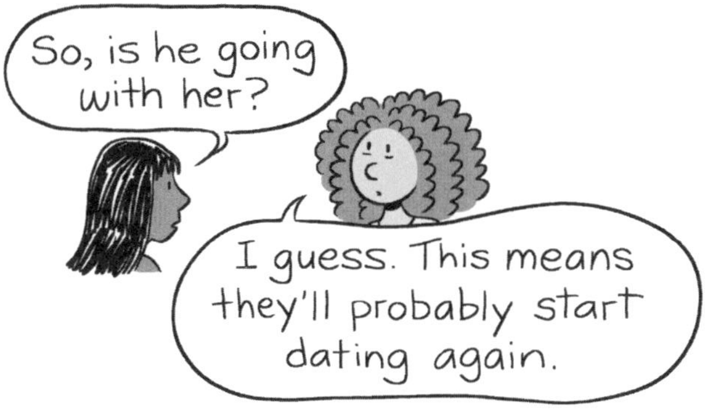
So, is he going with her?
I guess. This means they'll probably start dating again.

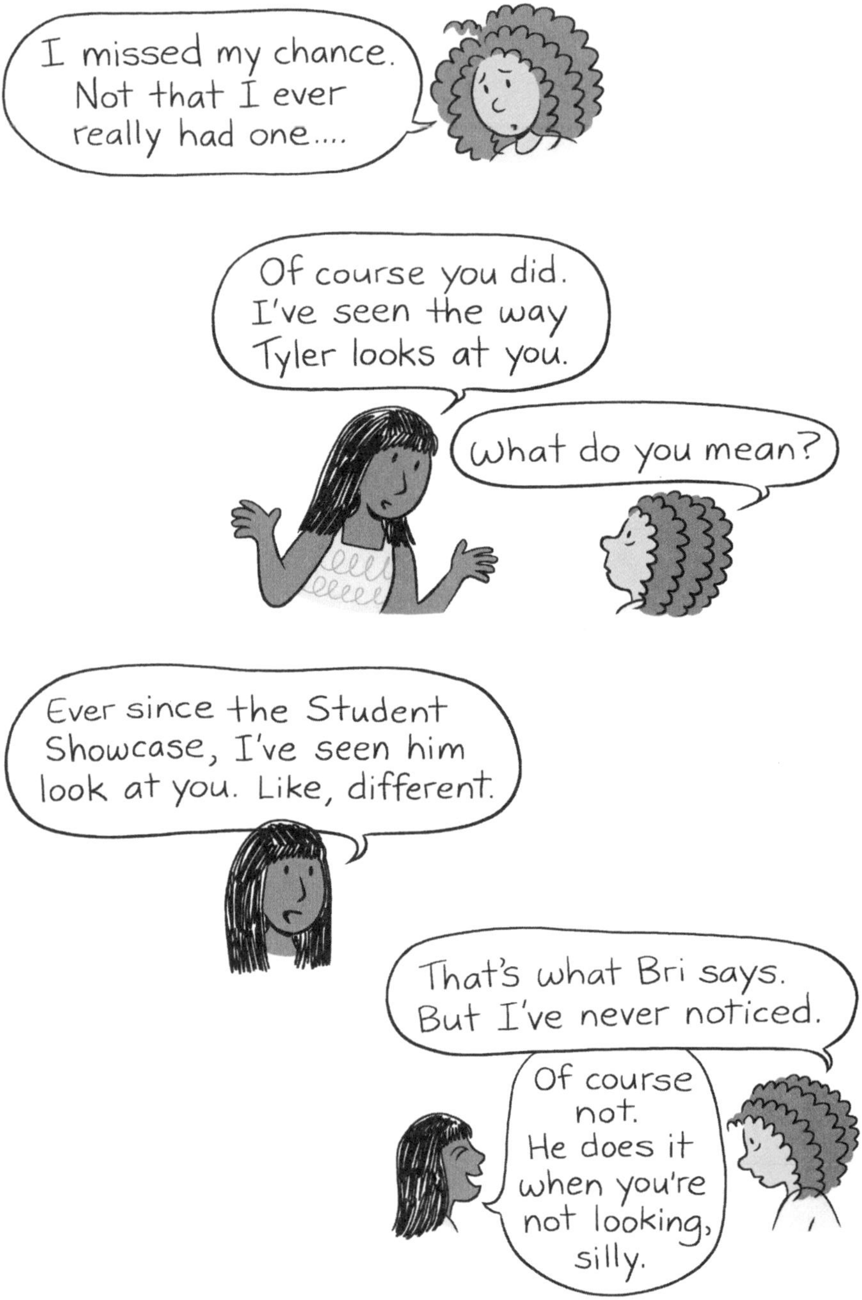
I missed my chance. Not that I ever really had one....
Of course you did. I've seen the way Tyler looks at you.
What do you mean?
Ever since the Student Showcase, I've seen him look at you. Like, different.
That's what Bri says. But I've never noticed.
Of course not. He does it when you're not looking, silly.

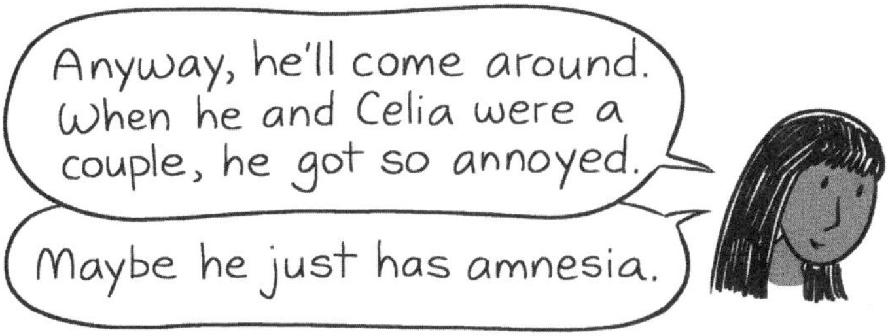
Anyway, he'll come around. When he and Celia were a couple, he got so annoyed.
Maybe he just has amnesia.

Emmie laughs, and I know she feels better. We head downstairs, where I convince Mamá (pretty easily) to give Emmie a vanilla concha from the batch she's baking for a quinceañera.

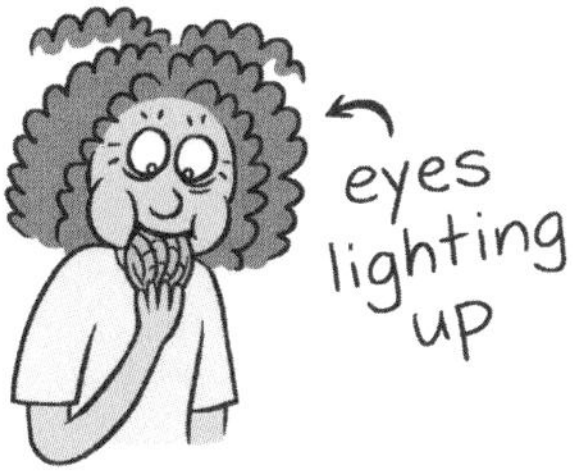
eyes lighting up

Mamá laughs.

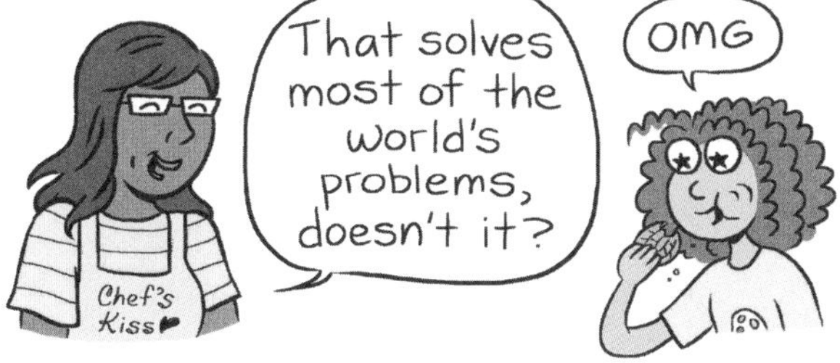
That solves most of the world's problems, doesn't it?
OMG
Chef's Kiss

Afterward, we ride our bikes to Brianna's mom's condo, where a frustrated Bri waits.

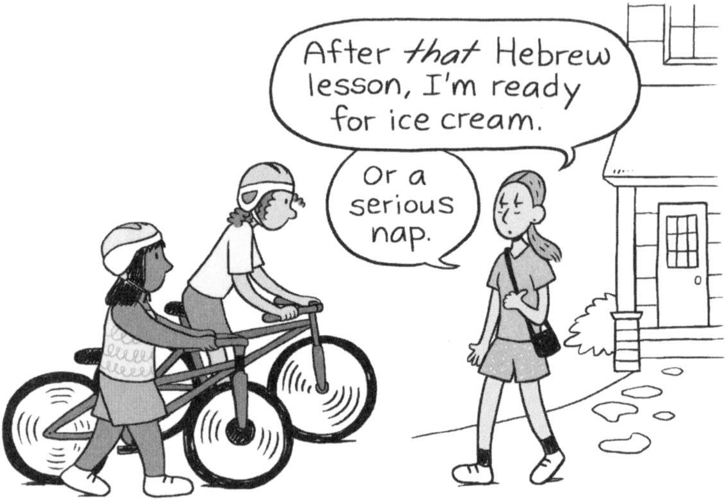
After *that* Hebrew lesson, I'm ready for ice cream.
Or a serious nap.

We ride our bikes to Taystee's.

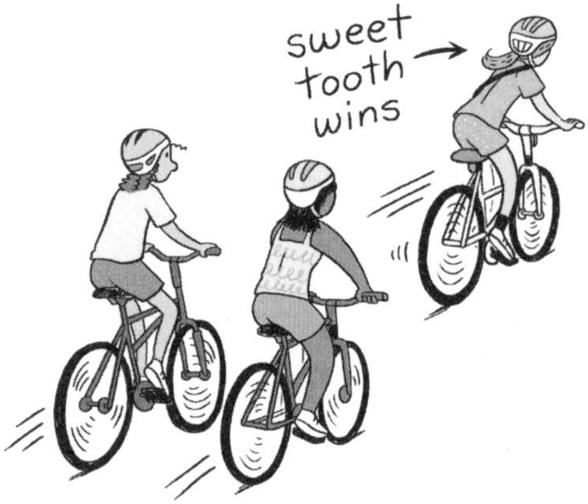
sweet tooth wins

When we get there, there's a small line. But this time, no one we know is waiting in it.

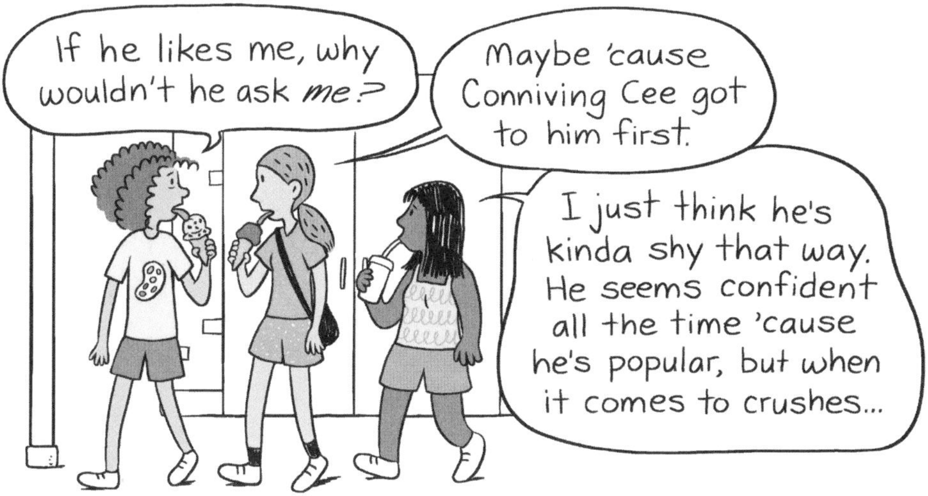
If he likes me, why wouldn't he ask *me*?
Maybe 'cause Conniving Cee got to him first.
I just think he's kinda shy that way. He seems confident all the time 'cause he's popular, but when it comes to crushes...

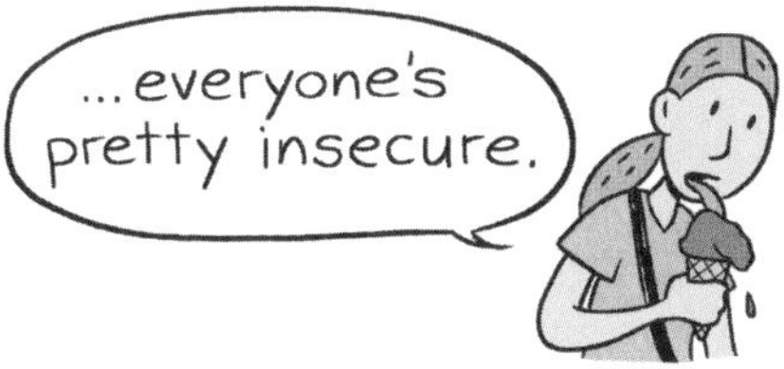
...everyone's pretty insecure.

I think of Ben. Maybe he is, too.

So maybe I do have a chance . . . ?

After we finish our cones, we head home in different directions.

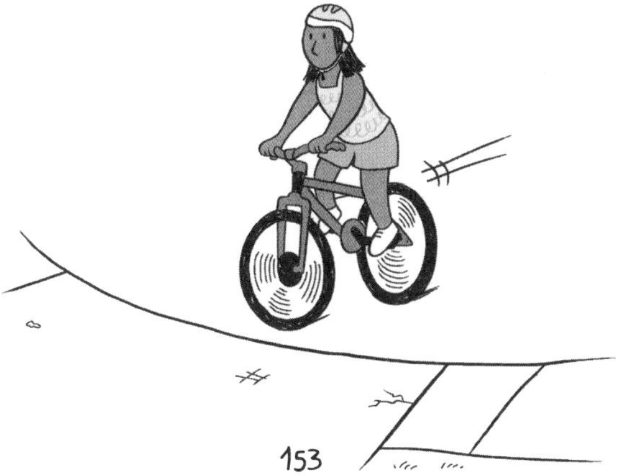

Sometimes I forget how high our driveway apron is. Popping my bike tire onto it, I nearly flip over when I see Leo coming out of his back gate.

Instead, I manage to stumble off my bike (not very gracefully) just as it drops sideways.

undies

OMG.
Leo rushes over as I manage to get to my feet.

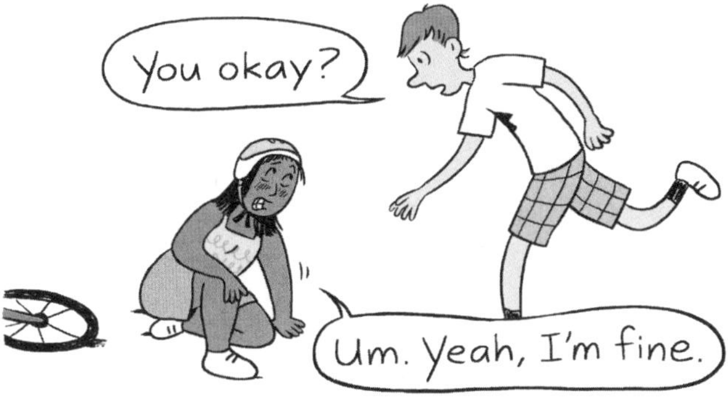
You okay?
Um. Yeah, I'm fine.

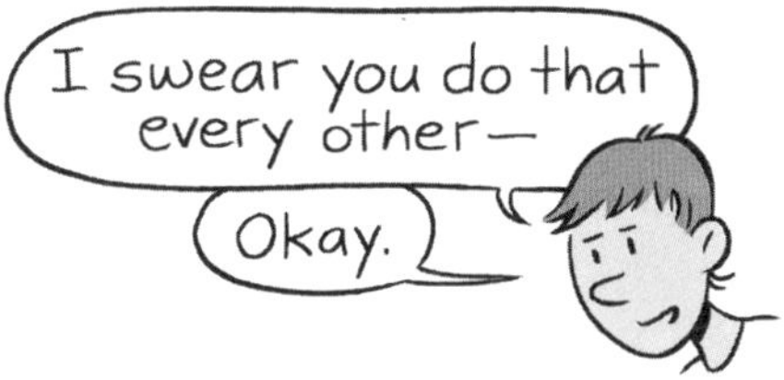
I swear you do that every other—
Okay.

We look at each other awkwardly. I try to give him a harsh look, but . . .

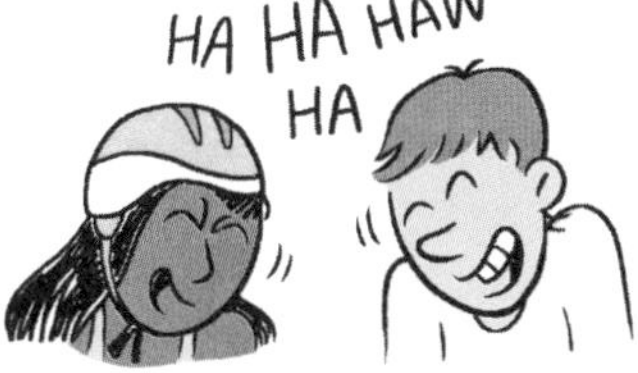
HA HA HAW
HA

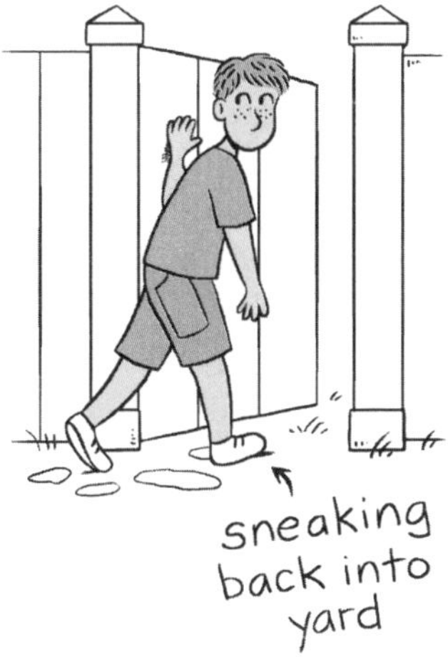
sneaking back into yard

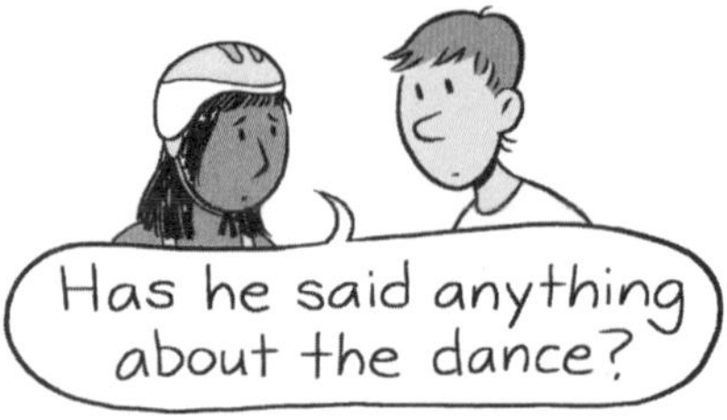
Has he said anything about the dance?

Leo gives me a funny look. He's no longer smiling or laughing.

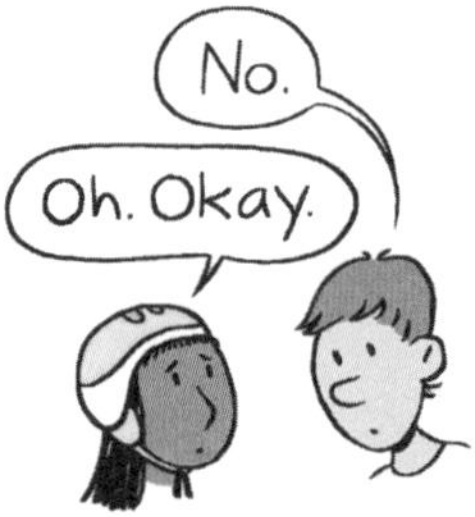
No.
Oh. Okay.

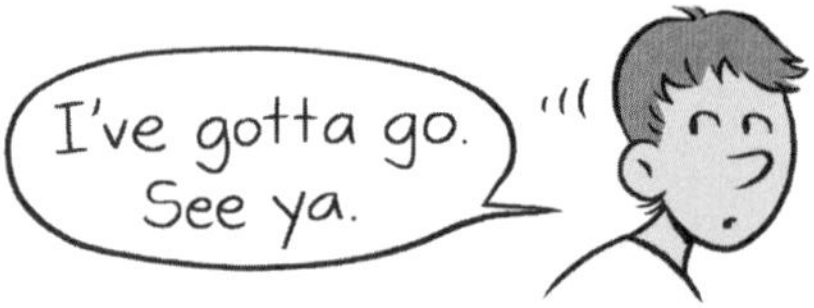
I've gotta go. See ya.

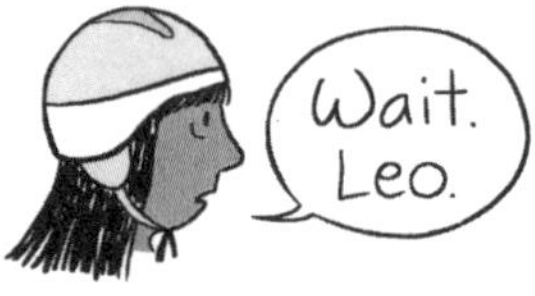
Wait. Leo.

He turns around.

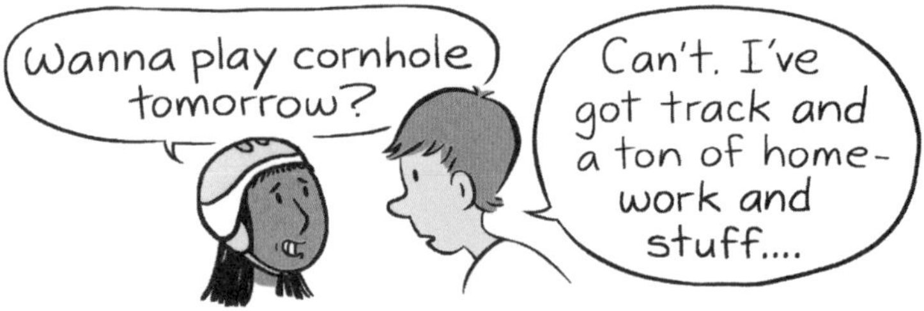
Wanna play cornhole tomorrow?
Can't. I've got track and a ton of home-work and stuff....

Okay.

I wave a half-hearted bye and head up the porch steps. Walking into the house, I accidentally slam the screen door.

SLAM.

Cachetona! You scared me.

Sorry.

I'm not even mad that she called me 'Cachetona,' I'm too . . . what's the word?

Distraught.

↰Winn Word

I head upstairs. Mamá's making my favorite dinner, pollo asado. But even the amazing smell doesn't affect me.

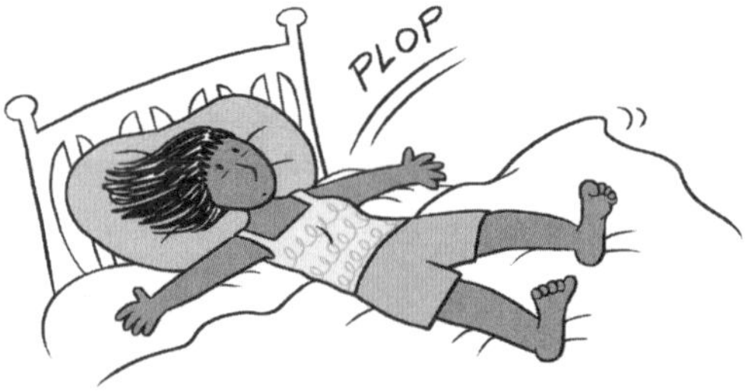
PLOP

Leo keeps avoiding me. I break my promise to myself and start worrying again.

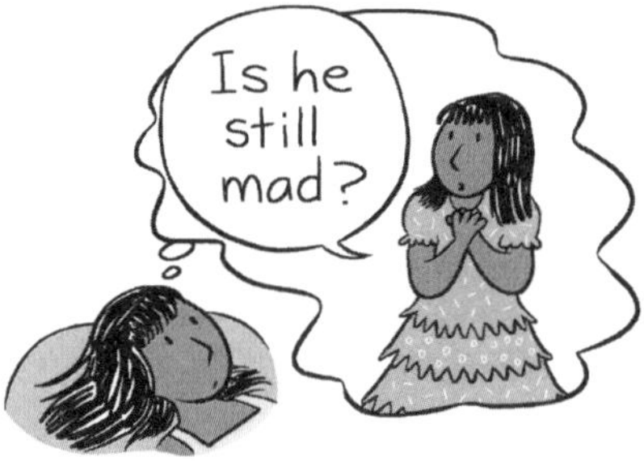
Is he still mad?

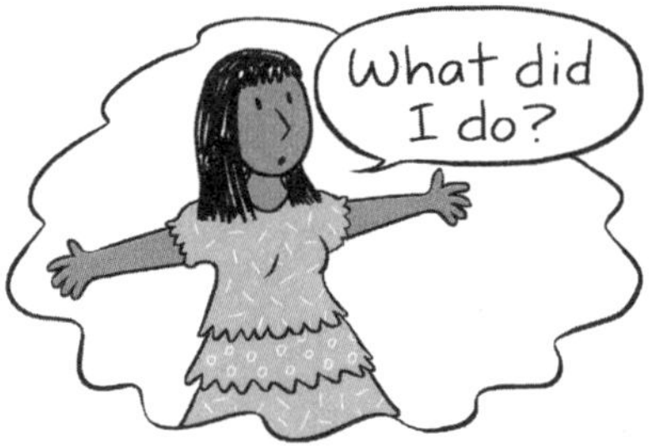
What did I do?

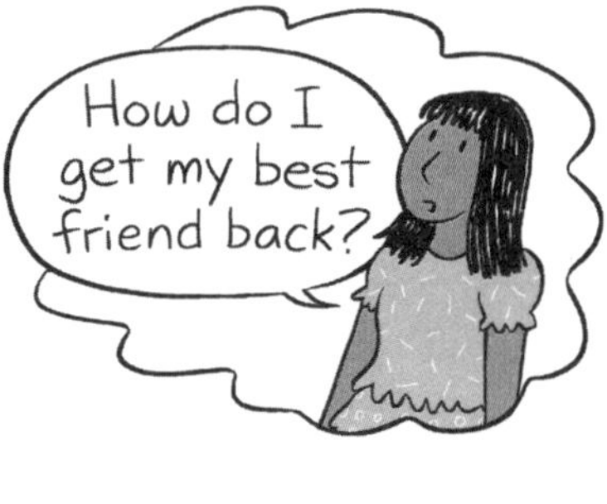
How do I get my best friend back?

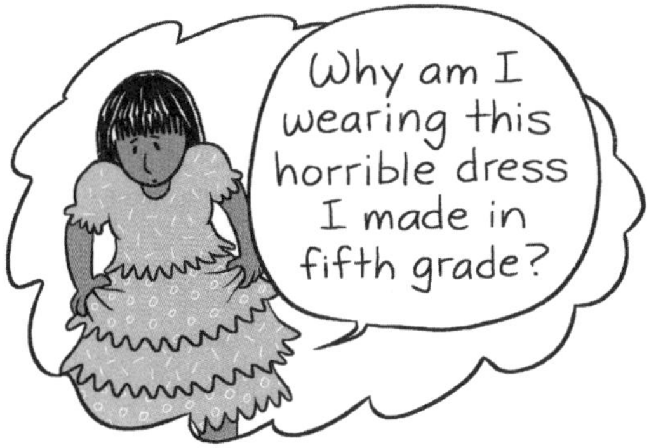
Why am I wearing this horrible dress I made in fifth grade?

It's the first time in a long time . . .

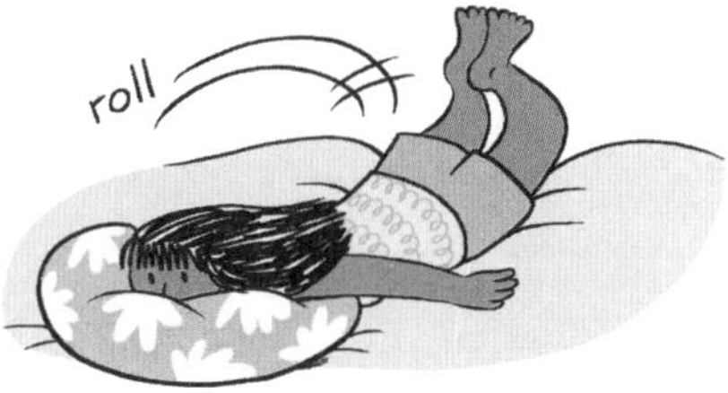
roll

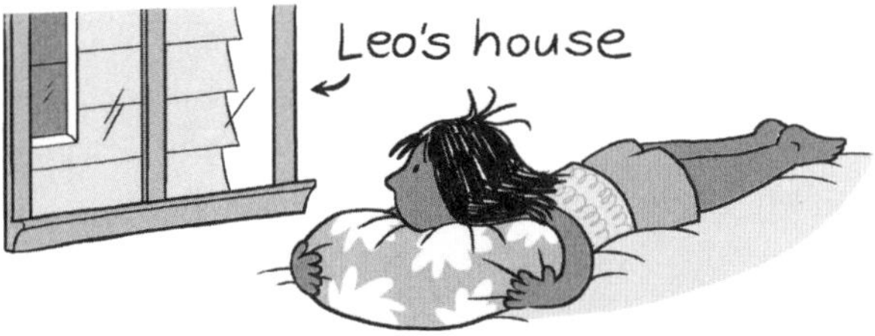
Leo's house

. . . I'm not thinking about Ben.

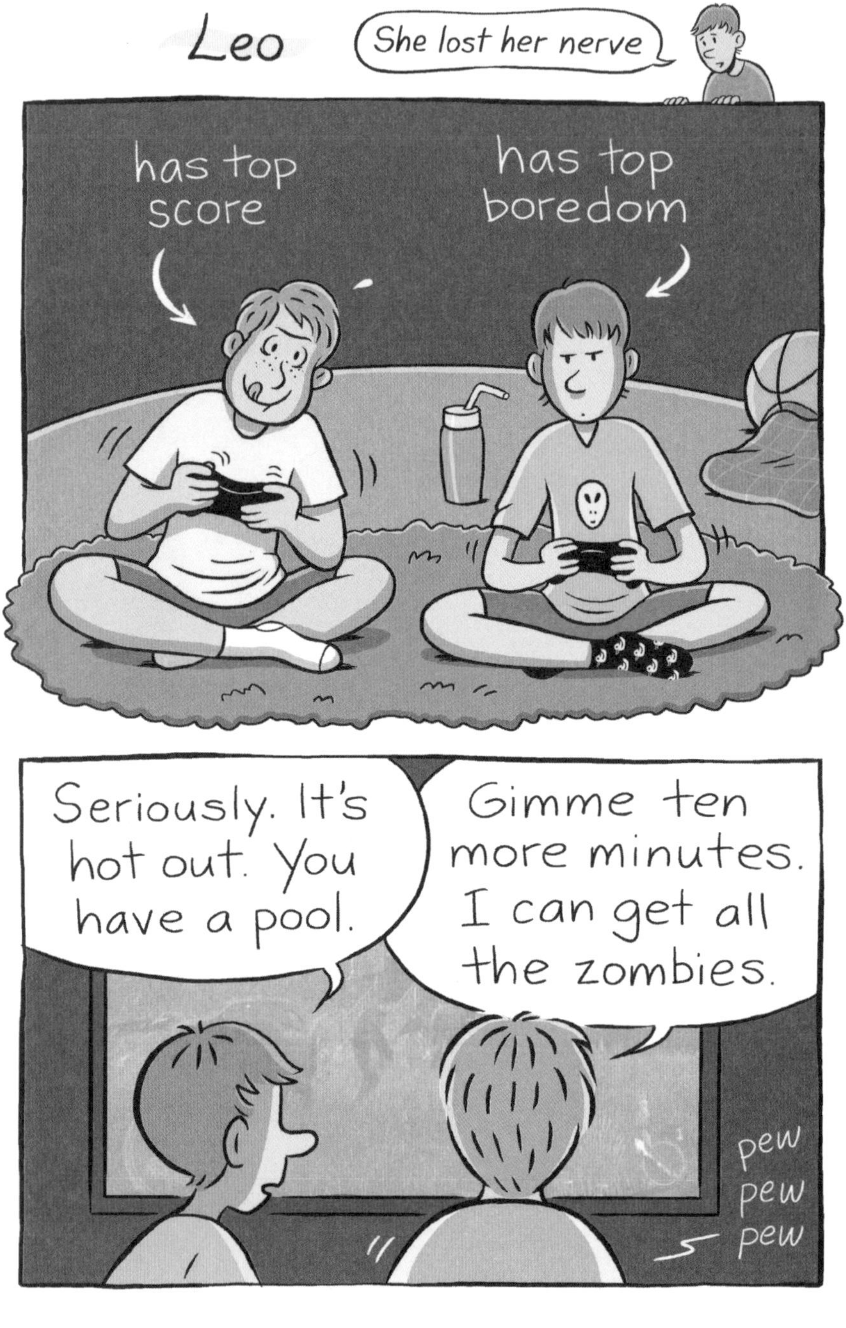
Leo
She lost her nerve
has top score
has top boredom
Seriously. It's hot out. You have a pool.
Gimme ten more minutes. I can get all the zombies.
pew pew pew

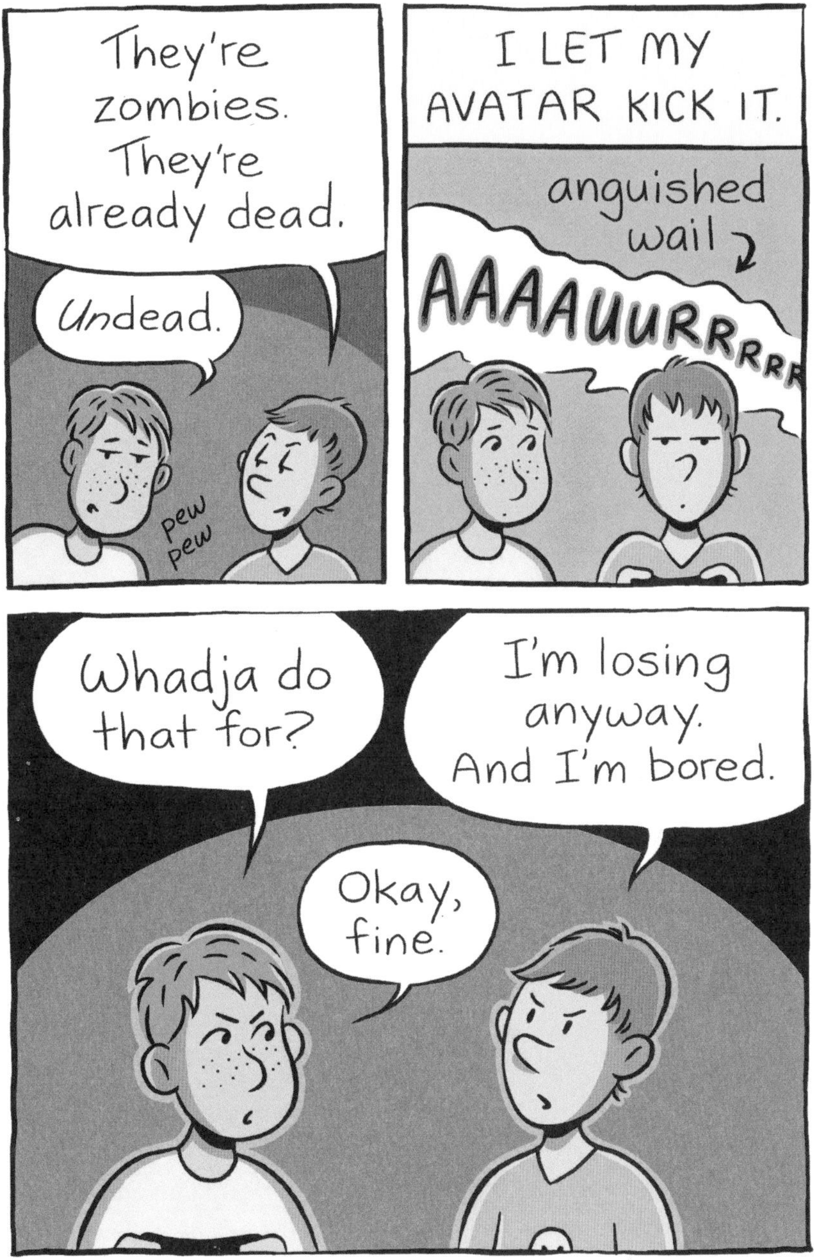
They're zombies. They're already dead.
Undead.
pew pew
I LET MY AVATAR KICK IT.
anguished wail
AAAAUURRRRRR
Whadja do that for?
I'm losing anyway. And I'm bored.
Okay, fine.

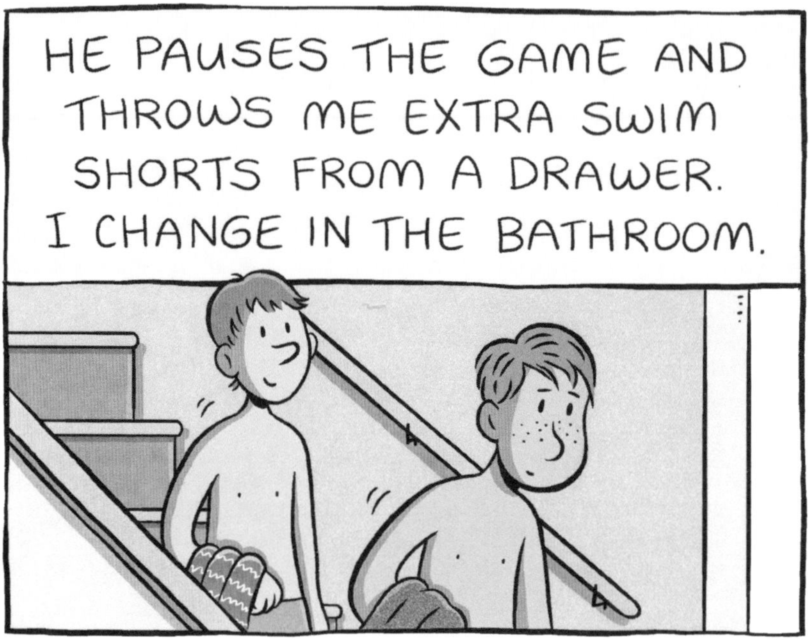
HE PAUSES THE GAME AND THROWS ME EXTRA SWIM SHORTS FROM A DRAWER. I CHANGE IN THE BATHROOM.

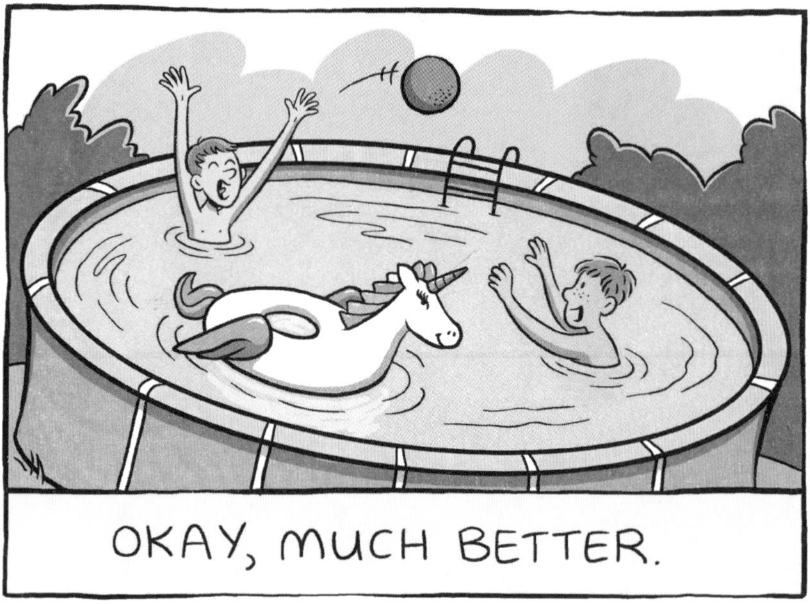
OKAY, MUCH BETTER.

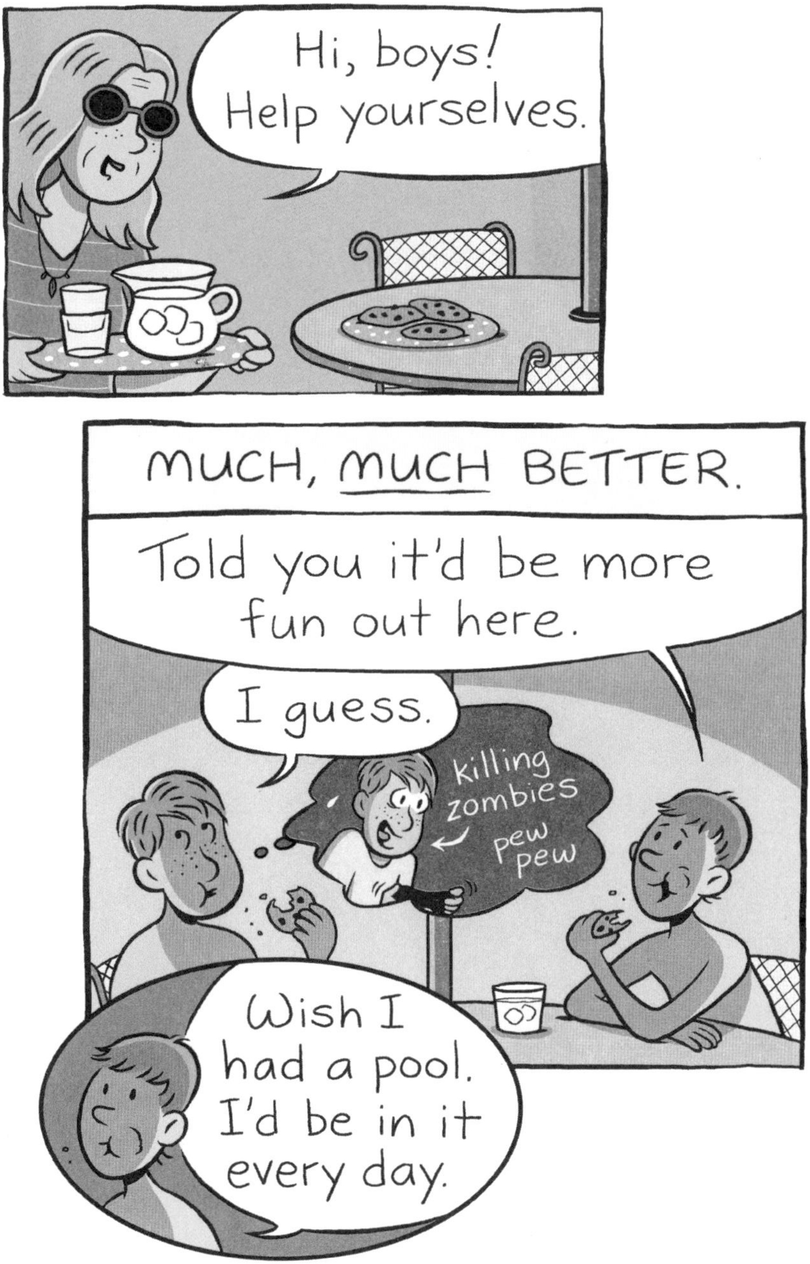
Hi, boys! Help yourselves.
MUCH, MUCH BETTER.
Told you it'd be more fun out here.
I guess.
killing zombies
pew pew
Wish I had a pool. I'd be in it every day.

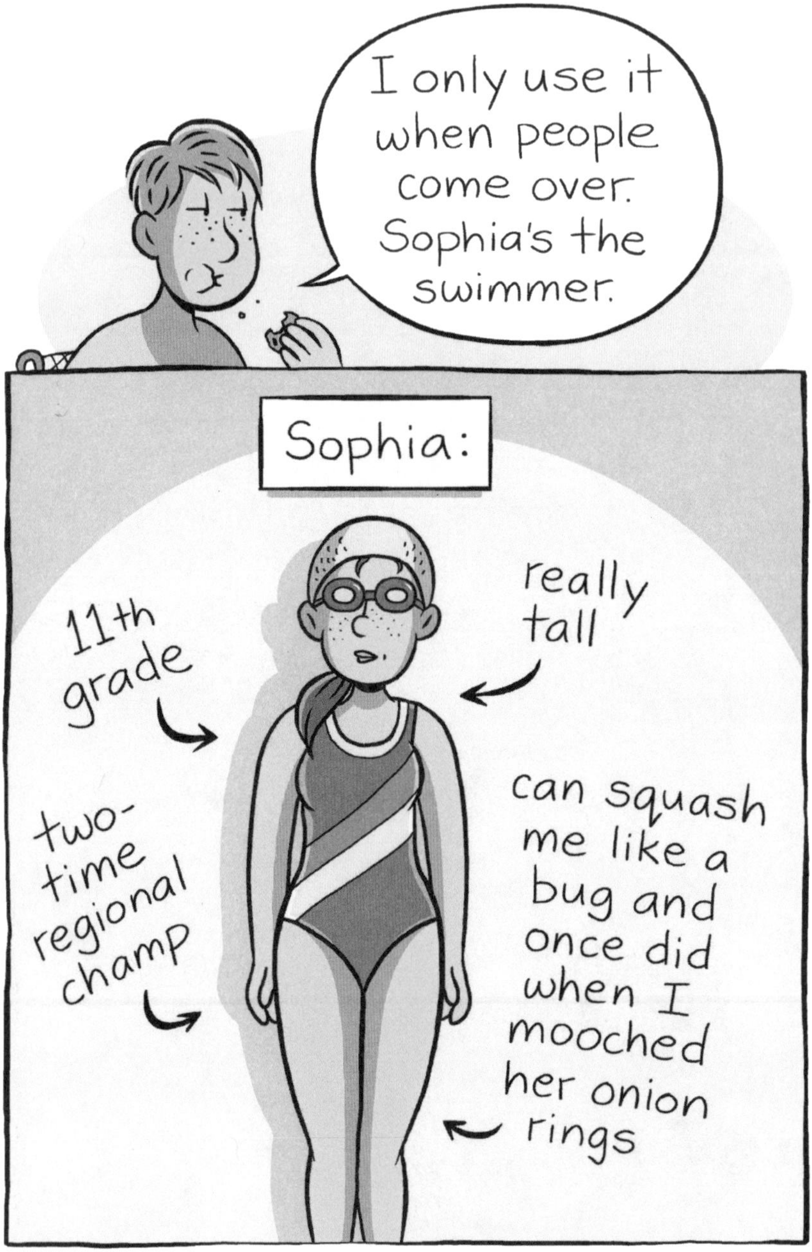
I only use it when people come over. Sophia's the swimmer.
Sophia:
11th grade
two-time regional champ
really tall
can squash me like a bug and once did when I mooched her onion rings

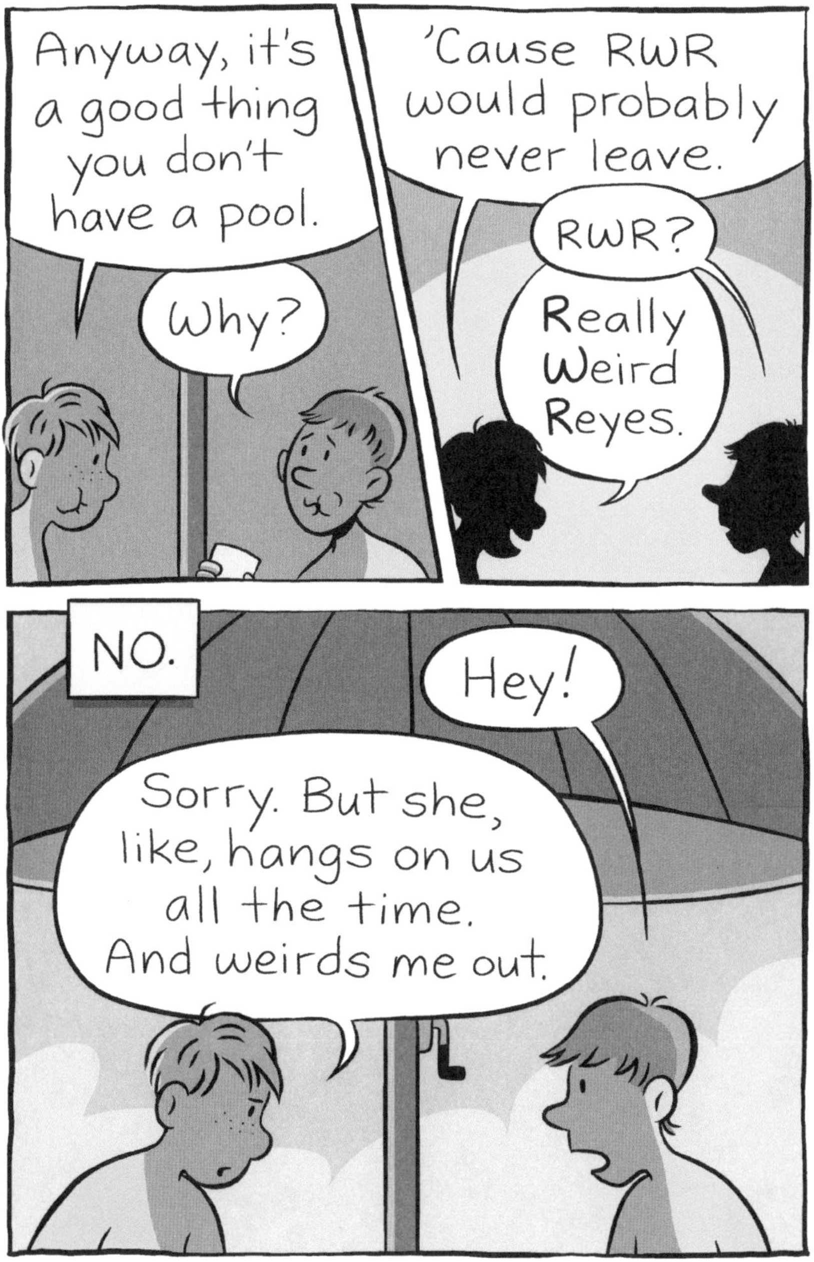
Anyway, it's a good thing you don't have a pool.
Why?
'Cause RWR would probably never leave.
RWR?
Really Weird Reyes.
NO.
Hey!
Sorry. But she, like, hangs on us all the time. And weirds me out.

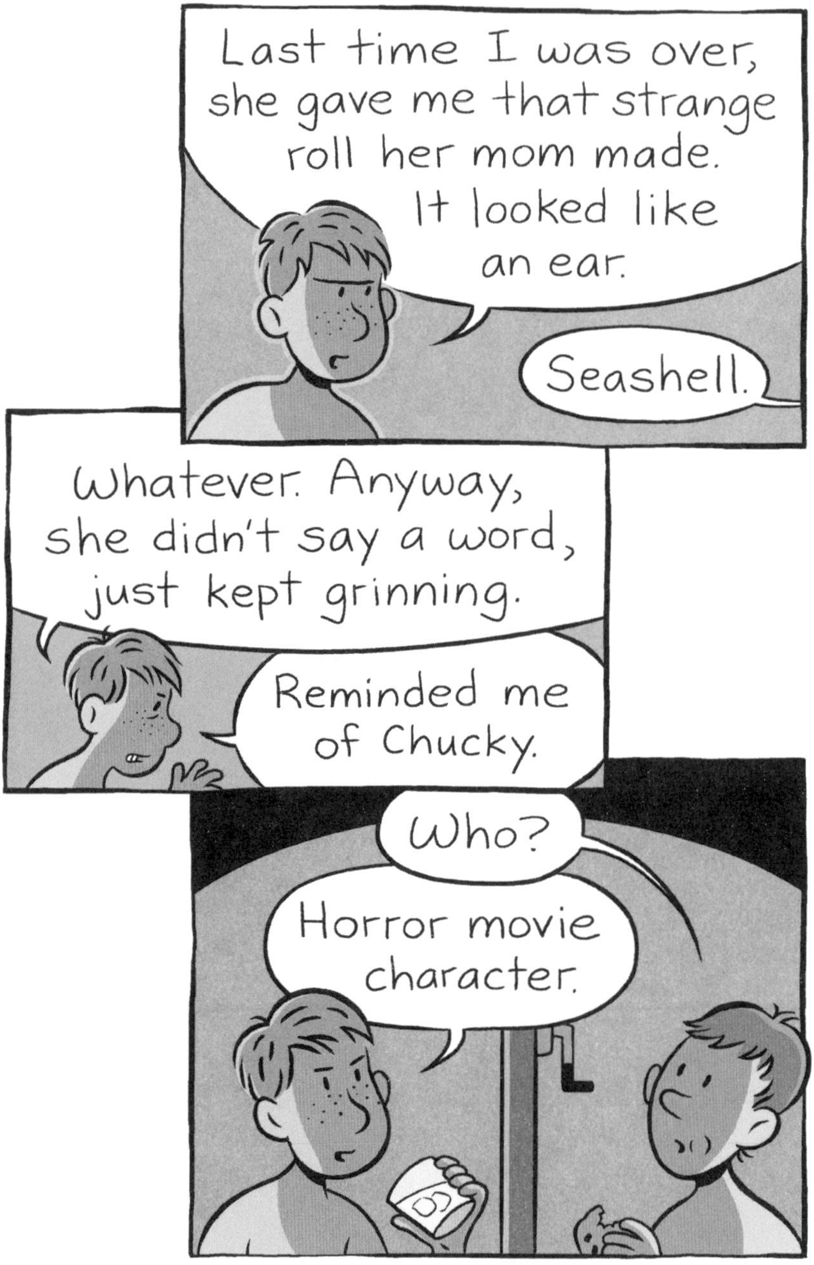
Last time I was over, she gave me that strange roll her mom made. It looked like an ear.
Seashell.
Whatever. Anyway, she didn't say a word, just kept grinning.
Reminded me of Chucky.
Who?
Horror movie character.

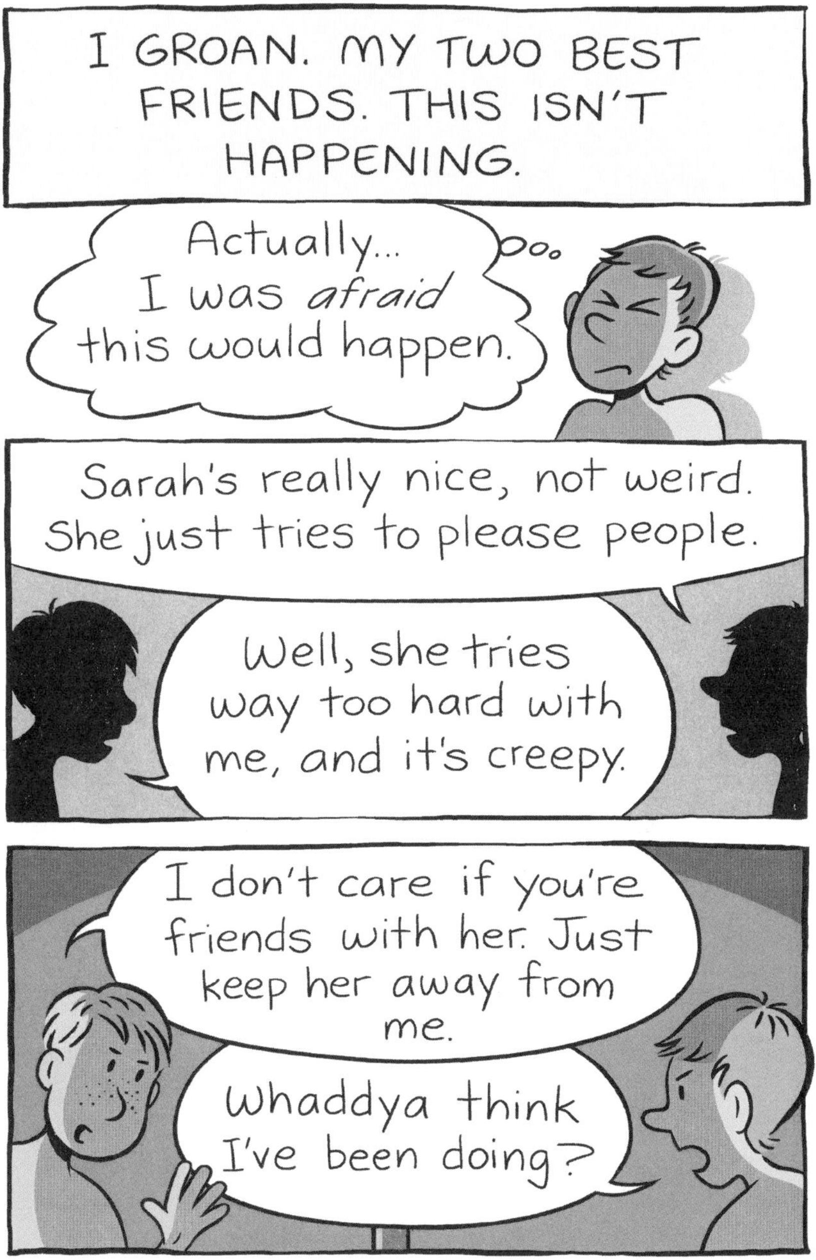
I GROAN. MY TWO BEST FRIENDS. THIS ISN'T HAPPENING.
Actually... I was *afraid* this would happen.
Sarah's really nice, not weird. She just tries to please people.
Well, she tries way too hard with me, and it's creepy.
I don't care if you're friends with her. Just keep her away from me.
Whaddya think I've been doing?

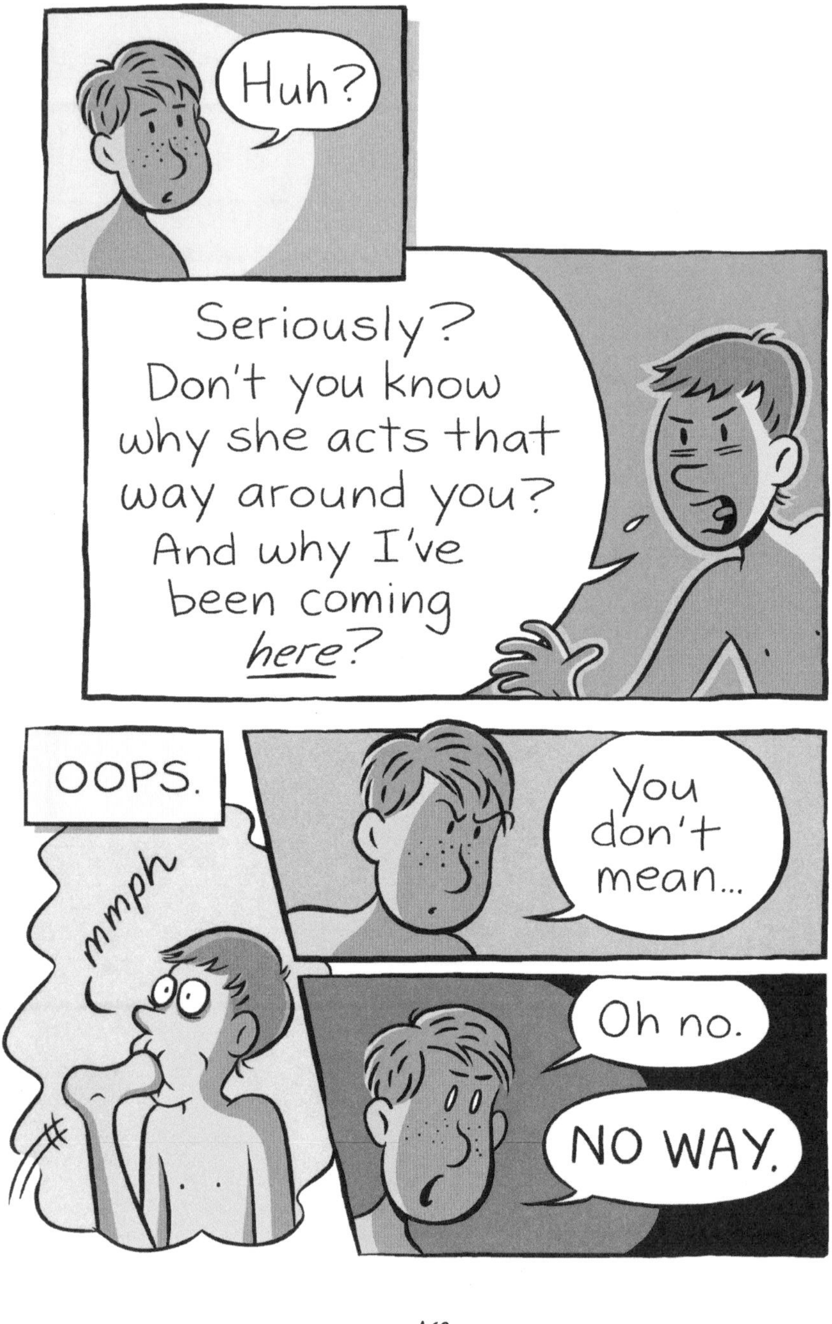

Huh?
Seriously? Don't you know why she acts that way around you? And why I've been coming here?
OOPS.
mmph
You don't mean...
Oh no.
NO WAY.

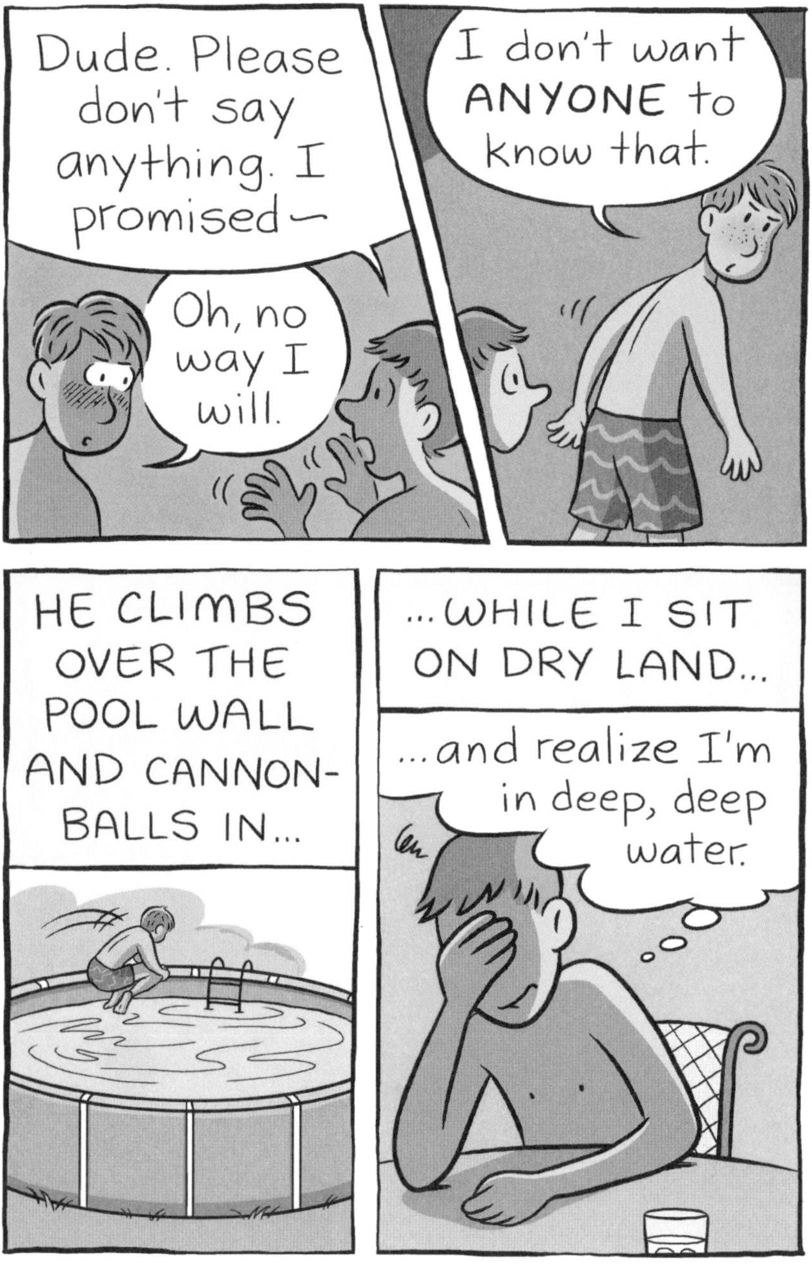
Dude. Please don't say anything. I promised—
Oh, no way I will.
I don't want ANYONE to know that.
HE CLIMBS OVER THE POOL WALL AND CANNON-BALLS IN...
...WHILE I SIT ON DRY LAND...
...and realize I'm in deep, deep water.

SARAH

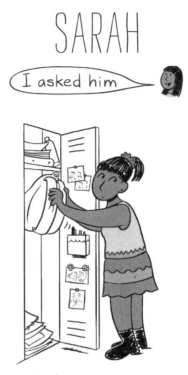

I asked him

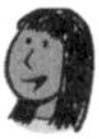

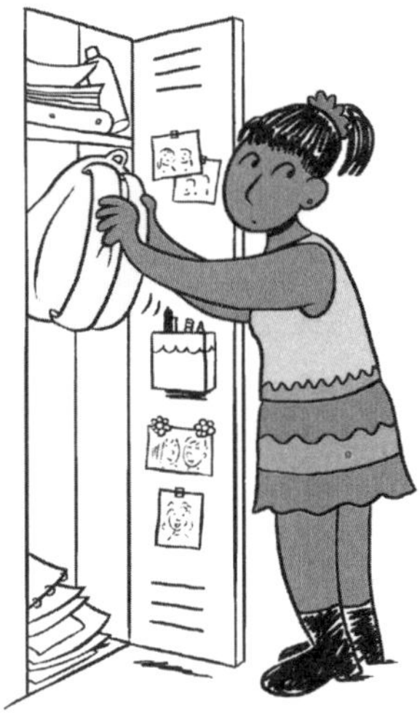

Friday. Morning of the dance.
And I don't see Ben anywhere.

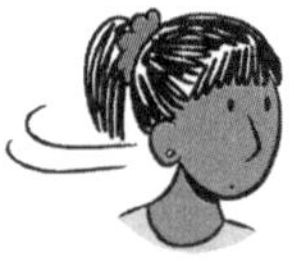

He's usually one of the first ones here, like me. Not 'cause he loves school that much, but 'cause his dad drops him off on the way to work. Leo told me Ben would rather get a ride and come early than sit on the funky-smelling bus.

bus odors:
lunch
feet
floor
"sprits"
(combo of body spray and armpits)

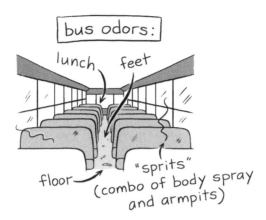

I'm early just 'cause my bus has the closest route. I usually see Ben at his locker around this time. Except when he's sick.

flashback:
gone for a week with the flu (aka longest week of seventh grade)

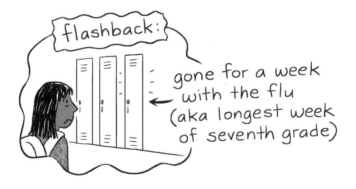

uh-oh.

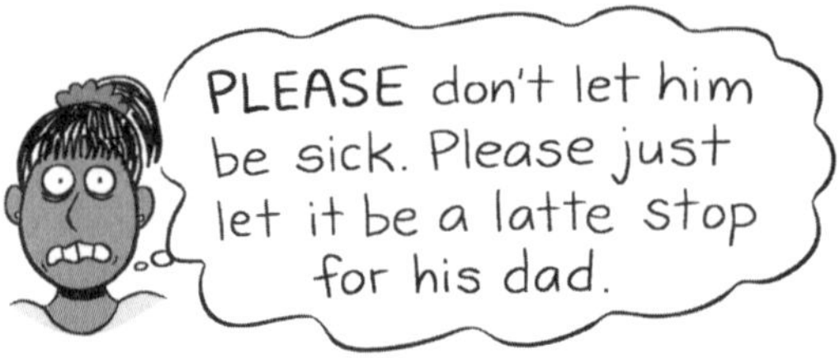
PLEASE don't let him be sick. Please just let it be a latte stop for his dad.

I wait a few extra minutes just in case. No sign of him. Soon the hallway gets crowded as more kids get dropped off.

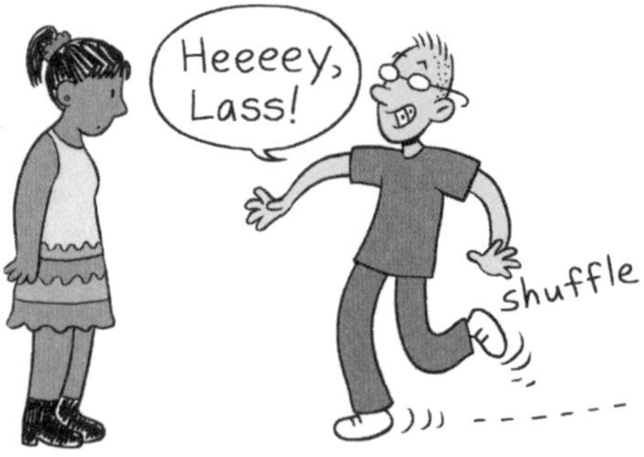
Heeeey, Lass!
shuffle

Joe jigs over. I'm so distracted, I barely register that he's right in front of me. When I do, I try to smile.

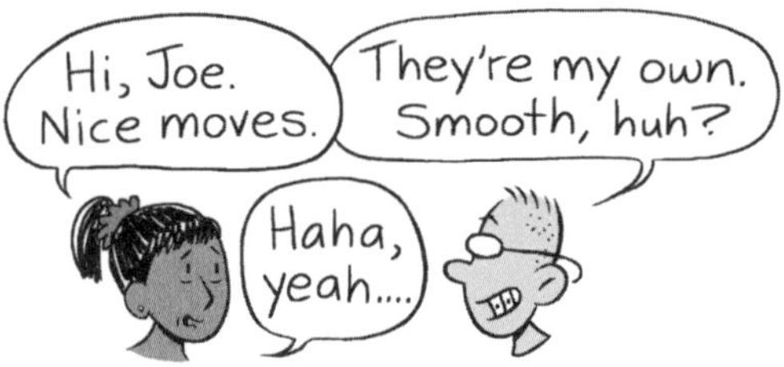
Hi, Joe. Nice moves.
They're my own. Smooth, huh?
Haha, yeah....

I keep looking down the hallway.

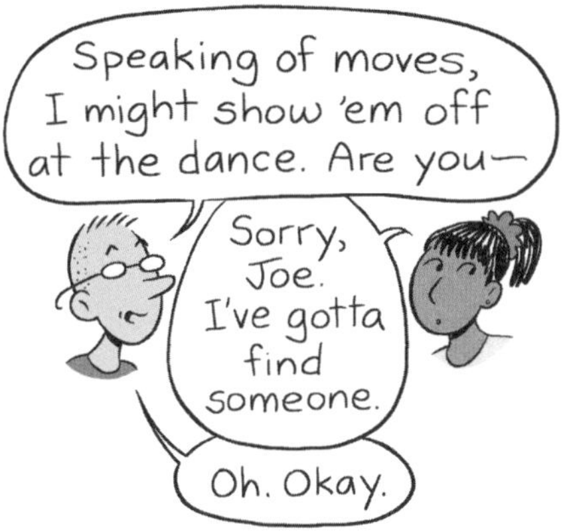
Speaking of moves, I might show 'em off at the dance. Are you—
Sorry, Joe. I've gotta find someone.
Oh. Okay.

I quickly close my locker door and race down the hallway, dodging people, backpacks, and angry hall monitors.

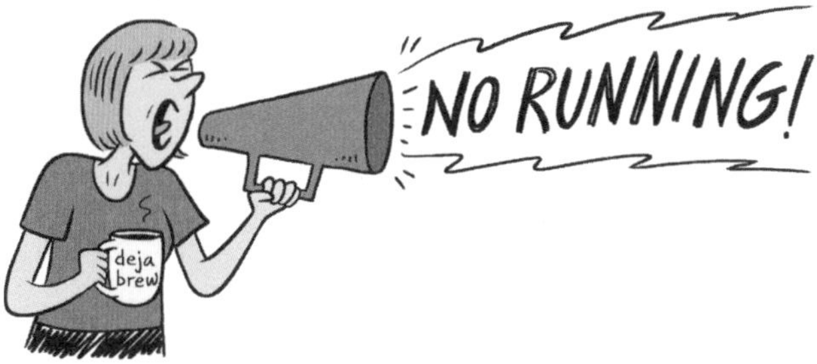
NO RUNNING!
deja brew

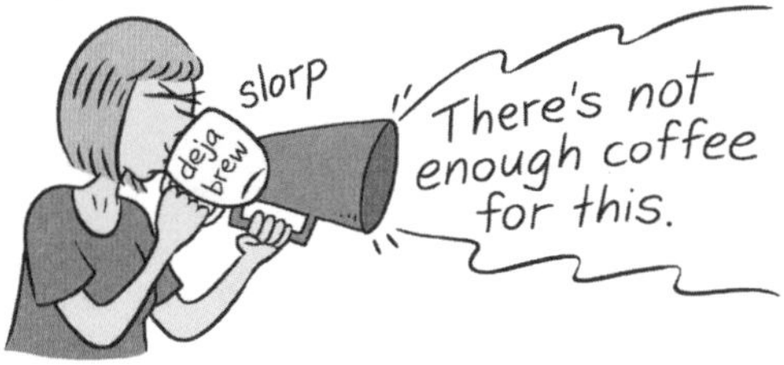
slorp
deja brew
There's not enough coffee for this.

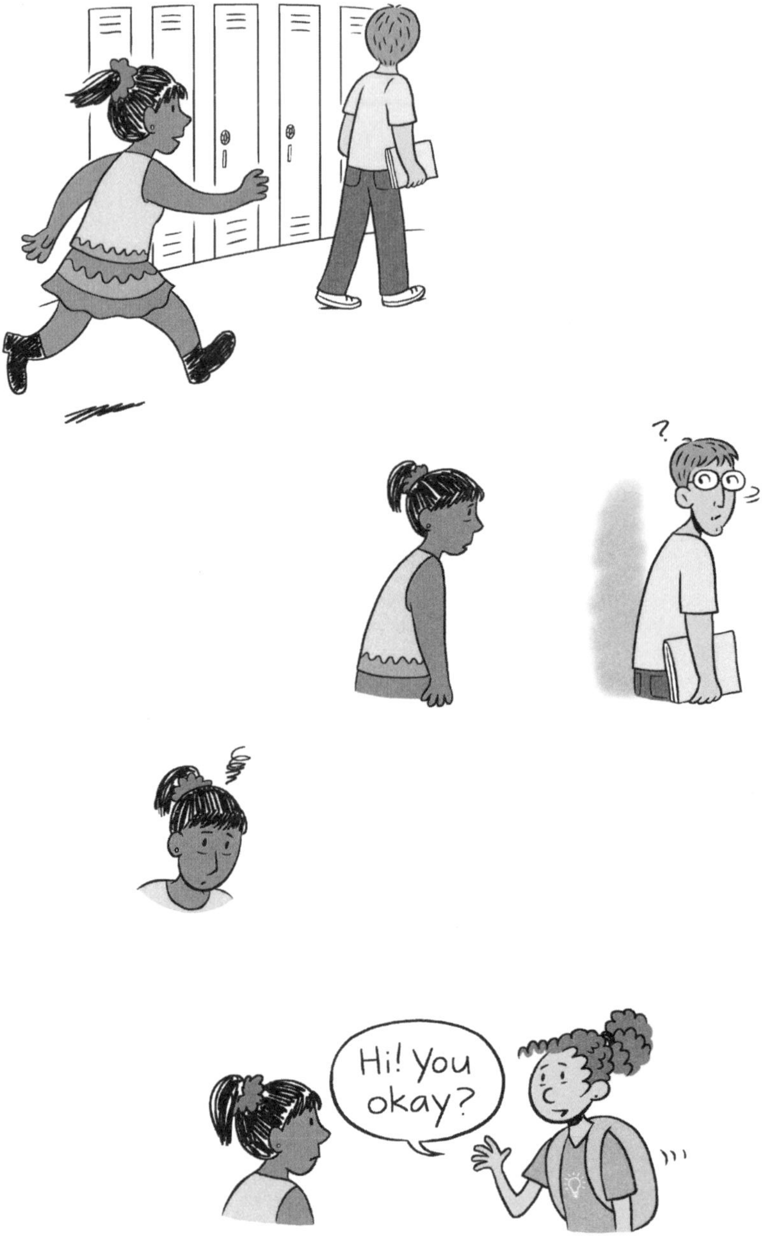
Hi! You okay?

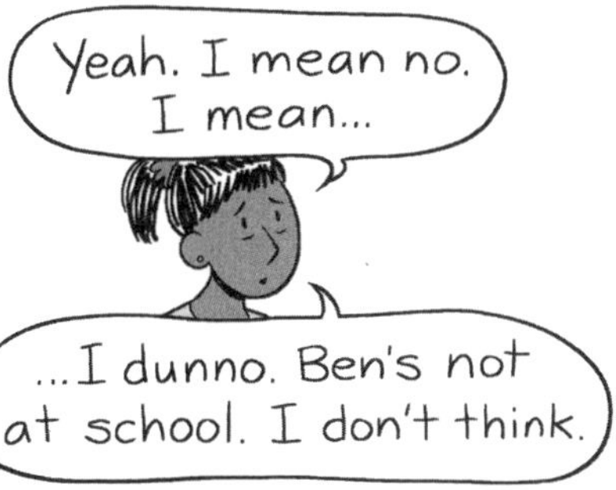
Yeah. I mean no. I mean...
...I dunno. Ben's not at school. I don't think.

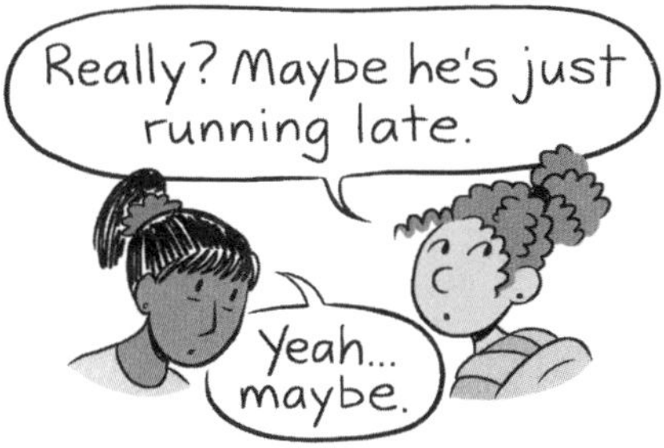
Really? Maybe he's just running late.
Yeah... maybe.

I try not to panic. I keep Emmie company at her locker while she puts away her stuff. Bri soon arrives.

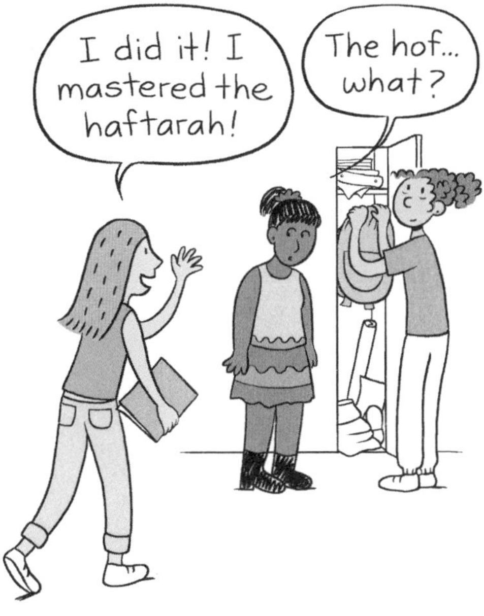
I did it! I mastered the haftarah!
The hof... what?

It's a Hebrew prayer. I finally had a breakthrough.

That's great, Bri!

You guys will be impressed. That's *if* I don't have a panic attack and throw up on the altar flowers.

They laugh, but I'm still peering down the hall.

What's with her?

Ben hasn't shown up.

Oh, he's probably just running late or something.

Besides, it's Friday. Half the kids are tardy when it's nice on a Friday.

It is nice. Sunny and warm. All good signs for a great evening. No dark and threatening clouds to foreshadow bad events.

Like being ditched.

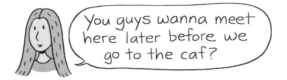

You guys wanna meet here later before we go to the caf?

Decorating. Instead of afternoon classes.

(sigh) Sure. Just wish I was looking forward to the dance. I don't wanna watch Tyler and Celia's PDA...

...where we eat our tater tots.

Even though I'm anxious, I try to cheer her up.

It'll still be fun.

That's right. We don't need *men* to enjoy the dance.

We have each other. And music. And lots and lots of neon llamas.

neon cut-outs
for the dance:

← Lakefront
mascot

Emmie and I smile. If anything, decorating will be fun.
The bell rings, and we head to our homerooms.

BRNNG

I don't see Ben the rest of the morning. But I try not to
worry—after all, I don't always see him around. We're on separate school teams. (Lakefront is so big, the classes are divided into
groups or "teams" with their own teachers.)

team names:

The Petri Dishes

Punctuation Patrol

Let's eat kids!

Later, I meet Emmie and Bri at Em's locker, like we agreed. We walk to the caf together, joking around. I'm trying to stay cheerful even though a big part of me is worried.

We decorate all afternoon. When we're done, the place looks unrecognizable. Our neon cutouts—glued to black tablecloths—cover the walls, windows, and even the tray counter. Colorful neon garlands and LED balloons dangle from the ceiling. Tin trays—filled with giveaway glow necklaces and wristbands—decorate tabletops where glow-in-the-dark punch and candy (regular but with neon wrappers) will be passed out. We also made a doodle wall that people can decorate using thick neon pens.

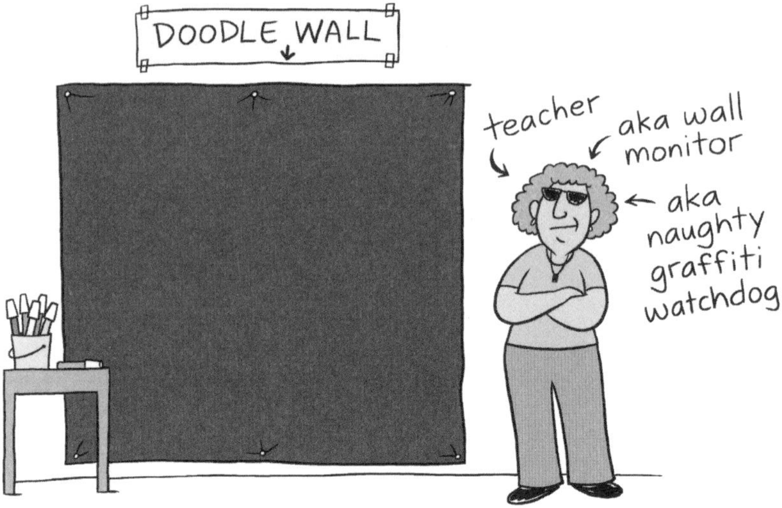
DOODLE WALL
teacher
aka wall monitor
aka naughty graffiti watchdog

And that's not all. We also thought of games: Ping-pong ball toss (into glow-in-the-dark cups) and a ring toss using glow bracelets and old bottles filled with sand and decorated with neon stickers.

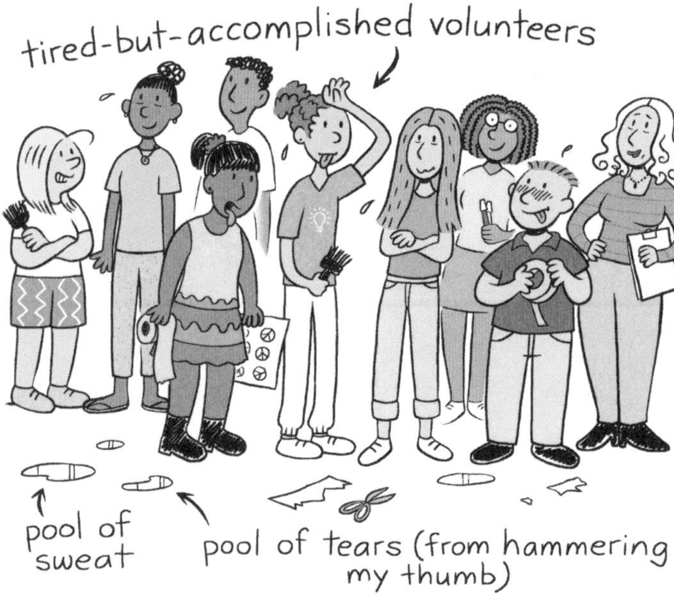
tired-but-accomplished volunteers
pool of sweat
pool of tears (from hammering my thumb)

By the time we're finished, we barely make it to the bus.

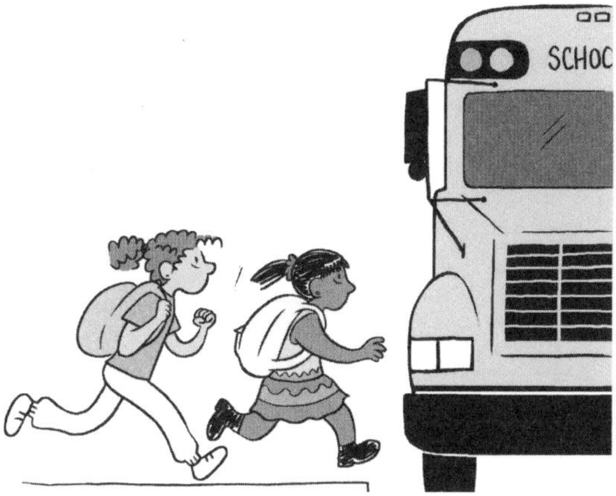
SCHOC

Emmie's coming home with me so we can get ready for the dance together. We sit down, catching our breath, and check our phones. Emmie checks for texts from her mom while I check for . . .

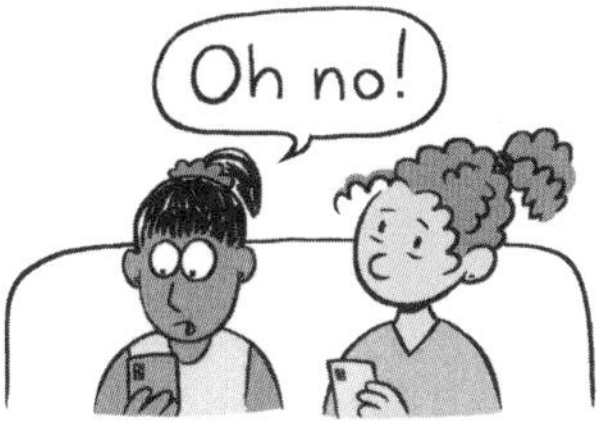
Oh no!

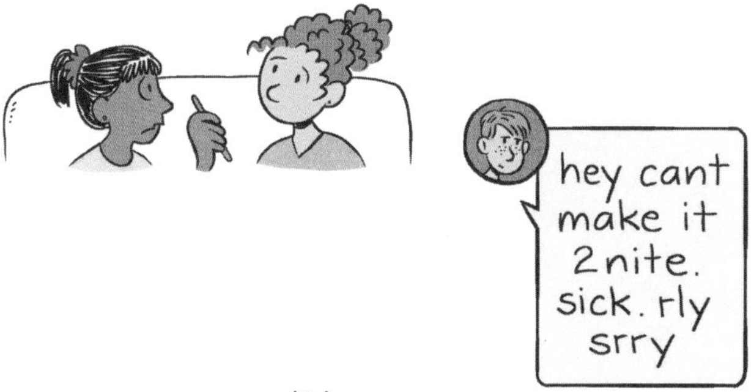
hey cant make it 2nite. sick. rly srry

My phone drops into my lap. I think I'm sick, too.

Ohh, Sarah, that stinks.

Yeah.

But hey! It'll still be fun, okay? We'll take lots of pictures of our decorations and tons of selfies, and we'll *dance* so much!

Yeah. Sure.

But I don't mean it. How can I have a good time now? I don't even know if he skipped school on purpose to avoid going with me or if he's really, truly sick.

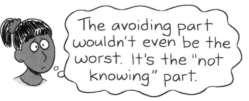

The avoiding part wouldn't even be the worst. It's the "not knowing" part.

My eyes fill with tears.

Reminds me so much of my dad. I'm never sure if he wants a relationship with me. There's always a little part of me that holds on to hope that he does. And I'm always left wondering.

Boys.

Yeah, I know. But there's Leo. He's great!

Not really.

I explain what's been going on.

I didn't really say anything 'cause... well, I thought it'd pass.

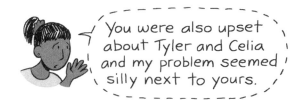

You were also upset about Tyler and Celia and my problem seemed silly next to yours.

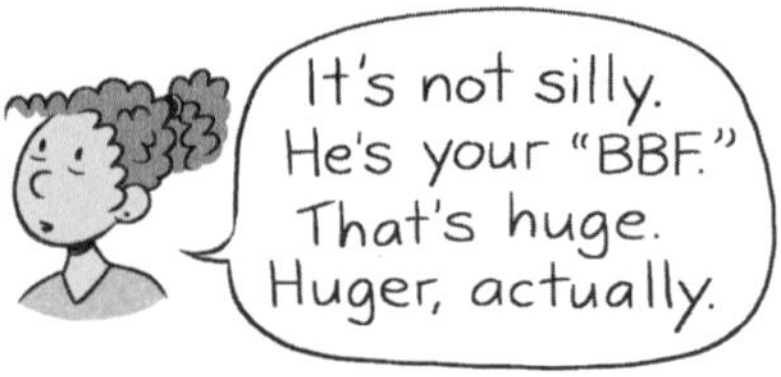
It's not silly. He's your "BBF." That's huge. Huger, actually.

She hugs me, which helps. A little.

We get off the bus and walk to my house.

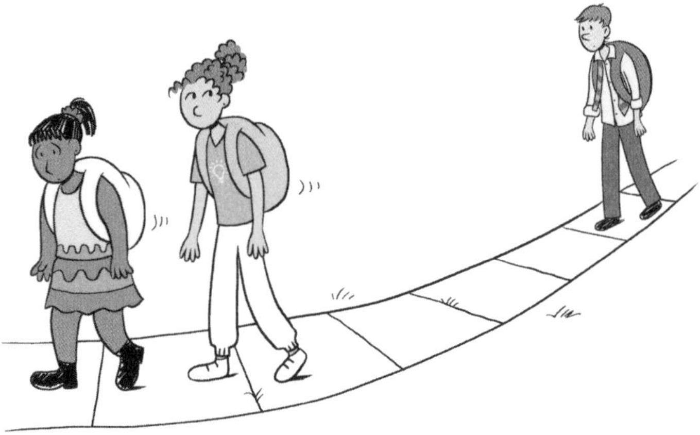

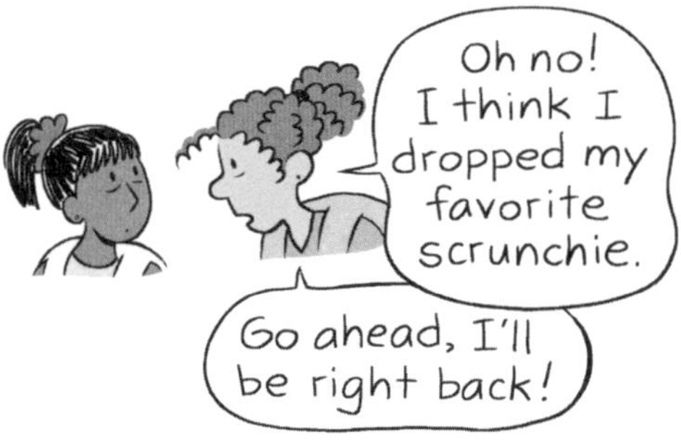
Oh no! I think I dropped my favorite scrunchie.
Go ahead, I'll be right back!

I don't say anything. I really don't feel like helping her look. I just wanna go inside and lie down.

And I **definitely** don't wanna go to the dance.

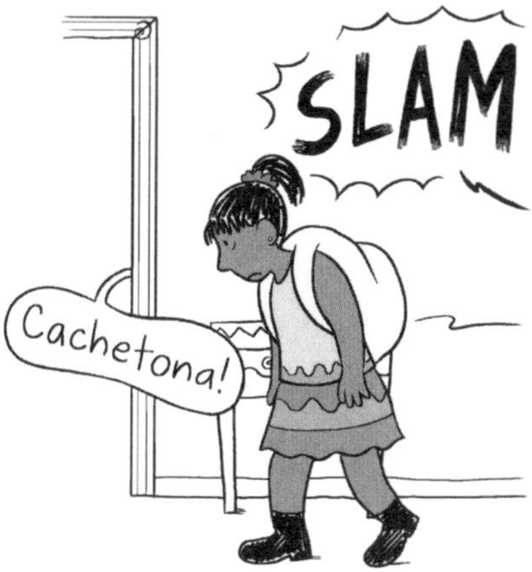
SLAM
Cachetona!

I plop on the couch and stare at the ceiling, smelling the irresistible scent of cooling donuts.

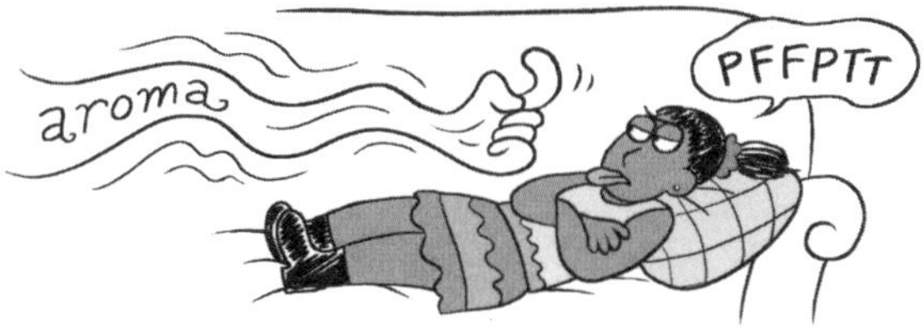
aroma
PFFPTT

At least I have Emmie and Bri, I tell myself. . . .

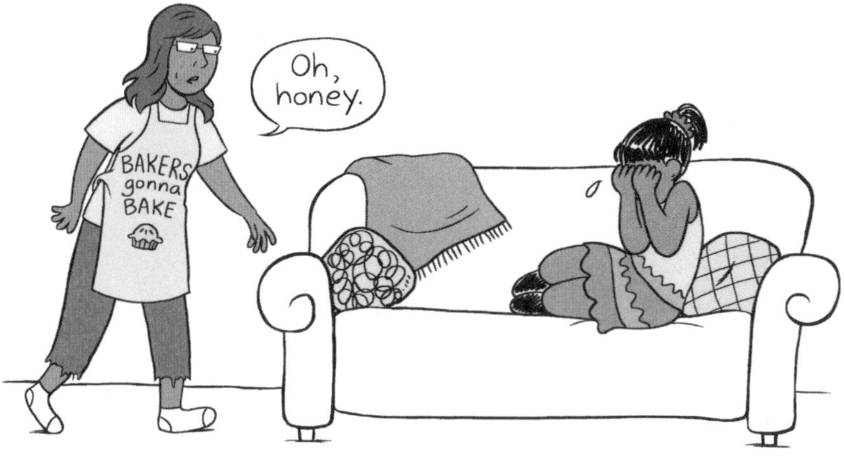
Oh, honey.
BAKERS gonna BAKE

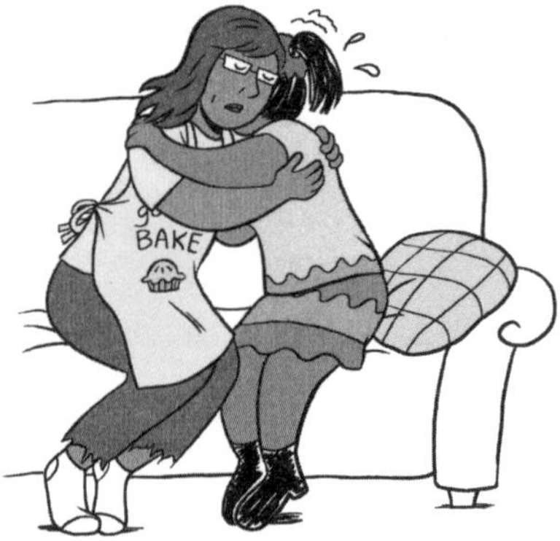
BAKE

. . . and my wonderful, wonderful mamá.

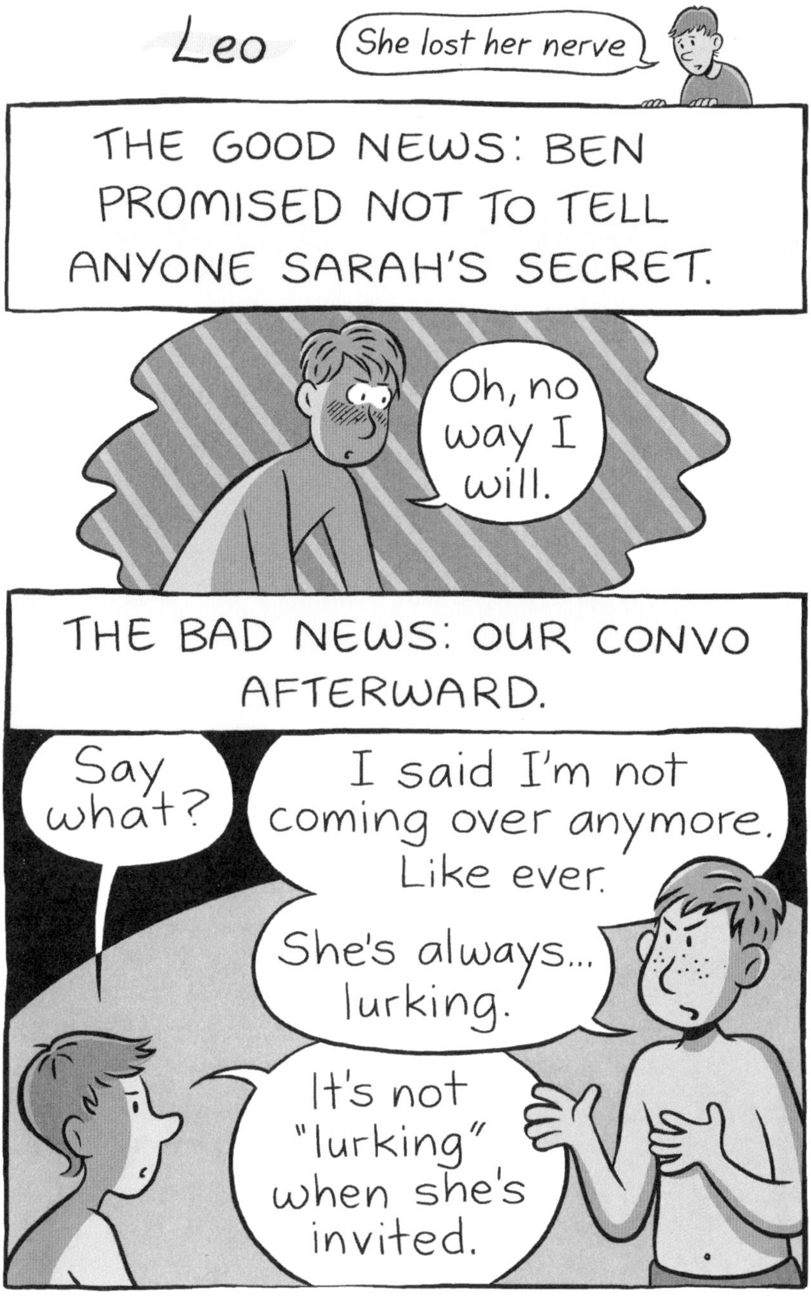
Leo
She lost her nerve
THE GOOD NEWS: BEN PROMISED NOT TO TELL ANYONE SARAH'S SECRET.
Oh, no way I will.
THE BAD NEWS: OUR CONVO AFTERWARD.
Say what?
I said I'm not coming over anymore. Like ever.
She's always... lurking.
It's not "lurking" when she's invited.

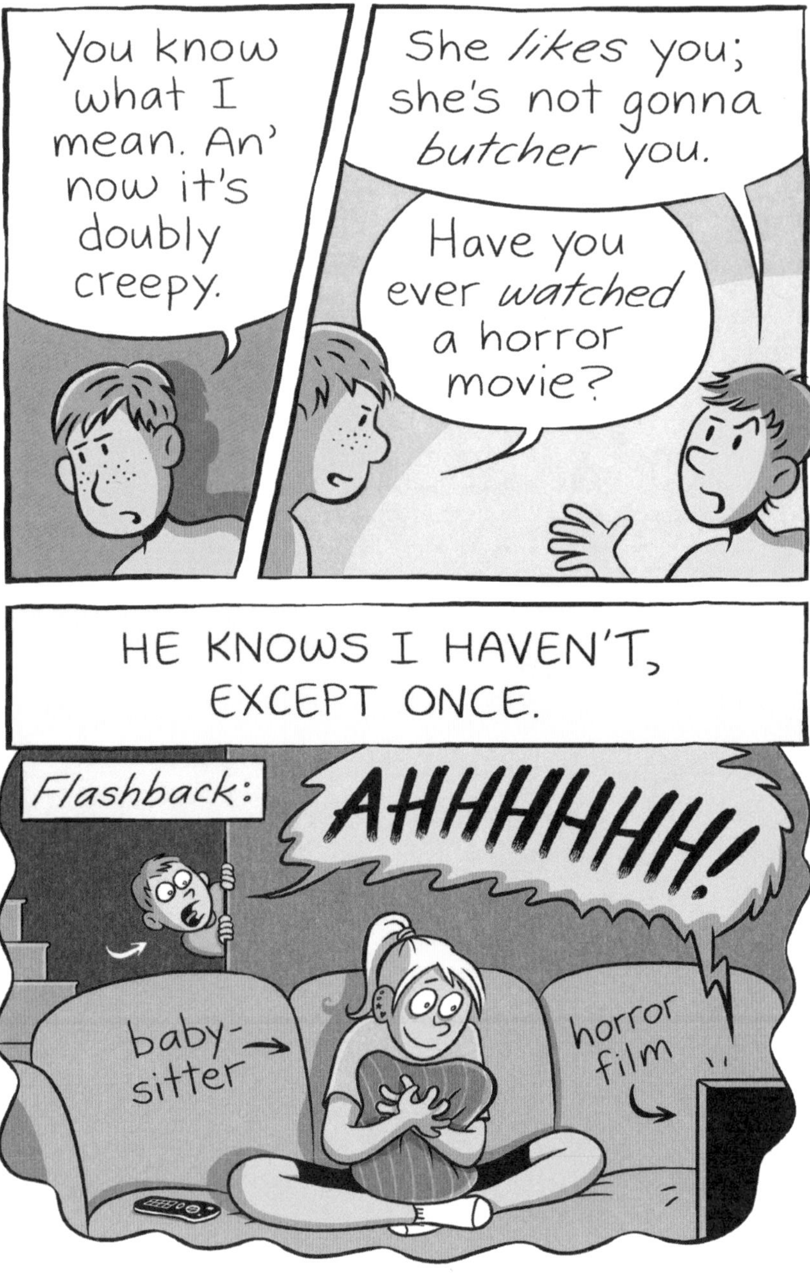
You know what I mean. An' now it's doubly creepy.
She *likes* you; she's not gonna *butcher* you.
Have you ever *watched* a horror movie?
HE KNOWS I HAVEN'T, EXCEPT ONCE.
Flashback:
AHHHHHH!
baby-sitter
horror film

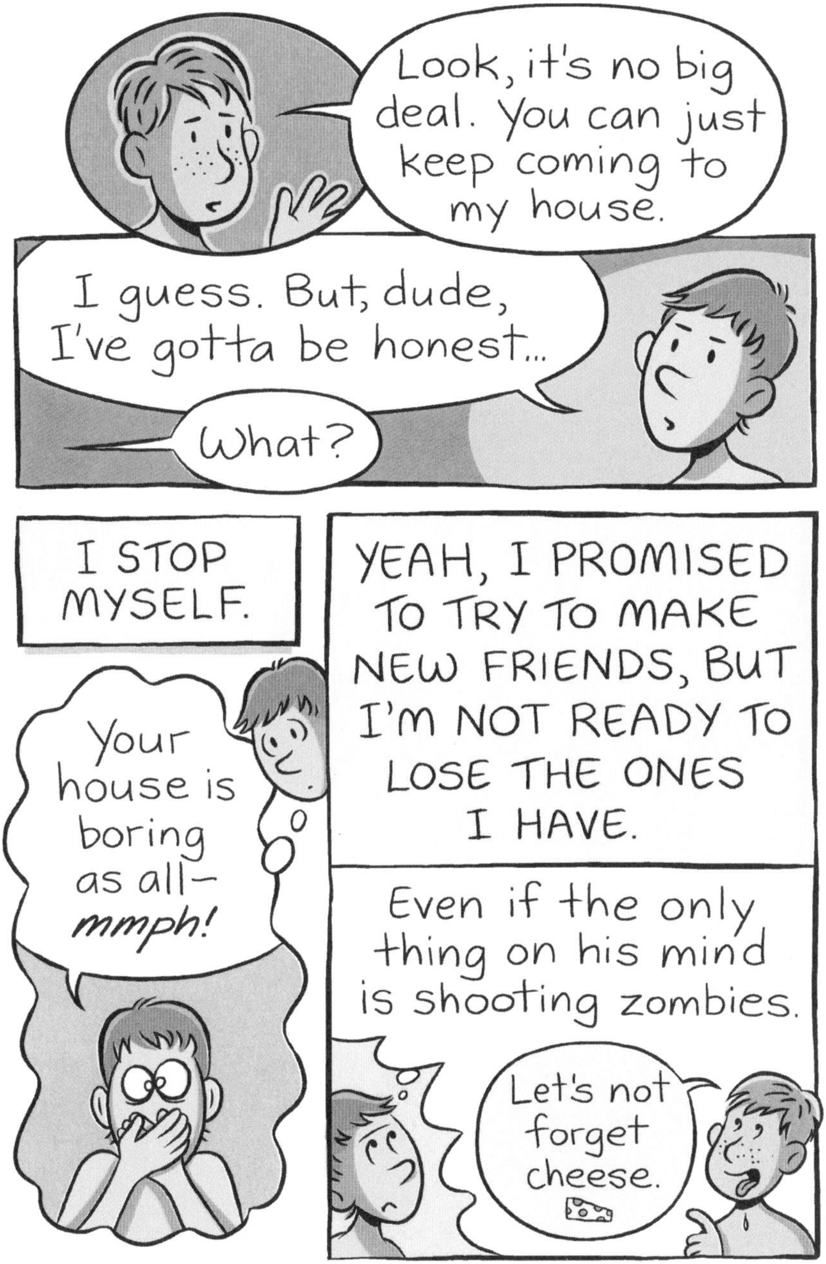
Look, it's no big deal. You can just keep coming to my house.
I guess. But, dude, I've gotta be honest...
What?
I STOP MYSELF.
Your house is boring as all—*mmph!*
YEAH, I PROMISED TO TRY TO MAKE NEW FRIENDS, BUT I'M NOT READY TO LOSE THE ONES I HAVE.
Even if the only thing on his mind is shooting zombies.
Let's not forget cheese.

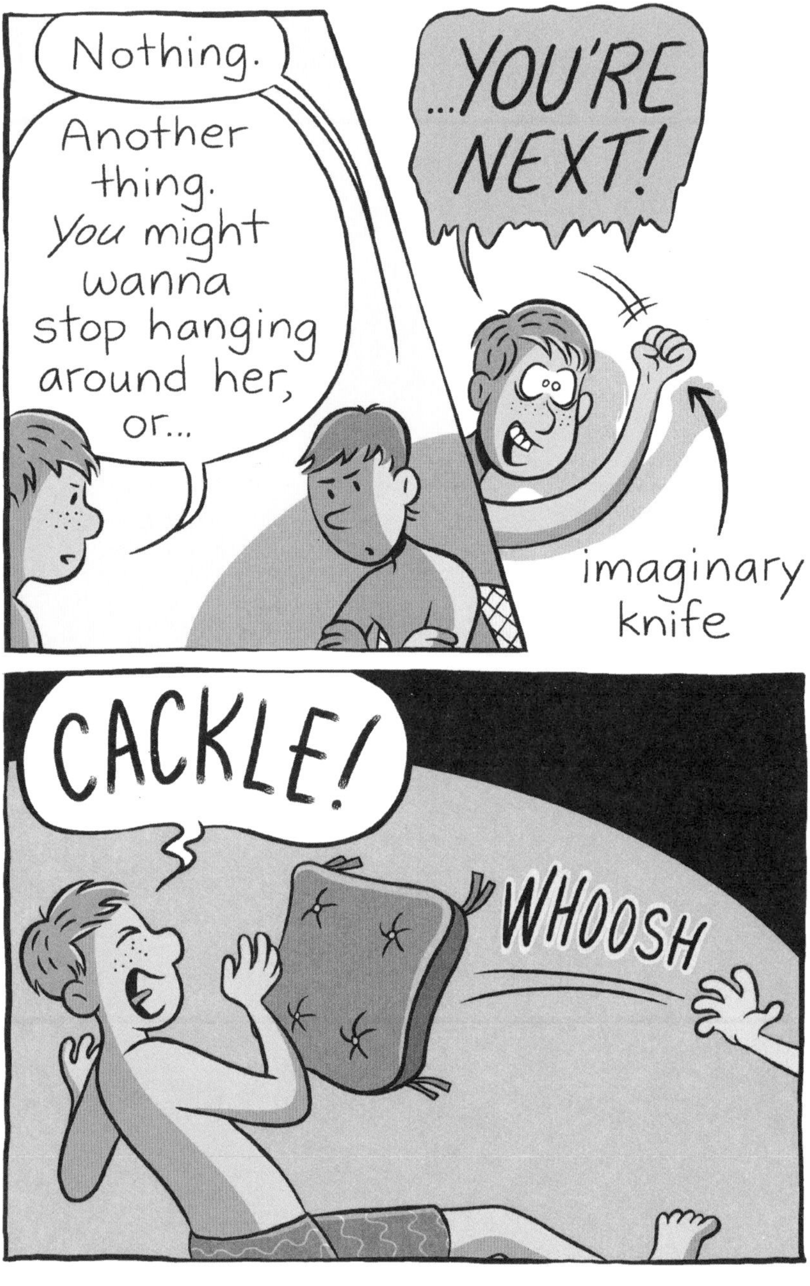
Nothing.
Another thing. *You* might wanna stop hanging around her, or...
...YOU'RE NEXT!
imaginary knife
CACKLE!
WHOOSH

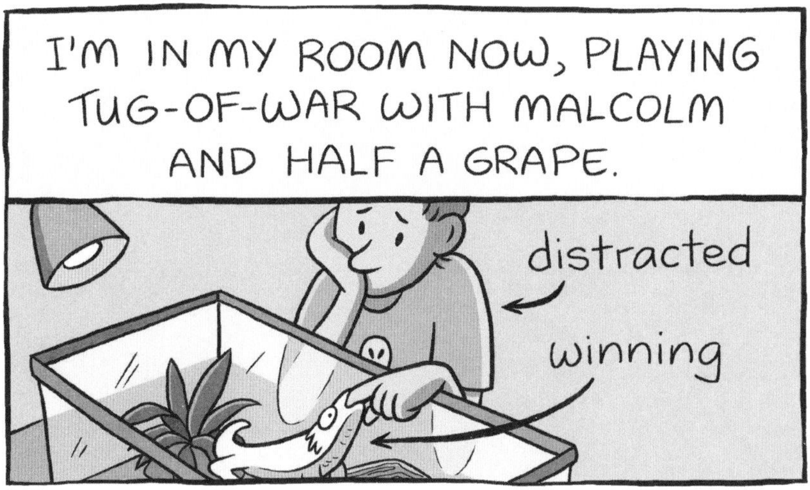
I'M IN MY ROOM NOW, PLAYING TUG-OF-WAR WITH MALCOLM AND HALF A GRAPE.
distracted
winning

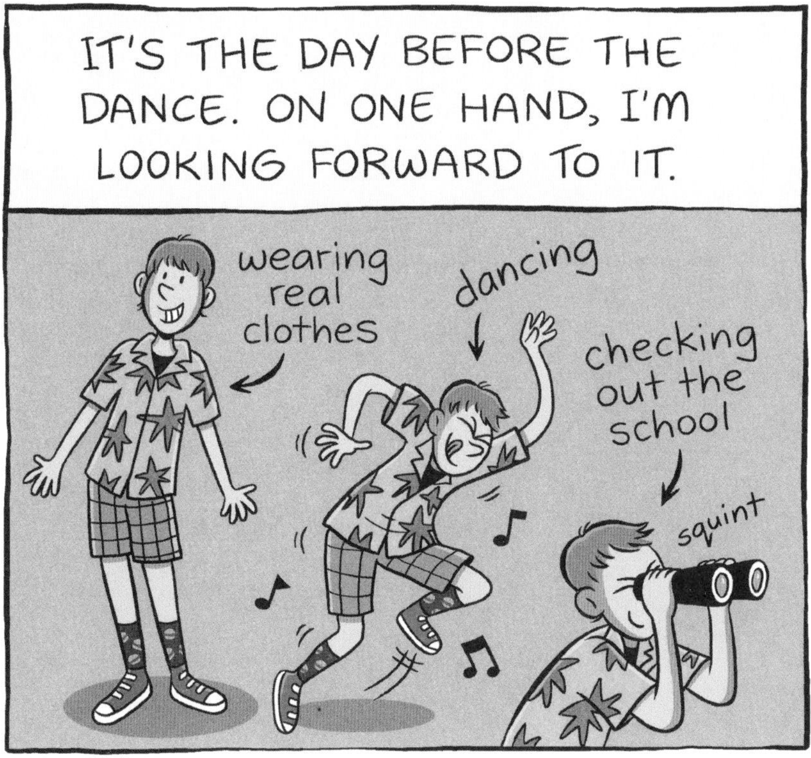
IT'S THE DAY BEFORE THE DANCE. ON ONE HAND, I'M LOOKING FORWARD TO IT.
wearing real clothes
dancing
checking out the school
squint

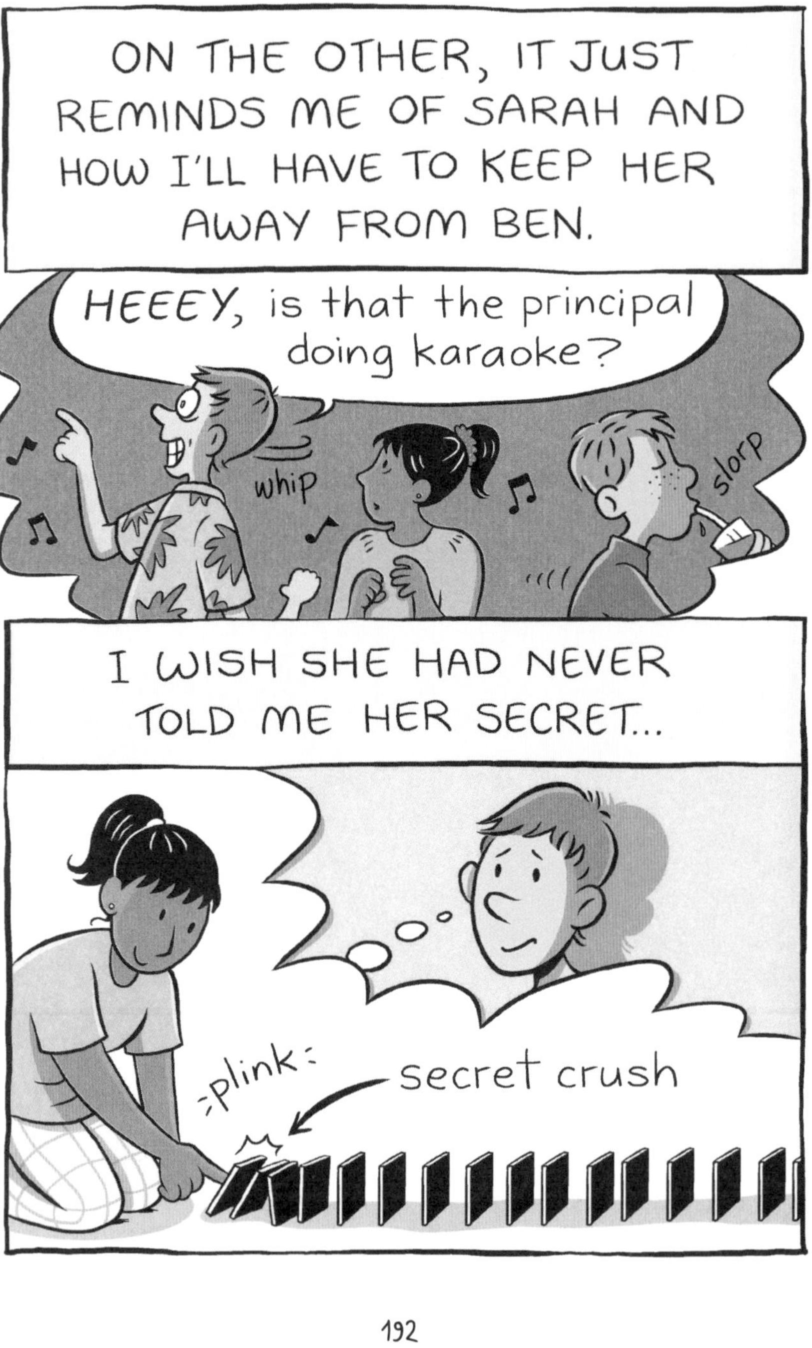
ON THE OTHER, IT JUST REMINDS ME OF SARAH AND HOW I'LL HAVE TO KEEP HER AWAY FROM BEN.
HEEEY, is that the principal doing karaoke?
whip
slorp
I WISH SHE HAD NEVER TOLD ME HER SECRET...
plink
secret crush

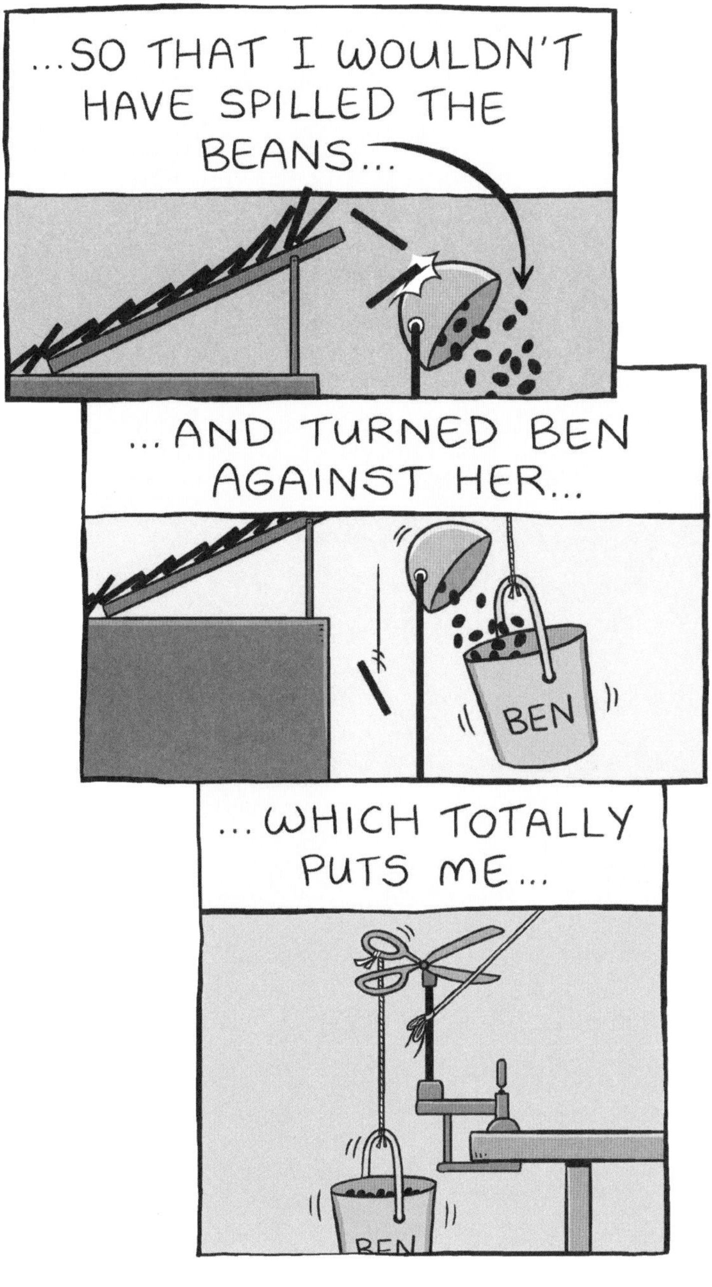

...SO THAT I WOULDN'T HAVE SPILLED THE BEANS...
...AND TURNED BEN AGAINST HER...
BEN
...WHICH TOTALLY PUTS ME...

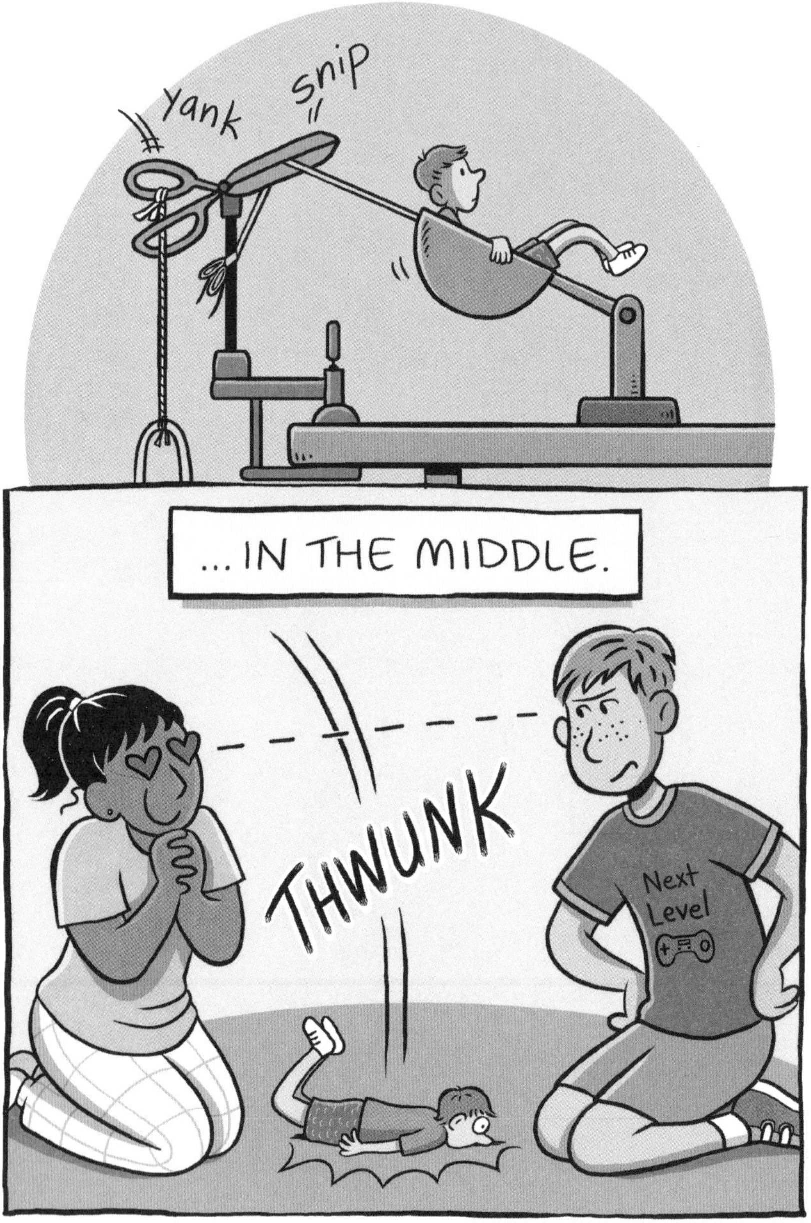
yank
snip
...IN THE MIDDLE.
THWUNK
Next Level

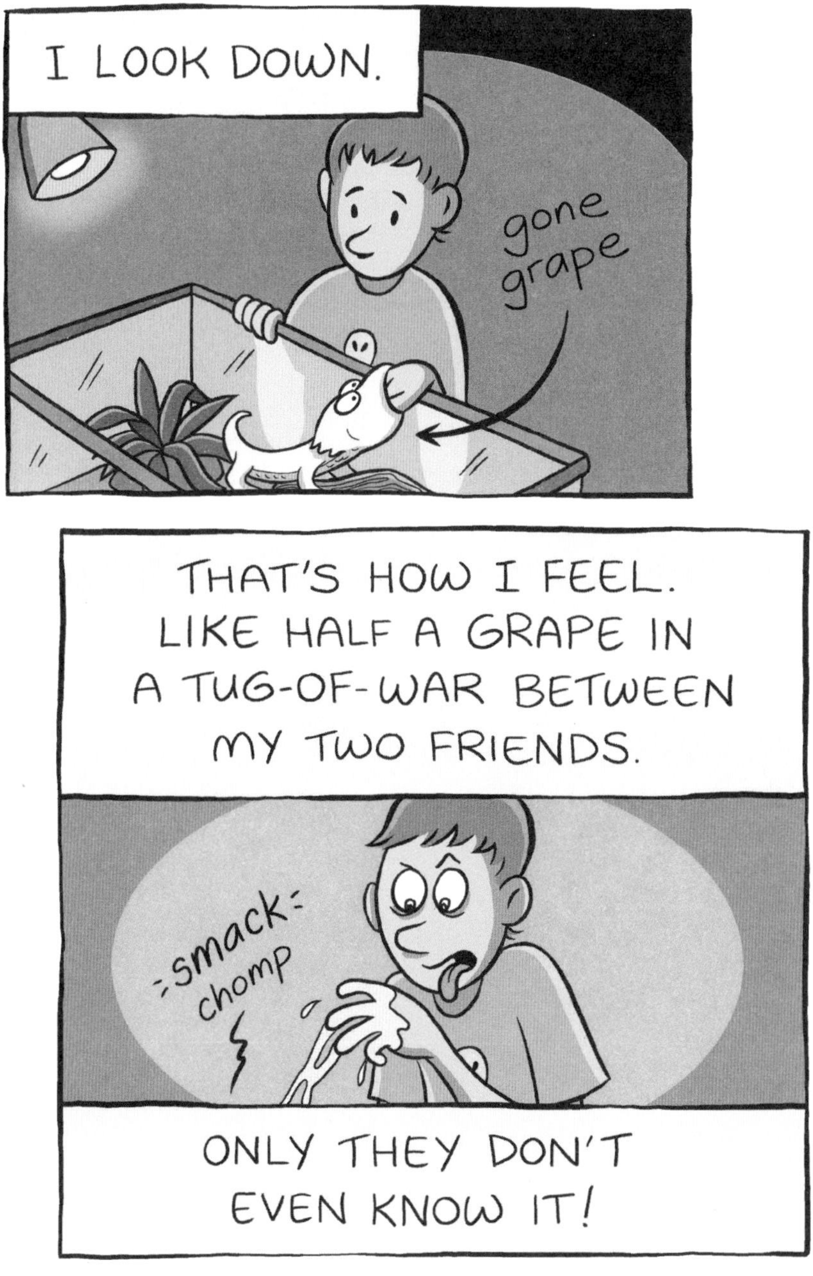
I LOOK DOWN.
gone grape
THAT'S HOW I FEEL. LIKE HALF A GRAPE IN A TUG-OF-WAR BETWEEN MY TWO FRIENDS.
smack
chomp
ONLY THEY DON'T EVEN KNOW IT!

SARAH

I asked him

I wish I'd never asked Ben to the dance!

my life →

rewind ↓

CLICK

I'm still on the couch. Mamá consoled me and then went back to baking, promising to save Emmie and me the largest donuts of the batch.

But I really can't eat.

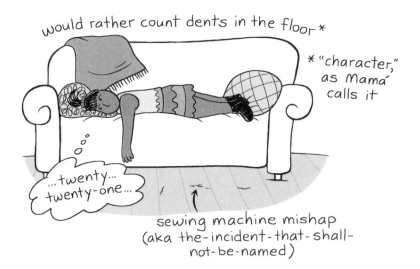

would rather count dents in the floor *

* "character," as Mama calls it

...twenty... twenty-one...

sewing machine mishap
(aka the-incident-that-shall-
not-be-named)

Soon, Emmie walks in.

Did you find your scrunchie?

I didn't really drop it.

Then why—?

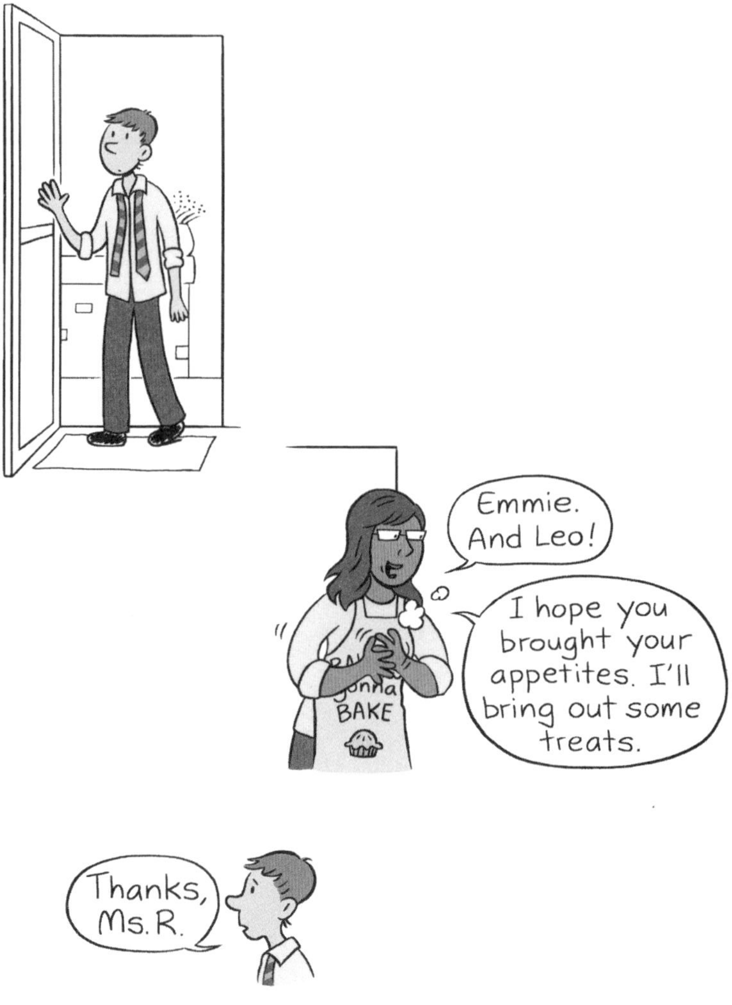
Emmie. And Leo!
I hope you brought your appetites. I'll bring out some treats.
Thanks, Ms. R.

Mamá must have some mystical power over us; I wasn't hungry, but suddenly I can hear all three of our stomachs growl at once.

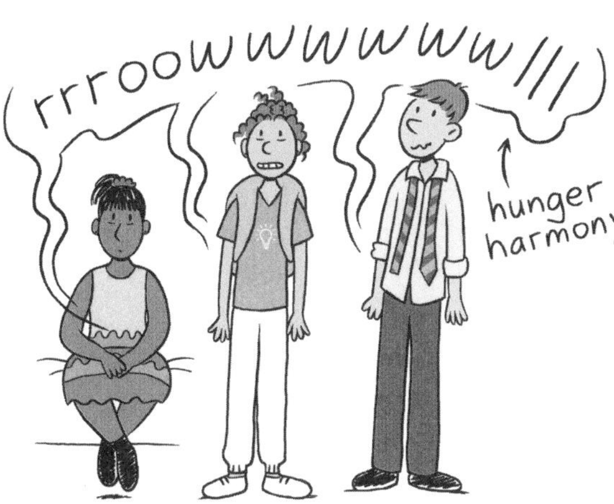
rrroowwwwwwwl!!!
hunger harmony

She smiles and heads back to the kitchen.

I stare at Leo, not knowing what to do or say.

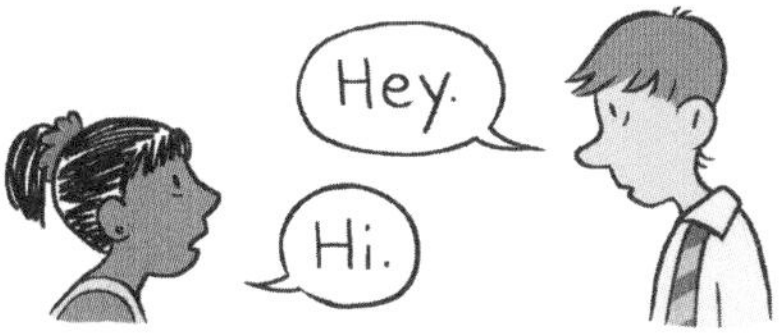
Hey.
Hi.

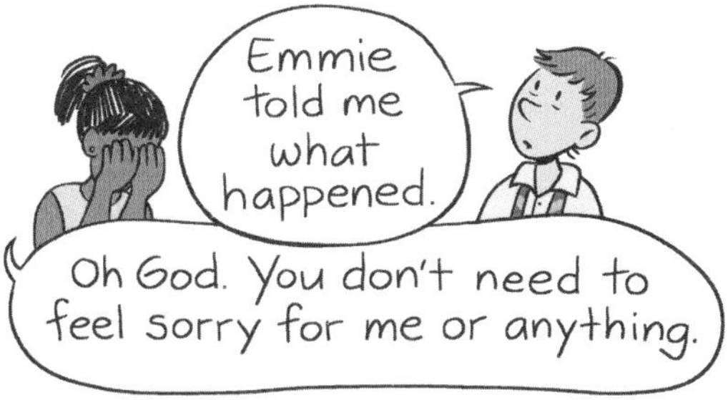
Emmie told me what happened.
Oh God. You don't need to feel sorry for me or anything.

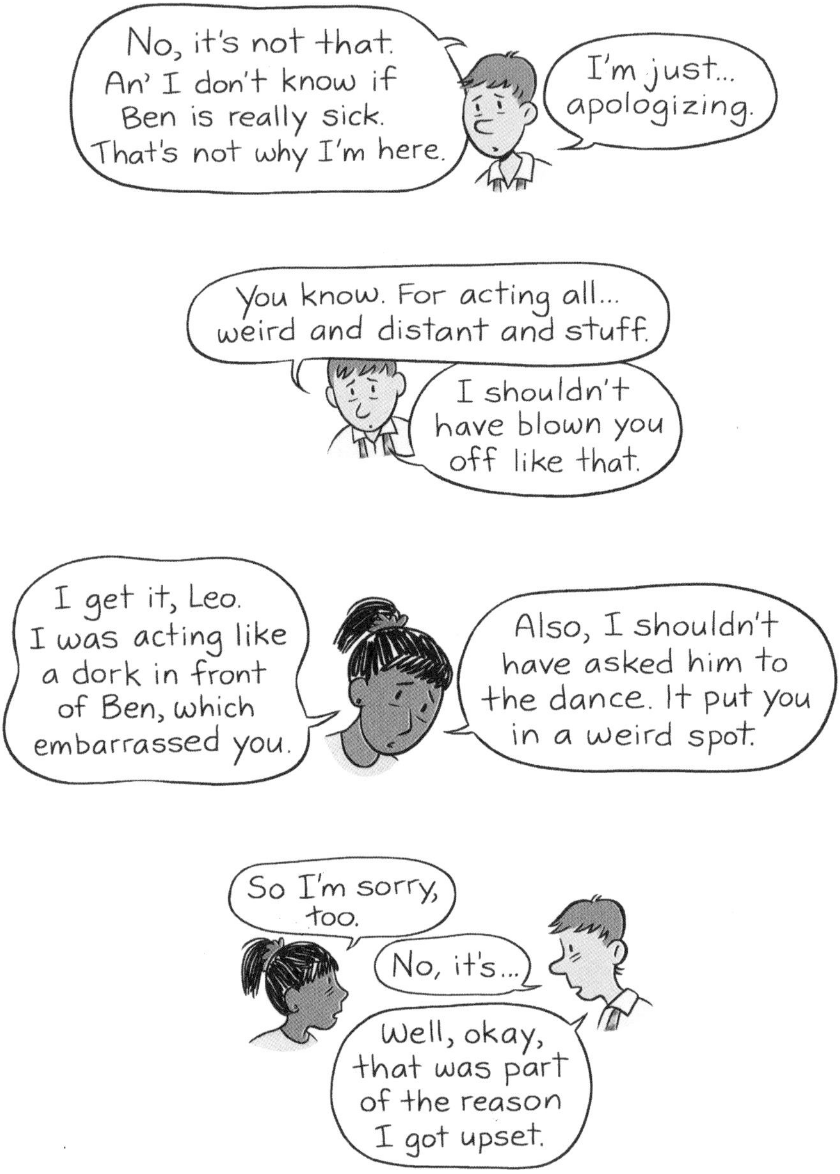
No, it's not that. An' I don't know if Ben is really sick. That's not why I'm here.
I'm just... apologizing.
You know. For acting all... weird and distant and stuff.
I shouldn't have blown you off like that.
I get it, Leo. I was acting like a dork in front of Ben, which embarrassed you.
Also, I shouldn't have asked him to the dance. It put you in a weird spot.
So I'm sorry, too.
No, it's...
Well, okay, that was part of the reason I got upset.

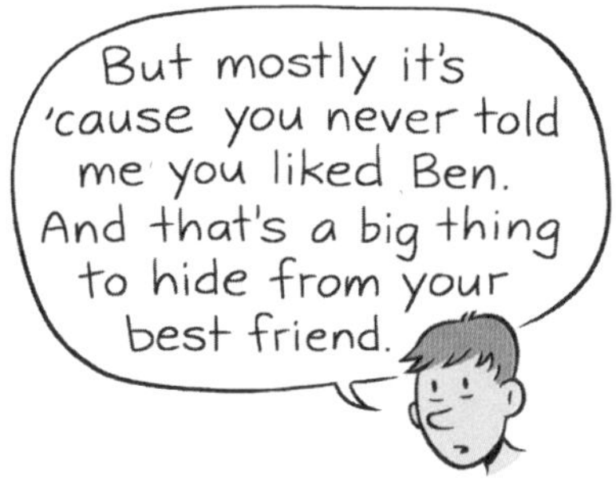
But mostly it's 'cause you never told me you liked Ben. And that's a big thing to hide from your best friend.

That hits me in the gut.

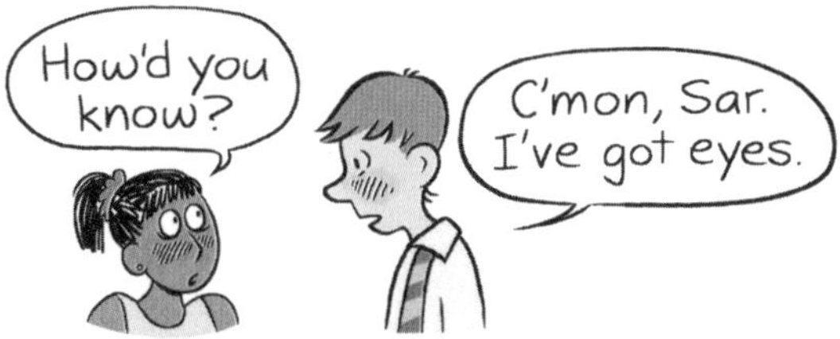
How'd you know?
C'mon, Sar. I've got eyes.

He guessed. I'm so embarrassed. But also relieved that it's out in the open. Still . . .

Something doesn't feel right. To completely **avoid** your best friend and not talk about the whole situation? That's not like Leo.

Then again, everyone seems to be changing all the time. Mamá says that's how it is for middle schoolers. One minute, you're a kid. The next, you're growing up and making questionable choices based on pure **feelings**.

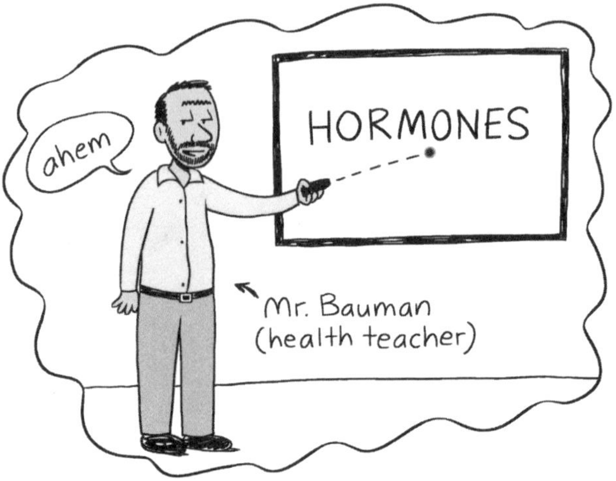
ahem
HORMONES
Mr. Bauman
(health teacher)

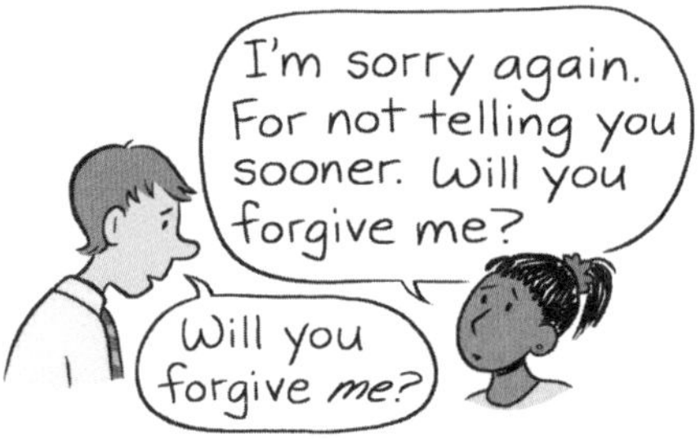
I'm sorry again. For not telling you sooner. Will you forgive me?
Will you forgive *me?*

I nod. He grins and leans down to give me a big hug. It's like a warm blanket. Even though I'm still upset about Ben, it feels so good to have Leo back.

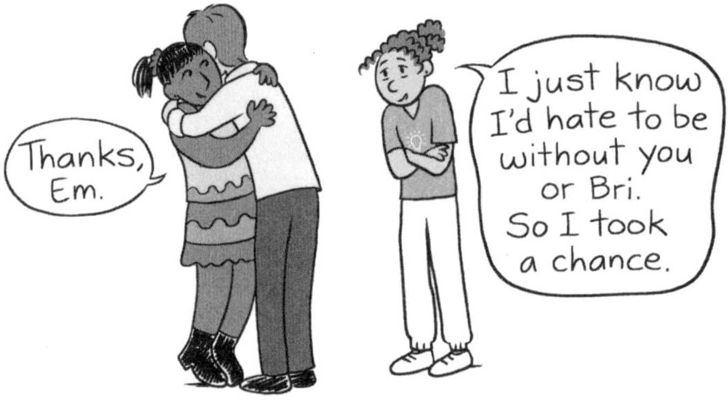
Thanks, Em.
I just know I'd hate to be without you or Bri. So I took a chance.

Even Emmie's changing.

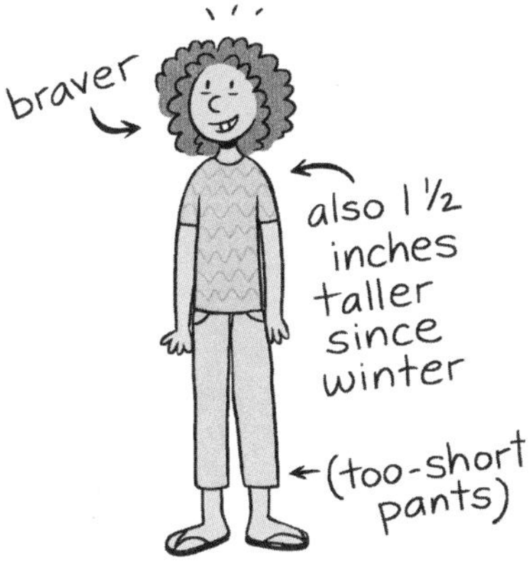
braver
also 1½ inches taller since winter
(too-short pants)

She and Leo glance at each other.

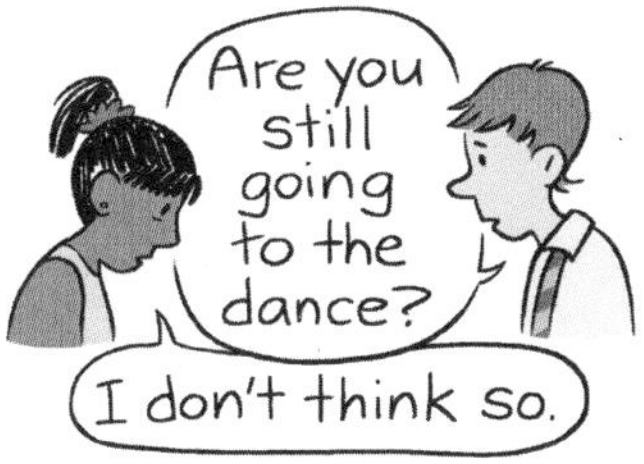
Are you still going to the dance?
I don't think so.

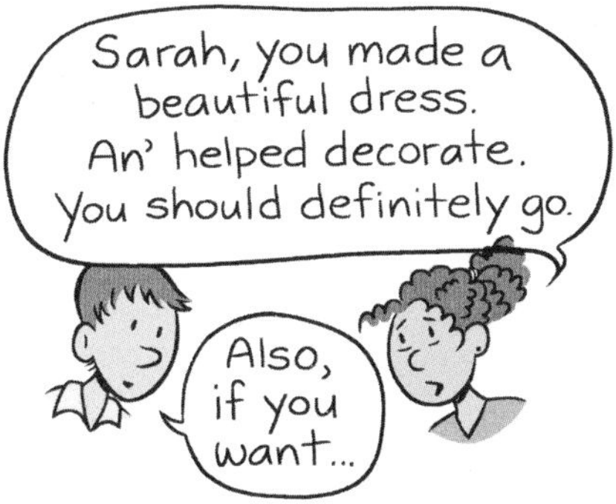
Sarah, you made a beautiful dress. An' helped decorate. You should definitely go.
Also, if you want...

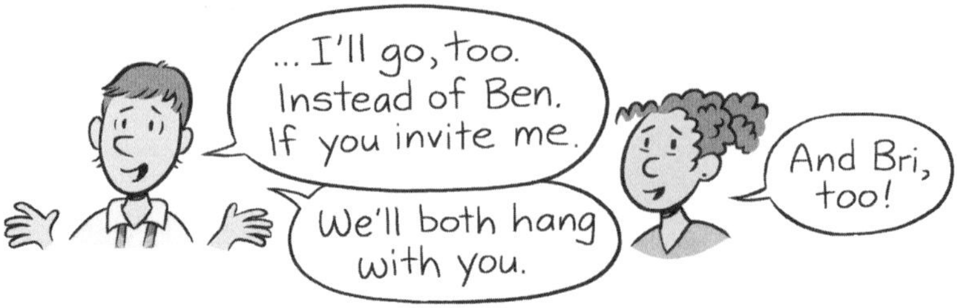
... I'll go, too. Instead of Ben. If you invite me.
We'll both hang with you.
And Bri, too!

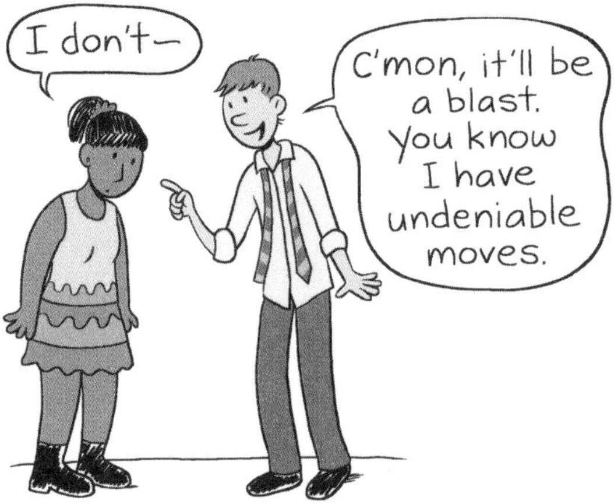
I don't—
C'mon, it'll be a blast. you know I have undeniable moves.

I laugh. I can't help it.

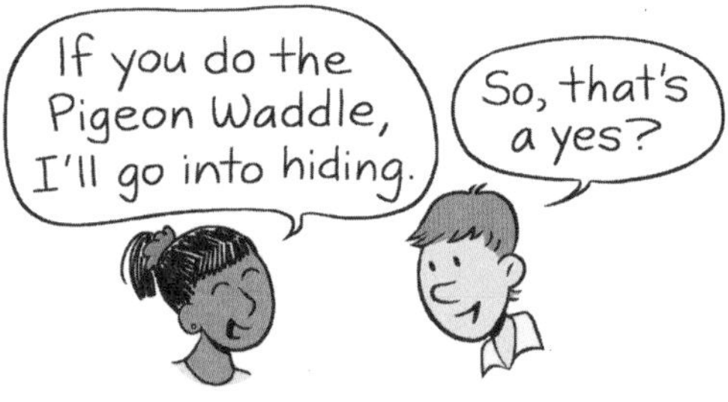
If you do the Pigeon Waddle, I'll go into hiding.
So, that's a yes?

I look at my two friends, who've never seemed so eager for an answer.

I'm still not sure it's a good idea, and I'm still upset, but I don't want to let them down. Also . . . I realize I don't want Ben to get the best of me. Whether he ditched me on purpose or not.

Okay.

They cheer, and I'm suddenly squashed in a hug.

warm, toasty sandwich

As if on cue, Mamá comes out of the kitchen with a pile of gigantic fresh donuts sprinkled with sugar crystals. Not sure if she overheard anything, but I don't really mind. Unlike a lot of other kids and their parents, I don't hide much from her.

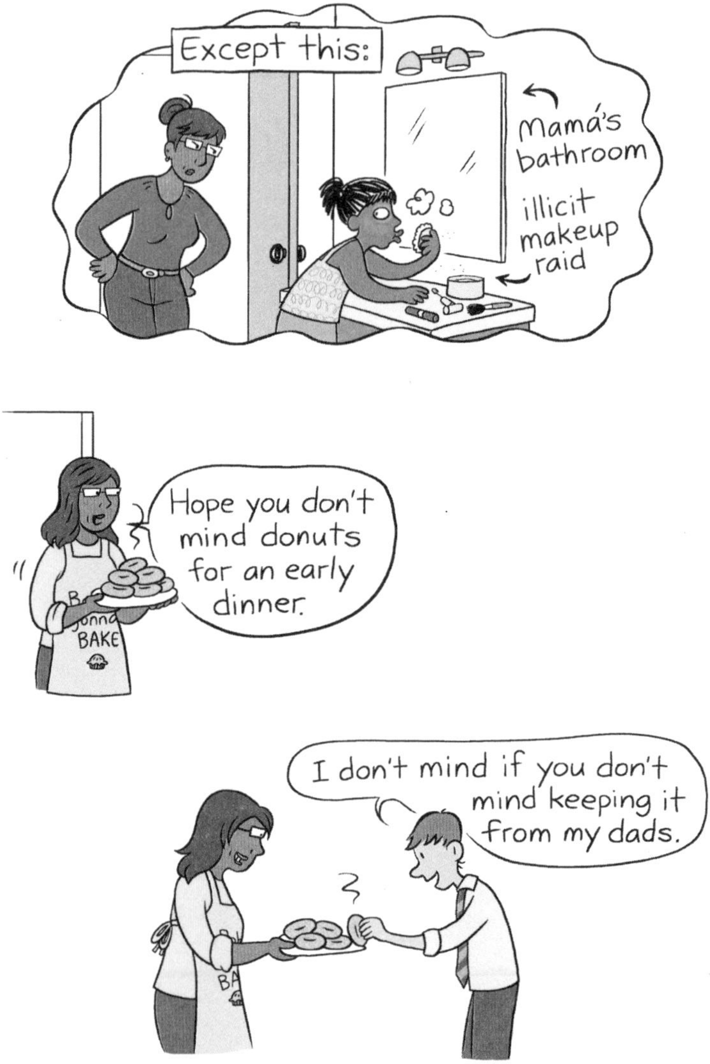
Except this:
Mama's bathroom
illicit makeup raid
Hope you don't mind donuts for an early dinner.
I don't mind if you don't mind keeping it from my dads.

Like Emmie's, Leo's parents are health conscious. But they're not as strict about it.

Same.

We take the donuts outside so we don't get crumbs on the floor. After we eat, Emmie goes back inside to use the bathroom. Leo stands up and dusts sugar off his pants.

So, guess I should start getting ready, huh? You want me to match you or anything?

No, silly, that's for proms. Just wear jeans or whatever.

Okay.

He starts running toward his house.
But stops.

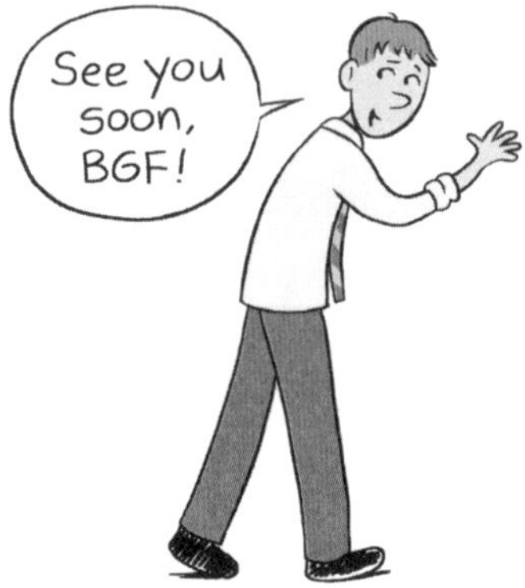
See you soon, BGF!

I start tearing up again a little. I can't help it.

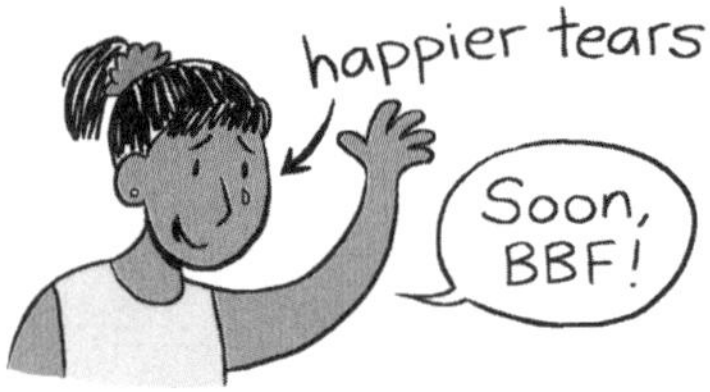
happier tears
Soon, BBF!

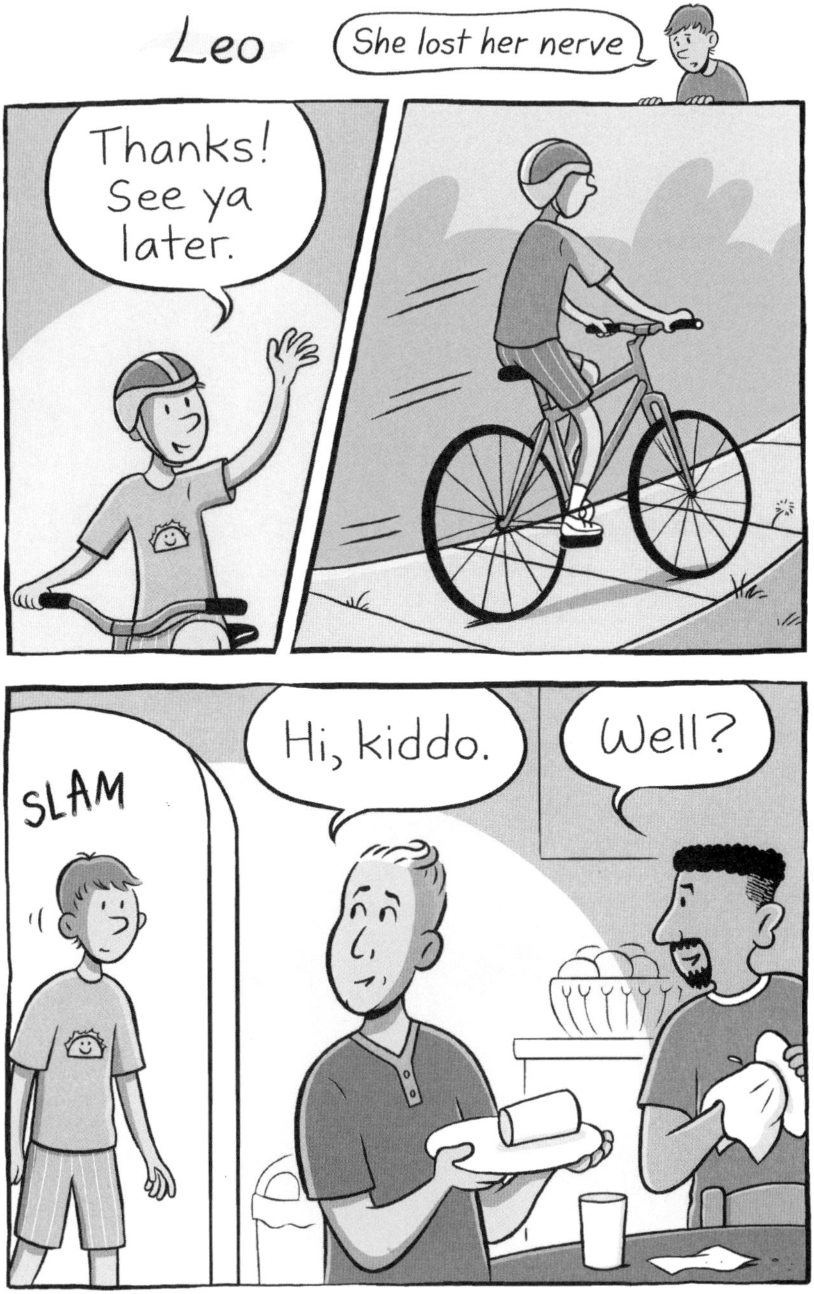
Leo
She lost her nerve
Thanks! See ya later.
SLAM
Hi, kiddo.
Well?

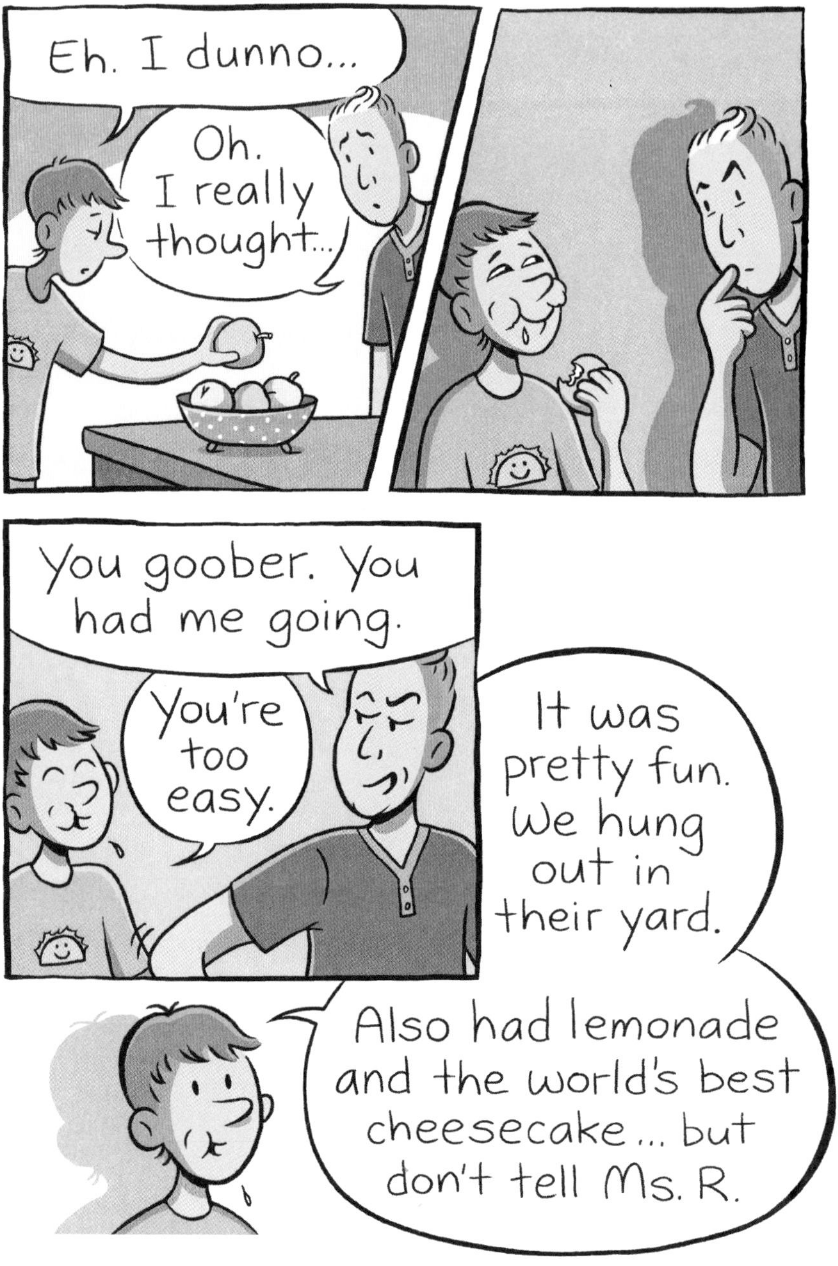
Eh. I dunno...
Oh. I really thought...
You goober. You had me going.
You're too easy.
It was pretty fun. We hung out in their yard.
Also had lemonade and the world's best cheesecake ... but don't tell Ms. R.

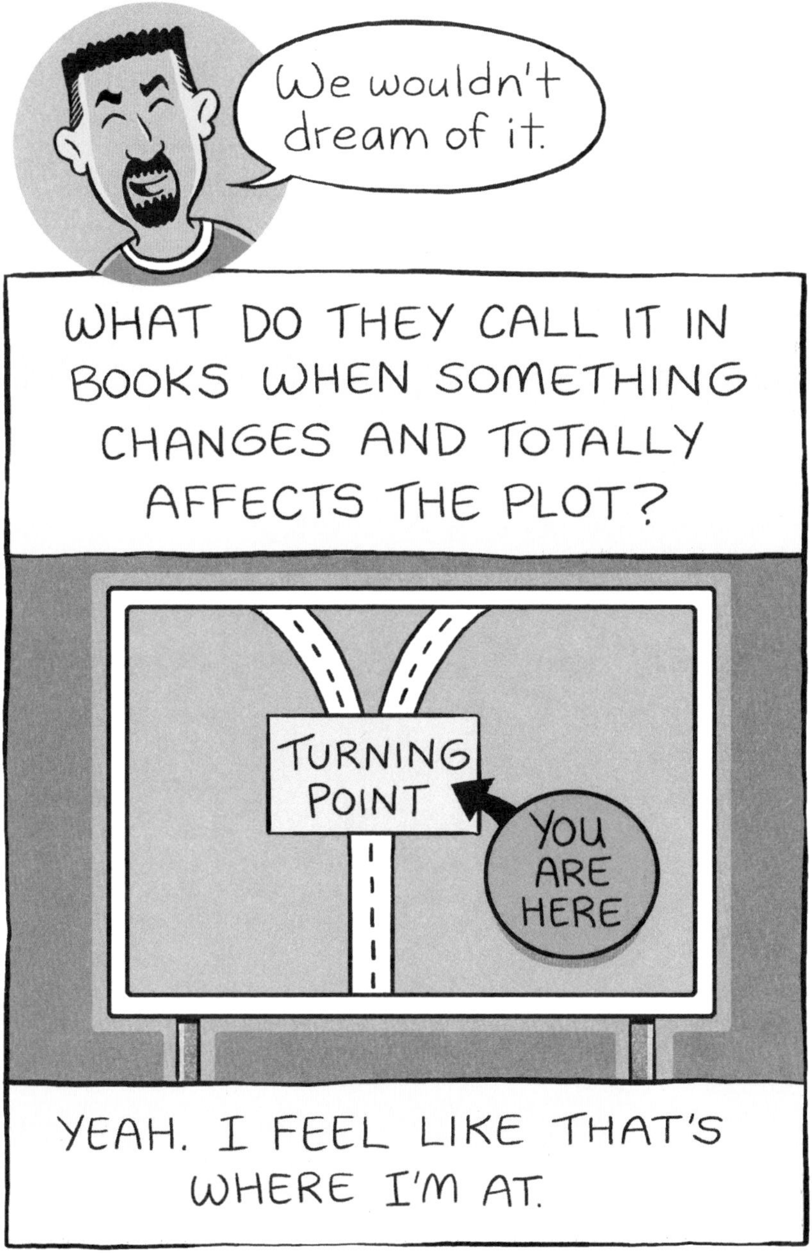
We wouldn't dream of it.
WHAT DO THEY CALL IT IN BOOKS WHEN SOMETHING CHANGES AND TOTALLY AFFECTS THE PLOT?
TURNING POINT
YOU ARE HERE
YEAH. I FEEL LIKE THAT'S WHERE I'M AT.

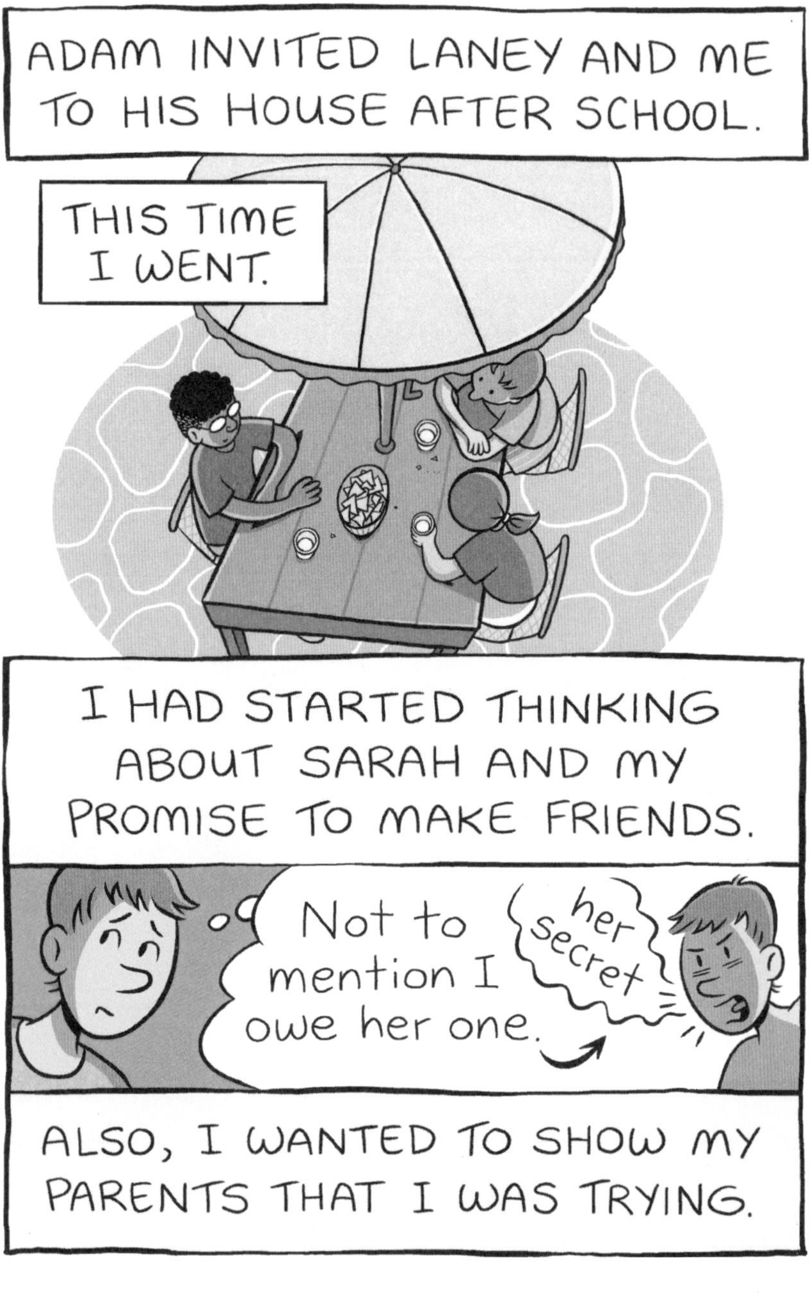
ADAM INVITED LANEY AND ME TO HIS HOUSE AFTER SCHOOL.
THIS TIME I WENT.
I HAD STARTED THINKING ABOUT SARAH AND MY PROMISE TO MAKE FRIENDS.
Not to mention I owe her one.
her secret
ALSO, I WANTED TO SHOW MY PARENTS THAT I WAS TRYING.

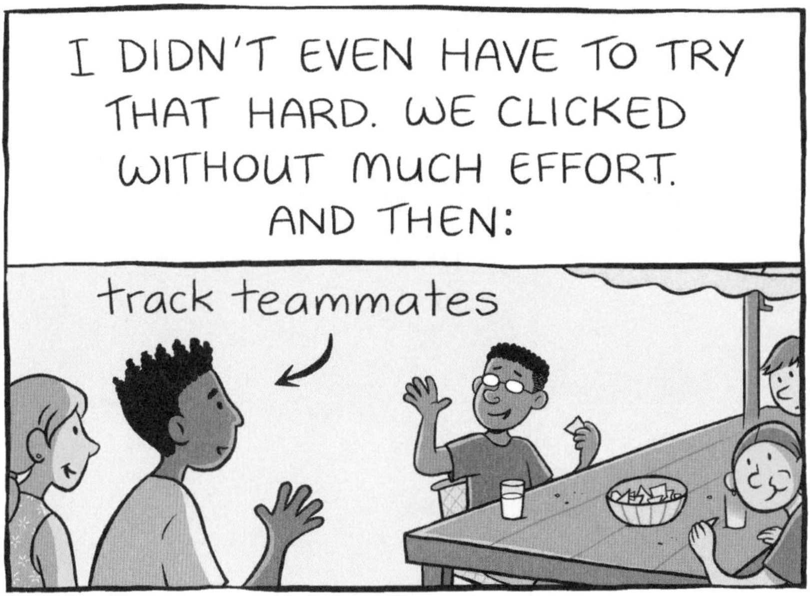
I DIDN'T EVEN HAVE TO TRY THAT HARD. WE CLICKED WITHOUT MUCH EFFORT. AND THEN:
track teammates

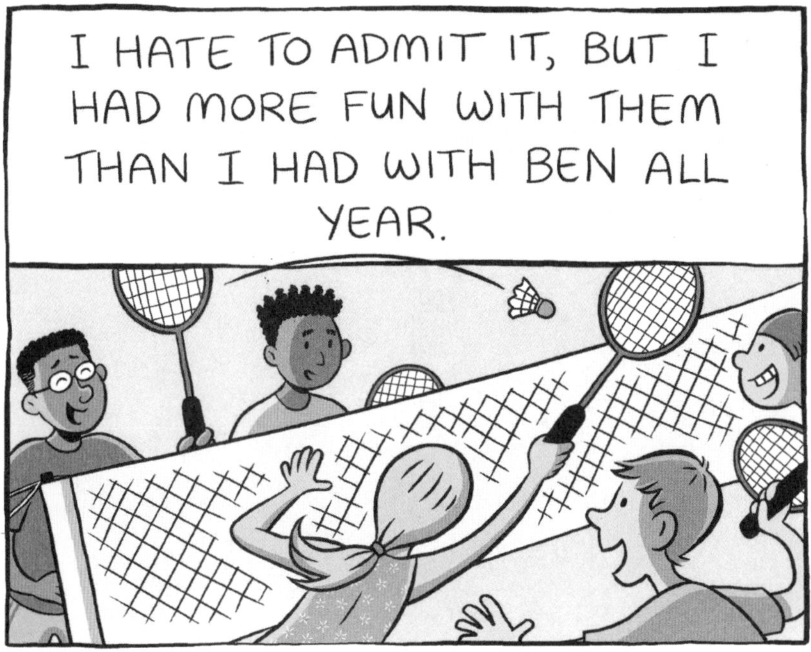
I HATE TO ADMIT IT, BUT I HAD MORE FUN WITH THEM THAN I HAD WITH BEN ALL YEAR.

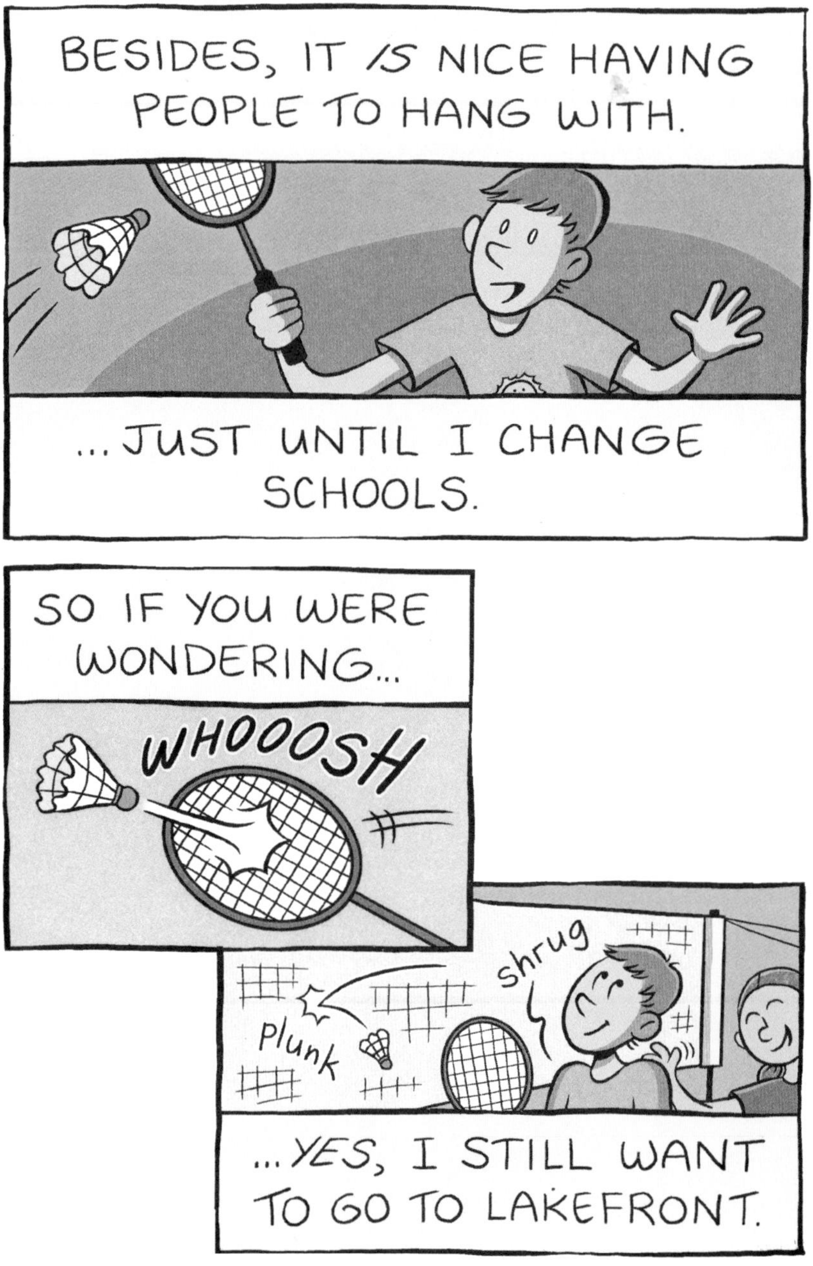
BESIDES, IT *IS* NICE HAVING PEOPLE TO HANG WITH.
...JUST UNTIL I CHANGE SCHOOLS.
SO IF YOU WERE WONDERING...
WHOOOSH
shrug
Plunk
...*YES*, I STILL WANT TO GO TO LAKEFRONT.

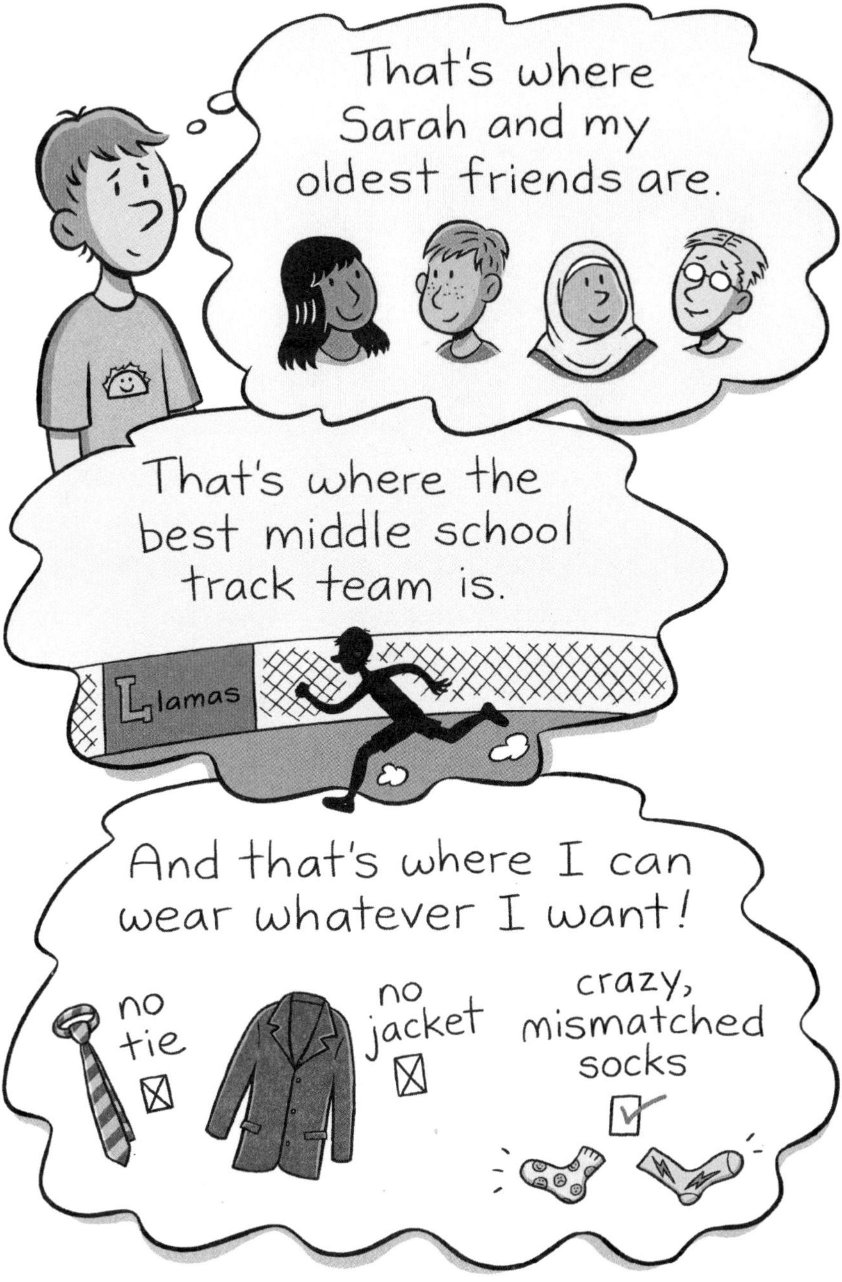

That's where Sarah and my oldest friends are.
That's where the best middle school track team is.
Llamas
And that's where I can wear whatever I want!
no tie
no jacket
crazy, mismatched socks

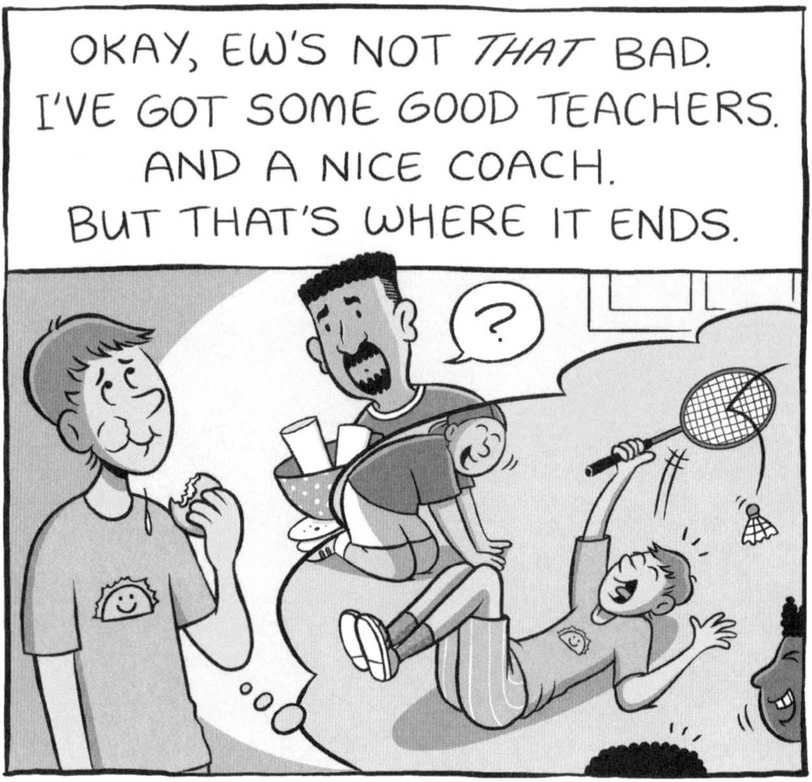
OKAY, EW'S NOT *THAT* BAD. I'VE GOT SOME GOOD TEACHERS. AND A NICE COACH. BUT THAT'S WHERE IT ENDS.
?

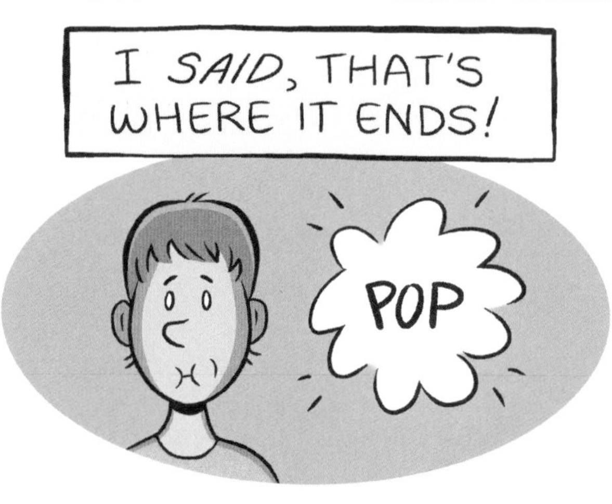
I *SAID*, THAT'S WHERE IT ENDS!
POP

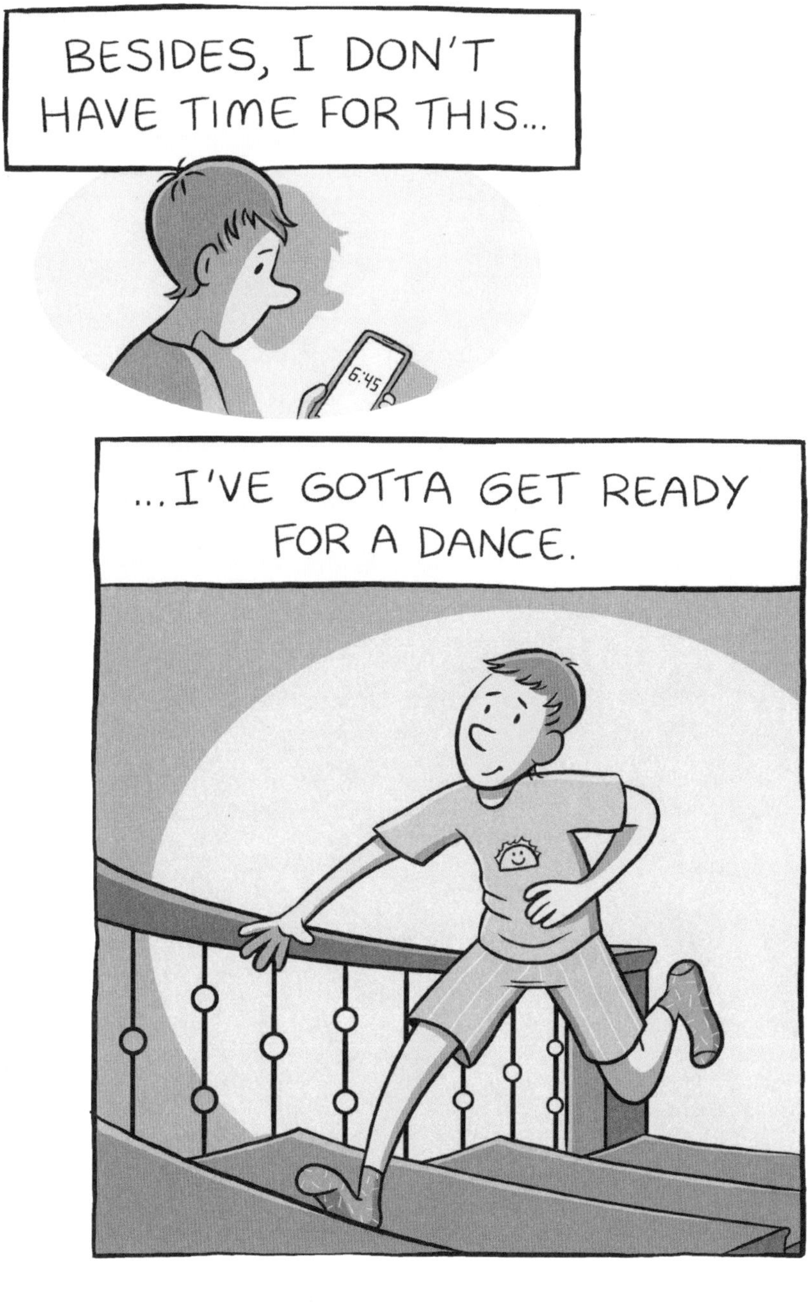
BESIDES, I DON'T HAVE TIME FOR THIS...
6:45
...I'VE GOTTA GET READY FOR A DANCE.

SARAH

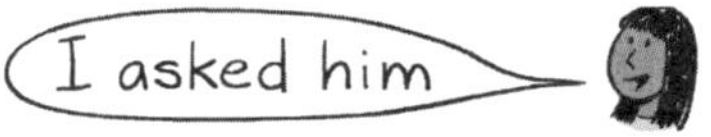
I asked him

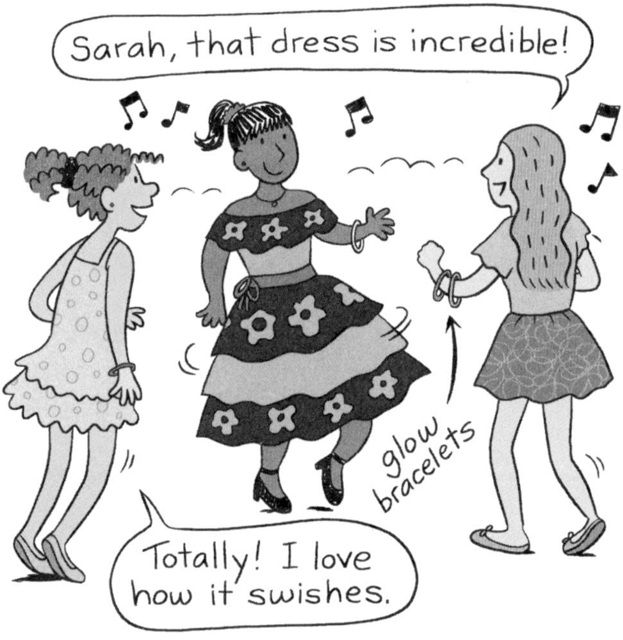
Sarah, that dress is incredible!
glow bracelets
Totally! I love how it swishes.

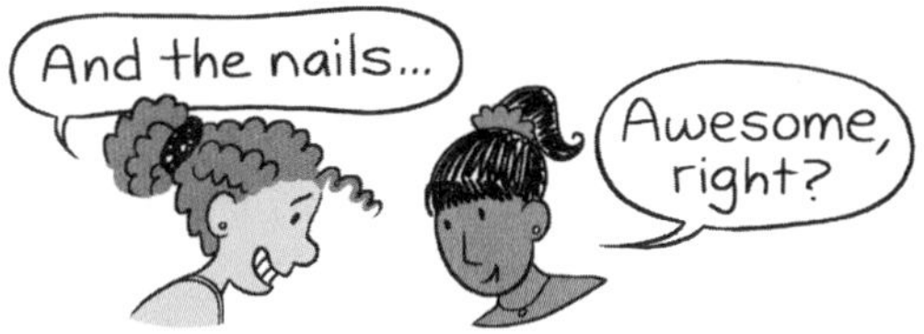
And the nails...
Awesome, right?

I had painted each of my fingernails a different color. And then I painted Emmie's like mine. In solidarity, Bri did hers the same way.

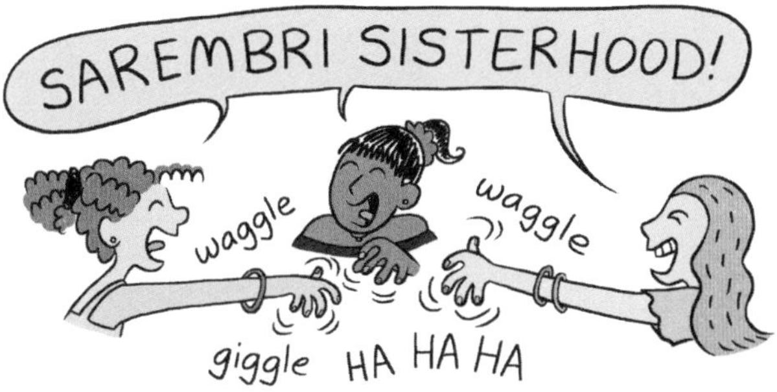
SAREMBRI SISTERHOOD!
waggle
waggle
giggle HA HA HA

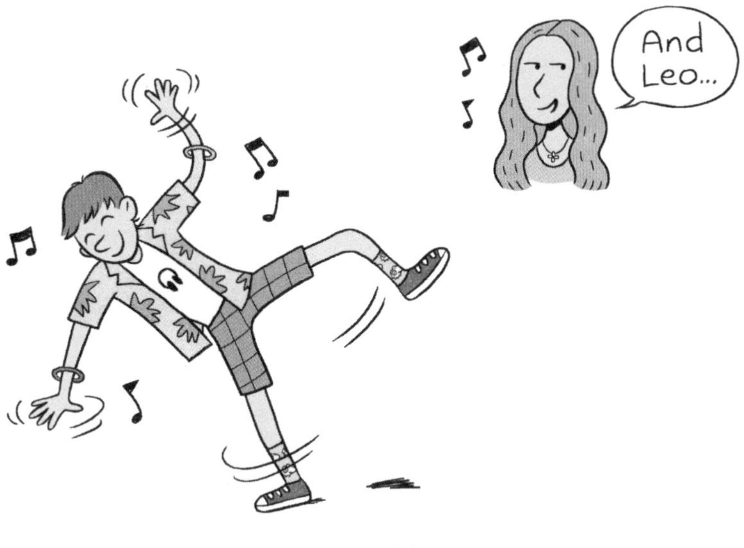
And Leo...

Never mind.

giggle

Leo didn't follow my advice to wear regular clothes. But that's okay. He's a lot like me when it comes to fashion. Outside of school dress codes, he doesn't follow any rules. Especially when it comes to matching.

Hawaiian shirt

odd-colored shorts

his Malcolm socks

I was worried he might be a little extra for Em and Bri, but they really get a kick out of him. Besides, he's so friendly and fun, it's hard not to love him.

SPLOOOOSH

wave of affection

I promise myself I'll never keep secrets from him again.

FOOMP

And he'd better not, either!

I have to admit, even without Ben, I'm having so much fun! It was definitely a good idea to bring Leo. Before we went to the caf, I showed him around. At first, he was excited to see it all, but in the end, I don't think he was that impressed. I mean, he goes to an expensive private school—I'm sure everything is fancier there.

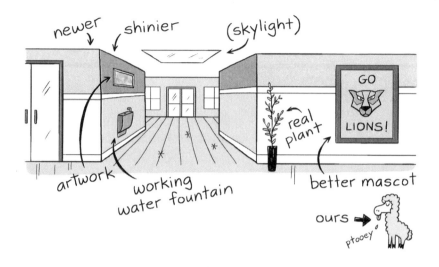

newer

shinier

(skylight)

artwork

working water fountain

real plant

GO LIONS!

better mascot

ours → ptooey

He was definitely happy to see some old friends. Although . . .
I noticed once he said hi and they talked . . .

Only a minute later:

Luckily, we got him dancing, and he was in his element. No Pigeon Waddle, but he still had some (ahem) unique moves.

Eggbeater

Jazz Rabbit

Duck Hustle

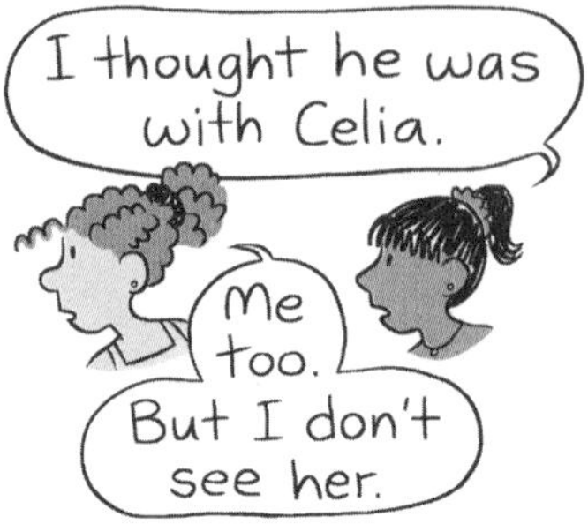
I thought he was with Celia.
Me too.
But I don't see her.

Tyler is having "glow" punch with Anthony and Joe on one side of the cafeteria. Joe is also tossing candy in the air and trying to catch it in his mouth.

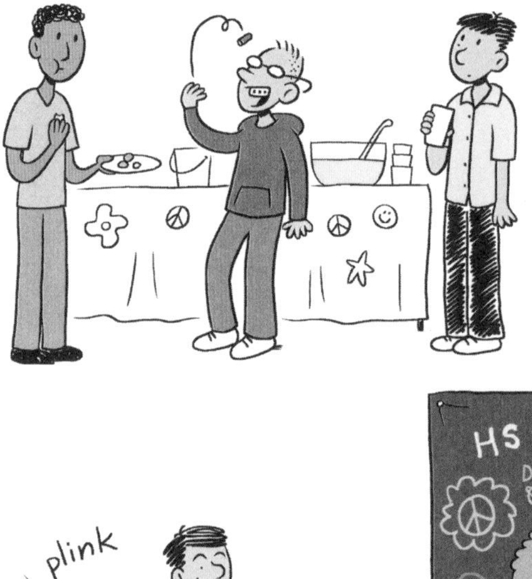

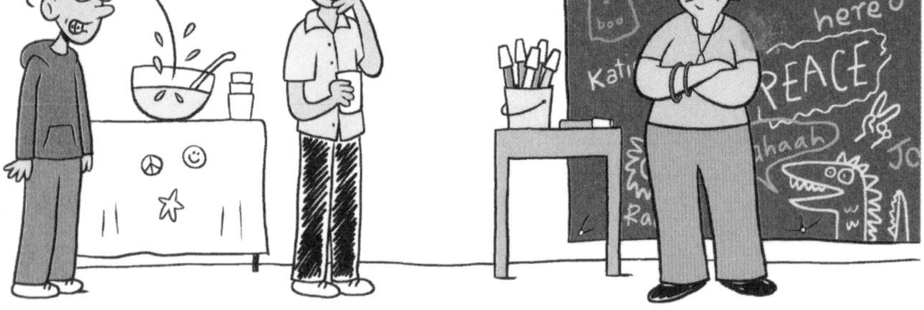
plink
HS + DZ
Dev/
Jaime wuz here
boo
PEACE

Look. There's Celia.

She points to the entrance, where Celia and her friends are checking out the decorations. Celia isn't looking very impressed.

too cool for everything

LET'S GLOW

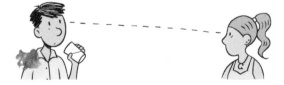

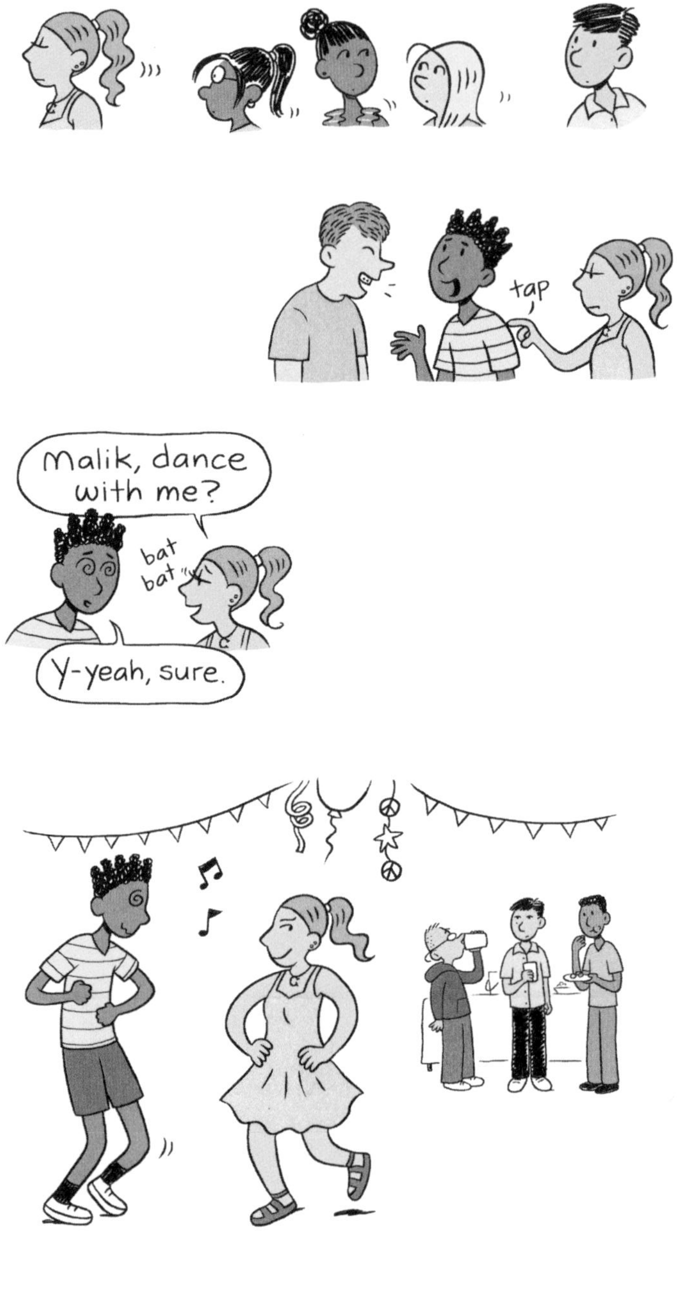
tap
Malik, dance with me?
bat bat
Y-yeah, sure.

Wow.

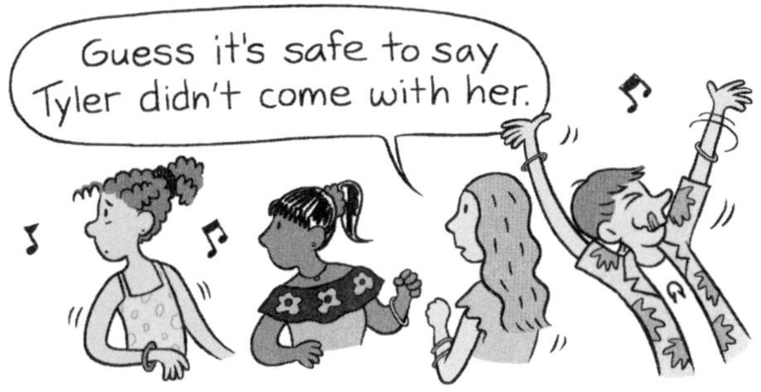
Guess it's safe to say Tyler didn't come with her.

We both look at Emmie.

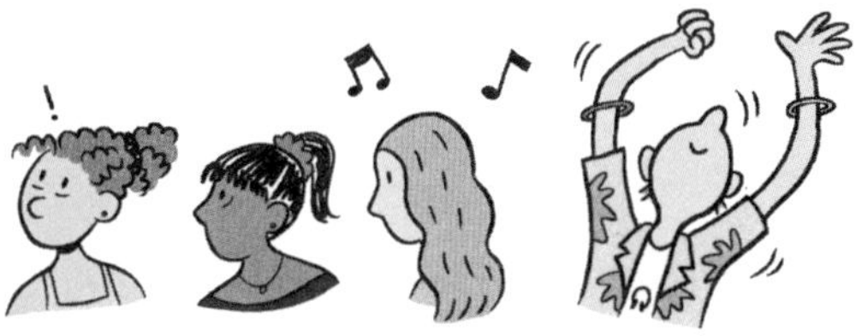

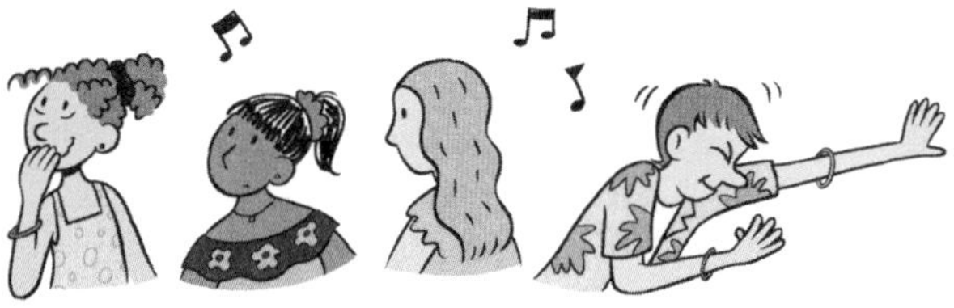

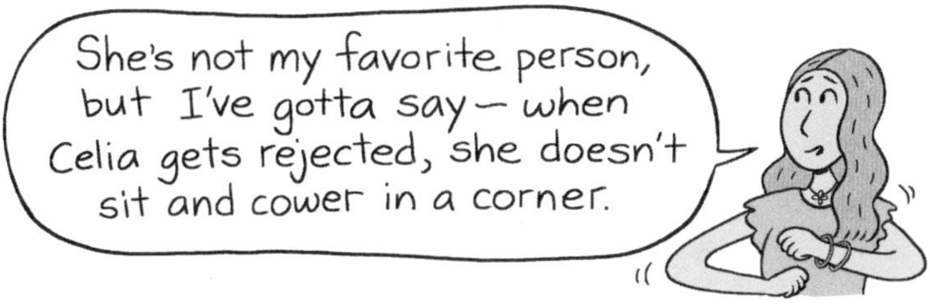
She's not my favorite person, but I've gotta say—when Celia gets rejected, she doesn't sit and cower in a corner.

That seems to spark something in Emmie. She kinda straightens up, glances over at Tyler, looks back at us, and . . .

I'll be back.

Where's she going?

Omigod.

No way!

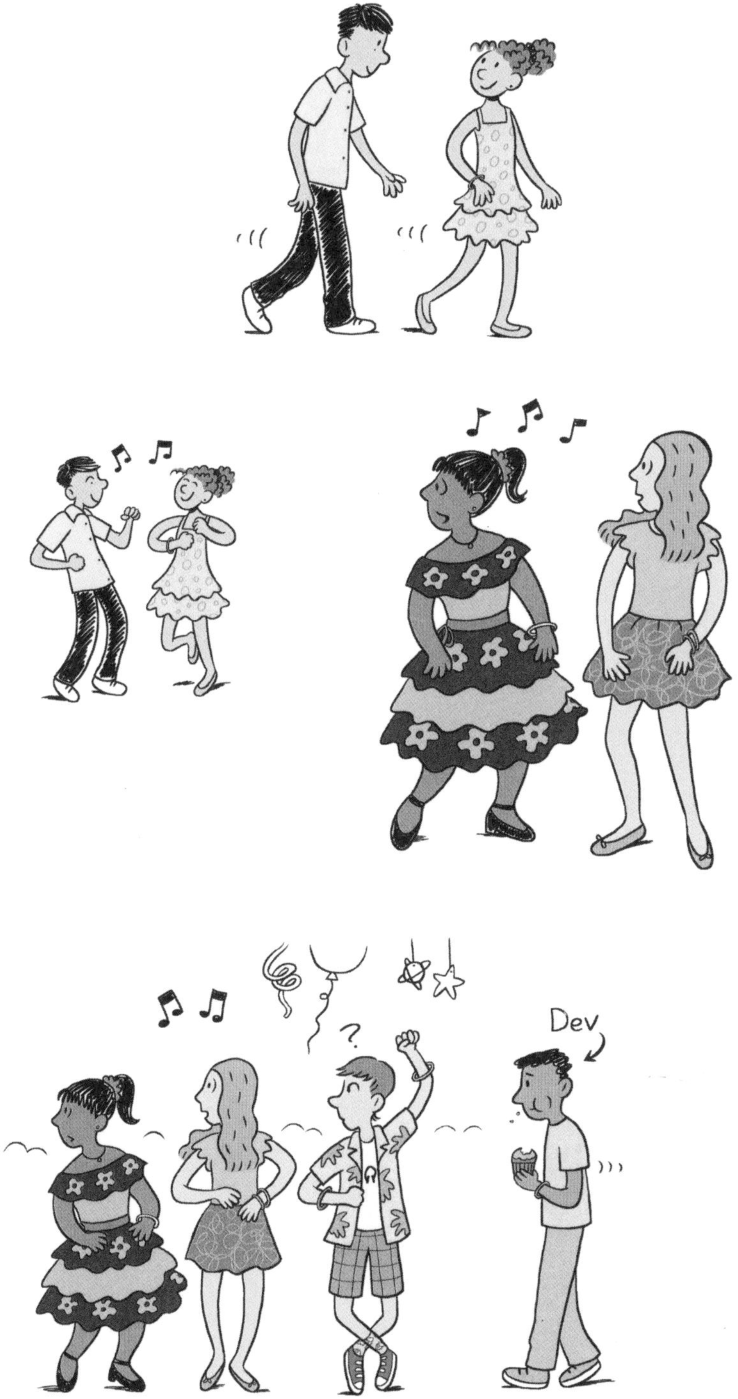
Dev

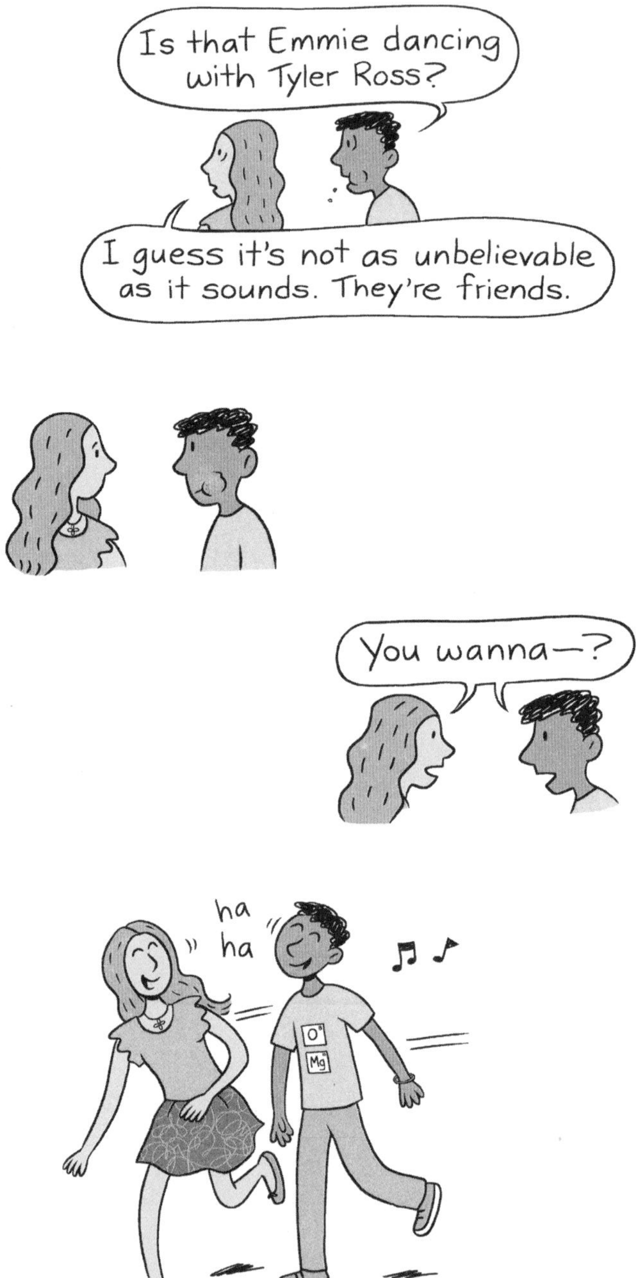
Is that Emmie dancing with Tyler Ross?
I guess it's not as unbelievable as it sounds. They're friends.
You wanna—?
ha ha
O
Mg

Leo and I look at each other.

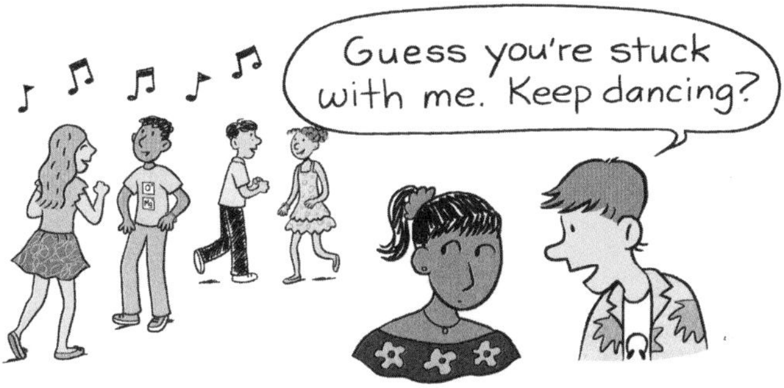
Guess you're stuck with me. Keep dancing?

He hints at doing the Pigeon Waddle till I play-punch him.

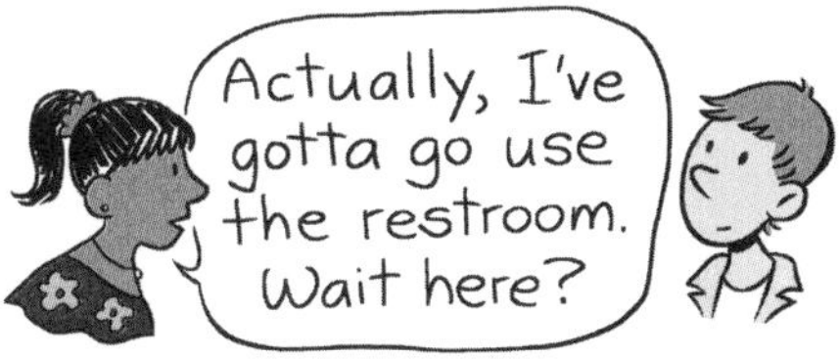
Actually, I've gotta go use the restroom. Wait here?

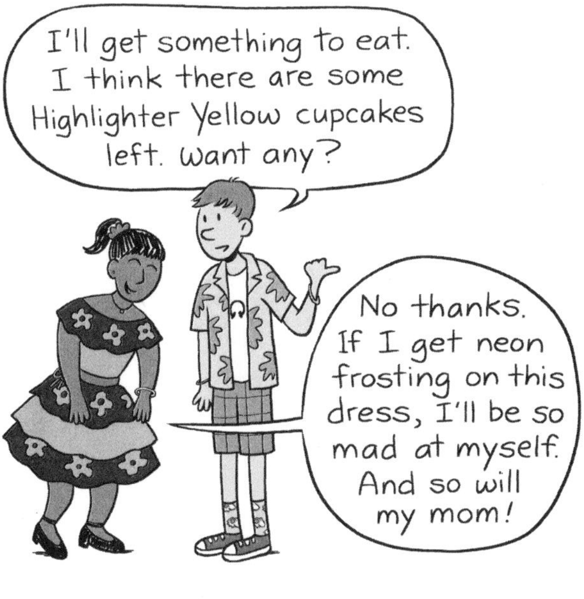
I'll get something to eat. I think there are some Highlighter Yellow cupcakes left. Want any?
No thanks. If I get neon frosting on this dress, I'll be so mad at myself. And so will my mom!

I head toward the cafeteria doorway when I hear something that stops me.

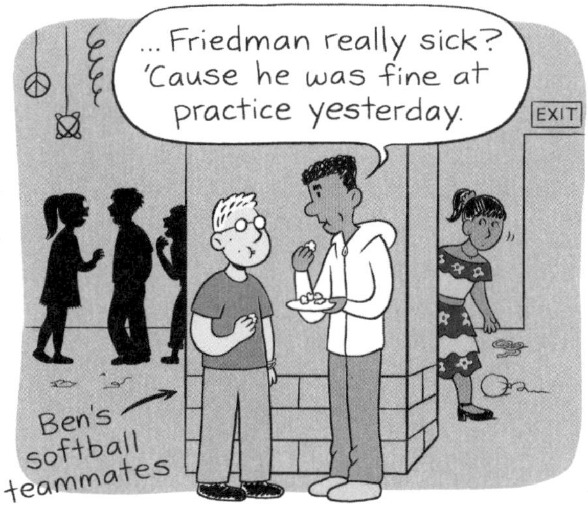
...Friedman really sick? 'Cause he was fine at practice yesterday.
EXIT
Ben's softball teammates

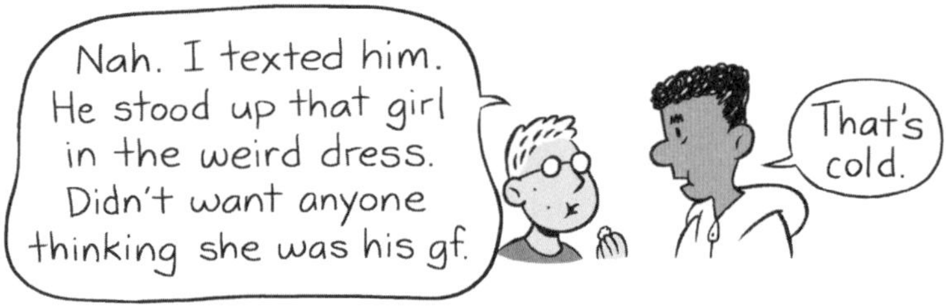
Nah. I texted him. He stood up that girl in the weird dress. Didn't want anyone thinking she was his gf.
That's cold.

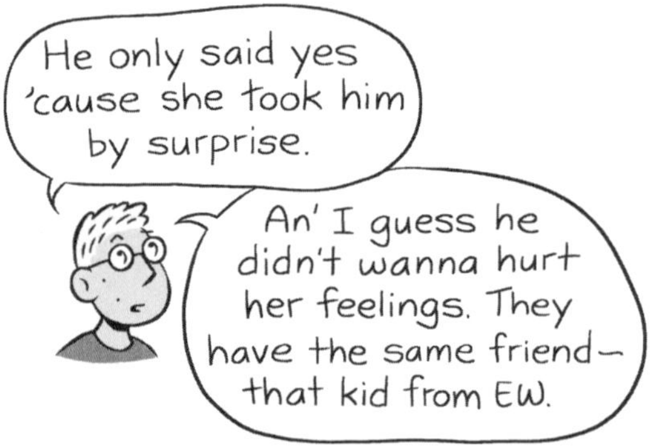
He only said yes 'cause she took him by surprise.
An' I guess he didn't wanna hurt her feelings. They have the same friend— that kid from EW.

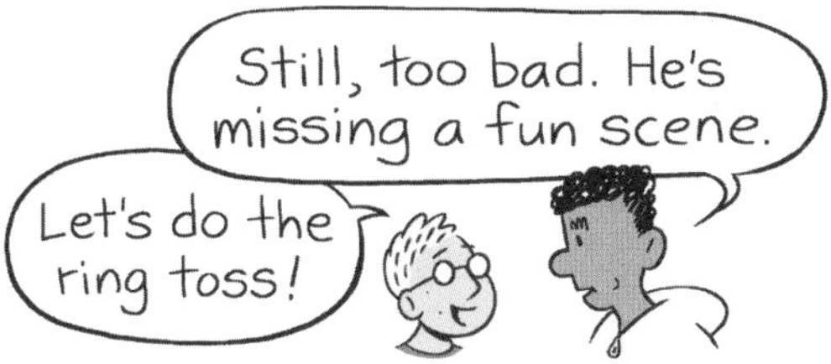
Let's do the ring toss!
Still, too bad. He's missing a fun scene.

They leave. But I can't seem to move.
So Ben really did blow me off.
It wasn't just a bad feeling.

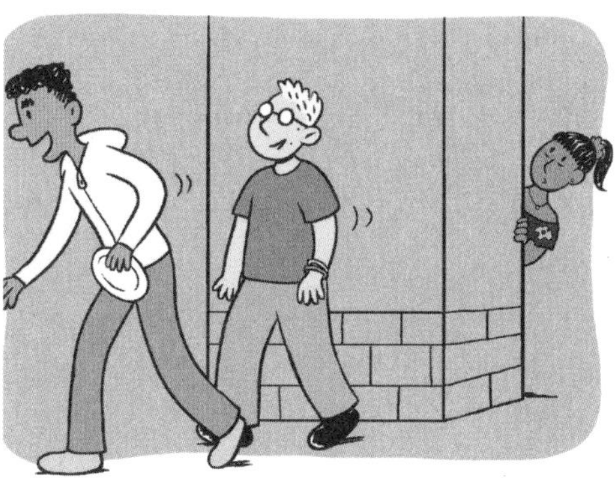

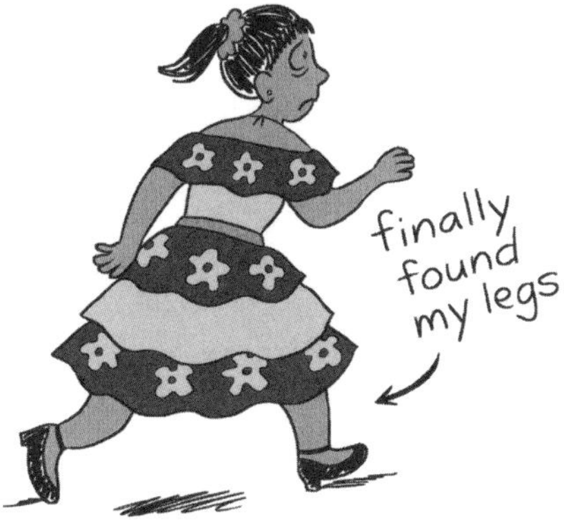
finally found my legs

I was wrong.

The "not knowing" isn't the worst part.

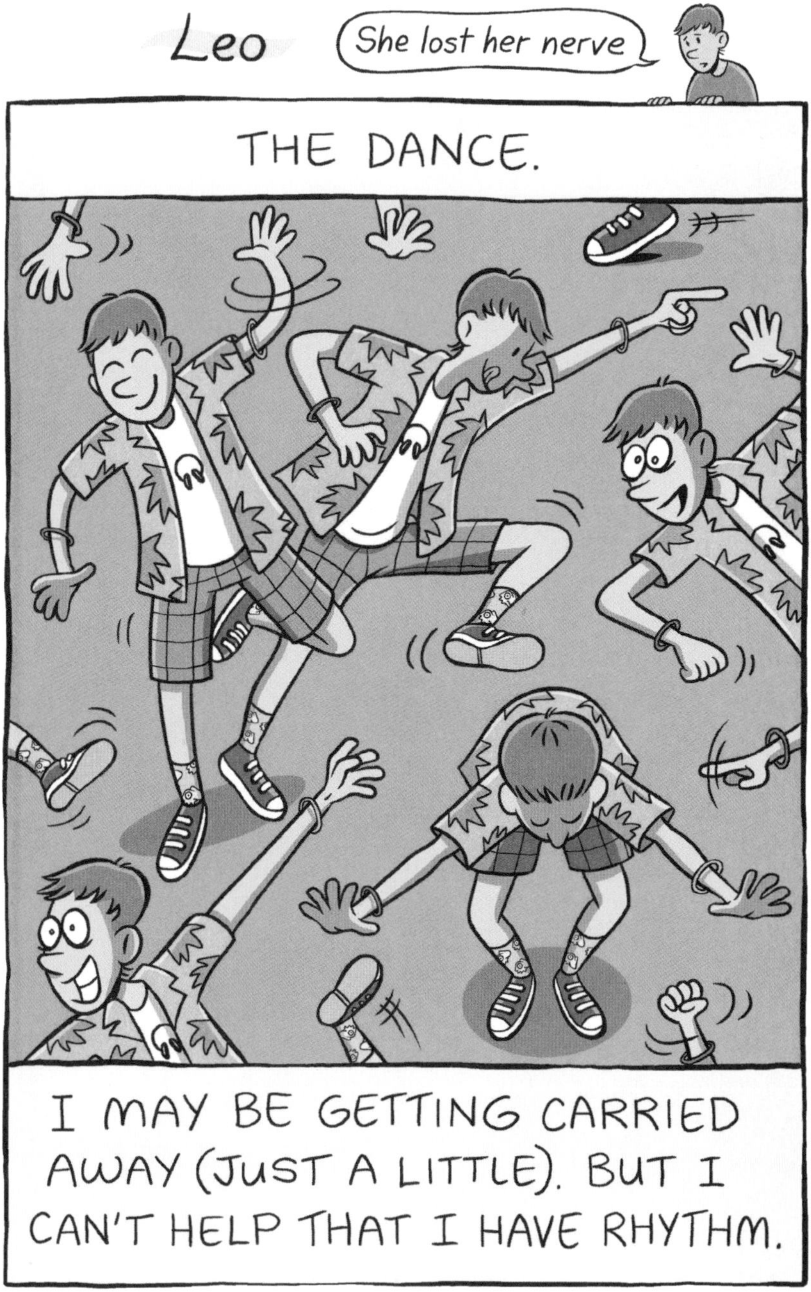
She lost her nerve
THE DANCE.
I MAY BE GETTING CARRIED AWAY (JUST A LITTLE). BUT I CAN'T HELP THAT I HAVE RHYTHM.

LEO'S GUIDE TO SMOOTH MOVES:
1. Circle your friends while doing the "slide-glide"*:
*invented and trade-marked
2. Spin around several times (just until you see stars).
3. Show off signature moves (aka squiggles, squirms, worms, kicks*)
*avoid teachers
shaka
4. Repeat.
5. Repeat.
6. Repeat until someone (aka Sarah) says:
STOP!
but I live 4 disco

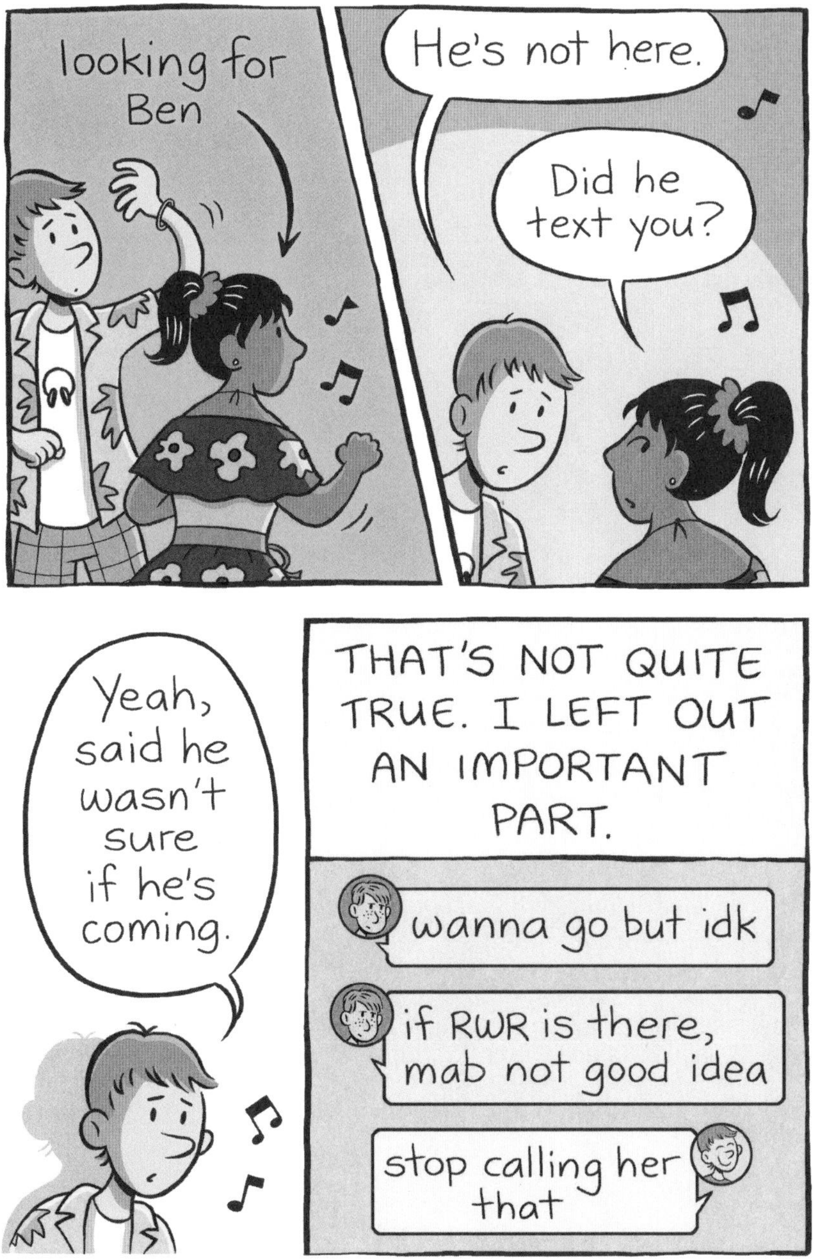
looking for Ben
He's not here.
Did he text you?
Yeah, said he wasn't sure if he's coming.
THAT'S NOT QUITE TRUE. I LEFT OUT AN IMPORTANT PART.
wanna go but idk
if RWR is there, mab not good idea
stop calling her that

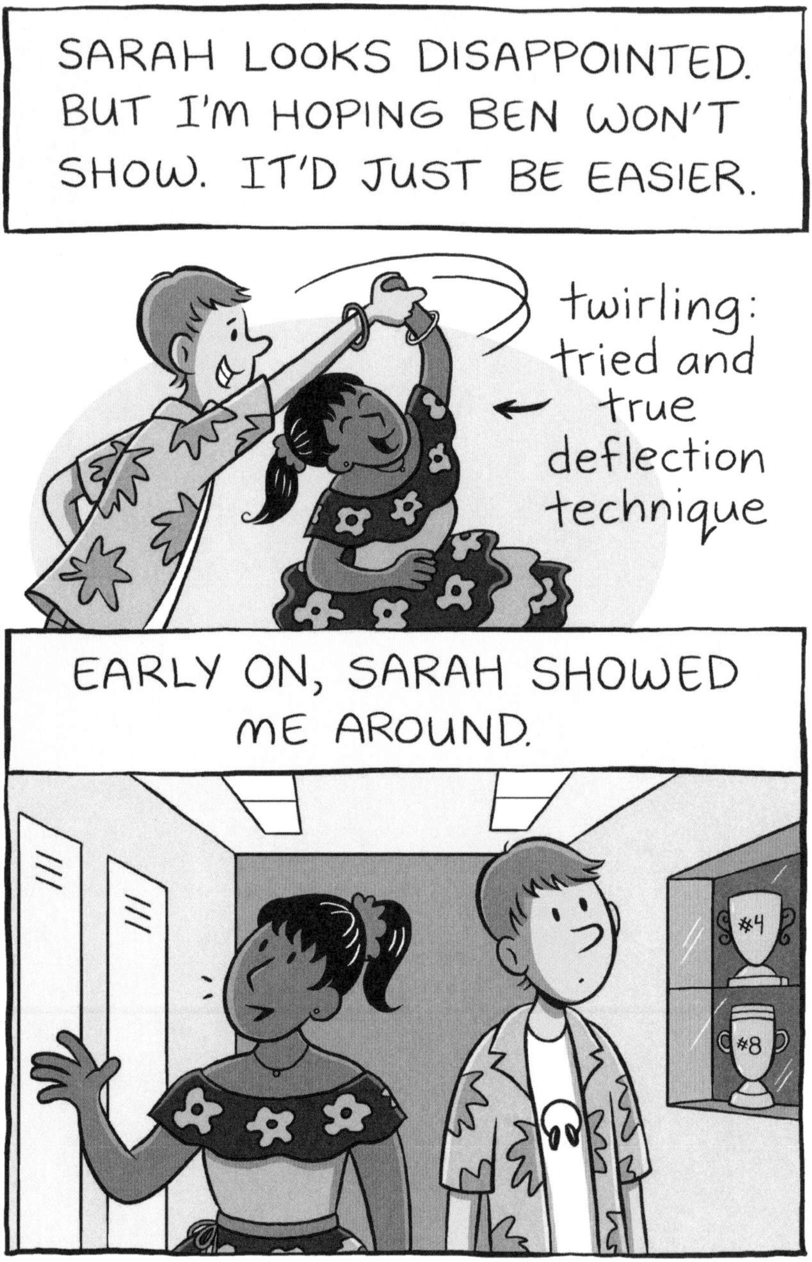
SARAH LOOKS DISAPPOINTED. BUT I'M HOPING BEN WON'T SHOW. IT'D JUST BE EASIER.
twirling: tried and true deflection technique
EARLY ON, SARAH SHOWED ME AROUND.
#4
#8

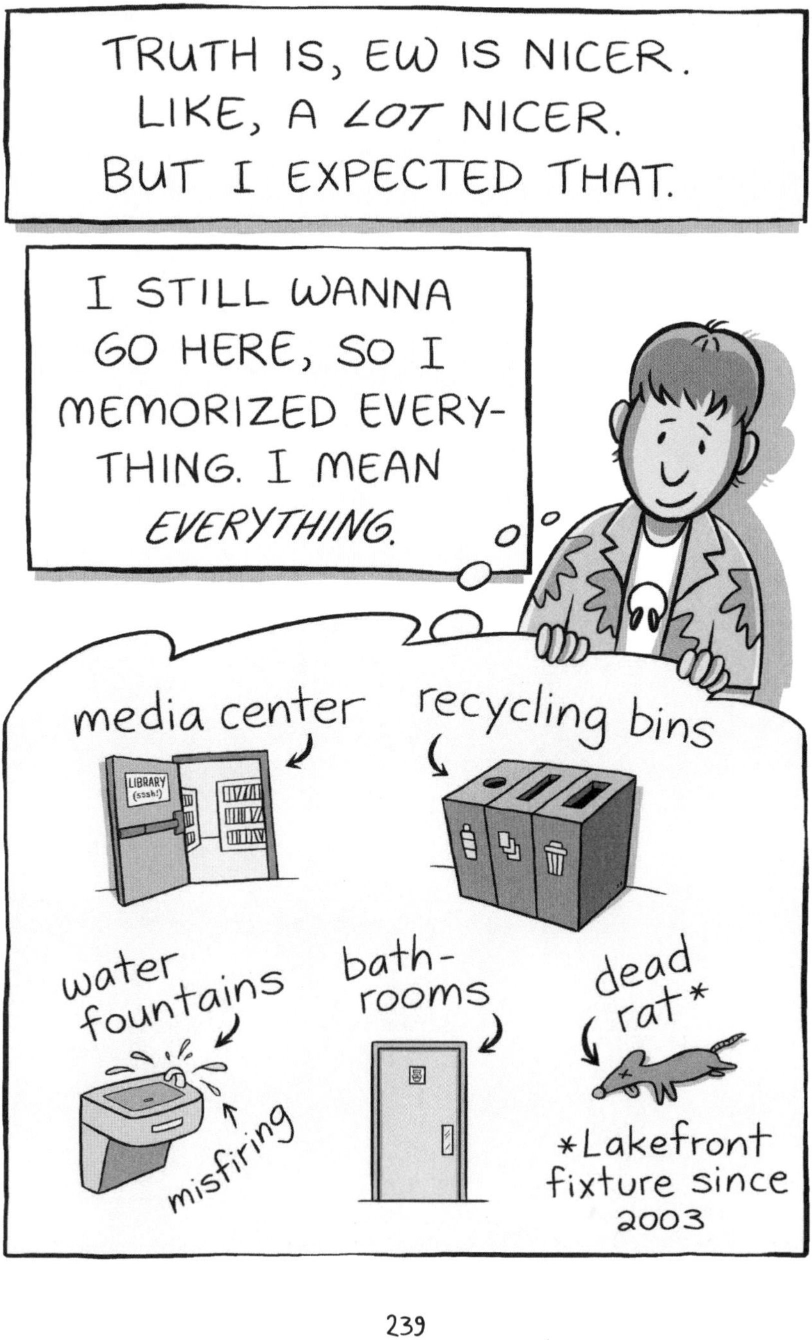

TRUTH IS, EW IS NICER. LIKE, A LOT NICER. BUT I EXPECTED THAT.
I STILL WANNA GO HERE, SO I MEMORIZED EVERYTHING. I MEAN EVERYTHING.
media center
LIBRARY (sssh!)
recycling bins
water fountains
misfiring
bath-rooms
dead rat*
*Lakefront fixture since 2003

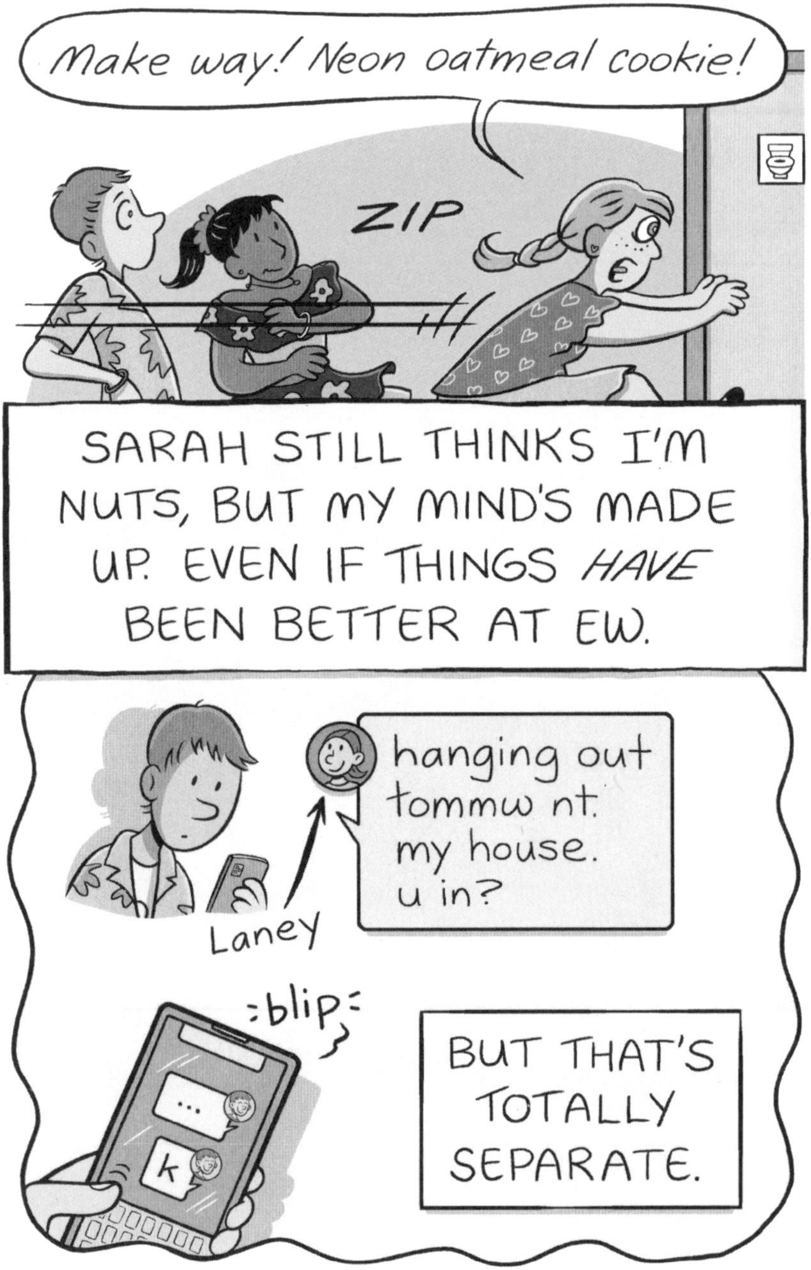
Make way! Neon oatmeal cookie!
ZIP
SARAH STILL THINKS I'M NUTS, BUT MY MIND'S MADE UP. EVEN IF THINGS *HAVE* BEEN BETTER AT EW.
hanging out tommw nt. my house. u in?
Laney
:blip:
...
k
BUT THAT'S TOTALLY SEPARATE.

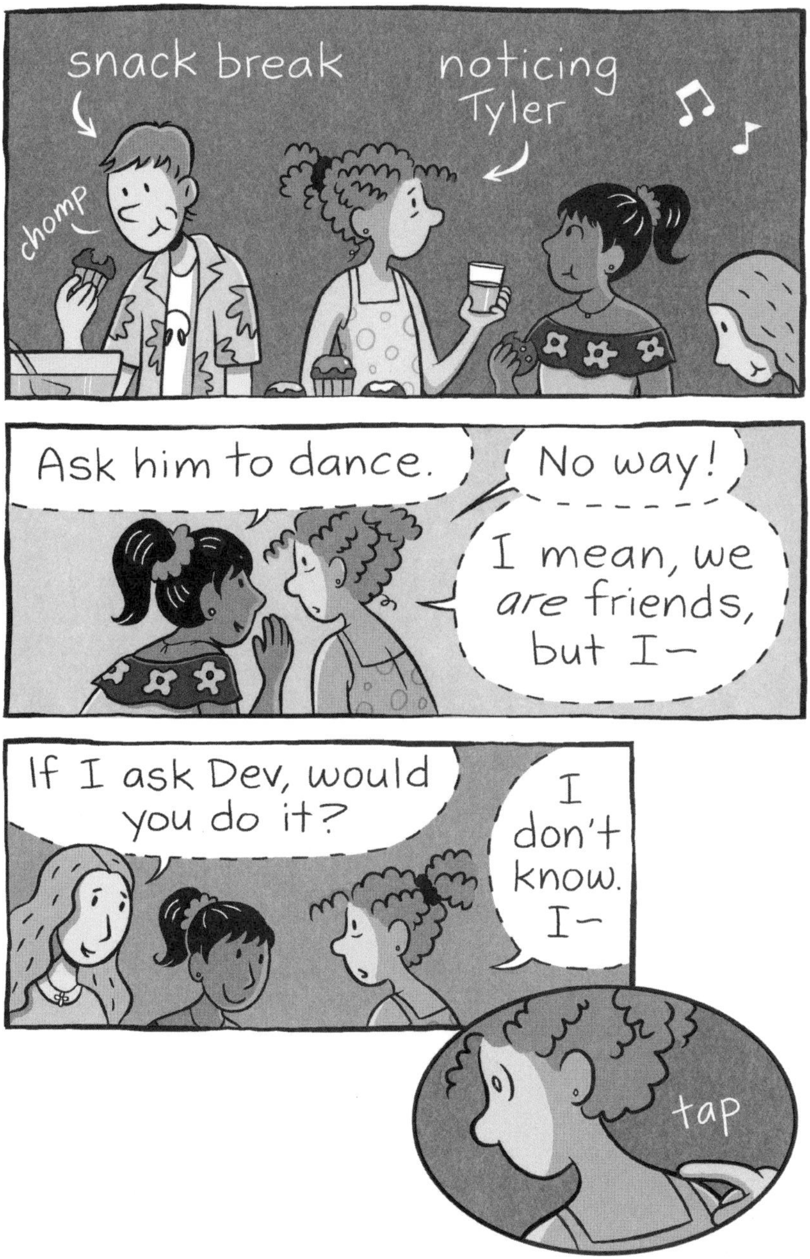
snack break
chomp
noticing Tyler
Ask him to dance.
No way!
I mean, we *are* friends, but I—
If I ask Dev, would you do it?
I don't know. I—
tap

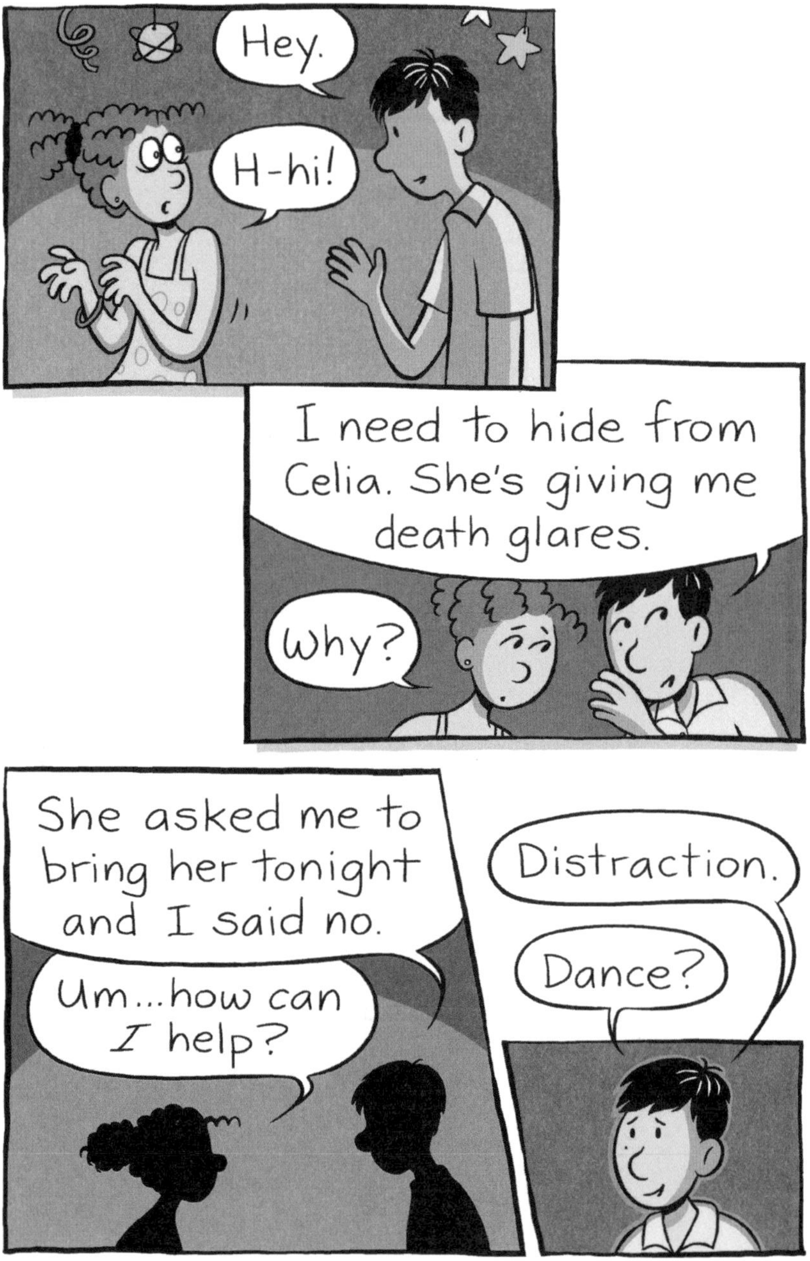
Hey.
H-hi!
I need to hide from Celia. She's giving me death glares.
Why?
She asked me to bring her tonight and I said no.
Um...how can *I* help?
Distraction.
Dance?

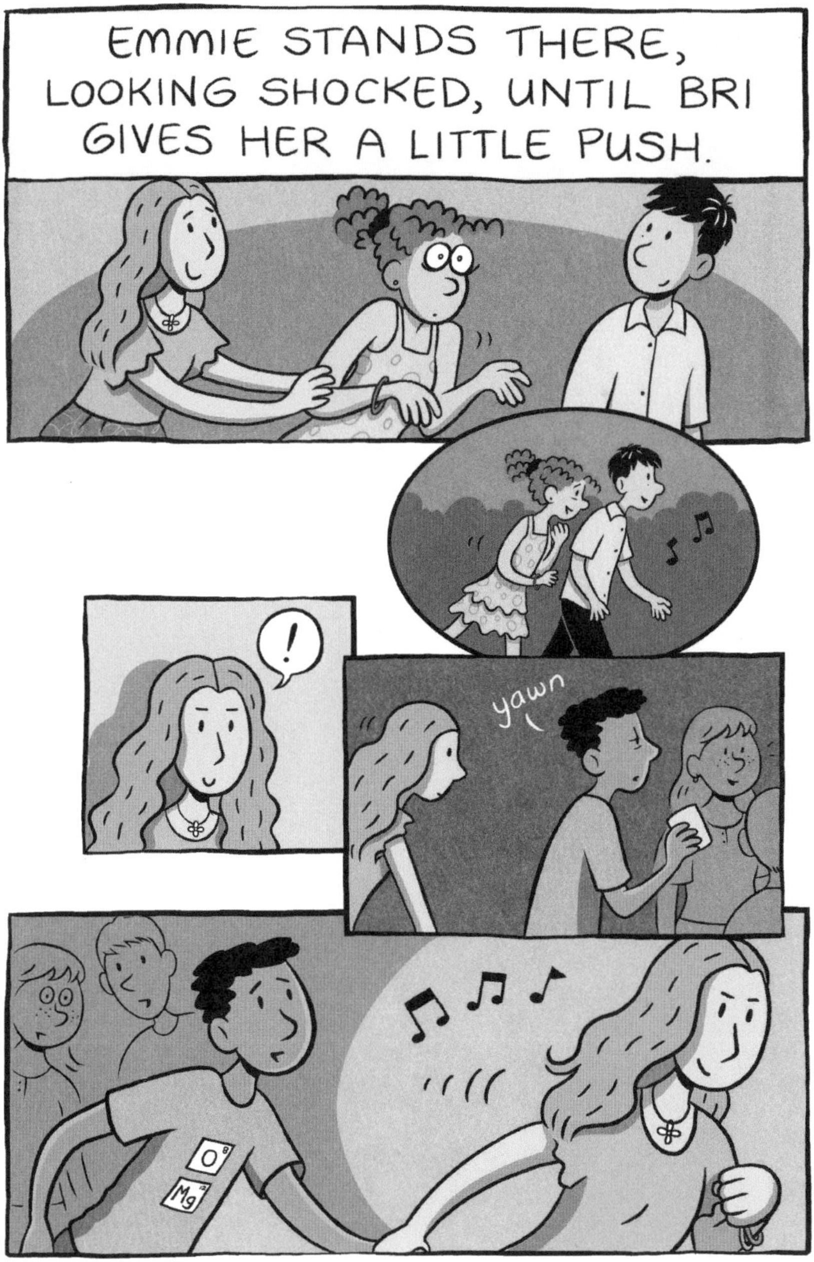
EMMIE STANDS THERE, LOOKING SHOCKED, UNTIL BRI GIVES HER A LITTLE PUSH.
!
yawn
O
Mg

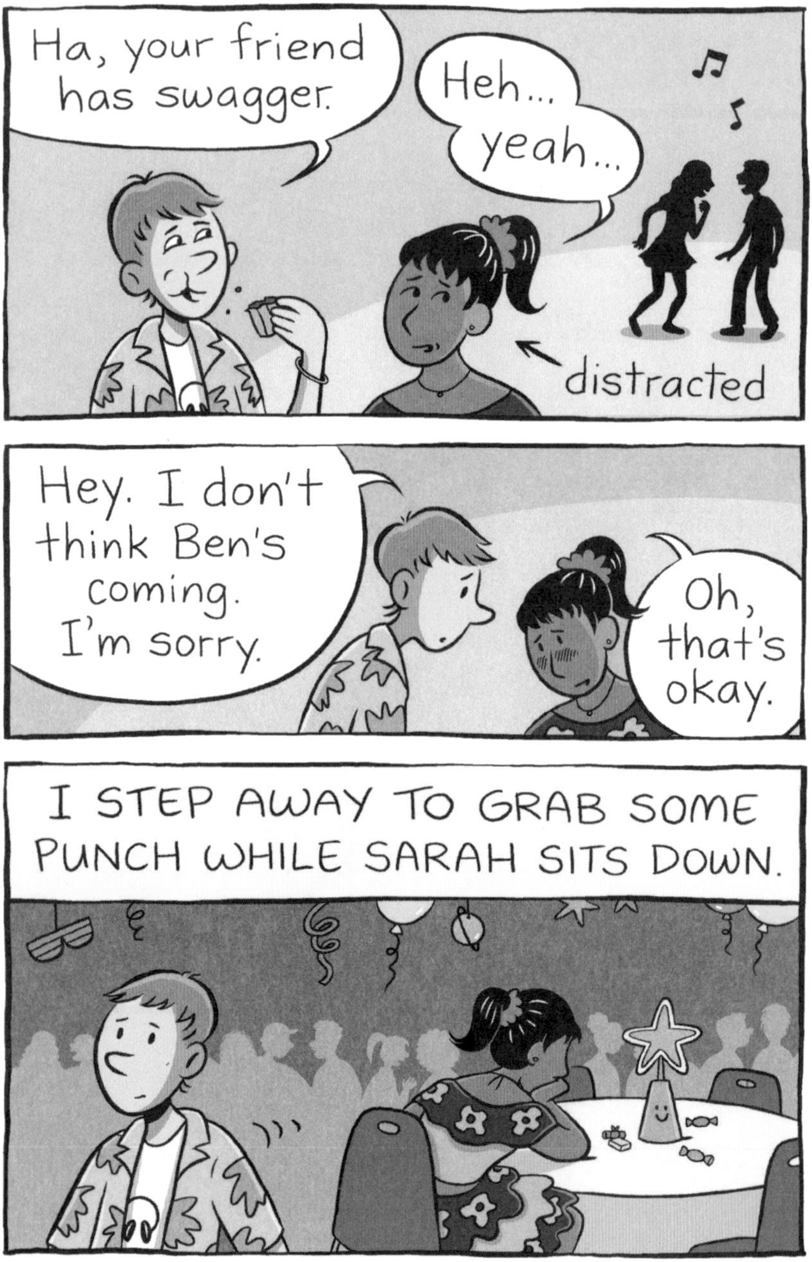
Ha, your friend has swagger.
Heh... yeah...
distracted
Hey. I don't think Ben's coming. I'm sorry.
Oh, that's okay.
I STEP AWAY TO GRAB SOME PUNCH WHILE SARAH SITS DOWN.

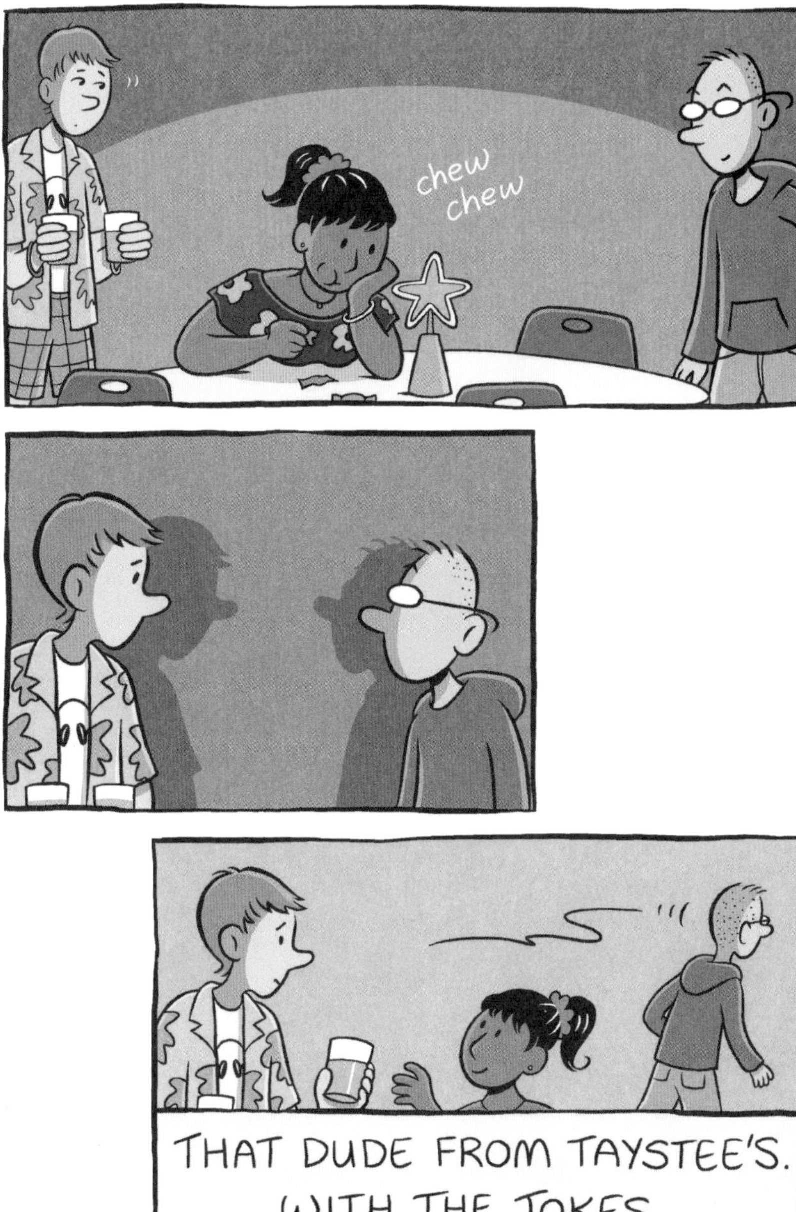
chew
chew
THAT DUDE FROM TAYSTEE'S.
WITH THE JOKES.

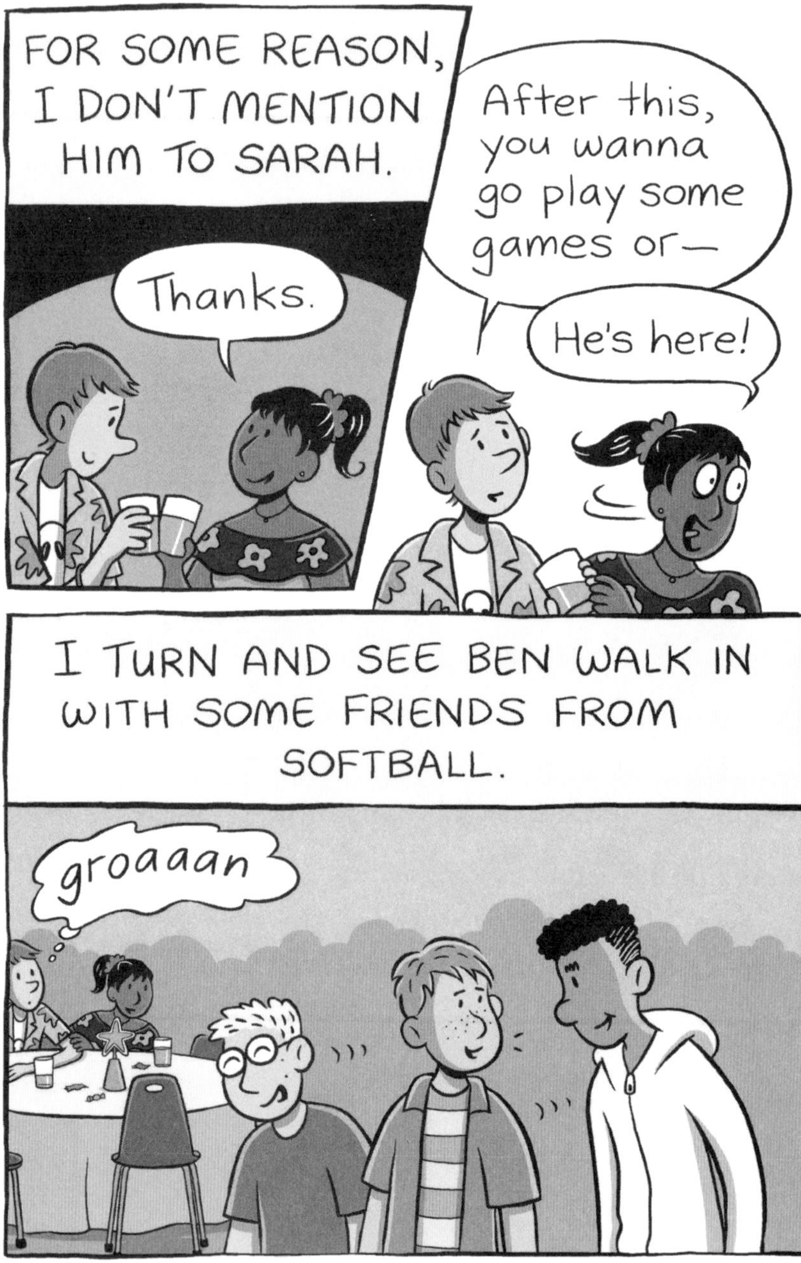
FOR SOME REASON, I DON'T MENTION HIM TO SARAH.
Thanks.
After this, you wanna go play some games or—
He's here!
I TURN AND SEE BEN WALK IN WITH SOME FRIENDS FROM SOFTBALL.
groaaan

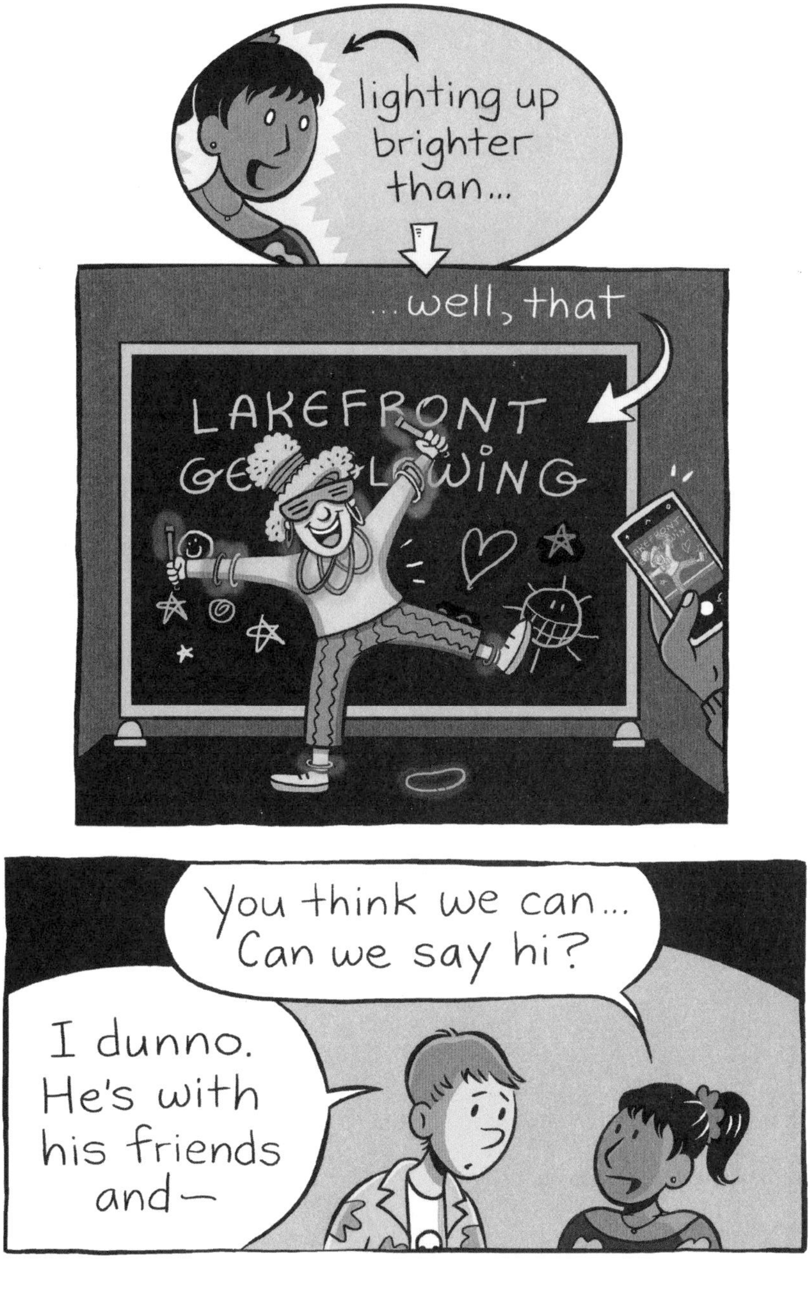
lighting up brighter than...
...well, that
LAKEFRONT GLOWING
You think we can... Can we say hi?
I dunno. He's with his friends and—

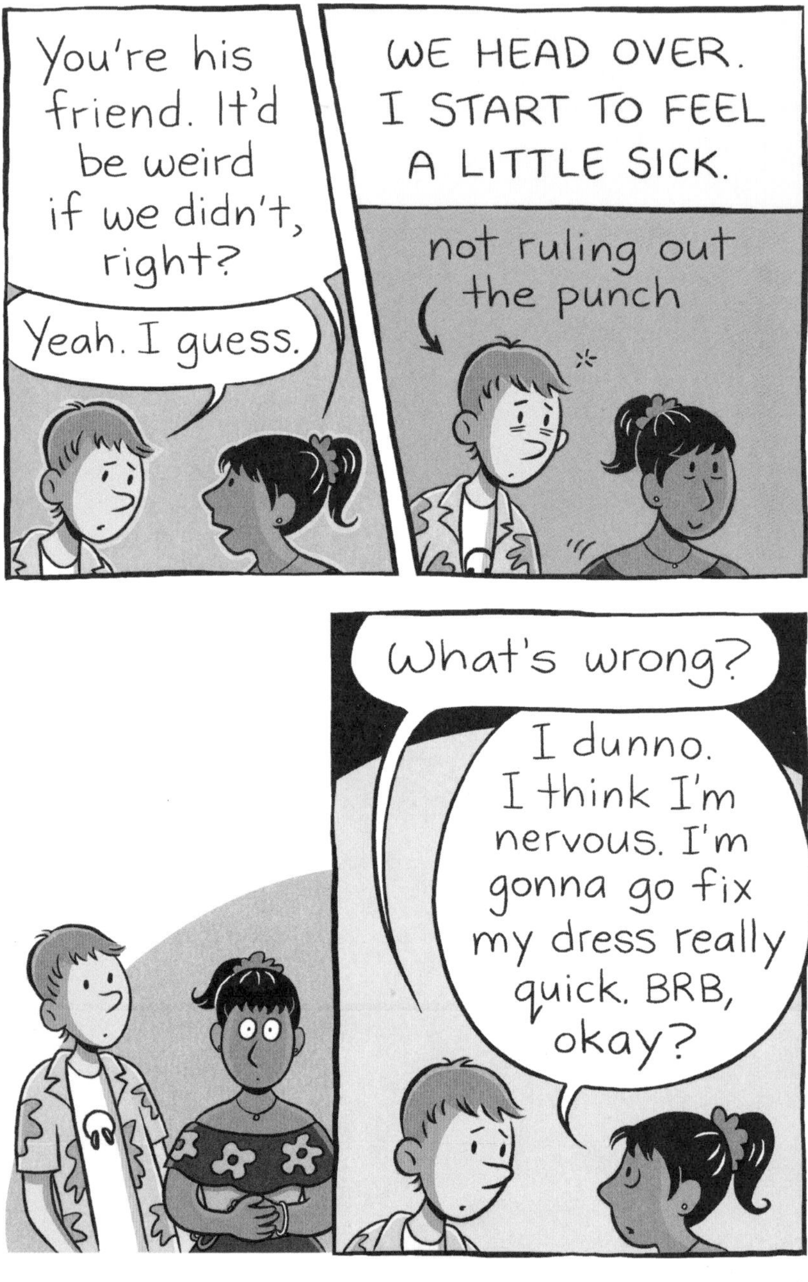
You're his friend. It'd be weird if we didn't, right?
Yeah. I guess.
WE HEAD OVER. I START TO FEEL A LITTLE SICK.
not ruling out the punch
What's wrong?
I dunno. I think I'm nervous. I'm gonna go fix my dress really quick. BRB, okay?

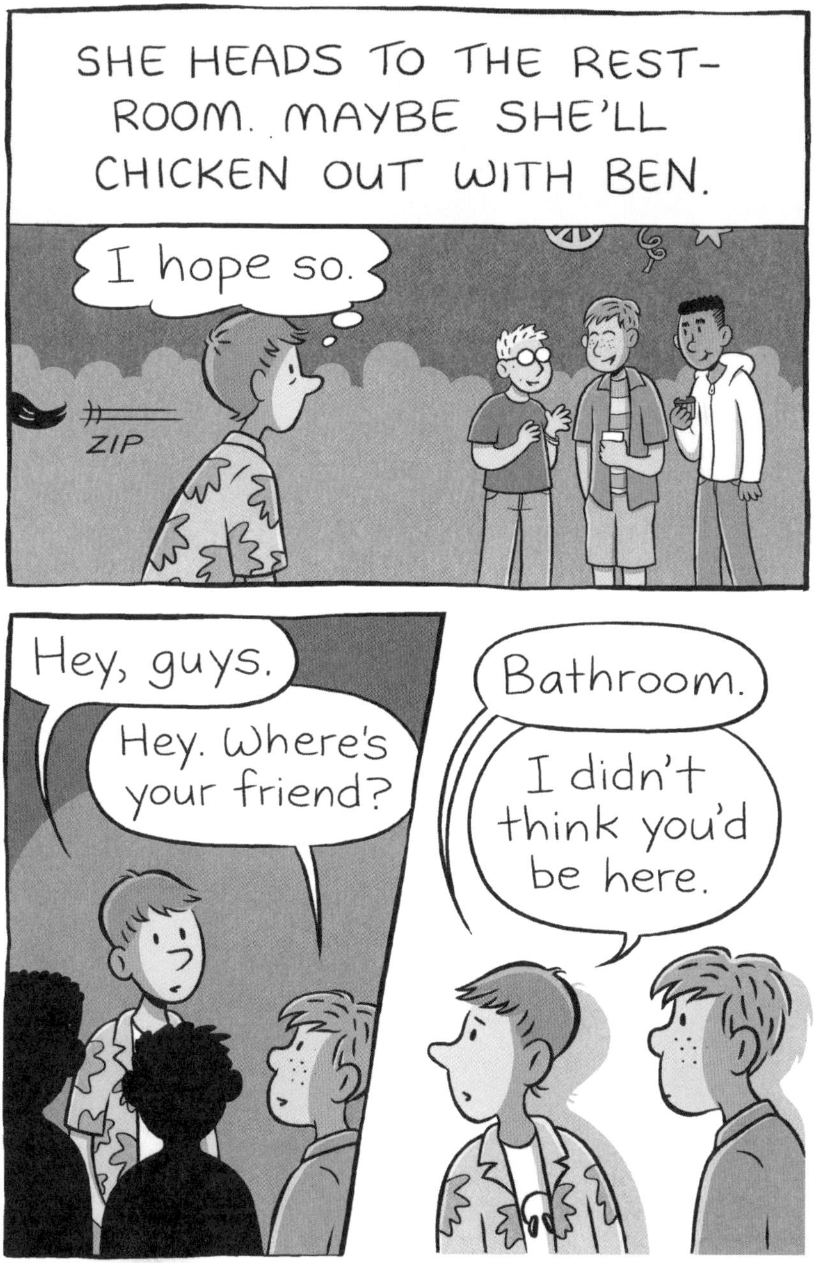
SHE HEADS TO THE REST-ROOM. MAYBE SHE'LL CHICKEN OUT WITH BEN.
I hope so.
ZIP
Hey, guys.
Hey. Where's your friend?
Bathroom.
I didn't think you'd be here.

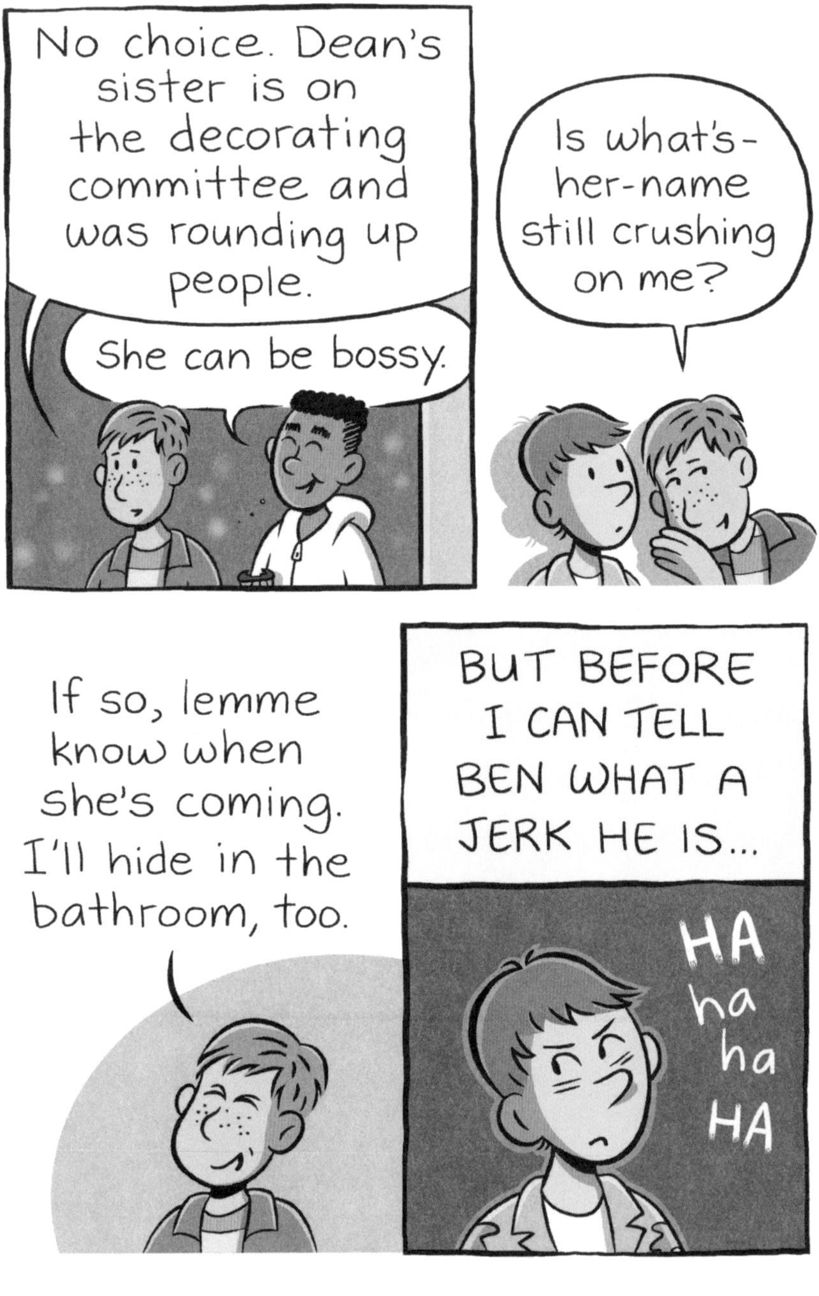
No choice. Dean's sister is on the decorating committee and was rounding up people.
She can be bossy.
Is what's-her-name still crushing on me?
If so, lemme know when she's coming. I'll hide in the bathroom, too.
BUT BEFORE I CAN TELL BEN WHAT A JERK HE IS...
HA ha ha HA

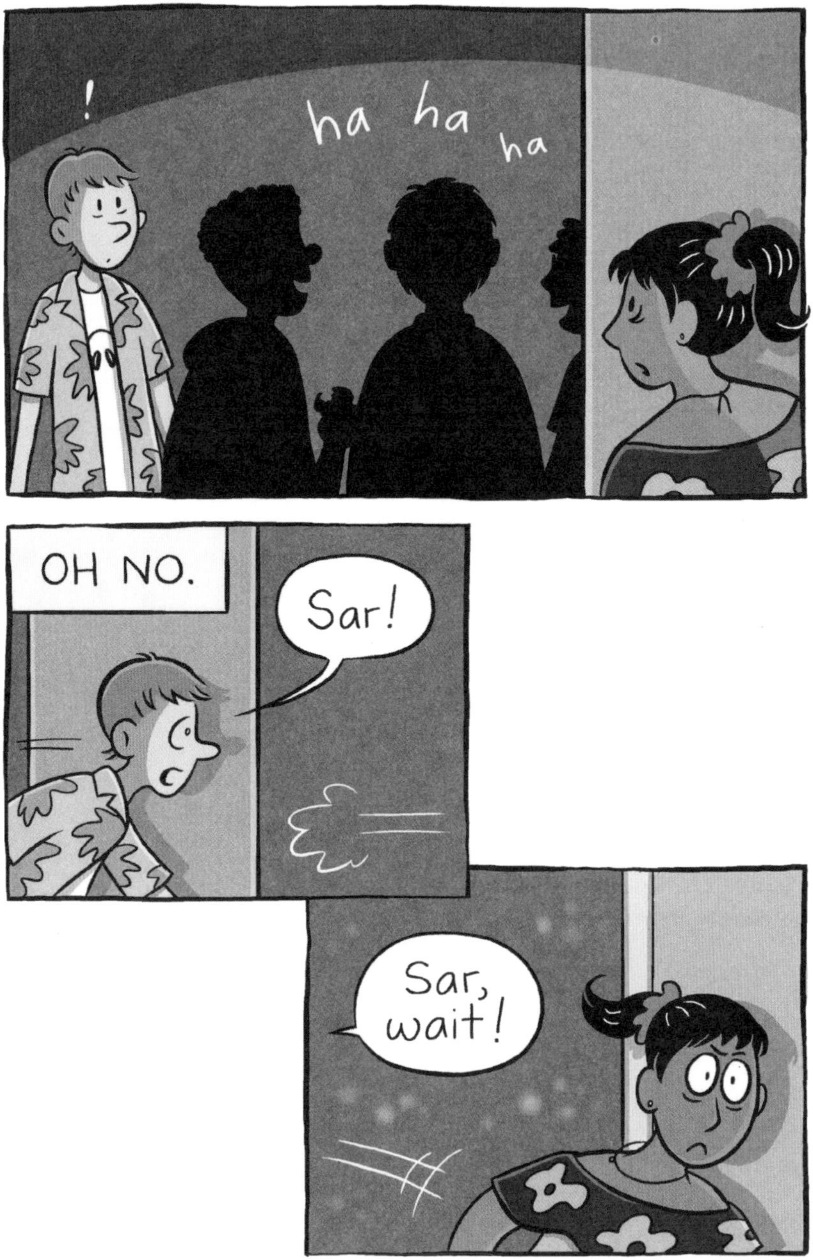
!
ha ha ha
OH NO.
Sar!
Sar, wait!

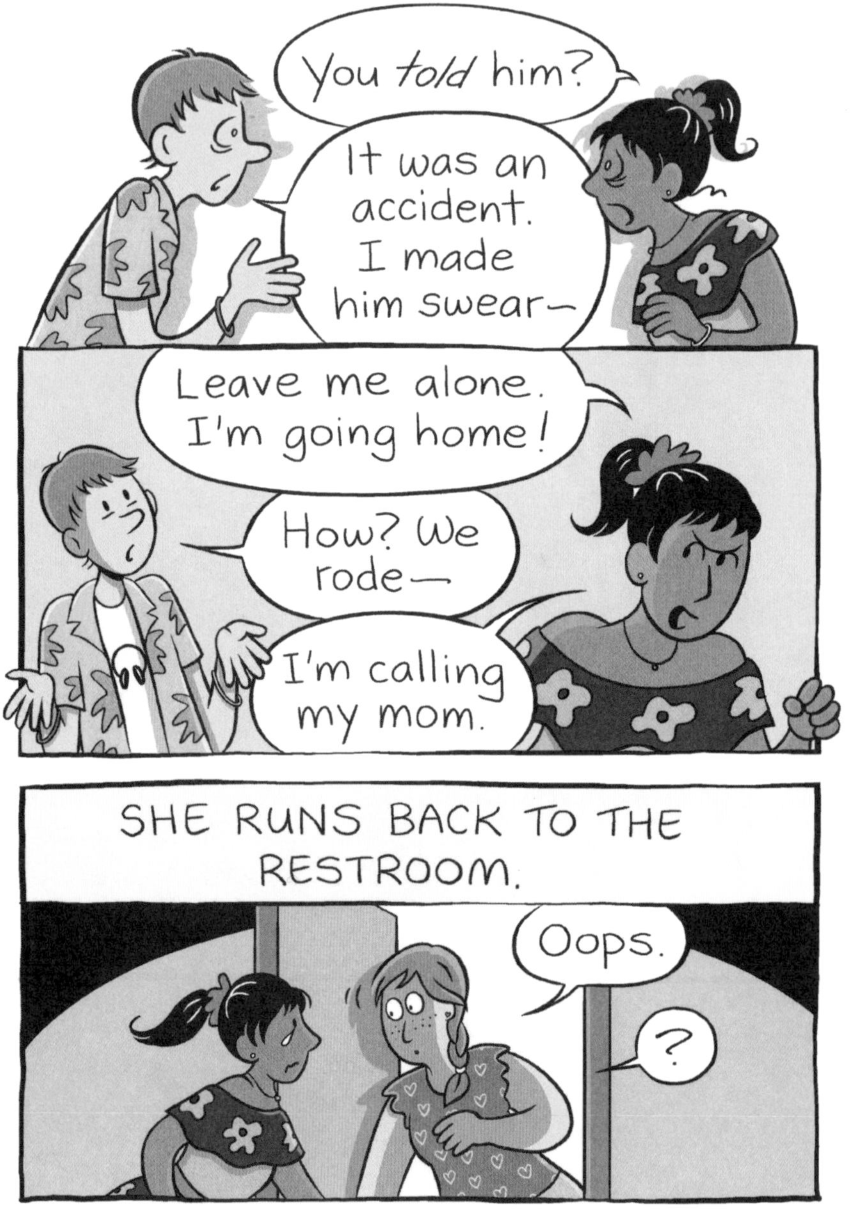
You *told* him?
It was an accident. I made him swear—
Leave me alone. I'm going home!
How? We rode—
I'm calling my mom.
SHE RUNS BACK TO THE RESTROOM.
Oops.
?

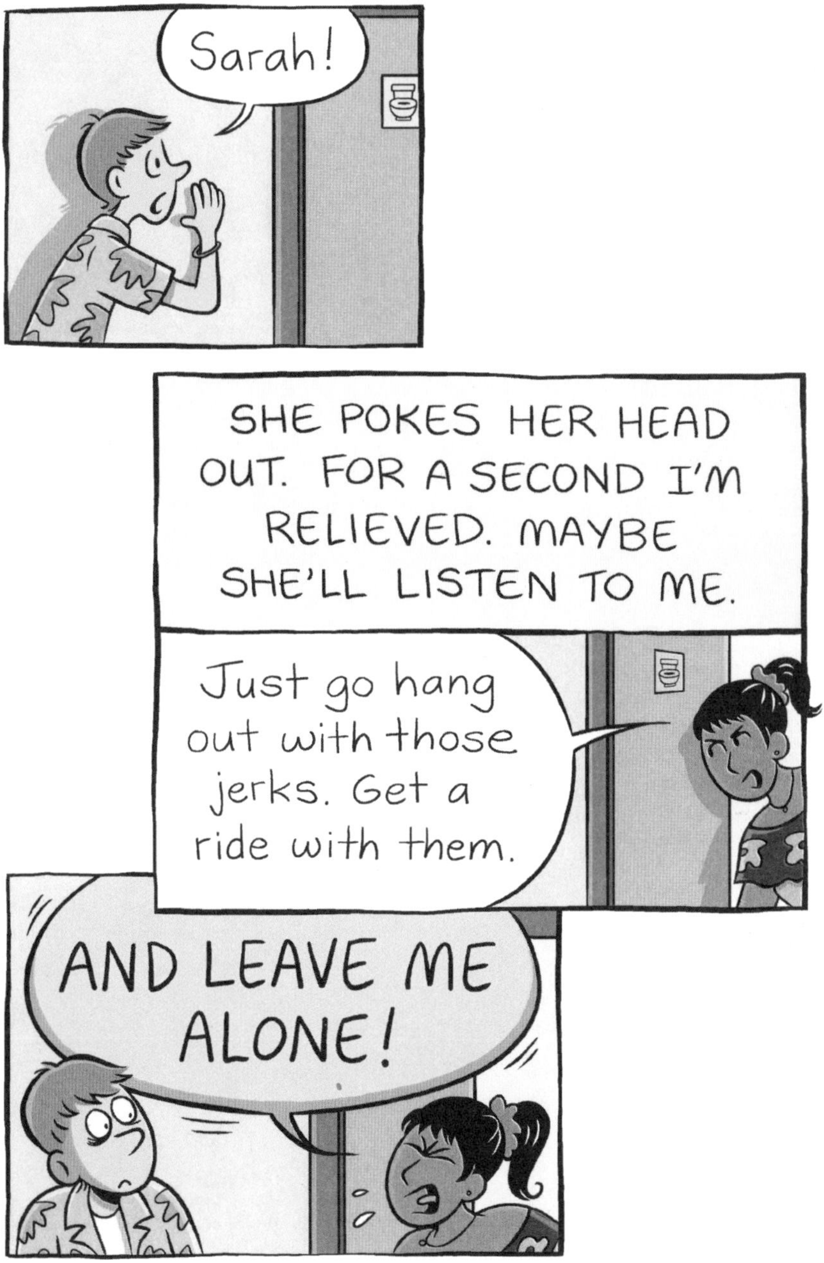
Sarah!
SHE POKES HER HEAD OUT. FOR A SECOND I'M RELIEVED. MAYBE SHE'LL LISTEN TO ME.
Just go hang out with those jerks. Get a ride with them.
AND LEAVE ME ALONE!

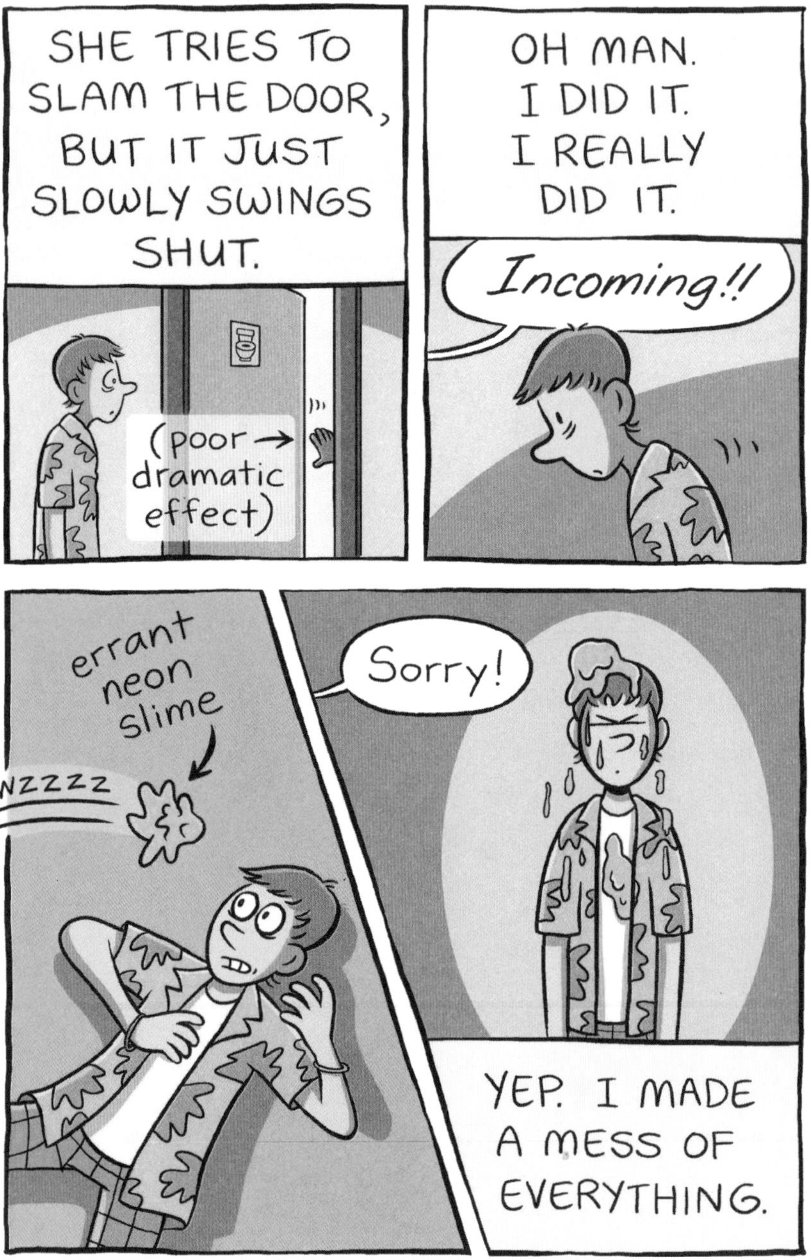
SHE TRIES TO SLAM THE DOOR, BUT IT JUST SLOWLY SWINGS SHUT.
(poor dramatic effect)
OH MAN. I DID IT. I REALLY DID IT.
Incoming!!
errant neon slime
WZZZZ
Sorry!
YEP. I MADE A MESS OF EVERYTHING.

SARAH

I asked him

For a while, I don't come out of the bathroom.

I wonder how many people do this . . . sit in a stall crying.
It's middle school, so I'm guessing a lot.

IT'S BEEN
0 DAYS
SINCE SOMEONE
HAS CRIED
IN THIS STALL.

I feel so humiliated. I should've known. My gut told me Ben didn't wanna go to the dance with me. I should've listened.

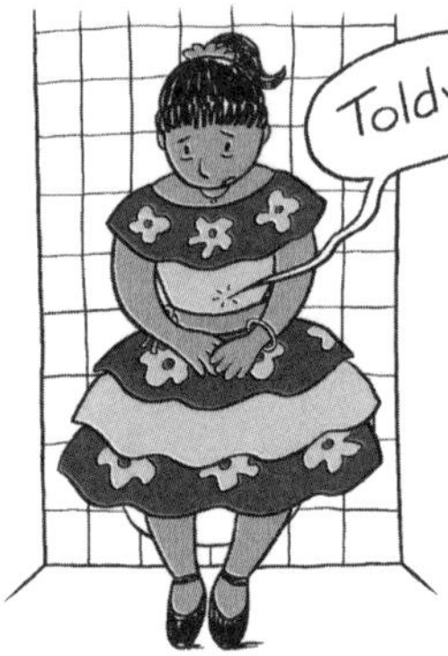
Toldya

Girls keep coming and going. I try to stay quiet. At one point, I hear a lone girl walk in, but I can't tell who it is. She's in the stall next to me for a long time. When she's done, I hear her washing up at the sink.

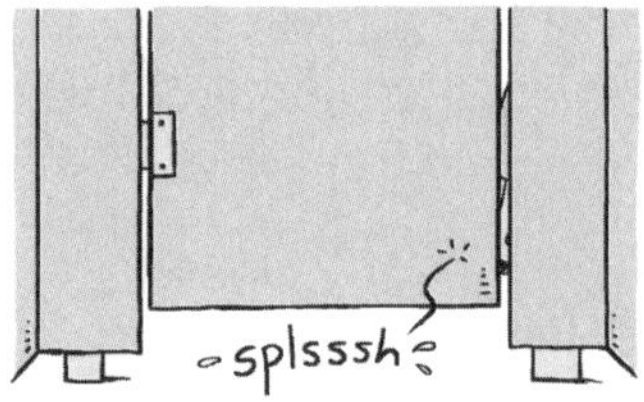
splsssh

Is that—?

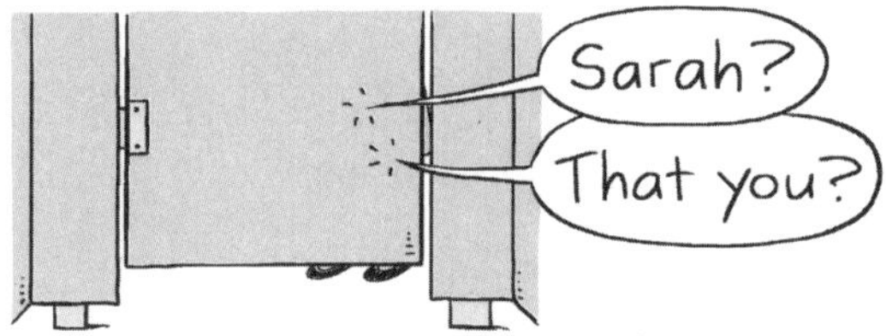
Sarah?
That you?

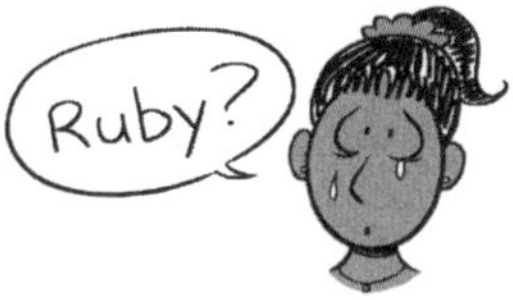
Ruby?

Ruby Donovan. She's in some of my classes and we both belong to poetry club. Well, she goes more than me. She's really passionate about it.

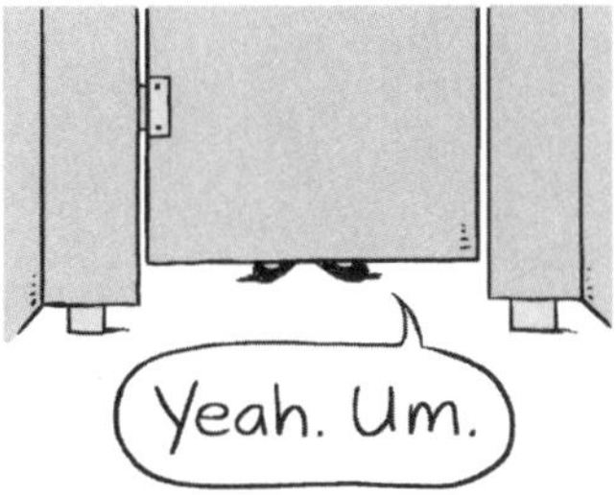
Yeah. Um.

She's also a lot better at writing than speaking. But that's okay.

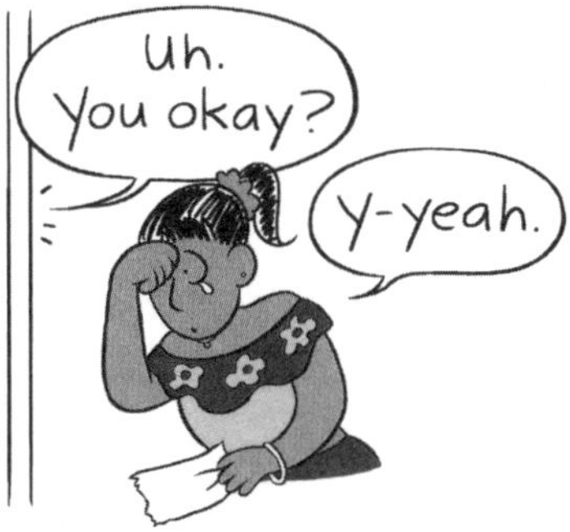
Uh.
You okay?
Y-yeah.

I flush the toilet and come out. I'm sure my eyes are all puffy. Between that and my usual chubby cheeks, my face probably looks like a big marshmallow.

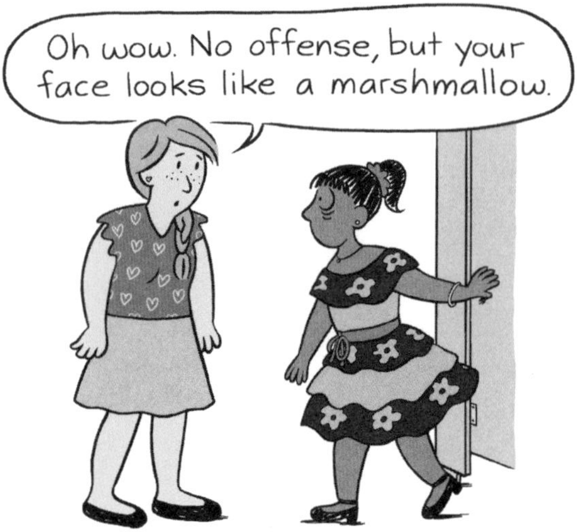
Oh wow. No offense, but your face looks like a marshmallow.

I burst into tears.

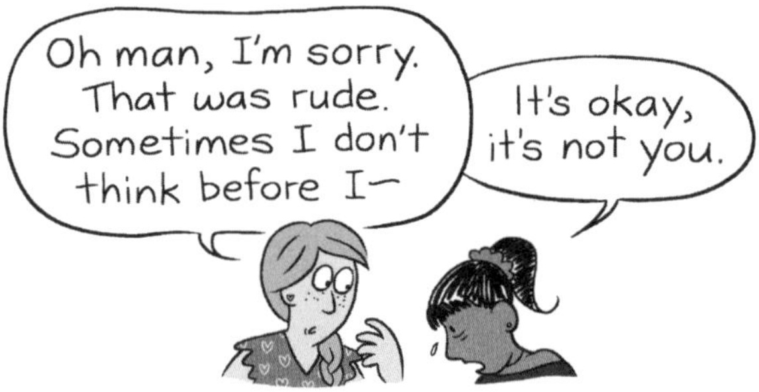
Oh man, I'm sorry. That was rude. Sometimes I don't think before I—
It's okay, it's not you.

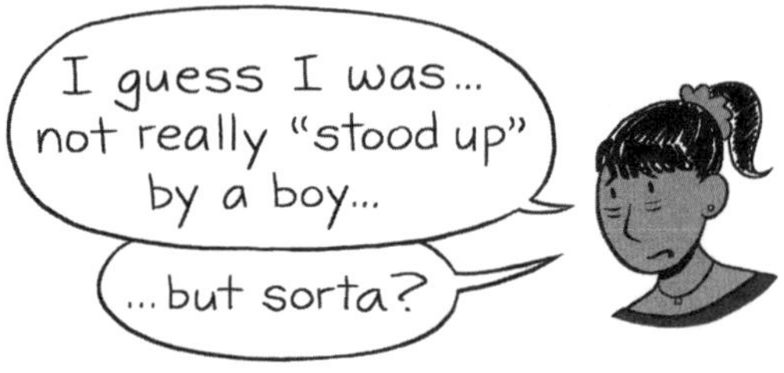
I guess I was... not really "stood up" by a boy...
...but sorta?

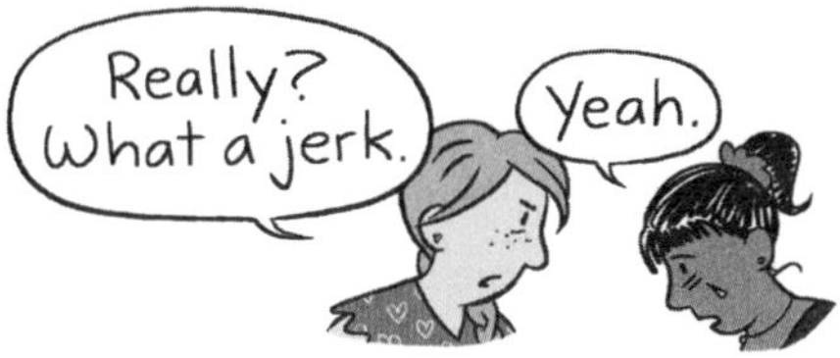
Really? What a jerk.
Yeah.

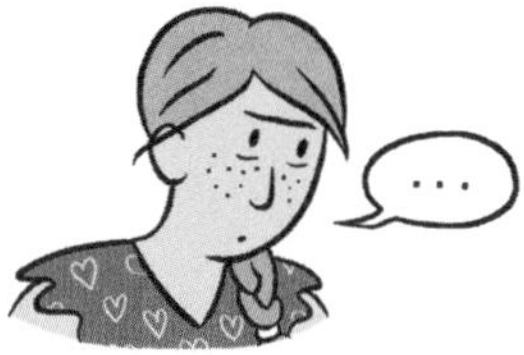
...

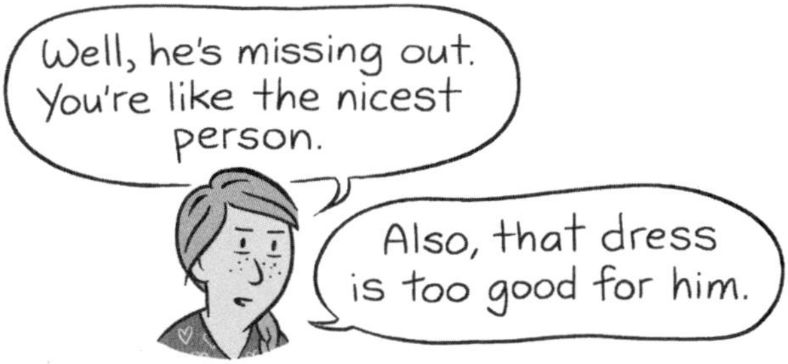
Well, he's missing out. You're like the nicest person.
Also, that dress is too good for him.

I laugh. I can't help it.

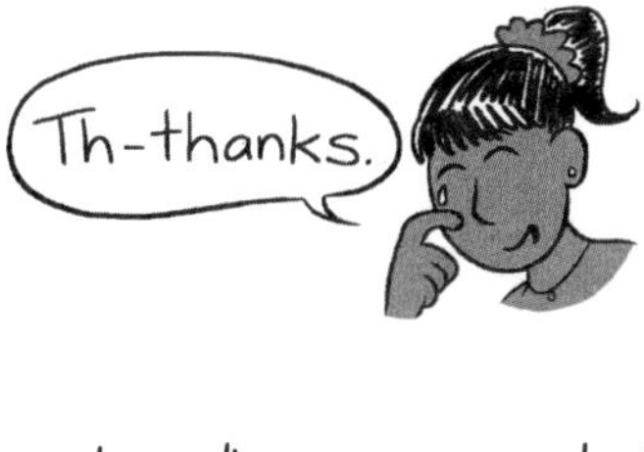
Th-thanks.

We stand there awkwardly for a second while I wipe my eyes a little too forcefully.

Ruby pauses, then takes my arm kinda gruffly and leads me to the sink. She grabs a paper towel and runs it under some water.

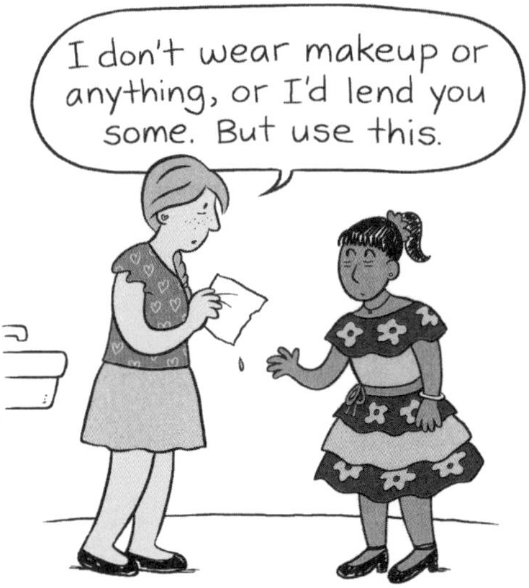
I don't wear makeup or anything, or I'd lend you some. But use this.

I take the damp towel and pat my sore eyes. She waits with me until they start looking a little better. Definitely less marshmallow-y.

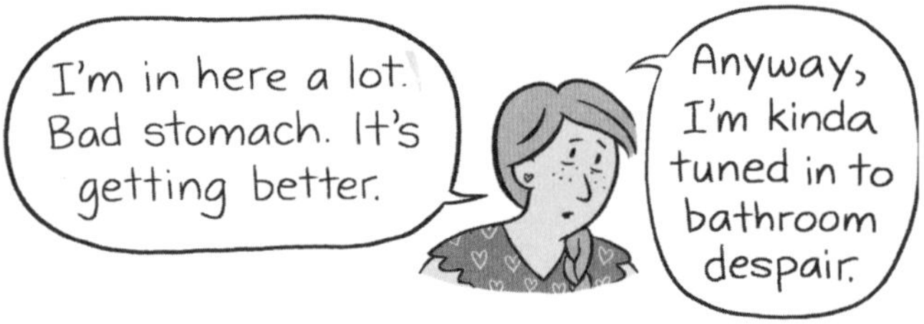
I'm in here a lot. Bad stomach. It's getting better.
Anyway, I'm kinda tuned in to bathroom despair.

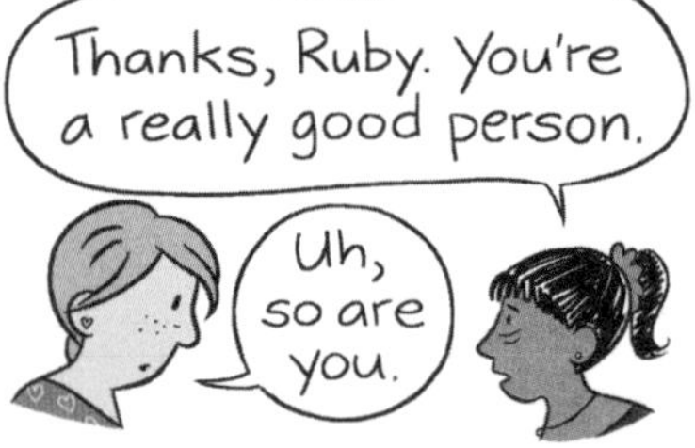
Thanks, Ruby. You're a really good person.
Uh, so are you.

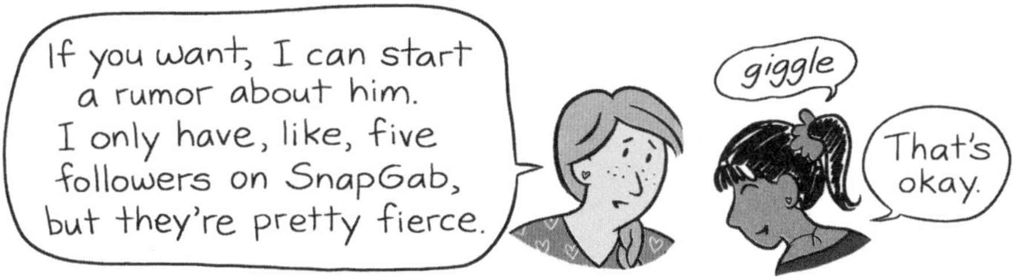
If you want, I can start a rumor about him. I only have, like, five followers on SnapGab, but they're pretty fierce.
giggle
That's okay.

We walk out together. I'm feeling a little more human. Ruby heads back to the caf.

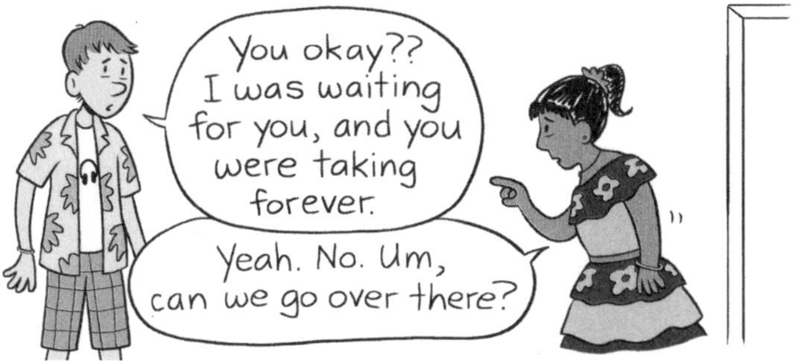
You okay?? I was waiting for you, and you were taking forever.
Yeah. No. Um, can we go over there?

I point to a back stairwell. We head over and sit down. I tell him what happened.

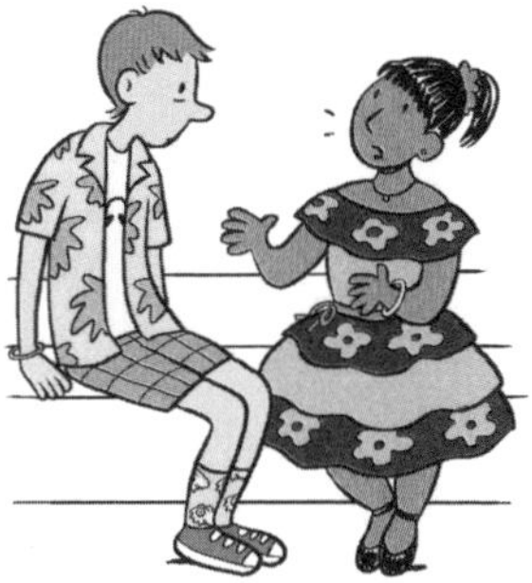

He doesn't say anything for a while.

It isn't lost on me that I totally put Leo in the middle. Normally, he'd take my side in an instant. But this is his good friend who blew me off, not some random seventh-grade dirtbag.

It's my fault. I shouldn't have asked him.

That seems to jerk him back into reality.

Forget him, BGF. Let's go dance.

But I—

C'mon. I'm gonna make you forget all about... who's-his-face!

He grins.

And I can't help it. I grin back. Not that I'm feeling anywhere near good, but Leo has a way of getting me out of my head.

We walk back to the cafeteria, and Leo pulls me onto the dance floor right away. I already feel a little better. Emmie, Tyler, Bri, and Dev join us. I notice Celia, dancing nearby, glaring at Emmie.

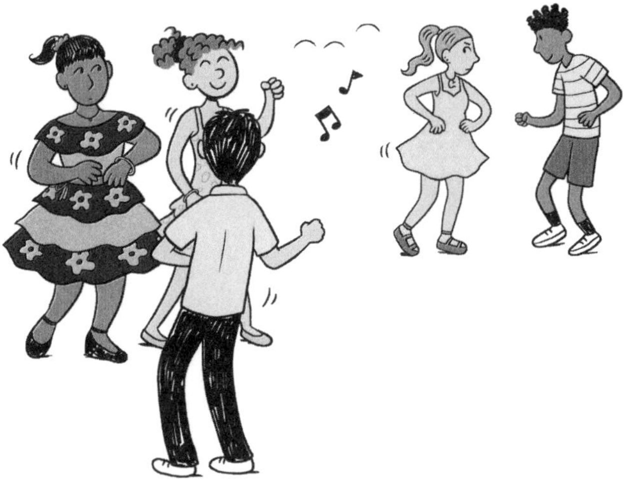

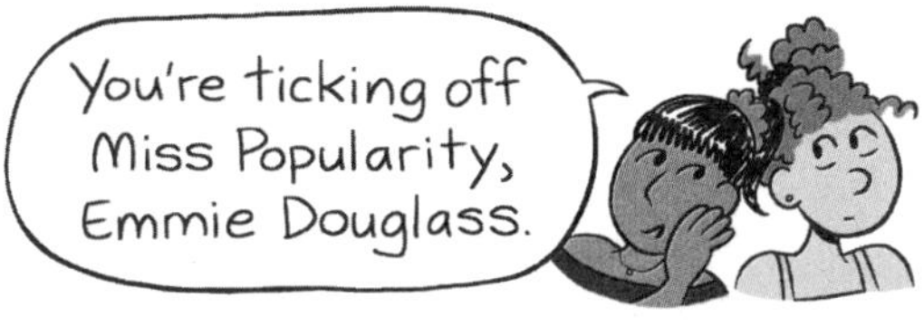
You're ticking off Miss Popularity, Emmie Douglass.

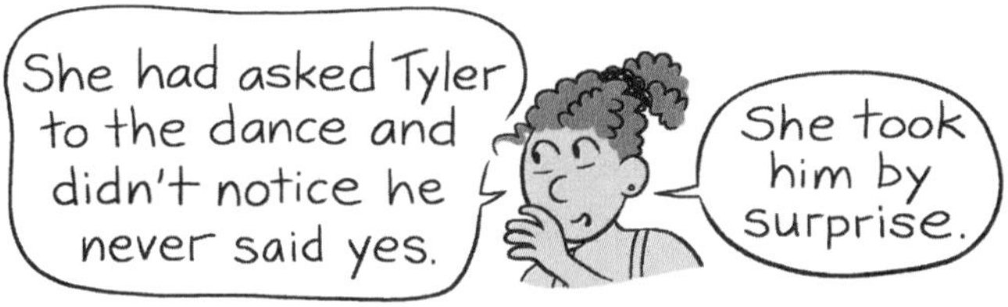
She had asked Tyler to the dance and didn't notice he never said yes.
She took him by surprise.

I swallow. "Took him by surprise." Sounds familiar.

Leo must've seen my face fall, because he grabs my hands and swings me around again. I squeal, laughing.

After the song ends and Leo goes to get some water . . .

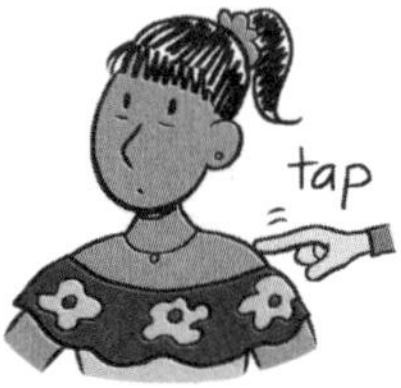
tap

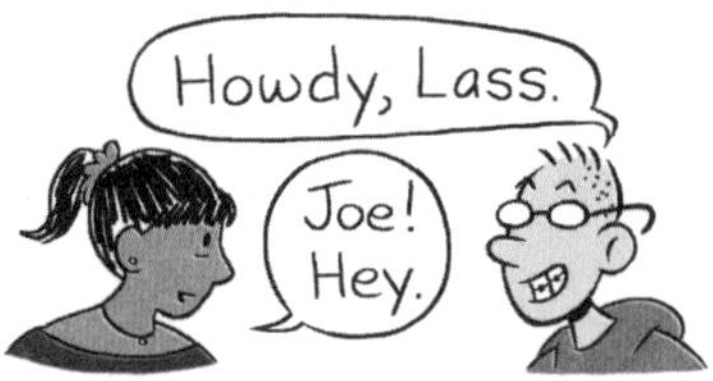
Howdy, Lass.
Joe! Hey.

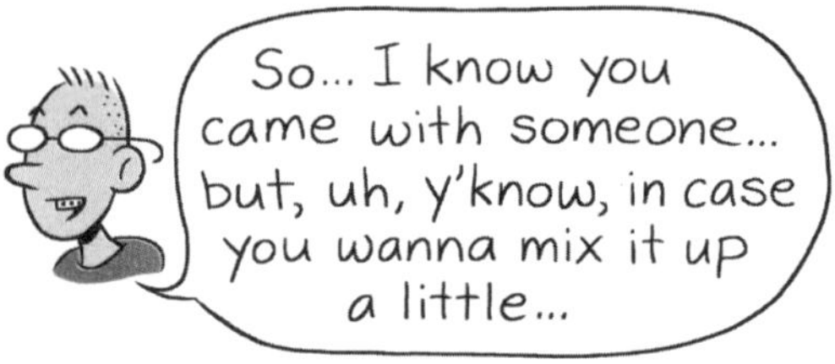
So... I know you came with someone... but, uh, y'know, in case you wanna mix it up a little...

He kinda stammers, and at first I'm not sure what he's trying to say.

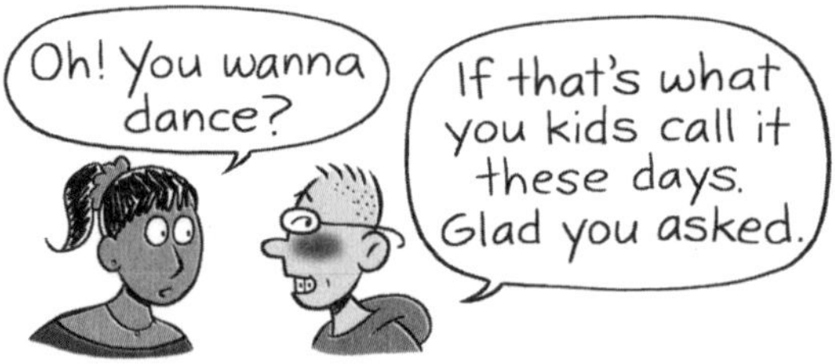
Oh! You wanna dance?
If that's what you kids call it these days. Glad you asked.

I laugh and we head to the dance floor.

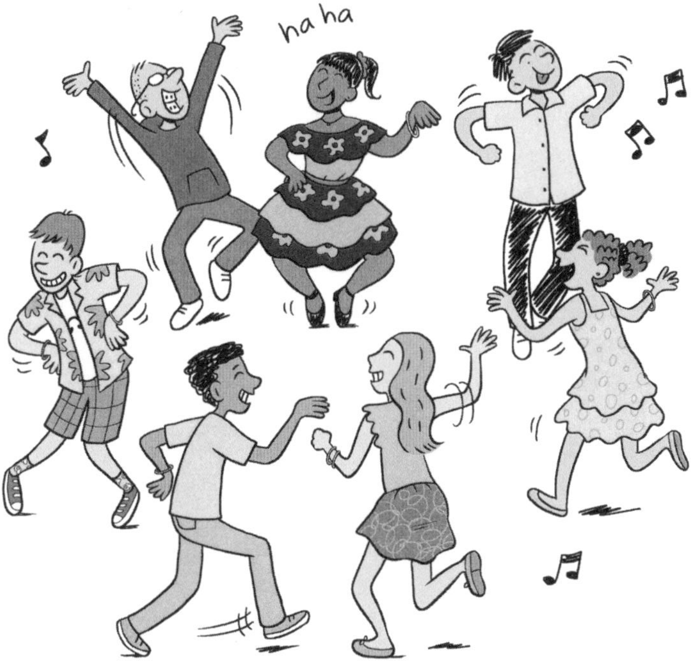
ha ha

As much fun as I'm trying to have, it still feels like there's a big hole in my heart.

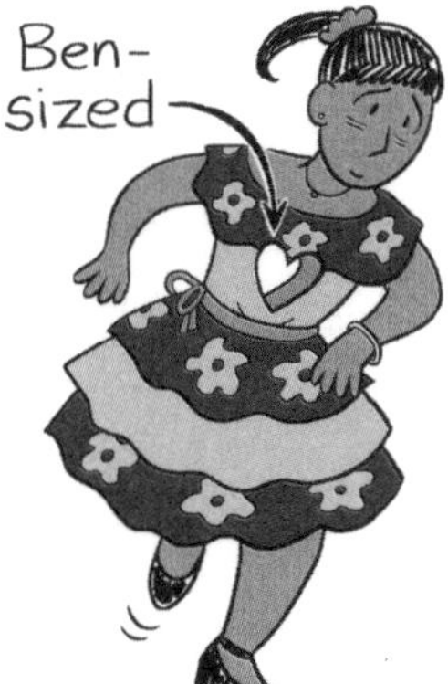
Ben-
sized

But I try to stay upbeat. I mean, that's what I do, right? I'm Sarah Reyes, nicest girl at Lakefront Middle School. Whatever happens, I smile through it.

crackle crrrack

Even if it's getting harder and harder.

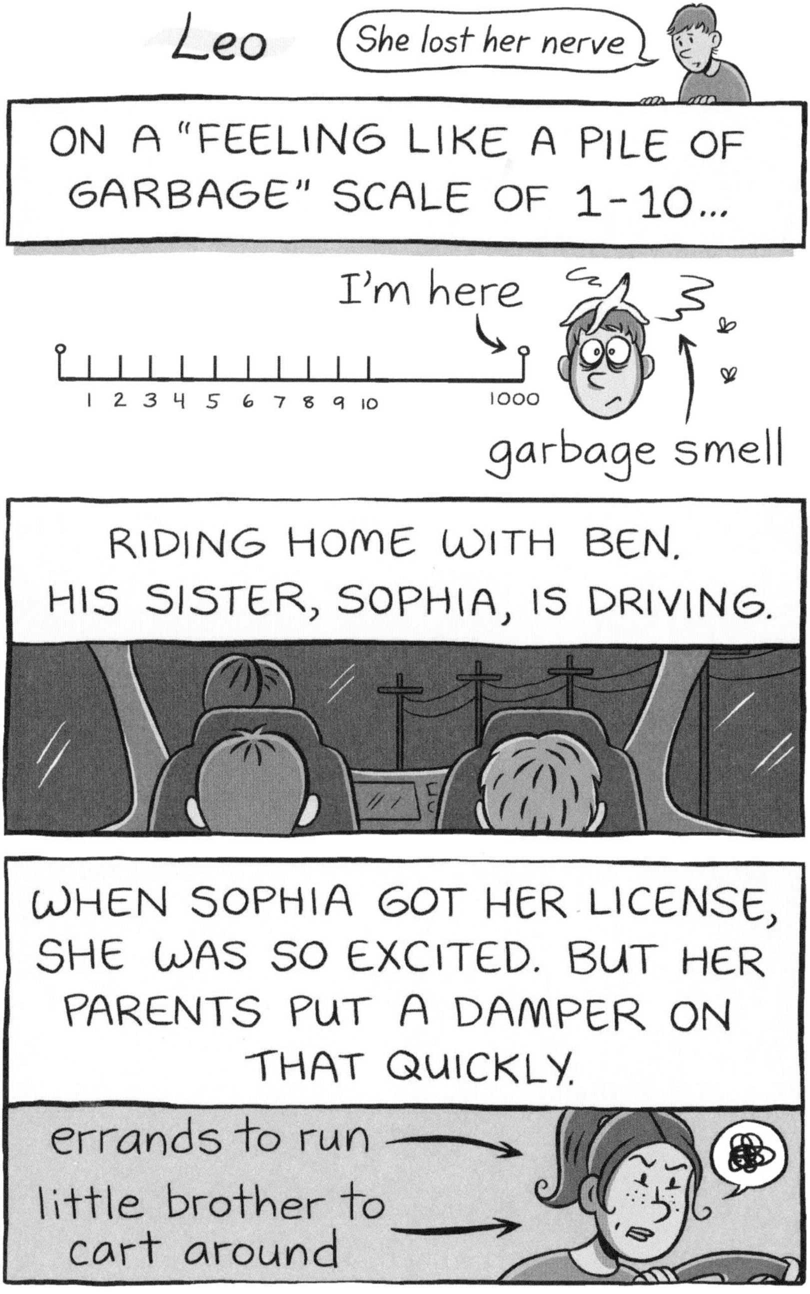
Leo
She lost her nerve
ON A "FEELING LIKE A PILE OF GARBAGE" SCALE OF 1-10...
I'm here
1 2 3 4 5 6 7 8 9 10 1000
garbage smell
RIDING HOME WITH BEN. HIS SISTER, SOPHIA, IS DRIVING.
WHEN SOPHIA GOT HER LICENSE, SHE WAS SO EXCITED. BUT HER PARENTS PUT A DAMPER ON THAT QUICKLY.
errands to run
little brother to cart around

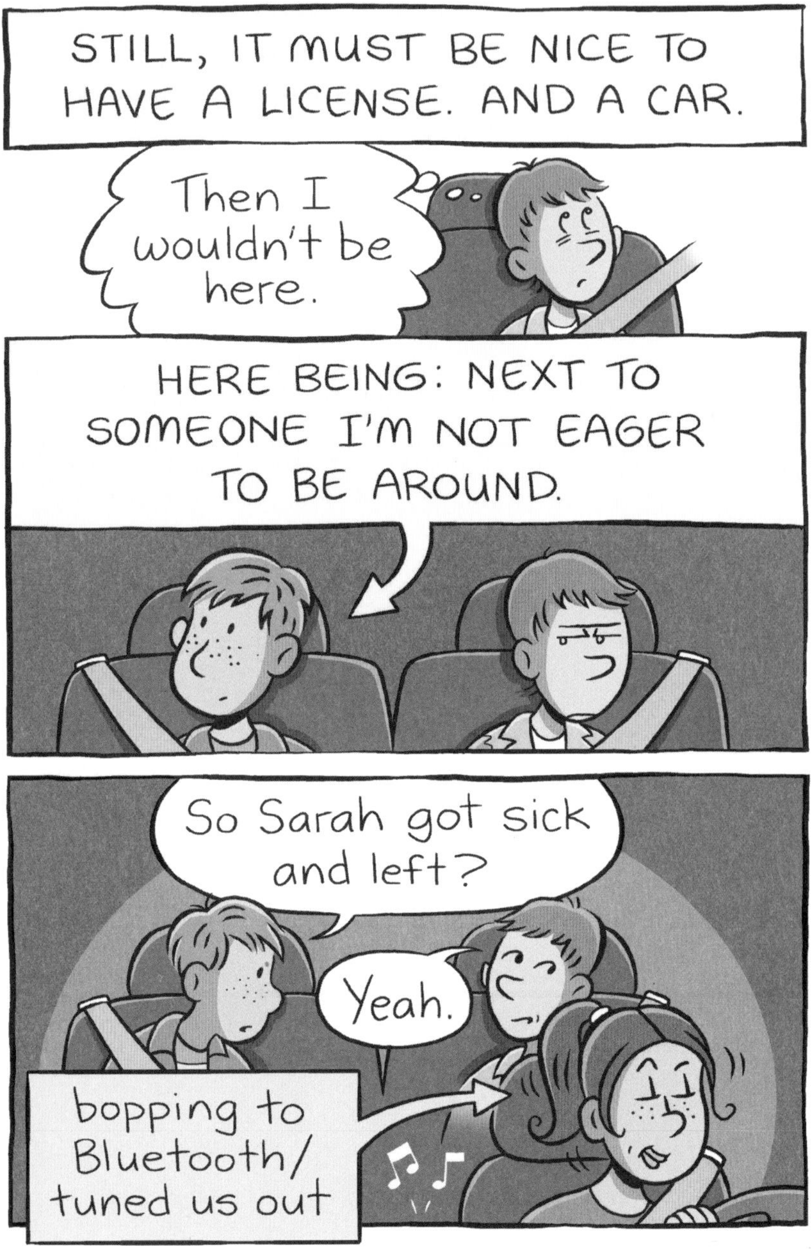
STILL, IT MUST BE NICE TO HAVE A LICENSE. AND A CAR.
Then I wouldn't be here.
HERE BEING: NEXT TO SOMEONE I'M NOT EAGER TO BE AROUND.
So Sarah got sick and left?
Yeah.
bopping to Bluetooth/ tuned us out

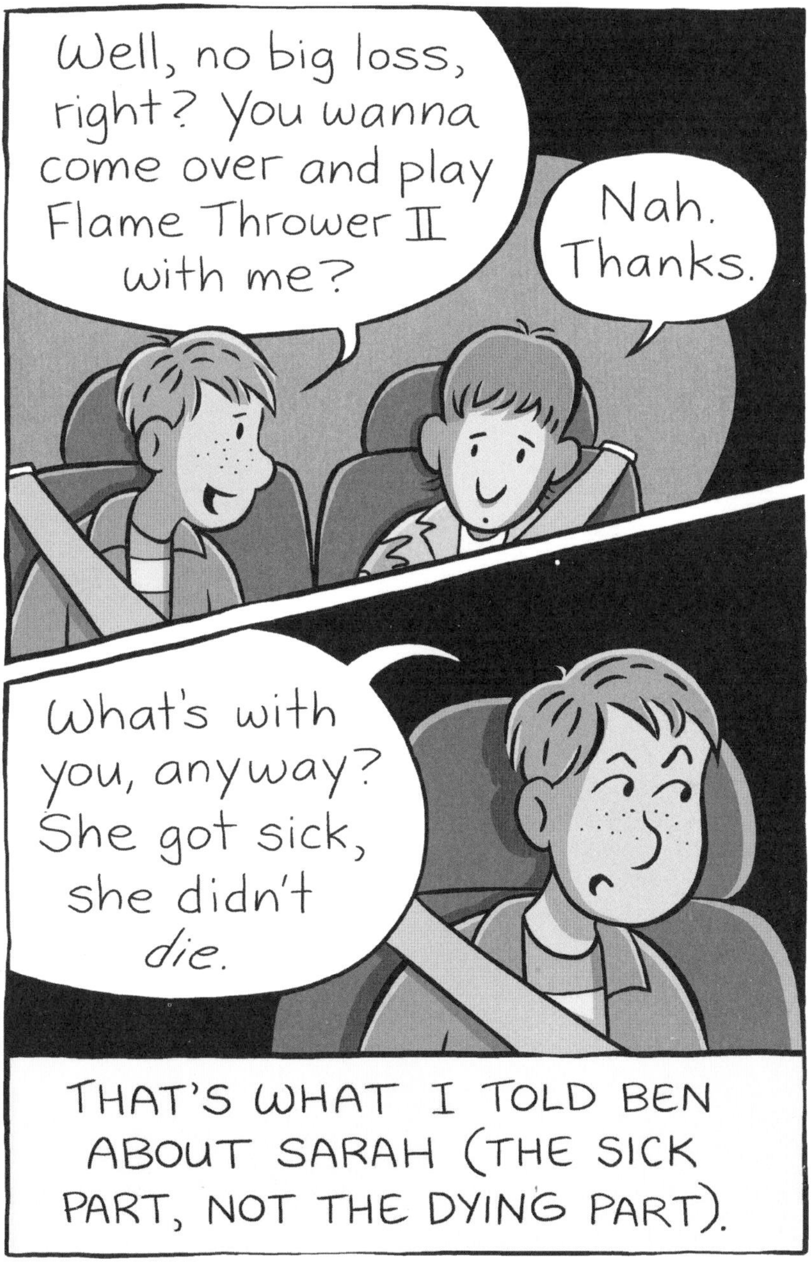
Well, no big loss, right? You wanna come over and play Flame Thrower II with me?
Nah. Thanks.
What's with you, anyway? She got sick, she didn't *die*.
THAT'S WHAT I TOLD BEN ABOUT SARAH (THE SICK PART, NOT THE DYING PART).

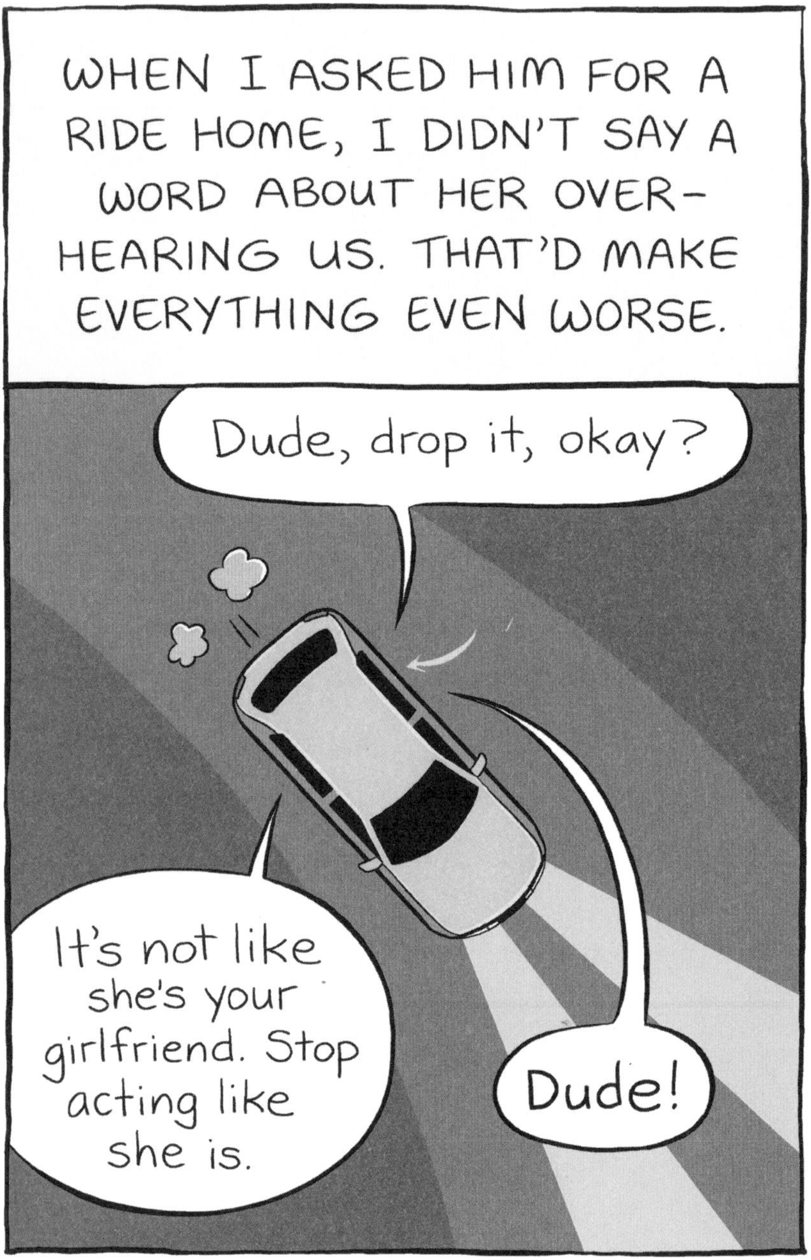
WHEN I ASKED HIM FOR A RIDE HOME, I DIDN'T SAY A WORD ABOUT HER OVER-HEARING US. THAT'D MAKE EVERYTHING EVEN WORSE.
Dude, drop it, okay?
It's not like she's your girlfriend. Stop acting like she is.
Dude!

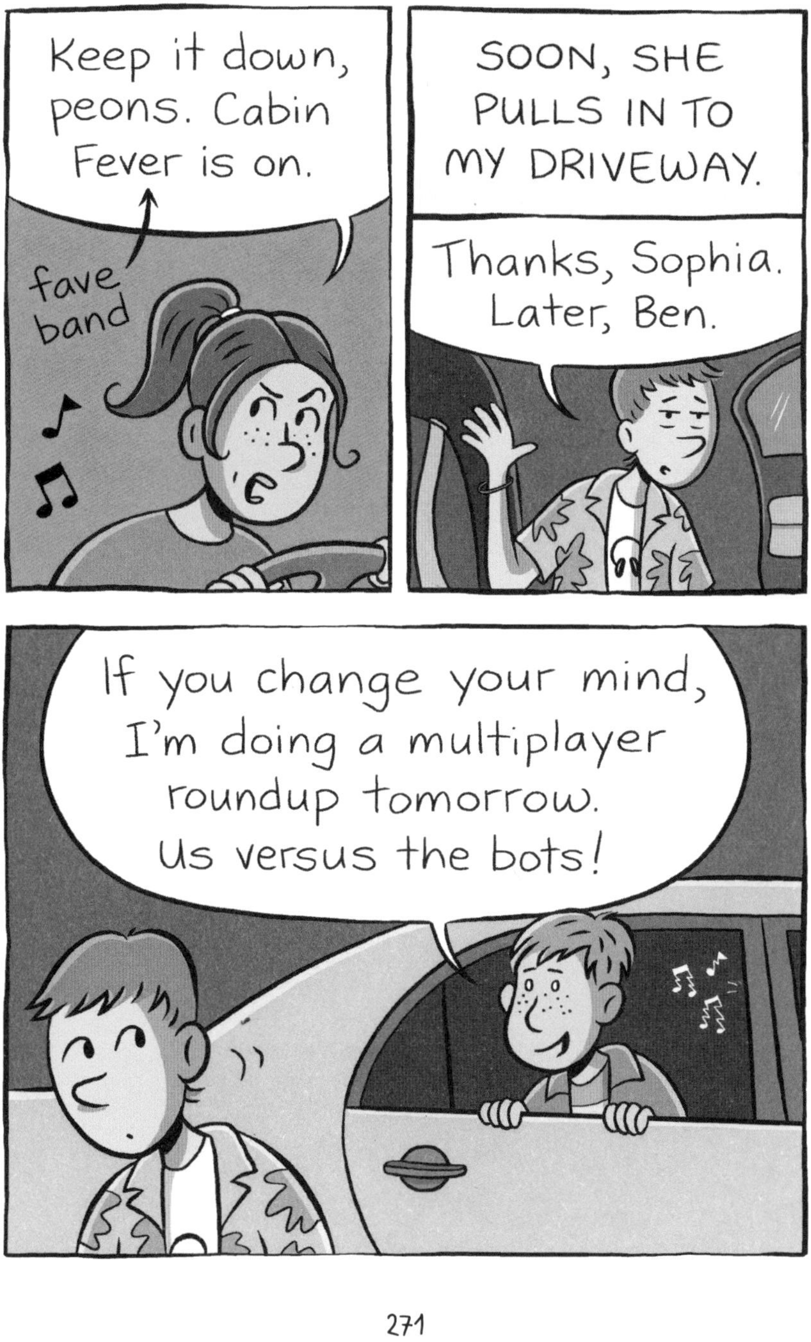
Keep it down, peons. Cabin Fever is on.
fave band
SOON, SHE PULLS IN TO MY DRIVEWAY.
Thanks, Sophia. Later, Ben.
If you change your mind, I'm doing a multiplayer roundup tomorrow. Us versus the bots!

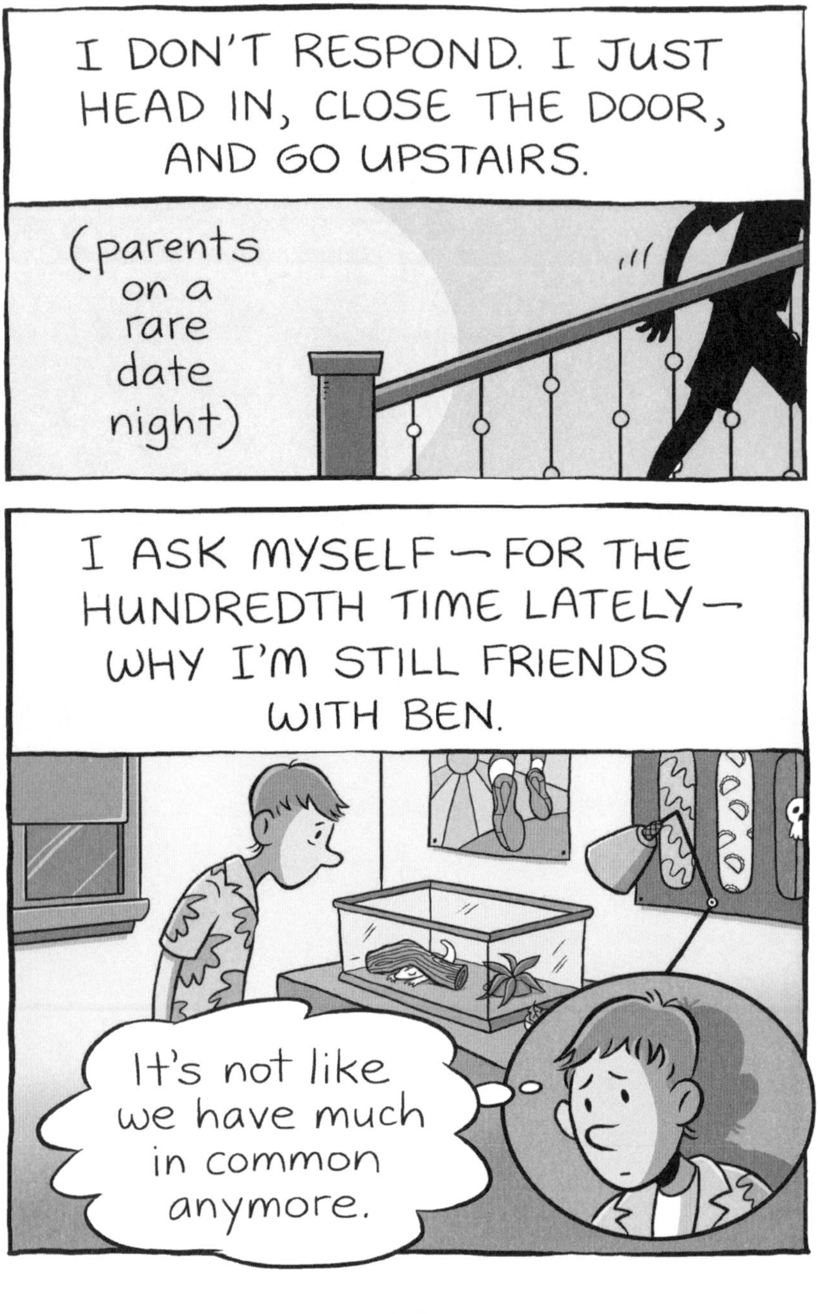
I DON'T RESPOND. I JUST HEAD IN, CLOSE THE DOOR, AND GO UPSTAIRS.
(parents on a rare date night)
I ASK MYSELF—FOR THE HUNDREDTH TIME LATELY—WHY I'M STILL FRIENDS WITH BEN.
It's not like we have much in common anymore.

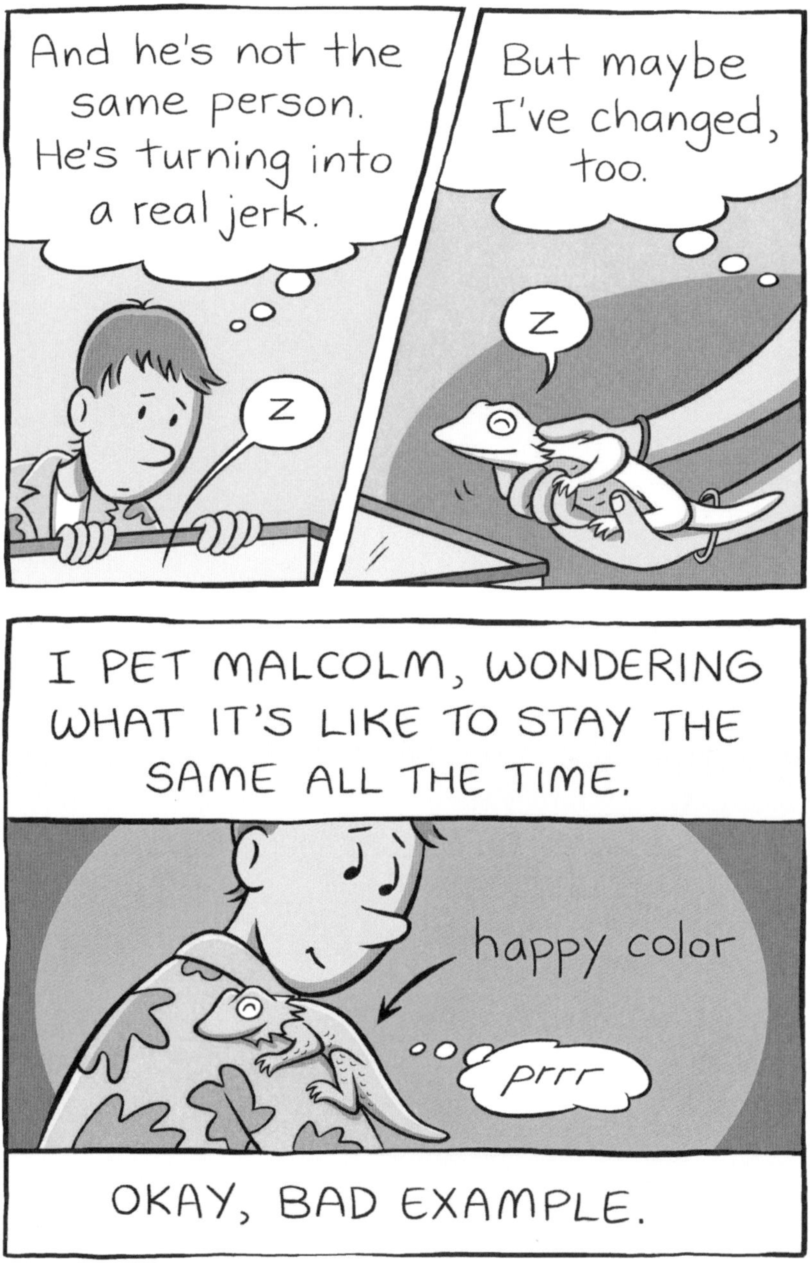
And he's not the same person. He's turning into a real jerk.
Z
But maybe I've changed, too.
Z
I PET MALCOLM, WONDERING WHAT IT'S LIKE TO STAY THE SAME ALL THE TIME.
happy color
prrr
OKAY, BAD EXAMPLE.

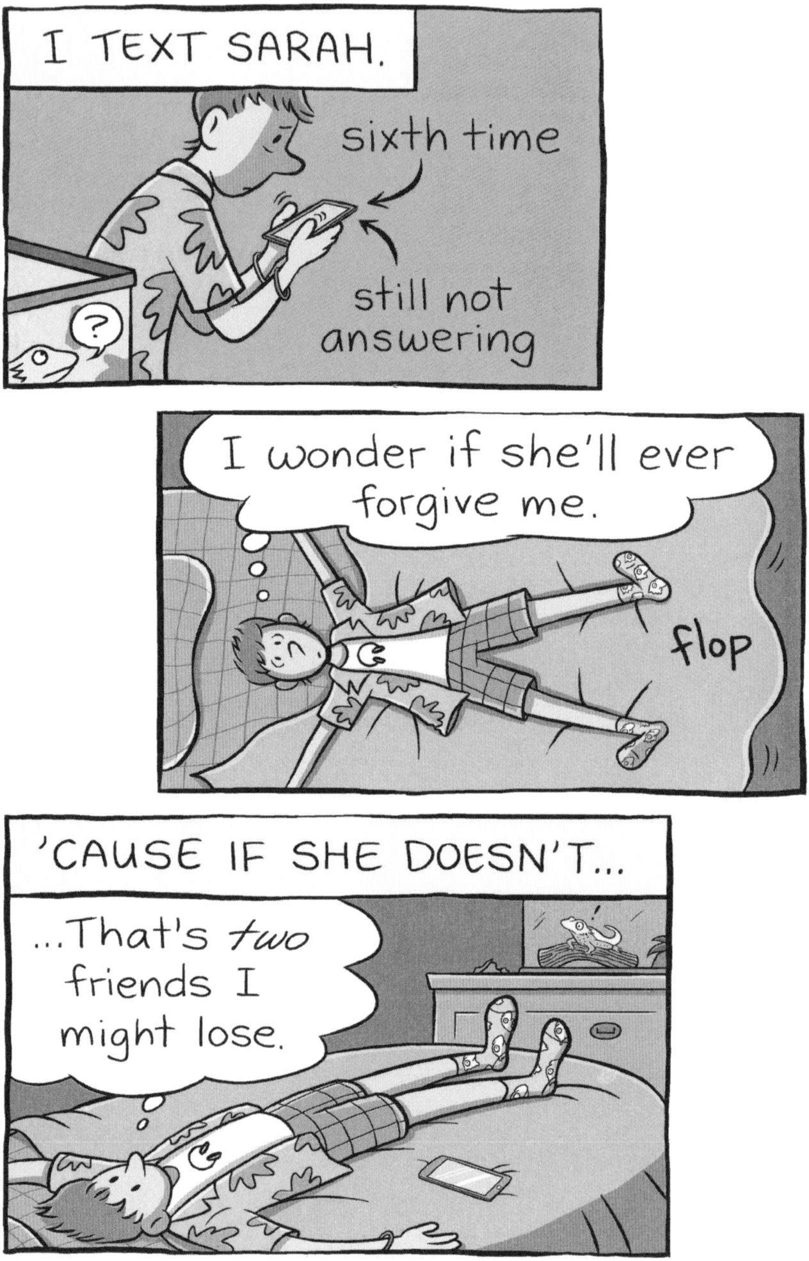
I TEXT SARAH.
sixth time
still not answering
?
I wonder if she'll ever forgive me.
flop
'CAUSE IF SHE DOESN'T...
...That's *two* friends I might lose.
!

SARAH

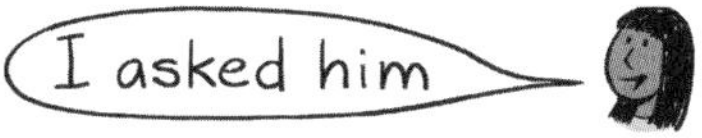
I asked him

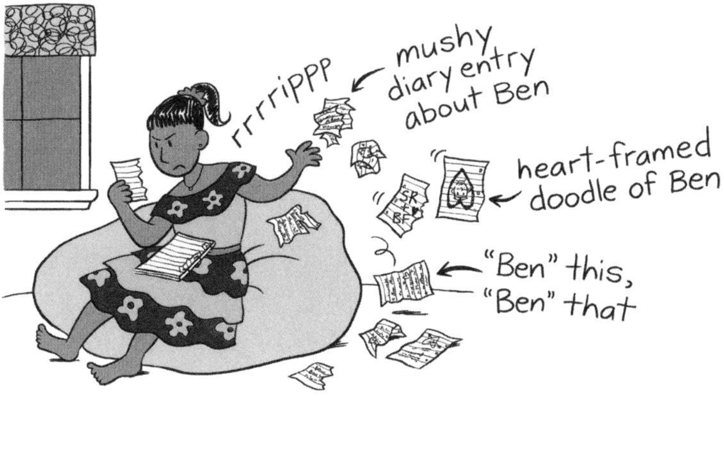
rrrrippp
mushy diary entry about Ben
heart-framed doodle of Ben
SR + BF
"Ben" this, "Ben" that

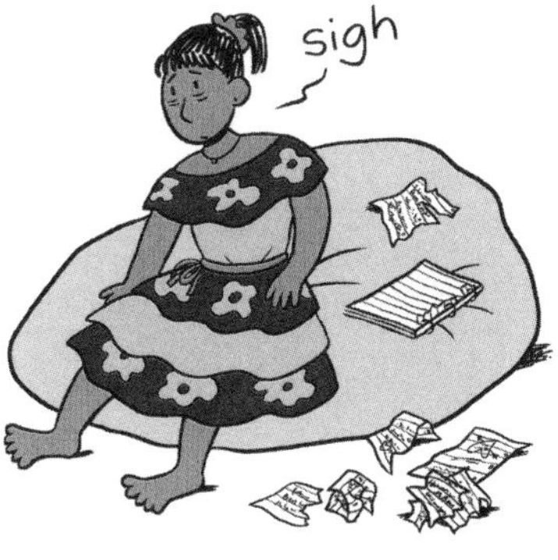
sigh

This was NOT the night I had planned.

I'm still so hung up about Ben. The only reason the dance wasn't a total disaster was 'cause Leo was there.

But something keeps nagging at me: the fact that Leo went from being my best friend to avoiding me to being my best friend again. It makes me feel . . . well . . .

fwuupp   head literally spinning

I don't think he was telling the truth. That he was upset 'cause I kept my crush on Ben a secret. At least, I don't think it's the whole truth. I mean, I know him. He's **not** an avoider. Leo likes to talk things out.

yap yap yap yak yap

...and talk, and talk, and talk..

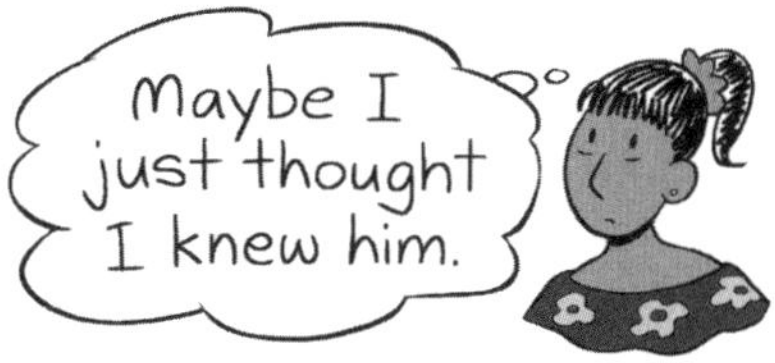
Maybe I just thought I knew him.

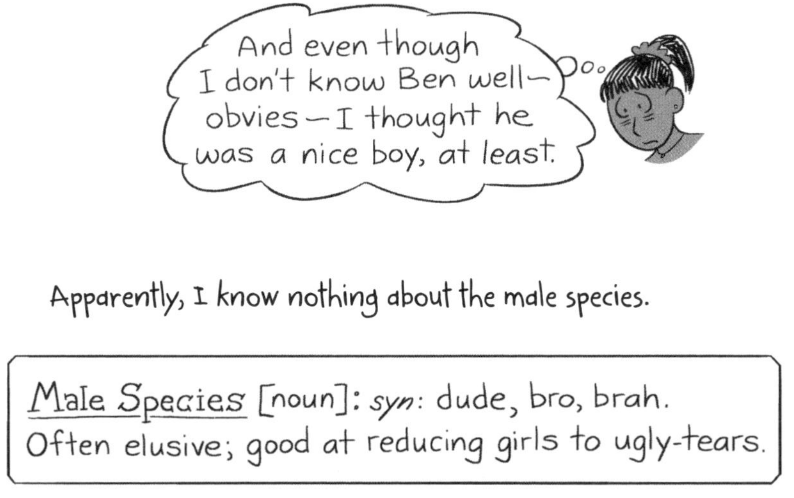
And even though I don't know Ben well—obvies—I thought he was a nice boy, at least.

Apparently, I know nothing about the male species.

<u>Male Species</u> [noun]: *syn:* dude, bro, brah.
Often elusive; good at reducing girls to ugly-tears.

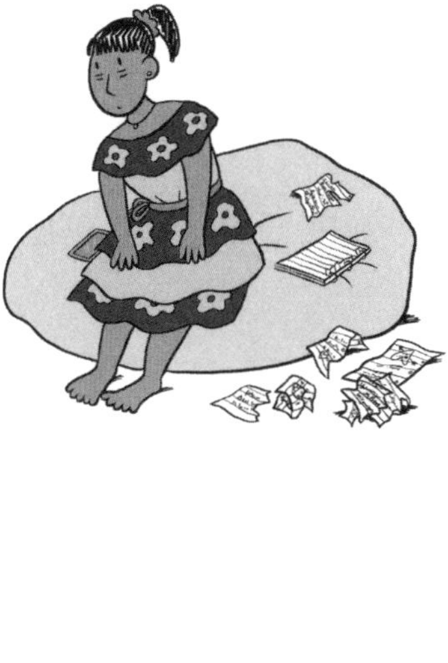

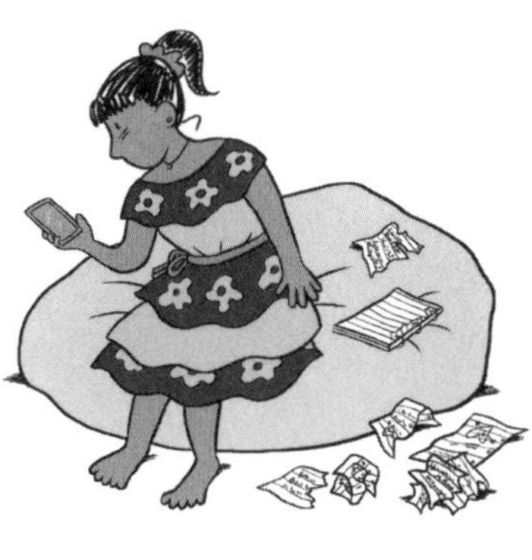

No. Sarah, you can't. Don't even think it.

But, I tell myself, I need to talk things over with someone objective. Someone male. With experience.

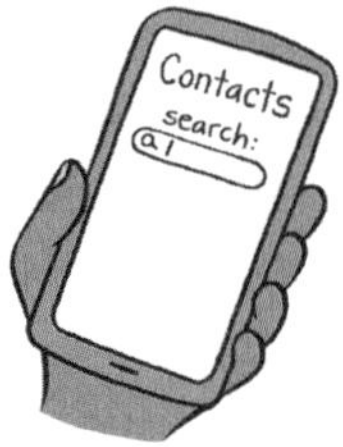
Contacts
search:

BAD, BAD idea.

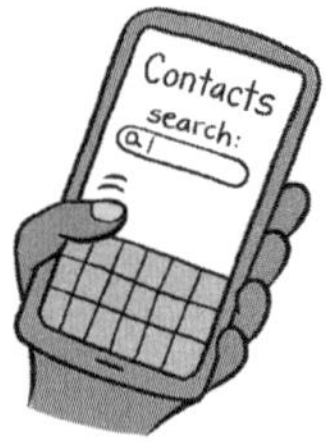
Contacts
search:

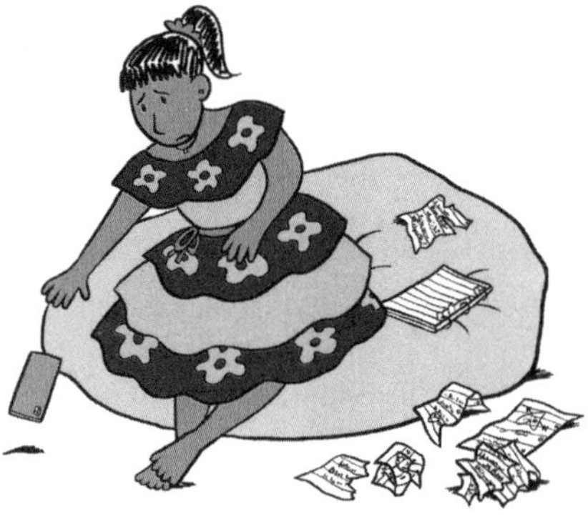

I can't.

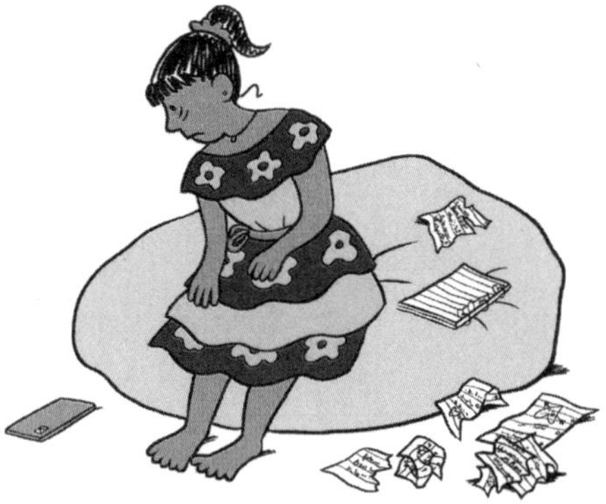

I've tried too many times in the past.

But this is what happens: either my dad's busy at one of his stores, distracted by Sheila and her three labradoodles, or just doesn't know what to say (pretty much like me, that last part).

Also, there's that other thing:

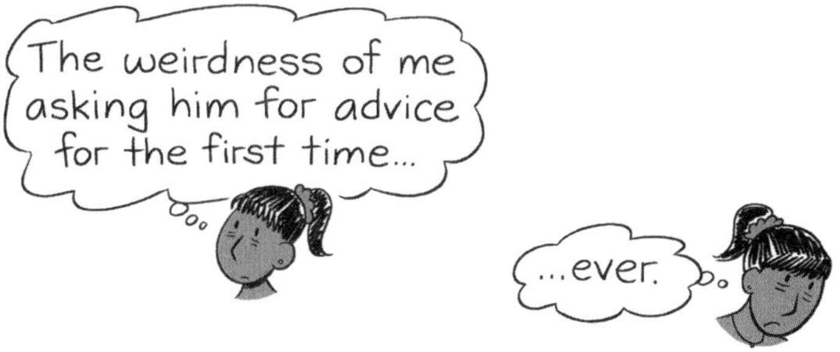
The weirdness of me asking him for advice for the first time...
...ever.

There's just no guy I can go to about all this.

Once in a while, I talk to Leo's parents if Mamá's busy or I need extra advice. But this is just too private.

I admit, sometimes I get jealous of Leo's relationship with his dads 'cause they're so hands-on. Yes, I have Mamá and she's great, but she gets busy. And tired. And I don't want to always bother her. At least with Leo, if one parent isn't around, the other usually is. And although he says they can be . . .

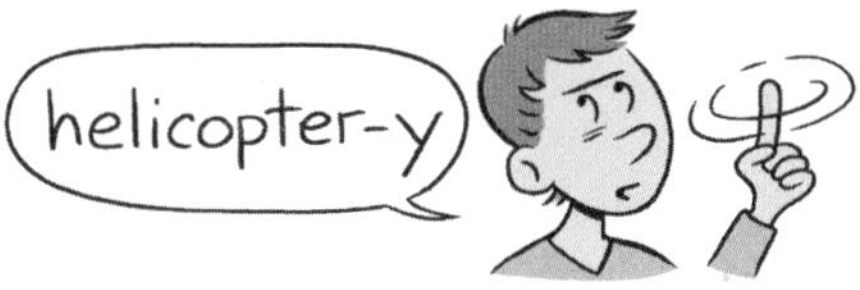
helicopter-y

. . . they are a loving team. Something my mom and dad definitely are **not**.

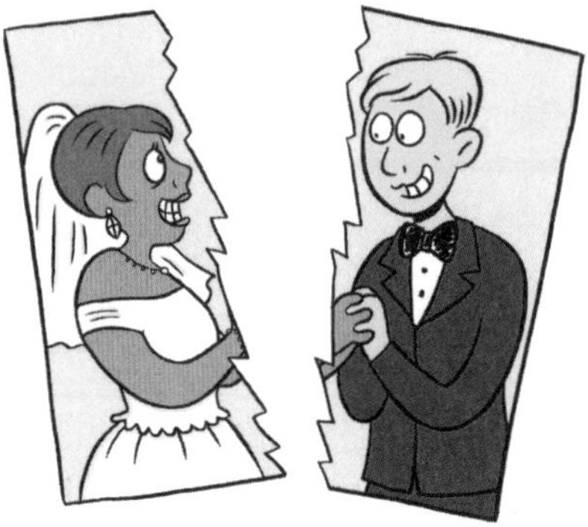

You'd think I'd cry. The fact that I can't (or won't) call my own dad. But I'm so numb, I'm almost—literally—petrified. So I just sit still. Really, really still.

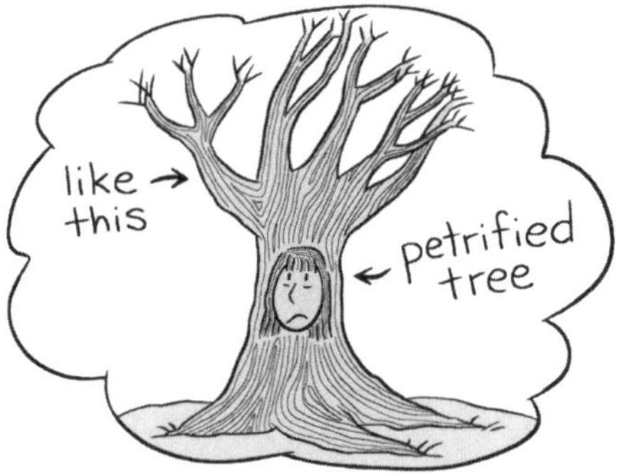
like this
petrified tree

Maybe that's good.

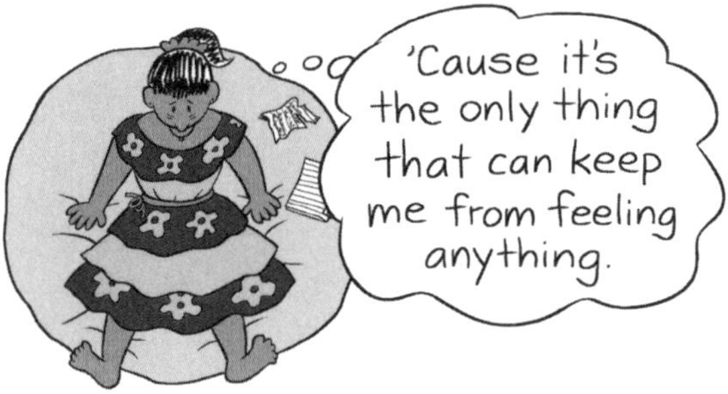
'Cause it's the only thing that can keep me from feeling anything.

Leo

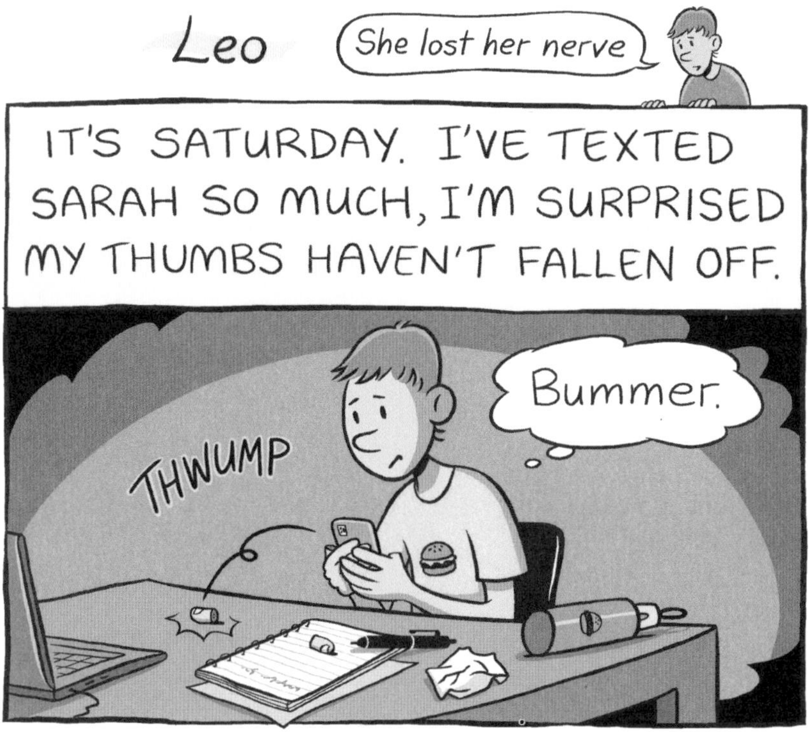
She lost her nerve
IT'S SATURDAY. I'VE TEXTED SARAH SO MUCH, I'M SURPRISED MY THUMBS HAVEN'T FALLEN OFF.
THWUMP
Bummer.

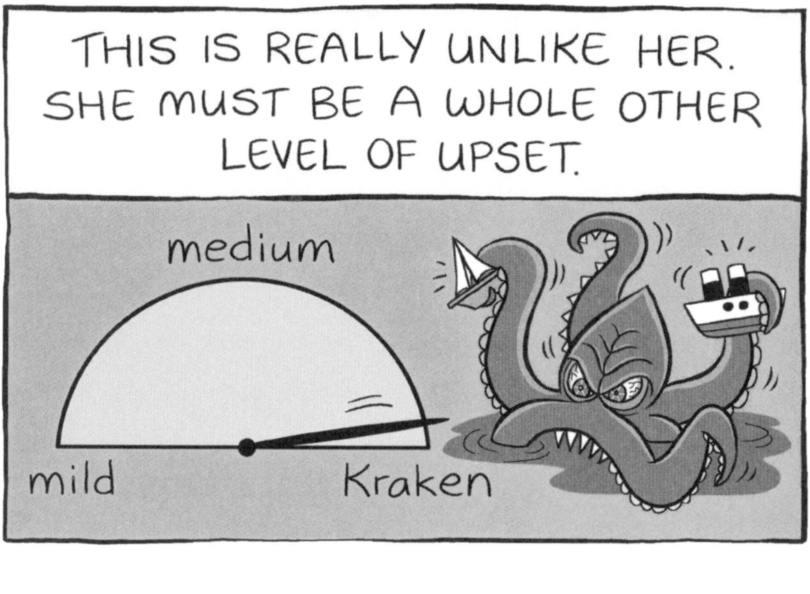
THIS IS REALLY UNLIKE HER. SHE MUST BE A WHOLE OTHER LEVEL OF UPSET.
medium
mild
Kraken

I REALIZE I HAVE TO DO SOMETHING DRASTIC OR I'LL LOSE MY BEST FRIEND.

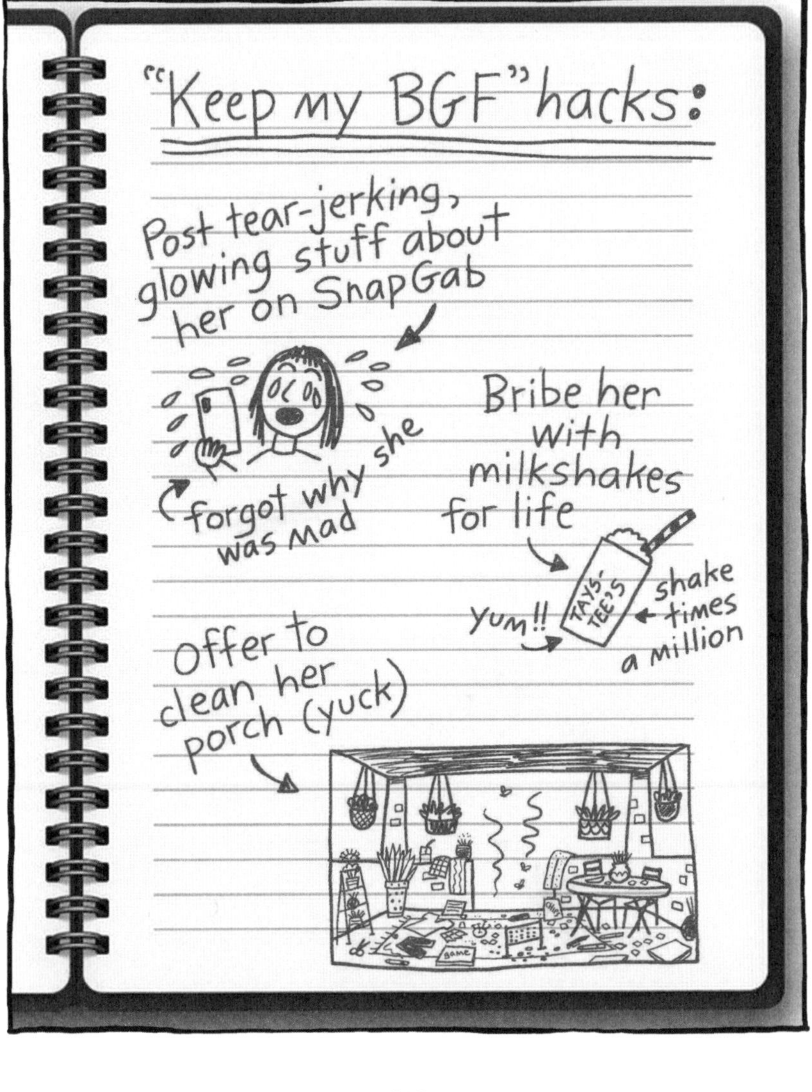
"Keep my BGF" hacks:
Post tear-jerking, glowing stuff about her on SnapGab
forgot why she was mad
Bribe her with milkshakes for life
TAYS-TEE'S
yum!!
shake times a million
Offer to clean her porch (yuck)
GAME

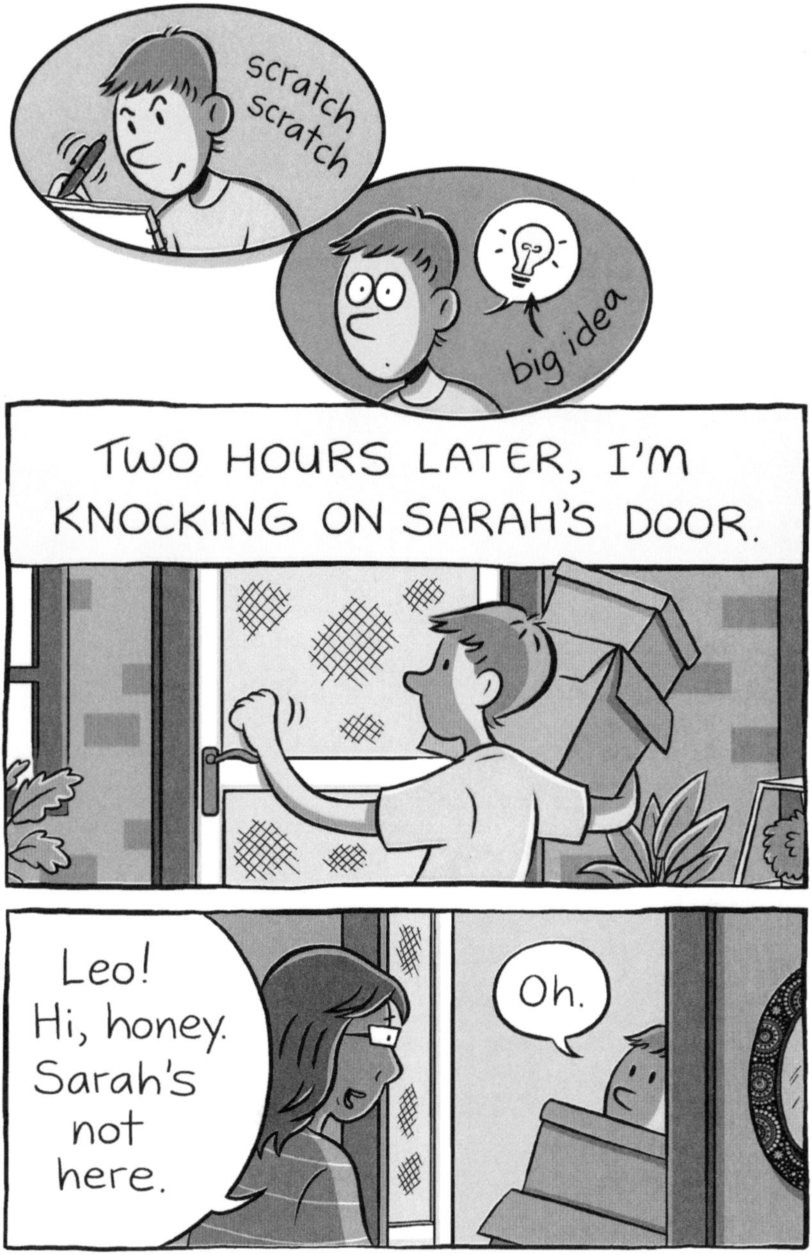
scratch scratch
big idea
TWO HOURS LATER, I'M KNOCKING ON SARAH'S DOOR.
Leo! Hi, honey. Sarah's not here.
Oh.

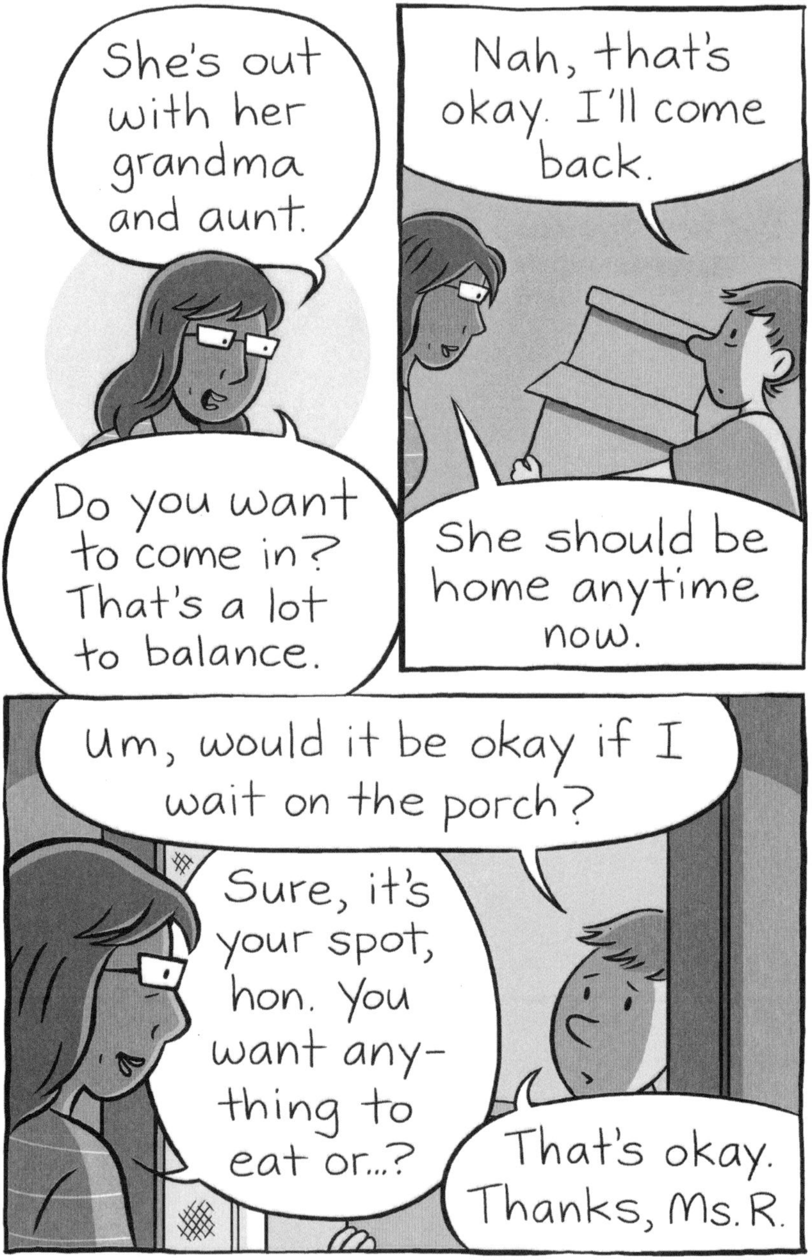
She's out with her grandma and aunt.
Do you want to come in? That's a lot to balance.
Nah, that's okay. I'll come back.
She should be home anytime now.
Um, would it be okay if I wait on the porch?
Sure, it's your spot, hon. You want any-thing to eat or...?
That's okay. Thanks, Ms. R.

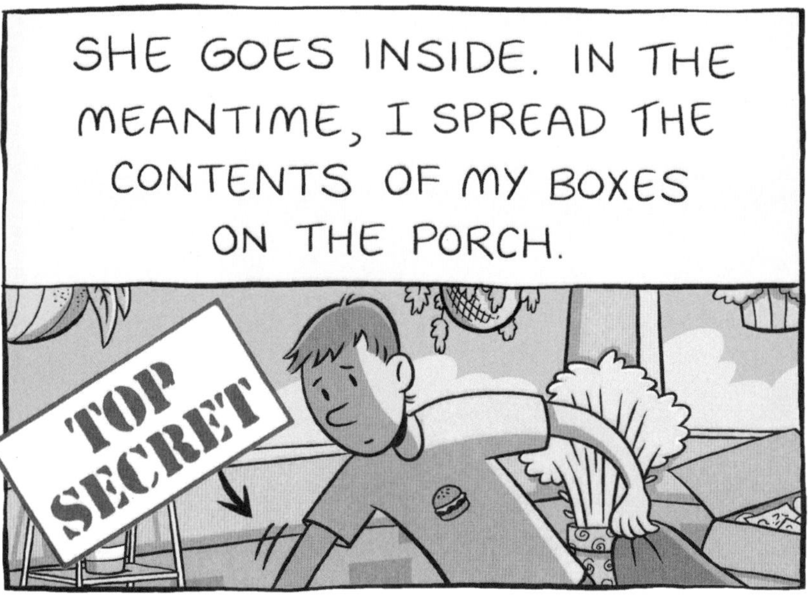
SHE GOES INSIDE. IN THE MEANTIME, I SPREAD THE CONTENTS OF MY BOXES ON THE PORCH.
TOP SECRET

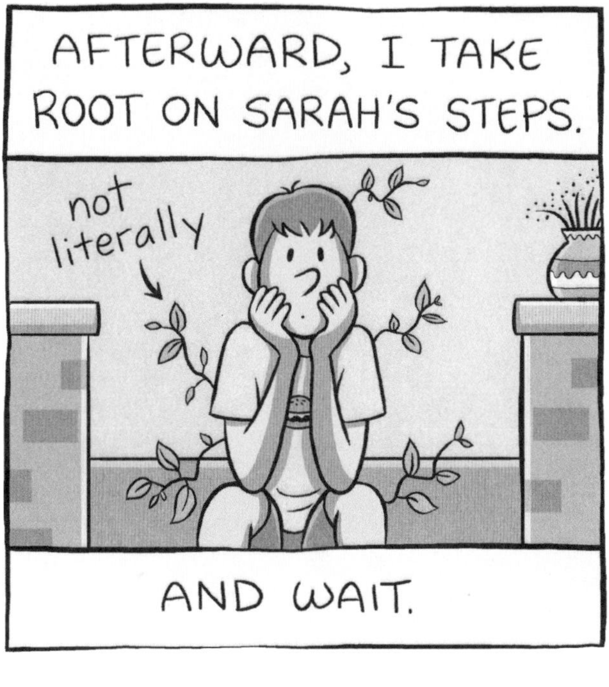
AFTERWARD, I TAKE ROOT ON SARAH'S STEPS.
not literally
AND WAIT.

SARAH

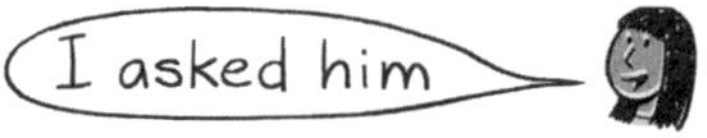
I asked him

Mamá finds me.

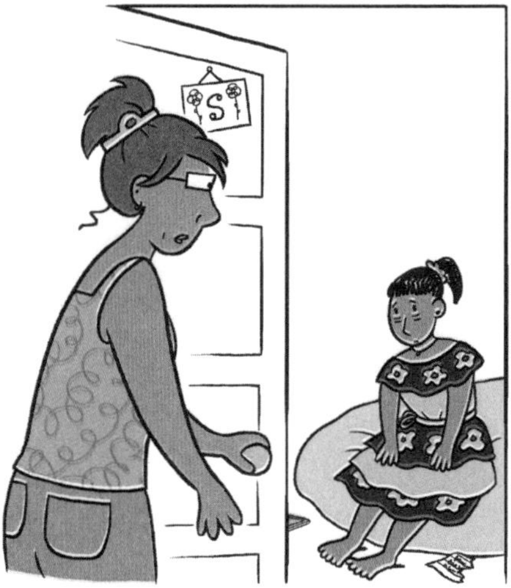

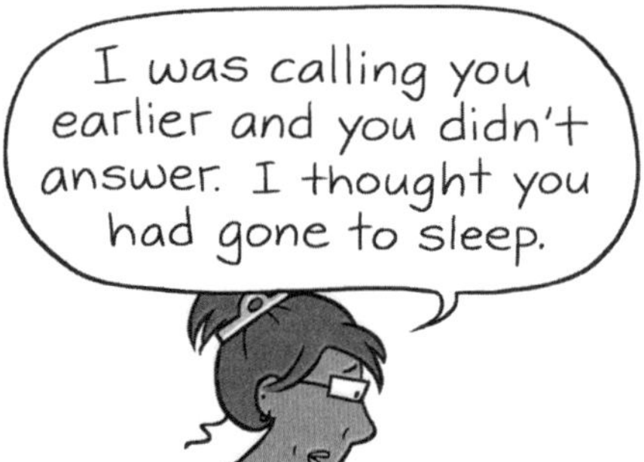
I was calling you earlier and you didn't answer. I thought you had gone to sleep.

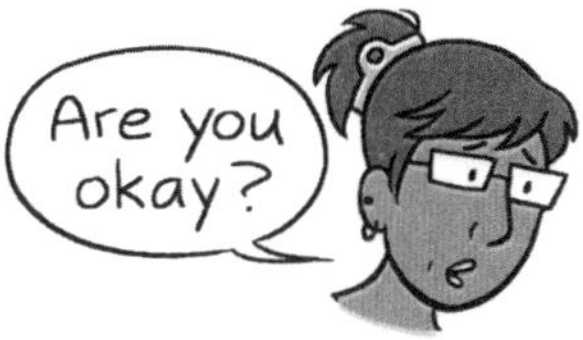
Are you okay?

I say nothing.

Mamá sits next to me on the floor.

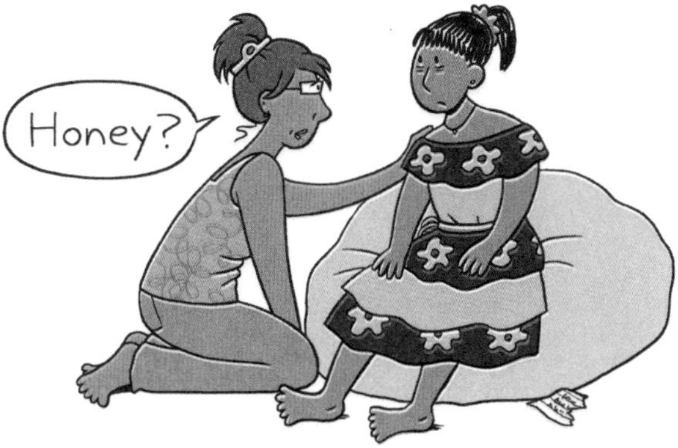
Honey?

I find my voice. Barely.

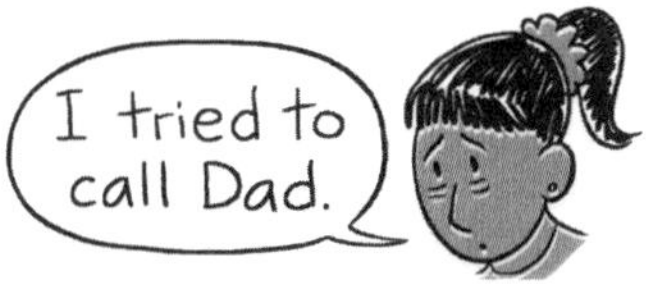
I tried to call Dad.

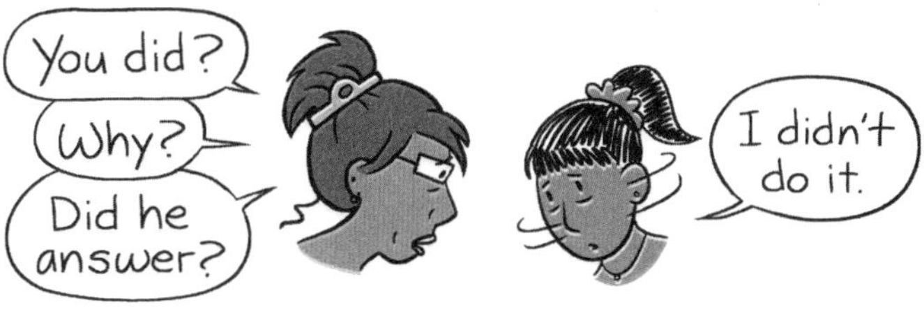
You did?
Why?
Did he answer?
I didn't do it.

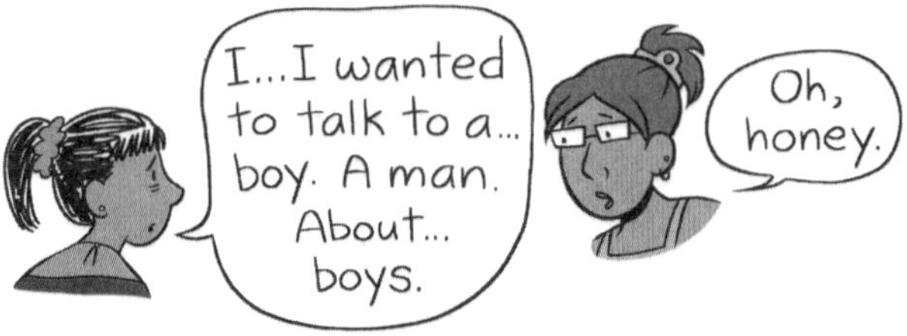
I...I wanted to talk to a... boy. A man. About... boys.
Oh, honey.

Mamá sighs like it's her last breath.

Then she reaches over and hugs me.

I can't even cry. It's like I wasted all my tears on a boy who couldn't care less about me . . . and now I have no tears left for my own dad.

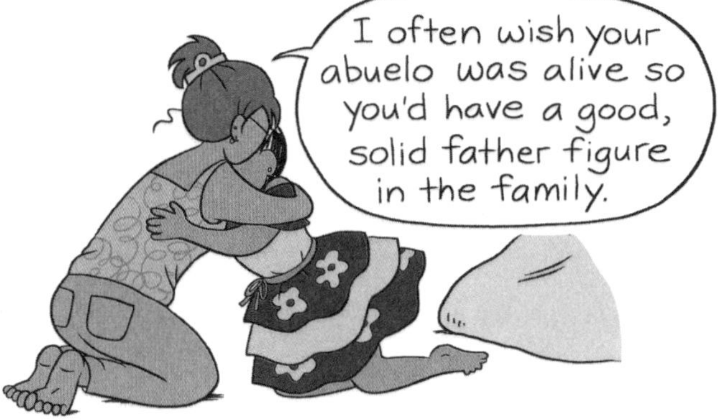
I often wish your abuelo was alive so you'd have a good, solid father figure in the family.

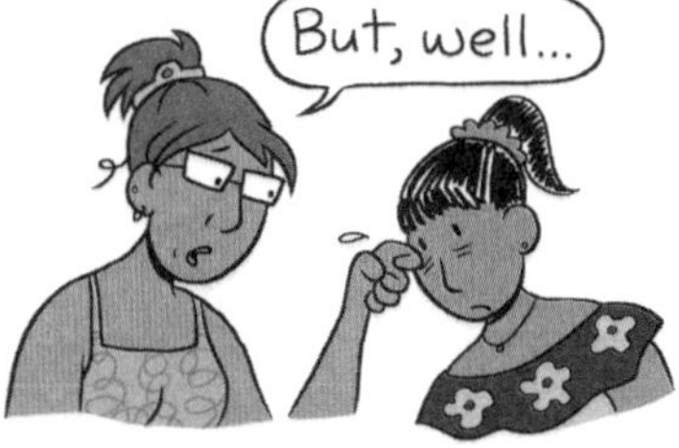
But, well...

Her words trail off.

We're so quiet, I start to notice other sounds.

clock ticking

laptop humming

highway buzzing

heart breaking

Mija, I don't have all the answers.

But I do know one thing.

I look at her.

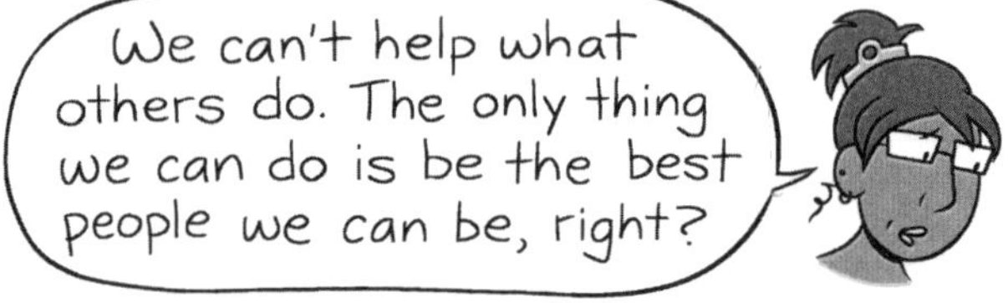
We can't help what others do. The only thing we can do is be the best people we can be, right?

I nod a little.

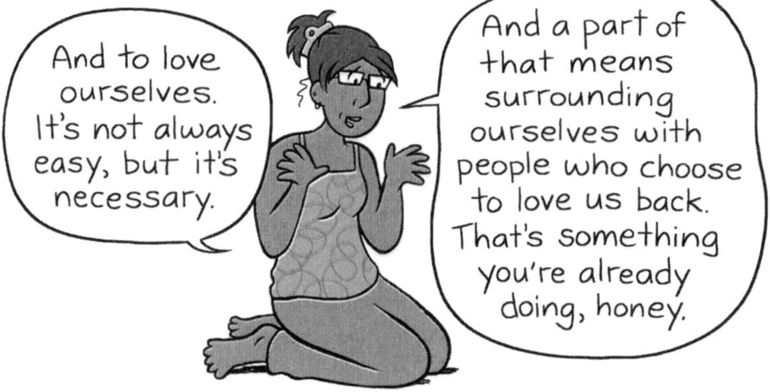
And to love ourselves. It's not always easy, but it's necessary.
And a part of that means surrounding ourselves with people who choose to love us back. That's something you're already doing, honey.

Sniffling, I think of Tía Elena and my grandma—people not of my choosing but who I'm lucky to have in my life.

I think about Emmie and Brianna. Friends I chose who chose me back.

And I think about Leo.

Mamá's right. I can't help it if some people aren't willing to share their lives with me. But I have plenty who do.

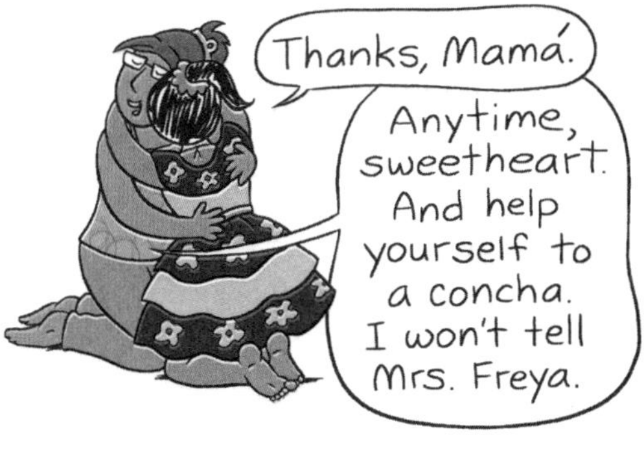
Thanks, Mamá.
Anytime, sweetheart. And help yourself to a concha. I won't tell Mrs. Freya.

I think I know what to do now.

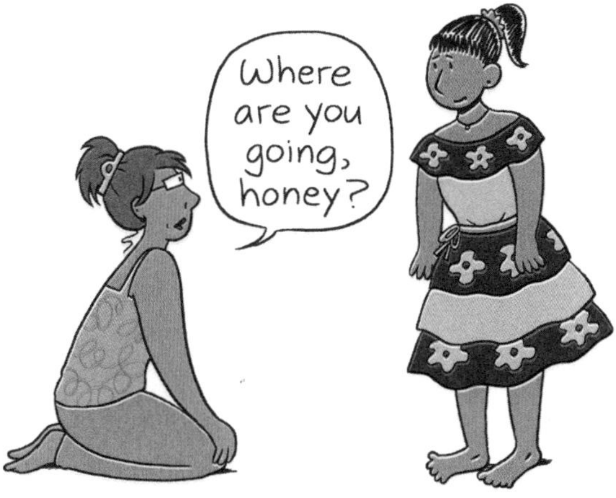
Where are you going, honey?

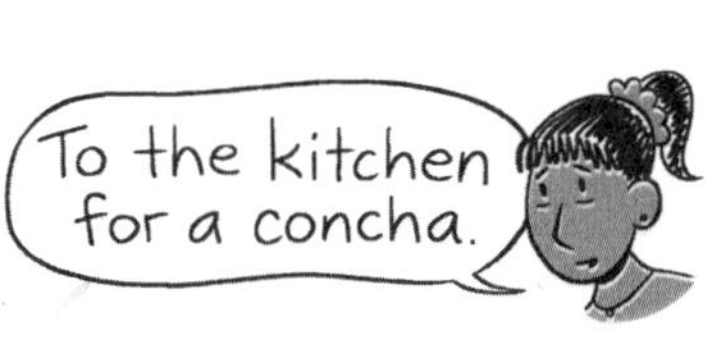
To the kitchen for a concha.

Mamá chuckles and squeezes me as we head downstairs.

And then...

...to Leo's.

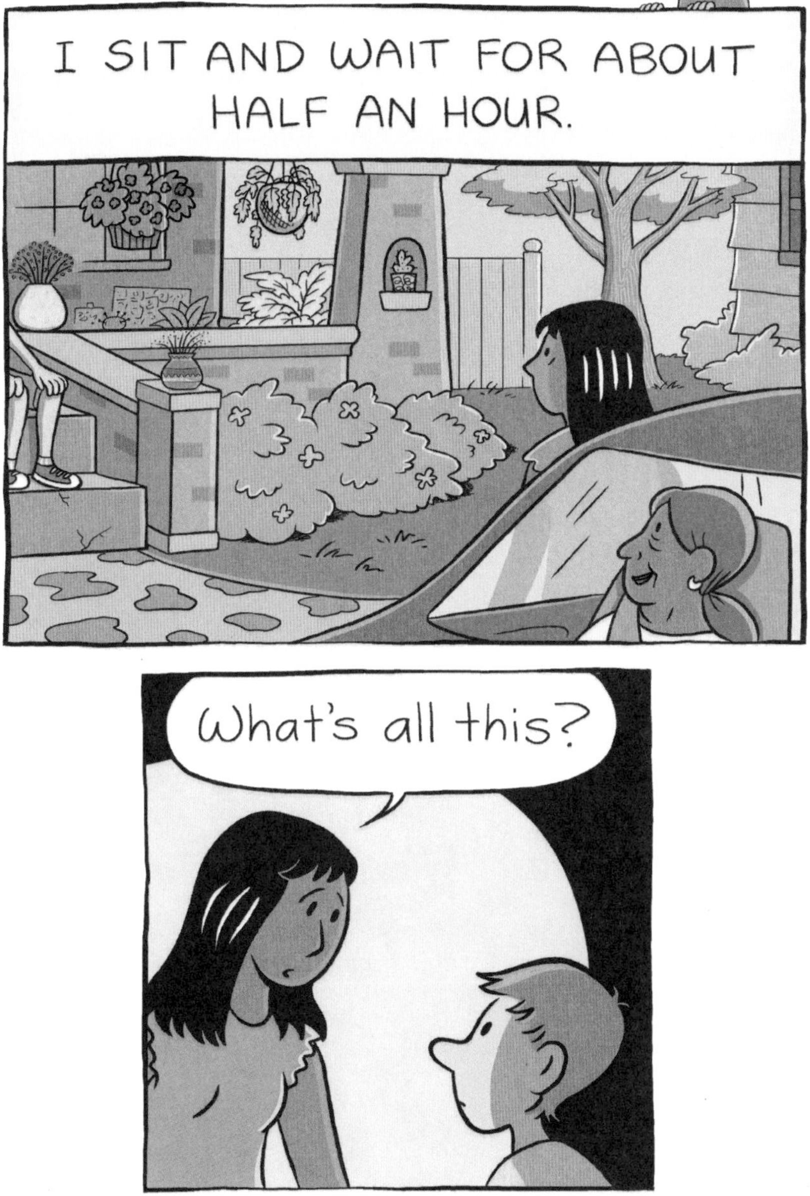
I SIT AND WAIT FOR ABOUT HALF AN HOUR.
What's all this?

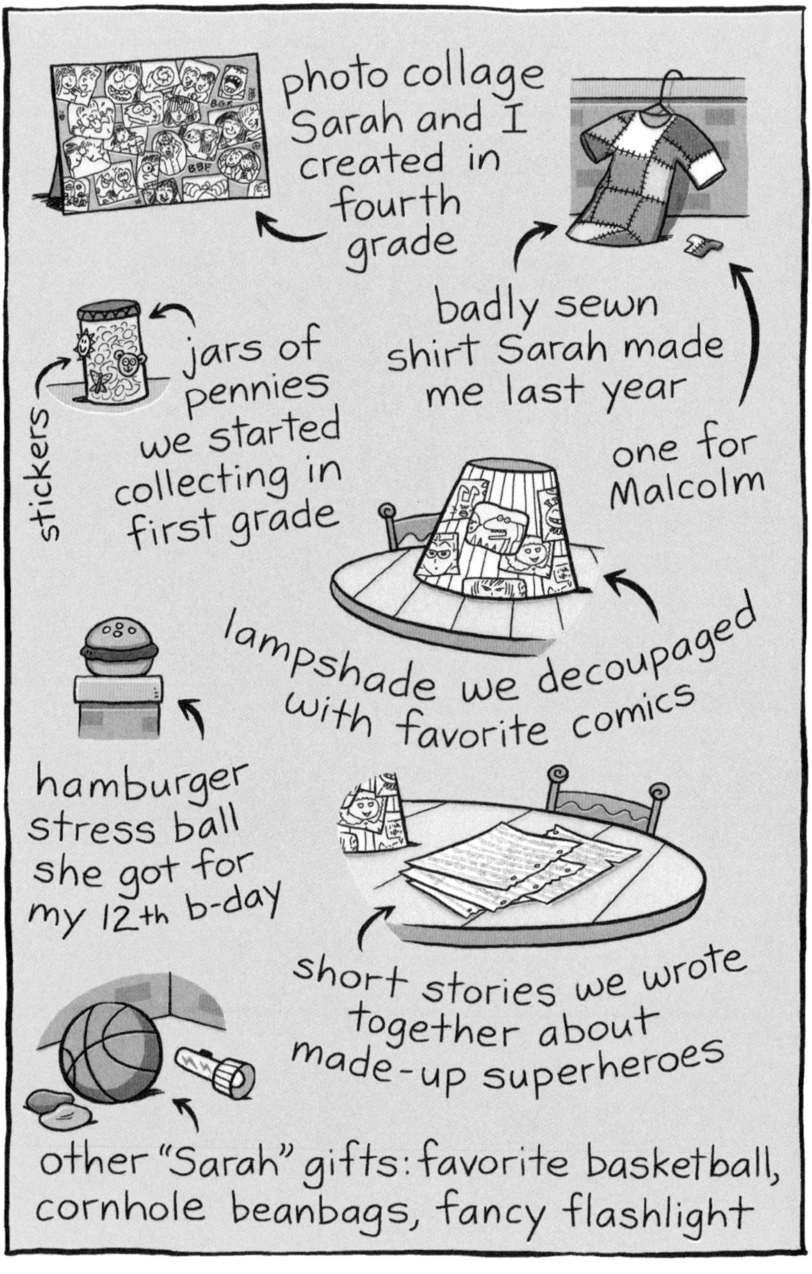
photo collage Sarah and I created in fourth grade
badly sewn shirt Sarah made me last year
jars of pennies we started collecting in first grade
stickers
one for Malcolm
lampshade we decoupaged with favorite comics
hamburger stress ball she got for my 12th b-day
short stories we wrote together about made-up superheroes
other "Sarah" gifts: favorite basketball, cornhole beanbags, fancy flashlight

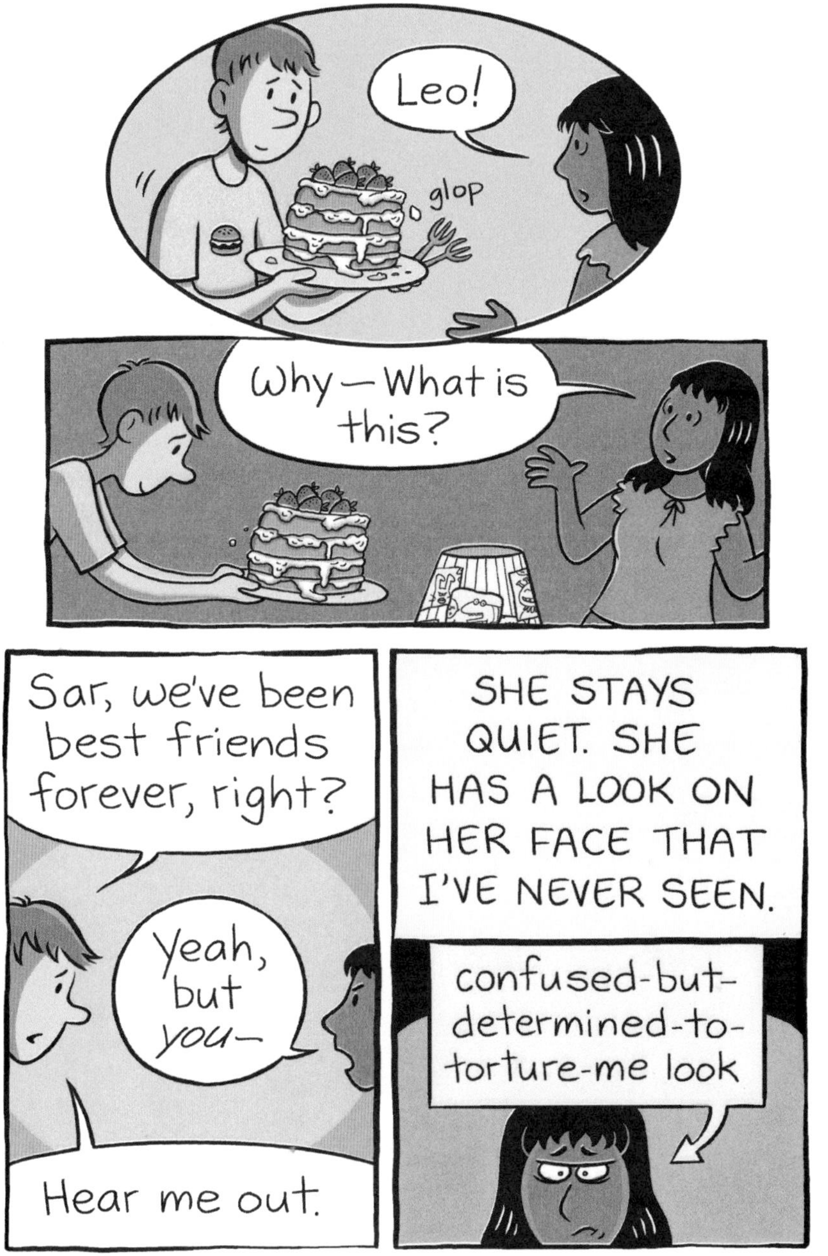
Leo!
glop
Why—What is this?
Sar, we've been best friends forever, right?
Yeah, but you—
Hear me out.
SHE STAYS QUIET. SHE HAS A LOOK ON HER FACE THAT I'VE NEVER SEEN.
confused-but-determined-to-torture-me look

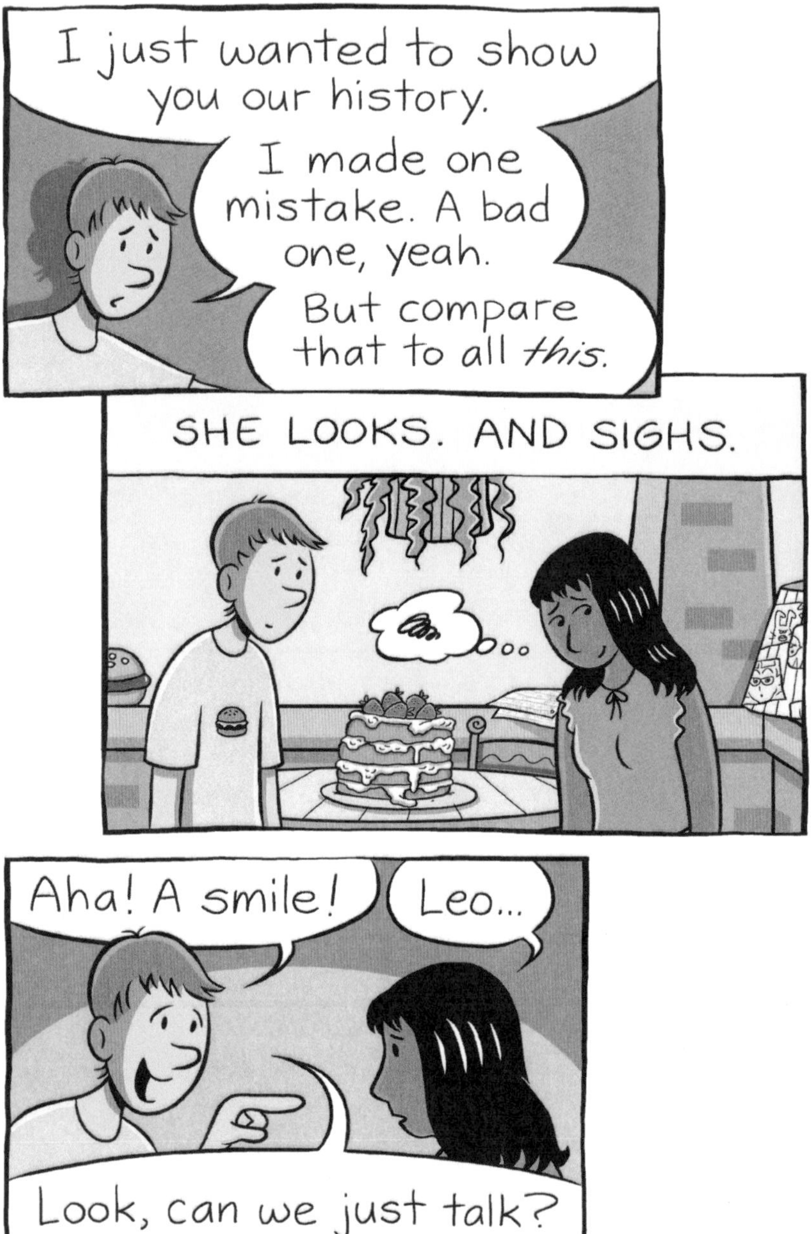
I just wanted to show you our history.
I made one mistake. A bad one, yeah.
But compare that to all *this*.
SHE LOOKS. AND SIGHS.
Aha! A smile!
Leo...
Look, can we just talk?

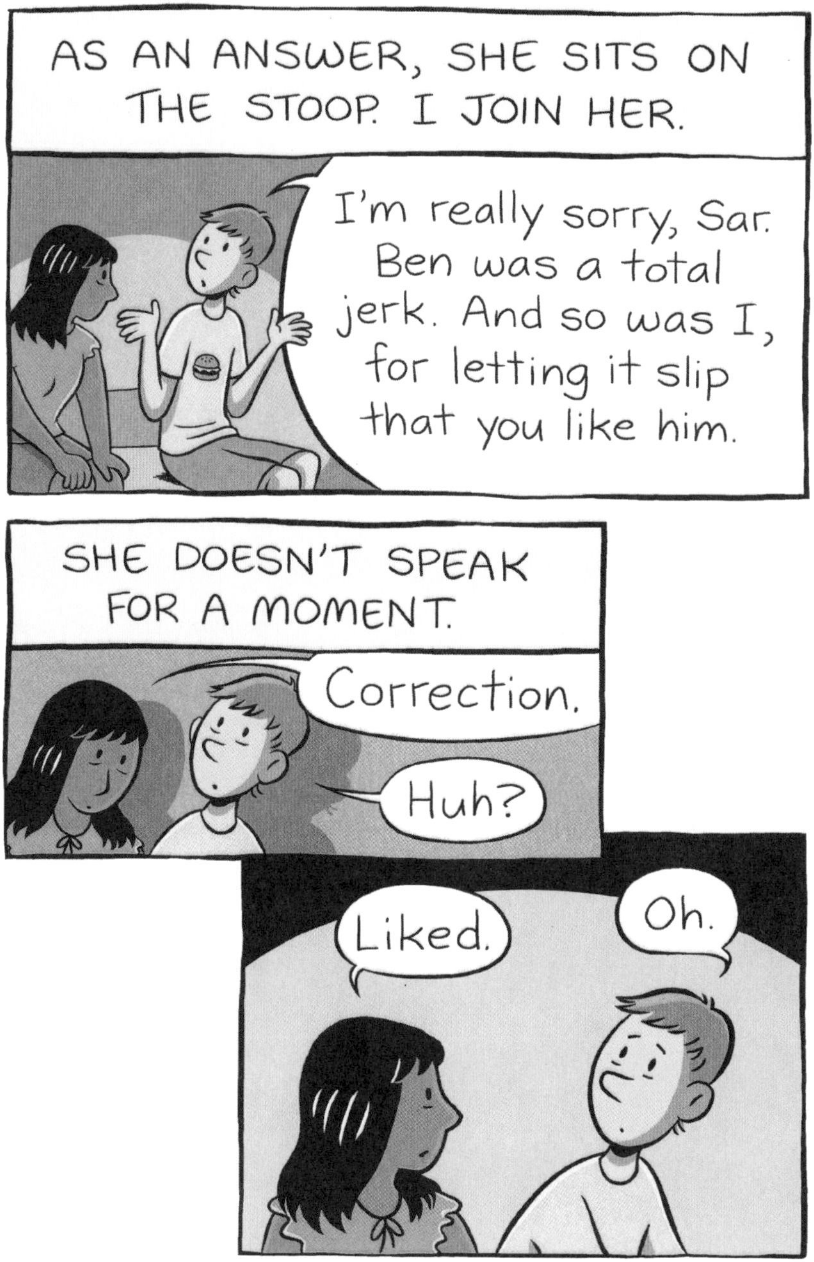

AS AN ANSWER, SHE SITS ON THE STOOP. I JOIN HER.
I'm really sorry, Sar. Ben was a total jerk. And so was I, for letting it slip that you like him.
SHE DOESN'T SPEAK FOR A MOMENT.
Correction.
Huh?
Liked.
Oh.

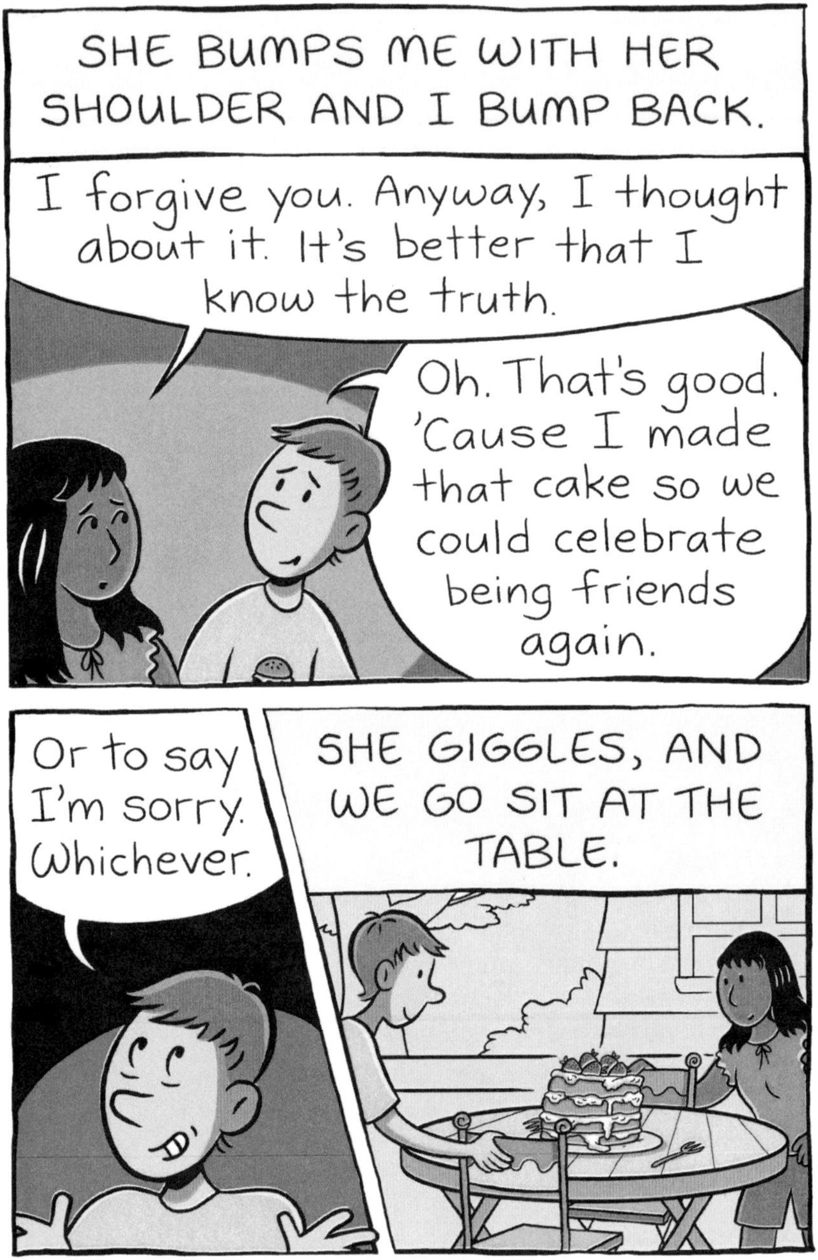
SHE BUMPS ME WITH HER SHOULDER AND I BUMP BACK.
I forgive you. Anyway, I thought about it. It's better that I know the truth.
Oh. That's good. 'Cause I made that cake so we could celebrate being friends again.
Or to say I'm sorry. Whichever.
SHE GIGGLES, AND WE GO SIT AT THE TABLE.

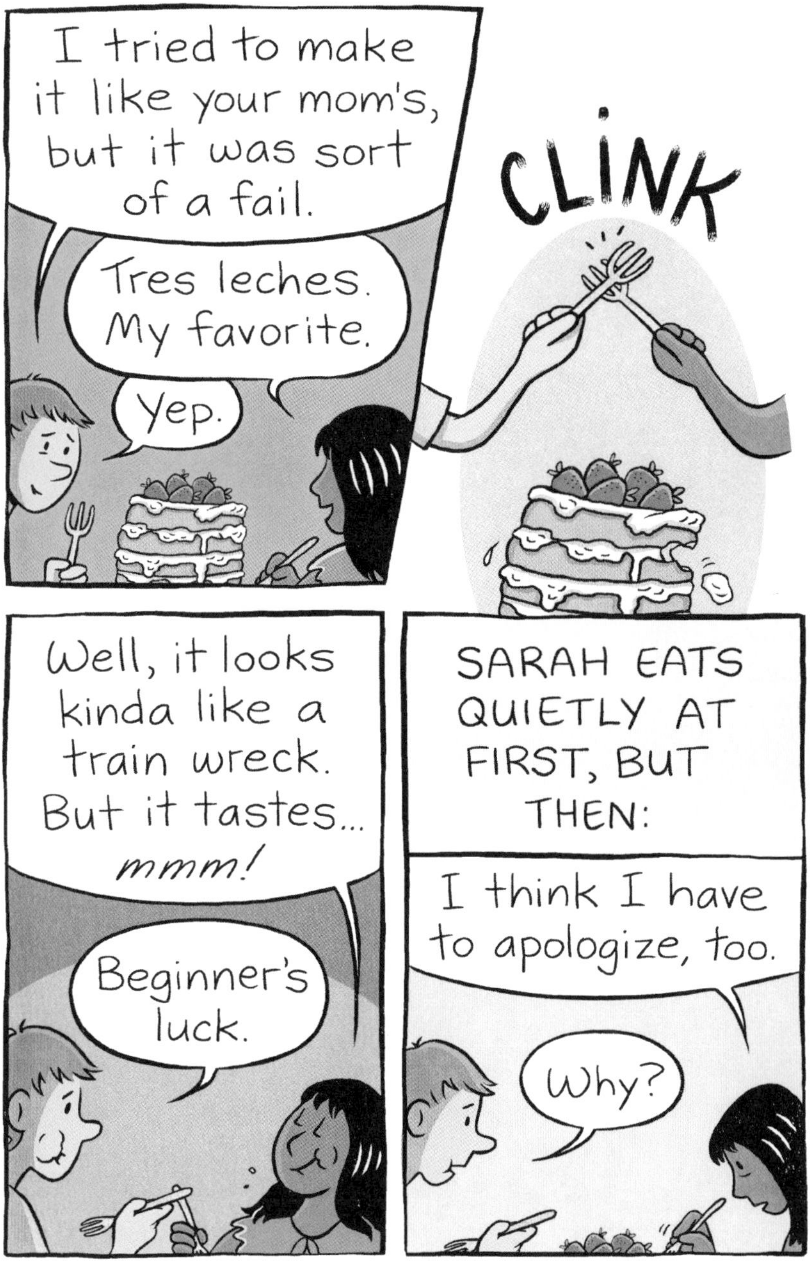
I tried to make it like your mom's, but it was sort of a fail.
Tres leches. My favorite.
Yep.
CLINK
Well, it looks kinda like a train wreck. But it tastes... mmm!
Beginner's luck.
SARAH EATS QUIETLY AT FIRST, BUT THEN:
I think I have to apologize, too.
Why?

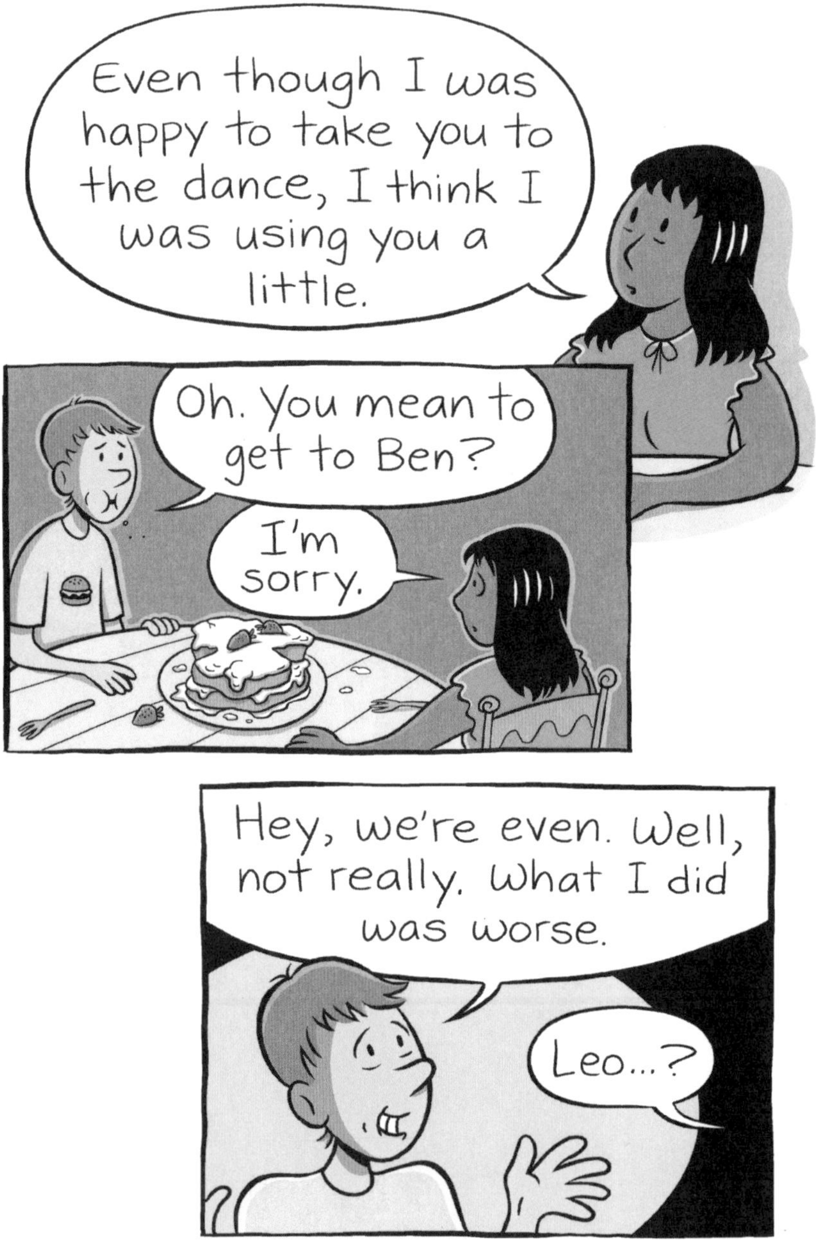
Even though I was happy to take you to the dance, I think I was using you a little.
Oh. You mean to get to Ben?
I'm sorry.
Hey, we're even. Well, not really. What I did was worse.
Leo...?

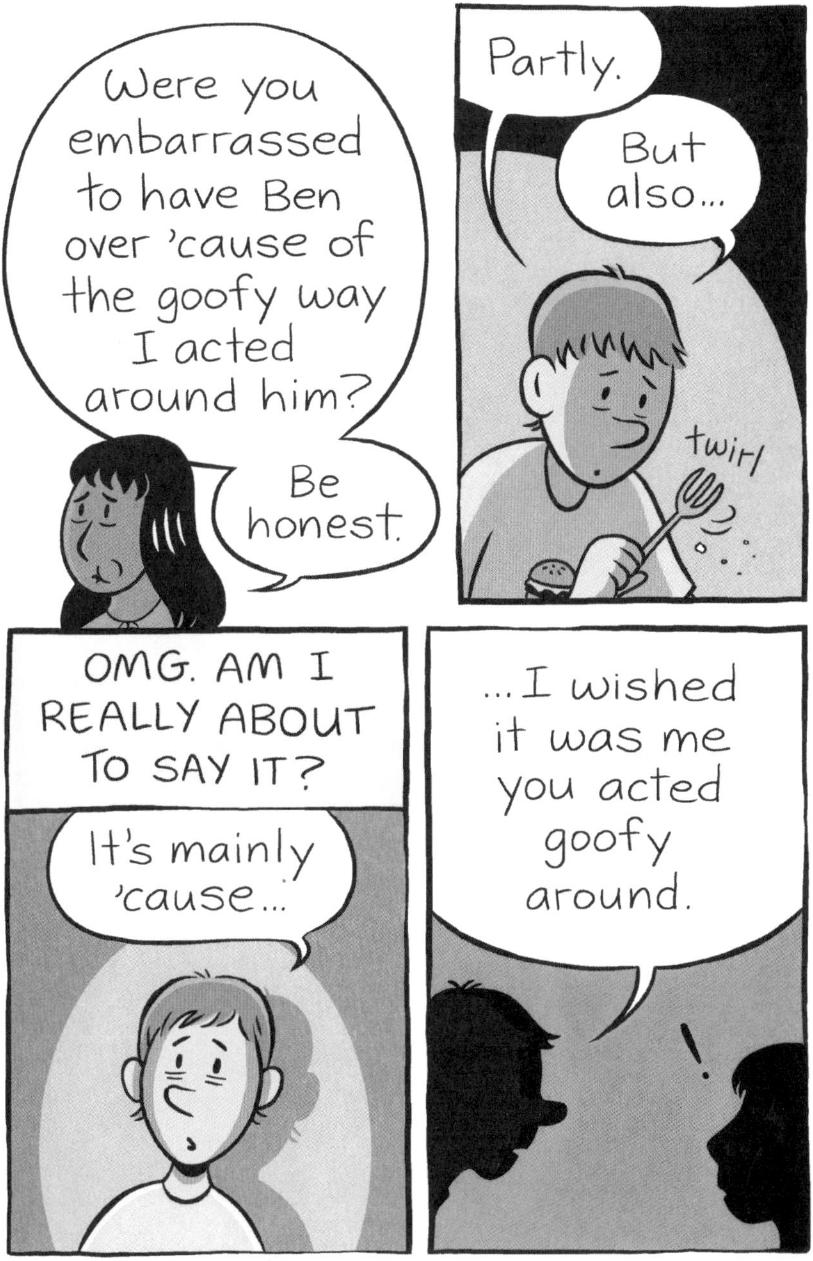
Were you embarrassed to have Ben over 'cause of the goofy way I acted around him?
Be honest.
Partly.
But also...
twirl
OMG. AM I REALLY ABOUT TO SAY IT?
It's mainly 'cause...
...I wished it was me you acted goofy around.
!

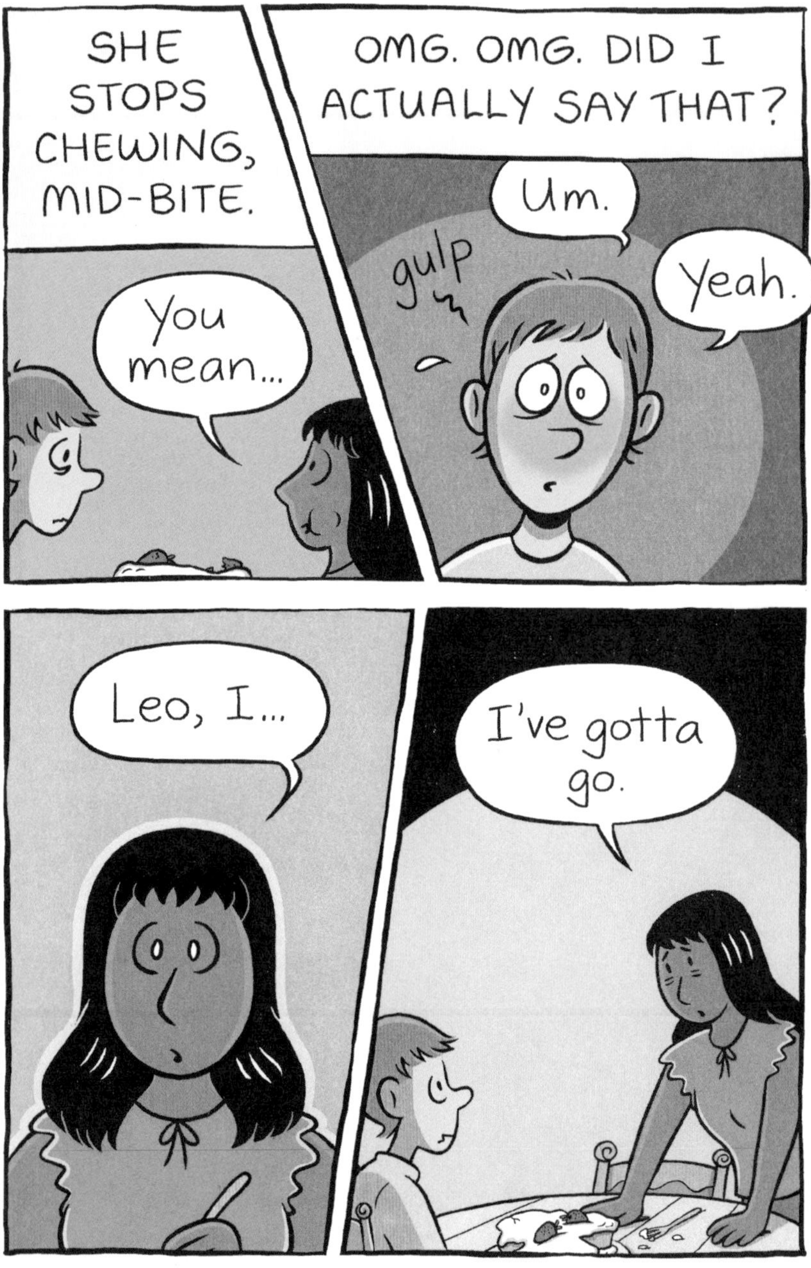
SHE STOPS CHEWING, MID-BITE.
You mean...
OMG. OMG. DID I ACTUALLY SAY THAT?
Um.
gulp
Yeah.
Leo, I...
I've gotta go.

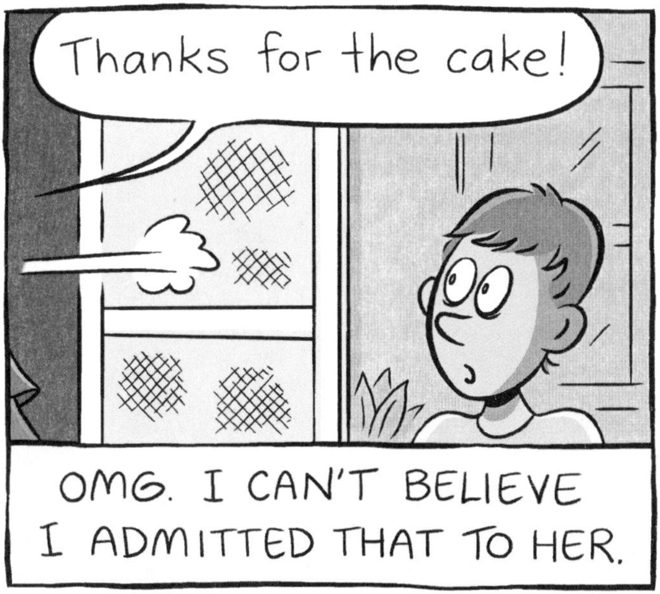
Thanks for the cake!
OMG. I CAN'T BELIEVE I ADMITTED THAT TO HER.

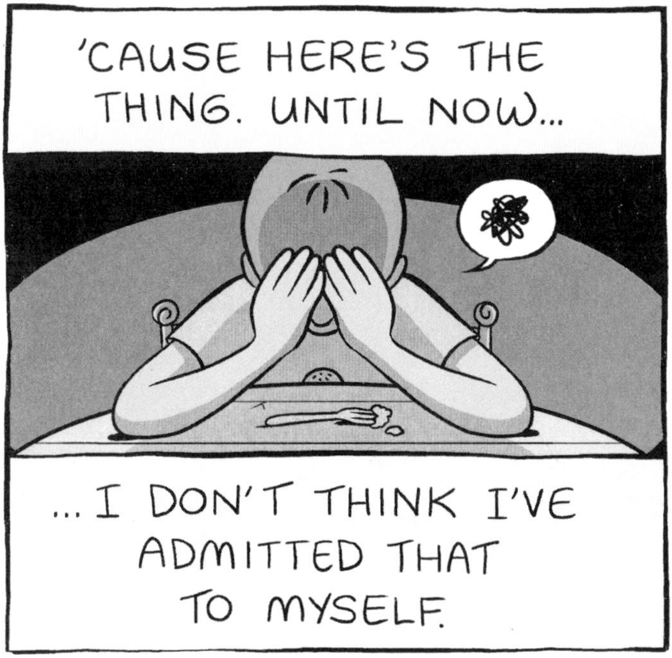
'CAUSE HERE'S THE THING. UNTIL NOW...
...I DON'T THINK I'VE ADMITTED THAT TO MYSELF.

SARAH

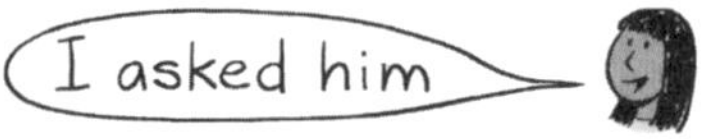
I asked him

For once, we're sitting on his stoop and talking.

(hey, change can be good)

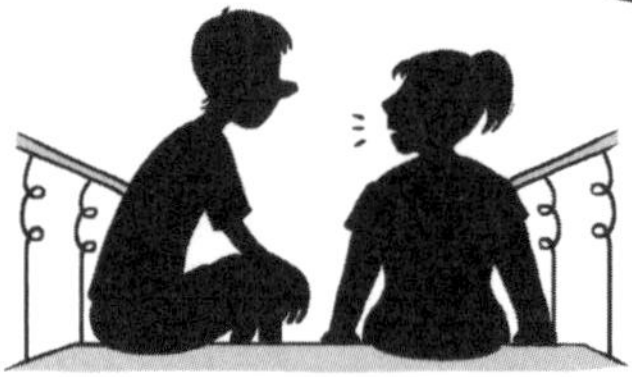

I told him about the (failed) call to my dad. And how bad I'm really feeling about everything.

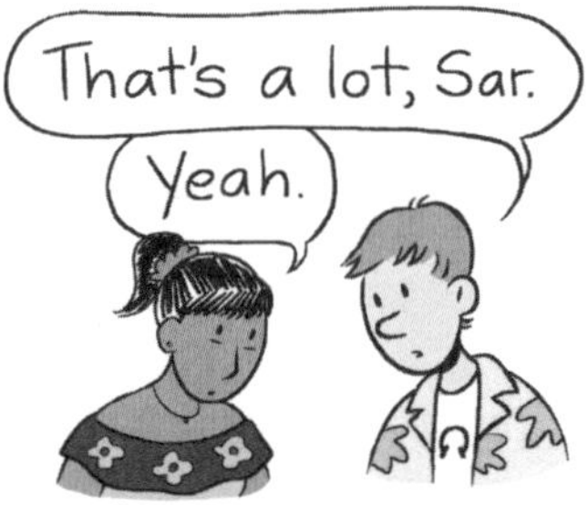
That's a lot, Sar.
Yeah.

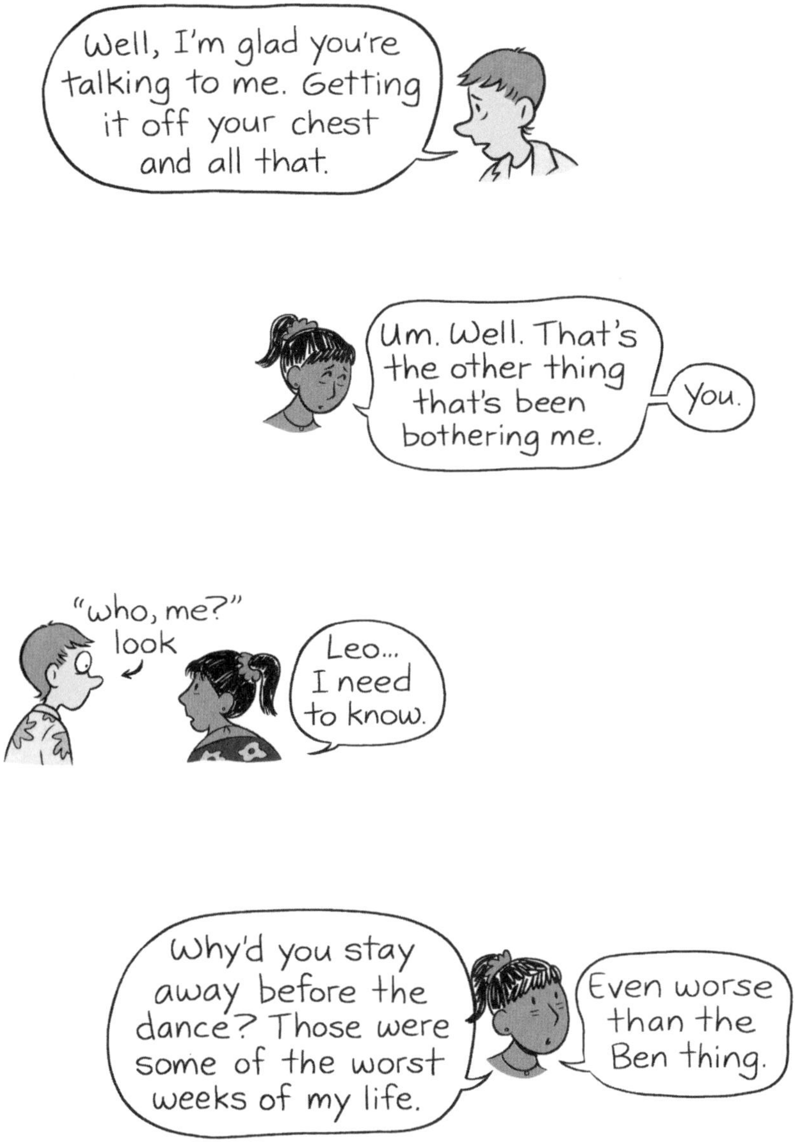
Well, I'm glad you're talking to me. Getting it off your chest and all that.
Um. Well. That's the other thing that's been bothering me.
You.
"who, me?" look
Leo... I need to know.
Why'd you stay away before the dance? Those were some of the worst weeks of my life.
Even worse than the Ben thing.

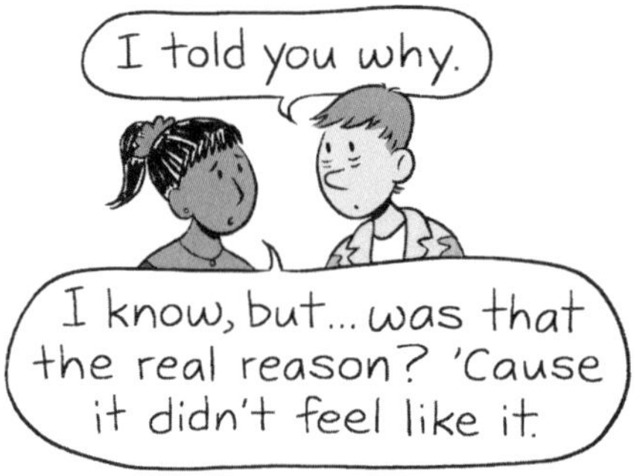
I told you why.
I know, but... was that the real reason? 'Cause it didn't feel like it.

He doesn't respond. I try not to say anything, because it looks like he's gathering his thoughts.

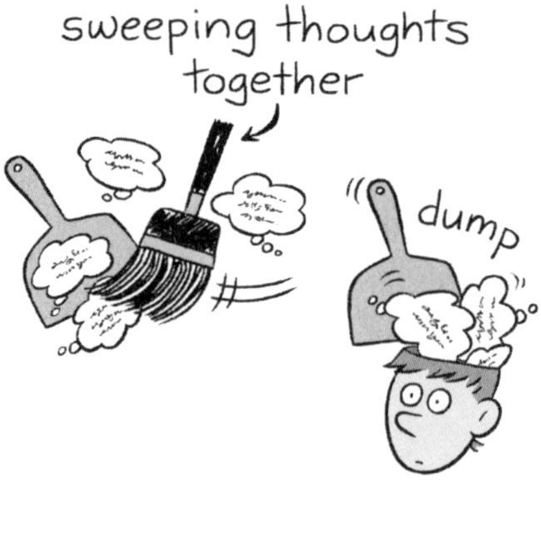
sweeping thoughts together
dump

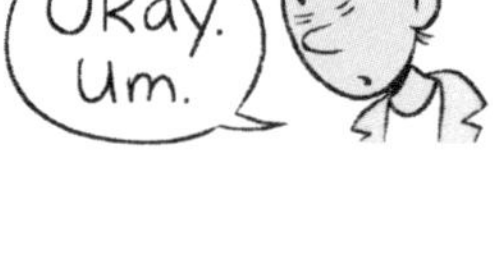
Okay. Um.

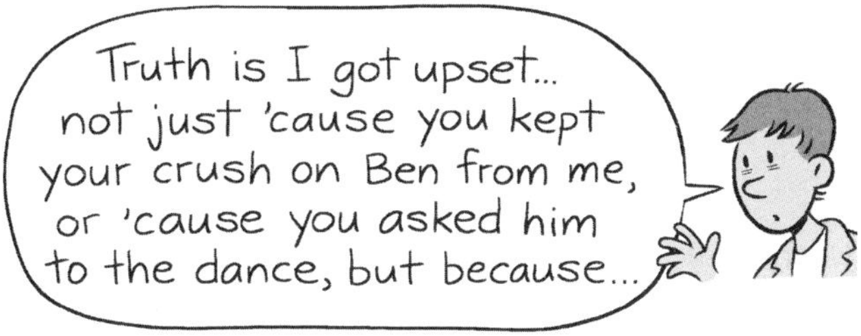
Truth is I got upset... not just 'cause you kept your crush on Ben from me, or 'cause you asked him to the dance, but because...

He exhales.

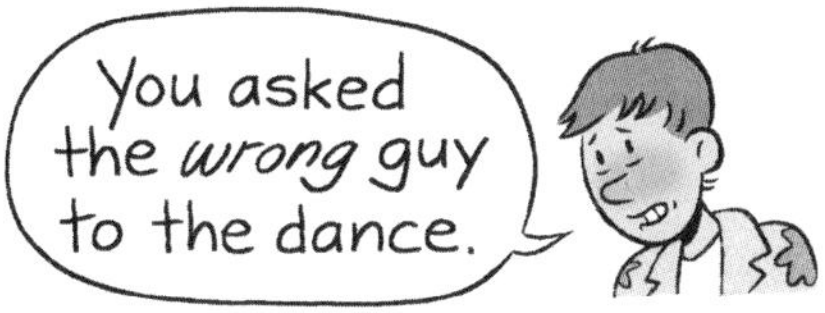
You asked the *wrong* guy to the dance.

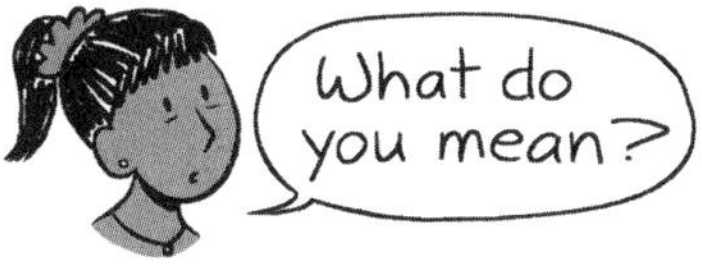
What do you mean?

He just looks at me and raises his eyebrows.

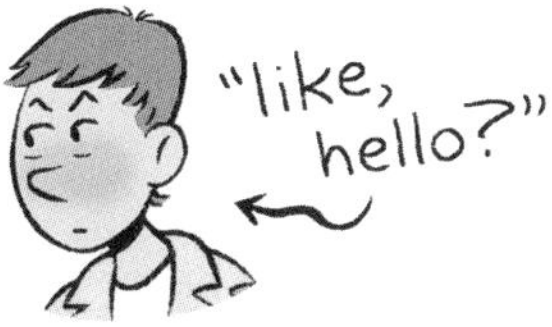
"like, hello?"

Which doesn't register at first.

Then . . .

rubber chickens

Ohhh!

CLUNK

Y-you mean...

Yeah.

I didn't even realize it until you asked Ben. It hit me like... I dunno.

Anyway, after that, I kinda needed some... distance.

It was wrong and I'm sorry. But I thought I was... I guess... protecting myself?

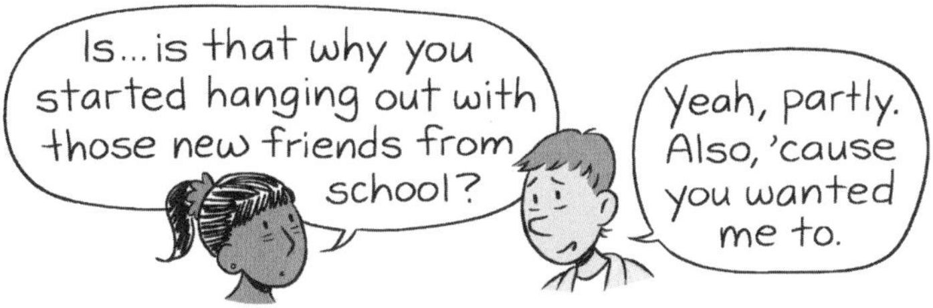
Is...is that why you started hanging out with those new friends from school?
Yeah, partly. Also, 'cause you wanted me to.

I feel a huge urge to run inside my house. But I don't.

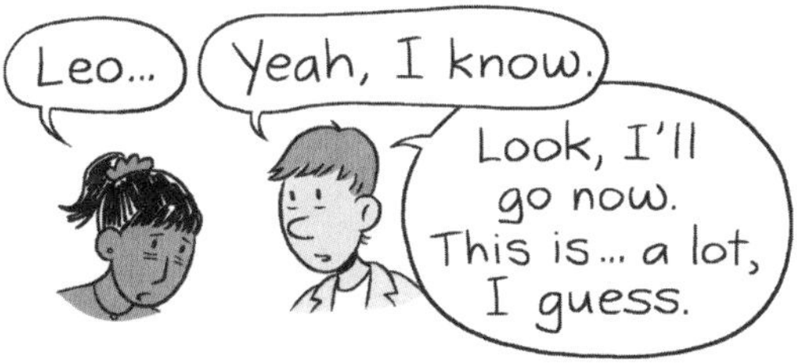
Leo...
Yeah, I know.
Look, I'll go now. This is... a lot, I guess.

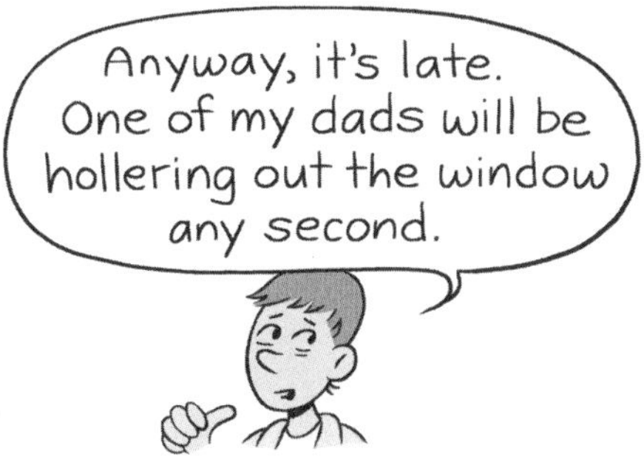
Anyway, it's late. One of my dads will be hollering out the window any second.

He gets up and heads inside.

Neither of us says bye. Or does our usual BBF/BGF thing.

Instead, I go home.

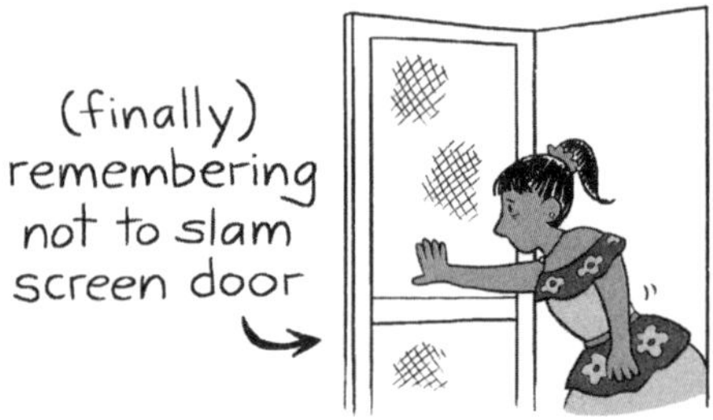
(finally) remembering not to slam screen door

Despite everything that's happened tonight, I fall asleep super quickly. Feels like all my feelings formed a giant brick in my head and knocked me out.

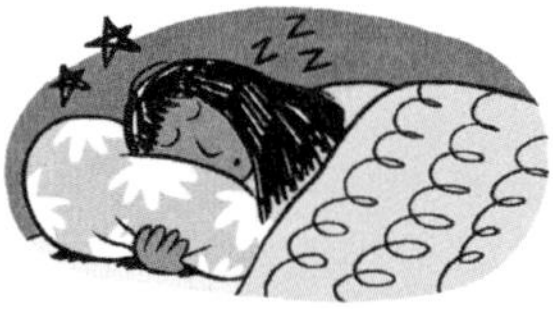
Z Z Z

I spend the weekend avoiding Leo. Luckily it pours, which helps. I try not to think about our habit of watching lightning shows from my porch. Instead, I stay inside and help my mom bake, do my homework, read, and sew while watching TV.

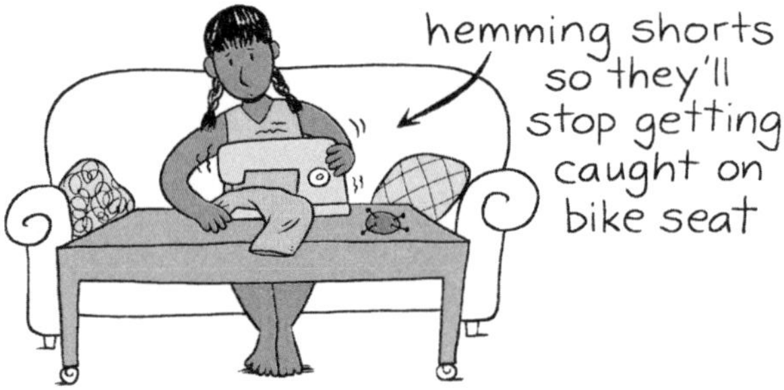
hemming shorts so they'll stop getting caught on bike seat

The next week, I go to school and actively hide from Ben.

I also keep my distance from Leo.

He hasn't texted me. I guess he's trying to give me space. It's not like I don't miss him, but how can I face him? Leo's like my brother. I've never seen him any other way.

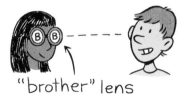

"brother" lens

His new friends come over after practice a few times, although I haven't noticed Ben coming around. From my window, I see them eating snacks in his yard and playing cornhole. Not that I'm spying.

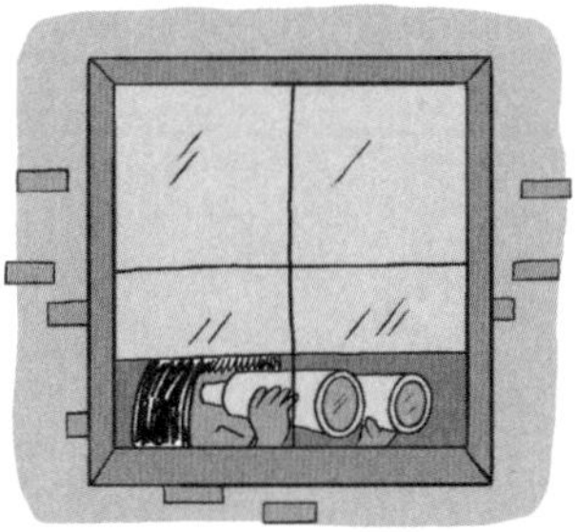

I just don't know what to do.

One day, Emmie and Bri corner me after art club (and Bri's Science Olympiad meeting).

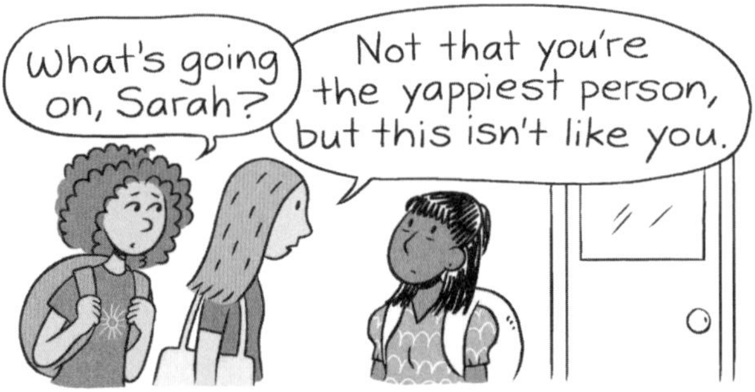
What's going on, Sarah?
Not that you're the yappiest person, but this isn't like you.

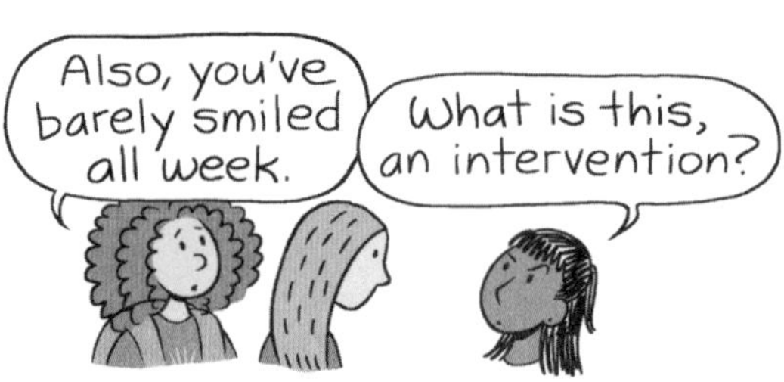
Also, you've barely smiled all week.
What is this, an intervention?

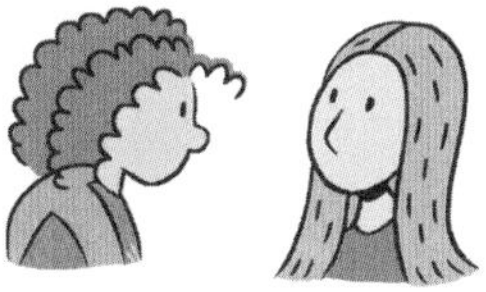

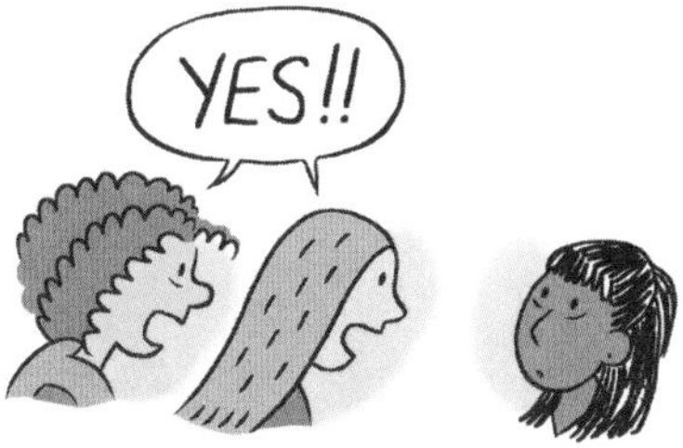
YES!!

I sigh.

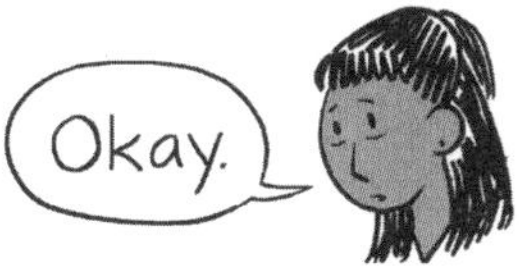
Okay.

We sit down on the stairs and I tell them about Leo.

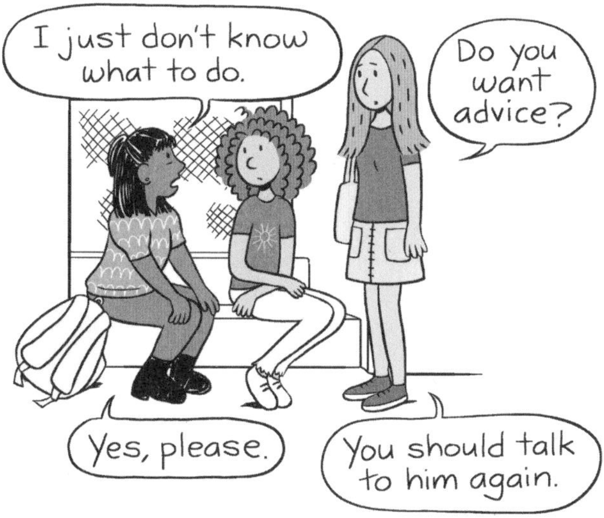
I just don't know what to do.
Do you want advice?
Yes, please.
You should talk to him again.

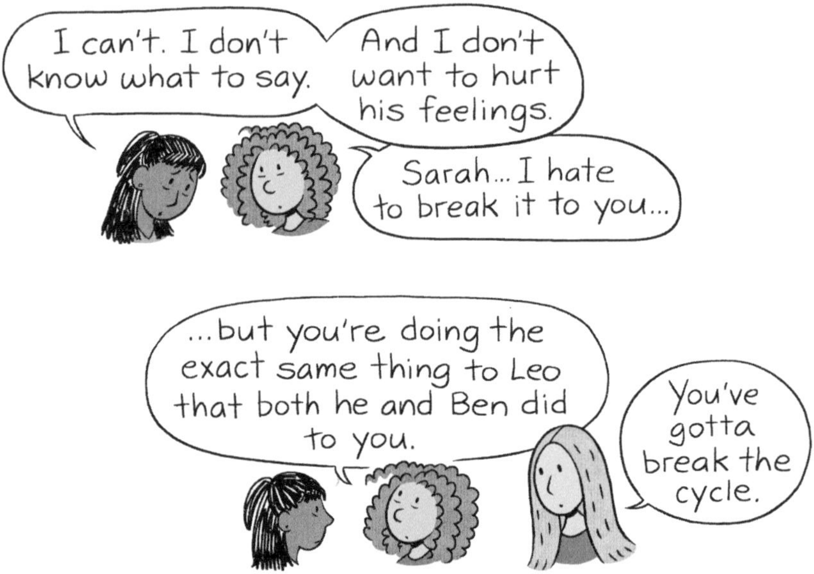
I can't. I don't know what to say.
And I don't want to hurt his feelings.
Sarah... I hate to break it to you...
...but you're doing the exact same thing to Leo that both he and Ben did to you.
You've gotta break the cycle.

I nod slowly. They're right. Of course.

So the next day, I text him.

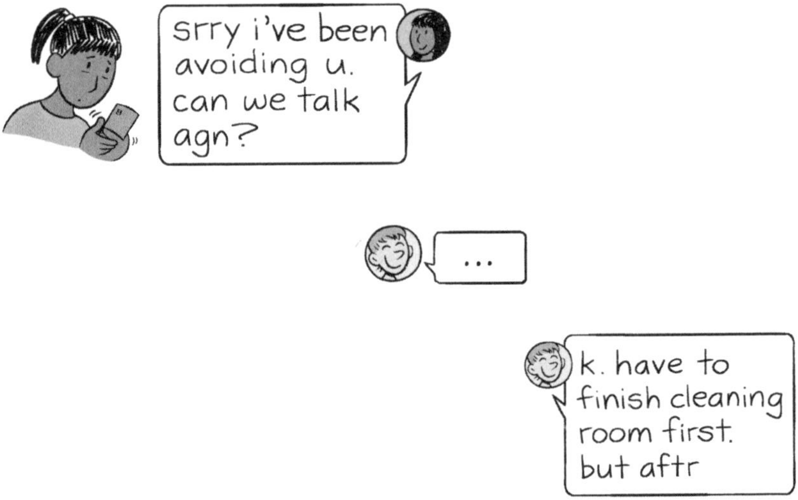
srry i've been avoiding u. can we talk agn?
...
k. have to finish cleaning room first. but aftr

I wait on my stoop.

After a while, I get kinda irritated that he's taking so long.

Which is a weird realization: I'm not nervous, just impatient. That's when it hits me.

I can't wait to see him.

This makes me wonder for the first time . . .

Could I ever see Leo as...

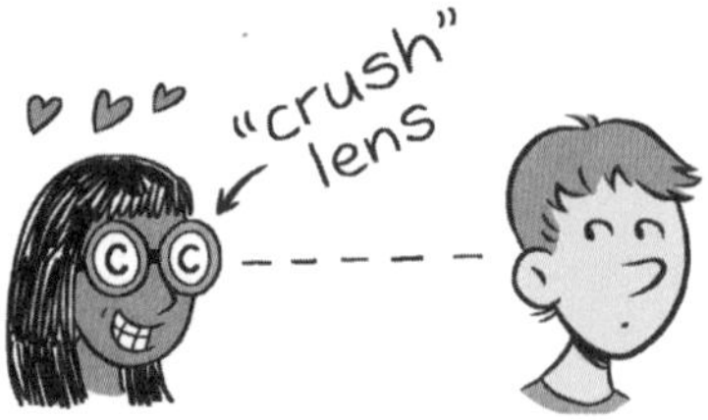
"crush" lens

I get the "ick" chills and shake it off.

But . . .

Okay, honestly, I don't know if that could ever happen or not.

Only thing I do know right now . . .

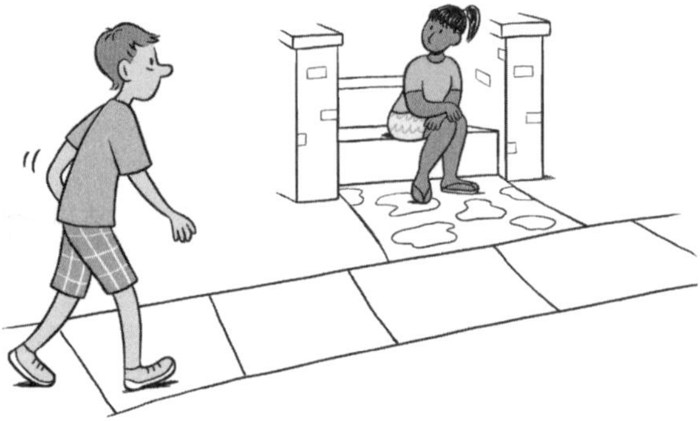

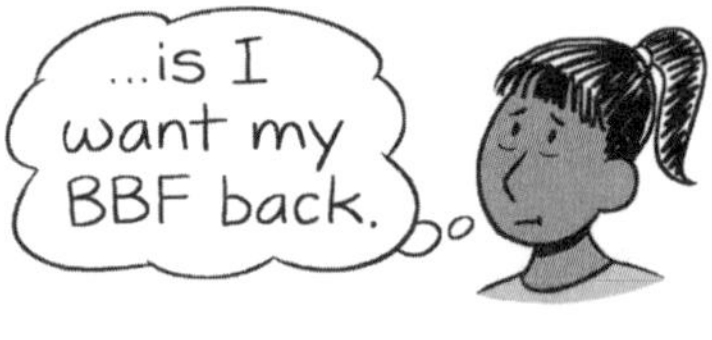
...is I want my BBF back.

Leo
She lost her nerve
IT'S BEEN A WEEK SINCE SARAH STOPPED TALKING TO ME ... AGAIN.
no new messages
this is getting old
AND ABOUT WHAT HAPPENED: EMBARRASSED ISN'T THE WORD.
embarrassed
mortified
humiliated
Wish I could change color and blend into a wall

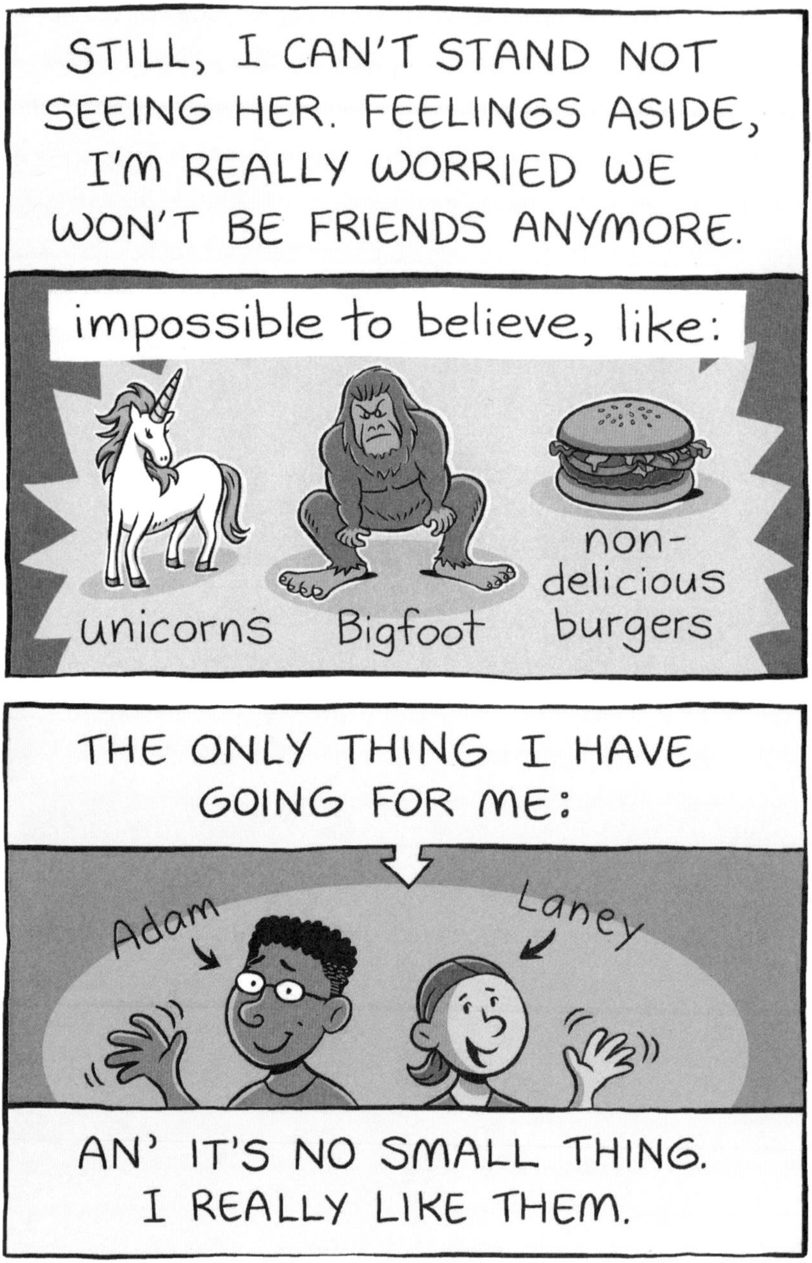
STILL, I CAN'T STAND NOT SEEING HER. FEELINGS ASIDE, I'M REALLY WORRIED WE WON'T BE FRIENDS ANYMORE.
impossible to believe, like:
unicorns
Bigfoot
non-delicious burgers
THE ONLY THING I HAVE GOING FOR ME:
Adam
Laney
AN' IT'S NO SMALL THING. I REALLY LIKE THEM.

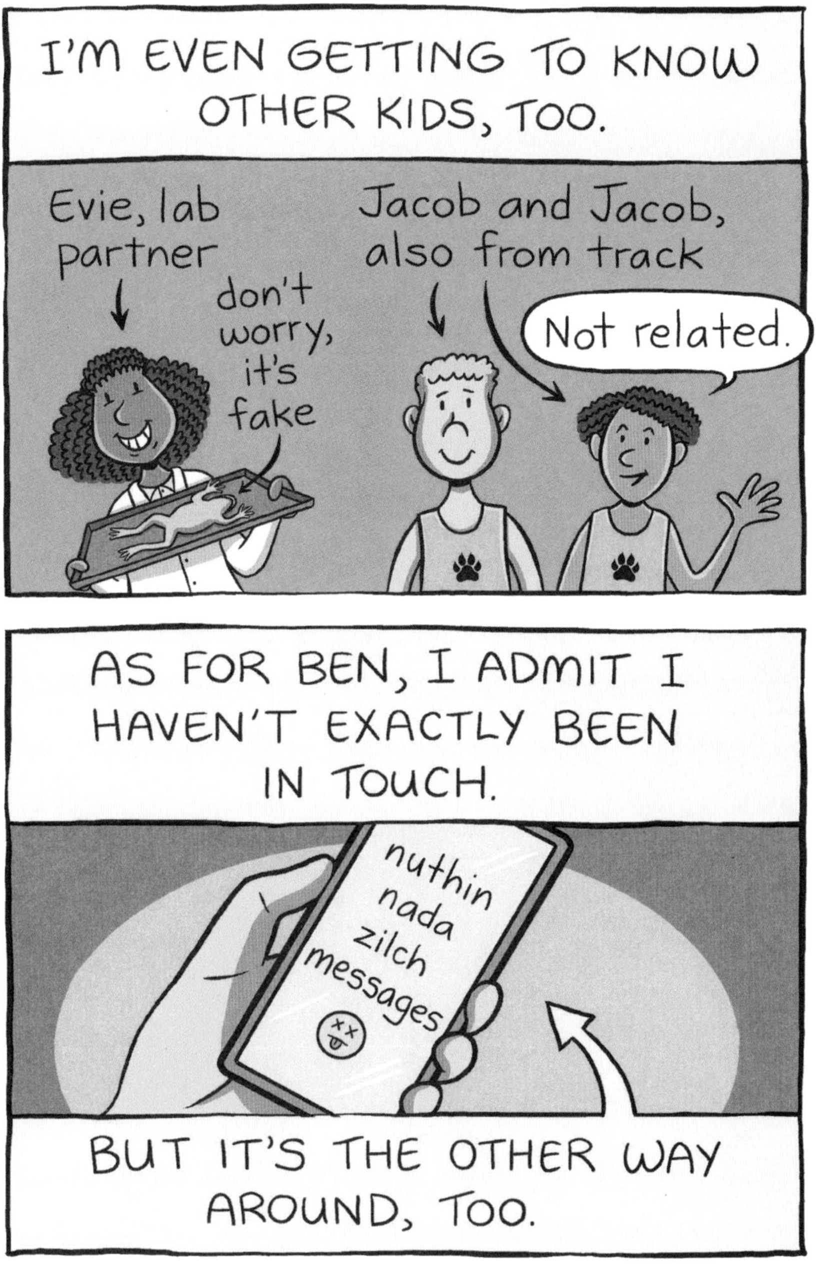
I'M EVEN GETTING TO KNOW OTHER KIDS, TOO.
Evie, lab partner
don't worry, it's fake
Jacob and Jacob, also from track
Not related.
AS FOR BEN, I ADMIT I HAVEN'T EXACTLY BEEN IN TOUCH.
nuthin
nada
zilch
messages
BUT IT'S THE OTHER WAY AROUND, TOO.

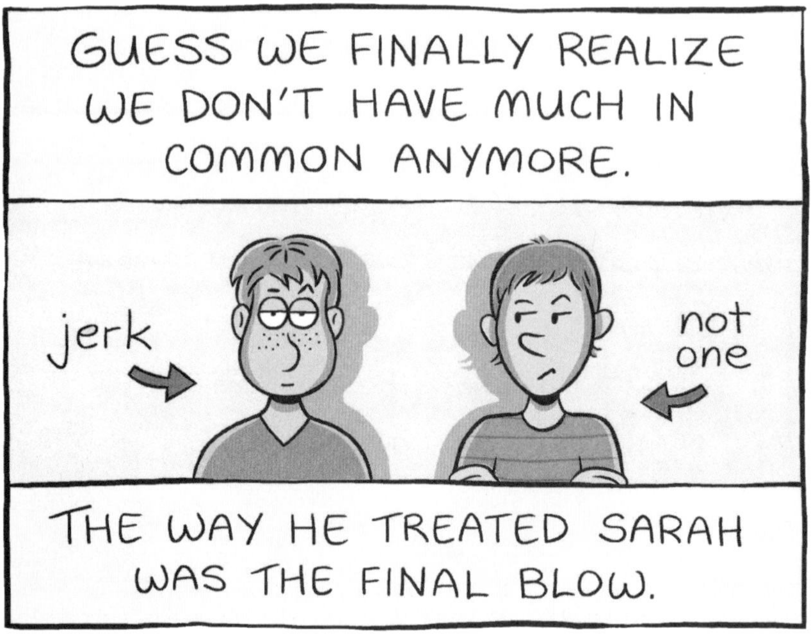
GUESS WE FINALLY REALIZE WE DON'T HAVE MUCH IN COMMON ANYMORE.
jerk
not one
THE WAY HE TREATED SARAH WAS THE FINAL BLOW.

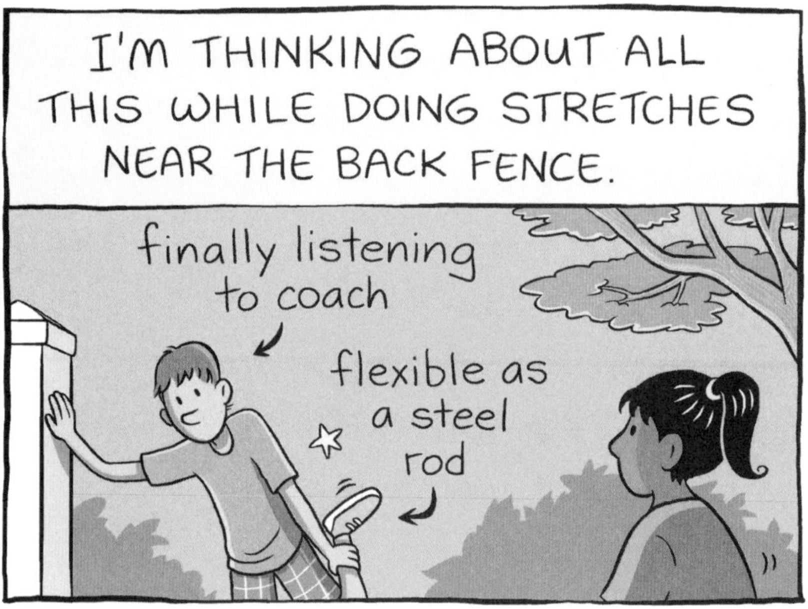
I'M THINKING ABOUT ALL THIS WHILE DOING STRETCHES NEAR THE BACK FENCE.
finally listening to coach
flexible as a steel rod

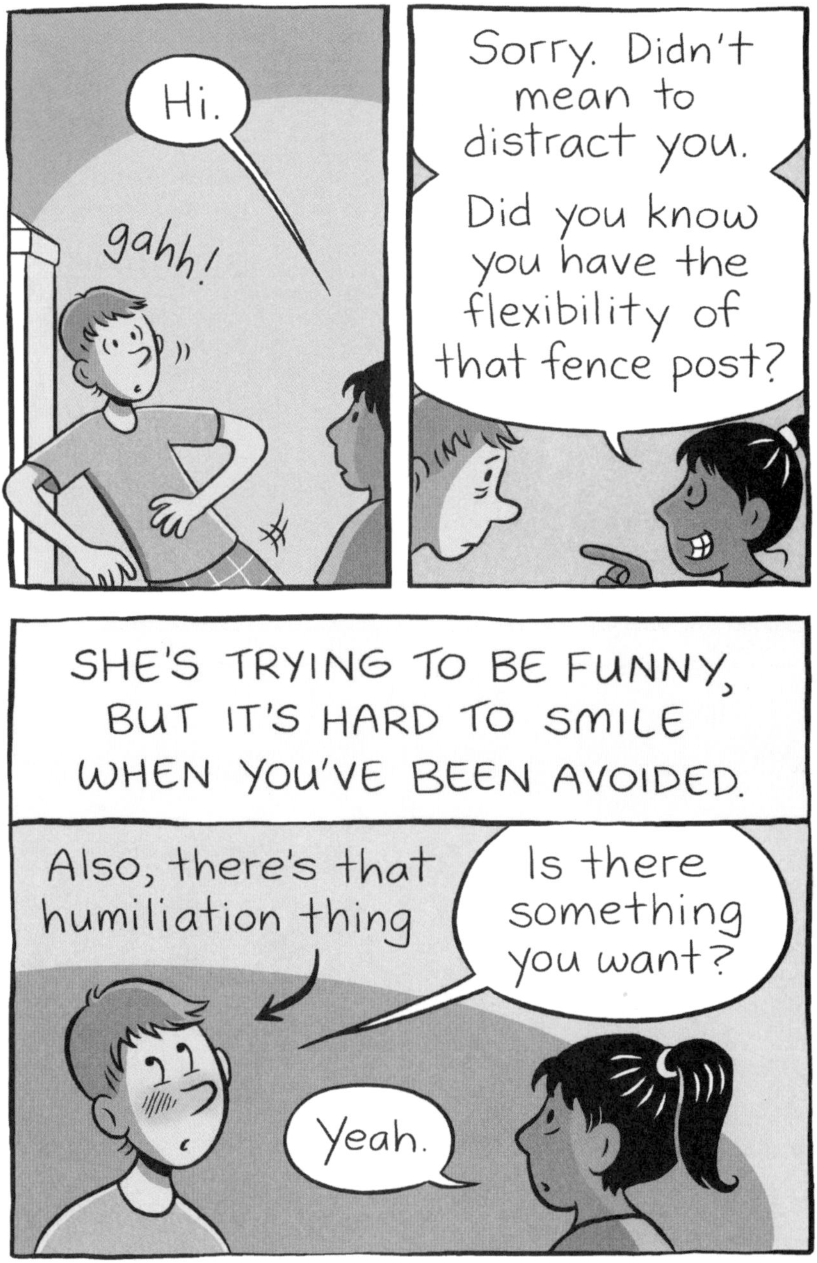
Hi.
gahh!
Sorry. Didn't mean to distract you.
Did you know you have the flexibility of that fence post?
SHE'S TRYING TO BE FUNNY, BUT IT'S HARD TO SMILE WHEN YOU'VE BEEN AVOIDED.
Also, there's that humiliation thing
Is there something you want?
Yeah.

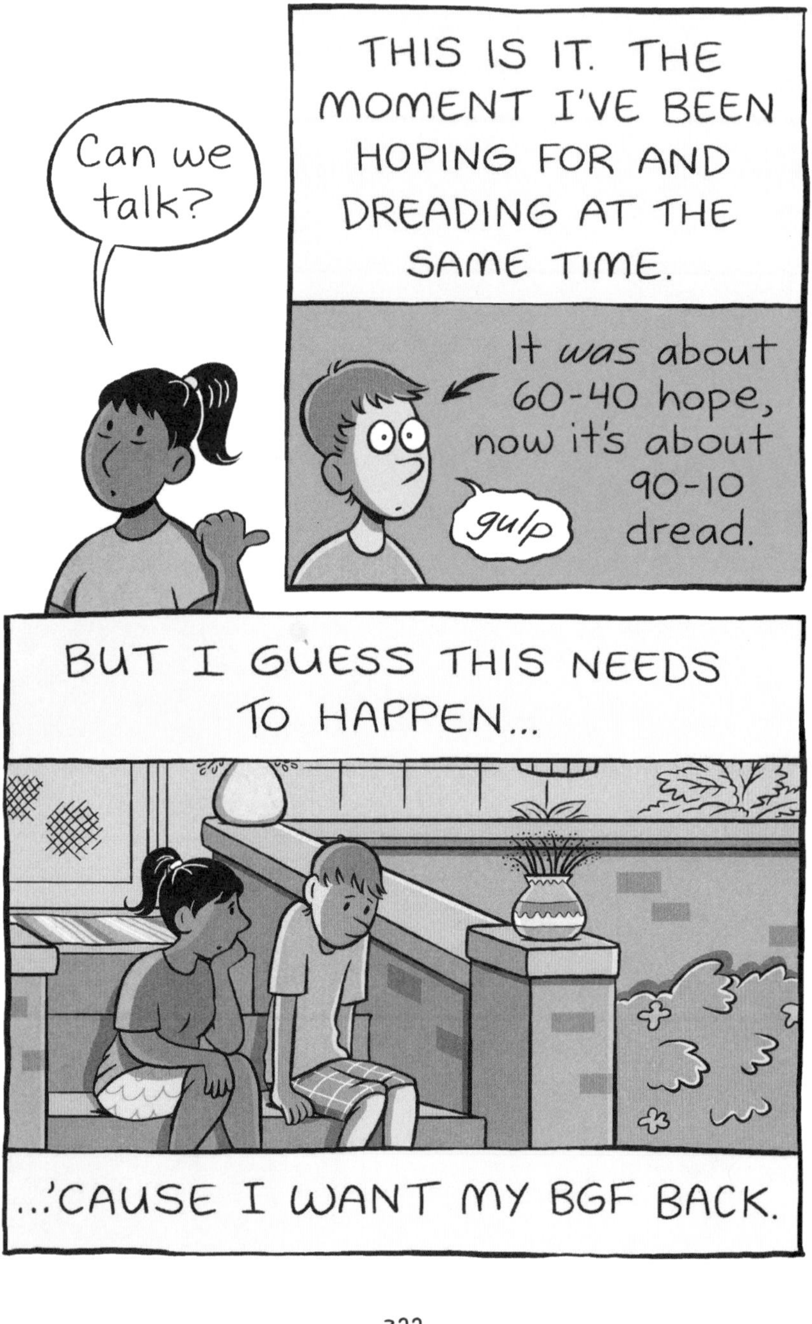
THIS IS IT. THE MOMENT I'VE BEEN HOPING FOR AND DREADING AT THE SAME TIME.
Can we talk?
It *was* about 60-40 hope, now it's about 90-10 dread.
gulp
BUT I GUESS THIS NEEDS TO HAPPEN...
...'CAUSE I WANT MY BGF BACK.

SARAH AND LEO

 The (shared) End

I want my BGF back.

I want my BBF back.

I'm really sorry I avoided you.

I, uh, get it. I'm glad we're talking.

I just... I want to be friends again, Leo. I don't want things to be weird.

Same.

He pauses. Then he stands and faces me.

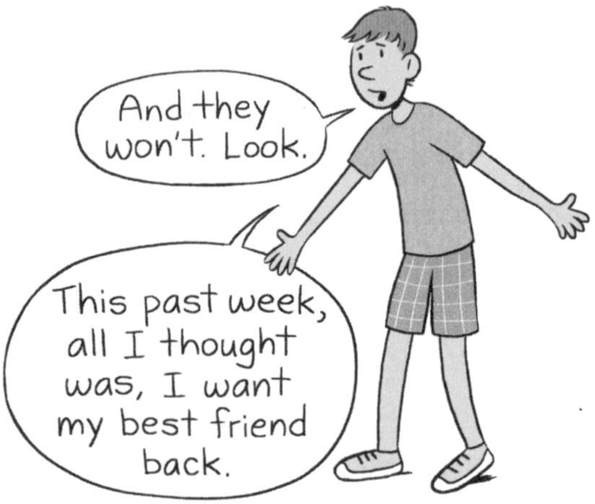
And they won't. Look.
This past week, all I thought was, I want my best friend back.

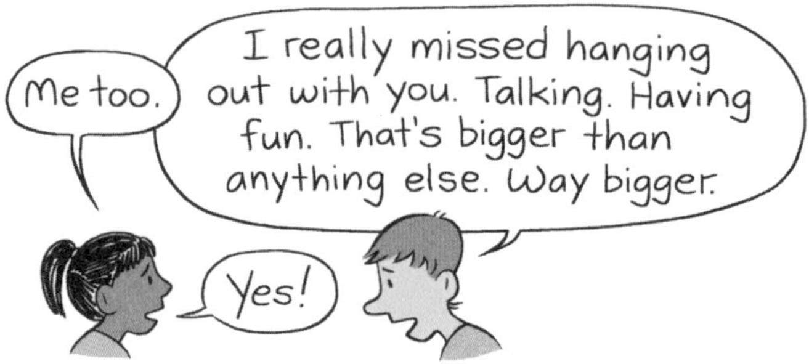
Me too.
I really missed hanging out with you. Talking. Having fun. That's bigger than anything else. Way bigger.
Yes!

We smile at each other. And I think maybe we have a chance to be friends again.

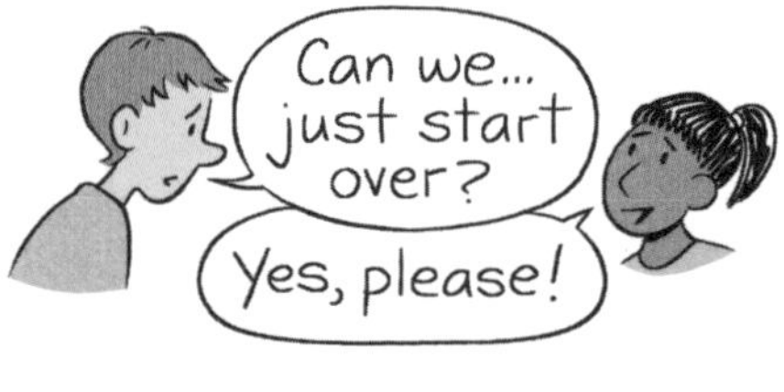
Can we... just start over?
Yes, please!

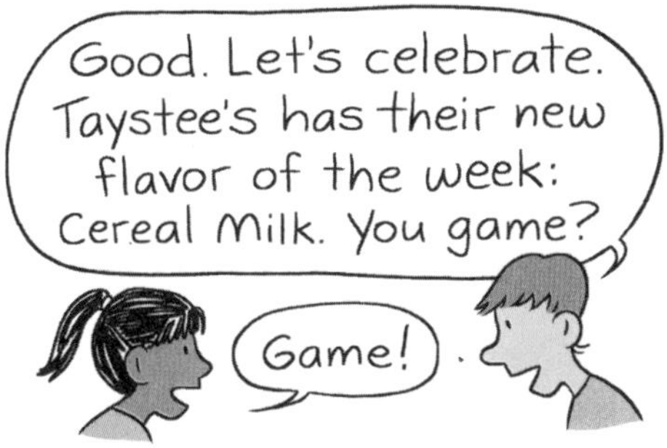
Good. Let's celebrate. Taystee's has their new flavor of the week: Cereal Milk. You game?
Game!

I go inside, grab what's left of my allowance, and tell my mom where we're going. Leo waits on the stoop.

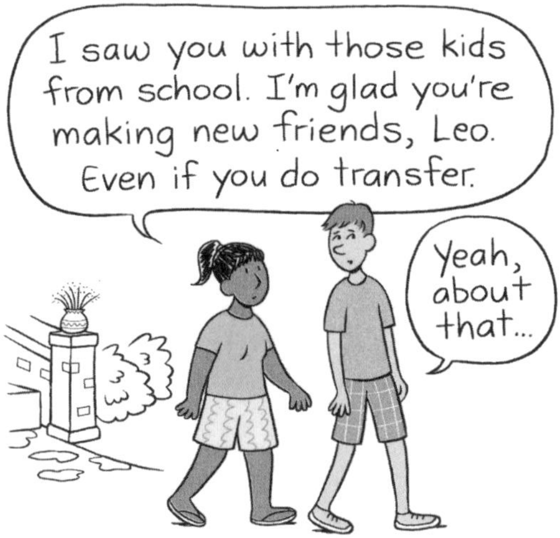
I saw you with those kids from school. I'm glad you're making new friends, Leo. Even if you do transfer.
Yeah, about that...

He kicks a stone down the sidewalk. We watch it bounce a few times and land in a crack.

I've been thinking. I might give it another year or two.

I stop.

Wait. What?

Yeah.

It's actually not so bad at EW. Especially with Laney and Adam there.

Plus I really like some of my teachers this year, and Coach....

I'm sorry. I know I've been saying all along that I wanna go to Lakefront.

Are you mad?

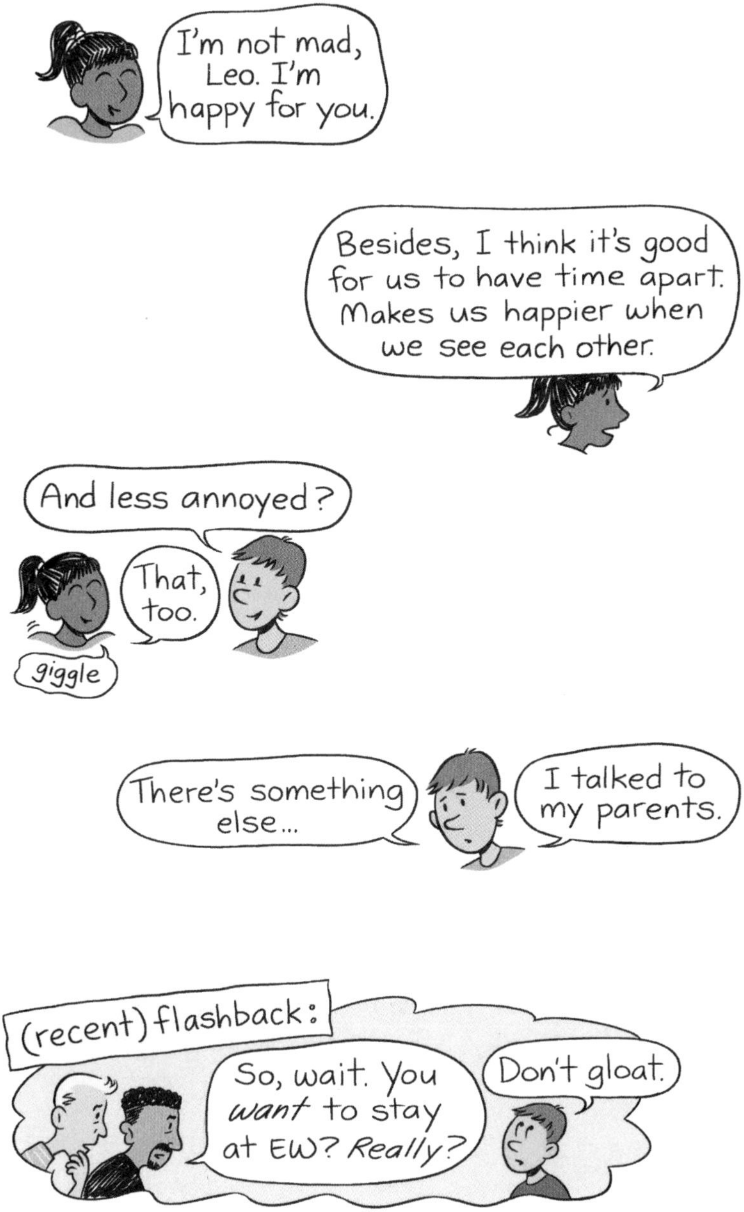
I'm not mad, Leo. I'm happy for you.
Besides, I think it's good for us to have time apart. Makes us happier when we see each other.
And less annoyed?
That, too.
giggle
There's something else...
I talked to my parents.
(recent) flashback:
So, wait. You *want* to stay at EW? *Really?*
Don't gloat.

Honey, we're not. Despite what you think, we didn't switch you out to be mean.

We did it because you weren't flourishing.

"You were distracted and unfocused."

pfft

Stop, Leo.

We were worried. We thought EW was better suited to your needs.

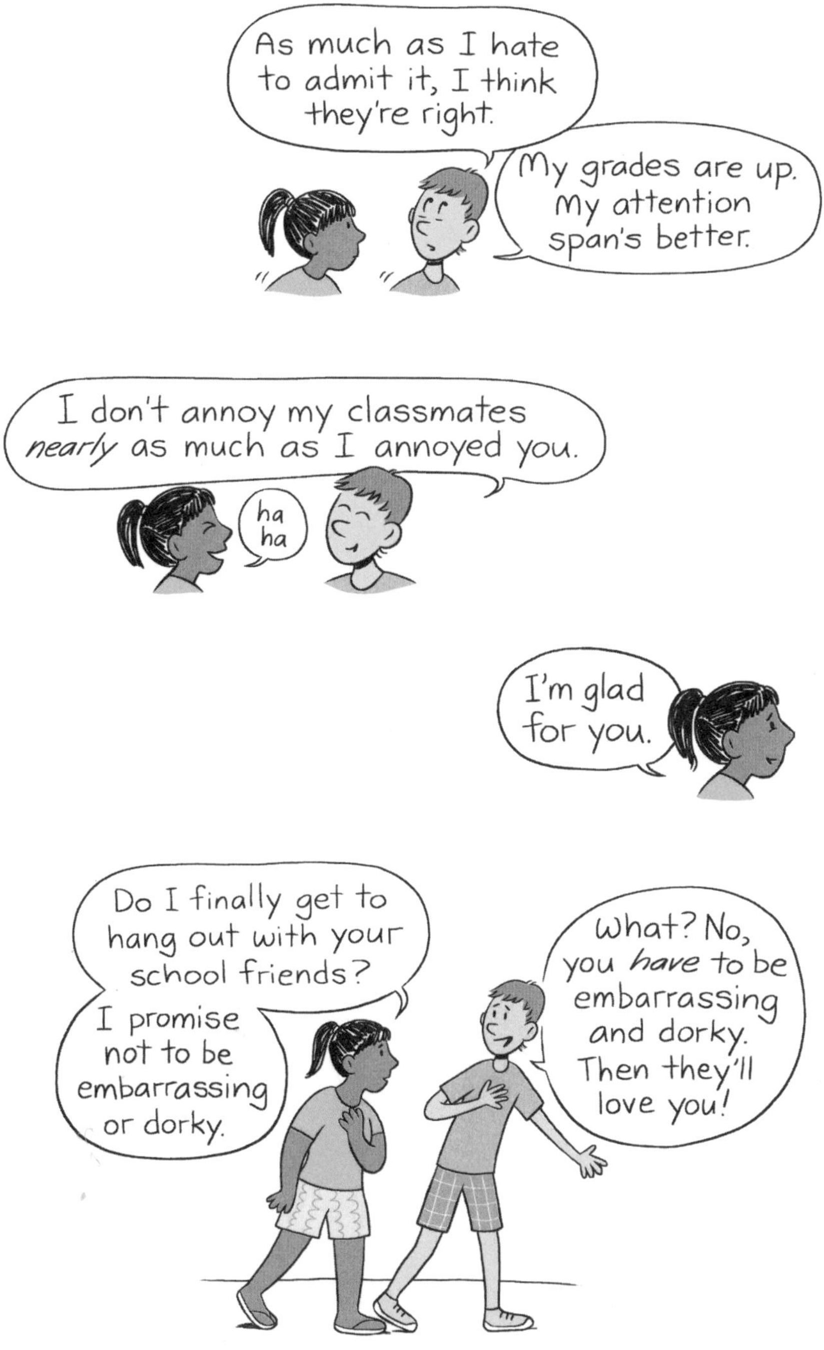
As much as I hate to admit it, I think they're right.
My grades are up. My attention span's better.
I don't annoy my classmates *nearly* as much as I annoyed you.
ha ha
I'm glad for you.
Do I finally get to hang out with your school friends?
I promise not to be embarrassing or dorky.
What? No, you *have* to be embarrassing and dorky. Then they'll love you!

I laugh, linking arms with him.

I do wonder if things will be weird between us again. I hope not. Even though we agreed to start over, everything is different. Leo admitted his feelings and he can't undo that. It'll always be out there.

But then I glance at him, and he smiles in that Leo way I missed.

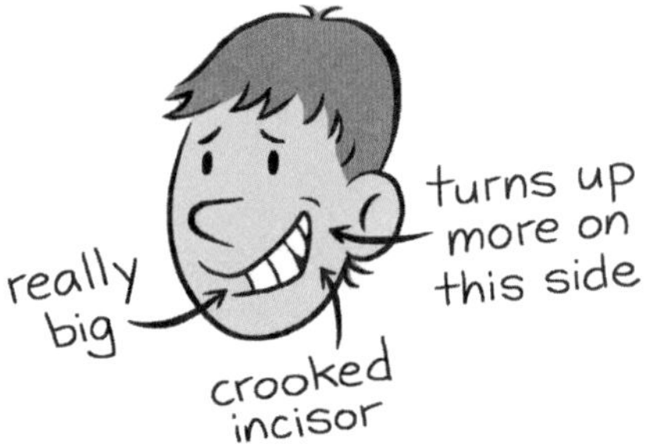
turns up more on this side
really big
crooked incisor

And somehow, like always, I know we'll be okay.

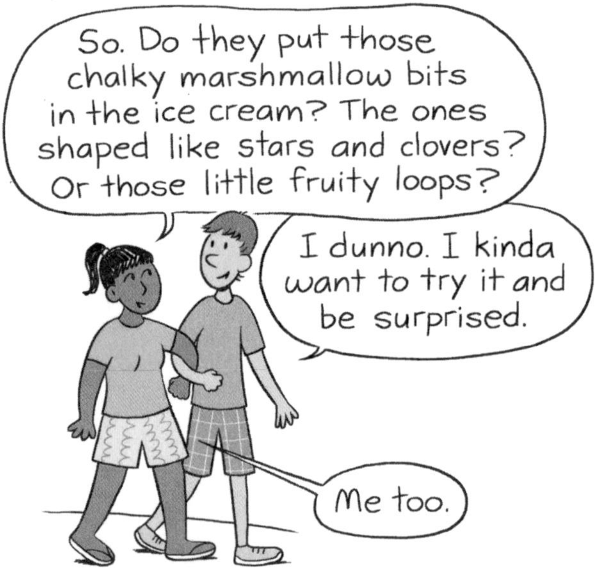
So. Do they put those chalky marshmallow bits in the ice cream? The ones shaped like stars and clovers? Or those little fruity loops?
I dunno. I kinda want to try it and be surprised.
Me too.

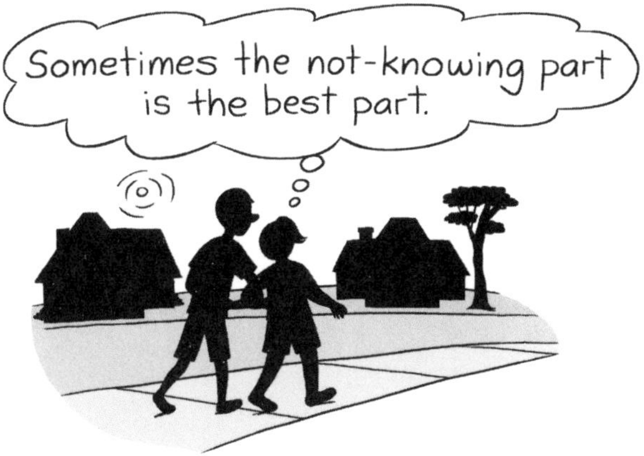
Sometimes the not-knowing part is the best part.

EPILOGUE
SARAH

We walk into Taystee's. It's super crowded. But then, it's Saturday afternoon and about nine thousand degrees out.

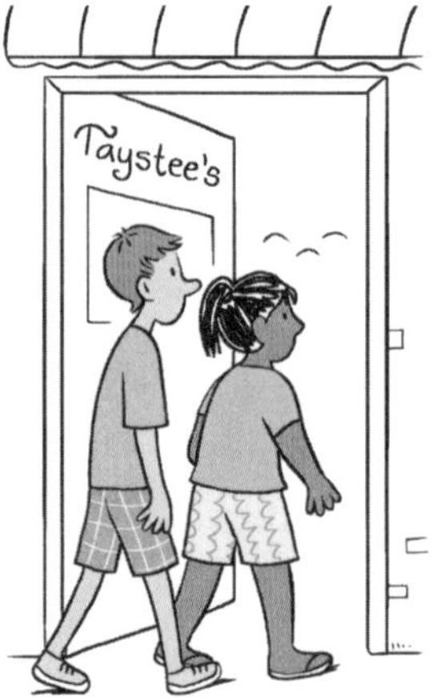
Taystee's

I see Joe sitting with Tyler and Anthony. I remember how his dancing helped cheer me up. I wish more people knew what a nice person he is . . .

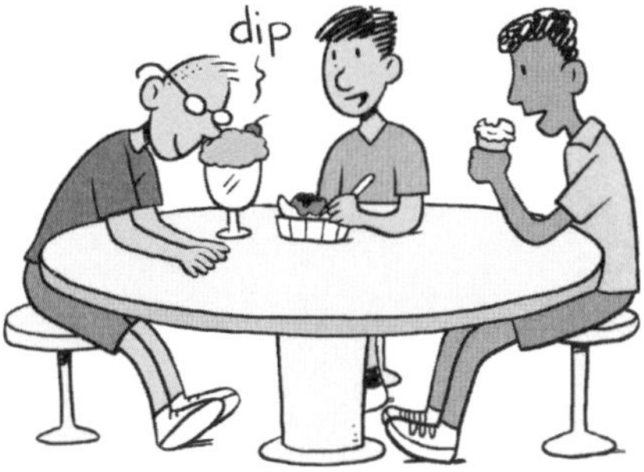
dip

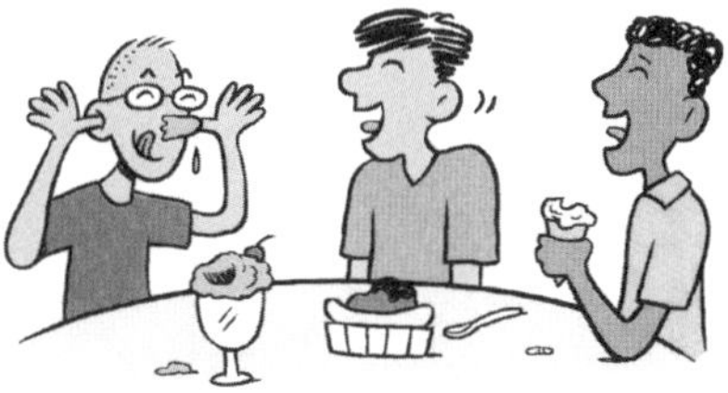

. . . under all that "class clown" stuff.

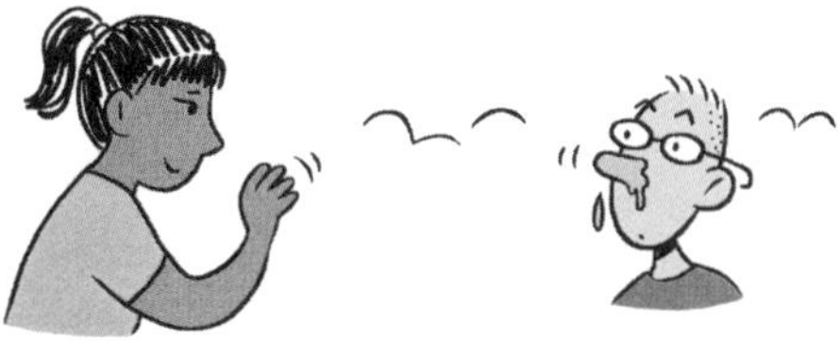

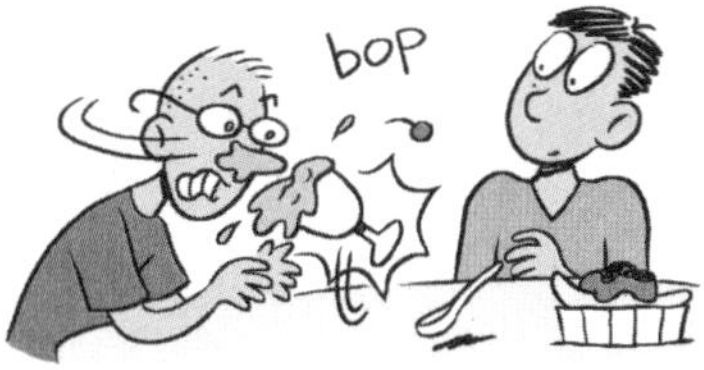
bop

Then I see someone else.

Leo notices him, too.
I don't think Ben sees us. He's engrossed in conversation.

(probably about Ninja
Robot Assassins III

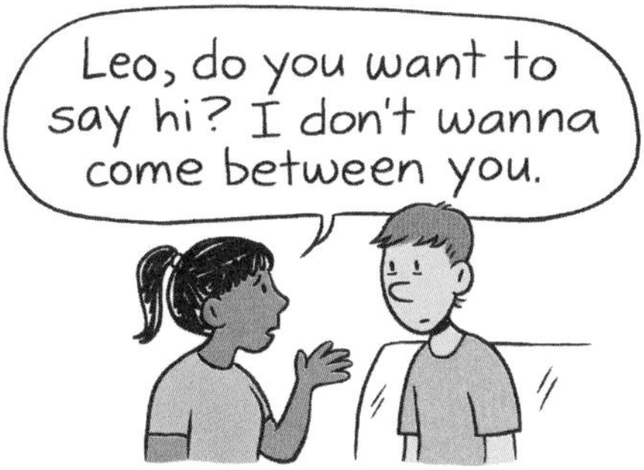
Leo, do you want to say hi? I don't wanna come between you.

He doesn't get a chance to answer because it's our turn in line.

We both order Cereal Milk on waffle cones.

After we pay, he glances at Ben.

Who's spotted us.

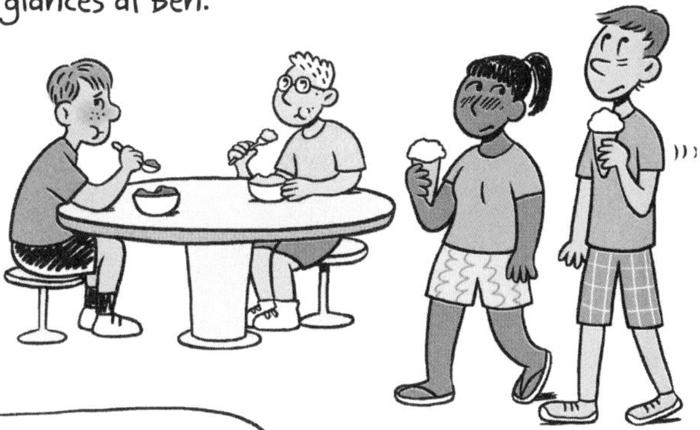

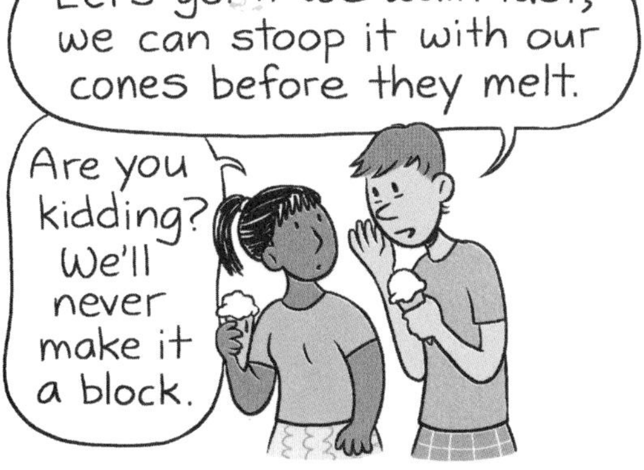
Let's go. If we walk fast, we can stoop it with our cones before they melt.
Are you kidding? We'll never make it a block.

But we leave anyway, our cones already dripping before we escape the air-conditioning.

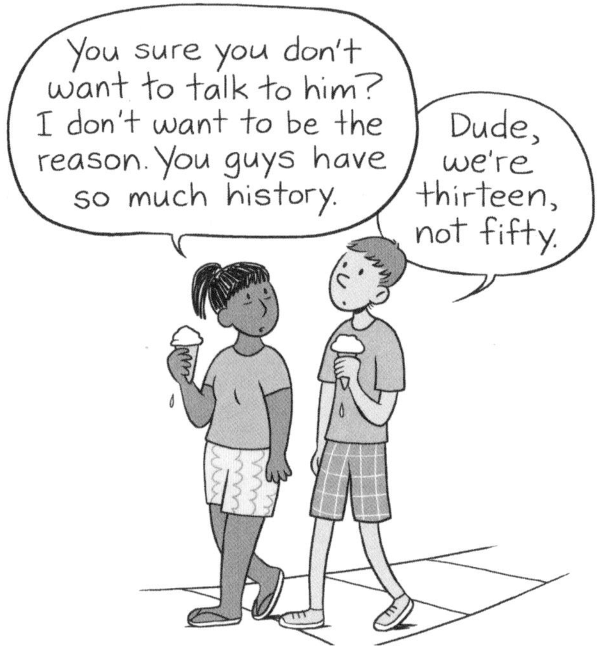
You sure you don't want to talk to him? I don't want to be the reason. You guys have so much history.
Dude, we're thirteen, not fifty.

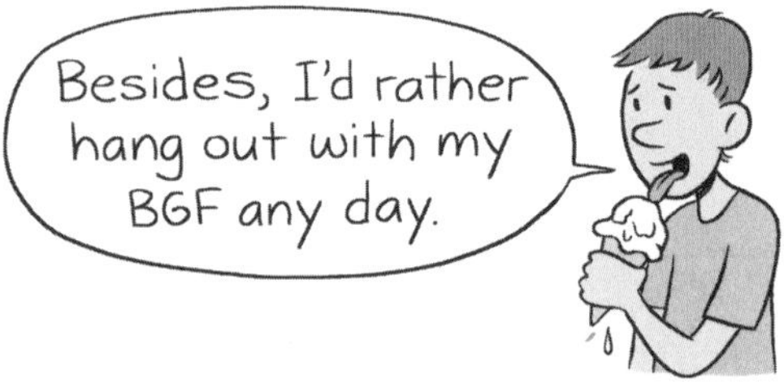
Besides, I'd rather hang out with my BGF any day.

Somehow, we make it to my stoop with most of our ice cream intact. We sit and lick our cones (and hands).

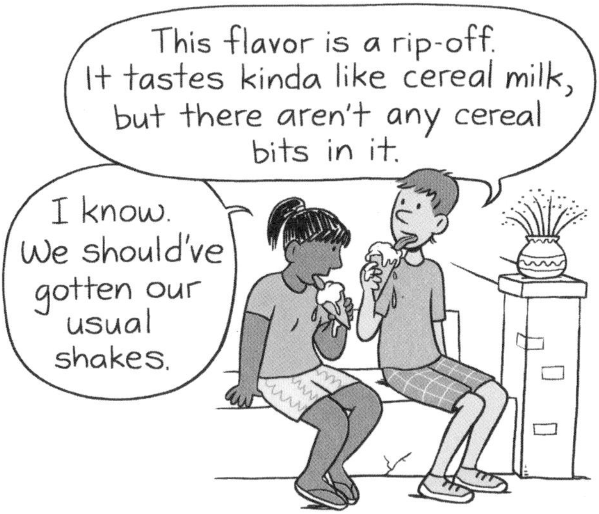
This flavor is a rip-off. It tastes kinda like cereal milk, but there aren't any cereal bits in it.
I know. We should've gotten our usual shakes.

As I lick, I feel something bumpy in the ice cream. I pick it out with my fingers and look.

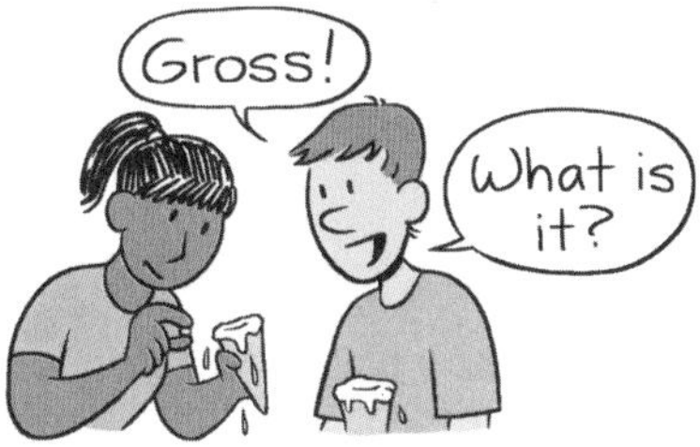
Gross!
What is it?

I inspect it.

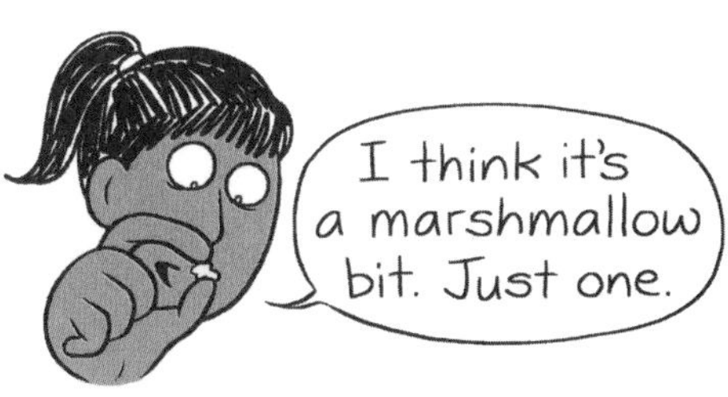
I think it's a marshmallow bit. Just one.

I look closer.

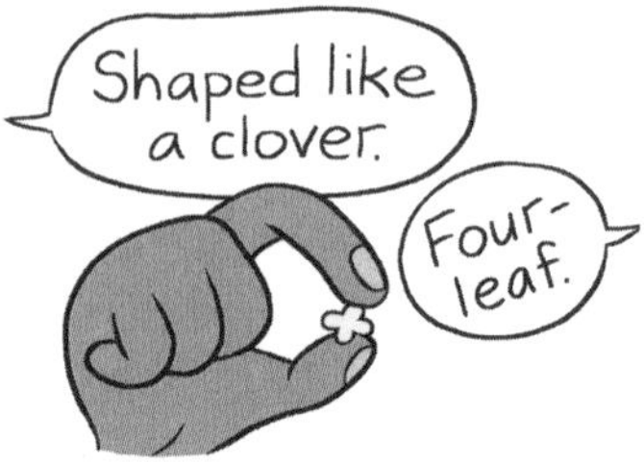

Shaped like a clover.
Four-leaf.

He pulls something out of his scoop.

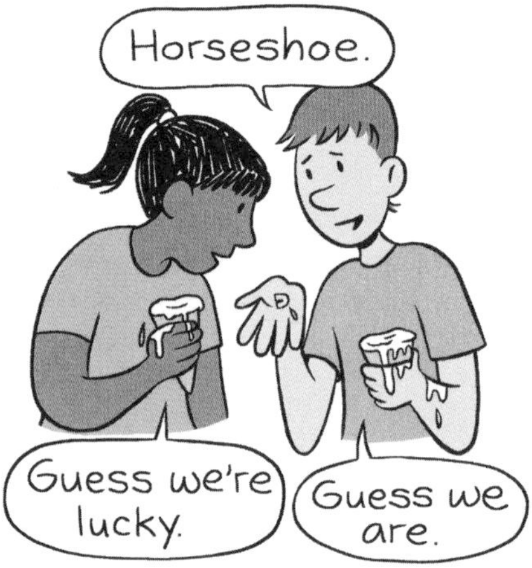

Horseshoe.
Guess we're lucky.
Guess we are.

We lick our cones silently. I start to daydream about our vast thirteen-year history.

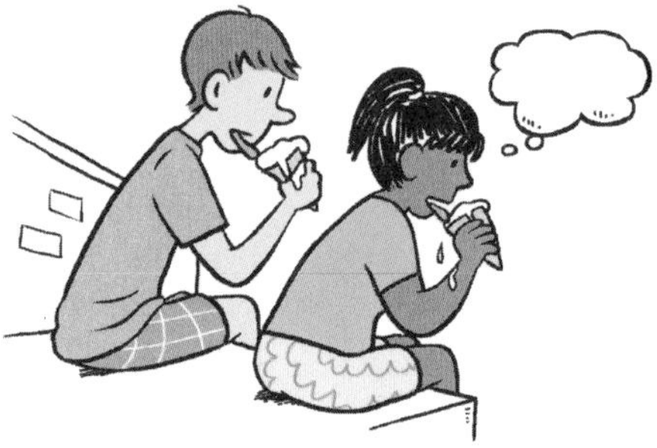

And I think, going forward, whatever decisions we make . . .

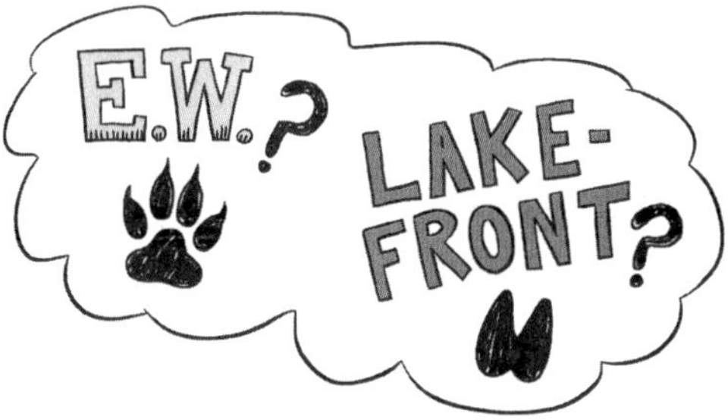
E.W.?
LAKE-FRONT?

. . . whatever crushes we have . . .

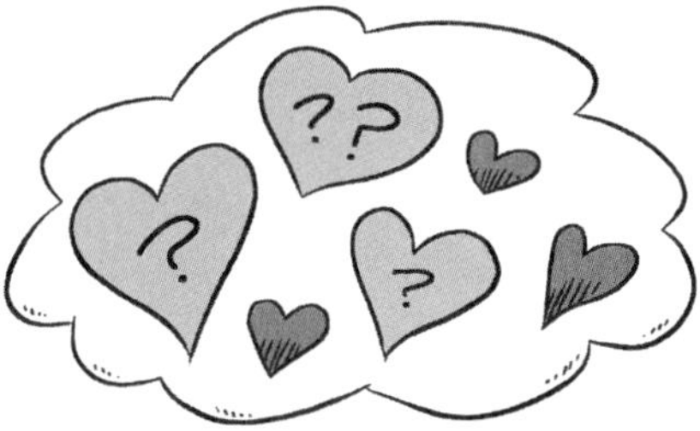
?
??
?

. . . and whether we're brave or not about our choices . . .

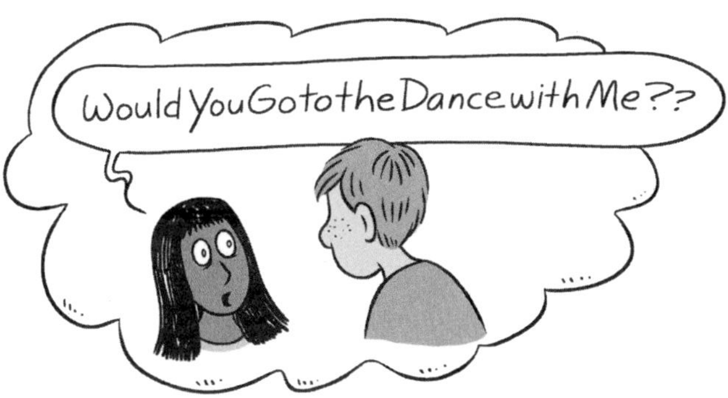
Would You Go to the Dance with Me??

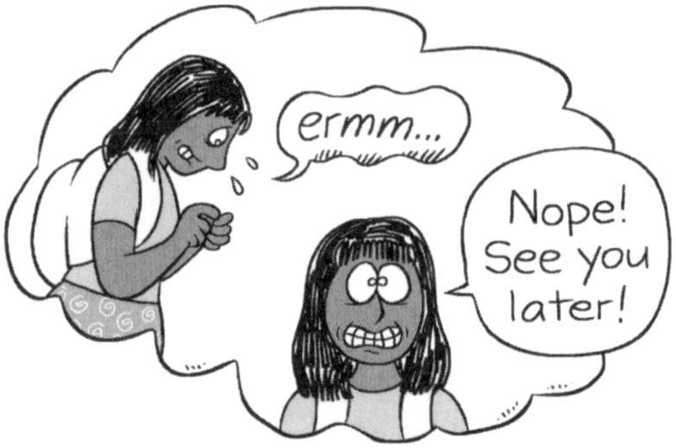
ermm...
Nope! See you later!

. . . as long as Leo and I are honest with each other . . .

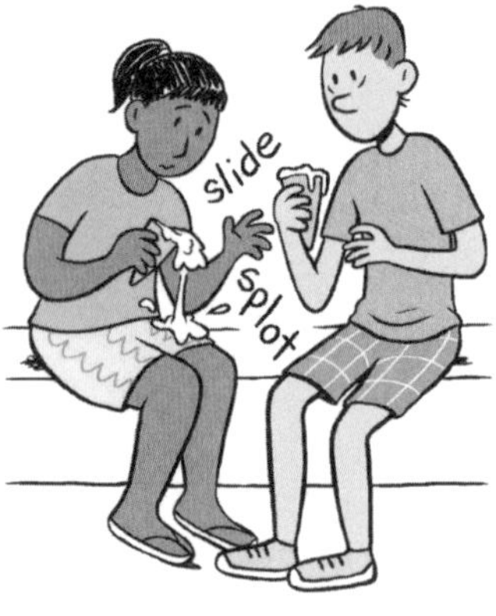
slide
splot

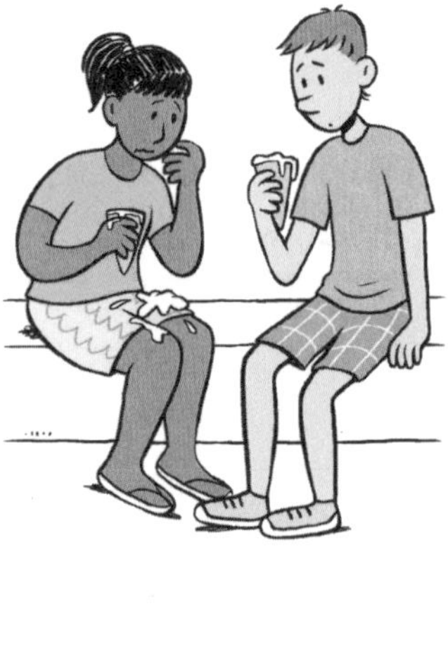

. . . it'll always work out in the end.

ACKNOWLEDGMENTS

So many people to thank! These books really do take a team and I'm lucky to have the best team behind me.

Lots of thanks to my fabulous editor, Donna Bray. She and I have worked on so many of these books, we now have an enviable flow. I always trust her feedback and ideas, and these stories wouldn't be the same without her.

Also, so much thanks to my incredible agent, Dan Lazar, whose judgment I trust unwaveringly and whose immense support I'm always grateful for.

To Laura Mock and Amy Ryan, total creative superheroes. I so appreciate their talent, enthusiasm, and artistic eye(s).

To Taylan Salvati, Vaishali Nayak, Robert Imfeld, Jon Howard, Gwen Morton, Patty Rosati, and the rest of the hardworking, supportive team at HarperCollins. They raise the bar on excellence.

To my wonderful mom, who gave me so much of her talent and all her perfectionism. Thanks (I think).

To my family: Mike, Mollie, and Nikki. Simply said, you are the best and I am the luckiest. Can't forget the fur baby, Rosie, who I thank for all the stress-cuddles.

Last but not least, I'm eternally grateful to all my readers: without you, these books wouldn't be possible. Keep those main character suggestions coming (Sarah was a clear winner)!

Rosie waiting on her cuddles